MW00333508

VOICES OF THE STARS

ROWENA WHALING

Spiral Gate Books

ISBN (trade paperback): 978-0692802052

Voices of the Stars copyright © 2014
by Rowena Whaling
All Rights Reserved.
Cover art by Claudia McKinney, Phatpuppy Art
Author photo by Carla Rey Lankford

Spiral Gate Books

Dedicated To

"Bobby Whaling and Yvette" – who gave my spirit a home in which to dwell and a childhood filled with love, awe, and phantasy... to my beloved Ember – Keeper of the Fire of my heart – who helps me in countless ways... And to Mystic, who shares the Mysteries...

Thanks To

The Great Teachers who inspire... to Solitaire who took my hand at the beginning... to Lord Serphant for sharing The Dream, to Katherine Lohr, who gave the gift of hypnosis to me, to Silver RavenWolf who elicited from me the promise to write a novel, to B. Willie Dryden who walked a long part of the winding path with me, to Carla Ray Lankford who captures beauty, to Kia for your help and love, to my sisters Dahlia and Gwendolyn and to all of my family and friends of the Village of Dragonstone who have shared the Magic with and encouraged me:
Avalon, Covenant, Denise, Divana, Eagle, Eclipse, Ember, Fle, Gwyddyon, Jacquelyn, Ken, Lazarus, Mystic, Pat, Persephone, Raymond, Star and Witness... to Wanda, Patricia, Kay, Gypsy Ravish, John Wisdom Gonce, and Jack and Lesley Montgomery, for your help and support... To Corinda Carfora and Anthony Ziccardi for believing in me

And to my sister Anastasia... who showed me *the other side of the mirror.*

Special Love to: Meghan (Ashirah), Mikie, Mightor, Miss Pusskins, And Chance...

Author's Note

These histories are, of course, translated from their original languages into our commonly spoken tongue. You will note that I have used the device of capitalising many words that are not normally capitalised in the English language. The reason for this is to keep the reader's thoughts set in the characters' understanding of the Sacred Nature of all Creation, and that every endeavour under the Sun is a reflection of what the Gods taught us to do "In the beginning" – at the Cosmogenesis. Thus – Hunter, Weaver, Healer, Seer, Priest/ess and so forth will also be capitalised to remind the reader of the respect accorded these vocations and pursuits. All Magical actions or psychic phenomena such as Dreams, Visions, and Casting of Spells, as well as all Divine names and principals such as Love, Death, Time, Night, etc. are likewise capitalised, as opposed to dreams – as in an aspirations. Please note, too, that I have used British spellings. Oh, yes – and as the plural of "Wolf," I have used "Wolfs" – just because.

On names... Pendragon is the traditional spelling of what is understood to be the surname of Uther, coming from French romances written six to seven hundred years after Post Roman times. However, the gist of this novel is that Morgan's Histories tell the "true" stories and not the layers of legends added long after the fact. The fact is that Brythonic and Old Welsh descriptive names were broken down into the two or three words that they mean. As an example, the modern name Johnson would have been written and spoken as John's Son in the Brythonic tongue. The name of one character in my book is – Rhodri ab Naw Caw which means: Rhodri = Circle or Wheel ruler... Naw = "Legendary son of Seithved," seventh son of a ninth son... Caw = full of joy. The Ap – means from or son of. So, in the case of Pendragon, I am using Pen Dragon. Pen means chief or high and Dragon (Draig or Dragwn), of course, means Dragon, but the title Pen Dragon was used to denote Chief battle Commander. The Brythonic or Old Welsh name reads as Pen Draig or Pen Dragwn.

On proper pronunciation of Brythonic words... the absolutely correct pronunciation is unknown. However, for some sense of clarity, you might try using Welsh rules of pronunciation. There are many good sites on the internet to help with this, as well as to bring a little joviality into your day. This will help greatly in the reading of this book. As an example, understanding why Annwyn (Ah-noon) rhymes with 'Moon' in the opening poem "My Mother taught me how to thread a needle..."

Every time I travel in Wales, I and my companions have uproarious fun trying to pronounce the Welsh street, town, or farm names written on sign posts along the very narrow, low stone-walled Welsh country roads or, for that matter, along the modern motorways, too. It's impossible, of course, to pronounce them using English rules! We always get a bonus laugh when hearing the way the words are actually supposed to sound in the beautiful, lilting Welsh tongue.

Have fun!

Rowena

Introduction by
Jack Montgomery
Author of "American Shamans:
Journeys with Traditional Healers"

In these days of "Games of Thrones," The Lord of the Rings" and "Hunger Games," it is hard to imagine what new mythic, fantasy saga could possibly be told, and even it told, would be interesting enough to draw and hold a jaded fantasy reader's attention. There are two basic types of fantasy novels being produced nowadays: one that are the sole product of the author's imagination like the Lord of the Rings and those with a connection to a defined historical or mythical person or period. While both types can be enthralling, the ones with a historical connection can be enchanting at a deeper level as they have an anchor in the common memory and can inspire further research and study. "Voices of the Stars, is an enchanting saga which is built thematically upon the Arthurian legends and yet is not explicitly tied to those 13th century stories. For a historically based novel to work as fiction, it must go beneath the surface of the historical events and probe the shadowy depths of the agendas, motives and passions that generated those events. "Voices of the Stars" accomplishes this task in several ways including character development, thematic harmony and poetical/lyrical addendums.

What makes a good fantasy novel truly enchanting is the depth of character development that draws the reader deeply into the lives of the characters and lets them feel empathy for their situation. Author Rowena Whaling has done a magnificent job of character development in "Voices of the Stars" as she develops the story of Morgan of the Woods and in the words of the main character "weaves, entwines and spreads like the gossamer threads of Arachne-ultimately and forever changing the meaning of events as they truly were."

The elements of magic, myth and the supernatural are also woven together into this epic story with great care to create a unique harmony of the historical and the mythic that carries the reader into the mist-shrouded world between the worlds where Druids chant, dragons fly and the god and goddess make their ethereal presence known. There are also the all-too-human elements of love, violence, sex, relationships and betrayal to mention a few that let the reader further enter into the inner world of the characters. This literary treatment gives the characters humanity and makes them believable.

One further positive literary element found within "Voices of the Stars" is the author's use of epic poetry and songs throughout the texts. The author, a gifted songwriter and musician has been producing her own musical magic for decades and weaves this element into her storyline with literary grace and elegance.

All of these elements combine in Whaling's epic story to create a story that will excite you, prompt tears of joy, or simply arouse your sense of wonder. "Voices of the Stars" takes one on a spiritual as well as literary journey and will inspire you to read more about the Arthurian legends as well. The second book of the trilogy"Rowena of the Glen" continues the saga to a new time and place. Whaling is to be commended for her masterful work and I am certain that she will eventually have a place among the great fantasy novelists of our time.

Oh Lady of the withering Dream
The potent Art remains...
Yet is ever receding
From Mankind's world of fame...

Oh beauty of the Moonlight's beings
Your shadow's kiss now wanes...
Forgotten abandoned Enchantments...
In ruins they lie unclaimed...

Oh, Lady of the countless Stars
Do men forget your dance?
They march to the drums of War Gods
Devoid of all romance...

Oh why is this thing happening?
Will you ever return again?
Oh Radiant Light – to spin and twirl
To ancient Love's refrain...

Voices of the Stars

My Mother taught me how to thread a needle...
'But first,' said she,
'We must put thread to spool...
By three, then seven, then thirteen twines...
By three, then seven, then thirteen Times...
With fingers do we wheedle...

By three, then seven, then thirteen twines...
By Hum and tap and spoken rhymes...
By three, then seven, then thirteen Times
By hand we make what is needful...

By three, then seven, then thirteen twines...
By the Magic of Annwyn
By three, then seven, then thirteen Times...
Beneath the thirteen silver Moons...'

Prologue

In the dark and loathsome hours immediately proceding the Death in battle of Mordred, son of Morganna (she called Le Faye) and of the mortal wounding of Arthur, the King, the three ladies: Vivianne, Lady of the Lake; Nimue, the Enchantress; and Morgan, Priestess of the Great Goddess and daughter of the Seer, Igraine – retrieved Arthur from the bloody battlefield and laid him upon a pallet. By Saxon ship they travelled to the port from whence a punt could cross the marshy Waters of the Inland Sea to bring Arthur home to the Isle of Apples. There, it is said, that by their Magics, they even now keep him suspended 'twixt Death and life in waiting for a fairer Time for the King to return to these Fair Isles of the Britons – to once again bring back the old ways.

But Morganna grieved excessively and she fled Northward to the Snowy Mountains of Gwynedd. There she saw a strongly built house which was pleasing to her, so she conjured upon the house and family which therein lived a great Charm of invisibility and forgetfulness so that no one passing should ever see it again. And what is more, with her Spells and Incantations, all that ever existed of that house, family, and Animals would be forgotten by any who had ever known them. Furthermore, if a Hunter or a wanderer should, by chance, happen upon the house and walk into it, he would immediately forget that it had happened. That family and their Animals, Morganna turned into her servants. And there, Morganna Le Faye grieved and waited...

What lies within these vellum pages is a history written in the tongue of the Britons which I, Morgan, have written down in order to preserve the truth of these matters – because, it is a fact that legends of the simple folk, as well as songs and poems of the Bards, gallop into fancy like Warhorses to the smell of blood. What begins as a simple circle Weaves, entwines, and spreads like the gossamer threads of Arachne – ultimately and forever changing the meaning of events as they really were. So, now, in my very old age of eighty-three years, but still of clear thought and memory, I have completed the writing and compiling of the truth as it happened; through five generations of histories, the length and breadth of the Isles of the Britons, even through the continent which lies across the Eastern Sea. I shall give it into the hands of one whom I would trust with my very life and all I hold Sacred. With Divine assurance I know that these histories will last through the millennia...

Morgan

When my Mother Igraine was fifteen years, she was married to Gorlois, the Dux of Dumnonia, and later had two daughters by him. The eldest was Morganna and seven years later, she gave birth to me, Morgan. In a very eerie way, both of her daughters resembled her exactly. In Times to come, my sister and I would be confused in legend and in lore. Even now, as I am nearing the end of my life, this has begun.

Now, it so happened that my Mother Igraine was of the Old Dark Tribes; those here long before the Romans had invaded, or even before the Clansmen had arrived upon our shores. People of the Old Tribes are of smaller stature and much darker than either of the fair skinned or light eyed invaders of our lands. My Mother Igraine was, already in her fifteenth year, darkly mysterious and exotic: black hair, black eyes and lithe as the Faye – or so it is told – and was acclaimed as being exceedingly beautiful. And so, I suppose, were we.

When the Dux of Dumnonia first laid his eyes upon Igraine, he Loved her and would have her as his wife. He was a Briton of the Clans' and Roman blood who lived in the Roman style. His fortress lay upon a rocky promontory facing the Western Sea in the land of Dumnonia. Now, he honoured the ancient Goddess of the Old Tribes and their Spirits of Tree and Stone and Spring. But then, he also respected the Druids and the Gods of the Clansmen. However, being a military Commander allied with Rome, he himself worshipped and made sacrifice to the Eastern God Mithras, as well as the Sky Gods of the Greeks and Romans.

Beyond the deep Love Gorlois came to have for my Mother Igraine, she represented great political gain and riches for him. You see, she was the daughter of one of the wealthiest Chieftains and most respected blood lines of the old race, who were not – in spite of commonly held opinion – impoverished savages hiding and living in the secret Woods and Mountains of the wilderness, wearing flea-ridden and filthy Animal skins. No, far from that...

Had not the Clans travelled for centuries and thousands of leagues across many rich and intellectual lands in search of the mysterious Isles of the West? ...the Isles of the Hanging Stones and of gold... and of the people first descended from the Gods inhabiting the land which had once flourished beyond the Western edge of the known world? ...of that which was "the Island of advanced civilization, science and the known Cosmic Mysteries, the Island which sank beneath the Western Sea and whose people sent out one hundred boats in all directions to preserve their race of God-like ones, as well as their vast knowledge?"

Or, so the tale is told.

But, I did say that I would write of true history.

It is unfortunate that there is little written history of my race. However, when the Clans arrived upon our shores, they did find culture, gold, and Mysteries. And, although my Mother's people have chosen to live by themselves amoungst the Spirits of Tree, Stone, and Spring, they have maintained their wealth – wealth beyond counting.

So, when it came about that the Dux of Dumnonia had built his fortress, the unfortunate fact was that it lay on the edge, but within the lands of the Tribes. This he had not realised until he fell victim to numerous raids with arrows that flew with deadly accuracy through the Sky like silver Birds, from distances unbelievable. From these attacks he could find no defense.

Then, one Day, there arrived at the outer gate of his fortress a procession of men and women of the Old Dark Tribes. They were dressed in a splendor of gorgeous robes, short loin coverings, and head pieces – some of feathered crowns or Stag's heads with antlers. Others had Wolf's head helms and all had perfectly rendered golden bracelets, neck torques, and earrings. There was so much gold and golden amber – pieces as big as the fists of Gorlois – that he could only stare and shake his head in wonder at the sight. This was quizzical to him. They had been the aggressors; had shown their might and now came in all their dignity trusting that Gorlois, too, was a man of honour – and so he was. Gorlois opened his gates to welcome the peacemakers.

They had come, not in early morning as would have been the Clannish custom, but just as the late afternoon Mist was rolling in from the South. They appeared as quietly as Deer, stepping from the Tree line of the Misty Forest. The Sun was low enough in the Western Sky to light the Sea like a great Fire upon the Water.

In the years to come, Gorlois, whenever describing and retelling this story would always say, "So, the Sun didst cast His rays upon this peaceful embassy like the radiance of Apollo himself."

You see, the Tribes count their Days as beginning at sundown and ending with sundown – just as do the Clans – to honour the Great Mother, from the Dark Waters of whose womb all Creation has sprung. The Tribes hold that at sundown each Day, all things return to the Chaos of un-manifested potentials, to become again a great soup from which, at the next Dawning, a new Creation arises which BECOMES, – lives and breathes – until the next sundown, when all things UN-BECOME and return again to the Great Mother.

At the very front of the procession, Gorlois saw a man who seemed to him to be their Chieftain. At the man's right was a woman, perhaps twenty years older than he. This woman was the Tribal Grandmother. Then Gorlois turned his eyes to the man's left and there he saw Igraine. His breath left him. Her forehead and high cheekbones were painted with black dots. She was adorned with nine delicate five-pointed Stars tattooed just above the center of where her beautiful high breasts touched each other. Her fathomless black eyes were lined in powdered coal. A black Serpent was tattooed round one of her ankles and on the other was a band of gold with shells and bells hanging from it, which covered the top of her slender foot.

My Father, in his eloquent way, was later to tell this story many times: "I feared to cause offence... but try as I might, I could not keep my eyes from Igraine. Her beauty and grace rivaled that of Aphrodite."

Igraine spoke the language of the Cymru as well as the older tongue of the Tribes. So, when Gorlois had asked her name, she had spoken it. He found her voice to be as sweet as of the Birds of Rhiannon.

And thus began the parlay. It was explained to the Dux that he had built the outer walls of his fortress around a Sacred Well that had been worshipped at and used for Healing from Times unknown. "But war," they said, "was not for cultured men and women... not when a peaceful solution may be attained.

"The Sacred Well must not be imprisoned behind your walls and gates – it needs be open to all! How can we make this come about? What price would you name for us to come to agreement in this matter?"

Gorlois missed not a heartbeat, nor did his eyes stray from Igraine. He said, "No amount of gold or riches could be as fine as she – I would have Igraine as my wife and Lady of my fortress.... *If* she be willing."

This, they had not expected! A sharp intake of breath was heard and a murmur went through all present. The Chieftain then responded "This is not a matter that can be decided here nor now. All of our decisions – especially those of this measure of gravity – are made by council. We will return to you, Lord Gorlois, with our answer at the New Moon."

Now, Igraine was a Seer of her Tribe. She had been taught and initiated by the Tribal Grandmother, who, Gorlois would later learn, was revered and respected above all in honour and opinion.

After they had returned to their Forest home, what was lingeringly and torturously discussed over and over again amoungst them was whether their beloved Igraine could be given in sacrificial marriage to this Roman – Gorlois, called Dux of Dumnonia.

The things they struggled over were these: Could they let their precious daughter of the Tribe be held captive by this man? No, they could not – unless it be by her own will, for doing so would profane their long-held tradition, which deemed that a woman's body was hers alone to command. If Igraine refused, should they summon all of the Dark Tribes to war against Gorlois? This solution would be at the cost of much bloodshed and many lives! Or, if not, would they simply abandon the Sacred Well? They talked with Igraine to see what she would say, for after all, it *was* her decision to make.

Igraine was powerfully loyal to her people as well as to the Goddess, so she thought about it and prayed to her Mothers of Earth, Stars, Moon, Sun, and the Seas and to the Great Mother of all things everywhere – the One who dwelled always within her heart. She made sacrifice; she went on a fast of only Water and the juice of berries. She deprived herself of sleep for three Nights and three Days. She went out into the wilderness with little covering, for she had no fear of the Wolfs and other Animals that therein lived and they held no fear of her. After all, thought she, "Am I not one with them in Spirit?" She was accustomed to communing with them – not only in this world of form but also in the Otherworldly Realms of Trance. So, she gave herself over to Vision and sought their counsel.

Each one, in turn, reminded her of the Mysteries and of the rightful way of things:

Igraine's Vision
The Hind was first to approach her. She spoke...

"Listen well, Igraine: We mark the year's beginning at the dark Time, when all the World has gone to sleep or died; when the Trees have lost their leaves of red and gold and have turned to brown and grey and when the Grain and Herbs have withered into their slumber. We count that at that Time the Goddess Herself has gone to rest from all her glorious works upon the Earth. It is to honour Her that we end and begin our year in the Time of falling leaves.

"Humans cut down the Grains and their seeds are gathered, else they fall to Earth. Either way, the seeds must be shed...and thus ensure that all living things will thrive come the next Summer.

"Do you understand, Igraine? All worthy things require sacrifice. It is simply the way of things."

The Hare appeared...

"We, too, honour the Great Mother, at the beginning of whose darkness and slumber comes the season of rest and celebration – and of sharing our bounty of stowed food. For everyone, this is the season of staying within our sheltering homes, reflecting and planning for next year's endeavours.

"But as the cold of Winter falls, your men hunt us, to fill your cauldrons with our meat, to flavour the Grains, Fruits and Vegetables that were culled at the gathering. They tan the skins of Deer and Boar to make the boots that your people need. Your women use the wool from shearing the Sheep to Weave the cloth that will become your clothing. Even do the Wolfs and Bears sacrifice their furry hides for the warmth and covering of Humans.

"This is our way of life. We must sacrifice for the good of others. *We understand*! We are all One! Everything under the Stars has a cost, Igraine... For all things needed or wanted, a price must be paid..."

"Yes, yes. Hare is right!" exclaimed the Owl. We tooo must hunt to live."

Then Raven whispered...

"These are The Mysteries, Igraine. These knowings are our very life and breath.

"In the beginning, at the first moment, when the first spark was struck and the first vibration sounded, the Cosmos began. Then Creation sprang forth and rumbled with a great rumbling which continues to rumble until this very Day as all spreads out from the center, wherein lies the connection and the power of the ONE.

"All Rituals of life and every endeavour under the Sun are Sacred, Igraine. The Gods taught us how to do everything by their example at the Time of Creation – in the Land of Myth – which exists in the Eternal Present. As They do, so do we.

"For to us, you see, everything we do is an expression of Magic and Love for the Great Mother. When we eat, we are only imitating how the Gods ate in the Time of the Origin. When we work, we are doing the work that the Gods taught us to do. When we mate, and when Humans make Love, we are copying the great embrace of the God and Goddess at the First Time... the ecstasy of whose climax was then and is ever happening. For only by that coupling can the Cosmos remain alive. As I know you understand, Igraine, all things are connected. We must all honour the cycles of life in order for the life of all Creation to continue. We must fulfill the works and responsibilities that They have outlined for each of us so that we may each fulfill our destinies. For long generations before us and after we are gone from this realm, the Well has been and will be a part of the proper order of things.

"Every Time a Sacred work becomes un-Sacred, or a Sacred place is abandoned, the Magic of our world unravels just a bit more. Humans must keep the Sacred places of Spirit protected and venerated. This is imperative! The Spring – or Well of Nodens, as Humans call her – is such a place as this. She has been cherished for thousands of years. We of Animal kind have drunk the Sacred Spring's Waters, as has the land around her. The Human Tribes and countless generations of their Ancestors have come to Her for Healing and Magic. Yet now the Well lies beyond the reach of those who need and would honour Her –

imprisoned behind walls of Stone..."

Grandfather Oak stretched his boughs in the Wind and spoke thusly:

"Humans do not look forward to the next vibrational change on a Cosmic scale. Because when this happens, it will end all that exists. All of Creation will be drawn back to the Great Mother and will wait in Her womb for the next Creation to begin.

"My work is to go through the annual cycles of sprouting, leafing, colouring, and bearing acorns – then fading and lying barren, until She awakens all the Earth anew.

"Humans have a Great Work as well. Besides your everyday tasks, you must keep the cyclic Holy Days by feasting, performing the Rites and – along with the Gods – reenacting the Creation Myths, in honour of Them. As long, it is said, as we all continue to turn the great Wheel in this fashion, one cog at a Time, our world will go on and we will prosper."

"Sleep well, Igraine," said the Voices, "and rest now, child, from your Visions..."

Years later, when I was a child, my Mother Igraine told me that at that very moment – when the Voices had become silent – the Crystal that she was holding in her hand began to Hum. She also told that she felt the vibration of the Crystal go through her and connect her with all and everything, and that that was the first Time she had truly understood the meaning of "We are all One." So, she Chanted over and over again, the Chant of Enlightenment:

We are all One... We are all One... We are all One...
The Earth, the Stars, the Moon, the Sun...
We are all One... We are all One...
Of feather and fin, of scale and skin
Of fur and blood and bone...
Of Herb and bough, of Sky and cloud
And bogs and sand and Stone...
Of Lightning's blaze, of Thunder's rage
Of all things yet unknown...
We are all One... We are all One... We are all One...

At the end of her Time of Vision, Igraine returned to the Tribe to relate to them what had been told to her and what she held to be absolute truth.

She addressed all who had anxiously gathered around to hear her, saying: "The Sacred Well of Nodens must be tended!"

She told them that she must offer herself as wife to Gorlois, but that he would have to allow Sacrifices to be made to Nodens' Well, and to the monolith that stood within the Well's enclosure.

You see, it had been the custom of the Old Ones, from Time out of memory, to place a monolith within the Stones holding the bubbling Waters of the Springs, rising from beneath the Earth. These monoliths have long been held to be indwelled by the "God of the Well" – in this case Nodens – or by the Spirit of the Spring.

Igraine explained that by agreeing to Gorlois' offer, she would thereby become Guardian of the Well. But, Gorlois would have to vow upon his sword that never again would he hold prisoner the Well and the Stone. What is more, he must agree to leave open the gates of his courtyard, wherein was the Sacred Well, during the light of every Day from thence forward, so that people of the Tribes, as well as all others who wished to, could come for Healing, Blessing, or Divination. Lastly, he must agree that he would allow Igraine to perform the cyclic Rites and Festivals of the Tribes, upon their proper Times, within the outer courtyard of his fortress. If all of these conditions were met, then she would live with him in peace. And, according to his custom, she would vow to be faithful to him – giving her body to him alone – for as long as he lived.

Her decision was very hard for the Tribe to accept, for it was a departure from their Time-held ways. But, because Igraine had received these messages from the Spirits, the Tribe was compelled to honour her decision.

So came the appointed Time... It was the sunset leading into the Night of the New Moon, the first sliver of silver light as seen in the Night Sky after Her darkness – the Time of beginnings, of planting seeds and hailing the approach of the returning warmth.

Igraine – adorned in her Sacred painted symbols, clothing, and jewelry – walked out at the front of the peaceful procession with the Chieftain and Grandmother of her Tribe to approach the fortress of Gorlois.

They made to him their offer. Their beloved Igraine would give herself to Gorlois as his life's companion. With her, they would give gold and more gold, amber and pearls and much more of that which they knew the Romans held to be of great account, for their Tribe had almost unlimited resources. They would also pledge their peace upon his house, if he would agree to all the conditions laid out by the Spirits in Igraine's Vision.

Without hesitation, Gorlois agreed.

As I said before, Gorlois had Loved Igraine immediately. It was with a true and abiding Love that he welcomed her into his home and did never abuse his position with her. He honoured, revered, and accorded to her his respect, in the same manner as did the Tribes-folk and the Clansmen.

All of these things I know in the way of true history, not legend, for they were told to me, Morgan, by my Mother Igraine, who was there.

Part One
Foundations

Chapter 1
Igraine of the Tribes

Morgan

When Igraine had first come to live with Gorlois, his fortress Courtyard was terribly unkempt. The ground was muddy, rutted and pockmarked from the wheels of wagons and the hooves of Beasts. Along the interior walls were old stables, Goat and Sheep pens, and ramshackle huts filled with trestles covered in Barley, Oats, Vegetables, Apples and Mushrooms – some rotting – and were all attracting many Flies. Large, soggy, flea-ridden piles of hay and straw – which stank of mould, as well as slop buckets, which simply stank – were scattered here and there to feed the Animals, such as the Pigs and Dogs, who were left to walk about the courtyard freely. The Sows had made nests for their Piglets, which nests apparently were allowed to remain the whole year long. In the midst of all this filth stood Nodens' Well.

Gorlois, true to his word, immediately saw to correcting the sloth of his workers – cleaning up the courtyard and repairing the Well. He lifted the Well's monolith, which had fallen, and then returned it to its place within the Stones encircling the Spring. He cleaned out the hollow iron pipe that allowed the ever moving Waters of the Spring to run freely into a Stone-lined trench, to flow beneath the outer wall and toward the village. Then he helped Igraine to create a comfortable and pleasing garden setting around the Well. Nearby, Gorlois built shrines dedicated to the Cymric and Roman Gods and to the One who he worshiped, Mithras. In a distant corner of the courtyard, between a Thorn and an Apple Tree, my Father built a small, covered, Christian chapel. There, upon the Altar, he kept a bowl of Christian Holy Water – which was quite amusing to my Mother, because it had actually come from the Well of Nodens and had then been consecrated by sitting beneath the light the Full Moon for three Nights. He tied two pieces of Wood together in the form of a Christian cross and hung it upon the back wall. He thought this to be polite. "For, my dear Igraine" said he, "I promised to keep the Well open to *everyone*. Perhaps some Christian family will have need of respite also." My Mother later explained to me that my Father had put it there, away from the other shrines so as not to create discomfort for those who would not mix their God with the Old Gods. Thus did Gorlois open his gates to all who would come to worship and to Heal at Nodens' Well.

And so life went on, peacefully, honourably, and equitably between this Cymric-Roman and the people of the Dark Tribes.

After some Time had gone by, Gorlois could not be satisfied in his heart that he had done all that he could have to please Igraine, for never had she asked anything of him. One Day, early in their life together, he said to her, "Igraine, it is my wish that you would ask something of me – anything – just for your own pleasure. The pact that was made for our hand-fasting was an act of selflessness on your part. I know that you only agreed to stay with me to protect Nodens' Well. I hope that you will never regret your decision. Please allow me now to give to you your heart's greatest desire – even if that is to go back to your home and family."

Igraine's answer was this: "My home is here with you, Gorlois. Not only because I am honour-bound to tend the Well, but because... do you not know that I Love you?"

"Oh Igraine, will the Gods never cease adding to my good Fortune? I am a very wealthy man. I would send to the ends of the known world to acquire whatever gold can purchase for you, my little Bird. Please, just name it."

My Mother told me that she had not had to consider what was her deepest desire – for she already knew. She said, "I wish to become literate! To learn how to read and write, in Greek, Latin, and even the language of the Clans! I wish for you to find a Scholar who could teach me. This is my greatest desire!"

"I should have known. It will be done."

True to his word, as always, within a year my Father had employed a man from the Greek Isles, who arrived with a full coffer of clothing and personal goods, all appearing to be new – no doubt from my Father's largess. His name was Demetrius. And because of my Mother's exceptional intelligence, it took her only three years to accomplish all that she had wished to.

This had all happened before my birth, even before Morganna's.

Igraine
I did truly Love my husband. It mattered not at all to me the difference in our ages. He was a wise and passionate man. Never did I want for anything. Never did my eyes or heart wander toward another man. Gorlois was everything to me. Except, of course, for my Love of

the Goddess; my resolve to be Hers *first* never faded.

Then one Day I realised that I was with child. Both Gorlois and I would have another with whom to share our joy.

Now, it was the custom of the Romans, and a wise one indeed – for so many babies died in early infancy – to wait three full Moons' Dances from the time of their birth to choose a name for a child. You see, a child was not considered a complete *being* until its name had been given. This I understood. I am told that it is a thought of many peoples – that within it's naming is the power of a thing.

A great feast was planned in honour of the naming of our child.

Gorlois, as a Roman, would normally have the privilege of naming his first child. Although in practice, usually it was only the male children thusly honoured – as the Romans attributed less value to daughters than to sons. That, of course, was not the way of my people. But Gorlois, having had a Roman Father, was raised primarily in Roman fashion. His Mother, though, was of the Cymric Clans, who hold women in the same honour and esteem as their men. Regardless of Roman culture, Gorlois' Mother had ruled her house alongside her husband. It was my understanding that my husband's Father and Mother Loved each other well and had no problems coming to terms with these differing philosophies.

But, as completely kind and genuinely thoughtful as Gorlois was, this was *one* Roman custom upon which he would insist. Or, at the very least, he *hoped* that his loving wife would defer to him in this one thing. Of course, I did.

I knew in my heart that Gorlois was hoping for a son. I think all men do.

Still the Voices whispered in my ear, "Morgan, Morgan"... always, "Morgan."

But, son or daughter, everything must be made ready for the naming celebration.

So, on went the preparations for the Great Feast, which made everything aflutter in the entire household.

There were strange and exotic foods, which had to come from far across the Eastern Sea. Many great delicacies were to be served to our guests, such as wines from the vineyards of Gaul, Fruits called Oranges, Figs and Olives – all of which had been very difficult to obtain, especially given the short Time that was had from birth to naming.

The Hunters were all awaiting the perfect hours to hunt so that the wild Boar, venison, and great Fowl would be brought to the Fires in proper Time to be prepared and roasted for the feast.

Everything was in fine order; the long trestle tables were to be clothed in long cloths of woven wool. Silk cloths of great value had been purchased – or given to us as gifts – to drape across the trestle tables here and there as ornamentation and some to hang along the walls; for silk, rather than tapestries, had the delicacy of an infant.

All was done in honour of the babe. Gorlois spared no expense.

Many people were coming to the Feast, for my husband was a renowned and noble man, who was respected by all. There were so many for whom arrangements must be made – such as places for them to sleep comfortably. And then after the Great Feast, there would be those who would remain at the fortress for several Days and for whom enough food and drink must be laid in. It was all an amazing ordeal, but it was Gorlois' wish.

Coincidentally, a dear old friend of Gorlois named Aquila – which means "Eagle" in the Roman tongue – happened to have come to our land about three weeks before the naming of the baby and had already been in contact with Gorlois. When Aquila had learned what was to happen, he was ecstatically happy for this blessing in Gorlois' life.

Now, Aquila travelled with a man named Yagouth – whose name means "Bull" or "Brute Strength" – and was the name of an ancient God of his people. He was a man from the mysterious Desert lands of the East. Aquila and Yagouth posed in the guise of master and servant. But anyone with "the Sight" or even common sense who observed them looking into each other's eyes would see the great Love and desire that was between them. Those who knew them more intimately knew that they shared a bed. But they shared much more than desire and a bed – they shared a Love and devotion which comes perhaps once in a lifetime. And, it was a Love that I could "See" was as deep as Love could run – in this they were very blessed. So, when they arrived on the Day of the naming and I met them, I instantly had a very good feeling for both of these lovely men. They told me that they had brought a gift of great value across the Seas and Mountains from the distant lands of the East. I thought this was such a kind gesture on their part, although I had no idea what the gift could be – assuming perhaps it was something of gold or coin from Constantinople. I did not know – at that point, it did not matter.

Finally came the Day of the celebration. It was a beautiful, sunny Day and so it was decided that the opening festivities be held in the courtyard.

It was the custom for all of those who had a gift or a Blessing – a prophecy perhaps – to give it to the parents or Father or the child.

The line of gift givers was long. Aquila, when it came his turn to speak, approached Gorlois together with Yagouth. Aquila made a gesture to Yagouth who then retrieved a black leather bag that was tied on his belt. When he opened it, a hush fell over all gathered. I am sure everyone thought it to be gold, but when he emptied the contents of the bag into his hand, there was a silk cloth as delicate and beautiful as one might expect from the farthest Eastern lands. He then peeled back the four corners of the cloth to reveal the largest and most exquisite pearl anyone in attendance had ever seen! A Sea pearl – so lustrous was it that it picked up the light of the Sun and could be seen from across the courtyard. An intake of breath came from many people as Yagouth held it out to Gorlois.

"Please accept this token of our esteem for you, my friend, as our gift for your beautiful little daughter."

Gorlois exclaimed "It is a pearl!" At that moment, Yagouth said the word for pearl in his native tongue, which sounded very much like the name Morganna in my husband's native tongue of the Cymric Clans.

My husband said "Morganna... That then, will be her name!"

This was very quizzical to me, because I had wanted to name my daughter Morgan, although this was a name of the Clans. In fact, I had heard the whispers in my ears all through the Time of my carrying the child, and even before... "Morgan, Morgan"... You see – Morgan and Morganna mean the same thing to the Clansmen – 'the Swirling Sea'. And now, here was this, a pearl from a faraway land, a pearl from a swirling Sea.

Still, the Voices kept whispering in my ear... "Morgan, Morgan."

Six and a half years later, I was pregnant with our second child. Although he never said so, I knew in my heart Gorlois again wished for a son. But, our second baby, finally born at the end of my hard labors, was another girl. Gorlois came into my chamber and the worry and fear he had held on his face vanished and a great indulgent smile replaced it. He said, "How beautiful she is!"

I replied "They are all ugly little red things when they are born."

We laughed. But she had a full head of hair – black hair, dark as Night. She did have a pretty face for a newborn... *and* she came out looking exactly like Morganna, who her Father adored.

"My darling wife," said he, "you must take what is your right – to name our second child."

This had been my heart's intent, even if she *had* been a son. So I said "Morgan... I would name her Morgan.

"I know what you think, my dear husband – you think our daughters' names too similar. But you see, Morganna was named 'Pearl' in the tongue of Yagouth, whereas this little one will be named Morgan, which in your Mother's tongue means, 'Swirling Sea' – the place of the origins of all that exists.

"My people's Myths say that – 'Before the Great Goddess awoke into her conscious awareness, She was a Swirling Sea of Chaos, without form or order. Then a sound arose – the Great Vibration – and all things in the Heavens and upon Earth came into being.' My people's legends say that these Wisdoms travelled across the Western Sea with my

Ancestors, from the 'Island that sank beneath the waves'."

My husband smiled. He loved it so when I told him the Myths and legends of my people.

Thus my darling one came to be named Morgan and soon she grew in beauty to match Morganna's.

And so it was that Gorlois and I now had two beautiful daughters. We had wealth, comfort and between us, a loving and equitable arrangement. Gorlois was very good to me and I was kind and comforting to him. Within my heart, there continued to grow a great affection and Love for him. And in his heart, I was the passion of his life. Thus it was for the rest of his Days upon this Earth.

But, Gorlois was many, many years older than I. Betimes I wondered and worried what would happen to me and my daughters – and Nodens' Well – upon his Death. I would seek the Goddess' help and protection whenever that eventuality would come about. As for now, he still seemed young enough to me.

As the years went by, I taught both of my daughters the Arts of Healing and of Magic, because this was my right and my Sacred duty. But as she grew, Morganna became more and more of a trouble and a threat. There was a sinister way about her. I hated to think this of a child of my flesh, but it was truth! I had the *Gift* – and the *curse* – of the "Sight." I was able to "read" her thoughts – up to a point – at least when she was very young. Yet as she grew older, I no longer could. She was the only one I had ever encountered that I could not "read"! She frightened me. Oh, not that I was afraid for myself. Perhaps my fear was for everyone...

Morgan

It came about that when I was past my third year-turn, my Father became very ill and many people were in fear of what would happen to all those who depended upon him, should he die. His illness lingered and two years later, he still lay in his bed, withered. All the Magics and herbal remedies that my Mother knew how to use were keeping him alive... but not making him well. He was wasting. More slowly, albeit, because of her work, but not Healing. "Sometimes it is just a Time for someone to die" or so it is said. Death is, in itself, I believe, a blessing for that person – so that they may be refreshed in the sweet Fragrant Fields of the Netherworld and there cast off the failures – and successes – of this life. There, too, does their Spirit hold their attained Wisdom deep within – in order that they may re-form and bring that forth to this Earth to live again.

"For how else," my Mother bravely explained to me, "could we ever reach complete Spiritual Enlightenment?"

But my sister and I only knew, or cared, that our dear Father was lost to us already.

Igraine
The Politics...

I feel that it is important to write of certain events at the beginning of my history. For, during my first years with Gorlois and the hundred leading into them, much had happened in the way of political events on these, Our Fair Isles, as well as on the continent across the Eastern Sea. These things I came to know because Demetrius, the Scholar, taught me events of the world as well as to read and write.

The Romans had pulled out of Britannia – as the Romans called it – quite some years ago, but still there were some of The Caesar's Roman Elite Guard living amongst the Britons, as well as the many people who had chosen to convert their culture over to the Roman way – and their Gods to the Roman Gods. Many of these Roman-influenced Britons lived in great Roman-styled villas that they had built. Within these villas, amazing murals were painted on many of the walls, as they had been in the living areas of Gorlois' fortress. They had warm bath chambers. Tiles of painted clay of various colours – which had been fired in great ovens – were then set in pieces onto their floors to form beautifully elaborate scenes of their old Myths and Gods. They lived a life of grace and luxury. It was from a family such as this that Gorlois had come.

Rome – as powerful and advanced in government, law, road building, and military strategies as she was – had long ago fallen into decadence and moral decline. Demetrius told me that she was but a pale shadow of what was once the brilliance and beauty of the ancient Greeks. Why, even, had the Romans taken most of the Gods and Goddesses of the Greeks and called them their own – renaming them and 'demoting' many of the Goddesses – this, due to their expansion of "Father-ruled" society. However, between the beginning of the Britons' Romanization and now, Rome had turned her eyes Eastward to Constantinople, which had by my Time become the new Rome. It was the city of the Emperor Constantine, who had fought by the old "pagan" sign of a flaming cross.

It was during his reign that there was much Chaos and competition amoungst various religious groups and factions – those who honoured the Old Gods and the old Greek and Roman Rites, as well as thriving influences from the far-flung Roman Empire. And then there were the Christians – a rapidly spreading mass of diverse theological ideas and so many different sects! – each with their own collection of Holy Writings and one disagreeing with the other – even as to who or even what Yeshua was. A fine mess it was.

As a response to all of the infighting that that engendered, Constantine decided that there should be ONE Universal Religion for all

Romans to follow – a Christian one. It was finally mandated that it was illegal for anyone in the Roman world to worship other than as outlined by his universal 'Catholic' Church.

After centuries of Roman rule over Our Fair Isles, she was forced to abandon her dream of ruling the entire Western world. So, in the year of four-hundred ten – as Romans reckon it – Roman rule, Roman law, and Roman troops left the land of the Britons.

The Legends...

Legends abound of Martyrs, Mystics, Bishops, and Monks and of their great and Magical works. Some are even now developing. The oldest I have heard tell of on these, Our Fair Isles, is of a small group of men and women from Old Jerusalem, who had come to these Isles long ago; some call them early Yeshuites, but it is also said that they were really Jews, before anyone even thought of themselves as Yeshuites. It is also told that these men and women had come with a man named Yosef. It was so long ago now that the details have fallen into a haze. It is known that they established a House of Worship on the Isle of Apples within the Inland Sea, just beneath the Tor – not far from the Red and White Springs within the lands of the Order of the Goddess. The legends of these people tell that Father Yosef was a wealthy tin Merchant and a close relative of King Yeshua of Jerusalem. It is also said that they were good, kind, and charitable people, even so to the much more primitive Marsh Folk living near to their settlement. Some of their descendants remain, even until today. It is also told that Father Yosef planted the Thorn Tree, which still grows near to the Red Spring.

It is ironic that when the Romans all became adherents of the "Universal" religion, and The Caesar converted them from their old "Pagan" ways – some in name only, of course – they began to persecute these original followers of Yeshua and to try to change their customs. They called them heretics! But to go on with their legend...

Perhaps, it is closer to the truth to call them "Histories," for these were very literate people and much concerned with keeping accurate genealogies.

This same Yosef was said to have returned to Old Jerusalem and there to have rescued the two Miriams along with several other family members and good friends. On a ship they sailed to the Northwestern shore of the Great Sea, which is *called* Mare Nostrum, "Our Sea," by the Romans, where their descendants have remained and flourished until this Day.

By the Time of my writing these histories, there are not as many now in Briton who follow the "Universal" religion as there had been in my Grandmother's youth.

Yes, there are many legends of diverse Christian folk. But all this is another story, for someone else's book, and written by more informed hands.

Of Vortigern...

Amoungst the Cymru Chieftains who had achieved the highest stature by their wealth and power there came to be a leader, a Warrior, one who stood above the rest in ambition and who especially disdained The Caesar and the Pontifus Maximus.   He was a determined traditionalist, who would stop at nothing to restore Gwynedd – and all of the Clans – to their pre-Roman Clannish culture.   His name was Vortigern. He had fought a few battles against those who would fell his cause, for many Dux – of a staunchly Roman bent – would try to take over the lands and diminish the powers of the Clan structures. These skirmishes were fought from South of the White Chalk Giant, all the way up to the lands of the blue Painted Tribes, North of Emperor Hadrian's wall. But there he stopped. These Tribes are very old. They had been there already when the first Clans arrived on these Fair Isles. There was a Time when they wrote in fanciful symbols, which are still carved into large Standing Stones, dotted around their countryside – even on the wild Islands off the West and Northeast coasts of the mainland. Although, if they still understand these symbols, they are not telling anyone what they mean! These are the wild men and women of the Picti and are much feared. No, Vortigern would not go far into *their* lands, for they are the fiercest of all Warriors. So much were they so that even the Roman Legions and their "Britannian" troops – as they were called in the Days of Rome's full glory – had feared to face them.

However, Vortigern's vision had met with hard opposition amoung most of the Romanized Britons, for it had been three hundred years since the Romans had come with their military mastery, their excellent roads and luxurious lifestyles, and many of the Romanized Clansmen were determined to carry on Roman society, even though Rome herself had abandoned them.

It came about that when The Caesar heard news of Vortigern and what he was trying to do, he liked it not at all. The idea of Vortigern trying to place himself as a sort of 'King of the Britons' was very threatening to him, for he feared that, if left unchecked, this could lead to some powerful "Barbarian" army coming to the gates of Rome with a desire for blood! So, The Caesar, with the backing of the Pontiff, sent a great Warrior to fight against Vortigern. This was a man they called in the tongue of the Britons, "Garmon" and in the Latin, "Germanus." He was a cruel fighting man and a great Commander.   He was also the Bishop of Auxaire in Gaul.

Now, to explain... The "Universal Church" had – in the land of the Gauls – much more successfully established itself, with its Churches and

Bishops, than ever had it done on our shores.

Many of its Bishops were made, not by their devotion, but by purchase. Families with the most wealth, political influence or favours could buy the Bishopric and all the wealth and lands that went with the position for their sons. This had little to do with these prospective Bishops' Spiritual Enlightenment or their good works toward their God, the ill, or the needy – but all to do with their political station. In this very way had the Commander Germanus been appointed Bishop of Auxaire – Bishop by the Grace of Gold! We thought this shameful. However, the shame was not ours.

Caesar Theodosius, who was in Constantinople with the Pontifus Maximus, called a great convene. This convention resolved to send Germanus to lead an army to Our Fair Isles to accomplish the eradication of Vortigern and his lofty plans. Germanus was militarily backed by The Caesar's personal "Élite Guard," who had the distinction of fighting under the banner of the Royal Purple Dragon. Up until that Time, the traditionalists and the Romanized Britons had often fought side by side against their mutual antagonists – the Eire.

Enter the Saxons...

A Time came when Vortigern found himself short of trained Warriors, so he hired Saxon mercenaries from the Continent to augment his troops. This was originally for fighting off the raids of the Eire, who were plaguing the Western Clans. He gifted these Saxons with large plots of Earth on which to live in return for their services. So it was that the Saxons eventually set up a small Kingdom on our soil.

The Saxons were eager to be given this land, for Our Fair Isles are far more habitable and our soil richer for farming than much of theirs.

Those Saxons were a fierce and violent people who have their own Gods, to whom they are fervently devoted. These are mostly Gods of war and machinations; but also do they honour Goddesses: of the Stars, Earth, Moon, Fire, and Ice.

One reason for their fearlessness and ferocity on the fields of battle was due to their belief that, if they died whilst in battle or with sword in hand, they would immediately be swept away by Woden's Valkyries, "Choosers of the Slain," into the halls of their "Paradise" – albeit a much more "earthly" place than the Christian's Heaven.

Understand, these people were from a vast area of land stretching from South to North. Not all of them were actually Saxons. Although they all worshiped Odin – or Woden – they did, according to how far North or South did they originate, call this Paradise by different names. I am relating this because of the fact that although everyone on Our Fair Isles referred to them as Saxons, their two strongest leaders, the Commanders of their sizeable army, were actually from Jutland.

These leaders were the infamous Hengist and his brother Horsa.

As long as Vortigern paid his Saxons their mercenary stipend and allowed them their land and self-governance, they were quiet and kept to themselves. So they did live peacefully with us … at least at first.

These plans of The Caesar had all remained secret until Vortigern "heard it in the Winds." For it was said that he had a powerful Druid-Wizard as his advisor.

Understand, Vortigern had not the numbers of Warriors he would need to win this fight, for the Britons still loyal to Rome would stand against him. So, in all of his egotism, competitiveness, and visions of grandeur – and against the counsel of his Druid – he hired yet more Saxons to go up against the Roman army alongside his loyal Clansmen.

The hero of the ensuing Roman victory was a man called Uther the Pen Dragon... The name Uther means Terrible and Wonderful. So, his name meant "Terrible, Wonderful, Chief Dragon." Of course, he was not born with this title – it was given to him *after* this battle.

News came to Gorlois three years before his Death that Germanus and the Roman army were calling all their loyalists to arms against Vortigern. Of course by that Time, Gorlois was already ailing.

The tales that arose about this battle were fascinating! One was that Germanus had won against the "Pagan" Clans, by raising a great and deafening battle cry of "Hallelujah." With this Magical Incantation – or, by the power of the God's name alone – the battle was quickly over. But then, there were other strange tellings, too.

There was a man – a wise and good man – named Ambrosius Aurelius, who was the greatest of all the Romano-Britons' Dux. He was the Britons' Chief Battle Commander. It was he who led the command on the field, under Germanus. Yet it has always been said that the victory had gone to Uther, the Champion who had slain Vortigern. Many have wondered at the details of how this may have come about. The title of "Pen Dragon" was already, rightfully, Ambrosius'. He had not been felled in this battle and his honour and reputation continued to grow after that Time. How and why, then, had this well-earned title been transferred to his younger brother Uther? This is something that has aroused much speculation. All I know is that even as I write his name upon these pages I am sick with hatred of this Uther!

I must rest. I will continue my writings at a later Time.

Morgan

A note regarding perspective and interpreted observation...

There is something I must interject at this early part of my compiling of these Histories. It is about the way that different people *interpret* and therefore *remember* so very differently the same observed events, actions, words, inflections, innuendos, motives, Time, place, *who* said what, or even who was present at any particular happening. Much of it has to do with the passage of Time, failing — though well meant — memory, or simply personal agendas. Perhaps it is simply that people are so different one from another. This has ever been quizzical to me. Yet, I dare say that I, too, fall prey to these very things myself. This is why I have asked everyone to write down their histories as soon as possible after their happening.

But to continue...

The Celebration of Treaties...

It was more than three years from the Time of the Hallelujah battle, when the Romans and Britons who had fought in that battle finally agreed upon mutual terms of settlement — and chose a fortress at which to have their Victory celebration and to make their peace treaties.

It was decided that the feast would be held at the fortress of the Dux of Dumnonia — my Father.

This was a glorious honour! Dux Gorlois had been a great and respected Commander, and even though he must now be carried from bed to chair, his Wisdom was still honoured and respected. It seemed a good compromise as well, due to his obvious sympathies toward *all* of the Britons. And, he was one of the wealthiest of them. This feast would cost a fortune in gold! And gold my Father had aplenty.

Many men were seeking to marry one of Gorlois' daughters, so that in due Time they may gain land and power — for that was the Roman way.

Now, the daughters of the Tribes and the Clans are in no way considered inferior to their men. They were not then; they are not now. In matters of law, inheritance, wealth, or the bonds and rights of marriage, women have their say — and their *way* in all things — as much as do the men. This is an equitable and peaceful way of living. However, it was and still is not so amoung the Romans — nor those who would follow their social rules. These men had embraced the Idea that their Sky Gods were the rulers of the Heavens, with Goddesses having been relegated to inferior positions. This, of course, went right along with their male-dominant society... women are considered by them possessions. They are *owned* by their Fathers — and *owned* by the men they have married — or been given to in marriage. Should they be the sole heir of their Father's dominion, the man who marries them becomes the owner of it *all*. The wives have nothing to themselves. Their *sons*, not their daughters, inherit at the Father's Death. These women have no means of support, other than by whatever good graces their husbands — or sons — will lend them.

Therefore it was no surprise that rumour spread like a Fire in the Wood that Gorlois had two of the most beautiful daughters in all of these, Our Fair Isles. And that his wife, Igraine, who was also very beautiful, would soon be up for the taking as well, because, when Gorlois died, she would be fair game in the thinking of these men.

I must say that this attitude is *only* amoung the truly Romanized men of the Britons, for it has ever been the way of the Clans and the Tribes to honour the Great Goddess... and any man who honours the Goddess, must also honour women, for we are the fleshly representation of the Goddess on Earth. These men remember their Mothers' teachings. Women of the Clans and of the old Dark Tribes are well treated. In this we are alike.

The Honours...

When it came the Night of the great Feast of Treaties, no expense was spared.

Great tables had been spread with gold and silver plates and tankards. The hall was lit with many torches, which had been fragranced with Herbs. Beautifully woven cloths and tapestries graced the tables and the walls.

Igraine came out to greet and welcome all at the Well of Nodens, which lay in the path of entrance to the fortress. She was arrayed in all of her exotic Tribal finery. For, on this Night she would stand as a free woman in her own right, before these men who might have it in their thoughts to capture her one Day.

As the banquet began, each guest was seated in their respective places, according to rank.

Then, when all others were seated, Gorlois, as grandly as he had the strength to do, ever so lovingly introduced Igraine to this assembled company.

"Hail and welcome, my beloved wife, Igraine of the Tribes, you of the greatest beauty, you of Wisdom beyond all I know, Sacred Priestess and Seer of the Great Goddess, Guardian of the Well and *owner* of all that is mine."

There was a rush of whispering across the great hall and then silence, for in this declaration, Gorlois had named her heir in her own right of his fortress, lands, titles, and his responsibilities toward the village folk who depended upon the Dux of Dumnonia.

It was unheard of that this be said by a Roman. But, Gorlois was not only that, but a Clansman, too...

The silence was profound... but then, beginning with one voice, that of Ambrosius Aurillious, a cheer arose and spread across the whole assembly.

When the cheering subsided, Igraine settled into the chair of honour on Gorlois' right side.

The crowd settled, too, as each man became acutely aware of

Igraine's great beauty and poise.

Gorlois continued his say... "Igraine of the beautiful eyes which are like black mirrors, into which anyone who looks may see eternity... Igraine... you whose eyes peer into Otherworlds – and can see into the hearts and intentions of all who look back into them – bring forth your noble kin so that they may be welcomed by my comrades in arms."

Igraine, at Gorlois' request, had invited some of the most noble men and women of the Old Dark Tribes, so that these Romans could see how it was with her blood – that they were of high culture.

They entered in elegant, graceful form, and did cause another stir amoung the feasters. This Time however, it was with appreciative applause.

When it came about that all the military men had become well drunk with mead, wine, and beer – and bellies were stuffed from feasting upon well oiled and fatty beasts, oysters and Dolphins from the sea, Apples, Grains and other such savories, Gorlois – always the gracious host – said:

"Uther, the Pen Dragon, let us honour you with a toast!"

Lot of Lothian stood, albeit waveringly. He raised his voice and proclaimed, "Uther, The Pen Dragon!

"...Let us all raise our tankards to the champion of the Hallelujah battle. You, who rid us of the tyrannical Vortigern! Vortigern... He who turned brother against brother, son against Father, and cousin against cousin."

His voice trailed off. For, what could be said about this great loss, which still smarted the hearts of those present.

Silence. But then another cheer arose.

"Uther! Uther! Speak! Tell us the story of how it was upon that Day when you bested Vortigern and ended the war." Tankards and fists began to beat upon the tables in rhythm. It ceased not until Uther stood.

"Oh, my brothers in arms, I will tell you how it was upon that fateful Day. He began to bellow in his thunderous voice, so that all did hear his words.

"Army like the dashing Sea, with its clashing surge...
Horses curveting anxiously with frantic wild-eyed urge...

Until the Earth did shudder with their mighty tramp...
All loathsome gore... I could not see... using bodies as a ramp...

I smote him with my sword 'til I severed trunk from head...
The Saxons turned their tails and fled the field in dread...

His head did tumble down... rolled 'cross the putrid ooze...

His eyes and lips in question froze 'How ever could I lose?'...

Oh, hideous sight my eyes beheld... still he sat upon his mount...
From whence his head once did sit, blood gushed up as a fount...

Of a sudden the stage fell silent... save the Ravens as they wheeled...
A horrid waste of kith and kin lie slaughtered upon the field...

So Warriors late of brazen boast hath ye won or hath ye lost?
All dear remembered fondnesses... oh, wretched, wretched cost...

Thee hailest me thy Champion, oh thou greedy Gods of war...
Whilst Pale Ones haunt our hearth Fires... pray thee honour me no
more..."

The mood waxed heavily sad. After a respectful pause and trying yet
again to keep the celebration "celebratory," Gorlois – always the
diplomat – turned attention toward Igraine once more.

"My dear beloved, to allow my friends – these great Warriors and
Chieftains – to experience some of the ways of the Tribes, would you
mind, my dearest Dove, singing for them and perhaps have your ladies
Hum and dance for them? For your voice is as beautiful as the song of
any Bird and the grace of your people is stunning."

She answered, "My dearest husband who has been so kind to me and
whom I Love exceedingly, I will do this for your excellent company, as
it is your wish. And I, as well, would be pleased to entertain those
gathered here."

Once again all eyes were upon Igraine.

A strange instrument sounded from within the midst of her people
and then quiet but steady drumming began and a drone of Humming
voices came in softly beneath Igraine's voice. She opened her mouth
and with the most beautiful and beatific expression on her face, sang a
song of loveliness – her voice stretching to the heights of the Stars above
and plunging into the souls and hearts of all who were listening. When
she gazed at them, each one was captivated by her Enchantment. But
within the beauty, her hidden Magic was thus; "Do not dare to try to take
from me what is mine..." but in the blessing of her song, the words
continued: "do be Healed and prosperous... and I bid you peace and the
fulfillment of the desire of all of your hearts."

This is where my Mother had made her fateful mistake. No matter
how well trained – how adept – be anyone in the Arts of Magic, mistakes
can be made. One who practices the "Arts" must very carefully consider
the words they speak or even the thoughts they think when in that state of
Magical consciousness. Of this, my Mother made very sure to warn to

me later. For, you see – when she granted the desires of the hearts of all present, a chill ran through her to pierce to her very bone. For there was one especially honoured at that feast – the one now named Uther the Pen Dragon, the fervent desire of whose wicked heart – from the moment he first saw her – was to lie with Igraine. He cared nothing for anything else; not for peace, not for wealth, not for Gorlois' fortress or lands, nor his own honour or his family's good name. As consumed by lust as are Ravens feasting upon corpses after a battle was he – eaten to the marrow with desire to lie with her and to have her as his own. There would be no turning back for Uther!

Therein began the great trouble.

Gorlois looked up when Igraine had stopped singing in the middle of her blessing song. She looked stricken. She realised the mistake she had made, but it was too late. The words had been spoken; the words of power, the words of Magic, the Words of Making. There was no taking them back! She said, "Oh!" and an expression of fear crossed her face. Now, Gorlois had never seen fear on the face of his wife, so he looked in the direction of her staring and saw that the focus of her distress was Uther. Gorlois tried to stand so that the true extent of his fading and failing heart might not be known – so as not to let his weakness show – for there could be danger in that... and so that he would not embarrass himself. He held to the arms of his chair and his servants helped him as he stood.

He said, "My dearest, what is the matter?"

Igraine was taken aback, as she knew not what to say, but she pointed her Magical finger from which a line and a ray of her power hit Uther in the heart, knocking him back down onto the floor – chair and all. For Igraine knew that Uther had risen in his lust; and for this Igraine despised him. She said, "*That* man would do me ill, dishonour you, and cause great calamity."

Gorlois was very angry for he knew that what was spoken through the words of his wife was always absolute truth. There was a great rush and a great rumble around the hall. Arguing broke out, for Uther had been their battle's hero, but others knew Igraine spoke the truth, and all knew of Gorlois' sense of honour. But they really did not yet know the *honour* of Uther. Opinion was split, but eventually most of the younger Dux' and Roman Warriors sided with Uther. They said that it was only the *word of a woman* that was being accepted by this besotted old man, honourable as he may be. Then, most of those got up and left. As Uther and his young friends were storming in anger from the fortress, Uther loudly proclaimed, "I *will* have Igraine! And now, I will destroy you, Gorlois, for this disgrace you have caused upon me in my hour of Honours."

They rode from the outer courtyard in great haste; hooves thundering across the bridge, throwing up Stones and turf along their way.

Almost speechless with shame, Uther's brother Ambrosius Aurillious, with moist eyes, said, "My Lord Gorlois, please hold this not against me or my Ancestors, for as I live, I do not approve of my brother's intent or actions. And to you, kind Lady Igraine, great Seer, I hope that you will 'See' a good end to this, for I am grievously sorry."

"My good Sir Ambrosius Aurillious, I 'See' that when your Time comes, you will go to your Ancestors with all honour, for you have lived a life worthy and true."

Of course, again, all of this has been related to me by my Mother and others who were there to remember these events. For all I, Morgan, can remember of these things were my Mother's haunted eyes on that morrow.

There is one other thing, though. I found this page tucked within some other correspondence of my Mother's. Perhaps it had been forgotten with Time.

These were Igraine's own words:

Late in the Night, when the raucousness and confusion had died down and all was at some sort of peace, Aquila, along with his companion Yagouth, who had come all the way from Gaul to attend this high event and express their respect for Gorlois – asked to speak with him. And so Aquila and Yagouth were allowed into Gorlois' bedchamber and I went with them.

Aquila said, "My dear and old friend Gorlois, we have talked together, Yagouth and I, and have come to the agreement that we cannot leave you here under the threat of siege. We are not Warriors, but we simply cannot leave. Our hearts will not allow us to abandon you in this Time of danger! We must lend our support and aid to you in any way that we may."

But Gorlois said, "My dear and very old friends, you are not Warriors. Aquila, you are a Philosopher and Yagouth you are a Holy Man – and both of you are Merchants, not Warriors. You only bear your personal daggers to protect yourselves. What good would you be in battle against well-armed and battle-seasoned Warriors? I do not mean to offend you in any way, but simply – look around you. There is a large Roman guard whose charge here is to defend me and my fortress and they are all well trained. Their commission from the Gods and their superiors is to fight, to slaughter, and to be slaughtered – to stand in bravery. I am well protected. Besides, my lovely Igraine and the Goddess she serves, as well as the Spirits of the Well, will protect Igraine and our daughters. But, you, on the other hand... I fear for your lives if you stay. I would not have that grief and that burden upon me while I am so ill. Please take your leave of me and go in your Gods' peace. Go with my gratitude, my friendship."

So it was that Aquila and Yagouth, two Days later, having taken their leave of us the Night before, packed up their belongings and were about to leave our fortress. It was very early in the morning, but I ran out into the courtyard with only a blanket wrapped around me and said, "Please wait! Would you not allow me to share with you the blessing of Nodens' Well, and allow the Spirits who dwell therein to hear your wishes? – for I hoped that you would experience and take of the Waters. Even, I humbly ask that you allow me to say my words of power so that you may have safe journeys – and a long, happy and prosperous life together. For you are good men of your words and our gates are left open to all who would come with open hearts to receive the blessings of the Well."

They looked at each other, smiled broadly and said, "We would be so honoured, Lady Igraine."

Yagouth did this in a position of his hands being placed palms together in front of his heart and bowing forward toward me. I assumed that it was a custom of his people and was greatly pleased by this.

So we walked together to the Well and the shrine and I did as I had done hundreds of Times here since my marriage to Gorlois – I performed the Words of Power. I Chanted and sang for them.

These men already had many blessings in their lives. But they drank the Water of Nodens' Well and I could feel the Spirits of the Ancestors, the Gods, and the Great Goddess around us. I believe that Yagouth felt them too. I cupped my hands and poured Water over each of their heads and Chanted the Words of the Making and then I asked them to turn their hands palm up – for this is the feminine side, the receiving side – and I poured some Water from my hands into theirs and Chanted another blessing for them.

We bade each other a final farewell and they rode away. But, as I watched their leaving I had an easy heart because I knew that all things that had been asked of the Spirits that Day would manifest and these two beautiful men would live long, happily and prosperously with each other.

I wish that all things could go that way for people, but of course, that is only I as a woman speaking. For I do know well that we learn from the wicked and the evil things that others do – and that we ourselves do. We learn from these things and if we be smart – if we be wise – we allow our own mistakes as well as those of others to bring us closer to Spiritual Enlightenment. So, the good and the bad must fall upon everyone at some Time, but I knew that these men would have much more good than bad.

It was cold outside in the courtyard that morning though I was warm in my heart. But my thoughts went back to my own situation here and a shiver of doom went through me and a great sadness began to overtake me.

I went back to my husband's chamber. He was sleeping on his great and beautiful bed. And though we had each our own chambers, usually I curled up to him at Night under his great wool and skin blankets. That morning, I snuggled up to him and found some peace, but from then on I awaited what foul and wicked circumstance was about to befall my household.

Chapter 2
Gwyddion, The Merlin

Morgan

Now there was in Gwynedd a very renowned Magician and Druid. He was the one whom the Clans called "The Merlin," which means the *Hawk*. This title signified their recognition of him as having attained the greatest knowledge, power and prestige of all the Druids. His name was Gwyddion.

Only in some – not all – generations did the Druids now give this distinction to one of their own. Although there had been a Time, before the Romans outlawed the Druids – for fear of sedition – and killed most of their generation, that there had *always* been a Merlin in Briton. However, the Days of the Druids' glory had been crushed. Now that Rome had quit their rule over "Britannia," the Druids were rebuilding their numbers and their Universities. So, to be named "The Merlin" was quite an exceptional honour.

To speak truth as it was, this title had been bestowed upon him not only because of his celebrated triumphs in association with Ambrosius and Uther, but – and mainly so – because of his work as Architect, Seer, Counselor, and Magician to Vortigern and because of the splendorous fortress he had designed and built in the Snowy Mountains of Gwynedd for him. Nothing made by the hands of man – save the ancient Hanging Stones and Henges which, it is told, were built by the God-men of lore – could compare with it; not even did the wonders of the Roman Builders upon our land compare. His fame had grown and spread throughout these, Our Fair Isles. His brilliance, inventions and discoveries went far beyond the ken of his contemporaries!

Gwyddion's unusual education had not been gained in the formal setting of a Druidical University, but rather solely Master to apprentice. Indeed, his Master, Brennos, had come through a long noble lineage of Druidic Masters. Brennos had apprenticed with Ea Kunagos, who had been apprenticed to Calleach-oidhche, who were of the line of the last acknowledged "Merlin" of Briton, Bran y Doeth. Now, each of these Druids – having been trained underground, both figuratively and literally – had needs been trained so due to Roman persecution.

After Brennos had accomplished twenty years of pure Druidical education, he had vowed to himself never to stop gaining knowledge. His interests had turned to the great Greek Scholars and Philosophers and toward whatever other books of the Sages he could acquire. Even by word of mouth did he seek Wisdom – including that of the old Dark Tribes and of the Order of the Goddess on the Isle of Apples. The gaining of knowledge Brennos had continued until his eyesight failed him and he became too feeble of body to travel.

So, while Gwyddion trained with Brennos, he had been exposed to many diverse Sciences, customs, forms of worship, and profound otherworldly activities – at all of which he proved to be an amazingly adept student! Although Gwyddion's acquiring of this vast and varied knowledge, which was known to not be *purely Druidical* – and despite his very young age – the great Council of Briton's Druids had unanimously named him "The Merlin." And so it was...

Truthfully, the sum of his diverse education and experiences set his path somewhere between the traditions of the Great Goddess of the Tribes and the practices of the Gods, Goddesses, Magic, Mysteries and lore of the Druids. Perhaps because of this, Gwyddion was respected by all. We were not, after all, *so* very different.

Much more surprisingly, he was, as well, revered by the Roman Britons – many of who had, at one Time at least, theoretically been devout Christians. His Wisdom was unchallenged.

At the Time of Gwyddion's having first been considered as a candidate for the esteemed position of The Merlin by the High Council of Druids, he was still in the service of Vortigern. But there had been storms brewing in Vortigern's camp and increasing tensions between him and Gwyddion.

At the Time of the staging of the "Hallelujah" battle, Gwyddion abandoned Vortigern and allied himself with Ambrosius and Uther. This was just past his nineteenth year-turn. He was still very young at the Time of the "Honours" of Uther, being then only twenty-two. He had by then served Uther and Ambrosius for three full years. But, The Merlin had little taste for accolades of slaughter and so had begged off the victors' feast. He had gone instead to see his old teacher Brennos, in Gwynedd.

After the Feast of Treaties...

It came about that after Uther's riotous, angry threats at the Feast of Treaties, he dispatched a messenger to The Merlin.

Uther wrote: "Meet me on the Full Moon in Pisces... at a certain place in Gwynedd, near to Brennos' Cave. I am in urgent need of your help."

He told Gwyddion the truth of all that had happened, for Uther knew there was no fooling The Merlin.

You see, at Times, Gwyddion had the opaque silver grey eyes of an old man, who should not be able to see, but this was all *illusion*. He was not an old man and he had eyes like pools of deep water, like silver spirals were they. He could look into the eyes of anyone and See what was truth and what was lie – or so did Uther believe. There was no point in Uther's trying to hide from him exactly what he had done or what he desired.

So he said to him, "Gwyddion, you are known as The Merlin of these Isles and respected above all other Magicians. I want – no, I *need* – for you to create a great Magic for me, for there is someone I desire more than anything... even more than I desire to become the next High King. I desire Igraine. I lust for her Night and Day. I must have her!"

The Merlin responded, "What is this – to become *King*?"

"It has been decided in secret council that since the Romans have gone from us and seem never to return, we must indeed have a High King to maintain order within our lands, so that we and the Clans may protect ourselves – as a unified force – from the Eire and Saxon invaders. We want a High King! There must also be a council... of course. And in these secret talks we have spoken of *my* becoming that King. But even as much as I want to be High King – far beyond my wanting that, I want Igraine."

"Just exactly *who* is *us*?" asked The Merlin " and – forgive me, but, why *you* and not *Ambrosius*?"

"Ambrosius is too soft of heart. He grows old... slower on the field. And..."

Uther's voice trailed off lacking a good answer.

"Old? By only nine years beyond your own age, Uther! How dare you try to usurp him? And how dare you ask me to do your bidding to satisfy your lust!?"

Just as Gwyddion had spoken these words, a Bear crossed the path in front of him. It stopped. It looked straight into his eyes... and the Owl, Chronos, who The Merlin carried on his shoulder as companion, blinked and hooted. The Bear did not try to do harm – and in the shimmer of a Star, was gone. But, Uther had seen nothing.

Now, when Gwyddion told Uther what had just happened, he was speaking in the tongue of the Clans, which was of a less formal nature than that of the Roman. Uther repeated the word for "Bear" – in Latin – which sounded much like "Arthur." At the hearing of this name, The Gwyddion felt a chill run up and down his spine. It broke through his head and out of his toes and down into the Earth! Then his legs grew long and gnarled and down went they... down and down into the soil and Rocks did they grow and entwine with all that lurks within the Earth, like the roots of a mighty Tree – for Gwyddion was *becoming* a Tree. Then his arms raised and his fingers grew and extended. Up went they, up and up beyond the Moon and into the milky band of Stars.

When Gwyddion, The Merlin was thusly Entranced, the "Voices of the Stars" whispered in his ear, "Gwyddion... Gwyddion..." in a shimmering of sound, the untold many spoke as one.

"Gwyddion, you must listen to what Uther is saying, for he *will* be King and it is true that the other Britons want this. It is also true that waves of invaders from the Northern and Teutonic Tribes will try to overtake and forever change the ways of *all* the peoples of these Isles. Uther is a coarse man, but he *is* a man of his word.

"Gwyddion, we must make you understand that there are great Magics afoot here that go beyond the ken of men. You must listen and obey. In return, we will give to you the greatest of all Gifts – *the knowings* of the Cosmic Mysteries – as well as a lifetime of great purpose.

"It is true; the land needs a High King. Uther has the blood. His Mother was Elen of the ancient lines of the Kings of the Britons – pure of blood back to the beginning. Uther's – and your – Father was known to the world as Flavius Claudius Constantinus – named Emperor Constantine the third; the second of Briton.

"Igraine is a great Seer, beloved of the Goddess – and *would be* counted as royalty of the Old Tribes, if they held such notions. Together they will make a King who will unite, in blood and mutual respect, *all* the peoples of these Fair Isles – such a King as will never be forgotten: Arthur – the Bear – and you will be his mentor and counselor! You are the *one*, Gwyddion, to bring this all about! You must agree to quench Uther's lust for Igraine with his oath that what issues from that Night's doing is yours! Also, he must then leave Igraine as a woman who owns herself *as well as* the fortress, the Sacred Well, the shrine, the wealth, and lands and is responsible for the folk who therein reside.

"Mesmerize him, Gwyddion! Look deeply into his eyes with your silver spirals – use your 'Grym Hudol' – your Magical Powers – and he will agree! Once you have his oath, you must leave – on this very Night – and rush to Igraine.

"When you explain to Igraine what is at stake, she will agree. For, without these great Magics, Uther – left to his own devices – would storm Gorlois' fortress, kill him, and rape Igraine. She would feel bound to take her own life for being forced to submit to him against her own will. But you must remind her that she is sworn to be Guardian of Nodens' Well and has two young daughters, all of which would be in great peril were she dead! She must be persuaded to agree to bed Uther under her own terms. This she will do. You must see that this all comes about."

When the Starry Voices released The Merlin, he came back into himself, with Uther staring at him. He looked around. It was full dark whereas it had been Dusk at what seemed a moment before. Slowly recognition returned to him. They were standing in a Wooded Glen near an oval Ritual Hill, where had been in the distant past a monolith placed at its Northern edge. He noted seven Stones standing in a circle, with seven Oaks trained to grow over the Stones. Gwyddion remembered then, that they were standing in the great Valley of Gwynedd, just a few leagues from the Snowy Mountains where Brennos lived in his Cave.

As Gwyddion stood there in that Glen, another great tingling came through his body. He shivered as he heard the echoes of a Well bubbling up in great bubbles, "gu-glug, gu-glug, gu- glug" – his blood ran cold.

"By the power of three!" said he.

But, was this dread or anticipation? He knew that this was not business for this Time, but for a Time and a Time and yet another Time to come.

So, Gwyddion, The Merlin, looked deeply into Uther's eyes and outlined the terms of his bargain exactly as the "Voices" had instructed him to do. Uther agreed and gave his word of honour not to break the pledge.

Then Gwyddion told him, "Meet me on the next Full Moon, at Gorlois' fortress in Dumnonia, where your desires will be fulfilled."

"But why so long? My heart will burst with the waiting."

"We will do this my way – or not at all!"

"Not at all? I will take her with or without your help, Gwyddion! You are my Councilor, not my master to tell me what I will or will not do!"

"Indeed. Why then do you seek my help?"

Uther had no better answer to this query than the plain truth.

"I wanted her to Love me. I thought that you could use your Magics to make her Love me."

"Uther, do you not know that real Love has a life of its own? I have not the power to make her Love you and if I did, I would not do it – for things such as this lie far beyond the boundaries of my ethics and honour."

"So be it, then. But still – I will take her!"

"Uther, my brother, have you ever feared me?"

"No, I have never felt the need."

"And I have never thought you a fool. But cross me in this and you will have committed your life's greatest folly! Then we both will have been proven wrong."

Incredulous, Uther stared at Gwyddion.

"Have you just threatened me?"

Uther had spoken these words in anger. But then, feeling defeated, he relented;

"I would indeed be a fool to cross you, for many reasons; not the least of which would be to lose your friendship. I will do as you have said and meet you on the next Full Moon. Gwyddion, I pray you, let us never be torn apart, over this or anything."

But by Gwyddion's reckoning it was all too late for that.

Gwyddion knew that the events before him were momentous. He also knew that the travel he was about to undertake would be terrifically taxing. So, remembering what Brennos had taught him, he first cleansed himself in the water of the bubbling well. Then he began.

Gwyddion ran all the way to Dumnonia. He did not own a mount of his own for he had always walked everywhere he went. This peculiarity was just one more elusive thing to add to his mystique. And in his unfailing practicality – which might seem in direct contrast to his peculiarities – he knew that Uther would do nothing, such as giving him a Horse, to aid him in reaching Igraine. So he ran.

Even though he was twenty-two years and in the fullness of his physical strength, it took all of twenty-five Days and Nights to reach her, for the way was ragged and heavily Wooded.

Years later, he shared with me, Morgan, all that had been going through his thoughts whilst he ran and ran. He said that it was as though his whole life had re-played itself in his thoughts, over and over... and that the memories were bittersweet.   These were the things he remembered, the events of which he wrote.

Gwyddion, The Merlin
On The Way to Igraine...

In my youth, I had been called Gwyddion, the Bastard. Oh, not by the Clan folk of Gwynedd, my homeland, who placed no stigma upon that condition, but by the Roman household in which I had spent my early childhood – my Grandfather's house. My Mother, Alexandra, whom I Loved so, lived under his protection, as did I.

My Mother was of noble birth. As I heard the story, she had Loved a Warrior of high distinction. He Loved her, as well, so they had planned to marry in the Roman fashion. But he was sent somewhere far away for battle and never returned to her. She did not hear from him again. He never knew that he had left her with child. No one knew who he was, not even his name, for she would not tell it.

Because of the details of my birth, I, Gwyddion the Bastard, was given none of the training that the other boys living in my Grandfather's house were given. This, in itself, did not matter much to me for I cared little for the Arts of War. However, for the lack of any meaningful endeavour, I was exceedingly bored with my existence. After my regular chores, there was nothing for me to do but to talk with my Mother and watch her Weave or tend her Herb and Flower garden. That part of those Days was my only joy, for I did Love my Mother well. However, by the Time I turned my eighth year, my Mother's ladies, as well as the other boys in our household, chided me that I was like a "baby clinging to my Mother's bosom." This saddened and embarrassed me, so after their cruel words, every Day I would go into the Woods alone and talk with the Animals, Birds, and Trees.

One Day, I wandered farther afield than was usual and came upon a Cave. Someone lived there. I slowly crept to the opening and called out, "Anybody here?"

A deep and old-sounding voice said, "Come in, my boy, I have been waiting for you."

The old man was nearly blind, but he got on well enough. "Finally," thought I – "an adventure!"

We talked for hours, of Herbs and Crystals, Rocks and Wells... and of how all these and everything else in the world around us have a life force of their own. We also spoke of lands across the Seas, far, far away – with very different Gods from ours. I drank in his every word. To my great amazement, when I looked through the Cave's opening, wondering if it would soon be Time to return home, the Sun had all but fallen beneath the Earth's edge.

I said, "I have to go!"

"Well then, you will have to come back," quoth he.

And come back I did, most every Day, for the next six years. That was the beginning of the Magic... and the path from which I would never stray.

Well, Brennos – for that was his name – not only taught to me the Arts Magical, but we spoke much of construction, Engineering, Architecture, Mathematics, and Astronomy. He told of the great Stone edifices in the East. We talked of Mysteries and wonders unthought-of on these Isles, at least by me. He taught me to read and write in the Greek tongue, which was still the language of the intellectual – as well as in the tongue of the Clans.

As the next six years flew by, I learned what seemed a lifetime's worth of knowledge from him. None of this was ever known to my Mother or Grandfather. They thought me a wild and weird child. But regardless of what my Mother's opinion of my weirdness was, what little of life we shared was spent in the richness of companionable Love.

One Day, while walking through the Wood at the foot of the Mountain, near to where Brennos' Cave and my Grandfather's villa were, three men with a large sack came and overtook me. I struggled to get away from them, but they were too strong – too determined. They captured me, threw me in the sack, and took me away! To what place, I did not know! As you can imagine, I was very fearful. I forgot all the Words of Power Brennos had taught me to use in just such a situation; I forgot everything for fear of my life.

"I was still but a boy," thought I as excuse. Although it was true that at my age of fourteen years, some were counted as men – some fought in battles!

"I must get control of my emotions so that I may be cunning in the face of my adversity" I told myself.

I had been captured for reasons unknown to me and taken toward the top of a Hill, into the presence of a military Commander named Vortigern.

He and his Architects had been trying – and failing – to build a fortress there. When they released me from the sack and my eyes had adjusted to the light, I found that I was standing amidst his foolish Counselors – so called Magicians and Architects. They were speaking of their great calamity.

It seemed that every Day the Builders had placed the foundation Stones to a certain height, then left their work for their evening's rest. But every morning, when they returned to work, the whole structure had collapsed during the Night before and slid down the Hill! No one had an answer as to why this was happening... or how to correct the situation.

So, at his wit's end, Vortigern had resorted to bringing there a Soothsayer – of questionable reputation – to Divine the problem. This old man – after cutting open a Hare, so as to look into its entrails – told Vortigern that the Old Gods were angry for not having received their portion. He said that a blood sacrifice must be placed beneath the cornerstone to appease "Them." But, not just any blood would do... it must be that of a boy who had no Father of this world! Vortigern had sent forth his henchmen to find this child – under penalty of Death, if they did not return with such a boy.

After thinking much about it, I came to the belief that the three men sent out to find such a boy had twisted the meaning of the decree and, for the sake of expediency, had stolen the first bastard they could find: Me.

Of course the first thing they asked me was, "Who and where is your Father, boy?"

To which I answered, "I know not who he was, but as to where, I think he lives not in the realm of flesh."

They heard in my words precisely what they wanted to hear; for this is the way of Humans, as I have come to learn. As educated as I was in every other way, I was still naïve to the evil ways of men.

Believing that I had nothing to lose by it, I called them all fools! I said, "Lord Vortigern, how can you, an intelligent man, believe this nonsense? Allow me to look at the bottom of this Hill to see if can be found the source of this problem."

Amazingly, he did!

In the years that have passed by, many legends have grown up about this event; that I became his great Counselor because, as I peered into the Otherworlds, I saw beneath Vortigern's Hill two fighting Dragons: a white one and a red one. And, Seer that I was, I saw the outcome of his final battle as well as the eventual fate of the Britons.

The truth of the matter is that he was trying to build his fortress on very unstable ground. For, when I went down to the bottom of the Hill to look around, I noticed that there were Rocks that every Day slid down the Hill. Something from within the Hill was shaking it – not enough to feel this whilst standing upon it, or to destroy it, but something in its nature was moving it just enough to tear down what they had built up on it the Day before.

I have gone back to that place several Times since those Days and still, small rocks slide down that Hill every Day. Curious that.

So, I went back up and said to Vortigern, "There is no need to kill me, sir – to sacrifice me to these Dark Gods your Magi are making offerings to."

I looked at him and could see within him. I saw that, illustrious man that he was – educated and supposedly wise – still, he was a very superstitious one. So, I told him the fanciful tale of the Dragons fighting in a chasm beneath the Hill for they were loathe to allow his building above it and that their rumbling fight was what was causing the falling down of his fortress.

"Your fortress, Sir," said I, "will never stand on this Hill... you must change your plans and move it!"

He followed my advice, thereby sparing my life. This was very unfortunate for the Soothsayers though! Doomsayers!

As soon as his superstitions were placated, I surveyed a site nearby, where the fortress would indeed stand. And there did I design and oversee the most splendid fortress in all of Briton.

Ah, yes, well did I remember.

And on I ran to Igraine...

Again, my thoughts traveled to the Time when I had arranged in my second year with Vortigern to get word to my Mother that I lived and where I was. A messenger arrived soon after that from my Grandfather's villa, saying that my Mother wished to see me. Vortigern, not wishing to cross her Father – who was a very influential man – allowed me to go to her, but only under heavy guard.

So very welcome to my heart had been the sight of her lovely blue eyes, that, whilst there, I forgot all else. It was upon that blessed meeting – when I could hold my dear Mother's face in my hands – that hope for my future was revived. From that Day forward I knew that my fate was not to be forever in the hands of Vortigern. I was almost at my sixteenth year-turn by that Time.

News came some Time after that from my Grandfather's house that my Mother was ill. Vortigern again allowed me go – again under guard – to see her.

It was then that she told me the name of my Father. She called him her beloved "Victor" – although I did wonder at that Time, whether this name was his actual name or a descriptive. This was all that she would say of it.

Next my memories travelled to the hour of my dear Mother's Death, whereupon she would have no one else beside her: not her Father, nor her ladies – but only me. She had not the need to send word this Time, for I had felt her imminent demise. Vortigern allowed me, for a third Time and under guard again, to leave his fortress without him.

When I arrived at my Grandfather's house, I found her feeble and pale, holding onto life by the thread of Love which bound her to me. She motioned for me to come close and put my ear to her lips. She whispered, "You must know the ancestry of your Father, so that perhaps you may find him, for I think he is not dead, but has just not returned to me. He told me that his name was Victor... and that he was the son... or perhaps he said grandson – my memory fails me – Oh, yes! – of Macsen Wledig. My Victor already had two sons here in Britannia, by his wife, Elen, of the Clans. Or, was that the name of his Mother? I cannot remember... When we met, he was already a widower. These two other sons – your half brothers, are Ambrosius Aurillious, Britannia's much revered battle Commander of current fame and, as to the name of his youngest... my memory fails me once more. Oh, no – now I remember... His name is Badraig Constantius."

This shocked me almost beyond belief... for bastard or no, it put me in the direct line of Macsen Wledig himself. And I had brothers! I knew not what to make of this revelation, or if anything would ever come of it.

I looked into my dear Mother's eyes as she bade me again to place my ear close to her lips. She said "My dearest Gwyddion..." – her breath coming now in laboured hoarse gasps – "If ever you should you find your Father... please tell him that I have Loved him always. And as for not returning to me, I forgive him... or would understand. You have been a good son, Gwyddion, and I have always known there is greatness within you. I grieve that I must leave you; the rest of the world means naught to me. Know that I bring the Love I hold for you with me into the land of Hades... or perhaps, if I dare to dream, into the Summerlands where I may be with you again. I will watch over you here in the land of flesh and bone. Call to me, Gwyddion, when I am dead... Find me in the Otherworlds, where I know you travel. I will try... someday... to come to you. Be listening for me, my son... I must leave now... my beloved..."

Her gasping abruptly stopped with one more ragged intake of breath. Her eyes, staring at me and filled with the most Love I had ever known, froze into her last expression.

I closed her beautiful eyes. Upon their lids I placed two gold coins to pay the Ferryman, as was the custom of her Father's house.

"Mother, oh Mother..." I could not help it: I wept and wept. She had been the Love of my life, but I took heart in the words she had spoken to me: "I will try... someday... to come to you. Be listening for me..."

The memory faded...

But just then – from somewhere on the Wind – I heard her voice.

"Gwyddion..."

Astounded, I said, "Mother... I have not heard from you in all these years! I Love you. Mother? Mother?"

But, no one answered. And although in my heart of hearts I still believe she had really spoken to me out there in the dark, brambled Woods, I realised it could have been only the exhaustion of my body, the remembrances of her Death, or my longing for her that had tricked me.

And on I ran, remembering...

The next Night, exhausted and needing sleep so badly and yet so agitated that sleep would not come – my thoughts went back in memory to another Time while I had still been with Vortigern. On that Night as I lay fretfully trying to sleep, I was bidden by my "Voices" to use the deep breathing techniques which Brennos had taught to me – to slow my heartbeats, so that within my awareness the shadows and images could shift and I would feel a numbing of my body and thus enter into the realms of Spirit. I obeyed. And then I had had a very disturbing Dream.

I saw into the past, remembering the Time and place of an imminent battle... even could I see and smell the fear of the people there. I had crept to the other side of the Valley from Vortigern's troops, where I stood hiding behind a line of Trees... awaiting my opportunity to approach Ambrosias Aurelius and his younger brother.

Now, I was a man of my word, always taught to be forthright. However, subterfuge is part of the very fiber of Magic. I had learned from Brennos that there are events and reasons which sometimes give good cause to go beyond the necessity of telling the whole truth.

Because of such an event, I would betray Vortigern.

I had stayed with him only until the pre-Dawn of what I had "Seen" to be his last battle, when I would lead him up to that which would Spell his doom... even unto his Death.

How confusing, yet clear, can Dreams be; shifting Time and place.

...And on and on I ran to Igraine...

There were Times when my legs were aching so badly that I thought I could take not another step. But I must. There were Times running through the great Woods of this land that the moisture rose so heavily that it rolled like a frozen Mist from the River to fill the entire Forest, so much so that I could not see an arm's length ahead of myself. There were Times when I ran right into Trees and thorny brambles – Times when my Owl Chronos was so cold that I must cover him in blankets and skins and hold him to my breast. Yet more Days and Nights came and went – Times when the ache in my side was so severe that tears rolled from my eyes, only to freeze upon my face, making me even colder.

But on I ran to Igraine... and to all of our destinies.

Upon the next Night's restlessness, I remembered my abandonment of Vortigern and the scene of the great battlefield where, upon the next Day, Uther the Pen Dragon distinguished himself as Champion of the famed Hallelujah battle, where the Roman-led Clansmen met their kinsmen who were fighting on the side of Vortigern. This battle was near to my nineteenth year-turn.

They had met at that most Roman part of the Britons' lands, several leagues Northeast of The Snowy Mountains, in Gwynedd. The Roman army was lead by Germanus of Auxaire, a man I did not like; a man of cunning and ruthlessness in battle. A Bishop was he, as is said "by the grace of gold!" Nevertheless, he was sent by the Christian Pontiff to end the perceived threat of Vortigern and his attempts to throw off Roman influence amoungst the Clans.

In the pre-Dawn madness preceding the battle – after five years of my life spent in service to him – I slipped away from Vortigern's camp, abandoning him to his Death, Casting about myself a Glamour, so that none seeing me would recognize me, or else, they would never see me at all. At that, I slowly walked out through their ranks, never to look back!

Regardless of what my lofty position in Vortigern's service had been, I was, in fact, his captive and forbidden to leave his company. Even though I could read in this man a great ambition and dishonesty, I had always known that it was in some way written in the Stars that I stay with him for the Time being.

To myself, I thought, "Uther, now I do your bidding, though not by my will alone, but by that of the Gods."

...And on I ran...

In the deepening twilight on the evening of the last Day, a sleepiness overtook me – one which I could not shake away – no help for it but that I lie down to rest awhile.

There is no recognition of Time – save the Goddess known by that name – in the Dream World, but still it seemed to me that no sooner than I had closed my eyes I was in another place and Time – in the future.

This was no Dream of foul digestion or an anxious heart... this Dream was beyond quizzical; it was prophetic – filling the deep chasm of things unknown, which are yet to be!

This is how it was:

First, there was a blinding white, then green, then blue light surrounding something which I could not at first discern. As my Dreaming eyes became accustomed to the light, an image of a cross was before me. How could this be? I was no Christian. But then no... not a cross, it was a sword, a wondrous sword which had appeared before me. Upon each side of its blade were words, written in Latin. I spoke and read the tongue of the Romans, but this writing I could not decipher.

I thought, "Many Times in my Dreams I cannot read... Wait... this means that I am Dreaming!"

At that I awoke, hearing myself shout...

"No! I am no Warrior!"

The entire world around me sent up a call of Voices ... but only those of Earthen and feathered ones. I blinked and looked around. Then I called out to the Spirits, "What Magic is this?... for this sword, it burns within my head and heart, the palms of my hands and the bottoms of my feet. What is this about? I am not a man of the sword! And yet I know that it is mine!"

There was only silence about me now and the eeriness of the creeping Mist. I called out once more, this Time imploring Them, "I beg an answer!"

But as ever, They would unveil the Truth only in Their own good Time. Not long thence forward, did I reach the fortress of Dumnonia.

Morgan's note:

I am compelled to interject this here...

Although Gwyddion had not written of it in his first memoirs, in years to come, he told me the details of his relationship with Vortigern and why – he supposed – beyond his fear at the first, he had felt an immediate distaste for the man... of how the events of his life had played out leading to the final drama and how, in fact, Vortigern lost the battle against Uther and Germanus.

Quoth he: "During all the Time I acted as counselor for Vortigern, he kept looking at me in a way that made me feel quite uncomfortable, yet realisation had escaped me, for at fourteen and fifteen years – even until I had nearly turned my nineteenth year-turn – I had been an innocent. Although this was beyond the years that most boys had developed in this way, I had not yet engaged in a sexual act with a woman or a man. With these things I did not fill my thoughts or heart, but only with the Divine Mysteries. Really, I had no Time for such things, even if I had been so inclined. But, alas, I was not. I think that I believed that my Magic would be eaten up by the giving of my semen to another. At some point in Time, I began to become aware of a lust burning in Vortigern toward me.

"Before his last battle, in fact the very Night before, Vortigern summoned me to his pavilion under the guise of needing my counsel.

"He was drinking excessively. He asked me to join him in drink. He knew that I did not drink strong drink, nothing of Vine, Herb, or honey that had been fermented. I liked to keep sure of my thoughts and in command of my self. But Vortigern insisted. And so, for this one Time in my life, I did agree to drink a small glass of wine... into which Vortigern had put Herbs known to greatly lower inhibitions. What fool he! I was well versed in the Herbal Arts and could tell every ingredient by the first smell alone! Of course, when he could not see, I spilled it upon his carpet.

"He walked over behind the chair in which I sat looking at charts that lay upon the table boards. He put his hands on my shoulders, leaning over me to look at some diagrams I had just drawn. I felt the sick chill of fear. No, worse – a foreboding! Vortigern reached down and touched my chest. He rubbed downward on my body with his hands, and then he lifted me into his arms and kissed me, full on the mouth. He put his tongue between my lips. He was greatly aroused sexually and breathing roughly. As he held me to his body, I felt a very hard and persistent throbbing of his manhood.

"Morgan, truly I tell you, I was terrified!

'So Vortigern, you would have me as your catamite,' thought I...

"But then I thought, nay, I am too old to be considered a catamite – although I am nearly a man, yet in this way I am as a child...

"Fretfully, I reminded myself: 'I must remember my Charms and Words of Power...'

"And so did I say a word of the Druids' Magic – one that I am forsworn ever to repeat or to write upon vellum. This word was of the "Un-Making," which stopped the moment, immediately!

"I used the 'Grym Hudol' of my spiral eyes to look deeply into those of Vortigern's. I placed within the man's thoughts that which echoed through his body and created the effect of removing his ability to feel sexual desire! I had Cast a Spell of impotency upon him, which emasculated him and lead to his loss of prowess in battle and ultimately to his death.

"For, it is one of the greatest of Mysteries that the Fire which burns at the base of the back-bone – coiled like a Serpent – either sleeps in waiting or rages by will. It is the Fire of Creation – of sexual power and of Magic.

"I had said the word that would remove the ability of that Fire to burn within Vortigern, dooming him to his death. And that is why I, Gwyddion, later to be called The Merlin, left him to his own devices on that Night before his last battle."

Gwyddion's writings continue…

Finally, I reached Dumnonia.

Igraine had known that I was coming. She had felt my presence growing stronger and stronger, although in fact, she had never met me. She knew of me as Gwyddion The Merlin, for I had by that Time been so named.

She ran to the overlook of the fortress and there saw my approach. Staggering in a run, favouring my right side and holding my owl Chronos, whom I had wrapped in the warmth of my cloak, close to me, I had seldom been so relieved to reach a destination. Igraine called out that the inner gates be opened quickly and she herself ran out to greet me. Her attendants aided me into the fortress.

She said, "Sit ye down, Lord, and calm thyself, for I feel a great turmoil within thee. Please allow my servants to bring food and drink for to recover thy strength, as well as to wash thy feet with fragrant oils, for so exhausted does thou seem."

I did allow and appreciate her kindness.

But as I was attended to with these courtesies, I said, "Igraine, Guardian of the Well, Daughter of the Goddess, great Seer, I pay homage to thee, but let us, as peers speak casually to one another."

She smiled and I became aware of her great beauty for the first time. No wonder Uther has lost his mind over her.

"Lady, there is great Magic afoot of which I must tell you, yet I know that you will like it not. But it was the "Voices of the Stars" who spoke all to me and I am honour bound to speak it to you and to bring you to Their way of thinking."

And so I told her...

Igraine was sorrowfully troubled at the news that she was being asked to willingly give herself – her body – to this man whom she hated! She became very angry and said, "How can They ask this of me? I have sworn – and will keep my promise – to Gorlois; that as he lives I will never give my body to another man."

"Igraine, you can see that he is very close to Death."

"But you said that Uther will be here in three Nights!"

"Think on this matter. Go within, Igraine. Your perceptiveness has already confirmed all I have told you, else you would not have said; 'How can They ask this of me?'"

Igraine lowered her head in acknowledgment of the truthfulness of my words.

Then I asked if I might speak with Gorlois.

"Oh, but you will not tell him that Uther comes for rape? He must not be killed! I could not bear it. If Uther comes to murder my husband, I will kill him or be killed in the trying, regardless of the cost."

"Igraine," I reasoned, "what then, would become of your little daughters and all that Gorlois has held precious? Calm yourself, dear Lady – for your husband's life force will not long be within his body no matter what you do. You know in your heart that it is Time to let him go...

"So I ask once more, may I speak with him?"

She replied, "Of, course my Lord, The Merlin."

I entered the great chamber where Gorlois lay catching his breaths in much weariness. I looked about. I felt and saw many Spirits present to comfort this beloved man.

There was a wonderful feeling of luxury here. There were carpets and great wall hangings that had come from the East, with quizzical geometric designs, some with grand depictions of the Greek and Roman myths woven into them. The floor had cemented upon it the tiled mosaic patterns that the Romans favoured so much. Its central theme was a Sky God with white hair, up in the clouds. Jupiter, they call him. I looked at the furniture. It was all hand turned and inscribed by the Tribes of the Old Ones along with some by the Clansmen who were both famous for their beautiful carvings. No expense had been spared – nothing missed for comfort in the chamber of Gorlois. There was a large and comfortable bed, set with great pillows and beautiful woven blankets in the center of the room, upon which lay the dying Gorlois.

He looked at me.

"May I speak with you, Lord Gorlois?"

Gorlois called me to him and asked, "Who are you, my son?"

"My name is Gwyddion and I am called The Merlin."

"Then I am most honoured to have you here. May I assume you are here on some mission of great import? May I also assume this means that my death is nigh?"

"Yes and yes, Sir."

"I expected as much. Then sit here by me and tell all."

So, I told him that Uther his enemy would be coming, but that I had tricked him into a vow of coming only to kill Gorlois and that for great payment which I had offered to him, he would leave Igraine as mistress of her own house, Guardian of the Well, of the folk who lived about, and of all the wealth Gorlois and Igraine had. I made no mention of the price Igraine must pay for her freedom.

"He has vowed it so," said I.

"I thank you so much for that, for with or without the aid of Uther, my Death is imminent."

"But, Lord Gorlois, when I told Igraine of these matters, she said that if Uther comes to kill you, she will murder him or else die for the trying."

"No! This must not be, for I am almost dead in any case. Call my wife to me, for I must tell her this. I would take my own life, but I do not have the strength. When will Uther be here?"

In three Nights, at the Full Moon..."

"Call my beloved wife to me, please?"

So, I ran to Igraine and told her all he had said... but that I had not mentioned the rape. She put her head down and thanked me for that.

"But, come with me now Igraine, for Gorlois wishes to see you."

Igraine and I went quickly up to the magnificent chamber of Gorlois, whereupon she leaned next to him in the bed, holding his hands in hers, kissing him on the cheek and murmuring sweet words of Love. Only some did I hear, wishing not to intrude upon their privacy.

I realised then, with astonishment, that she truly did Love this man who was so much older than she. And, that her Love for him was as a handfasted lover, not only as husband or Father.

As I moved closer to them, I did hear the rest of their whispered words.

"You have been so good to me, Gorlois, and I Love you so very much. What is it you would have me do? I cannot take your life from you. No, never could I! But you are no longer strong enough to take your own and I would not have you die in pain."

"I am already in pain, my Dove."

"But still, why do the Gods make me watch this? And yet, I would not leave your side at the hour of your Death. Oh, what will we do? I am in much grieving sorrow over the loss of you already."

Gorlois said aloud, "The Merlin holds secret powers within him, as great as your secrets of Herb, Root and Stem – and of yours as a Seer... Both of you possess the Magic of your different traditions. My darling one, I have heard that by just looking into his eyes, I may fall asleep peacefully and quit my breathing and the beating of my heart. This is a High Druids' power. Would that satisfy your wishes as to the way of my Death? If so, know that it would please me well; save that the last thing I wish to see in this life is your lovely face."

"Oh, my husband, must it really be so?"

At the risk of un-welcome intrusion into their privacy, I interjected...

"It is the most peaceful way Igraine – and this you know. Can you be so brave, for the sake of Gorlois and your little daughters?"

When Igraine had agreed and made herself ready, I looked into Gorlois' eyes and then allowed his eyes to look upon his beloved wife for one last Time... I whispered an Incantation, whereupon the greatly honoured and beloved Gorlois, Dux of Dumnonia, whilst beholding the vision of his beautiful Igraine, breathed in his last breath and his heart stilled. Then, Igraine simply took her fingers and closed the lids of his eyes.

She wept. Tears of sorrow rolled down her face. But because she was, after all, a powerful Woman and had the heart of a Warrior, her tears were brief. She knew what she must do and there was little Time.

She said, "Leave me alone and I will speak to the Goddess and to my Spirits. I thank you for saving my husband from Uther's blade and allowing him a sweet Death... But now I must go to those who guide me, to get Their counsel, before I agree to do what you have proposed."

Morgan's note...

Little did they know that my sister Morganna had followed them up the stairs after she had heard everything The Merlin had told Igraine in their initial meeting, for Morganna was a devious one and already strong in the Magics.

My sister, who was twelve years at that Time, was always sneaking about trying to hear what she was not supposed to hear. So, when The Merlin arrived, she had hidden herself in a concealed corner of the Great Hall and listened to all that had been said.

She was a jealous one, too – perhaps because our Mother favoured me over her. Igraine had given to both of her daughters the training of the Arts, for it was her charge to give to all who came forth from her womb the knowledge of our people's Wisdoms. However, she lived in constant trepidation of the wickedness she 'Saw' within Morganna – a wickedness that she did not find in me. And so, although our Mother tried to be kind to her, Morganna, who had the Sight too, knew that I was our Mother's favourite.

Morganna did Love her Father, for he – who did *not* have the Sight – treated his eldest daughter with much Love and gave to her all manner of expensive gifts – anything that she desired. They shared many happy hours together, which she did never have with our Mother Igraine.

So, when my Mother led The Merlin up the stairs, Morganna followed behind them and Cast upon her feet a Charm of silence, so that even the great Igraine and The Merlin did not "See" through her Magics.

This is even now a frightening thought to me, that she could conceal herself from those two. But, she had done it. There is no denying it. She heard all that had transpired between her Father, her Mother, and The Merlin. Morganna was there, too, at the Time of her Father's Death... although this was not a fitting thing for a twelve year old child to experience. She watched as The Merlin said a prayer to all the Gods and Spirits who surrounded Gorlois so that They may bless him and carry him into the Otherworlds in peace and honour. She then slipped back to her chamber, and with all she had heard of Uther and of Igraine's giving herself to Uther – who intended murder upon her Father – began to devise a very wicked plan for her future. Morganna understood very well what The Merlin had up his sleeve!

I hold this knowledge, because Morganna taunted me with it on the Day after our Father died. I was but five years, yet I will never forget the horror of those few Days. It was very much increased by my first realization of just what and who my sister really was. Of course, these things I never told my Mother. It was many years before we would all come to realise the immensity of Morganna's plan.

Gwyddion continues...

The next morning after I had rested, I indulged in bathing in the Roman baths of the fortress. Clean clothes had been brought to me and were laid upon my bed, ready for my use. Only then had I felt truly refreshed.

Igraine's attendants brought all manner of food and drink of which I might partake. I had been treated with all honours. If it has not been mentioned afore this, I have eaten little of the rich foods and meats that are common fare amoung the more affluent Britons. I prefer to eat a diet of Fruits, nuts, Vegetables, Fish – and when available, flat breads or raw Grains with honey. But I must say that upon that morning, I left behind my discipline of good health and enjoyed that meal as much as any I can remember.

When finally Igraine came to me, she said, "Those who give me Counsel have confirmed that all you have told will come to pass and that I must offer my body to this wicked and disgusting man, who would have slain my husband and raped me. And so, Merlin, for the sake of this household and my Sacred duty to Nodens' Well, my children and my honour, I will do all that you bid me to. But know this: What issues from my womb of this mating will be yours – as this was your bargain with Uther – for as long as it lives."

Any fool could have read Igraine's thoughts... that she would "... strangle this unholy thing, conceived in hatred and violent lust, on the Day of its birth."

"No Igraine... You must do no harm to the babe!"

"But I will! I will not raise what issues from this wickedness! This decision is what my own heart, as a woman and as a Mother, inclines me to. And I am that, too, Gwyddion! I am a woman made of Earth and I have feelings and a heart. I will carry this child to its birth, for to keep my promise to you, but after, if you come not soon enough to save it, I will kill it. Know this!"

"Oh Igraine, have you not heard a word I have said? This boy – your boy – is to become the greatest King ever known in Briton! He will unite all the Clans and Tribes of these Fair Isles. Oh, not in a unity of subservience, but of mutual trust and protection. I have Seen it all, Igraine. He will be a kind and generous King. A King who will not tear down the Old Ways. Is this not what you and your Dark Tribes have always longed for? ...to be left alone in peace and safety from all who dwell around you?"

Her only response was, "But, he will be Uther's!"

She lowered her face into her hands and wept.

"Oh, Gwyddion, these are not the circumstances under which I would have met you. I have even Dreamt that you and I will be good friends one Day. Please excuse my bitter attitude, but this is the worst of all Times for me."

It was then that I came upon an idea... Or perhaps, it came upon me.

Later that same Day, I went into the nearby village and found the perfect solution. Upon returning to Igraine's fortress, I brought the conversation up once more.

"Lady, please believe me, I have your best interests in my heart. And I should like very much to become your friend, too. To this end, I have a suggestion for your consideration:

"With Gorlois gone, the Roman Guard and their wives will soon leave this fortress. Your husband's troops must go on to their next command. They will only be allowed to stay long enough to salute him unto his funeral pyre. When they do leave, you will be bereft of help here. You and your daughters will *need* help without a husband or attendants. Might I bring a Roman Briton man – whose Mother was of the Clans, just as was Gorlois' – who also has a wife of the Tribes, along with some of their folk here to help you run your lands and household? I have met them only today; however I feel that they are of good honour and most congenial people. And it would serve you well to have some friends here to comfort you in your loss."

"Yes. I thank you, Gwyddion. I will trust your judgment in this matter."

Unknown to Igraine, I had sought this childless couple because I knew Igraine's vengeance upon Uther would be terrible.   The arrangement, which I had proposed to them was, that I would awaken the wife's womb with my Druid's Magic, on the Night of the Full Moon, so that she would become with child. This I would do in exchange for their help. They must agree to go to Lady Igraine's fortress with me, to offer their services as keepers, to help her run the fortress and lands. But always and only, must they keep me – and no one else – informed of any happening of import in the fortress, as a protection to Igraine, her daughters and the babes which would be born. I assured them that they would not be my spies... only would they keep me abreast of matters so that I might ensure the protection of all.

So, with the Fates' indulgent blessings, it all came about.

On that very Night, whilst Uther lay with Igraine, this same man and woman had sexual intercourse. I blessed their union as the "Voices" had bidden me to do. I touched the woman's belly so that she became pregnant... as did Igraine.

Morgan

My memory of that Night...

As I, Morgan, remember the happenings of that fateful Night and those times... *and* as I later learned them from my Mother Igraine and others, it all transpired as The Merlin had said it would.

On the Night of the Full Moon, Uther arrived with his armed guard and stormed the fortress, but he met no resistance. In fact, the gates were open wide and a great pyre was alight in the outer courtyard... weeping and quiet sobbing were heard all around. Uther then realised that he was too late to have his complete revenge upon Gorlois. Young as I was, this I read in his thoughts:

"Gwyddion, Damn it!"

Though I was but five years, I had glimmerings of the "Sight" already.

Now, Uther was, above all things, a Roman Warrior. He could not – would not – humiliate and dishonour himself by creating any more of a ruckus than he already had at the pyre of a fellow Roman Commander – a Dux, no less. Even though he had come here to murder this man who was his mortal enemy, he quickly signaled the order to his men, to still and dismount their War Stallions.

The pyre had been burning for hours...

There, across the courtyard from him we stood. Painted and adorned was Igraine, holding the hands of her two daughters. We were, all three, steadfast in quiet strength and dignity.

Uther waited in silence. But his eyes were always upon Igraine. All present waited for hours, until the pyre had consumed Gorlois' body completely and had almost burned to cinders and ash. This was the measure of respect held for Gorlois.

Just as the Moon approached the zenith of the Sky – the Full Moon in the month of Planting – Igraine sent Morganna and me with our caretakers to our separate bedchambers. She told them to stay with us, to watch us and under no circumstances allow us to depart our rooms.

When my sister and I were being taken away, Uther approached Igraine.

She then said to him, "I will not give to you the satisfaction of raping me Uther, for I will give myself to you willingly. But, all the promises which you have made to The Merlin you must again confirm to me so that I may know that you will keep your word in these matters. Only then will I give myself to you in a way which you will never forget."

Uther trembled. He was a little bit afraid of my Mother, and so should he have been.

He replied, "Then you must promise that this is all you will do to me and that you will not kill me this Night or any other Night or Day, nor curse evil down upon me – and that you will allow me and my company to leave at will. Do we have this agreement also between us? For, oh! Igraine, I have desired you so greatly from the moment I first saw you that never do you leave my thoughts. Your face is always before my eyes. I only want to share this needing with you. You are a Fire overwhelming me. And indeed, I will give myself to you in a way that I have never given myself to another. I think this Night is one that you will never forget, either."

"I am sure of that, Lord Uther," said Igraine, as she forced a smile to her lips.

She whispered into his ear, "Come, all is prepared."

They went up the winding stairway to her bedchamber, which was next to where my Father's had been.

When Uther walked into her chamber, what he saw there were all the trappings of the Old Dark Tribes. There was a Roman mosaic on the floor. But instead of the usual scenes of Greek or Roman myths, it was full of Doe and Stag, Wolf, Serpent, Bear, Bee, Dolphin, Raven and Swan, all dancing in a mighty circle. Entwined with spirals and knot work was it, which seemed more ancient than those of the Clans. Her walls were covered in frescos of the twisted Elder Trees of the Dumnonian Woods, filled with Birds of all sorts. The ceiling was covered with five pointed Stars. And there were images of shadowy Idols on an Ancestor Altar, set into niches in the Stone walls. These were all stained in blue, as if echoing the black dots on Igraine's forehead and cheekbones. Her whole bedchamber was as an exotic sensual phantasy.

The fragrance in her room was always intoxicating, yet soothing. It was the same perfume Igraine always bathed in... the same she must have worn on the Night Uther had first met her.

Uther lost himself... He began to tear off her clothes. She allowed him. He stripped her naked, he stripped off his weapons, his armor and his own clothes. They stood naked before each other. He was a finely built man and quite handsome... She loathed him! But she kept her word and used her skills at the Art of sex in such a way that he could not prolong himself and he came to his rapture quickly.

He said, "Nay, not so quickly, Igraine – you must wait and give yourself to me again for that was not enough. I was promised that my lust would be quenched this Night."

"Alright."

In a very few moments he was at it again and she fulfilled his every desire, just as she had promised.

Finally, in a couple of hours, he was well spent.

She then turned to him showing her loathing, raised her arm and pointed her first finger of Magic... and said, "Now, you will go... and you will never attempt to look upon my face again. You will leave me a woman who owns herself and fulfill all that you have vowed.

"As for this child we have made; it belongs to The Merlin... while it lives."

A horror came over him... for Igraine was terrifying in this, her Dark Mother aspect. And he realised somehow that with this Night's passion he had sealed his doom. He obeyed her. Fearful even to look upon her again, he dressed, put on his armor, and fled her presence.

Then Uther gathered his guard and they hastened away on their war Horses... whose breaths were steaming in the chill of the Night Air.

Uther rode forever into the Mists and out of our lives. Thus was the beginning of the undoing of Uther the Pen Dragon.

I remember that I had cried that Night – quietly so that no one else would hear. I cried until I thought my heart would break open and spill out onto my chamber floor! Even though only five years, I did feel my Mother's great pain and anxiety upon that Night, although much of what happened I did not understand – not until many years later, when my Mother finally told me of the horrors of that Night. For the sake of my Mother's dignity, did I never tell her of Morganna's actions. I was evermore careful not to allow those memories to flow through my thoughts, lest she know.

Foolish tales have arisen now in my old age, that my Mother was a weak woman who had fallen hopelessly in Love with the man who had slain her husband.

Weak woman?!!! Forgotten by these stories is the beauty and power which was that of Igraine. But, these legends, and many more in my Time, are those written by Saxons and Christians. However, beyond these, I have "Seen" into the future, far beyond my lifetime and it offends me greatly that Igraine, the great Seer, Healer and Guardian of the Well, will be remembered as a woman of weakness; a pawn in the games of men. What can I do about lies and stories that will be told? Except to write and compile my histories in truth; in the earnest hope that they will come to light, linger and live for centuries upon centuries, even millennia upon millennia.

A note from Morgan...

Note these words – which I added to these histories when first I found the following pages so many years later – which had been left conspicuously on Morganna's bed in her chamber, beneath the woolen covers, right where she knew that I would find them. That being on the occasion of our Mother's funeral – which of course, Morganna did not attend.

Morganna Le Fay – Memoirs of an evil girl

I am Morganna, the daughter of Igraine the Seer and of Gorlois, the

Dux of Dumnonia. I stood that Night at my Father's funeral pyre as the great billowing smoke fled its way to the Stars... carrying with it my Father's Spirit. I stood stoically. I was resolved within myself to shed not a tear, for that was unseemly. I looked around. Many people of the Dark Tribes had come to honour my Father for the kindnesses he had shown to them and the Old Ways. The drums of the Tribes were pulsing and their women were Humming.

Away from them stood a troop of Roman Guard, lined up perfectly, geometrically. And they as well, stood silent and still. These men were my Father's compatriots. A great Commander had he been, when still he had his strength. It was way beyond that Time now... the proper Time for him to die and go to his Gods.

But, my Mother, out of her obsession for keeping the life within his body, had fed him her Roots and Herbs and said her Words of Making, so that he had lingered and lingered in his suffering. He was each Day less of the man he had once been. And I think, perhaps, he had made his Spirit stay within his body to please her – more for her than for me. I hated it, and I hated her for her meddling.

I had Loved my Father. He was the only one whom I had ever Loved, save for my Wildcat, Terror. Or Tear-Her... An amusing pun, is it not?

I have a sister, Morgan, who is seven years younger than I. She had passed her fifth year-turn by that Night. She stood there, too, by my Mother.

There were those of his household who were wailing for my Father and others who were quietly weeping, for he was beloved by many.

Whilst I stood watching the billowing smoke, I thought, "So, it is done!"

With the rising smoke from the pyre of my Father Gorlois, the last of the foolish sentiments of kindness and empathy went out of me forever. Now I was free. Free to be who and what Creature I would be. Never again would I allow anyone or anything to keep me in hesitation from whatever I wanted.

My thoughts had been interrupted... A large man – Uther the Pen Dragon and his Guard – came into the funeral scene, raising a ruckus of sound and dust disturbing my Father's honours. It seemed that when they realised what was happening, they, as Romans, dismounted and stood quietly in honour of the Dux of Dumnonia.

I was resolved to show no grief. I clenched my teeth together and stared at Uther, focusing on my hatred.

My thoughts shouted: "You have come too late to do your wickedness toward my Father. You have come too late to seek your revenge. Or, have you? Will you seek your revenge now upon my Mother, then? No, not revenge upon Igraine, but lust!"

For I was there hiding and heard all that passed between The Merlin, my Father Gorlois, and Igraine, at the hour of my Father's Death, three Nights past. And I knew of all their lofty plans.

How clever a girl I am, thought I, to be able to fool the great Igraine and the Druid – Gwyddion, The Merlin – for none did even realise that I was there.

But count my words; I will have my revenge upon you some Day, Uther – not for disgracing my Mother, for she will go willingly into your arms this Night – but for your threats against my Father and against our house.

So, I stood and glared at him. His eyes never left Igraine and in them I could see the Fire of a great lust. So be it, then.

When all was over – my Father reduced to ash – my Mother put me, a young woman of twelve years, into the charge of the children's caregiver, Rhonwen, who was instructed to keep us, my sister and I, locked in our chambers for the Night. As if some foolish old servant could keep me, Morganna Le Fay, from escaping and from the seeing of all the events that took place on that fateful Night. I went willingly, but as soon as the hallways were clear, I Cast an Enchantment upon her, so as to make her fall asleep – completely into a deep Trance, so that nothing could awaken her.

I had great power, this I knew. Just by looking into someone's eyes, whilst hissing words of power with my Serpent's tongue, could I numb almost anyone into doing my bidding.

It has been said that only the great Merlin had this skill. But this was not so, for even at twelve years, it was mine as well! For the Magics that Igraine had taught to me I had learned very well, practiced much, and added to them, until I had gained even more strength in some of the Arts than she.

My Magic arises not from the same source as hers; my powers come from that which lurks in the shadows – on the other side of the mirror. And of this I will write no more.

But these things Igraine did not know and that is how I could deceive her so. A Mother's crippling Love – or hope – blinded her. Also, have I kept my own counsel. I am a good secret keeper. This has served me well in all of my life thus far.

So, just as we had done three Nights before, Terror and I crept to my Mother's bedchamber and with the Glamour of invisibility, I hid myself – even from the great Igraine.

Thus it was that upon that fateful Night, I watched as Igraine was stripped of her clothing and dignity, while Uther, whom I hated, stood before her naked with his huge, throbbing cock standing straight upright. He – filled with foolish desire for a woman who loathed him.

I watched as my Mother used the Arts of Lovemaking and of sexual ecstasy, which she had learned so well, to inflame and bring Uther to one after another thundering, Earth shattering climax! I became greatly aroused watching Uther with my Mother. She was very beautiful. I wanted Igraine! She was desirable. I looked just like her, only of course, I was younger.

I had been born old and was far beyond other girls of my age in the knowing of and acting upon sexual desire. Why, I had already had many young women, a few young boys, and several older men as well, in these ways.

It was very interesting to me to watch Igraine with him. It struck me then that it was like watching myself perform these acts of sexuality. How I wish that I could do just that – watch myself. I will work on that; perhaps Magically I may attain the ability to watch myself from beyond my body, for I do like to watch sex, as much as I like having it.

Even though all of these thoughts and anguishing desires were filling me, I was still aware enough to know that the child of The Merlin's plans would come from this coupling. But, he would NEVER be the heir of the Dux of Dumnonia – for I would never allow that to be! After all, I was my Father's "Pearl"... his rightful heir. No one will take it from me; must needs I kill them all! This I vow by all the Gods and Spirits that be – wicked or nay.

"SO BE IT!" said I, and snapped my fingers.

At once everything around me began to spin and whirl. I felt faint, as though I would vomit, for the chills and heat of the Sight were upon me. I braced myself against the cold Stones... Falling... falling...

I saw that beyond what was happening here in this chamber, there was something else afoot. What was it? Aah! It was Gwyddion, The Merlin, and his damned scheming!

As the developing Vision surrounded me, I began to understand his plot:

There was a Roman man and a woman of the Tribes in the near village – the light and the dark, the fair and the dusky – also coupling on this same Night of the Full Moon. You had arranged it, Merlin. Yes, and I can see now what you are doing. I feel the energy of your touch of blessing on this woman's womb, so that she will become with child on this very same Night as Igraine. Yes, of course, I see the child of this couple being born on the very Night that Uther's bastard will be spawned.

But wait! I see Igraine with a cord in her hands, which she has taken from beneath her pillows. She has it in her heart to strangle that which will be born of her unholy making with Uther. But you, Merlin, you will never let that happen, for you want this child. You would make him War Chieftain and High King. I see it as clearly as I see your handsome face.

Then the Vision shifted.

Now I see you running, Merlin, you are running... running... But this is not a thing to be... No, you were on your way here to Igraine...

I see a Valley in Gwynedd... A bubbling Well... An evil bargain struck... A burning sword... I feel the terror of a battle... The downfall of the great Dragon... I see a fair-haired boy with a circlet of gold upon his head.

Then swiftly moving darkness carried me... Where?

No! Spirits, I want more! Then my Spirits left me and the Visions faded.

Slowly I returned to the dim light of my hiding place and to an awareness of where I was. Terror was rubbing against my leg in distress. I scratched behind his ears to quiet him.

I wondered for a moment, in my daze, if The Merlin's political ambitions would go as far as to bring about the births of these two boys... – yes, they will be boys – at the very Time of Mithras' birth... and of course, that of the Christian God's. For, as they tell it, both of these Gods were born on "The Longest Night," in the cold month of Luis, the Rowan.

Shameless Gwyddion... Would you fool men into equating your "King" with a savior? Do you manipulate even the tides of birth?

But I had to admit with a resentful admiration, "What a delightfully wicked plan this is, Merlin..."

But secret it is not! For I have been taken into your thoughts by what Dark Spirits ride me. Do you feel me there? Well, there I am! And I know what you are thinking. I know what you have done. I have been shown the design of your great intrigue. In fact, I have stolen your 'Gifts' of the Arts. Yes, the abilities to deceive, to swoon people into oblivion and forgetfulness – these I have learned from your thoughts, Gwyddion, The Merlin. Someday my powers will eclipse even yours... I have only to bide my Time!"

Yes... I knew the artful schemes of The Merlin. And I was very, very proud of myself.

It was upon that moment that I began to plot an entanglement of Divine proportion – for my own eventual triumph.

Gwyddion
My recollections of the Births...

There was a man named Markus – whose Father had been Roman and whose Mother had been of the Western Clans – living in the nearby village who was handfast to a woman of the Tribes, named Tangwen. They were good people – and of the same bloods as Uther and Igraine! The dark and the light... His colouring was just as was Uther's... And Tangwen's as Igraine's... How perfect!

Now, I arranged with them that they, too, were to couple on this very

Night of the Full Moon of the Alder, which of course is in the month of planting seeds!

But theirs was no ordinary Lovemaking. There were crafty acts about on this Night. Had the Voices led me to this plan, too? Never will I be sure, for I had awakened that morn with the whole idea in my thoughts. Well, no matter... there it was! I approached this childless husband and wife to ask if I might lay my hands upon her belly, to stir within her womb the ability to conceive, so that Tangwen would become with child that very Night.

I would also make sure that the two boys would be born on the same Night.

But I wondered; what was prickling at the back of my neck?

Morganna continues...

Three Days later, as the Full Moon waned, there arrived at my Mother's house the very same couple I had seen in my Visions, along with some of their people. And just so, as The Merlin had arranged, they came into our lives and offered to stay at our fortress and be of service to my Mother in whatever way they might.

"We merely came," said they, "out of gratitude to The Merlin... and compassion for you, Lady Igraine, and for your daughters."

To my Mother they seemed very kindly and she immediately liked them.

So, all was set in place. The machinations of Gods and Spirits, The Merlin's, Igraine's and mine, began to unfold like a drama. Good, then... Let the game begin!

The months went by uneventfully and in relative peace, with no further communication from The Merlin and with both women progressively bulging like un-milked Cows. Then, the Time was upon them for the birth of the babes.

It was, of course, right on Time that The Merlin showed up to await their arrival and to put his protections into effect; this, I believe, so that Igraine's son would not be strangled. What he did was very cunning:

The Night my Mother went into her birth pangs, her ladies were called into her chamber. The Midwives, who would help with the birthing, were there to comfort and reassure her – not allowing entrance to any male. The Grandmothers of her Tribe all stood vigil as they burned sweet Herbs and Hummed in an eerie drone. As Igraine's pains became closer and harder, some sang sweet songs whilst others quietly Hummed and Drummed, for within their Humming and Drumming great Power is raised. This soothed her. Their wishes and Incantations were intended to let her feel only the joy of giving birth.

But Igraine said to them, "No, I would feel all the pangs of this birth. Let my joy come after this child is born." – "...and dead," she silently thought. And so they obeyed her.

Meanwhile, The Merlin went to see Tangwen – and as he had prearranged with her, touched his hand to her great belly to cause her Water to break – and on came her pains. He lulled her as had the Grandmothers done Igraine, so that she might have an un-eventful birthing and that the babe would be strong and live.

The boy that my Mother gave birth to looked like Uther. I knew this because again I had snuck behind the wall hangings. He had the golden skin, lighter hair, and blue eyes of many of that race of people. He did not look like Igraine, my sister, or me. In fact, he looked as Roman as he could look – as much as babies look like anything, the ugly little things...

But, the other baby born in our fortress that Night – Tangwen's boy – came out looking like one of the Old Tribes. He was dark and black eyed. He had a head of black hair that was already full – whereas the screaming little thing that my Mother had birthed had only a little bit of scraggly blond hair on his head. And so, the two boys could not have been more different, one from other.

The Merlin quickly went to Igraine and asked if he might see the babe.

She said, "Yes."

When he saw that Igraine's child looked like Uther, fear filled the chamber! *His* fear... I could smell it!

Again he reached into his 'bag of tricks'...

At that moment he made a great Enchantment, so that everyone in Igraine's chamber, except for the babe, would fall to sleep and thus would they remain until he snapped his fingers to awaken them. He made it so that when they awoke, they would have forgotten everything which had transpired since the moment before the birth, with none ever being aware that he had Spelled them into forgetfulness.

He then rushed to the other birthing chamber with Igraine's baby held fast in his arms – he, who would one Day be King. Gwyddion lay Igraine's boy on Tangwen's breast and took *her* child to Igraine – without even the knowledge of Tangwen and Marcus, or the other well-wishers who were waiting just outside the chamber door.

Just so, did Merlin the Enchanter, by his machinations, successfully switch the babes.

My Mother, when she awoke, saw everything as it had been before.

Then she looked, for the first Time, upon the babe in her arms – who she thought to be her own – and saw that he looked just as had her daughters when they were born.

She hesitated – her plan had been to have everyone leave the chamber and then to strangle the child, then to tell The Merlin that he had owned the babe for as *long as it had lived.*

Then, the babe turned his head, grabbed hold of the nipple of her breast and began to suck with a mighty suck. Tears fell from Igraine's eyes. A great Love for this child began to form within her.

When The Merlin reentered her room, he could feel it too.

Igraine was crying. He asked her, "Must I take this baby now before you kill it? For our bargain was that your child, who I myself must name, was to be mine when the appropriate Time arrived, to be fostered and trained to be a King! If he is in danger by your hand, Igraine, that hour is now!"

I laughed in wonder at his gift for manipulation – and at just what The Merlin would do next.

Then Terror and I turned our attentions elsewhere, for it had been a long Night. As for the rest of it, I would sleep very well, for I knew that with these revelations, I had the weapons that I would someday need to tear down the walls of The Merlin's fortress.

Gwyddion

Once I had switched the babes and returned to stand in Igraine's birthing chamber, she looked at the babe in her arms. He had just grabbed her breast and begun to feed.

She looked up at me and began to cry inconsolably. Sounding alarmed, I asked, "Igraine, what is the matter?"

She answered, "I must do something... for I swore to myself that I would not allow your plan for Uther's bastard to succeed. I would kill this child of his... And yet, now... he is so small and defenseless, Gwyddion... so like my daughters were."

Her voice trailed off.

"Oh, Igraine... Igraine... Love this baby boy. You have not another son – look at him; he looks just like you, there is very little of Uther in him."

"Do not speak that name in my house, I loath myself for just now evoking it!"

"Excuse me Igraine, but I swore an oath to foil any plan which would bring harm to this child. Let us compromise, you keep him and give him a name of your choosing. *If* I have your word that no harm will befall him by your hand, then to no one will I speak a word of his parentage. All will believe him to be Gorlois' son. But upon his twelfth year-turn, he must become mine to foster and to teach. It is then when I must give your son the name that he will carry as King of the Britons. Will this arrangement satisfy?"

She answered, "Yes, Gwyddion, we will do as you suggest" and then smiled. "Thank you, Gwyddion; I will name him Bedwyr, from the tongue of Gorlois' Mother." I smiled as well – but I smiled because I had accomplished the will of the Gods.

I went to the chamber where Igraine's true son was lying in the arms of and suckling upon Tangwen. She and Markus thanked me for the safe arrival of their son and for the easy labor which she had gone through.

"You are most welcome. But now, I will ask something of you, in return."

"Anything," they replied.

"I must name your son upon his 12th year-turn, when I will come back to take both of the boys born this Night, to foster and to teach. This plan must remain secret amoung we three alone. In the meanwhile, name him anything you wish as his childhood name, but know that the name which I give him upon his leaving home and coming with me will from thence forward be his true name."

"This is fine and good with us, Gwyddion, The Merlin."

They lovingly looked into each other's eyes.

"His name we have already chosen."

Then out of their very mouths came: "We will name him 'the Bear'."

I started...

"What is this?!"

"Well, you did say that we could name him as we wished."

"So I did... The Bear..." My voice trailed in thought... "Arthur."

It was then that I knew with all certainty that the Weavers would have their fingers in the happenings of all things concerning Arthur, the future High King of the Britons.

I left shortly after the births.

Chapter 3
The Children

Igraine

I, Igraine, will tell you about my daughter, Morgan. We called her 'Morgan of the Woods,' because ever since she was a little girl, she Loved to go for long walks in the Forest. That was where she was most at home. She would splash in the Streams that wind like Serpents through the Woods. She would talk to little Birds, repeating all of their songs and chirpings and Butterflies would alight on her hands and hair and would hold themselves majestically still in her presence. Even those Creatures which crept and crawled through the sodden leafy ground were her beloved companions.

Once, from a distance, I watched as she spoke something which I could not hear. Then slowly, she swung her long silken black hair back and forth. The Butterflies followed her motions.

There was another quizzical thing about her – Bees seemed to Love her and never would they sting her. They buzzed around her always, as if speaking with her. When she thought that no one was listening, she buzzed back to them in a similar way.

Morgan flowed like a breeze through the leaves of the Trees and her eyes were aware of everything around her.

As the years went by, her ability to communicate with the Animals, Insects, and Birds – even with the Trees and Flowers – seemed to grow and grow within her. Yes, she had a special gift in these ways.

Morgan was a beautiful child; not just to look at but Enchanting from the depths of her Spirit. Although my two daughters looked almost exactly the same, Morgan's being was different. Transcendent? Was that it, even then? There was a glow about her whole body; even the feel of the Air was changed, as, and after she walked by. Sometimes I watched as she raised her hands to the sky and I could see the Magic coursing from her fingertips upward.

Her voice was sweet as a Nightingale, exquisite in speech or song and her laugh was as winsome and light as a bubbling Spring.

Morgan was one with all of Nature and Creation. She Cast Love upon the Earth with her every footfall.

Morgan, my lovely daughter... my beautiful daughter. No matter the season, long Days would she go wandering amoungst the Snowflakes, Blossoms, Heather and Herbs or Leaves of red and gold. Sometimes I would become anxious for her as the deepening purple shadows of twilight would fall and she had not yet returned... foolish Mother. I knew the Spirits watched over her. But when it seemed she had been gone too long, I would wait for her from the lowest battlements, then suddenly she would appear from out of the Mists of the gloaming as if a specter – not wholly of this world.

Both of my daughters were beautiful, of course, but my "Morgan of the Woods" had the heart of the Great Goddess and HER blessings were within her.

As for Morganna...

Well, it would pain me to compare them so, for I hold, even yet, a Mother's Love and bond for Morganna – Goddess help me!

Yes, Morgan was always smiling, always happy, except on that Night, standing in front of her Father's funeral pyre. She held my hand so tightly. She had Loved Gorlois well, but it was me she was worried about, for my daughter Loved me with a great, abiding Love, as I did her. She was later to say that she was unaware of anything but my feelings of grief and overwhelming anger. She *was* only five years old.

She followed my gaze toward the unseemly clamor of armed Warriors galloping into the courtyard. And Morgan saw me stare – a vehement stare – at one man. He was Uther the Pen Dragon. But Morgan did not understand... not completely, and so thankful for that I have always been.

Only later, when she was older did she learn the truth of those heart-shattering, profane, and portentous events.

So, Time went on, and I, Igraine, continued to raise my two daughters – as much alike in the way they looked as were different beneath the skin.

As for the two young boys, they grew up, played together always and became the very best of friends.

I named my son Bedwyr "man of strength," thereby blessing him with strength of body, skills, heart, and Spirit.

Tangwen and Markus named their boy "The Bear."

Bedwyr and the Bear did everything together, including being trained in the Arts of war by Bedwyr's Father, as was the custom of Warrior Fathers, and both were trained very well. But Bedwyr, my son, excelled. Although he was of smaller stature than The Bear, who grew straight and tall, Bedwyr bested him in all of the Arts of war. The Bear was excellent – Bedwyr was better. The Bear was a thinker – Bedwyr, an experiencer. Bedwyr had the Gift of the Sight – the Bear did not, but he was never jealous. He was a pleasant boy, always courteous.

In any case, the boys were best of brothers and the best of friends... they swore always to stand by each other, although there was no blood between them.

Now, Bedwyr was not as handsome in a traditional way as was the Bear. Oh, he did have charm and a very good sense of humour and he was far from ugly; he was just more *ordinary* in his looks. That was quizzical, because it was often said that my daughters and I were beautiful... and well... although I disdain speaking of who his true Father was, I will say that he *was* a handsome man – and let that be enough on the topic of his Father!

None of this mattered to a Mother. All I know is that from the first Time I held the ugly little squirming dark thing in my arms, he had simply been my beloved son.

The Bear was not taught to read, for his Mother was illiterate, and his Father was more concerned with his physical prowess. He did, however, learn very well all of the battle-tested formations and strategies of Roman warfare.

Yes, the Bear was brilliant in his intellect and so hungry always for knowledge. Because of this, my sweet Morgan felt sorry for him.

All the children seemed to get on with each other very well, at least in the early Days.

Even Morganna, who was the eldest, paid attention to the two boys. However, I often wondered about her motives in this, for it seemed to me that it was more as if she was always watching them, not unlike her Wildcat stalking a Rat! The strange thing was that even at a young age, I could not read Morganna's thoughts the way that I could read everyone else's around me. This distressed me... what secrets had she learned that went beyond the teachings of my people?

The thing that began to concern me as the years went by, was that when I looked into The Bear's eyes and read his heart, I found within him a great developing Love for my beautiful daughter Morgan. Even by the Time he was only seven years, it was there. I thought; how sweet is this, that they have grown up together, have become great friends... and there he was falling in Love, with a child's Love – or was it more than that?

When the Bear had reached his eighth year-turn, Morgan was nearing her fifteenth and was becoming a young woman. Her breasts had formed, she had a curve to her hips, and she was beautiful!

It seemed to me to be a bit precocious, because usually boys have no interest in girls at that age.   But I dismissed it as just a childish infatuation.

I was wrong. That was by no means the last time that my judgment was faulty regarding my children. But what could anyone have done to change what the Weavers had already spun?

Many times I would watch them go into the Woods together. He followed her everywhere that she would allow. She did not mind. She told me how she had tried to teach him to speak to the Animals, but he would just smile at her and say "Morgan, you are the one with the Sight and the one who knows of all things mysterious. I however, who have no Sight of things unseen, am the one most blessed, to be able to walk along in the presence of one so wise and beautiful of countenance. Please Morgan, just tell me the stories, will you, of the Dark Tribes?"

And so she did.

She told me of her asking him if he would like to become educated.

"Bear, would you like to learn to read and write?"

...and that he had answered, "Morgan, it would be the second greatest desire of my heart."

"The second... what is the first?"

"That is something I may never be able to tell you – or mayhap I will some Day."

They left it at that.

Morgan told me later – much later – when the significance of the Bear's words were completely understood, that had she realised what was brewing in his dear heart, she would have gone to the Lady of the Lake earlier.

You see, it was like this...

When Morgan reached her fourteenth year-turn, she had a choice to make.

It was a tradition amoung the Tribeswomen that a young woman of her age, whose Mother was a Seer or Healer, would be asked to decide whether she would stay within the Tribal villages to serve in one of these vocations – or, if she had not these Gifts, to marry and make a family of her own. Or, she could ask to be accepted by the Lady of the Lake – in which case she must travel Eastward to the Isle of Apples on the Inland Sea – to the University of the Order of the Great Goddess – where she could become well educated in the Arts of literacy. There also to be taught the Cosmic Mysteries.

I had raised my daughters to follow as many of my family's traditions as was possible in our unique circumstances. This was one of them. They knew that they were expected to make one of these same choices upon reaching the appropriate age.

Morgan came to me herself when she knew it was Time to make her decision. She was heartbroken to leave me. She wept in my arms and said, "Mother, I would not leave you for anything! Must I truly go?"

"Morgan, it is Time. You were not chosen by your Father to inherit this great house, for although he Loved you well, Morganna was his firstborn – and in his family the eldest always inherits. Upon my death, I plan to honour his wishes in this.

"What do you choose my darling... to marry? Or would you go to the Grandmothers of my Tribe, to live primitively and learn more deeply the ways of Nature, to go within the Drumming and the Humming, to enter the Other Realms, to learn the Healing secrets of the Tribes and to Divine where the Herds will be for the Hunters? There you would also learn to 'Sing the dying to Death' and the newly dead to peace. For these are the ways of the Tribes. I know, Morgan, that for these Arts you are well suited.

"The problem with this choice is that you have been raised in a much different culture and environment than that which is amoung the Tribal folk. You are used to many comforts that are not to be found there. I was but fifteen years when I came to Gorlois' house and it was, at first, a difficult change. I think it may be even more difficult to go from this life to theirs.

"There is another choice Morgan; you may ask the Lady of the Lake if she would accept you as a postulant, to dedicate yourself to the Order of the Goddess on the Isle of Apples, where you would receive a long and excellent education... however, once committed to remain at the Order, you may not marry. Oh yes, you may have lovers, however you will never live beneath their roof or share the intimacy of a long life with them. So choose carefully, Morgan."

"Mother, please, I beg of you to allow me one more year to contemplate these choices?"

And so, I allowed it...

When her year had passed, I again asked for her decision.

Morgan surprised me. Perhaps, I had seen only her talents, not her innermost desires. For truly, I thought she would wish to go to the Tribes. Instead, she said, "Mother, if I must choose between them, I would choose to go to the Isle of Apples and there become a Priestess of the Goddess. For there I may continue my literary studies and learn more of other places in *this* world. I do respect and embrace the Arts of the Walkers, but I believe that the Spirits will allow me to approach Them wherever I may be.

"Mother, will you try to arrange this for me? And promise that, if I am accepted, you will come to visit me often? I know that you would be so greatly honoured there."

"I will send word – and I will come as often as I can Morgan. You may also beg leave of The Lady to visit your family, for she holds none captive on the Isle."

Thus came the Day for Morgan to leave...

On the Day that Morgan left, the Bear wept bitterly.

He had formed for her a necklace of Stones and shells – it was quite beautiful. When, at the last, he felt sure enough of having his emotions under his control, he approached her.

"This is my gift to you Morgan – may it ever serve as a bond between us. For you have been like a... sister to me."

He had choked on the word 'sister.'

"And Morgan, I Love you."

She accepted the necklace. I could see that it touched her heart, for she Loved the Bear, as well.

By that Time, to my astonishment, the Bear could read and write – in Greek, Latin and to some extent the language of the Clans. He had amazed Morgan with the swiftness of his learning and I knew that Morgan must have felt good about her part in his accomplishments.

Her intended parting words to him were, "I give to you my Love and blessing, Bear."

But then her eyes – her beautiful eyes – clouded over and they looked like the "Swirling Seas" and whirlpools into infinity. Whenever this happened, she drew everyone into them; and what words came from her mouth were not from her own thoughts:

She whispered to the Bear, "You will be 'The Bear of the Britons'... Like the Great Bear in the Sky."

Then her eyes again became her own.

Morgan put the necklace around her neck and kissed the Bear on the cheek.

I am not sure that she ever knew that she had spoken thusly to him.

She had whispered to the Bear alone, so that no one else would hear. However, I had heard – and there was Morganna, staring from a distance. I knew not ever what *she* did or did not hear.

Then Morgan left... and took half of my heart with her.

The Bear was devastated!

Thinking back now after all that has come about, of course her words spoken upon that Day make perfect sense, but at that Time they had puzzled me. I wondered what they meant... "Bear of the Britons"?

At that Time, Morganna was near to her twenty-second year-turn, but she had forsaken all other choices and simply refused to leave. She said, "I will stay in my Father's house, *as is my right*, at least until I decide what will be my adventures in this life."

There was no persuading Morganna otherwise. Of course, she had chosen to ignore the fact that I had been named "owner of this house." Nevertheless, I allowed her to remain.

Morgan travelled to the Isle of Apples, was presented to the Lady and petitioned her to become a dedicant of the Order. The Lady graciously accepted her.

In less than one year it came about that, in addition to becoming a "Huntress Maiden" initiate, Morgan was given the responsibilities that had been those of the old Beekeeper – as the former one had recently passed through the Veil. Morgan was sorry for the loss of the old woman – who had been so kind to her by allowing her to help in caring for the hives. But since the "Taker of Breath" – who visits all in good Time – had come for her, Morgan found her comfort in knowing that the old woman would have chosen her to take her place, if she had had good enough warning. As it was, Morgan had always wished to be a Beekeeper. Now her wish had come true.

In the blink of an eye seven years had flown by. Besides her becoming the Beekeeper of the Isle of Apples, Morgan had become a great and renowned Enchantress and Seer.

Yes, I was very proud of my Morgan of the Woods.

Regarding Bedwyr…

My son, Bedwyr – in addition to his prowess in all the Arts of war, had proven himself to be a great Hunter – and, as I have said, he had the 'Sight.' He had the Gifts of the old people, but his greatest gift was the gift of Love and the object of his greatest affection was The Bear. He Loved me, too, and Morgan, of course.

But he was cautious of Morganna. She was 13 years older than he and there was somewhat more that caused him to keep a distance between them.

Bedwyr did well enough in his studies of reading, writing, and speaking properly. I taught him to speak in the old tongue of my people, and he had also learned some Latin. But he was not proficient in these things the way the Bear was. It is interesting how two people can be so different. Yet in their Love and devotion to each other they were the same. I knew that theirs would be a lifelong bond.

The Bear

The very first memory of my life is of Morgan, not of my Mother or my foster brother Bedwyr, but of Morgan – kind, Enchanting, beautiful Morgan. I was sitting on her lap in the children's quarters looking up at her beautiful face as she, in her whimsical and wonderful way, was telling a story to us. I remember that Bedwyr was sitting at her feet. There was a chill in the Air along with the sweet and pungent smells of Cedar, Pine, Juniper, Apple, and Rosemary. Ah, yes, it was the Night past the Longest Night, upon which we had celebrated the pinnacle of darkness and the return of the Sun God's rule. The Son of the Great Goddess… Igraine had also reminded us that upon that very Night four years past, had Bedwyr and I been born. The floor rushes of our chamber had been strewn with fragrant Herbs and greenery. Long ropes of Cedar branches had been braided by Igraine and the household servants. These she had hung from the doorposts and had had her attendants wind them around the crossbeams.

Upon this Night of my first remembrances, in the chamber all the torches were lit and their flickering cast dancing shadows all about the Stone walls. The three of us were wrapped in pelts for warmth. Morgan shared her hot honeyed wine with us.

Her tale that Night was one told by the Old Tribes – the small Dark People of the Woods – of whom she, Bedwyr, Morganna, and their Mother, the Lady Igraine, were kin.

I do precisely remember that this story was about a very ancient God named Nodens.

She began: "I would tell a tale to you... a tale of great mystery... of fear... of Sacrifice... and of joy.

"Now on these Fair Isles, Nodens is the God of Healing and Divination, of Brooks, Streams, Springs, and Caves. He is a secret God... an old God – a God of dark and silent places. The God of deep and still Waters.

Then she lowered her voice, whilst we were rapt in attention and said, "Each God has a purpose and function. And, each one represents principals of Cosmic Creation. Do you understand?"

She looked into my eyes and probably read the incomprehension. Her eyes twinkled. She smiled and tousled our hair.

Well no matter...

Hers were big and long words to us and filled with the promise of so many things yet to learn.

She continued: "Sometimes he is the Son, betimes the Brother or the Consort of the Goddess. But all is aright with this," quoth she, "for such things as blood ties are different in the realms of the Gods. And as everyone knows, the Great Goddess is Mother of all."

I remember being completely amazed when next she said, "Nodens disappears – or dies, some say – at the end of every year-turn. Then He retreats into his Cave of Madness and into the depths of his darksome Wells. All the while, the Sun is retreating and the Leaves of Red and Gold are falling from the Trees. When Earth has turned to brown and gray, all the green around us descends with Him into Her Cauldron of Chaos, there to return to the Mother's womb – awaiting Her call at Winter's End."

I frowned...

"Oh, but not to worry, Bear, for He will spring forth again, all in the proper time. The great wheel must turn to continue Earth's cycles."

Then Morgan sang a song of ancient words and haunting melody... still today, it pierces my heart.

>   "For Everything She changes, changes, changes...
>   Will change and change and change again...
>   And all will return... return... return..."

Of course, this does not rhyme in my written language. But when she sang these words in the tongue of the Old Tribes they were melodious as the song of Birds.

Morgan continued to Weave her tale of mystery. We, Spellbound, hung upon her every word.

"Now, Nodens knows that, as we watch Earth's bounty wither whilst He has retired for the cold and dark Time – we will worry and fear that the end of all life is at hand and that the light will not return. Also, that the Grains, Apples, and wild Berries would not grow and the Beasts of the Fields and Forests hunger and die. Even would the Bees, without Flowers, perish and no more should we have honey or mead to nourish us and warm our hearts.   Then, alas, would we all die without sustenance. For indeed, do not even his Brooks and Streams freeze over whilst Nodens sleeps?

"Oh, dreadful hour...

"So, in His boundless Wisdom and Love – recognizing our grief, long and long ago He *Spelled* the Evergreens to always remain green – as a beacon and a promise, that nothing is lost forever. All things in Green Nature rest, but for the Evergreens, which seem never to sleep at all.

"And this is why it has been our custom to 'Bring in the Greens' and to hang the halls and hovels with Evergreen and Holly, as Mid-Winter's Eve draws nigh – whilst we all await the returning of the Light.

"All of these things happen to remind us that although She changes Her cloak and Her faces, the Goddess never dies. For, in just the blink of an eye beyond the depths of the Longest Night, a newborn God arises to become the Sun Mother's son. The Sun God waxes! The light returns! Hail to the Sun God!

"But what of old Nodens? Does He return with the newborn light?

"Well, no – not quite yet. A Day comes at about the Time of the new milking of the Ewes when the small creeping furry ones come out from their dens and logs and just about at that same time do we, too, have a feeling of a quickening within.

"Nodens yawns and stretches. He breaks free from the dark icy deep, to emerge refreshed; a young God.

"It is at the Time of The Stirring when we celebrate our Festival of the Returning Light. And here does end the tale of Nodens."

"Oh Morgan, tell us more!"

So Morgan continued, for even with children small as we, she could not but help to teach the meanings of the Sacred Festival cycle of Igraine's blood kin.

I cannot say that I remember the rest of the words she uttered, or that I did not fall to sleep in her arms, however, Bedwyr and I must both have been snoring.

"Can you guess what happened next?"

At this change of her intonation I awoke or recovered from my reverie.

Morgan laughed again. I remember thinking that her laugh sounded as beautiful to me as the bells on Lady Igraine's ankles.

"To go on with my story...

"Nodens is the God of Healing Wells such as the one my Lady Mother, the great Seer Igraine, watches over in our fortress' courtyard."

"Oh..." said we.

"So, if ever you should become very sad or ill of heart, my dear ones, seek out a Well of Nodens, for there you shall find comfort and solace. Should you come upon a Sacred Well by chance, you must pay homage to Him and offer a sincere offering. Also ask of Him the desire of your heart. For those who approach Him with pureness of heart and honest intention will be blessed *three Times three!*"

But what I hold in my heart from that Night was looking up into Morgan's beautiful face. I thought that the Goddess must look very much like her.

In years to come, many have said that both Bedwyr and I listen long and hold our council in patience. I do believe that this we learned from our long listenings to Morgan's stories.

Of my relationships...

Now, Morgan and her Mother Igraine, as well as her older sister Morganna, were stunningly similar in the way of their looks. But Morganna had an expression that was very different from her sister's. Even from my early years I felt as if Morganna was always watching me – but not watching me in the way of Love, as did Morgan. Morgan's smile was as beautiful to me as Apple blossoms and her voice... it was sweet as the Birds of Rhiannon. But the smile of Morganna was more alike a sneer. And her voice was like the rasping caw of Crows and Ravens. Now, take me not wrong, I did indeed Love Crows and Ravens – for they had a great squawk which made me thrill with admiration of their might and power. But to hear the voice of Morganna was different. She was to me as a Nightmare and her every word an evil omen!

Morgan was proficient in the Art of languages. She had learned Greek, Latin, and the tongue of the Clans. Igraine had taught her as had she taught Morganna and Bedwyr.

My Mother, Tangwen, could neither read nor write and cared little for either. As for my Father, what was of value to him was that we learn the ways and Rites of Warriors. He taught Bedwyr also, of course, as a courtesy to Lady Igraine. And so, Bedwyr and I grew up with most of our focus being directed toward the skills and tactical Arts of warfare... and of course, of hunting.

Bedwyr... He was – and always will be – the brother of my heart. I Love him very much, although we share no blood between us. He was dark, small and lithe like his Mother and sisters, yet he did not have their beauty. What he *did* have was the *Sight*. This too – it seemed to me at that Time – he had inherited from Igraine.

More of the Dark Tribesmen and women have that Gift than folk of other races. Many of the Clansmen – and women, of course, such as their Druids and the "Seers," have powerful Gifts of the Arts too, but somehow it seems when they mix with Roman blood, much of it goes away. Perhaps it is more their focus – or lack thereof – than blood. However there was one blazing example to the contrary... the man called Gwyddion, The Merlin.

He was more of the race of the Romans than the Clans... or so it was whispered. For his Mother was half of the Clans and the other half Roman. Rumours told that he was a bastard and so none really knew what blood his Father had. Although, because of his look, his Father had to have been a Roman, and a pure Roman. Nevertheless, *he had the sight* and great powers! He was well educated by one of the old Druids, it was told.

He had visited Igraine's fortress two or three times in my childhood. I remembered him especially well from one visit. It was Igraine he had come to see.

At that Time, I had thought of all Druids as very old men, with long white beards, and so, was surprised that he looked so young! Morgan, who seemed quite taken by him, told me that Gwyddion, The Merlin, was considered the greatest of all Druids – "by his works" – and that many other Druids had spent twenty years to come to "Know what he knew," while he was yet a boy. For all the years leading up to The Merlin's first visit, Bedwyr and I were very busy being honed in the skills of physical combat with sword, spear, and bow. We learned how to use our long shields as an offensive weapon as well as a defensive device. And although many of the ranks of foot soldiers still used an axe as their only weapon, little training was given to us of these, for Marcus had higher ambitions for us. He knew that, due to Igraine's late husband's position, honours, and holdings, Bedwyr would be highly placed at the tables of Briton's Warriors and that I would always be allowed to stand at his back, for he would insist upon it.

I was somewhat gifted with sword and bow, but never could I best Bedwyr. Even though he was much smaller than I, he was quick, cunning, and *he* had the *Magic*. He had great prowess in bearing weapons. He was magnificent! But then, I had thought, he *was* Igraine's son.

Marcus knew many of the Roman military formations and the function of all the mighty Roman war machines: the siege towers, battering rams, the scorpio – or dart thrower, the catapults, such as the onager, which was amusingly named "wild ass" and the older – but still in use – ballista. We learned all the names of these and how to put them into action. Now, these I was interested in. The tactics and calculations of the battle formations fascinated me, for I was a thinker and was always pondering many diverse things.

As an example: I was greatly interested in the histories of all the peoples of these Islands and beyond. Most of the common people living in the villages and countryside surrounding us knew naught of history at all beyond the time of their own grandsires. They simply gave it no thought; or in some cases could not even fathom the concept of it! To these, three hundred years may as well have been in the "Time of the Giants"!

The exception were the educated wealthy. Although, as I had been told, with each generation that passed – since the Romans had lessened their presence and then withdrawn – there were even fewer of *these* who were literate.

Of course, there were still the Bards and the Initiates of the Isle of Apples, as well as the few Druids which were left in Briton, who could all read and write.

And then there were the people of the Old Dark Tribes, who remembered and repeated their histories by word of mouth from one generation to the next.

At the Time of my childhood there was yet another culture of people living around us. With the influx of the later Romans, there began to be brought Ideas of a new religion. These were the people of the Roman "Universal Church" – the only religion sanctioned by the New Rome. They worshiped a new Sky God who had sent a Son to Earth who had been sacrificed. It was very much, in that *one* way, like all other religions. However these people were different in the fact that they had but *one* God and they claimed that their God was the *only* living and *true* God... that there were really no other Gods at all! They held no respect or regard for the Great Goddess – or much for women, for that matter. These people were not like the original followers of Yeshua, who were kind and respectful of others. Therefore, those who honoured the Old Gods were very suspicious of them.

The Universal Church kept a hold upon the Christians of our lands until there came a Monk from Rome, named Pelagius, who turned the thinking of most of the followers of Yeshua in the lands of the Britons.

Of course, it was Morgan who had taught all of this to me. How else could I have learned it?

A note from Morgan...

There are still Warriors, many of whom had been The Caesar's Commanders, who live here and are ready at the call to do the political and military bidding of Rome. But most of these have never given up their secret "Rites of Mithras" – Roman law or not!

In so many ways what had been Rome was truly gone from these Islands.

What was left of the vestiges of Rome were the Roman Britons, who had learned to live in the style and luxury of their Roman society.

By the Time of the writing of these, my histories, most of the people living in the lands of the Britons have gone back to the "Old Religions" of their Forefathers.

The Bear

Yes, I was a thinker and all my thoughts haunted me Day and Night. Very old thoughts for a child, I was told... very precocious. Morgan said that I had great potential to become wise and learned. However, I knew that I would never become *that* unless I could learn to read and write. By the Time we were past our seventh year-turn, Bedwyr had already been taught by Igraine to read and write. I must admit that I felt envy of this. Certainly not directed toward Bedwyr – and not an evil envy, but only a longing. There was a sadness coming over me. I felt that my true gift was to think and that my thoughts would be best written down. But how would I learn to read?

One Day, Morgan asked if I would like to go for a walk in the Woods with her.

"Just the two of us?"

"Yes, my dear one, will you come with me?"

I was thrilled, for I could never get enough of being with Morgan, even at seven years. This of course, has never changed in all of my life.

But to go on: We went for that walk in Morgan's Woods and I saw her chirping and tweeting with the Birds. It always thrilled me to see that they responded to her. It seemed to me that they would copy what she did. They would look at her; one even alighted on her finger... a wild Bird! She held it close to her face and it snuggled close to her. And then we walked farther and there were insects buzzing and creaking all around us and she copied their sounds. Then a Hare came right up to her! She called him "Mortimer" and fed some wild lettuces to him, which she had tucked away in her kirtle.

Morgan seemed to me like the Spirits of the Trees. Although she was *real* – I mean that I could reach out and touch her – she sometimes seemed ethereal, otherworldly, but always completely and utterly fascinating. We walked farther into the Wood and she named the Herbs for me and what their uses were and I listened to her every word ... but then, of a sudden she said, "Let us sit down here Bear, for there is something serious I must ask you."

So I made myself look very stern and serious. She smiled and poked her finger to the tip of my nose. We laughed.

Rays of Sunlight filtered though the branches above and fell upon her head, face, and hands; she did indeed look as one of the Twyla Y Tag – who my Mother had told me about – might. Then in her gentle and nonchalant way, she brushed my ragged hair away from my eyes and said to me quite suddenly, "Bear, would you like to learn to read and write? I could teach you... Igraine has taught Bedwyr and Morganna and I. I think that it is the greatest gift she could ever have given to us."

Then in a moment of boldness, I blurted out, "Yes! Yes! It would be my second fondest wish in all the World."

She looked at me quizzically and asked, "What would be the first?"

I cast my eyes downward and then looked straight into her eyes and replied, "No, Morgan, I cannot tell it; for it is a secret I must keep. Perhaps someday I may be able to share it with you, but not on this Day. However, take me not wrongly, I am thrilled and honoured, that you, one of the ladies of this great house would offer to teach me. Yes! And I thank you!"

"Bear, you need not speak so formally to me, we are like brother and sister. And I see within you greatness, though the 'Voices' have not yet let me know of your future or how it will play out. But I do know that you must have the Art of literacy. It is very important.

"So, would you like to tell everyone – or keep it a secret just between the two of us for now?"

And because I was shy for some reason about it – or perhaps, because to share a secret with Morgan was beyond a thrill – I said... "Morgan, oh yes, let us keep it a secret just between us two."

She smiled and laughed. And that laugh was like the echo of the bubbling Spring which was just beyond our sight.

"Then it will be our secret. And when you have accomplished this, then you can surprise everyone."

And so it came about that we would sneak away as often as we might without anyone knowing of it and Morgan taught me how to read and write the Greek tongue first – because it was the language of the intellectual – and then she began to teach me Latin, for she said, "I do feel that Latin will be very important to you in years to come."

She also began, but did not have time to finish, teaching me the tongue of the Clans. She did not have time to complete this task, because, when I was almost in my ninth year-turn, there came one of the worst Days of my life.

It was the Day that Morgan left. She left our house, left her Mother,

her brother, her sister and left me, to go to the Isle of Apples to become an initiate of the Order of the Great Goddess.

Our parting was short and bitterly sad for me. I had only a few Days to reconcile my feelings to the fact that this was what Morgan wanted.

I hurriedly made a necklace for her... "A child's gift," I chided myself after she was gone.

Then she was gone.

After our goodbyes, I ran deep into the Woods... Morgan's Woods... And there I stayed for many hours of many Days – and I admit that I cried and cried and cried.

But lest I make it seem that Morgan was the only one that I Loved, let me speak of Bedwyr, the brother of my heart and my best friend. I Loved him as dearly as one could ever Love a brother. I do not know what life would have been like without him, certainly never as rich. We were almost mirror opposites of each other and it worked well, each of us admiring the other for the gifts and talents that we personally lacked. Never was I jealous that he was far more proficient in the Arts of war than I *and* he had the Magic *and* the Sight, which I did not. But then, of course, *he* was the son of the Great House of Igraine of Dumnonia.

We had much fun together. We would go hunting and fishing and did all the silly and mischievous things that boys do whilst growing up. And so went the next three years.

Then, on the very Day of our twelfth year-turn – despite the Snow and Ice that covered the rocky cliffs upon which Lady Igraine's fortress stood – the great Merlin arrived to take Bedwyr away to foster him. He was to teach him the skills and Mysteries of the Druids and the movements of the Stars, new ways of Healing and much more.

He stayed with us for three Days, to celebrate the birth of the new Sun God, in our fashion.

In that year the New Moon came on the very Night of the birth of the new-born Sun God... "The Child of Promise." This was portentous.

Gwyddion, The Merlin, who had every right to, performed the Druidic Ritual of the "Cutting of the Mistletoe" with a Golden Sickle, which he had carried all the way from the Snowy Mountains to perform this Rite at its proper Time. The New Moon after the Winter Solstice was the proper Time. It came upon a different Night each year, so it was an amazement to us all that they coincided on that year. And so was Lady Igraine's household blessed with the "New Mistletoe." He actually allowed us to watch as he climbed the Tree upon which it dwelled! I have wondered about that many times, but have never asked *if* we should have been allowed to do this.

To my astonishment and blessed relief, The Merlin offered to take me along with Bedwyr.

To be fostered by the great Merlin! That was a happy Day. I was sad to leave my Mother, sad to leave my Father and Lady Igraine too, for she was always kind to me. But I was so very excited and thrilled; for I had heard that the Great Merlin lived in a Cave in the Snowy Mountains, very far from where we were, far enough away to be a grand adventure.

We packed up a few of our things. I took my writing implements and the one book that I owned. We took our bows, arrows, some clothing, sturdy boots, blankets, some foodstuffs – and we left – never to be the same again.

Just so ended my childhood at Dumnonia.

Bedwyr

As a boy growing up, I knew of myself as Bedwyr of Dumnonia... the only son of the great Gorlois, conceived very shortly before his Death, as well as of my lovely and powerful Mother, Igraine of the Tribes; woman in her own right – Mistress now of the fortress and holdings of her late husband.

I had two sisters; one six years older and one thirteen years older than I. And then there was my brother of the heart, the Bear.

My sister, Morgan, was such a lovely girl. I Loved her well. I remember that even in her youth she was always writing everything down. She encouraged me over and over again, "Bedwyr you can read and write. Write down your thoughts and feelings."

But to me, feelings were something felt – not written about. It was hard for me to make the connection of that.

As to my family...

I Loved my Mother very much. But of my siblings, though I Loved my sister Morgan and tolerated Morganna – the one I Loved best was the Bear, although he was not brother of my blood. I admired him in all things, even though he was not of my rank and station. But such things as that do not matter to a boy, nor would it ever have mattered to me, for I Loved him with a great passion. He was truly like a brother to me. We were exactly the same age, born on the same Night. Together we learned war and hunted and all such things as boys do.

Now, so many years later, I am writing these early events and memories, just as Morgan has ever prompted me to.

But I am a man of few words and all that I can say is that the Love which I felt for him as a child has only deepened and strengthened as the years have gone by.

I am finally, now in my fortieth year, writing upon these pages the remembrances of my youth, so that Morgan may add them to her collection of histories.

I have written on other pages the important experiences of my life: the grand moments, the great battles, learning of my lineage, the true nature of my birth and that of the Bear's – he who would become Arthur,

High King of all the Britons, of my championing him and of all the adventures we had with The Merlin, of the intrigues entwined in Arthur's wedding, of how I have stood in Arthur's shadow all the Days of my life – and have been much more than happy to do so. All have, or will be written. And I will give them to Morgan.

But I tire very quickly of expressing my thoughts, so Morgan, forgive this of me, as I know you will want to compile all these different pages in some chronological order. But these memories I will let be for now. I am weary this Night and haunted by Dreams unfulfilled.

Many things are afoot: Many virtuous, some evil, many painful things, Morgan, *many* painful things. This is all that I will say for now. Perhaps tomorrow I will continue.

Please keep this with all of your notes and as I have said, I will write more, so that by the end of my month of resting here on the Isle of Apples with you, you will have much of what I have felt in my weary, sometimes triumphant life. But above all, of the joy in my life for the honour of service – and Love I have born for the great one, Arthur.

I close now – Bedwyr.

Chapter 4
Morgan of the Woods

Morgan

Perhaps it is now Time for me to write upon these pages of the beauty of the Isle of Apples, this place that I call my home...

There is an ancient Hill rising from the Island, the steep sides of which – at some Time lost in memory – people had adapted into a great spiral pathway twining its way up to the summit. On top of it, there are Standing Stones which our Ancestors had lain up there. There is also, in the center of the circle of Stones, a great clear green Stone. It is said that this is not a Stone of the Earth, but one which fell from the Stars, and it is greatly revered. This Hill is called The Tor.

Everywhere you look on the Tor there are Wildflowers mingling with the Mosses and Ferns. Everything smells so sweet in Summer that the Butterflies, Bees and Glow-flies Love to linger there – all of which adds to the Enchantment of this place.

Here upon the Isle, we have a long Time of the pink and white blossoming of the Apple Trees at Winter's End. And then, a longer Fruit season than in most regions of Briton.

Even though it is not so many Days walk East of here, on the plains where the great Hanging Stones are, the Winters seem much colder and harsher. Perhaps it is the Winds which make it seem so. No matter the cloak, the chill pierces the bones!

I have heard stories of people and children being carried off by the Wind Spirits up into the Clouds never to be been seen again. I doubt these tales' truthfulness.

This place, which has become my home, is called the "Island of the Inland Sea" by some –because, for much of the Time, Water comes from the great Western Sea inland through Rivers, Streams and canals – some of which were handmade – to completely surround it.

Each morning, and then again each evening as the Sun disk sinks below the horizon, the reedy Water and all the land – save the Tor – is hidden within deep Mists. They cover the Water as well, so that when you stand atop the Tor, you feel as if you are on a Mountain of the Gods. You can see nothing *but* beautiful rolling Mist which, it is said, holds a powerful Enchantment. It is also said that "Within the Mists, all the secrets of the Cosmos can be found." And, if one can truly become one with the Mist, then one would feel the experience of being one with the ALL.

I have gone many times to the center of the Stone Circle where the Green Star Stone is and where are laid the offerings to the Goddess. Betimes I feel that I see the Star Stone glowing – although perhaps that is with the Vision of the "Sight" and not with the vision of my eyes.

Our land is also called the Isle of Apples. This is for two reasons: The first being our many orchards, which are filled with Apple Trees. They are native to our land and they flourish on their own, with very little need of tending.

Within each season they provide a different source of usefulness.

In the Time of Red and Gold Leaves, none surpass the Apple Tree in colour. Once the Apples are picked, the Earth Goddess leaves behind the pallet of Her greatest beauty.

Then come the Snows. From Sun rise to set, each bare bow and branch glistens with a crystalline glow, each defining their own exquisite silhouette, due to the heavy moisture in the Air of the land within the Lake. Even on Moonlit Nights through the dark of Winter, they glisten.

Near the Moon of Planting, the Apple Blossoms come in all of their glory. Some of our oldest Apple Trees – those which will in late Summer give small green Fruit – bloom with white blossoms of fine fragrance. Then shortly thereafter, the Trees that will later produce somewhat larger and more colourful Apples, blossom in the most delicate colour of pink – although these Trees are a bit less fragrant.

During Harvests, along with the Grains and Vines, the Apples come into their full glorious fruiting. Even beyond the obvious delights of taste and fragrance – it is said that the Apple is one of the foods of the Gods – they being one of the most healthful foods one can eat. They also provide much vigorous exercise for those of us who must pick them, warding off sluggishness through the Feast of The Longest Night, the Winter Calming, and beyond.

For Time out of memory the Apple has been a *symbol* of the Great Goddess. The Fruit of the Apple is as sweet as Love. Their shapes and colours are beautiful. And when you cut an Apple in half, you will see a five-pointed Star! – an ancient symbol of the great Star Goddess – and I am told, a symbol of protection, from ours even to the most distant and ancient of lands. Try opening an Apple now, if there be one wherever you are. Take a knife and cut through it across its middle. Do you see the Star? It has always been there. The Star in our tradition is also a symbol of the four earthly directions – or the four Elements – topped by "the Aether" – or *covered* by Spirit. These have long been held as Sacred Wisdoms.

Our Island has been a haven of Goddess worshipers for perhaps as long as Humans have stood upon this ground. Perhaps, even, before my Ancestors arrived here.

I believe it was for all of these reasons that The Merlin was beguiled by our Isle. Who could not but be?

Oh yes, as I have been writing this page, I just now remembered a certain conversation which Gwyddion and I had shared. It was this:

Many travelers have come to ask our Wise Mothers profound questions; for their Wisdom and Knowledge of the Mysteries is renowned. One question which seems oft repeated is: "Why are there so many different Goddesses worshiped – and sacrificed to – in the world of men?"

Well, *I* think... and Gwyddion agreed the answer to that just might be that long, long ago, before the world was made, the Great Initiator had spit forth Divine Powers – Male and Female, which had then become *Self Aware* – or perhaps, better said, Conscious. Perhaps, at that Time, they knew *what* They were, but not *who* They were.

Then came the sequence in the great Creation for Worlds, living beings of Stone, green, and flesh to come to be.

What if, at that Time, these Divine conscious beings sought out the *others*... those of the Worlds of form? What might this interaction have caused?

We theorized that perhaps each culture of this world had – *and has* – its own particular needs, each according to their own way of living. Perhaps it was that when these new beings of flesh and blood called out to the Great One, these male and female Spirit Beings wished to aid them along their way. Perhaps then the Two wished to become many... many Goddesses and Gods to answer many diverse peoples' needs. Perhaps this attraction was shared between the Gods and the worlds of men, such that they *formed* together, each their own identities out of their mutual need or desire... such that a hunting society might worship the White Moon Goddess or the Stag horned God; whereas a fiercer people might call to the Eastern Goddess Ishtar or the Alban Cailleach. Nomadic people of a landscape of harsh desert or a farming people might call to Sol, Re, or Apollo. Do you understand my words?

Of course, these are merely speculations.

Think of it, though – why should the Gods not be able to show many faces? Even we as Humans show ourselves in many differing ways to many different people. A Mother, for example, always shows herself as

Mother to her children. To her lover, she is quite the different person. If that lover works a farm with her, then during those endeavours she appears – and acts yet a different person than while entwined in passion. To her own Mother, she is ever child. To a friend she is confidant and merry-maker. If she be a Healer, Seer, or Wise Woman, to one in need she is ever seen as a Crone – and this regardless of her age. We are all – and all perceived as – different people at different times according to different needs or desires. Why, then, could not the Gods be?

But, as I said, this is just what *our* thoughts were.

There is no denying that all people want to understand the Gods and Spirits. It is within us all to feel the draw of the Great One. Yet we commune with the many. Even those who acknowledge but one God still have their Angels and Saints – be they friend or enemy.

Some may like to call Them sister Goddesses or Brother Gods. Or, some may like to call Them mirror or shadow images of each other. Really – what difference does it make what we *call* Them – only *that* we call Them. For are we not all the progeny – the Creation – indeed the substance of the Great ONE?

Thus goes the ancient 'Chant of Enlightenment':

We are all ONE... We are all ONE... We are all ONE...
Of root and stem of heart and drum...
Of bone and Stone and blood...
Of feather, scale, of skin or fur
Of HER we are the sum...
We are all ONE... We are all ONE... We are all ONE...
The seasons change, we dance our dance
From birth to shroud to dust
Time passes by – We live, we die
From breath to death we must
We are all ONE... We are all ONE... We are all ONE...

...Of course it sounds much more melodious in our original tongue.

It is said in our Mystery School that everything in Creation *IS* the Goddess. We only see the separation of things because we are Human.

Oh yes, I know, I am wont to linger on the Mysteries over much. So is The Merlin and thus, of these things we can talk for hours and hours.

Oh!... I have diverged from the topic of my writing.

So, to continue where I left off – about our beautiful Isle of Apples.

We are not totally isolated here. We have the little Marsh Folk's punts to take us from the Isle to the land which surrounds it. We have contact and friendly relations with the peoples who live beyond the Tor and the Order's lands in the nearby villages, as well as with the two hermits who live round about and the women who live at the small

Christian Monastery, which are all within walking distance.

Our closest neighbors are the Marsh Dwellers. They are a strange people, who are probably distantly related to my race. But as they have developed different customs and traditions over the millennia, no one really knows for sure who they are or from whence they have come.

There is some trade between us – they buy the honey of my Bees and some of the wonderful cheeses and other things that we, the women and men of the Isle, produce.

They, as well as many other people living near and far, desire our woolens – for our White Faced Sheep are acclaimed to be some of the best kept in all of the lands of the Britons – and we are known to be expert Weavers. We spin Magic into our every yarn. For, we are taught when first we arrive that to Weave is to be like the Great Goddess AIXIA, – She who Weaves Her Magic into the *tapestry* which is *everything* in Spirit and form – so when spinning the yarn itself, we "Spell" the Magic of Healing, protection, and prosperity into it. So, it is much prized.

Now, much of what we Weave, we use ourselves. But as there is always an abundance, we sell some of our woolens to others. This brings into our coffers great amounts of gold and other goods. People come from near and far away, hoping to acquire some of the "Magic Wool." We trust that they are blessed by it.

However, what is kept a secret is that we also hold back enough to give to the needy who surround us.

Near the bottom of the Tor, there is a wonderful, spectacular, and miraculous thing that happens. Not too many paces, one from the other, are two Springs which, it is said, come from far away beneath the surface of the Earth. They run through their separate passages and corridors through the ground for hundreds of leagues, as their Waters touch the soil, roots, Stones, and minerals on their way to the bottom of the Tor.

One of them, which lies just at the base of the Tor, goes through the chalk lands, where it picks up the white residue from its passages and tunnels, and bubbles up a milky white. Some take this as a symbol of the life-giving semen of the Son/Lover/God – without whose fecundity our great Mother Earth would not return to us at "Winter's End" to awaken the blossoms, buds, and sprouts. However, others like to say that the white Water is the milk of the Goddess' breasts.

The other Spring, which is not so many paces away, goes through the rocky clay lands. Her Waters pick up a red hue. Her flow stains all that it comes into contact with. We liken this Holy Water to the menstrual blood of all women, and therefore the creative life force of the Goddess.

There was – and still is – a small Church and women's Monastery close to our Order's lands and very close to the bottom of the Tor. We get on well with them and aid them in any way that we can. But beside the few, here and there, there are not as many Christian folk on these, Our Fair Isles, as there once were. After the Roman rule had ended, their numbers had fallen dramatically – when "the law" no longer dictated what one could believe or practice.

However, of the Christians still practicing their religion, some goodly number have moved into our immediate area. This is because of a great legend, which has been added as yet another layer of Mysticism to our already immortalized Wells. You see, the Yeshuites – or as they are now called "Christians"– have set up their own shrine near the Red Spring, which they call the Chalice Well. They say its red Waters symbolize the Holy Blood of Yeshua. This adds to the many quizzical and sometimes disagreeing stories surrounding their mythos.

One is that when the God-King – the Christos – was yet a little boy, a relative of his took him on great travels, in many directions of the known world. He is said to have been a wealthy tin Merchant – as well as a great Magician.

Legends say that one of these journeys was to the land of the Britons – to the Isle which lies within the Inland Sea. Upon this first visit, Yosef – for that was his name – and the boy spent the Night near the Red Spring. Of course, this was nothing unexpected as our Red and White Springs had been destinations of spiritual pilgrims for millennia.

The legend goes on to say that Yosef left an offering to the Well and the Land, then stuck his much beloved and long used staff into the Earth near to it. When he awoke upon the next morning, a Thorn Tree had grown in its stead. Some people say that this Thorn is still alive, and can be visited on the grounds of the little Monastery – where it stands always "dressed" with ribbons and the like.

I believe it was for all of these reasons that The Merlin was so beguiled by our Isle. He was so taken with this place.

I could go on endlessly telling of the wonders of this place that I so Love, but now I must put down my quill and away this vellum, for the hour is late.

Chapter 5
The First Battle

Gwyddion

And so it was that after my capture by Vortigern's men my life was spared by my own cunning – spared that is, from sacrifice by his Necromancers.

I was just past my fourteenth year-turn at the Time of my capture. Thereafter, for near five years, I was compelled to stay with the great Vortigern, designing and overseeing the building of his famed fortress and aiding him in attaining the power and influence he was to achieve.

For the sake of clarity – and posterity – Vortigern's true name was Vitalinus. This name means 'order.' Vortigern, in fact was a title, meaning something akin to "Overlord" or "High Lord."

However, after his defeat, he was known to the Western Clans as Gwr-teyrn Gwyrddeneu – "Vortigern the Thin." This was a reflection of the hard, lean – "thin" – years that followed, caused by the loss of so many of their able-bodied men in that battle.

As those years I spent with Vortigern's company rolled by, I took note of all his foolish endeavours; his ever more entangled alliances with Saxon mercenaries of war – whom he had first hired to bolster his forces when fighting off raids of the Eire upon lands of the Westernmost Clans – and his ever-accumulating debt to them.

Running short of funds, Vortigern had made a pact with the Saxon Kings Hengist and Horsa to hire the expertise and dreadful might and skill of their battle-honed Saxon Warriors – in trade for the best and most beautiful, arable land on the Eastern coast of Our Fair Isles!

I watched as more and more Saxons settled in with their folk. Soon they were becoming a mighty nation of their own – and a danger!

Finally, even Vortigern began to see the folly of having so large a Saxon host nearby. It was for this reason, I believe, that he further entangled himself in unsavory political negotiations.

He even went so far as to put away his first wife Sevira – the Mother of his sons – to make a marriage alliance with Hengist, who would proclaim himself King of the Saxons – here on Briton's shores! By marrying Hengist's daughter, the Princess Rowena, Vortigern sealed the bargain.

At least in this one thing, he had done well.

Oh, Rowena... she was fair of face and countenance, with long golden braids reaching to her waist. She was taller than most men around her. And she threatened their inherent sense of superiority, simply by her imposing presence. She was also intelligent and politically astute. I wondered how much Vortigern could ever hope to tame – much less receive Love from – this strong and self-assured woman.

On the great Wheel spun...

Soon Rowena became with child. I could not help but wonder; would their half Saxon children ever come to rule the West? No one could know the foreboding in my heart.

In my fifth year with Vortigern, everything in the West seemed to be reaching a climax, for you see, besides invaders and marauders, there were two factions in our land – one was the Clansmen who would go back to traditional Clannish ways, and those who were Romanised Britons – wanting to retain their Roman lifestyles and law.

It had always been Vortigern's agenda to reestablish the power and rights of the Clans, restoring their original borders and age-old traditions – throwing off any remnants of Roman rule, while at the same Time unifying them under one acceptable battle Commander... Vortigern, of course!

A noble idea... I must admit that I agreed with these sentiments, but not that they be carried out by Vortigern, who was a ruthless, vain, and haughty man. He was also what one might call a charmer. Oh, not in the ways of true Magic, but of guile. So much was this the case that he even coveted the position of High King over *all* the Clans.

When the Winds of gossip and espionage reached the 'ears' of Rome, it was inevitable that it would cause trouble... Trouble it caused! Vortigern's lofty ambitions proved to be very threatening to the New Rome. The Caesar would not tolerate this. For you see, already had several loose confederacies of Teutonic forces attacked the city of Rome herself – most notably that of Alarick, King of the Visigoths. Then, too, did other "barbarian hoards," as Rome called them, threaten the might of Roman Armies in ever more far-flung Roman Provinces – and betimes the "hoards" had prevailed.

Vortigern knew that if he and his followers were to stand up to the might of Rome, they would need outside help – namely from his old friends, the Saxon mercenaries.

So it was that when these political tensions had reached a boil, a mighty Roman army was sent to Briton.

This imminent battle, which was to be staged on the morn of the Ides of December – the Full Moon of that month – was to be commanded by one Germanus of Auxaire who had been sent to Briton – funded by the Church's Pontifus Maximus – under the auspices of The Caesar in Constantinople. At his command was the most feared and highly celebrated legion in the entire Roman world – Caesar's Elite Guard – fighting under the royal banner of the Purple Dragon... Germanus' directive was to thwart Vortigern's campaign completely.

From the Continent they came – along with those from the West and South of our own lands, and others from the Snowy Mountains within Vortigern's own territory – all travelling or meeting upon the great Roman road Northward.

Those Roman Briton loyalists' forces were stealthy, for they had been notified of the Caesar's Guard's chosen field of battle long before Vortigern had got word of it and had therefore travelled the selfsame road three Days before Vortigern's troops had. As far as I know, Vortigern never suspected their presence, for they had gone to great lengths to post Archers as lookouts along their way, lest someone warn Vortigern, and to sweep the road behind them with branches, so as to camouflage their passing.

The so called "Britannian" troops, led by their Dux and Lords – most of whose families were former Clansmen – were called to service by Dux Ambrosius Aurelius, the Britons' highest Battle Commander, at whose side was his younger brother Badraig, later to be called Uther the Pen Dragon. The combined Romano-Celtic-Gaulish troops were a force to be reckoned with!

Ambrosius Aurelius and his younger brother had already come to fame far and wide as Champions of Warfare and staunch defenders of the Roman lifestyle. Their reputations were those of honourable men. Never had a charge of rape or unwarranted cruelty been laid against them by their defeated foes – or by their women. I was so very anxious to meet them – especially in light of the revelation from my Mother that we were half-brothers

In retrospect, I must add here an aside:

As I have previously written, the name Uther means 'terrible, wonderful' and '*Pen* Dragon' means '*Chief* Dragon.' But, this title was not given to him until *after* the upcoming battle, to commemorate his success in it. Uther's baptismal name – for his parents followed the new religion – was Badraig Constantius. In later years, his birth name was forgotten altogether and Uther forbade the calling of himself by any name other than "Uther" or "The Pen Dragon"!

Now you may wonder if my whole life was a wretched existence during those years. I assure you that it was not. For, any situation of life, regardless of how loathsome, can be tolerated – or may even, in some ways, be made to seem fair – if one can engender a positive attitude, that is – which I have always tried to do.

I had made a few good friends in Vortigern's camp who helped to brighten my circumstance. For them I was grateful. Notwithstanding this, my solitude has always been my best comfort. For you see, I am never *really* alone.

Oh, it was not that I was ill-treated – in fact Vortigern provided many things for my comfort. The quarters allotted to me were far more spacious and luxurious than ever I needed or wanted. Always did I have plenty to eat – richer foods than I cared for, in fact. My clothing – vestments of my office, as Vortigern called them – were always made of the richest of fabrics.

About my sixteenth year-turn he had had matching breeches and a cloak made for me out of the finest woolen cloth that I had ever seen. The breeches were of a practical weight, enabling me to move freely in them. The cloak was truly magnificent. He had said – when giving them to me – that "You are a man now and have grown half an arm's length in height and filled out into your lean muscular frame since first you came to be with me. It is well overdue that you wear a man's clothing. I had them dyed a blue to match your grey-blue eyes, Gwyddion. Also, as part of your Year-turn gift, I am giving to you a brooch of silver and Sapphires, crafted of the traditional knot work of two entwined Dragons. May they serve to remind all others of your insight in determining what had caused the crumbling down of my original fortress, and of your brilliance in designing the one that now stands. May they serve as a reminder to *you* of my great esteem for you."

I had thought this peculiar – a Commander of war forces, a haughty King, making note of and lauding my physical characteristics... Of course, to understand why he would care to dress me in such a manner, one must understand Vortigern's predilections toward grandiosity.

Not long before I left his company he had gifted me with a twisted golden neck torque with Wolfs' heads on each of its ends – a beautiful thing it was. I had thought at the Time that I should have appreciated it. But its weight around my neck only served to remind me that no matter how he showered me with gifts and honours I was in fact and truth a captive enslaved to him.

I had always suspected that his gifts to me were vainglorious attempts at showing the world of his contemporaries that he owned and ruled me, his great Magician. I wondered "Am I as an Idol in his Temple, to dress, feed, and flatter whilst binding me upon his personal Altar?" His gifts tasted bitter as weeds.

Through my years in Vortigern's service, I had learned by

observation the ways of men. But somehow I had never developed their appetites and desires. I had lain with neither woman nor man. For, not only had I feared that somehow the power of my true fortress – my *self* – might be abdicated in favour of such base desires, but I simply had not had the Time to be involved in such things – for so busy had I been kept in Vortigern's service.

Then one Night came when Vortigern forced my hand by an act of great disrespect toward my body – even though he knew that I was not like other men in the ways of lust!

This happened upon the Night before the battle. It was the last straw in the bale. I abandoned Vortigern to his defeat.

The details of this encounter and of my abandoning him, I have shared with my Lady Morgan of the Woods. As I know that she keeps written a history of all who are entwined in this web of Arthur's world – and because even now it pains me to elaborate, I will leave it at that.

However, I have learned in my life that things in this world turn and change their colours like the seasons of the Trees – one year's ambivalence becomes the next's breathless desire.

But perhaps, that is another story, for another telling, in another Time.

The Night before the Battle...

The Night before the battle, I walked the camp closest to where Vortigern's pavilion was. Only he and the wealthiest Chieftains had covered areas in which to sleep – with the most influential of those camping closest to Vortigern.

As I walked on I saw the banners of Gwynedd flying proudly above each of the great Chieftain's tents. First was that of the house of Enniaun Girt. And over there, just beyond them – to the North of and closest to Vortigern – was the pavilion of Cunedda ab Edern and his sons. To his South were the three sons of Cadell Ddymllwg – whose names now evade my recollection.

And on and on they went...

Soon I found myself precariously close to Vortigern's pavilion. I feared recognition so I pulled my cloak hood forward, hiding my face from onlookers.

Smoke from a couple of hurriedly stacked Balefires that had been set with damp logs filled the chill Night Air, wafting through the surroundings like the tentacles of a giant Squid. Strange that this smoke should hold a beauty of its own, yet it did. All of these things were filling me with the eerie sense that, just beyond mortal man's grasp of this world of form, lurked dark, hungry Spirits awaiting their harvest of dead souls from the killing fields of the morrow. Of a sudden the smoke overcame me – I choked. My eyes began to tear and burn. I realised that more aid was needed from my cloak – I pulled it up to cover my mouth and nose, cautiously breathing through it.

I laughed to myself at that. I well knew this feeling of suffocation, although not in a literal sense, but in the sense of Vortigern's overpowering presence.

Ah, yes – Vortigern... and Vortigern's pavilion. Always must this vain man have more and better of everything than all those around him. Here he was, about to go into a bloody battle, yet he must show his pretention by hauling to the camp luxurious accommodations for feast, audience, and reclining: Sumptuous bedding, floor and table covers from Byzantium, silver plate and golden goblets with Rubies encrusted upon them. Yes, I knew his pavilion well; for it was here that he had sealed his doom.

Most of the other men, boys, and wives slept outside beneath the Night Sky – for there were always women who refused to let their men go alone into battle – foolish as that was. So, too, there were the whores who always followed armies – in hopes of plying their trade.

Some of the men were trying to soothe and reassure their women. Some were bolstering the courage of their sons for what would be on the morrow. I looked around and saw them, shifting from side to side nervously trying to get some sleep.

Listening to the sounds of whispered voices, fretful in prayer and supplication, the crackling of the Fires, the weeping of women and the restless whinnying and whickering of the Horses – who assuredly felt the mood of the Night – made me think that it must have been obvious to anyone who was at all perceptive that the camp itself was filled with foreboding and the static tension of fear.

I saw their faces. They were forever branded upon my memory.

Many of these men I had known for all the years that I had been with Vortigern. Some of the younger men, as old now as fifteen years, I had known as children playing with their toys when the world was to them a less mad and more beautiful place.

Memories flooded into me from everywhere I looked. There was one-eyed Cadeyrn, son of Bryn, who had first reasoned with Vortigern not to sacrifice me but to listen to my words. He had been perhaps... thirty-five years then... and very handsome. Now he seemed much older, grey and battle scarred. His three sons would fight and perhaps die beside him on the battlefield.

Over there was my friend, Gwynn ab Gwynn, shivering beneath the blanket which his beloved wife Meryl had woven for him especially for this Night to keep him warm. As for the morrow, it was to cover his Horse's back, "So that," said she, "he might sit more steadily on the Roan in battle." He and I used to have long and interesting talks with one another about timber construction of houses and buildings and better ways of letting the smoke of hearth Fires escape, as well as of the possibilities of stacking chests and affixing them to the walls, so as to hold clothing and other precious belongings – and of many other such innovative ideas. I did enjoy those conversations... Might he survive tomorrow's massacre? And if he did, what would he think of me for my deserting them at the last hour? Would he perceive this as the slinking away of a coward? Yes... just so would it probably seem to him.

Lying peacefully in slumber upon his pallet was Baldric the Bard. He, of course, would remain well behind the lines, to chronicle this battle in such a poetic and biased way as to make it seem that all the glory had been on Vortigern's side – regardless of the battle's true outcome.

There was sweet, young Gwendolyn, handfast only two months, weeping quietly in the arms of her beloved.

And so it went, on and on. I wondered which ones would soon become ghosts? I comforted myself with the knowledge that all things pass with Time and that these memories would soon all become merely specters of my past. Or, so I tried to tell myself.

This was to be no surprise battle. The old Clansmen and Saxons on Vortigern's side, as well as the Romans and Britons on Ambrosius and Germanus' side, all knew that, with the Dawn, rest would cease and the Day would turn to agony and Death – for if this Day did not bring Death to themselves, it surely would to their sons, brothers, friends, or lovers. This would happen even if the battle's victory and honours went to their own side. Grief was inescapable.

Even did I walk as far as the Saxon camp. At its entrance – serving as a boundary between themselves and the Clans – was erected a lintel of wooden post and beam construction. There were two huge, rough Tree trunks, still in their bark, serving as posts, with a heavily carved wooden beam laid across them. The carving was of two Horses rearing and facing one another. This was the device of Hengist and Horsa's long and well-established family line. Two torches, their flames whipping in the Wind, stood on either side of it. I walked through.

Inside the camp were many crude pavilions flying banners of Animal hides with standards of Boar's and Wolf's heads and cruel looking Dragons – identifying the other family divisions of these Teutons. Many of these had been intentionally splattered with blood. In the center of their camp was Hengist's and Horsa's pavilions, which were far more elaborate than the others. They flew their Horses standards, which heralded them as "Kings" – as they did by then proclaim themselves.

I saw and smelled the evidence of blood sacrifices to the Germanic War Gods. Animal? Human? Who could know?

I kept seeing men make the sign against Evil Enchantment or Black Magic as I passed them by. They feared me. I was no friend to these men.

But friend and foe alike, all knew that with the Dawn their world would be cast into an orgy of maniacal Chaos – a great feast of Death and horror.

Their camp was close to the path that would lead me out of sight to cross the Valley to the Roman army.

The two great armies faced each other on opposing Hillsides across the great Valley. Both were alight with the red glow of camp Fires. The Hills faced each other North and South, so that neither side would have the advantage of the Sun's rays in the other's eyes on the morn.

This Valley lay at the Northeastern corner of Gwynedd.

There I was, creeping in the Night, under a Spell of invisibility to Uther and Ambrosius.

"So, this is it, then," thought I.

Thus was my destiny irrevocably changed. Never again would I be Vortigern's counselor, Magician, captive, or fetch.

I slipped away from Vortigern's encampment, knowing that he was doomed to fall in this battle, by my doing. Now would I have blood on my hands... not blood of sacrifice but blood of betrayal and murder. So be it!

Truth was, I felt little guilt. Vortigern was a wicked and evil man. So I told myself. Yet, there was a sickness in the pit of my stomach. There was also great relief, to be rid of him.

I had come to the edge of the Valley.

Upon that pre-Dawn twilight, a heavy Mist was creeping along the Valley floor, as was common in these regions. It was hard to tell what kind of Day it would be.

I crossed the Valley to the other side.

Then I, Gwyddion, feared by many as "Vortigern's Great Sorcerer," hid behind the Trees, trembling. I did not declare my presence to a soul – for this side was, in essence, a Christian army. Although I am sure that history will tell it true – for so well known a fact it is – that most of the Warriors who were on the Roman army's side were in actuality still worshippers of Mithras, or of other more ancient Gods – and were Christian in name only. Still, I felt that in this instance, caution was better than valor.

Whilst I hid in the Wood, thinking of all these things, the sun began to peek over the horizon. I then observed the first clash of battle that I was ever in my life to see – a life which would thenceforth hold no innocence from slaughter.

The Battle...

Germanus' and Vortigern's armies stood upon their opposing Hilltops, each facing the deep, dark Valley below.

Germanus' ranks were filed in perfect Roman formations – save for the conscripted peasants, strung out in front of his "official" army.

This Valley had long ago been de-Forested for the sake of farming. It was rare indeed to find such an idyllic location – protected as it was from the Winds. Idyllic, that is, for farming – as well for battle.

I will tell you how it was on Germanus' and Ambrosius' side upon that early morning.

The Cavalry waited at the very rear – mainly on the left and right flanks, but some as well behind the Vanguard Foot Soldiers. They were donned in resplendent armour with fancy helms and outfitted with long swords and spears. Even their mounts were resplendent with their silver buckles and ornaments, which held together their leathern harnesses, ingeniously wrapped around them, securing their richly coloured, woven and tasseled riding blankets. Some even had what are called saddles, made from soft-formed leather. These, too, were fitted with silver and gold buckles. Why, I even saw a few Horses who had metal protectors around their eyes, to save them from easily being blinded by enemy lances and swords.

In front of the Cavalrymen, in all positions, were the Foot Soldiers. They were dressed in what armour they had, with the wealthiest – mostly clad in what I thought to be ridiculously heavy, shiny armour – leading the hoard.

All of this was intended to intimidate their enemies, I suppose.

The Archers, in turn, stood just behind the Vanguard's front line. Long Shield Carriers would protect them from the first three or four rounds of enemy arrows.

The conscripted peasants positioned in front of the "official" infantry were weaponed with only axes, hoes, or wooden pikes for to defend themselves with – or so as to kill the enemy, should they prove so lucky. They awaited the onslaught of Vortigern's Bowmen. These peasants, as always, would feel the brunt of the first call – as they were considered the "expendable ones."

In actuality, it was Ambrosius Aurelius who led this army. Although Germanus had been sent to command, he stayed back astride his mount upon a Hilltop vantage point with the two highest ranking of Caesar's Guard and a command Flag Carrier who would signal his orders – thus placing Ambrosius and his brother at the front lines of Cavalry.

That which Vortigern faced gave the appearance of a multitudinous throng. A fearful sight was it for him I am sure – for he had lost his battle lust because of what I had done to him.

His own iniquities along with all the Gods and Fates had led him inexorably to this moment and I am sure he realised his doom.

The first signal was called by Vortigern himself. I heard a blast from one of his mighty curled war-horns and then he shouted, "Archers, loose!"

Then came through the Air a mass of straight arrows with deadly metal points and perfectly ridged tail feathers. Way up into the Sky went they, into a great arc, then falling into the front lines of Germanus' army.

I watched as the peasants, without shielded protection, went down screaming as arrows pierced through their mouths, their necks, into their guts, some into their loins. In the case of one man – I saw an arrow enter through his eye, into his skull, then breaking through to lodge with the pointed end of the shaft protruding from the back of his head. He went down stiff and straight as a board falling from the side of a barn.

Quizzical, all this... It was a puzzlement. For, although totally real, these things were so horrific that I could not actually process them in my thoughts as such. It was all as a Night-terror to me.

As I have told, Ambrosius' Archers were standing in wait near to the Vanguard's front edge, behind the Long Shield Carriers. Just as Vortigern's Archers had loosed three rounds, Germanus' signal was waved. Then, from Ambrosius came the shouted command, "Notch, draw, loose!" At this, his Shield Carriers all as on with impressive precision crouched to a kneeling position so as to give clear shot to the Archers. Their shields gave a deep "whump" as they hit the ground in unison. I thought I felt the impact through the earth beneath my feet... Quick as lightning, the archers returned three rounds of arrows. After the three rounds had been loosed, the Archers, as they had been instructed, fell to one knee behind the Shield Carriers, who stood once again in "Testudo" formation – shoulder to shoulder with shields forming a wall in front and angled above them to deflect enemy arrows – this, to protect themselves and the Archers. Three more rounds did the Archers loose in this same manner. When this had been accomplished, Ambrosius' Warriors themselves divided their formation – opening an aisle through their midst, one rank at a Time – all the way back past the Cavalrymen – through which all the Archers quit the front. After the last of the Archers had got through, the Warriors again closed their ranks. This Roman precision was as a dance, so fluid in motion were they.

You see, excellent Archers are far too valuable – and hard to replace – to endanger them any more than is necessary.

It was after this maneuver that Ambrosius hollered "Charge!"

The un-slain peasant forces began to run down the Hill toward the deep Valley floor and the men on Vortigern's side did the same. I watched breathlessly as they came closer and closer.

Of a sudden with a great and horrific clash, came they face to face, chest to chest – being skewered by javelins and swords. The sheer force of their meeting was unbelievable! I saw arms, legs, and heads flying off in all directions, blood gushing out of them and quickly making the field so slippery with blood and gore that many Warriors could not stand their ground.

With so many coming down the sides of both Hills to collide in the middle, pretty soon the fighters began to fall into a great spreading mound of slain and wounded bodies. Bodies upon bodies... resembling a great wave upon the Sea was this heap of carnage, growing higher and higher. Yet, because in this arena there was nowhere for the wave to crash and diminish, ever more dense did it become. Soon the bodies were so buried by one another that even those who had been pulled down without wound fell in Death for the lack of Air to breathe – or for the sheer press of weight.

So high was this wall of bodies becoming that when the Cavalry was flagged to ride into the fray, they were forced to jump the mound of men, but their War Stallions could not jump that far or high. So they landed – or fell – upon the fallen Warriors of friend and foe alike.

When the riders behind the first few lines of Cavalry saw what was happening, many of them tried to pull up and stop, which caused them and their mounts – and many more behind them – to fall or be pushed into the ever growing mound of agony.

From the distance I heard a cacophony of sounds – not only the panicked crying and begging of the wounded caught in the lengthening Death mound and the high-pitched screams of their Horses; but yet another nonsensical layer...

Was that a joyful sound?

As it so happened, when Germanus of Auxaire got Wind of what was befalling his Warriors, he commanded that a rousing Chant be raised by all waiting to enter the field of combat.

"Alleluia! Alleluia! Alleluia!"

I was later told that this was an invocation of his God. Even so, was this a jest? His men were dying from his farcical lack of good strategy! Who could be joyful in this impossible predicament?

Yet there it was again and again...

"Alleluia! Alleluia! Alleluia!"

All of this I saw from where I stood hiding in the Wood. Although I wished with all my heart to turn away, I could not, for I was held in the grip of morbid fascination.

So, this was war!!! I thought "How can Warriors later jest and boast of their escapades of valor on the battlefield? How can anyone glamourise war?" In all truth and fact I loathed even the Idea of war! I did then and do now. Yet there I was... Watching...

I began to feel faint, the world around me spun, my gorge rose, and in helplessness, I vomited uncontrollably.

"But, wait," thought I... "I have some power over this. Vortigern cannot win this battle for I have removed all possibility of that! The battle lust can no longer exist within him, for I have "Spelled" it from him. The fighting will cease at the moment of his Death. I must move quickly, so that there is less carnage on this field than there will assuredly otherwise be."

My resolve was set. In that perfect moment it was Time for this to end.

Using the intensity and compelling *desire* for victory that I held within me, and the strength of my *directed will*, I stirred and awakened the powers of the Element of Fire and of the Beings who work within its Realm of heightened passions.

I then, from deep within myself, drew up all of my "Grym Hudol" – my Magical Power – and called to all the powers of this Earth. "I stir thee... Awaken and come into my left hand!"

As I held it out with fingers splayed, all came into me with a jolt and a quake. It swirled around my heart. My hands felt like glowing hot embers. I felt the power of Gods coursing through me!

There I stood with something akin to a great Tempest roaring in my ears – whilst imagining the Death of Vortigern. When I had completely entered within the Time and place of that which I was Envisioning and "saw" it unfolding before me, I threw up my arms toward the Heavens and shouted, "AS I SEE IT... SO BE IT!"

No sooner than I had spoken those words the battle turned – and seeing this, the Saxons began to flee the scene.

Then thought I, "Those being killed now are the men of the Clans. This is not what I wanted! These men and women are my kindred!"

I cried aloud, "Oh horror, will you never end?"

But I had pictured the scene and had Cast the Magic. I must now wait... It would prove to happen just as I had "Seen" it.

My eyes were drawn back to the writhing, screaming wall of carnage in the low of the Valley – which had been heaping ever higher in the absence of my attention. Now it was totally impossible for even the largest and most brilliant of all War Stallions to jump it. It was then I saw it... the emblem of Ambrosius... the Pen Dragon banner, rapidly approaching the wall of bodies. "Whatever will they do?" I asked myself. Then, to my amazement I saw a lone Horse and rider burst forth through the midst of his brother-Warriors. I held my breath as I watched him and his steed tromp upon the bodies of the living and the dead – surmounting the mound to reach the other side. Then this daring rider pushed forward amidst the shocked and miraculously dividing army of the Clans toward the person of Vortigern! There came he through the midst of them, with his great sword held on high, swiftly approaching Vortigern, who was caught in the press of his own Warriors' fumblings. But it was *not* Ambrosius who galloped so fleetly – it was his younger brother Badraig, riding in his stead.

"What is this?" – thought I.

I will never know how it came about – I mean the mechanics of the thing. It was as if the Spirits of the Four Winds had parted the soldiers side to side so that Badraig had a clear running shot.

Then he reached Vortigern and with his heavy long-sword lopped off his head with one great blow. It fell off his shoulders and rolled away... Just like that! All of Vortigern's men stopped whatever they were doing and watched as it rolled and rolled along the putrid ground into a pile of dead bodies. They looked back in horror as they saw that his corpse was still sitting astride his Horse.

Stillness...

A great fount of blood was gushing from his neck where only a moment before his head had been. A foul of gore, a Spring of red – then his body fell to his left onto the ground.

The battle was over.

All the men who had followed Vortigern lay down their weapons; only a few more of them were killed before the Romans realised what had happened.

When Ambrosius caught up to his brother and saw Vortigern dead he raised his blade high and shouted the command, "Halt! Stop! Lay down your arms! Cease your fighting, my Roman compatriots! My Britons! For that we may mend our quarrels without further violence."

The field became quieter. All of the clash, the hitting of metal upon metal, the war cries and the hollering of commands by the men on both sides stopped. They stood still and silent.

Oh, but then... their faces showed recognition of the Nightmare of this; for all that could be heard now was the moaning and the wailing of the men who had been badly injured. These slain and injured men – and women – were their kindred. Their brothers, their sisters, their Fathers, their sons. Swords had plunged and cut, arrows had pierced and axes had chopped. Arms and legs were gone. Torsos were hacked in twain, with entrails trailing across the ground. Men lay flattened by Horses.

I looked up to the Sky; it was a clear and sunny Day. "Funny that," thought I, whilst the Ravens went wheeling above. The great carrion Birds awaited their Feast of Death.

I fell to my knees and then raised my hands up again, this Time in supplication to the Great Goddess. I prayed, "Great One of all beauty and comforts – and to every God and Spirit watching over me; I beseech Thee, keep my eyes from beholding this abomination ever again!"

However, my prayer was not to be answered in the affirmative by Them. For, many more battles would I be obliged to observe in my life; but always, I watched from a distance.

There was a truce agreed upon. There were prisoners taken of the wealthiest ranks on Vortigern's side. They would be well treated until their houses could raise their ransoms.

Of course, this was not so for the Saxon Mercenaries that Vortigern had paid to be a major part of his army. For, when the Saxons realised that Vortigern had been slain, the remainder of their hordes fled. But they were recognizable – for they had a look in stature and clothing which was much different from that of the Clans, so they were hunted down and killed... no prisoners taken. They and their brethren were given a great lesson by the Romans upon that Day – too bad that the lesson was not remembered.

Only one of their leaders had fallen. Their great leader Hengist escaped – not to be heard from again for some Time.

As for the Clansmen... Ambrosius and the Roman forces allowed all of their men and women to return to their home territories, with their word of honour that this would be the end of their rising up in arms against the Romano-Britons.

Now, with most armies, it was commonly done that the women would be captured and raped by the triumphant side. But Ambrosius – because most of these people were related to one another and because it was just the kind of man that he was – sent out an order very quickly.

"No rape or rapine! You will let the women find their dead on the field with no harassment and when the women find their Loved ones and are weeping over their corpses, you will tell them that they may take whatever gold or silver rings or torques and blankets that they wish from their corpses, but then they must go and take no more."

For, as it has always been in war, the winners take the bounty of Horses, swords, shields and any other weapons or armour they may find. This is their right.

Ambrosius ordered his soldiers to mercy-kill all of those who were mortally wounded, which was a gesture of kindness and of honour.

The Birds continued to circle above, waiting until the soldiers finished stripping what was left of value from the corpses. Then the Ravens' Feast began.

When the Roman troops had come back to their camp I sought out Ambrosius and Badraig – of whom the men were already Chanting "Uther, Uther!" I approached them with a gesture of peace. When I had explained to them who I was and what I had done they welcomed me to their company. For as they said, they were "fain to have Vortigern's illustrious Counselor and Magician in their company." So, they found a place for me and provided clothing and all else that I would need.

Thus ended my Time with Vortigern.

Later on that Day I went to the battlefield to Heal all those that I could.

I came upon the wounded and slain, perhaps having fought as enemies – perhaps as compatriots – lying all together now upon the bloody field... Who were they? I mean, to me... Were they friend or foe? I suppose it did not matter.

By evening twilight on the next Day, those corpses not taken away to family graves had been stacked into many great piles and were being burned. The stench was almost unbearable.

Here and there around the site were other Fires, roasting meat. Hungry Warriors must eat. But from whence came the meat?

I admit it – I vomited several more times that Day, although I had eaten nothing. Now only yellow bile came from within me. When my body had no more to give, I could only gag and retch, unable to control the impulse.

Yes, a wretched deal it was! Why could all this not be settled hand-to-hand, sword to sword – or by whatever rules of combat seemed good to the opponents – between the two adversarial leaders themselves – winner take the field? Why was the world of Man so greedy and unreasonable, to have disputes come to this – this Nightmare whilst fully awake? War... Oh, Fool's endeavour!

Near the end of the stacking of bodies, I thought I saw sweet Gwendolyn's lover thrown upon the pile. I could not be sure that it was he, for his face was so mutilated. Had she too fought? Was she lying beneath him ready for the pyre?

Then I wept. I wept for Gwendolyn and all the grievers left behind. When my weeping was done, I heard the "Voices" – chastising me: "Gwyddion, Gwyddion, how can you be such a hypocrite? Was it not your machinations that orchestrated this ghastly killing of Vortigern? Was his head not lopped off by the Blade of this Uther at your doing – by parting the Warriors on the field? You yourself have done this. His blood is on your hands."

I recognized in Them the Voice of Truth. I began to say something back in my own defense... but they were gone... as always.

Many stories – mostly contradictory – have been told over the years past of how it was upon that Day. I suppose that is the way of things in this world.

One newly growing rumour is that Germanus of Auxaire – not Uther – had won the battle against the Clan loyalists by his own powerful Incantation of "Alleluia," and of course by the rousing, thunderous volume of thousands of Christian Warriors' Chanting these words all at a Time and of one heart.

However, as is well known that, in terms of religion, there is no "one heart" amoung the Romans – much less Britons.

Oddly enough, that story goes on to say that when Germanus' army Chanted their Alleluia Chant, the entirety of the enemy forces turned, one upon the other in a God-inspired confusion. Then, any left alive fled in cowardly retreat before the Roman Cavalry could reach them, with Vortigern escaping to his fortress and into the arms of his Saxon Princess; where the Magic of Germanus – or the power of God sent by

Germanus – descended from the Heavens to completely consume Vortigern by Fire, thereby causing his Death. Funny that.

When all that I could do for the wounded had been done, I and a small contingent of Cymru men and women brought the tightly wrapped and bound corpse of the mighty tyrant Vortigern home to Princess Rowena, so that she may bury or burn it as she would. She chose a pyre.

Actually, I had tried to convince Uther and Ambrosius not to display Vortigern's head on a pike, as this is a nasty and un-healthful thing to do. But they would not let me take the head to Rowena... it was Uther's prize.

To go on:

Princess Rowena asked of me that I *make* the Fire. I said yes and so I did!

Now, it is a known fact that when one is an Adept of the Arts Magical, they must always mind their thoughts, words, and will. For, their Grym Hudol can take over when their emotions rise, thence causing things *to be*, whether consciously intended or not.

I was thinking only to light a torch from a small Fire designated for that purpose – which stood far across the courtyard – then to touch it to the pyre, thereby igniting the bottom course of logs.

All I really know is that of a sudden I realised that Vortigern was truly dead and gone from my life – and yes, I suppose it was not until that moment that it had fully dawned upon me – the anger and frustration that I had felt toward him for all of those years churned my gut and turned to rage.

I cannot say what really happened next, only that of a sudden there was a great conflagration at the pyre. Yet I was still standing at the smaller Fire, from which the torch had been lit.

When Princess Rowena's attendants revived me from my faint, I could remember nothing after my lighting the torch. They confirmed my remaining at the small Fire. But, with looks upon their faces somewhere between awe and dread, they told me that in the instant of my lighting the torch a great Flame had leapt from my hand, across the courtyard to engulf Vortigern's pyre.

Who knows? Tales abound of those Times. I suppose this is why Morgan has had us write our histories as we remember them.

Chapter 6
Endings and
Beginnings

Gwyddion

My life with Uther the Pen Dragon in the years that followed...

All that the "Voices" had whispered into my ears – of the bidding that I would be asked by Uther to do – about Igraine and of the babe – came to pass.

Now, in my old age, I have heard tales of how it was because of his betrayal of Gorlois that Uther had lost his Kingdom. But he had not even been King at that Time.

At the Celebration of Treaties, Uther had been honoured for his role in the winning of the so-called "Alleluia Battle" by killing Vortigern; yet in truth, he was not the Commander of that battle. No, it was much later that he had become a "King" of sorts. But news travels very slowly across this Island, so I can understand how people might have confused events.

In the fifth year after the so-called "Alleluia Battle," Uther's, and my, renowned brother Ambrosius Aurelius died. I knew this had happened before anyone told me so, for upon that Day I looked up into the Sky and to my amazement beheld a great Comet. Like a Dragon with a Fiery red tail it was, signaling the Death of one of Briton's greatest sons. I grieved mightily. Ambrosius was a good man and a true hero. I had Loved my brother well.

Events transpired in such a way that after Ambrosius' Death many battles against the marauding Eire were fought and won by Uther, the Champion. The Time came when all the Dux and Chieftains seemed to fall under his charismatic sway and almost unanimously decided to make Uther Great War Commander over all the Clans of the West, the North and the Roman-styled Britons alike. They called him a King.

So it seemed that the wish and The Dream that had been born in Macsen Wledig had finally come to pass. So it seemed.

But Uther was a man who allowed his emotions to rule him, and little by little, over Time, this became evident to everyone.

He meant to be a man of his word, but he gave too many pledges and promises to too many people, which were impossible for him to keep – much as I believe he would have wished to do so. He drank too much and he talked too much when he drank. In his drunken stupors he would offer *this* to this Chieftain or *that* to that Clansman... many Times his offers conflicted.

I had stayed by Uther's side, to watch these events unfold, for I had a great stake in what was to be the future of Uther the Pen Dragon's son, Arthur. For it was *he* who would become the true High King of these Fair Isles.

I acted as councilor to Uther for over fourteen full years, although my frustration kept mounting, for he rarely listened – or acted – upon a word I said. I believe that he kept me around because he Loved me in his own way. I stayed by Uther's side, watching these events unfold – and as much as my honour would allow, I helped him to patch things up when he made stupid and foolish mistakes. But finally there came an end to it.

The Time came that, because of his debaucheries, his power and his prowess began to wane. He grew fat and began to lose battles. This caused much disgruntlement against him amoungst all the other Commanders and nobility and even amoungst the common people.

One Day when I was reading a book in my chamber, my thoughts were interrupted by a feeling of impending doom. Uther... Where was Uther? Something made me get up from my repose. I grabbed my cloak and staff, ran out of Uther's fortress and began to run South. To whence I did not know, but I ran. From morning to near Sundown I pursued my fear. Finally I came to a small grove of Ash Trees on the edge of where the trail began a serpentine course into a more deeply Forested area. I stopped. "Yes, this is the place..." I thought to myself. I caught my breath and stood watching from behind an old Tree. Uther would be here soon.

It was the evening of the rising of the Dark Moon. The Sun had already fallen well below the line of Treetops and twilight had begun. Twilight.. my favourite Time... an Enchanted Time... A 'tween Time... neither Day nor Night. A Mist was rising. I began to feel a prickling on the back of my neck.

Then I saw him coming, riding his great Warhorse in a panic. He had a look of terror upon his face. His Horse, whose mouth was foaming, was stumbling over rocks, for Uther was leading him off the path and into unknown terrain.

That was when I heard other movement. Six riders were in quick pursuit of him. Uther was being ambushed by some of the most powerful men in the Kingdom. I recognized them...

Uther seemed like he had aged thirty years in the more than twelve since that fateful Night of his mating with Igraine. He was an older man now – old beyond his years. His face had a deep expression of sorrow and resentfulness upon it – and a bubbling anger was in his heart. He was a cynical man. I read his thoughts: "Look at all I have done for this Island – look at all I have done for them and now they seek to betray me – to kill me. I wonder which ones they are?"

"I have heard that they fight amoung themselves already, of who would be King when I die... When I die! I am not dead!"

But they came ever closer and the evening fog grew thicker.

I began to run swiftly toward him. But then, it seemed that I turned into the Hawk that is my namesake. My consciousness left me and I flew into the heights. I encircled Uther and peered down upon the scene. Had he seen me?

Then one man, who was the swiftest, caught up to him.

Uther took out his sword – the sword of the King. It had been made for him. It was very beautiful and he kept the blade as sharp as a blade could be. He withdrew it, held it up and said, "Come on then! If you would be King, if you would have me not be King, see if you can defeat me. I am Uther, The Pen Dragon! I am the terrible, wonderful King Dragon! – the Chieftain of the Dragons!... Come and get me if you will!"

They closed in on him. Just then his Horse stumbled and he was thrown to the ground. His sword flew from his hand. His Horse staggered and fell over his left leg and crushed it. Uther howled for a moment in agony, for he was sorrowfully injured – but then he stopped. He knew that he was trapped. But he would not show fear. If this was his Time to die he would die like the great Warrior that he was.

They stood around him, with their swords pointed at him, and they threw accusations at him – no doubt trying to make themselves feel better about killing their King. But Uther said:

"I am an unarmed man. I lie injured beneath this Horse – what fairness is there in this? Which one of you will claim that you bested me in battle? You cannot truthfully say it and you would be dishonourable in the sight of the Gods if you did."

They looked at each other, and almost with one voice said: "True, there is not *one* of us can claim this, Uther."

Uther gave them a crooked smile and said "Ahh!" – in understanding. Just then all the blades at once were pointed at the center of Uther's chest and plunged into it. His expression was one of surprise

– just for a moment – and then his expression did not change.

Therein was the end of Uther, the Pen Dragon, so called "King" of the Britons – and the end of The Dream that all had shared – or so they thought.

The men looked at each other and as if at a word simply walked away to leave him where he had fallen. There would be no hero's pyre for Uther... No Warrior's salute... In fact, one of his former compatriots spat upon his corpse!

Then I ran to Uther's body from my hiding place in the Oaken thick – from whence I had been watching this disgraceful assassination. The men who were abandoning their former "King" to the "Feast of Ravens" saw me approaching and became horrified. For in fact, all knew that I was the King's Magician!

By this Time in my life I had attained such great fame that a fearfulness and a dread of me was held by each and all – except of course, for those who Loved me well.

I said to the assassins, "So be it then, if this is how you will have it. But remember – forget not – that Uther died as King of the Britons. Remember always..."

They looked quizzically at each other then replied, "What difference does this make now? There be no heir of his blood!"

As far as anyone yet knew, that was true. Of course, no one knew of Arthur – the boy called "The Bear." For, even though Uther had a voracious sexual appetite that seemed as though it could not be quenched, never had there been so much as a rumour of a child of his loins being born.

I replied in a stern voice, "I tell you *remember*! Remember that *you* named him King. *You* called him Pen Dragon!"

As I said these words I stared into each of their eyes. There was a blazing and a searing which emanated from my eyes, etching directly into theirs an indelible thought.

"You named him King."

It has been said that a couple of these men went mad – for Day and Night all they *could* do was to remember and repeat my words over and over, "You named him king. You called him Pen Dragon."

The rest of them kept their sanity, but every Day, even if only once, they remembered that *they* had named Uther "King." Never did they forget. This was to be useful to me in the future, because of Arthur.

The reason why it was so important that they all remember that Uther had been murdered as King and had not been bested by another Champion was this: It has been, for Time out of memory, the Clans' custom that when a King dies without an heir of his blood, the one who bests him in battle and defeats him has the best claim to become the next King.

When these men had fled the scene, I buried Uther. Atop the mound of soil covering his grave, I heaped a pile of Stones and began to mark it by placing the King's Sword upright amoung them.   Something restrained me.   I wondered if Uther's sword could be the "Flaming Sword" of my Vision. I did not believe that it was, but perhaps... I thought it would be a fitting emblem for Uther's rightful heir, the next King – King Arthur. So I wrapped it in skins, and took it with me to hide with Brennos, for I had decided that it was Time to go back to the Snowy Mountains, so as to rest awhile in his Cave of Wonders. So, instead of the sword, I tied two sticks together with vine in the shape of a cross and placed it to mark the place of Uther's final rest.

So it was that, in the eleventh year of the Bear's life, the man from whose lust and greed he had been conceived, had died.

My brother Uther was gone... And indeed, I did shed some tears.

Return to the Cave of Wonders...

Brennos and his Cave had been the saviours of my boyhood. The measure of comfort I felt then and have always felt there with Brennos is one of the greatest treasures of my life. So, immediately after Uther's slaying I began to wend my way back to Brennos.

It took several Days of walking to finally arrive at Brennos' Cave. When I did, I called out as I had done when a child:

"Is anybody here? Does anybody live here?"

The very old voice of my teacher laughed and said, "Come in, my boy – I have been waiting for you!"

We embraced, both joyous in our hearts. I was "home" once again.

"Come and have some wine with me!"

I replied, "Thank you so much Master Brennos, but I do not drink the Fruit of the Vine which has fermented. However I would take some hot Water with honey, if you have it."

"Certainly" said he.

I remember that we lit two wall lamps inside the Cave as darkness fell. The light from these gave sparkle to the Crystals embedded in the walls surrounding us. Oh yes, this was a Magical place – for Brennos was a Magical being.

I told him of Uther's decline and Death and reminded him of my Vision of the "Flaming Sword."

He sat silently in amazement at all the happenings which had been maneuvered into place by the Weavers – and was in awe of those things which he then understood were yet to take place.

I pulled out of my travel sack the great sword of Uther's that I had taken from his side on the Day he was slain. I unwrapped it from its leathern covering, so as to show it to Brennos.

"Brennos, when I hold this Sword in my hands I feel the fading of power – the dwindling of a Dream. I feel what is left of the Spirit of Uther, my brother. But I do not feel that this is the Flaming Sword of my Vision. For one thing, it does not appear the same as did that one.

"This Sword is a Roman Long Sword and it has not a cruciform hilt. And it holds not the heat of true power.

"These things, in themselves, would not bother me – for Visions are not always solid, but are shifting things like as seen through Water – though at other Times Visions are as clear as the Crystals here in your Cave. Still, I trust my Visions.

"I believe that the only flame it has ever held was the passion of Uther. But now Uther's flame has been extinguished through his own folly.

"I think this is not the sword of my Vision – what think you, Brennos?"

Brennos, of course could not see the Sword well, so I placed it into his hands – for, although mostly blind, he had vision as clear as the Eagle of Rome – through his "inner eye."

He said, "No, I do not feel the power of the Gods coursing through this Sword."

"Still, I would leave it with you Brennos, if this is alright, so that you might protect it, for I believe that it may prove valuable in assuring others of Arthur's true paternity."

"Of course it is alright, Gwyddion; I will keep it for you...

"However, the Time has come for me to tell you a great secret that was told to me by my master, who trained me to be the Creature that I am."

Well, my ears perked at this and I said, "Tell me!"

"Well, then, I will... this is what my master Ea Kunagos told me – word for word – I remember it clearly: 'There is an ancient Sword of Kings on these Isles, going back farther in Time than anyone remembers. Macsen Wledig himself wielded this sword. It was by and through this Sword that he won all of his battles. Its blade is of a metal sharper than any other known – which looks as if – and is stronger than – silver, but of course, is not. Where the blade meets the hilt of solid gold are two Dragons' heads, which extend from its sides. Each Dragon's head has precious Stones of red as its eyes. Where the hilt meets the blade, it is embellished with one great clear green Stone, which sits centered between the Dragons. Legends claim that the green Stone is a piece of the Star Stone that fell from the Heavens and now sits upon the Altar in the center of the ring of Standing Stones atop the Tor, on the Isle of Apples. It is said that when Macsen lifted the sword in battle, it glowed green, then flamed blue! Its name is Caledfwlch.

'Macsen Wledig came to his Kingship of Briton by right of his marrying Princess Helen who held the royal blood of King Hen Coel of olden fame, whose sword Caledfwlch had also been.

'But Macsen Wledig, when he knew that it was near to his Time to die, hid it away from all sight; for it is said, "He found not a man living of righteous intent, who would be King."

'Or mayhap he was simply too prideful to admit his waning power. It may even be that the Voices – which he would have thought to be Angelic – whispered in his ears that the true King must find the sword himself! No one really knows. Caledfwlch has been lost to the world of men ever since.

'It is said that only when the rightful King – or Queen – wields the "Sword of Kingship," will its flame glow – the sign that they cannot be defeated in battle. For, this is the Magic of the ancient sword, "Caledfwlch."

'Know this too; any imposter or usurper, who covets it and tries to wield it un-deservedly, will be struck down dead by a bolt from the Thunder Gods, the moment he, or she, holds it in their hands.

'Farther back beyond King Hen Coel, its glory enters into the Time of Gods, Heroes, and myth.

'The oldest myth of all says that Caledfwlch was first brought to this Island by Igraine's people – the Old Dark Tribes... that it arrived upon one of the first one hundred boats cast off from the Island that sank beneath the Waves... Who knows?'

"But, back to Macsen Wledig...

'He and Helen had a son named Flavius Victor. His son, in turn, was also named Victor. He was known in the Cymru tongue as Gwidr the Younger... Gwidr – or Victor – the Younger and his true wife had two sons. The eldest was Ambrosius Aurillious, and the younger was Badraig Constantius – known as Uther the Pen Dragon. Later, Victor begat you upon your Mother Alexandria, who was, through her Mother, Grandmother and Grandfather, also in the direct Royal hereditary line of King Hen Coel.

"Some say that Caledfwlch lies hidden in the protection of the Lady of the Lake."

Each Time Brennos said "Caledfwlch," my skin prickled and my heart quickened. My head inside felt as if it would explode with my eyes popping outwards. Everything around me became wavy and translucent. I knew this feeling well. It was "the sickness" – a bit of nausea, dizziness, and spinning... Such an unearthly feeling it is – as though I lie suspended betwixt two realms... un-grounded in either... apart... ill. It comes with the "sight." Then the "Voices of the Stars," once again, whispered into my ear.

"Yes Gwyddion, *that one* is the Sword of Kings, the sword of flaming truth. Caledfwlch... Caledfwlch is for the one and rightful King to wield.

"Ambrosius is dead now, Gwyddion, and so now is Uther. You know that *you* are the rightful heir in the line of Macsen and Hen Coel, through your Father, Victor – but also through your mother. Yes, Gwyddion, it is you who has the *truest* hereditary right to the rulership of Briton... Blood tells blood, Gwyddion – bastard or no. Only a true heir of Macsen's and Helen's blood will ever find the Sword of Kings. All other lines have died out.

"But you are not a man in the ways of other men. Even though you would be a wise and good King, you are not to *be* a King; that is not your fate in this life. No, but you will *make* a King, Gwyddion, The Merlin. You will *guide* a King – the greatest King of all – Arthur, the 'Bear of the Britons.' With you by his side, he will fulfill The Dream of your common Forefathers, Macsen Wledig, King Hen Coal, Constantine the Great – and many others!

"Brennos is right – only the true heir will ever find the Sword of Kings, for it lies well hidden in the safekeeping of the Lady of the Lake. You are the only one who can retrieve the sword of Kings from whence it hides. But remember, Caledfwlch must also accept its King. As a sign of this acceptance, the sword will *sing and glow*, first green, then with what seems to be a blue flame.   Once you have received this confirmation, you must put Caledfwlch back to where it was hidden.

"Then Gwyddion, you must contrive circumstances to fall in such a way so that Arthur will find Caledfwlch by his own hands and wield it by his own merit! Caledfwlch must be his.

"You see Gwyddion, by your finding the Sword, you will have claimed your right of Kingship. By replacing it to its place of hiding, you are relinquishing your Kingship to offer it to the 'one of righteous intent' who must next wield it. Remember, Caledfwlch must sing and flame in his hands as well as in your own. If the Sword of Kings rejects either of you, all will have been for naught and your mission failed!

"Remember, it would be best to keep the fact of your being the *first* rightful heir a secret from all save your most trusted allies – and even then, only if you believe it to be the better part of Wisdom to reveal this fact.

"After these happenings have been accomplished; you must devise a way for all the Dux, Chieftains, Tribesmen, Minor Kings and Queens of these Fair Isles to accept him.

"However, if you were to be without Uther's sword, they may be loathe to believe him Uther's son. So then, Arthur must have both swords!

"These tasks are for you alone to accomplish. Use your great powers of intellect and Magic, Gwyddion, to formulate a method wherein Arthur will be chosen as High King. This must be done!

"Fret not, Gwyddion, for we see the outcome before the beginning of a thing. You will not fail. Failure is not written in your Stars, Gwyddion!"

I fell to the floor with tremors.

Brennos was very concerned for my well-being.

"What is it?" he asked. "What is it?"

"Just a moment, I am coming back to myself."

"Of course... I understand. It is about Caledfwlch, is it not? Tell me, did the 'Voices' say that it is for Arthur?"

"Yes... for Arthur."

I saw my destiny unfolding before me.

Hmm... Caledfwlch... hidden in the keeping of the Lady of the Lake. When the proper Time is upon me, I must devise a plan.

After that first long and enlightening evening of conversation, I was offered a pallet on the floor, where I spent the Night in restful slumber.

His Ravens three...

When first I had met Brennos, he had lived with a Wolf named Ffrind. Ffrind had lived with him for almost twenty years. But some Time after my capture by Vortigern, she had died of very old age.

Now he had three companions who shared his Nights and Days with him.

The first of them had come to him about three and one half years before. I had met her on my last visit. She was a beautiful young Raven. He had named her 'Raven.'

He told me that after a year or so, she had flown out early one morning and had come back that Night with a male Raven. And so, Brennos named him 'Night.'

The two Birds became a mated pair and the three of Brennos and the Ravens got on very well together. Some Time later the two Ravens had had a nest full of fledglings, but, one of them – who was a female – did not learn to fly on Time or as well as the rest. So it was that when all the others left the nest, she stayed with her parents, and it was only by chance that she had stayed too long. Therefore, she never left at all. And so he named her 'Chance.'

To the first I said; "Hello, Raven, I trust that you have been well."

But to the second I said... "Why, who are you?"

"This is 'Night'" replied Brennos.

To my surprise, Night spoke back and said – "Hello." I laughed. Then the third little shy one – for she had not grown as big as her parents – came out and perched upon my wrist. I said: "Well, are you not beautiful!? What have you named this one?"

He explained why he had named her Chance and I replied, "We are all gifted by – and victims of – *chance*, are we not? Does she ever remind you of that truth, Brennos? For, as she perches here upon my wrist *I* am reminded: We are all in the hands of the Gods and the Mother of Fate. To us, all that comes about seems merely as if by chance. But I have come to see that The Weavers have plans in the works – unbeknownst to us."

"Yes, it is true. Speaking of chance, only yesterday – but before your arrival – someone else happened into my life... just by chance."

"Really?"

"Yes."

He went toward the back of his Cave – wherein it was darksome and still. He took a stick and held it out before himself. As he went further back I could no longer see him for the lack of light. But presently, he walked out, and there was an Owl – a beautiful young one – perched upon the stick.

He said, "Mistress Owl, meet Gwyddion."

The Owl said, "*Whooo?*" and we both laughed. But then of a sudden, into my thoughts, she spoke – in a voice that was both thoroughly feminine and mysteriously Owlish. Oh, how can I describe it? Wizened... old beyond her age, yet beautifully compassionate and patient. Why, yes... her voice was as I had always imagined the Faery Godmothers' in Brennos' fables to be – the ones he used to tell me when I was yet a boy.

"*Whooo* are you?" said she, and "Why have you come to Brennos' Cave of Wonders?"

Brennos later told me "Your eyes began to spin into those eerie silver spirals, as they are wont to do."

He stood and watched as the Owl spoke to me – and as I, his former apprentice, replied to her "I am Gwyddion. Many call me The Merlin."

"Merlin? A Hawk?" said she. "Then you should see very *clearly* why I have come here to meet you.

"It was only a matter of Time, our meeting. Do you not remember that we have been together for many lives and so will we be again and again and again? For all things foretold take place in the Night of Time – when Time as we think of it sleeps... The Time between... We are all but shadows *whooo* fleetingly pass through Her... Even *yhoou* – the great Merlin – *yhoou* will have your *Time* and then it will be gone. But the Time of greatness that will be remembered is the Time of Arthur, the King. The Boy called 'the Bear.' This Time is upon us! So I have come... just in Time. Soon we must go to get him. And I would travel with *yhoou* – if it be your will – for the rest of our lives."

Then my thoughts began to clear and I came into myself again.

Brennos was holding me, where I had fallen to the floor.

"What is it, my boy?"

"It is Time."

But I had used the Greek word "Chronos," which means "Time." So that is what I named her – this beautiful white Owl who was to be my life's companion.

"Chronos."

Then I knew that, indeed, it was Time for all foretold great events to begin.

I spent fourteen Nights there with Brennos, during which my strategy was formed. Then, with great sorrow at leaving him and leaving this place of solitude and of peace, I set out and began to wend my way Southward.

I would arrive just in Time to collect my charges at the boys' twelfth year-turn, which was still more than three months hence.

But first I thought I would go to visit Morgan. I had much to share with her for I knew that she was to play a great role in Arthur's life, and I trusted her completely.

She had very recently achieved her elevation to Enchantress on the Isle of Apples. I was very fond of little Morgan. Well, she would not be so little now – would she?

So, in Brennos' safekeeping – in his Cave of Wonders – I was to leave Uther's Sword until the Time came to make Arthur King.

Morgan

These are the things Gwyddion, The Merlin, related to me upon his first visit to the Isle of Apples. I wrote them down at the Time of that visit and am placing them here so as to be in sequence with his written words.

Gwyddion told me that on his travels Southward toward the Island of the Inland Sea, he had many adventures.

He first went into the deep Forests of Dumnonia – to the land of the ancient Dark Tribes, where he bade greetings and paid homage to my grandmother – the Mother of Igraine, and to the Old Grandmother of the Tribe, the very same who had been standing with Igraine when first she had met Gorlois. She was still alive. "So old was she! But I should not be surprised, for I have heard of other such Seers who have lived longer than even four generations."

Along the way through the lands of the Dark Ones, he had often felt that there were eyes upon him, eyes behind the Trees, up in the Trees and behind the Standing Stones. Unseen eyes were everywhere.

These people of the Old Tribes – my people – were called "the Watchers" by some. They watched – and listened – for everything. They had a system of sending messages and news as quickly as an Eagle flies over the boughs and Mists of the Forests, even to the length of these, Our Fair Isles. This was amazing to all others – even fearsome!

When finally they came – out of nowhere as it seemed – there were four small dark men standing before Gwyddion. They had said, in halting words of the Cymru – in Gwyddion's tongue – "Greetings, Gwyddion The Merlin, what finds you in our lands?"

He must have smiled within himself at the knowing that they feared him not. For he told me that, "These men were cunning and filled with old Wisdoms. By their very countenance they *commanded* respect, although did not *demand* it."

"I would pay homage to the Grandmother of your Tribe, and to she who is Mother of Igraine, the Seer, and Grandmother of Morgan, Enchantress of the Isle of Apples and of the ones called Morganna and Bedwyr...

"Bedwyr? Not the Bear?" they quipped; with knowing smiles upon their faces. "You will be welcomed, Gwyddion, The Merlin. Allow us to escort you to them."

Gwyddion told me that he had thought, "Even with all of my Druids' Gifts, I wondered – no, doubted – if I could actually find their village *without* escort. For the Old Ones have means of keeping to their own kind ... ancient Magics of keeping themselves concealed wherever and whenever they wish to."

With a bow he had said, "I thank you very much."

So, after going through all of the protocols that were known to him regarding their race, he was then taken to see the old Tribal Grandmother.

"As old as she was now and wrinkled, the twinkle had not dimmed from her eyes."

He told me that her eyes "...danced with Charms. You could read the intelligence behind them. Her thoughts were sharp as the end of a stick, sharp as the sting of a Wasp... and her tongue... well, sometimes it could be that, too!"

But she had been very welcoming and glad to see him. He shared what news of the outer world that he could with her and she shared with him their Tribal events.

Their culture, their Rituals and seasonal round made it seem to him as if they lived in a circle, with one season flowing into the other, one cycle of beginnings and endings returning to the Chaos then springing forth to life again, with no reckoning of the years.

Just so, I knew in fact, they did.

He was treated very, very well. They fed him and provided an Enchanting, canopied Tree house for his privacy and sleep. He rested there with them for two weeks. He went along with them when they hunted. Although he was of the habit of eating very little flesh – such as an occasional Fish – he realised that they were honouring him by their invitation and he would not offend them by abstaining.

It had been a good visit. So much so that when it had come Time for his leave-taking, he said that he had felt a sadness.

The old Grandmother of the Tribe blessed him and Igraine's Mother gave him a parting gift. The gift was a large, ancient golden brooch, with un-recognizable symbols etched onto it.

She had said; "We know... We understand... what greatness lies in my daughter Igraine's blood. Yes, I mean the boy... the boy who you will train to be to the one King for all peoples. This brooch holds – within the glyphs of our Ancestors – the formula to keep you from Death's grasp, so long as he holds the sword of Kingship."

He, in turn, gave to them a Druids' Blessing and cut off a lock of his hair and gave it to her, for he had nothing else to give.

It occurred to him that he would probably never see either of them again on this side of the Shadow Realms.

Now, I must add here that for Gwyddion to relinquish a piece of himself, such as his hair, to another, was a great showing of trust. For the Druids, as well as, in fact, most of the Magi of this World, are very cautious – or perhaps very wise – in their belief that to hold a piece of a person, such as their hair, skin, fingernails, saliva or the like, is to hold some of their power, which could be used to harm or control them. It was also a showing of the respect and Love held in his heart for them.

So, on he went with his journeying, until finally he arrived at the Isle of Apples, climbed the Tor and there found me – a woman grown – tending my Bees.

He had come up from behind me, thinking to surprise me, but I had grown in *Sight* as well as in body. I smiled from the inside out, knowing that this was Gwyddion, The Merlin, who had treated me so sweetly when I had been a little girl.

Never have I had need of covering myself with nets when tending my Bees and never have they stung me. I always move very slowly around them for their comfort. They buzz their buzzing then I buzz my buzzing back to them. We talk and sing with each other in this manner. Oh, I know, this has always seemed "wyrd" to others, but it is just the way we play with each other.

When Gwyddion came upon me, so as not to startle me he whispered, "Good Day to thee, my Lady Morgan of the Woods."

"Ah, Gwyddion!"

We embraced.

"My Bees will do no harm to you."

"Well, neither will Chronos my Owl companion do harm to you or your Bees. Morgan, my dear girl, let us walk together on this beautiful Day, if you might take some Time away from your duties?"

I giggled, "Why, certainly!"

"Will you be able to stay here with us for long, Gwyddion?"

"Perhaps for a while, for I have much to tell you Morgan, much that I wish for you to remember. I trust you implicitly, but these are things that, for the Time being, must remain between us two alone.

"Have you made a vow of any kind which would require you to share any information I give to you with the Lady Vivianne?"

"No, I have not. In any case she would honour my confidentiality with *you*."

So, he spoke to me then of all that had happened and of all things that were to come.

Of course, even from the great Merlin, some things are hidden.

He was, however, very careful not to mention Arthur or "the Bear" by name, always using terms like "Your brother" or "Uther's heir," for at that Time, even Igraine knew not of the boys being switched at birth. So, of course, I thought that he meant Bedwyr.

The few Days he thought to spend here actually turned into a few weeks, due to all he wished to share with me. He was also, I believed, revitalised through his taking in the serenity and beauty of our Isle of Apples. We did indeed have good Days together.

So, when all had been said and done between us and we were to part, we looked into each other's eyes and in the stillness of that moment, I read his thoughts – or perhaps it was his heart – which spoke of the pleasure it had been just to look upon my countenance – and of how much I reminded him of my Lady Mother Igraine. I blushed then and my own heart fluttered... But as to why, I have never known...

"Some Time, when I come again, Morgan, it must be at the Season of Sowing – at Winter's End – so that I might see the blossoming of the Apple Trees... or perhaps in Summer – to see the proliferation of beautiful wild and cultivated flowers that are tended here on your Isle. I have heard much of them from other pilgrims. One Monk told me – 'In Summer everything smells so sweet that the Butterflies, Bees, and Glow flies Love to linger there – all of which adds to the Enchantment of this place.'

"Oh yes, then there is the Apple Harvest when the orchards come into their full glorious fruiting."

I replied to him, "They also provide excellent exercise, for the picking of them is vigorous work – thus warding off our sluggishness through the Winter Calming and celebration."

"My sweet Morgan" he continued "this Cold Moon of Mid-Winter has shared its own beauty with me. Frosted branches, white covered cottages, Priestesses flurrying around in richly dyed woolen cloaks, and our warm conversations by the hearth-Fires, have all been indelibly etched upon my heart. I will never forget this, Morgan. So I suppose that I will be visiting you often."

His handsome face and his blue-grey eyes grinned...

Upon his leave-taking he formally bade 'Goddess-be-with-you' to the Lady of the Lake and began his Westward journey to Igraine's fortress – to my home – which stood atop the craggy Cliffs of Dumnonia, hanging high above the edge of the Western Sea.

Igraine

Through the next two years, after Morgan's departure for the Isle of Apples, life at my fortress had been prosperous and peaceful. All the children of my household, including the Bear, remained well, safe, and happy. And so, on went life until the boys reached their twelfth year-turn. It was upon that very Day that, once again, Gwyddion, The Merlin, came back into our lives.

Of course he had been back to visit with us as often as he could manage through the years that had passed, but those had been merely cordial and pleasant times, spent in good conversation and getting to know all of my household better. This visit, I knew, was of a much more purposeful and profound nature. After the proscribed greetings and polite conversations, he spoke with me about the agreement I had made regarding my son Bedwyr.

"I am sure, Igraine, that you remember your promise to me."

"Yes, I do... How quickly the Time has passed."

"Igraine, you know that it is customary for boys to be fostered."

"Yes... yet, I would never have agreed without being under duress..."

"Nevertheless, you did agree to it... I will teach him many things, Igraine. This was ordained by the Gods long ago."

"Gwyddion, he has been taught many things already. But yes, I am not betraying my word... I know that he will do very well with your mentoring. But it would break my heart to take him away from the Bear – for I know that they are beloved, inseparable friends."

Gwyddion smiled with a twinkle of joy in his eyes... or was that triumph?

He continued, "I was hoping to take them both with me. In fact, I had already spoken with Tangwen and Markus about this possibility when last I saw them."

"Oh, I see... that will, of course, be wonderful for them – but promise that you will come often and bring them back to us, for my Morgan has gone... and now the boys will leave too."

"You can be assured that we will come as often as is possible."

A side note:

I noticed upon that Day that Gwyddion did not say to me, "Well, you still have Morganna..."

I had seen the way he always looked at her. And it was with the same dread and horror as did I. But we did not speak of it...

Gwyddion
The Joyous Days...

Arthur and Bedwyr were just past their twelfth year-turn when we left Dumnonia.

After our leave-takings we wound our way down the difficult path away from Igraine's fortress. Standing high as it does upon its Wind-swept promontory above the rugged Dumnonian coastline, its mass of timber and Stone appeared all the more huge, looming above us as we descended toward lower ground. The boys could not refrain from looking back toward their home and Mothers left behind. No doubt they also suffered apprehension over what the future might hold for them, but they had bravely taken their leap of faith and there was no turning back now.

Our journey was long and hard but eventually we arrived at the spacious Cave I had prepared as our dwelling within the belly of the Snowy Mountains.

Now, our Cave had far less comforts than had the Fortress of Dumnonia, wherein Bedwyr and Arthur had lived since their births. You see, it was furnished very scantily.

The first thing I had done when I found the Cave was to contrive a means of hanging an oil lamp near the inside of its entrance – for when evening fell it was too dark inside for me to see my hand before my face. Then, near to where I had envisioned a table to be, I found a small natural shelf jutting out from the Stone wall, which was just the right size to place another oil lamp upon. Next I procured the services of a man and his wife who lived on a nearby farm. I left instructions for them – and silver too, of course – to first clean the Cave and then to lay rushes and flea-bane and fragrant Herbs upon its floor – which was very hard, it being Stone and not dirt – for softness and warmth. This would also help to keep out fleas and flies. The man, who was somewhat of a carpenter, had made three raised areas that would become our beds, two log benches and a trestle-and-plank table. That was it.

As far as keeping larger beasties from inhabiting our home until I returned, I had Cast a very un-welcoming Spell with them in my thoughts!

Arthur and Bedwyr spent the next five years under my tutelage. These were joyous Days – Days of peace, free from worry and concern, Days of Sunny or Cloud-dappled blue Skies, fishing in the cold Creeks of the Snowy Mountains in Winter and Summer, playing games of wit and skill... All the while was woven into those Days the knowledge and Wisdoms they must gain. Much of my Time was spent teaching them in the Woods; of root and stem and seed and Herbs, of Moss and Stream, of Trees and Flowers, of Stones and Caves – and of all Creatures of flesh and bone.

In my training of them, we practiced the ancient "Walkers' Arts," so that they both might learn to traverse the Otherworlds – there to meet the

Spirits, who were their *true* teachers.

With these Arts, Bedwyr had no problem, a fine and gifted student he was; a 'Seer' – but Arthur could only accept and understand these practices intellectually. I had taught them both equally, but the gates between Arthur and the Otherworlds seemed to be locked. This greatly disappointed me at first, but then I relented – for not all men or women have the Gifts of the Arts Magical. I realised that I must accept Arthur as the Creature he was. He was a good boy, brilliant, valiant, and a lover of nature and of the Goddess. In fact, he honoured all Gods and Spirits. But, to shift into the waves of other-consciousness... this he had much trouble with. So be it, then – as the Fates willed it.

They had both already been taught to read and use letters and I knew that Bedwyr's Father, Marcus, had trained them well in the games, skills, and crafts of war. Still, there was so much more that they must learn in order to be King and King's Champion, such as the matters of leadership and diplomacy... in these, at least, I had acquired proficiency.

Now, while it is true that I have ever disdained the butcheries of war, I had by then come to know that, in the world of men, betimes battles were a necessary evil. I have heard it said somewhere that for some things there is no good answer. During my years with my brilliant brother Ambrosius, I was privy to many conversations – and even a book that Ambrosius held in his possession – regarding Roman military tactics, maneuvers, and formations. This book was one of Ambrosius' most prized possessions. It had been a gift from Emperor Theodosius – the second of that name – in appreciation for his continued service and allegiance to the Roman Empire, given to him through the hands of Germanus of Auxaire on the occasion of the "Alleluia Battle." The information in the book I had committed to memory. True, at the time, I was only interested in these things from a purely intellectual standpoint, but the realization had later dawned within me that this would be very practical and excellent information for Arthur to have. Thus, thanks to Ambrosius' new book – *Epitoma rei militaris* – General Rules of War – written by one Vegetius, I was able to teach the boys something beyond what Marcus had imparted to them. These things we turned into fun games played by the three of us with makeshift props for weapons and shields. In this manner, they learned of 'The Wedge,' 'The Saw,' and 'The Orb' – offensive and defensive formations. Perhaps the most beneficial information of all regarding how Rome had achieved their military greatness was that 'training was the most important tactic to the Roman Army'. Every soldier was trained to fight hard and to improvise – not unlike an engineer; able to make use of whatever was to hand in any situation.

The main reason the Roman Empire was so successful in its military conquests is because the men were so tightly bonded, each man thinking of the next as his brother. It was unthinkable to them to fail their family, so men stayed by their brothers regardless the odds against them; fighting to the death, if necessary, to protect one another.

If only Arthur could eventually develop this kind of loyalty amoungst his troops, he could not fail, thought I. And so it proved to be in later years.

Yes, my life during those years was all about the boys.

Having taken upon myself the whole of their continuing education, it was clear that instruction in the ways of Love between a man and a woman were to be difficult for me to teach them. For, never had I lain with a woman – and as far as I could then see, I never would. I tried to teach the boys what I had heard of Love... But soon I realised that my attempts were an abysmal failure. They would have to learn of these matters in their own good Time.

In later years people said that I was not a man at all, but a Creature made of Magic – that my birth had been a thing of rare wonder, that I had not really had a Human Father at all. No doubt the silly rumours of Vortigern's camp were still being tossed about. These served my purpose well – for none would ever suspect that *I* was indeed the truest heir of Macsen's blood.

Through those years when the boys were with me, news had reached me that since Uther's Death, the Clans and their Chieftains had all vied with one another, each one seeking to take Uther's place as War Chieftain or King.

The Chieftains could come to no agreement. Petty disputes and squabbles went on and on, but all of their struggles were no part of my life in those Days.

The cycles of the Great Wheel turned – as always they do – and before I knew it, five years had passed and the boys were at their seventeenth year-turn.

One cold Day as we were all sitting and fishing by a Creek, with the mid-Stream's Water splashing and bubbling, with the Ravens above qworking, the ice at the edge of the Creek creaking and the Breezes pushing the last of the browned, fallen leaves to and fro upon the Mossy ground... on that most wonderful of Days, again I was taken... taken without warning or asking...

The Voices whispered my name, "Gwyddion... Gwyddion..."

I suppose that my face had turned white, for the boys were staring at me. Deeper and deeper into the Well of my self was I pulled until I heard them whisper again.

"Gwyddion, Gwyddion! It is Time."

And so it was.

I told the boys that we must go now.

Of all things, although he claimed not to have the Sight – and indeed it did seem that way – it was Arthur who said, "It is Time... Time to go? Will the world ever keep changing for us? I fear that this is the end of our youthfulness... of our beautiful boyhood together... I feel in my gut that there are things afoot that will change everything. Tell me, Gwyddion, tell us... There is something that you have been hiding... what is it – please tell us now!"

It was then, at last, that I told Bedwyr and Arthur the circumstances that had led to their births.

Bedwyr was heartbroken. Oh, not because he wished to be the son of the great Dux of Dumnonia, but instead for the fact that Igraine was not his real Mother.

Arthur, in his great Love and compassion said, "Oh my brother, what difference does it make? It is you she Loves far better than me; she will always Love you thus, as will I always Love you. There has never been a distinction between us before. You never made me feel like an underling, why should I now do that to you? Nothing changes, Bedwyr. Nothing will ever change between us. Nothing will ever part us – nor will anyone."

However, Arthur seemed to take the news of his own birth and of who his true blood family was as a tragedy... Arthur wept bitterly and often. He thought that Bedwyr and I had not heard him – but of course, we had.

"This means that Morgan is my blood half-sister..." was all he ever said to us about it.

A shiver and a foreboding came over me. Not of perilous doom, not of anything that would un-do the Love and friendship of the three of us – but of something in the future that would bring great grief to one, if not all of us. And because, by this Time, I held a great Love for both of the boys, I was sore distressed.

Back To Brennos...

When we awoke upon the next morn, with great haste the boys and I with Chronos began our journey toward Brennos and his Ravens three – to inform him of all that must now be done and to retrieve Uther's sword.

Chronos always reminded me that there was a Time for everything. Along our way she whoo-whoo'd in my ear each Night – Oh, not my physical ear, of course, but the ear inside my heart – and gave many Wisdoms to me. All along our journey to Brennos' Cave, I communed with her: "Advise me, my dear friend and companion. Aid me in this plan that I am to devise regarding the sword Caledfwlch and the making of a King..."

I kept asking... but as always, she kept her own counsel until she was good and ready to give it...

One Night, while sleeping beneath a rocky overhang where we were

protected from the Wind, I thought I heard Chronos say, "Whoo...
Whoo... Caledfwlch is awaiting yhoou, Gwyddion... For, there is a
riddle from Times long past, which says, 'He Whoo finds the sword is
the true Blood King – although he is never to *be* King – while yet, the
True King finds the Sword... He who solves this riddle is worthy...' As
you know, Gwyddion, Caledfwlch is the sword of the Kings – and
Queens – of the Britons from Times unknown. Those were the Days of
equality of men and women on this Isle – until the Romans ruled and
brought with them the un-balance...

"Now, a sword is a masculine symbol. Just so, is a chalice a
feminine. Yhoou know, Gwyddion, and yhoou believe – as the Dark
Tribes and the Clans believe in common – that there must be male and
female, light and darkness, breathing out and breathing in, to keep the
balance and to keep the world in motion.

"These Isles are becoming an empty chalice. Long held traditions
have been swept away by the Roman invaders. Now they, too, have left.
Our chalice has nearly been drained. We drift upon a Sea without
direction... Caledfwlch – in Arthur's hand – will fill that cup and revive
the Britons' pride of heritage.

"First, yhoou must find Caledfwlch, to fulfill the Spell upon it.
Then, by replacing Caledfwlch and spiriting Arthur to it, you are in effect
naming him as your heir and the next true King... But he himself must
retrieve the Sword of Kings from whence it hides, to prove *his*
worthiness...

"Then Gwyddion, yhoou must finally complete the balance of the
Sword of Power for all time, by etching into it its final symbols...
Caledfwlch has waited for ages to be completed."

I asked incredulously:

"What is this? I must alter the great Sword of Kings?"

"Whoo Whoo... Whoo Whoo."

"What did you say?"

" Whoo... Whoo... I said – yes, yes... 'Cosmos' and 'Chaos' must be
etched into the blade...

"Pick up that stick at yhoour feet, Gwyddion. Hold it as yhoou
would a sword, then turn your palm up... On the side of the blade then
showing, yhoou must etch 'Chaos.' Chaos is the Great Mother – the
Dark and Formless One, the Originator. Then, on the opposite side –
with it held palm down – must be etched 'Cosmos.' Cosmos is all that is
in form – the movement and manifestation of the Great Goddess – all
that lives in myth as her Son and Lover, the young God...

"To etch these into the blade, Gwyddion, yhoou must use only
yhoour Magic – only the "Grym Hudol." Use yhoour first finger of
power – or yhoour wand of Willow, if yhoou prefer – to direct that
energy which is capable of breaking sound and making light. Use it

instead of a forge and a chisel of iron.

"This Sacred act must only be done within the Magic Circle of the Lady of the Lake – only she may make a King with yhoou... And only the Great Mother's Priestess may seal the bond...

"Yes, Gwyddion, a Sword is just a Sword – an implement of warfare – but Caledfwlch will be the *symbol* of the Divine unity of Goddess and God – the tie that will bind all the peoples whoo dwell upon these, Our Fair Isles.

"By this Sword, as well as the Pen Dragon standard, must Arthur fight and win the battles which will restore order and peace to this land. While he holds it, he will be invincible!

"But, all this in its own good Time...

"Whoo, whoo... whoo, whoo..."

My body stopped its floating and I became more stable within myself. I looked at my wonderful Chronos. I thought I understood...

"Dare I ask more? You have told me this much – tell me... tell me what plan I must devise and where I can find the sword."

Silence...

I lay my head to rest that Night and listened to the howling of the Wolfs...

We reached Brennos to find him well. Arthur and Bedwyr fell under his Charm just as I had done as a boy. We had a wonderful – albeit short – visit, retrieved Uther's sword, and bid a good-bye to Brennos, promising to return whenever possible, then were on our way Southward to the Isle of Apples.

On the very first Night's rest from our hard travels down frozen, muddy roads, we were fortunate enough to come upon a mean round-hut with smoke issuing from the center of its Snow-burdened straw roof. We dared to knock upon its plank door. A suspicious voice spoke from behind it...

"Who goes there? What trade have you with me?"

"We are four weary travelers: One man and his Owl companion and two tired boys – none of whom mean any harm to you. We happened upon your cottage, saw the smoke of your hearth, and wondered if we could spend the Night inside, upon your floor. We have bread and cheese to share with you and I have a bit of green ribbon for your good wife – if you have one, that is."

"I have an axe in my hand, just so you know," said the man, "try no foolishness. Go away!"

"Well," thought I, "this may prove to be a bit bothersome..."

"Good man, you asked: 'Who goes there?' My name is Gwyddion... I am the one people call The Merlin of the Britons. Truly we mean to be no bother or harm. Please, will you give us shelter from this cold?"

"The Merlin? How do I know you speak truth? Do some Magic for me and I will let you in."

Now, I was taught that Magic is never to be done for foolishness or vainglory... Yet, we *were* cold and damp through to the bones...

"Alright, my good man, I will stop the Snow from falling... But you must open your door to see that it is done, as there is no opening in your wall for to see out of." Of course, unbeknownst to him, the Snowfall had already ceased. I said a nonsensical 'Magic word' and then told him to go ahead and look.

He pushed aside the wooden planks serving as his door, to see that it was indeed not Snowing anymore.

Poor ignorant man – what if I had been a robber?

But he had told truth – there was an axe in his hand...

He smiled a half toothless smile and welcomed us in.

"Hurry or all the warmth will leave my hut!"

We put our blankets down on his filthy straw-strewn floor. There were only two choices as to where our blankets would go – over or under us... We chose under – hoping all the while that they would not become too infested with Fleas or whatever other wee beasties might lurk there. However, in the case they should begin to bite, I always carry some oil of Flea-bane with me. We covered ourselves with our cloaks and were very grateful for the shelter.

As I was falling to sleep, from somewhere in the distance I heard a calling... "Gwyddion... Gwyddion..." – but this voice was *neither Chronos nor* the "Voices of the Stars." It was a mighty and deep sardonic voice... Of course this aroused me so that hours passed before I *could* sleep...

Then, I had another Dream...

Upon so many Nights, I Dream. Mostly they are inconsequential Dreams of things troubling me, or of secret desires, or of people who dwell in my thoughts of the long-ago past – or simply of those people and happenings that had been present in that very Day's events. Sometimes they play out in frolicsome – or terrifying – phantasy... These are just Dreams... But then there are the other sort – the Great Dreams – those which hold portents of things to come, or messages from beyond this realm of form. The Dream I Dreamt that Night was of this second kind...

It was like this:

We were searching and searching for something – somewhere. Where it was, my Dream did not reveal. But after long and long tiresome travel, through many Sun and Moon risings and fallings, we found ourselves at a barrier of Water. A Sea? A Lake? Then I noticed that it was filled with jagged Reeds. Beyond its expanse there was a great Hill winding up to the Stars. Its top was hidden in Clouds. It was beckoning – nay, beguiling us toward it. The bottom of this Hill was enshrouded in a heavy Mist rising from the Earth. It was eerie... frightening. Yet, so persistently was it luring us toward itself that we had no recourse but to traverse the perilous way. Only one man's length beyond the soggy shore could I see...

"How far is the winding Hill?" I asked.

An answer echoed...

"As far as the blood of these Fair Isles or as far as a Dream is away. As far as the realm of Gwyn ab Nudd."

"What? Gwyn ab Nudd"? He is Lord of the underworld! Are we to die then?"

The Voice answered:

"Arthur will... Arthur will die to the man he now is... As for you and Bedwyr – there will be no turning back from the path. The Question is: 'will you accept the quest?'"

"A quest? Is there a choice?"

"Always there are choices... and consequences, Gwyddion, The Merlin, this you know – everything has a cost."

As these specters faded, we were already across the gloomy reeds. When had this happened?

My next footfall was upon the opposite shore. Then we were rushed to the foot of a Mountain – its heights looming above us – or was it the same Hill I had seen moments ago? I could barely see for the Mist. But a vibration – a sound – was emanating from a Moss covered, hidden Cave opening into the bottom of the Hill. So loud was it that I held my hands over my ears, for fear they would burst – then I fell to my knees.

"HA-HA-HA!" thundered the great booming voice. No living man dares to enter into the opening of my Realm! Why have you come?"

"I cannot *remember* why..."

"Well then, Gwyddion, The Merlin, I will have sport with you... another riddle...

"He who will *never* be King, will *forever* hold the Sword of Power in *my* Realm... HA-HA-HA!"

We awoke in the morn, there in the ragged hut, not itching too badly. Although I did notice that Chronos seemed to be preening herself overmuch...

We broke our fast and bade the man farewell. Then we were on our way again through the Snowbound Greenwood.

That next Night, as we slept in the hollows of two giant Trees, I Dreamed again... I Dreamed of sweet Morgan. She was beckoning me. Next that I knew, I opened my eyes to a glorious new morn.

My Spirit began to lighten as the four of us continued. I knew that we must walk all the way from the Mountains to the Isle of Apples and that would have been too long a Time for me to be moody.

Many fine and wonderful talks and adventures had we after that –

making glorious plans for the future. As idealistic boys and men are wont to do, we spoke only of the great achievements and the marvels that lay ahead of us – nothing of the dangers.

Chapter 7
To Make a King

Gwyddion

Traveling to the Isle of Apples had been a demanding journey. There had been scant food for us to eat on our way – only that which we could hunt or fish.

When finally we had arrived, we found that the sisters and brothers of The Order had prepared a great celebration in honour of our arrival – complete with feasting, bonfires, tale telling, and songs. We were delighted. They had prepared meals of venison, Fish and foul along with delicacies of dried Fruit, baked Grains, honey and mead. Of these we were very appreciative, especially realizing that this was not their usual fare, for they of the Isle of Apples are like me in that they are very conservative in their own eating habits.

So it was that Lady Vivianne, with her uncanny foresight had already begun to make preparations – months ahead of the future King's arrival.

I continued to be stunned at Morgan's beauty. So like her Mother was she. How quickly Time passes! Let me see... Arthur and Bedwyr were seventeen years now... Hmm... That would make Morgan twenty-three years – a perfectly wonderful age.

Of course, my charges were also delighted to see Morgan... most especially Arthur.

When finally I spoke with Morgan alone, I mentioned the Dream in which someone was calling to me. She smiled and said, "Yes, I know... I am glad that I was successful in reaching you. You see, when I told The Lady that I sensed great changes in the Winds, she told me of the far-reaching events of the near future and of how Gwyddion, The Merlin, must now make a King.   Hence, my calling to you in the land of Dreams..."

"Of course... It was you who called me here! I should have known..." Then teasingly I said, "So how, then, would we begin to make a King, Morgan the Enchantress – here amidst your beautiful Winter gardens, bells and Bee hives?"

"Well, first," said she, "we must go to the Lady of the Lake."

"Ah, the great Lady Vivianne... I will be most pleased and honoured to speak with her of these matters."

"As a matter of secondary fact, Gwyddion, you should know that I am aware that the Bear – uh, Arthur – is my brother and our future King. In fact, I have known this for some long Time..."

We left it at that...

Auspiciously, we had arrived on the eve of the New Moon – on the Moon's darkest Night. I, who am Druid trained, believe, that upon the Dark Moon is the Time of banishing or of cursing. It is the Time to be rid of all obstacles in the way of attaining our needs or desires. So, after the feasting and celebrating had ended, in the Druids' way – within an Oak Grove in the Woods – that Night I performed my Magics which would thenceforth exist in the Other Realms, there to work on Arthur's behalf to remove all evil influences that might block his path onward toward becoming High King of the Britons.

On the second Night, with the first sliver of the New Crescent Moon visible, at last the *Making* Magics could be set into motion. This was the Time to *begin* the bringing of Arthur's Kingship into manifestation in the world of Men.

As was the Order's custom, our visit was to start with the boys and my resting, meditating, grounding to the Earth and all of Her Creation and just general pleasantness, before any business could be done. This was all the more important in preparation for the blessing of a new King. Quite frankly, it was a welcome relief, for the long trip in the cold of Winter had worn us all out.

Upon the eighth Day, it was Time to make our plans.

The Wind had begun stirring on the Isle; it was a steady blow. There was great power in the Air as Morgan and I walked to the quarters of the Lady of the Lake. Our footfalls crunched upon the Snowy Earth. From somewhere in the distance I heard the sounds of Wolfs wailing their Winter song. An Owl Whoo-Whoo-ted to Chronos from a branch of a silvered Tree nearby – I felt as though Magic was afoot everywhere.

Lady Vivianne was an older woman, of course, but not so old as to diminish her allure. She was dignified – austere even – yet hidden deeply somewhere within herself was a charming and intensely caring woman, filled with the Spirit of the GODDESS. I had the sense that if she were to let her guard down, she could be as playful as the Twyla y Tag... If she would only let it be so. I liked her very much and greatly respected her.

All the while that I had been on the Isle, Lady Vivianne had made sure that I was treated as her peer, by which I felt very honoured. After all, she *was* the Lady of the Lake. So, that morning I felt no compunction in asking, "My Lady Vivianne, I beg private audience with you..."

She welcomed me into her quarters.

"Yes Gwyddion, of course, with what may I help you?"

She and I spoke for hours upon hours of all that had happened to me and to the boys. I told her then that Arthur, and not Bedwyr, was Igraine's son. Of this news, she seemed not surprised! I told her of the "Voices," my Dreams, my years with the boys, of how Chronos had come into my life, of Uther's murder, the acquiring of his sword, and of many other things...

"As you know, Lady Vivianne, I must lead Arthur to find Caledfwlch before any of what work we are about can proceed. But I know not where it is.

"I *have* heard of an old legend – one which is held secret by a very few Adepts. My master Brennos told it to me and he in turn was told it by his master Ea Kunagos. This legend tells that Caledfwlch, the Sword of Kings, is held in the keeping and protection of the Lady of the Lake – by you – my Lady.

"Yet, in a worrisome Dream, when haunted by the specter of Gwyn ab Nudd, I was told that I must go into his Cave – the entrance to the Underworld – to find it. I can still conjure-up the look and the smells of His Cave – wherein my Dream insinuated that I would find Caledfwlch."

"Gwyn ab Nudd?" She laughed. "It is true then; All the Gods *are* ONE... Here, in our world of Myth, Nodens, 'the Water Maker,' is the God of deep and darksome places, of Wells and Caves – and of the Underworld. And to those who would play in darkness, He guards the entrance to the *other side of the mirror...*

"My dear Gwyddion, as to my holding Caledfwlch – no, I do not. However, I do know where it lies. Gwyddion think! Where is there a Hill that hides a dark and Mossy Cave at its base – a place where none dare to tread... neither Kings nor Wise Ones? Have you not heard these legends?"

"Of course! Have the doors of my thinking faculties been locked to the obvious? The dark and Mossy Cave from whence flow the Waters of the Sacred White Spring – here at the base of the Tor! It has ever been thought a dread place; indeed, an opening to the realm of the dead. One superstition says that: 'If one passes through the mouth of the Cave, they are held captive, albeit to a place of Beauty, a land of delights and eternal youth – realm of the Twyla y Tag... the Faye... or the Old Gods. But once there, there be no returning to the world of Man...' Yet I have heard darker myths as well... Tales of ragged toothed Phantom Hounds guarding the way out of the Cave of Gwyn ab Nudd... and that those souls, who through their folly, greed, and audacity have challenged the

Rowena Whaling

Lord of the Underworld and must pay the cost by forever remaining in his place of *Ever Sameness* – where one hour repeats the last, unto the end of the worlds.

'Nid a i Annwyn ond unwaith'... Which means in my native tongue, 'There is but one descent into Annwyn.' Every Human body contains the 'mewnol yn cael ei,' their inner being or soul – and that is what is held there in bondage! Then again, my Lady, some tales soften the blow – by hinting that there would be *one* way out. In Druidical teaching, what this would mean – if it were reality – is that although their soul has traversed through many lives and in many forms to attain to live as a Human – this one and only exit from the realm of Gwynn ab Nudd would oblige them to climb the ladder of transmigration again, to live all of their inner being's lives over, beginning with its lowliest form – a Snail perhaps – eventually to rise once again into the world of Man.

"But Lady Vivianne, I have always thought these stories to be but metaphor."

"Metaphor? Yes, of course they are, my dear..."

"May I confide in you, my Lady?"

"Yes."

"Although I be Druid trained, I believe not that man is higher or more valuable than Animals, Insects, Trees, Rocks or any others who share this Earth with us. Is it true that in your Mystery School, you teach just as I believe: that all beings of form are part of the great ONE, and are equal in the GODDESS' eyes?"

"That is true... Gwyddion, it is well known amoung the Britons, that you share some beliefs of every Tribe and Clan on these Fair Isles. Perhaps, in addition to your renowned abilities and Wisdom, this is *why* you have been accepted as The Merlin by *all* – not just by the Druids. In fact, I believe that you have given the title of 'The Merlin' a new meaning.

"You know as well as I, that all things in this world change, given enough Time and necessity. It is now the Time for all on these Our Fair Isles to become more tolerant of one another's beliefs. You, my dear, are the bridge to this new and much needed accord.   Without this compromise, Arthur's reign of peace and solidarity could never come to be."

I, always being shy whenever receiving praise, veered away from that conversation, onto safer ground...

"Uh-humm... thank you Lady Vivianne... But, my Lady – what of finding Caledfwlch?"

"Ah, yes... To find the Sword of Kings is not the most difficult part. The next heir in succession of the line of the true 'Blessed Kings' will always find Caledfwlch. For this is written in their Stars... However, only a true heir of *'Righteous Intent'... AND one 'Powerful of Heart'* will hold the sword of Kings, for only they can command the Blue Flame of Caledfwlch. Caledfwlch will *sing* for no other."

"I see... and so the story expands...

"But, why then, did Ambrosius Aurillious not hold the sword of Kings, for truly he was a man of *'Righteous Intent'*? No man have I ever known to be more honourable, fair minded, true to his own word or acting in justice to all men and women! As for being *'Powerful of Heart,'* fame of his great, compassionate, forgiving and benevolent heart gained for him the Love and respect of all. Surely the Gods found him to be a man of honour?!"

"Yes, Gwyddion, he was a man of compassion, kindness, and honour – a good man. No one could deny him these qualities. I know that your heart holds a great Love and respect for him. But, as to 'Powerful of Heart' – in this he had a dangerous flaw. He was loving, compassionate and forgiving *to a fault*! Did he not allow his younger brother, the one called Uther the Pen Dragon, to betray his fellow Dux Gorlois of Dumnonia without reprisal or consequence? Did he not allow this same brother to usurp his own rightful position as the Pen Dragon – and this done to the ultimate harm of the tentative alliance of peace and stability of his countrymen and women? No, Gwyddion, a true King may hold a powerful life-long Love and yearning for one person, but never would he – or she – shirk their responsibility to this land or people for personal gratification. Neither would they call a wrong a right because of that Love. 'Powerful of Heart,' could be said in another way... That being 'Power Over Heart'... Do you see what I mean?"

"Yes... Yes, my Lady, I do."

"Gwyddion, let us speak frankly, I know the living secret of the Holy line of Kings. I know that you – and only you – have the power, by right, to make Caledfwlch come to life – once again to the service of these, Our Fair Isles! Shh... Before you speak; I also know that the Stars have not written the journey of King for your life. However, once the sword is awakened, the true heir – in this case *you* – may pass the Kingdom into the hands of the one he deems worthy, and if Caledfwlch accepts that one, then he, or she, will make Caledfwlch flame. This is how Uther's son will wield the Sword.

"I am sure that you recognize the problem. All the rest of these details of a transfer of Kingship and so forth are too complicated to be understood – or accepted – by those who must give Arthur their allegiance now... *Only Arthur* must ever be *seen* as the awakener of Caledfwlch. So he must find the sword *after* you have held it and relinquished it back to the darksome, hidden Cave – when, speaking aloud, you must say that "Arthur, son of the Pen Dragon, is true and ever heir of the Sword of Kings." Then it will truly be his, until upon the Day in which Arthur, in turn, willingly names his own true heir by giving

Caledfwlch into their hands."

Finding Caledfwlch...

As great Dreams often do unfold in the Realm of the Middle World, what events seemed beautifully – or frighteningly – Phantastical, play out in everyday, ordinary ways...

Upon the Day after my conversation with the Lady, Arthur, Bedwyr, and I set forth to the Cave at the bottom of the Tor.

Oh, the beauty of this place... We drank from the White Spring and I told the boys to climb the icy spiral path until they found some green Moss on the uppermost Northern side of the Hill and a rare Winter blooming Herb with yellow Flowers, with which I wanted to make an elixir... "Take the going slowly, for the path can be treacherous at this Time of year." I used this subterfuge to keep them busy for quite a long while so that I might examine the Cave by myself.

To tell it true – it *was* a fearsome place and beautiful at the same Time. At first, I could see nothing, for so dark was it in there. When my eyes began to adjust to the dim light, I noticed that there were glimmers here and there against the walls. I lit a torch. Then, moment by moment, the walls seemed to come alive until I saw that the entire round arch of the walls and ceiling were encrusted with Crystals. As shifting illumination and shadows of torch light reflected off the milky white iridescence of the Spring Water running its path in the floor of the Cave, the blue-grey of the interior Stones as well as the clear, pale, purple, and pink coloured Crystals seemed to glint and bounce against each other. Yes, this was a place of beauty, so I wondered why there were such grim tales about it.

Then I saw them – Stone Creatures of gruesome visages, heads of twisted bones and cruel grimaces with sardonic smiles, protruding from the walls. "Wait," I thought, "These are only natural formations of the Rocks, simply exaggerated by the flickering light." Or were they? But then, deep throaty groans began to emanate from the Stone Creatures nearest my torch. Startled, I turned – shifting my torch toward the next and more hideous head. When I moved they began to silence, but then, the Rocks nearest my torch began to awaken. The groans were deafening... I mused: "Oh, it is just some sort of vibration caused by the heat!"

Now satisfied with this explanation, I began to move more deeply into the bowels of the Earth, toward an opening from whence the White Spring flowed into the Cave's main chamber. At that point, the ceiling dropped and the walls narrowed significantly, forming a tunnel-like passage. My breaths began to echo. Of a sudden I felt a great chill come about me as a gust of Wind rushed through the mouth of the Cave. When the Wind entered the narrow passage where I stood, it spiraled around its walls – or at least, so it seemed – then *it* began to echo too... and echo and echo. The low-pitched whispers magnified. They seemed to be calling to me. "Merrrr-liiin... Merrrr-liiin..." Beyond all reason, I thought to flee.

I was snatched from my panic when I noticed a very subtle greenish glow coming from somewhere further back in the passage. My wits returned.

The pungent odor of fear in my perspiration, mixed with the earthen smell of the Cave and the chill in my bones was unsettling, yet on I searched for Caledfwlch.

The passage split into two paths and then again into three – each of them looking the same. "How easily one could lose their way in this labyrinth," thought I, but always I followed the green glow.

I could not say how many twining branches of the passage I had passed or how long I had been at my task – but of a sudden, there it was! I had come face to face with Caledfwlch!

Someone, at some Time past, had stood the sword upright – its blade held amidst a pile of Rocks, its hilt leaning against the Crystal wall – with the green Stone facing the entry of this last chamber of the Cave. I reverently approached. When the light from my torch hit the sword's green Stone, it reflected onto the walls and ceiling about me. Then the small chamber's entire surface was lit with clear Crystals, all the colour of Emeralds. I looked down at my hand... even I was green...

I spoke to the Spirits of the Cave...

"Will you think me a thief if I take it? That is *if* Caledfwlch will truly 'sing' for me... The Lady of the Lake told what my Mother had also said: that I am the true and rightful heir of the ancient Kings of the Britons. But the 'Voices' told that it was not written in my Stars 'to be a King, but to make a King – Arthur.' If Caledfwlch does not *sing and glow* in my hand, I will leave it here, in your realm – the realm of the Old Gods. But if it does sing for me, then I am honour bound to give it into Arthur's hand... I just wanted to tell you..."

I held my breath. "How do I dare touch this ancient relic?"

My arm reached out to it... I closed my eyes... and then my hand grasped it... I pulled it loose from the Stones that were holding it and raised it into the Air...

Caledfwlch began to vibrate and Hum – or was that just the shaking of my hand? Then came the famed blue Flame... So it was all true!

I held it for a few moments, reveling in the Magic. It was like an old friend in my grasp. Of a sudden, the realization hit me – I could be this!... I could be High King of all the Britons... A surge of self esteem – or was it grandiosity? – hit me like a bolt of lightning. Yet I knew that I must give it up...

I said the words: "I, Gwyddion The Merlin, brother of Ambrosius

Aurillious and Uther, called the Pen Dragon, do claim the right of wielding Caledfwlch as true High King of the Britons."

At those words the Flames raged... The amazing thing was that there was no heat – only brilliant light...

"From my hand I hereby relinquish Caledfwlch to Arthur, son of Igraine, Great Seer of the Old Tribes, and of Uther, called the Pen Dragon. Only Arthur may find and retrieve Caledfwlch from these Stones, whence I replace it. I give my right of Kingship to him as my heir and name him High King of the Britons – which he and only he will be until the Day upon which he willingly gives Caledfwlch into the hand of the one he names as his heir."

The blue flame went dim as soon as I had spoken the words... Starstruck I had been – but only for a few moments. I replaced Caledfwlch into the pile of Stones, just as I had found it...

Hurrying, I followed my footprints down the twisting passage to the chamber of the Cave's mouth. I walked outside. The sun shone brightly – it was a beautiful Day. I squinted – my eyes adjusting to the brilliance of the light. I then busied myself by picking Mosses at the Stream's edge, until the boys returned.

They were longer at their task than I had thought they would be. By the Time they returned, the Sun Disk was sinking below the Hills. It was too late upon this Day to lead Arthur to *find* Caledfwlch...

That Night I could not sleep at all. I could not feel comfortable in my own skin, much less my bedding. Whims – or were they truly desires? – flooded through my consciousness... to have felt the power of Caledfwlch in my hand.... It could have been a beguiling thing... I could have kept it for my own... For a moment, I had been King.

Sleep finally came. I awoke feeling better – with determination. The Ghosts of "What if?" had fled...

"Chronos, how can I lead Arthur to the sword, yet allow him to find it? I know that this is something he must do by himself. Am I being like a Mother Owl, fretting to protect her Owlets? Will I ever be able to set him free from the nest? I think of every danger and every trap waiting to devour him... I think of every Wisdom I must yet impart to him... Yet, I know that the Time has come for him to be a man and a King on his own merit. This must be the hour of release."

Chronos, of course, only blinked...

Morgan had asked us to rise very early that next morning so that we may accompany her across the reedy Lake, to deliver some sacks of the Order's cheese stocks to a needy widow and her two small children, as well as to the old Monk who lived not far from the Lake's edge. I could not refuse her. And so, we four were up and away to the Marsh Folk's punts, while the Isle was still cloaked in pre-Dawn twilight. By the Time we had crossed the Water to the far shore, it was bright and cold, with the sunrise casting brilliant hues.

We spent perhaps three hours on the opposite shore and then returned on the waiting punt.   I had paid little attention to my surroundings – so deeply in my thoughts had I been of Arthur's task – until Arthur said: "Look, is it not unusual for there to be such a dense Fog on the Isle at this Time of Day? The Sky has become clouded and the top of the Tor is hidden from sight. Does it mean that a Storm is coming, Morgan?"

My head jerked up at that, and there it was – the scene of my Dream!

Slowly did the Punt-men pull the little punt across the Lake. Then, all played out, as it had in my Dream – yet without the Phantastical drama.

First, Morgan was carried off the punt by the Punt-men and then we were motioned to step off into the cold, ankle deep marshy Water.

As we walked to the foot of the Tor, I told the boys that I had investigated the inner chamber of the Mossy Cave the Day before... They began to tease: "Well, then did you go down into the land of the Twyla y Tag?"

"Yes, in a way I did. I *began* the un-riddling of a Riddle!"

"What?" said Arthur.

"Well, since you asked first, you may try to un-riddle it first... Go into the Cave and just see and hear what you will. Only bring a torch for to see and a long stick with you to scratch the ground with, in case your journey be long and winding."

Of course I knew that that would sufficiently prick his curiosity! I also knew that I had done all that I could, or should, to lead Arthur to the sword – knowing, too, that the True King will always find Caledfwlch. Now it all was up to Arthur.

It is my hope that Arthur will write the details of his finding of Caledfwlch in his history... All I will say is that after a couple of hours, Arthur came back to us with Caledfwlch in one hand and a long stick still in the other. His face shone with a beatific smile and a vague blue-green glow.

The Blessing of a King...

The Ritual Blessing of a future King was a greatly honoured tradition of the folk on these, Our Fair Isles. This tradition dated back into the Time before even the Druids had arrived here. Clan and Tribe alike would never accept a Chieftain or King without the blessing of the Lady of the Lake – blood or no.

The Lady's blessing would indeed add credence to our claim of Arthur's kingship amoung our prospective allies.

As I have said, upon the Night of our arrival the Moon was Dark, now the Full Moon was three Days away.

Now that Arthur held Caledfwlch by right, everyone living at The Order was told the news – Arthur had been promised the blessing of the Lady of the Lake. All who were to be involved in the Ritual became a-flutter with busy preparations.

The Ritual...

I will now describe upon these pages, which I call "The Book of Gwyddion's Histories," the Ritual acceptance and blessing of the future King of the Britons by the Lady of the Lake.

I suspect that very few have ever witnessed this Rite – as it has been held as one of the Order's deepest Mysteries. I know that this book, which I will place into the hands of Morgan with unquestioning trust, will be kept a secret until the Time she deems it necessary and honourable to share. If not for this trust, I would be hesitant to record this. Such is the esteem I hold for her.

This is as it was...

It was the Night of the Full Moon.

Let me here note that that evening and Day were unseasonably warm – such as had not been known in memory! This was a good thing, for Winter Nights atop the Tor can be brutal.

There were only six of us – Humans – who had been chosen to attend. Vivianne – Lady of the Lake, Arthur, Bedwyr, Makyr, Morgan, and I – were counted as six, but seven were needed for the Ritual. Of course, Morgan's beloved Bees–who had been invited to follow us there – were counted as the seventh.

First we were asked – on our honour and in dread of the Gods' wrath – if we could enter this Holy place in a state of perfect peace... of heart, as well as with one another. All of us bi-legged Creatures answered "Aye!" The Bees hummed... All was perfect.

We Humans were then anointed with oils, which had been coloured with red and white pigments. Ancient symbols of the Old Tribes who had "Vanished into the Woods" were written in blue woad on our hands and faces, along with nine Stars, in honour of their Nine Mother Goddesses. Upon only Arthur's forehead was painted a crude Stag's head, with seven tined antlers, as though it served as a primitive Chieftain's circlet or coronet piece. We were all robed in white garments, which had been woven from the wool of the Order's Sheep. They were to be worn for this one Night only. Of course the Bees were counted as living closest to Nature and thereby needed no anointing or special garments. And a good thing *that* was!

In silent procession, led by drummers and quiet Chanting, we climbed the spiral path of the Tor, up and up to the great Stone Circle on its top. That was where the green Star Stone, which had fallen from the Sky somewhere in these environs, had been moved in Times long past and placed to lay in the center to serve as an Altar.

The drummers – all but Makyr – and the Chanters, waited behind on the path. Far enough away were they for the words spoken to be unheard by them.

There were seven Sacred directions to work within which would enclose – in a Magical sphere of power and protection – the Sacred space within the Stone Circle. These must first be acknowledged and honoured. Then the four Elements of Air, Fire, Water, and Earth must be stirred or awakened, so as to focus their powers and attributes into our Ritual space, to aid in the work to be done.

When we entered the Temple of Stones, we formed a circle. Arthur stood at the East, with Caledfwlch at his side.

He raised his voice in solemn salute, saying, "I stir and rouse thee, Oh Spirits of Air, you who are and represent the Times of Dawn, earliest blossoms, birth and all new beginnings... You are the breath of life, the first breath we take and the last. You are the Wind and those winged Creatures who fly amidst it. From your Realm of the East comes the origin of thought, memory, inspiration, and our rational, analytical processes. You are the domain of Science, Mathematics, and Astronomy... You are sounds... the sounds of flutes, whistles, stringed instruments, and bells... You are the calling of Birds, the chirping of Insects, and the creaking song of the Trees, as well as the melody of bubbling Springs and Streams..."

With this said, Arthur was given a small bell, which he rang three times at the end of his invocation of Air. "We bid thee hail and welcome!"

Makyr stood at the South and stirred the Element of Fire...

She said, "To Fire who enters from the Southern gate, you who represents the Time of high-noon, Mid-Summer and the age of our young and strong adulthood...

"Fire is of Serpent and Cat, of Lightning and Thunder... Wherefrom comes the source of all energies and power... It is passion, invincibility, assuredness, conviction, spirituality, anger, blood, and lust and the Magical Cast of directed WILL! – The spark of Creation itself. And let us not forget, the fermented liquor of honey, Fruits, and Grains, the Spirits of which can make our hearts dance into wild abandon!"

Makyr clashed two flint Stones together once and made a great spark of Fire.

"We bid thee hail and welcome!"

Bedwyr stood at the West and bowed to the Element of Water...

He called to the Times of twilight, of Red and Gold Leaves, and of the age of silver hair and approaching Wisdom.

"Water, you of the Western realm are the Element of our emotions, wherein is found the place of compassion, Healing, beauty, and Love...

yours is the place of access to the Mysteries. You are the source from whence all life springs... Water is the Element of the Seers, the Siren, and the song of the Siren. Water is also the Element of our children's tears, our grief, our sorrows, and our regrets... Element of Water, you are the *place* of Magic, the Trance, the Dream... and the entrance to the Otherworlds... home of all Sea beings... the Whale, the Seal, the Salmon, and Eel.

He offered to the West a beautiful shell, filled with the Waters of the Red and White Springs, to honour and celebrate the presence and Magic of Water, in this our Sacred Rite...

"We bid thee hail and welcome!"

Lady Vivianne stood at the North... "Seat of the Elders... Element of Earth... The Times of Midnight, Cold Winter, and Death... The Realm of truly attained Wisdom..."

She Chanted:

"Of Tree and Stone and Flesh and Bone...

"Of health and wealth, of hearth and home..."

She stomped upon the Earth three Times, poured a handful of dusty soil upon the sacred ground in front of her bare feet and then she spoke again...

"The Forests, the Mountains, the Sands of the shores... all of Green Nature, Her Creatures and more. These things are of the Element of Earth..."

She went on... "Our good Times... Nights spent by our hearths with dear friends in laughter. The work of our hands in which we are well satisfied, the food we eat... The children we make, Love and teach – and sometimes bury – A life of honour to be remembered by a good name! All of these, too, are of the Element of Earth."

She reminded us that Earth is also our stability – our families and home – and that singular quality for which all wise ones seek – balance...

"To you and the Spirits who work within your Realm, I bid Hail and Welcome!

To the Air that we breathe, the thoughts that we Weave...
The Flames of our passion, our Spirit's conviction...
The Well and the Trance, our song of romance...
The Forests, the Mountains, the Sands of the shores...
To all of Green Nature and so much more.
We Hail and we welcome thee, Elements four!"

Lady Vivianne noted at that Time, that we had all entered this Temple of Earth and Stone by the Northeastern gate – to honour the Ancestors, for this was the place between Death and birth. Though, of course, the gate was unseen...

The intensity grew – the Air around us felt hotter. I began to sweat. The circle was filled with Spirits... I felt the life force of Animal and Human Ancestors and of other unknown Spirits who act as our teachers and guides... So many had come... The Trance was upon me.

Then Lady Vivianne asked me to bind us all to the "Pole of Destiny" ... to the beginning and the end, the Alpha and the Omega, to the core of Creation, to the center of the Cosmos, and to the Land of Myth, which is the *Eternal Present* of the Gods.

I knelt upon the ground, just to the West of the center Altar Stone, so that I was facing East... I placed my hands flatly upon the Rock... I said the words... thereby not only binding our circle, but representing the direction of Below:

"I bind this circle to the core..."

Other ancient and hidden words did I speak, which I am under an "oath of silence" never to repeat...

Then Morgan, half Entranced, was led to the Star Stone and was laid across it. How appropriate – Woman as Altar... the way it must have been "In the Beginning"...

Morgan's Bees encircled the space over her first and then the whole Ritual Circle... buzzing there to hail the Above!

It was then that Lady Vivianne called to the great White Moon Goddess – Goddess of the hunt and of all Creatures wild and free.

"Beauty of the Night!" quoth she, "You who shineth amoungst the Stars and within our hearts... I am your Priestess Vivianne... I call out to you to fill this mortal vessel with your Divine Love...so that I may utter your words of Wisdom...so that all within this Temple who Love and worship you may hear them... Oh, great and benevolent Mother, Hail and Welcome..."

How stunning it was to see her thus transformed – one moment a woman, the next a Goddess!

Lady Vivianne, as the White Moon Goddess, placed into Morgan the power of Her Divine Self by holding her hand above Morgan's belly... Morgan then became the Center – the 'within'!

Morgan began to glimmer. The Full Moon's shadows, which were cast betwixt the Standing Stones, became very pronounced – so that even though the clear, Starry Night Sky was very dark, the whole circle appeared as though torch-lit... but without the flickering... There was only the Moonlight's steady glow.

Then Morgan raised her beautiful voice in a song of evocation and praise to the GREAT GODDESS. And so haunting a melody it was...

The words she sang were in a language I had never heard.

When Morgan began to sing, all other sounds went silent – no Tree, no Wind, no Bird or creeping thing was heard – save for her Bees, which were buzzing in seemingly the same melody.

Or, was it all just the Magic – the Magic of place and of moment – that made it seem so? I will never know. But so it was!

A scabbard for Caledfwlch had been wonderfully crafted by Makyr. On it were symbols of great antiquity – unrecognizable to me – which Makyr had carved into it by her own hands and tools. Within each symbol was held a Magical Power. The scabbard was made of the finest leather, several layers thick – it was sturdy, yet flexible. An exquisitely beautiful thing it was – worthy of a King.

Makyr placed the King's scabbard upon Morgan's belly. She then returned to the South and began to drum with a steady, persistent beat upon a drum made of Tree and hide. My head began to swim...

Then, The Lady of the Lake Enchanted the scabbard with the words of an ancient Charm of Making:

"Anail nathrock
Uthvas bethud
Dociel dienfey"

By serpent's breath...
By life and Death...
I bind this Spell to the Making!

I noted with whatever part of my consciousness that was still capable of analytical thought, that Vivianne was speaking the Charm of Making in the ancient tongue of the Eire. The Charm is used relatively unchanged everywhere Druids intone their words of power... Even is it so in Gwynedd, where my native language is spoken. Was this yet another honour paid to Arthur and me? I thought "surely there were Charms of Making in the Old Tribes' tongue" – and of course there were...

Vivianne Enchanted...

Ati me peta babka...
Gatekeeper open your gates for me...

Sebet babi...
The seven gates...

Kadingir...
Gateway of the Gods...

Ina qereb...
Into the midst of...

Baraggal...

The Holy of Holies...

Edubba...
Of the House of the scribal tablets...

Tammabukku...
Dragons...

Ulmash...
Glittering...

Gibil...
Ones of Fire...

Nusku iqbq...
Words spoken... "Budding Branch"...

Etu...
Then to be dark...

Si g...
Then – to become silent...

Cacama!
Amen! So be it!

Of course, at that Time I had no idea what her words meant – but later she translated them for me, as best as ancient words of a lost tongue can be translated.

Of a sudden – when the old Chant had begun to resonate with *The Dragon* – as we Druids call the Earth's Energy – Morgan, with Caledfwlch's scabbard upon her belly, began to rise upward into the Air, leaving Time and place behind. She shimmered...

Then the Lady of the Lake proclaimed... Or was this the voice of the Dark Mother hissing?

"While Arthur wears the scabbard of Caledfwlch he cannot bleed out his life's blood unto Death. Cut he may be, for that is the Warrior's honour, but no limbs or vital parts can be severed. No killing wound can be inflicted upon him..."

Lady Vivianne repeated the Charm twice again, so that by the *Power of Three* all things would manifest; and that Morgan, while she lived, would also be bound to the Magic of Caledfwlch's scabbard.

Morgan's body slowly lowered and came to lie upon the Star Stone again.

I took her hand to aid her in standing. She wove back and forth for a moment, pale as a ghost, then came back into herself. She looked at me – and for a moment, some vague expression of longing crossed her face – then it was gone. I have often wondered what that look was about.

She let go my hand, then walked to the East to hang the Magical scabbard about Arthur's shoulders.

Then, from a buckskin roll she had brought to the Ritual and placed in waiting next to the Stone of the North, Morgan pulled out a beautiful woolen cloak, which she herself had spun, dyed, woven, and embroidered.

The dye she had made from Madder and Bluebells to render the wool a deep, rich purple. On the front and sides of the cloak she had embroidered emblems of all the Tribes and Clans of Our Fair Isles. Covering most of its back was a great Red Dragon – the Pen Dragon standard. Almost alive did it seem – stomping proudly as each breeze shifted the fabric of the King's cloak. It was fastened by a bronze clasp, which had been fashioned by one of the Metalsmiths of the Order. A Dragon and Eagle were cleverly entwined in knotwork about it, to form the closure.

Morgan tried to drape it over Arthur's shoulders – which she could barely reach – so he knelt at her feet to oblige her.

The Time had come for Arthur to place Caledfwlch across the great green Star Stone. When he did, the sword began to emanate a green light, as did the great Stone... But the green glow of the sword slowly changed to blue. The Wind picked up! The sword began to flame... blue flames!!!

From somewhere I heard an Owl hooting – Chronos responded. It was at that point that I realised that all the sounds of the Night had returned...

My Vision – here it was!

I had been told what to do, so I obeyed... I began to reach for Caledfwlch so as to do the task set before me... but then the Flames themselves lifted Caledfwlch... and turned her so that the side which had the large green Gem Stone where blade meets grip was facing the Earth – presenting the side of her blade which would be facing upward when Arthur held her in the underhand position...

I stretched out my right hand – first finger – and pointed it at the Flame surrounding the Sword, which Flame leapt between Caledfwlch and my finger. I felt the Gods' power coursing through me. With the Flame directed by my first finger I etched into the great blade of Caledfwlch the letters of the word "Chaos."

Then the Flame lifted her again and turned her so that the other side of the blade – the side with the Gem Stone – was presented. There I etched "Cosmos."

I proclaimed: "I bind this Spell to the Making!"

"That is it!" thought I. "It is begun!"

And so it was...

We ended the Ritual with a shared cup of the mead from the Honey Bees. We drank from the shell that Bedwyr had held in the West to honour the Element of Water, whereupon we were refreshed and energized with perfect and pure Love.

As we left the Circle of Stones through the Northeastern gate, I could feel its sides and even perceive a lintel lying across the top of them. That gate was nothing of the physical realm – yet was it so much more. All things on the Tor were as such. I think that no matter how the Sands of Time, or the trifling of men's hands, change this most Sacred of places, it will always be here for true seekers: The green Star Stone, the ring of Standing Stones surrounding it, the power, the majesty, and the Magic – these will remain forever – in Spirit if not left in form.

Such was the beginning of the making of a King.

We had no more Time to spend on the Isle of Apples and so upon the next morn we bade everyone farewell and took our leave. Arthur – although past seventeen year-turns – when kissing his sister goodbye, had moist, red eyes. He quickly turned as tears escaped them. This did not go beyond my seeing, recognition, and pity.

We were taken to one of the punts, moored near the entrance of The Order, on the Northern Inland shore. Through heavy Mists we left this Otherworldly land.

When the Marsh Folk's little boat finally bumped upon the mainland shore we exited into the world of Man. Now we must face the awesome tasks set before us.

Thank the Gods, the warmer weather held.

Meeting at Table Rock...

We travelled Northward again, however this Time not toward the land of the Cymru, but through the center of our lands and Easterly toward the coast, eventually arriving at a place far to the North, which was to become known as "Table Rock." On our way, Arthur's first recognition dawned of how vast was this land he was to protect and keep united in purpose.

I had sent a message ahead of us to all corners of these great Isles to Chieftains, Dux, Kings and Queens, and to the Old Dark Tribes as well as the Saxons of Hengist's now established Kingdom on our Eastern shore – even to the Picti, who were known for keeping to themselves – that there was to be mighty council, which I, The Merlin, was calling. The missives said: "There will be a great unifying purpose in our coming together. This council will be held two Full Moon's Dances hence." I also said that I wished for it to be held in the Southern reaches of the lands of the Picti – if that met with their agreement.

The territories of the Picti Tribes began North of where the Emperor Hadrian had built his wall, to keep them out of "Roman lands"... so fierce were the Picti in their battles! They would face an armoured line totally naked – which in itself was intimidating – but also, their skin and hair would be painted blue and black. Their unknowable symbols were tattooed in black, all over their bodies and faces, which fascinated me, but terrified their foes – especially their more superstitious foes, such as the Gaulish/Roman armies. Also, their hair was parted and twisted into pointed sections, with some sticky substance applied to it to hold it standing up on end – this way and that – or straight out to the sides of their heads! They were an unusual people to say the least! They were also very clever. As did the Cymru, they would scream on the battle lines at their enemies. But *their* screaming never stopped! Then to escalate this cacophony, there were their eerie pipes and wild drumming and their women – who fought side by side with them – as they sang or wailed and shrieked their battle songs.

I had been told that I was known of all over Our Fair Isles, even by the Tribes living on the Islands in the far West, North, and Northeast off the coasts of the land of the Picti. Apparently this was true, for somewhat to my surprise, many responded that they would come – and come in peace – to our great council.

When the Time of our unlikely meeting arrived, the Wind was howling. Great thunderclaps shook the ground. "So the Thunder Gods have come too" thought I. On that great stormy, windy Day, we met at the appointed place, not far from the Eastern Sea, where a mighty escarpment juts straight up from a hilly landscape. On top of this great rocky Hill, it is said that Rituals, as well as Tribal Councils, have been held from Times beyond memory. Near to that promontory, and down a long sloping defile from it, sits another great mound, atop which, at its highest point, was a very large flat rock... large as a Kings chamber and perfectly round. We all gathered there, in the rain.

I raised my staff – I thought this would be a good touch – and spoke, "Sit you down, and let us each be seated at the perimeter of this great round Stone which men call 'Table Rock' – so that no one will be sitting at its head. For we have gathered here today as equals – with all being due the same honour, respect, and tribute.   Despite our past disagreements or enmities, we all have today the opportunity for a united defense of our lands, from future interior wars and exterior invasions. Let us be pushed by the Wind. Let the Fires of our hearts free our Spirits. Let us put behind us the strife of the past. Let this cleansing Rain remove our enmities toward each other, for I have brought here to you, on this Day, the one unifying force."

The weather got worse and worse. Some of the men made the sign against evil Enchantment, but most respected and listened to me. They began to hold their shields and checkered woven cloths above their heads, for bits of ice were falling down from the Sky. But still they sat and listened. For this, I was grateful! Then, out into the middle of this stormy circle of Warriors and Elders, in his purple cloak, came Arthur... Tall and straight with golden hair, Roman features and piercing blue eyes was he – yet the look of the Clans insinuated itself upon him, as well. He was beautiful! I turned him around, very slowly so that each man and woman could see him. I said, "Behold – the King of unity!"

Some laughed and jeered, some got up enraged: "What are you trying to do, Merlin – pass off an unfledged boy to us as King?"

I responded, "No. This is no plain unfledged boy! He who stands before you is the son of Uther the Pen Dragon – made upon the Lady of Dumnonia – Igraine, great Seer of the Tribes. As to his mettle in training and prowess in the Arts of war, Markus, steward of the fortress of Dumnonia has trained him well. And I have bestowed upon him the Wisdom of the ages!"

I thought that sounded impressive... even if it be that I boast.

There was a murmur that went round the circle. The Clansmen, of one accord said, "Prove this to us – we have not found a High King, for there was no deciding factor in Uther's Death nor was there an heir of his blood or battle Champion to fill his place. Here we are all these many years later still bickering amoungst ourselves..."

"He *is* the son of Uther the Pen Dragon and nephew of Ambrosius Aurillious, the Good. He is the grandson of Macsen Wledig. And as everyone knows, Macsen Wledig's wife, Helen, was the only living heir of King Hen Coel of olden fame. Oh yes, he is the rightful heir. The bloodline of the 'Old Dark Tribes' also runs a current through his veins from his own Mother Igraine, who would have become the Grandmother of her Tribe had she not married Dux Gorlois of Dumnonia to tend and protect Nodens' Holy Well. Arthur comes from all the lines of old Briton's greatness. Only the Picti, who are our ancient neighbors of the North hold no claim to Arthur."

Then from the Picti: "We have never had a King over us – why should we want one now – especially one of Roman blood? Uther, the Pen Dragon was nothing to us..."

The women and men of the Old Dark Tribes sat in silence, listening.

Again, the Clansmen shouted, "Why have we not heard of him? What trickery is this? Uther had no heir of his blood." They were murmuring, arguing, almost coming to fists, some were standing and raising such a ruckus that it seemed the Thunder Gods were only booming in response to their accusations when...

I shouted: "Stop!"

I lifted my staff and pounded it down upon the Rock – it felt as though the entire Rock shook. Startled, they stopped. I turned, staring into each man's and woman's eyes whilst tapping my staff upon the Rock in a steady repetitious thumping – thereby mesmerizing them... They calmed and listened...

"Yesss... yesss... that is better... Let the rain wash away your apprehensions."

I continued: "Bastard born he was, but what meaning has that to us? I have protected and taught him in the ways of being a King since his twelfth year-turn, and before that he was educated in the house of his Mother Igraine of Dumnonia. Yet now, even more than claiming his rightful rule, he has a Dream – a Dream which I share and am committed to seeing the fulfillment of: The Dream of seeing all the peoples of these, Our Fair Isles – including the Old Tribes and the Picti, as well as those Saxons who *already* share our lands by rights – prospering and living in freedom from the fear of each other. An Isle united by purpose, whose people are committed to stand at the side of their compatriots against invaders. Arthur desires not to usurp leaders of Tribes or Clans that be, but to have their willing oaths of allegiance to this *alliance of peers* under the battle command of one Over-King."

Soon they began to acknowledge my words and began nodding in agreement...

"Gwyddion, The Merlin, we believe you! Our hearts are strangely at rest."

But still a few – stronger of will – said, "What Dark Magic of yours is this?"

At that I realised that I was indeed insinuating my will upon them. I snapped my fingers and returned each to their own true consciousness and will.

I answered, "It is the Magic of the Thunder Gods and Spirits of the Wind and Rain which have calmed you – so that you may listen to my voice." Which was *A truth...* if not *the whole* truth... "Now I shall prove to you his right and worthiness. Here in my hand I hold the sword of Uther, the great Pen Dragon."

They all gasped in amazement as I passed it, one to the other.

Some said, "Uther's sword has been lost for years..."

Then one voice cried out, "So you have known its whereabouts all this Time!"

Then yet another: "Well, but a sword alone can prove nothing. Everyone knows you were there, Merlin, watching from the Woods as Uther fell. You took Uther's sword!"

I retorted, "Ah, this sword may prove nothing ... but... Arthur, show it to them now!"

Arthur's purple cloak parted, he pulled it aside with his left hand, and there was the finely wrought scabbard – there was the dazzling gold hilt of the ancient sword of Kings. They all gasped. Arthur grabbed it with his right hand and brandished it aloft – the Gemstone began its green glowing...

I said, "Behold: Caledfwlch! – the lost sword, last wielded by Macsen Wledig."

Silence... Then there was a great bustle of conversation and arguing. I repeated, "Behold the sword of the ancient Kings of our Islands!"

Many would not look... until they saw the eerie green light on the faces of those around them...

For a third Time, I shouted "Behold!"

Then they all faced the sword. It threw out its blue Flame – flaming up to the Sky. And at that very moment – very fortunately for me – the Storm calmed... The Rain stopped... The Sun disk shone through a parting of Clouds... They all stood and bowed to the power, the might, the Magic and the goodness of Caledfwlch. The deed was done.

It was agreed that all would reconvene after one week during which Time they would consider whether to accept Arthur as Over-King, or no...

Still, there was some squabbling and even a couple of skirmishes as all camped in the environs. But finally, by the Time we all met again at Table Rock at the end of that week, Arthur, through the Games – which it seemed to me that all men have need to play – had proven to them his valor, might, intelligence, good heart, strong will, and leadership abilities.

So then, beneath a blue Sky, one by one they knelt in front of him to have him place the sword Caledfwlch upon their heads. They pledged themselves to the alliance and to Arthur – who would be High King and war Commander of these, Our Fair Isles.

Morgan's note...

I feel that I must add some words to Gwyddion's account of these happenings, for I doubt that what I am about to write has ever been mentioned – and surely not by him, for he would not. Perhaps he does not even realise... No, I am quite sure that, with all that Gwyddion has written of Arthur's beauty and handsomeness, nothing has been said about the look of Gwyddion and of his countenance.

To me he seems like the Angels Christian folk tell of. He is a man, yet more beautiful than a man should be – though nothing of his countenance is effeminate – no, not that at all. He is in fact very manly, in a lithe sort of way – yet otherworldly at the same Time. Yes, he is a handsome man, with square shoulders and a bewitching smile. He walks with self-confident determination. His blue-grey eyes are deep and shadowy, yet they sometimes sparkle with wittiness. Yet, it is not only these things that make him seem so enchanting. Perhaps it is the stuff of

Magic that fills his Spirit even more extraordinarily than it does my Mother or Lady Vivianne.

I often ask myself: "Am I confused by my great esteem for him? Am I infatuated with him? Is this the Love that comes from recognition or familiarity of one Creature for another of her own kind? Or is it the Love a woman holds for a man?" I do not truly think so, yet I do not know.   Perhaps it is all the *Glamour*...One Day I may come to understand my feelings for him. But as for now, I can only express my great respect.

Chapter 8
Vivianne, Lady of the Lake

Vivianne

I, Vivianne, am the Lady of the Lake. I have been elected such by the Council of The Nine High Wise Mothers of the Order on the Isle of Apples. This will be my position until my Death. Although, the longer I live, the more mistakes I make, the more Human foibles I demonstrate, the more I wonder how deserved is this lofty title.

I have been asked by my dear Morgan to relate my experiences, views, and feelings regarding all persons and events concerning Arthur and those involved in the making of the King. She has also asked me to write the sum of our Mysteries – in as much detail as my vows of secrecy will allow – for this she will add to her Histories. And so, I will.

To begin, I will write of some of the Great Mysteries of our Order and how they correlate to our Priestess Initiations...

We recognize in our GREAT GODDESS many faces and attributes. The people of all the lands around us do the same. Many other traditions place the Goddesses' faces into three stages of Being: The Maiden, The Mother, and The Dark Mother, Crone or Hag, as these relate to the phases of the Moon. They call the Crescent Moon the Maiden; the Full Moon the Mother; and the Dark Moon the Hag or Crone, referring to her as a Triple Goddess. Even their Goddesses who are not directly related to the Lunar Mysteries are placed into these categories. I do not know how long these ideas have been held – or how they may have been influenced by the Romans – for they do not seem to be so divided by out-lying or Northern Clans and Tribes.

We honour their beliefs, of course, but a long, long Time ago our Ancestors recognized that the two Crescent Moons, the Waxing and the

Waning, each have very different qualities. So, our Mysteries, our teachings and stages of accomplishments – as marked by our initiations – and our work within the Order, are based upon *four* faces of the Moon.

The Waxing Crescent Moon is personified as the Huntress Maiden, the Full Moon as the Mother, the Waning Crescent as the Enchantress, and the Dark Moon as Old Wise Mother.

Our young girls usually arrive here on the Isle at or near their fourteenth year-turn. They live here and are taught to read, write, and to understand rudimentary mathematics. They then begin to learn the Mysteries of the Waxing Crescent Moon – The Huntress Maiden.

The Huntress Maiden represents the first Bow of the Rising Moon as seen in the Night Sky after She has emerged from being hidden in darkness. She represents all things fresh and new: youth, beginnings, the Element of Air, and the Eastern Sky as the Sun rises at Dawn. She is eager, unafraid to explore the Mysteries of life. She is bold, enthusiastic, loyal and strong. She is the arising, the awakening, the freedom of wild Nature; forever young and beautiful.

In other cultures, She has had many, many names, such as: Artemis, Minerva, Idea, Athena, Aphrodite, Diana, and Bloudwedd – to name a few. She is a Warrior of the Spirit, ever alive and anxious for adventure.

Our girls study and practice these attributes for two to three years, along with their learning to read and write. When – and if – these postulants have accomplished their studies – AND we have seen in them a Love of the GODDESS – AND they have demonstrated a good sense of ethics, we will initiate them to the station of 'Huntress Maiden.'

Some of our girls may wish to leave the Isle at this point to become Healers and Herbalists in their families' villages. This they may do with our blessings.

But, those who have accomplished this training, and in whom we, the Council of Nine, see the quality of *devotion* to the GREAT GODDESS and Her Son/Consort, may stay with us and devote themselves to further learning and accomplishment.

However, there are also those who ask only to remain here with us as Huntress Maidens for the rest of their lives, with the intent of never going farther than their first initiation. I will say that in this there is absolutely no failure, shame or disappointment. You see, to my thinking, one's first Initiation is the most important of all, because it is at that point which one dedicates their life to the Love and service of the GODDESS and the Old Ways. These ones, who go no farther in training, but who remain with us, work as cooks, planters, Herbalists' and Healer's assistants. They keep everything clean, as well as share in the care of our Animals. They also assist in the essential works of Weaving and Harvesting. What is more, if they have other special talents, such as dancing, drumming, singing or storytelling, we honour these too. For, it is not good to always be working, learning or meditating. In fact, it is well known that we of the Order have many and many more fun-filled and joyous Times here on the Isle of Apples.

For those who continue their studies and practicing, the next step is to attain to the 'Mother' initiation.

The Mother represents the Full Moon. She is the source of life and Love. She is fertility, the Element of Fire, the South, High noon, maturity, Mid-Summer... She is the lover and as such she burns with passion and Her passion brings forth Creation. She is our Healing and comfort in life. She delivers the bounteous Harvest. She is the Great Green... the milk of devotion, which will sustain and comfort her children. She is the directed Will of the Cast of Magic – the teacher, the protectress, the fullness of life.

In other traditions, She is called Anu, Demeter, Madron, Brigit, Henwen, Hera, Juno, Frigg... and so many more.

When our initiates study and practice these attributes for yet two to three years more and have accomplished these qualities, they are initiated as Mothers. They then become the teachers and mentors of the younger girls. They either remain always at this level, or, in the case of those who excel in the Magical Arts, have the Sight, commune with the Spirits to an exceptional degree, or have the Gift of being Walkers Between the Worlds, they are taught the deeper Cosmic Mysteries, which, of course I cannot put into these writings.

These young women are nineteen to twenty-one or more years old when they begin their training as Enchantresses. The Enchantresses are taught only by the Council of Nine High Wise Mothers – or in some rare cases by extremely *Gifted*, older Enchantresses. This training will go on for as long as it takes.

The Enchantress represents the Waning Crescent Moon who is personified in the Maiden of twilight. She is the Goddess waning into the Dark Moon. She is of the Element of Water, the beginning of the pull of the Tides... the Priestess, the Poet, the Seer, the Siren. She draws all to her as she retreats into darkness. She is the great empathizer, and as such, may very well be vulnerable. The Huntress Maiden within her must balance her. The Mother must protect and keep her strong.

She, too, has been called by many names: Persephone, Siren, Circe, Ondine, Ariadne, Arianrhood, Dadb, Lady of Twilight and more.

There is one final Initiation possible: The Wise Mother...

The Wise Mother represents the attributes of the Dark Moon. She embodies all knowledge, Wisdom, Dark Mysteries, and Banishing Magic. She is transformation. She stands at the crossroads, passing on her knowledge to the next generation.

We Chant – "She is the end, the contraction, the fall... She is the Death and beginning of all." She is equated with the North, Midnight, old age into Death, deep Winter, and the Element of Earth.

Some call Her Hecate, Cerridwen, Cailleach, Aerfen, Morrigan or Scatach, and Hel...

I can say no more about the depths of this level of Initiation. Once again, I am bound to silence. However, it *is* commonly known that from the initiates who attain this status are chosen The Nine – The Council of High Wise Mothers of the Order on the Isle of Apples.

Beyond our initiations symbolized by the four Moon stages, are the GODDESS principals as embodied in the Nine High Wise Mothers, who form the spiritual leadership of our Order.

I will give here the names of our Goddesses Nine... Or rather, the Nine faces and names of the ONE ETERNAL GODDESS – as we call to HER in the ancient language of our Ancestors:

Waxing Crescent Moon:

"Shi-Zikru" – which name means Idea...

Full Moon:

"A-Ama" – Mother or Ripened Womb... In our Rites, She is sometimes invoked as "the White Moon Goddess".

Waning Crescent Moon:

"Mudi" – Enchantress, Secret Keeper, or Seer.

Dark Moon:

"Elat-Salamu" – To become Black ... She is also called "Night," "Death," and "Wisdom".

Star Goddess:

"Nana" – The Heavenly One...

Sun Goddess:

"Sud-Ma" – Sun Mother... She is also called Day.

Earth Goddess:

"Kia" – Terrestrial One... Also called "Great Nature" or "The Great Green".

Sea Goddess:

"Na-Amu-Ma" – Sea Mother... We understand that she is also "TIAMATU" – the Primordial Waters...

All of these Faces of THE GODDESS and the entirety of all Creation – in form, energy, and Spirit, are "THE ONE."

SHE is "The Weavers" – the Triple GODDESS of "Fate" – of Past, Present, and Future. SHE is "TIME" or "The Night of Time" – as in "Primeval Time."

SHE is the ABZU – "primeval source."

HER name is "AIXIA".

AIXIA, when read from left to right means Cosmogenesis, when read right to left means Cosmonemesis.

The GODDESS never dies; SHE only changes her faces... SHE is Eternal...

And then there are the God Mysteries: The God as Son, Lover, and Consort of the GODDESS...

These are the Gods of Light, Darkness, Sacrifice, and Shadow. They are: the Sun God, the Sacrificed God of Grain and Harvest – The God/Brothers of Winter and Summer – and the Dancing, Horned God of Ecstasy, lust, and wild, untamed Nature...

Lesser – or should I say more personal – than these, are the Dark, Shadow Gods: of Springs, Caves, Forests, Thunder, Rain, and the Nether-World.

Of course, as I have said, we also train Priests here at the Order. They represent the Gods in our Rites. They Smith and plant/harvest, as well as teach the other young male initiates and perform many other Arts and labours, such as poetry, carpentry, stonework, and Animal husbandry – all to the service of the GODDESS and the Gods – and to the great benefit of their sisters and brothers of The Order.

The Male Mysteries are as different from Women's Mysteries as are Men from Women... different – yet at the same Time, similar in nature.

As I have explained, the Mysteries of the Huntress Maiden – the Mother, the Enchantress, and the Old Wise Mother – are stages of our lives and growth – personifying the Moon. Each woman, in order to be an enlightened, healthy, and balanced being, must strive to hold elements of each of these phases of life within her psyche throughout the whole of her life – in as equal a measure as she is capable. This is also true for men.

Of course, the reality is that each of us – male and female – has our own gifts and capacities. Some will always be more Huntress or Mother, Enchantress or Dark Mother. This in itself makes for a more beautiful and interesting community.

It is just so with men.

The four stages of the Male Mysteries correspond to the Women's thus:

The Hunter: He who provides...

The Warrior: He who protects...

The Satyr: He who holds the power of ecstasy...

The Mage: He who has excelled in the Mysteries and/or meets the challenges of life and overcomes them by his Wisdom.

In order to be clear, I will give one example:

Let us look at the third phase of the Moon – the Waning Crescent. It conveys our deepest instinctual tides. For a woman, this is her Psychic and empathetic *pull*. For a man, their sexual *drive*.

Now, this is not to say that women are not sexual beings or that men do not have psychic Gifts – much to the contrary – yet these – the Enchantress and the Satyr – are each the attribute of a woman's or a man's most primordial, instinctual nature. It all plays out in this way:

For a woman to *attract* a man and to *entwine* him into her sexual *embrace*, she uses her psychic, intuitive, drawing-in nature. For a man to *embrace* his psychic/Magical abilities, he must use the Fire of his sexual energy.

Just so is it with the other three attributes or phases of life.

I do hope that whoever reads this will grasp these basic concepts – for on these, our Mysteries, I have said all that I may.

I know that The Merlin has written in detail of the events leading to Arthur's having been blessed and chosen High King of the Britons so I will begin with the next and most important sequence in Arthur's story... that being the Fertility Rites on the Isle of Apples.

However, I feel that before I begin this story, I must make note of how the significance of things held in great value for millennia can begin to fail – of how Time changes all She touches...

As a consequence of Rome's invasion, some of the peoples of this land have accepted that, by a crowning – and not only by the Great Rite, would a man be recognized as King. Yet, for longer than anyone can remember, it was only the blessing of the Lady of the Lake and the Sacred Marriage that was needed to make a King or Chieftain of the Britons. In all other lands it has been the same – only the GODDESS could make a King. With the advent of male-ruled societies, the Goddesses are being pushed into the background and now *men* make a King. Whatever will be, will be, I suppose...

Word had come, with the arrival of The Merlin, Arthur, and Bedwyr, of the meeting of the Chieftains, minor Kings, Queens, Dux, Tribal Elders, and the council of the thirteen High Druids – which had been held at an ancient meeting place called Table Rock in the Southernmost lands of the Picti. It told of how The Merlin had presented Arthur as the son of Uther the Pen Dragon – that, by his word, by the blessing of the Lady of the Lake and the showing of Uther's sword and the tale of Arthur's claiming of Caledfwlch, he was able to convince all assembled that Arthur was Uther's rightful heir. It also told of the eventual success of The Merlin's proposal of peace and *alliance* between all the peoples who lived upon these Fair Isles. It told of how Arthur had held flaming Caledfwlch on high... gaining the sign of acceptance by the Thunder Gods – along with the approval of all there gathered, that he be High King.

Although Arthur had been thusly accepted at Table Rock, he would never really be King until the "Summer Rites" and the Sacred Marriage had taken place. Afterward, he would be crowned High King with much pomp and celebration – with many words spoken and all of the protocols observed. But, even with all this, his Kingship would not be "official" until the moment a thin gold band was placed to encircle his head. Only then would the deed be done – Arthur would be High King.

So, now had come the Time to prepare...

Morgan was already being observed and considered by "The Nine"– which included me, of course – for the highest initiation of Wise Mother; and this perhaps within the next yearly cycle or two. This was a rare thing indeed, for it had only been three years since she had become an Enchantress. Usually, for a woman to be considered for this station, she would have passed her fortieth year-turn and have begun the Time of the cessation of her Moon Blood's flow. For, this Wise Mother Stage *represents* or symbolizes a woman past her bleeding and hence, birthing and fertility; of her having entered her Time of Wisdom of the Cosmic Mysteries.

However, having peered deeply into our oldest writings to find a precedent for such a thing, we, The Nine, could find none – yet found no actual *prohibition* of a younger woman's initiation into this station – save only that the candidate had attained the required level of Wisdom. After an Enchantress' becoming a Wise Mother, she would no longer be eligible to perform Ritual sex. She could lead these Rites and perform the function of Priestess in all other of our Rituals and deepest Magics. Of course, this in no way means that a Wise Mother could not continue to enjoy the sexual pleasures of the flesh...

As is our long-held tradition, the one to be 'Goddess' in the fertility Rites was chosen thusly:

From all of our Enchantresses, The Nine would discuss amoungst themselves the qualities, Gifts, and devotion of each, and from them, select nine names to seal into a chest, called the Bowl of Choosing.

Why it was called a bowl? I have no idea – except that at one Time, long ago, perhaps it *was* a bowl.

But, I digress...

So it was that at the beginning of our year, which was at the Time of Red and Gold leaves, Morgan's name had been sealed in the Bowl of Choosing, along with the names of the eight other Enchantresses who were deemed to be ready and worthy to fill the role of the Goddess in the Sacred Marriage with the man who was to be the Stag God for this year's Rite.

At the end of our next Festival – that of The Longest Night – The Nine would hold a three-Day council, in which none would leave the company of the others, to thoroughly compare the attributes of each of the young women whose names were retrieved from the chest. Then we would vote as to which one of the Enchantresses would have this Sacred privilege.

I, being the Lady, would always hold my vote until the last. We preferred a unanimous decision on this, however, upon some years the votes were split. Mine, being the ninth, could always be a tie-breaker.

The great problem was that I had already known, having been *told* by

Igraine, that Arthur – and not Bedwyr – was Morgan's true brother and that Gwyddion, The Merlin had raised him to be fit as High King. But that information had been for my ears only at that Time – I had promised to tell no one of it.

To place these events in their proper sequence for the reader, this choosing council was held *before* Gwyddion, Bedwyr, and Arthur had come to the Isle for the Ritual Blessing – and *before* any of my sisters of The Nine knew that Arthur and Morgan were half-brother and sister – or even that Arthur or Bedwyr would become King!

The Night before our choosing council, I, in a fretful fatigue, had finally fallen to sleep just before Dawn. I had a Great Dream. The Weavers appeared before my eyes, to tell me that Morgan must, without fail, be the chosen one. Even in my Dream I questioned the Wisdom of this – of the potential political implications, what with the over-sensitive morality of the Christians – even with some of the Clans... and then there was the heartache it would undeniably cause to Morgan – perhaps even to Igraine... or to Arthur??? The answer came as if a roar of the Ocean... as if the whole Earth shook... "I *AM* WISDOM!" After that I feared to question again.

So, when the Time came to discuss Morgan's qualities at the conclave, I held nothing back. She was, of course, my favourite. I had said all but that. I knew from the first round of discussion that Morgan was the choice of every one of the other eight. At the end of all talk, when everyone else's votes had been cast, I told my sisters of my Dream. Then I added my vote to theirs, to make it unanimous.

Yes, Morgan was just that exceptional. She had obtained – or perhaps, better said, had been *Gifted* by the Spirits – Mysteries and Wisdoms far beyond her years or even beyond the level of our Order's teachings; for there are indeed "Knowings" and abilities which are given to some few ascended ones directly by the Gods.

I knew that to lie with her brother would present a very difficult problem for Morgan. But what could I do? The Goddess had spoken... What will be, will be! Only the Weavers can know how they will spin our lives to the ending of a thing – or what blessing or calamity may come of it... Of course I said nothing to Morgan of this at that Time.

A week before the Rite, I told Morgan that she had been chosen to embody the Goddess/Lover in the Heiros Gamos – the Sacred Marriage. She cried inconsolably.

"Oh no, you cannot ask this of me! We were born and raised in the same household! He is my little brother of the heart, I have always thought of him as such, although I knew not we were of the same Mother. The Night the babes were born, I held them both in my arms. I played children's games with Arthur, my little Bear. I taught him to read and write. It was I who gave him the knowledge of Herbal lore, the

Forest secrets, and the myths of my Mother's people. It was I who sat awake all Night when he was but three year-turns and had the spotted fever. I wiped the tears from his eyes when he was six and had cut his knee, so that no one else would know that he had been crying. I..."

"Morgan, shh... The Goddess has spoken – not only once, but twice!"

Morgan replied, "Oh, my Lady Vivianne" – she having fallen to her knees in supplication before me – "Forgive me, my Lady, but are we not all Human and fallible, even you my Lady? Have you not taught this to us yourself?"

"Yes... This is true, I am fallible Morgan. What would satisfy your doubt?"

"I... Let me think... Yes, if you would call all of the Enchantresses here together and let us Divine Her answer once more by drawing lots, then, if I am chosen for the third Time, by the Power of Three, I will obediently submit to Her will."

She must have been in a terrible state of feeling, for really, she had no choice in this matter. But because my heart – yes, I do have one, although many may not think so – went out to her in her pain, I decided to prove the GODDESS' will – by the Power of Three.

I called the Nine and all the Enchantresses together, had the young women draw lots and the outcome was the same... SHE had chosen Morgan!

And so it was...

Chapter 9
Morgan and Arthur

Arthur

Two weeks before the Rite of Fertility, Gwyddion, Bedwyr, and I arrived at the Isle; I, for cleansing, preparation, and learning the secrets of the Sacred Marriage – Gwyddion to rest and refresh his Spirit and body – and for Bedwyr to work with the young Priests in preparation for the joyous Night.

Now, Bedwyr was not like me in that he was no stranger to the Sacred Pleasures – the acts of Love between a man and a woman. Igraine had spoken well with him of all the ways of pleasuring a woman. This, he said, she had done not long before he left with The Merlin and me at our twelfth year-turn.

Bedwyr had shared with me what she had said: "For to drink at the Well of a woman's body is an act of worship to the Goddess."

So, these pleasures he had enjoyed often and apparently with much relish, whereas I had never... There was, after all, a small village not very far from Gwyddion's Cave...

But Lady Igraine, not knowing that I was her son, had said nothing to me.

My parents – Tangwen and Marcus – had never had these talks with me. I suppose they expected that The Merlin would include this into my training, but alas...

No one told me which Enchantress had been chosen to lie with me on that fateful occasion. So it was – and always would be – that I, upon arrival and having been greeted by the Lady Vivianne, sought out my Morgan.

I had wandered the whole of the Order's lands, seeking her for the entire first Day, but to no avail... That Night I asked The Lady where I might find Morgan... She only said, "She is in solitude... meditating, I believe, my Lord."

It was strange to my ears to be called "my Lord" by The Lady of the Lake... I supposed I must become used to this.

Morgan was not at the bonfire that Night, either.

The next morning, after I had arisen, I hurried to the communal tables to break my fast. Even there, Morgan was not to be found.

"Oh, well, then," thought I, "she is probably already busy with her Bees." So I looked there. She was still not to be found...

Where then, could she be? Of course! She must be meditating at the Stone Circle on top of the Tor.

So I followed the great spiral path up, up, up — toward the top of the Tor. I became dizzy and disoriented half the way to the top. In fact, I barely made it there without falling off of the path. Not from the physical exertion — for I was Warrior trained. No, it was from some other "*Pull*"— which I had never felt before! Finally I did reach the top. There I found Morgan.

"Greetings and Love, my sister, have you been well?"

I kissed her on both cheeks and her forehead and then knelt at her feet.

"Yes, Arthur," she replied.

"Morgan, it is so good to see you. You grow even more beautiful every Day, it seems." I lowered my gaze for a moment... "I have missed you so."

"And I you, my Bear."

She had addressed me by my childhood name. I felt it smart. Could she not see that I was a man grown now?

There was an awkward silence between us... Or perhaps it was only I who was awkward. I turned my eyes downward again...

"Arthur, something is bothering you. Is it anything I can help you with?"

"Yes, Morgan, I am bothered. But, this which bothers me... well, it is a secret that I have held from all but Bedwyr. It is so embarrassing to speak of — and all the more so to say it to you. Yet, you are the only one who I feel will not shame me for it... except for Gwyddion that is. But he would be of no help to me in this matter.

"Oh, how impetuous I am, always rushing. My concerns can wait...

"How I have longed to see you, Morgan."

Morgan peered straight into my eyes, and she looked as sad as I had ever seen her... So beautiful was she, even in sorrow.

"Are you really alright, Morgan?"

"Oh, yes, Arthur..." said she, with a sigh of weariness.

"You are tired, Morgan. Well, then, please let us just sit here on this cool, Sunny Day and talk with one another while we have this Time alone. Let us speak only of pleasurable things for as long as you will, before I burden you with my troubles."

She smiled.

"Arthur, that is so like you – always kind and considerate. Of all the many things which I have Loved and admired about you, your selflessness and concern for others tops my very long list."

"I have always Loved you, too, Morgan, as much as I could ever Love! To learn that you are my half-sister changes nothing. I think you know this."

At that moment, I knew that she understood my meaning... She understood everything! The North Wind stirred... She knew... "Daughter of the Wind" that she was... She knew... Nothing more need be said of it.

And so, she veered our conversation toward safer ground. We spoke of shared childhood memories. Then, we spoke of Morgan's work and studies here on the Isle of Apples. How she had accomplished three stages of Initiation and that now she was an "Enchantress." I mused that she had always Enchanted me... She talked about her beloved Bees.

Thusly did we while away the afternoon and all too soon the Sun began to fall beneath the disk of the Earth. Twilight was upon us.

Then Morgan broached the subject of my concerns again:

"We are entering the hour of deep shadows and of darkness. This is the Time *between Times*. Once it is full dark, it can be treacherous coming down the Tor's spiral path with no torchlight. So speak to me of these shadows that you hold within you. You trust me Arthur, I know this and so you can. In this you pay me great honour. Nothing can be as bad as all that, for you have not within you a place for evil. Tell me what you will Arthur, my Love, for you will not be diminished by whatever haunts you. I want to help you if I can."

I lowered my gaze from hers, but she raised my head with her gentle hand and bade me not to turn away from her.

I blurted it out... "I have never lain with a woman! Oh, it is not that I desire men... It is just that... I can feel no desire for anyone but... with anyone who is not..." I sighed... "for anyone I have met since I left home!"

How could I tell her that she was the only woman I could ever desire? For as long as I can remember, it was only Morgan. As soon as my body began to change and to feel sexual urges... the Dreams of my Nights, which left me panting in a sweat, were always of Morgan. When, as a youth the flames within my waking body had to be quenched by my own hand, it was Morgan's beautiful face I saw behind my closed eyes. I had always believed that one Day I would make her my own. We would marry; have children and live our lives in true happiness. But then, thought I – "Where is the humanity? She is a Priestess, living on this Isle and I must be King – so far from her touch... And now, the ugliest of all the Trickster's tricks... Oh, Gods, you have dealt me treachery! She is of my own Mother's blood! Oh the dreadfulness of Fate, that she is my sister... Why do the Gods torment us so?

Like the feasts of Spiders... we hang suspended... bound in their silken threads... where ne'er they let go...

"Oh, but what folly of mine is this, to curse the Gods in this Holy place? Here – I whimper and moan like a puppy. Of course, other men will know her! And I will never – this, then, is the curse of Arthur, the King. All the rest I could accept, if only she could be near to me, even if only as sister."

Lost in thought as I was, still I heard her gentle voice call my name:

"Bear, I will always be with you, for you are in my heart and there you will stay, until I close my eyes in Death's embrace."

Had she been reading my thoughts again?

Well, so be it! I act like a clumsy fool when I am around her. I wish I could hide the truth from her.

Then, from somewhere behind my eyes I heard...

"Would that not be the greatest tragedy of all?"

What? Who had spoken those words to me? Were those the "Voices" of whom I had heard Gwyddion speak? Had they truly whispered this into my head? Could it be so – that I curse the Gods and then in their infinite mercy, they give the only answer I could live with? So then, I must tell her with my words, when the moment is right. Whatever we are to be to each other, it will at least be honest. We would have no dark secrets to shadow what fond closeness we might share.

Morgan

I enter here, into Arthur's writings, this page of my own, for the sake of continuity and to tell what my own thoughts and feelings were at that Time...

I said to him, "Arthur, let us speak without embarrassment or discomfort. If you are afraid that you will not know what to do, do not worry about that. As part of our training and worship of the Goddess, all of the Enchantresses are taught to be very proficient in the Art of sexual Love. In fact, you could have none better to teach you the ways of great pleasure – for yourself – as well as the women in your life with whom you are sure to share these skills."

"But, I want no one save..."

"Arthur! You ask for my help, but you do not listen... Your natural healthy desires will awaken to the Enchantress – or to ANY woman, and your body will take over and respond."

"You know this yourself Morgan? Have you... Oh, forgive me; I have no right to question... to ask you this. I say too much. I am so sorry."

I looked at Arthur – perhaps for the first Time as a man. I coolly appraised him. The first thing one notices about him are his stunning and compelling, beautiful blue eyes... Beyond beautiful! No one could look at them without becoming enthralled. He stood straight and tall, with wide shoulders and muscular arms. Yet he was lithe and agile as a Stag... A Stag... The King Stag... The Hunter... Yes, he looked like a God – the strong, but finely chiseled features of his face, his straight Roman nose. He had very light brown hair, streaked golden by the Sun, which rolled in waves pushed back from his face. He was very tall – taller than most men, which was surprising to me, as he was Igraine's son. But then, I remembered that Uther's blood was his as well. His hands and feet were large, which we Enchantresses were taught usually meant that he would be well endowed in his man-parts. I imagined that every woman's head would turn toward him at his approach – and that all of the other Enchantresses would be having fun with their bawdy talk and laughter, wishing that they could have been the one chosen as his "Goddess" for the Festival Night. Yes, why would any woman not want him?

I said, "Arthur, do you not realise how desirable you are to women? He looked at me with a question in his eyes...

"Am I, Morgan?"

We stood looking at each other in silence – my uneasiness growing. Was that a seductive tone I had just heard in his voice? What could I say to him, without crushing my beautiful little brother's heart? He whom I had so Loved since he was a babe?

Yes, I knew the significance behind his question...

"Arthur – trust me, you will be alright. Through your life you will bring many women to your bed, to give and to receive pleasure and to ease the pressures of being King. All will be well Arthur, please believe me."

But when I had spoken those words, a shiver went through my body. Was this truth or lie? Or was it only wishful thinking on my part?

Arthur

I, Arthur, have written of this – my most secret of secrets – because, when we were still children at Dumnonia, and Morgan offered to teach me how to read and write, it was with the promise that I would someday keep a book of my life and of my true feelings. I gave to her the promise that I would. I have always and always will keep my promises to her.

If you are reading this entry Morgan, I have probably died and am awaiting you in the Summerlands – for there, too, will I Love you beyond all measure.

Morgan

The Sacred Marriage...

The Days were coming closer and closer to the Rite of the Heiros Gamos...

Oh, what would I do? I do not really mean *do*... I had been well taught which things to do and say to inflame a man to passion and how to emit the scent of mating which all Animals awaken to by their very nature – but which many Humans have lost the ability to recognize. These are things that were well known by all women of our ancient Ancestors, but it seems that, as Time goes by, more and more people have disconnected from their instincts. It is said that only the Magi... the Adepts... and the wild Tribes upon the Earth now live by their instincts along with their thoughts. To live this way is one of the highest goals of all Mystery Traditions: To BE... and feel as one with the All and to know our Animal natures as well as our Godlike natures. Yet even more: To speak with the Green Earth, the bubbling and rushing Waters, to listen to all flying Creatures as well as those who walk, slither, creep and crawl. These things, I hope I have learned well.

But then, I am bothered... even mortified, to share these Arts with my brother Arthur. I myself am repulsed by the thought. Not so much perhaps, because of the blood shared between us – for in many lands brothers and sisters marry in Royal lines to keep the blood pure. This is a long accepted practice. But, although I Love Arthur as much as I could Love anyone on Earth, I cannot Love him in the way that he Loves me. What harm might this 'Sacred' act cause to him, to his heart, his life, his Kingship? How could things – feelings – ever be the same between us? Oh, GREAT GODDESS, Fulfiller of Desires, please let this play out to harm none, for I would do most anything to not cause harm to Arthur. Anything! Just ask it of me! If there be any way out of this, place your will or desire – any bargain that you might accept – into my consciousness. I will do it, whatever it may be! This I promise on my word as your Priestess and daughter.

Then came the Day!

I was secluded on the Day of the feast. Only Makyr and Lady Vivianne were allowed to be with me. I was Ritually cleansed, massaged and rubbed with oils of juniper, cedar and the musk of a she-Wolf. My robe, of softest buckskin, was made for me by Makyr, who was my closest friend on the Isle. It was beaded with dried red Tree berries and it felt gloriously sensuous. Red slippers had she made for me... But curiously, she had embroidered them – exquisitely – on their soles – with her name: Makyr. I thanked her for all she had done for me. Then I asked her why she had embroidered her name on the soles of the slippers. She threw her arms around me and held me very close to her body. She caressed my hair – which she had just scented – and kissed my mouth. "Because" she said, "with every step you take toward him tonight, you step on my heart, my dearest one."

I choked up and began to speak, but Makr gently held her fingers to my mouth...

"SHH... now... it will be alright. I know this is hard for you as well, Morgan – for different reasons. But, this Night's doing is your Sacred duty. I honour that. You must know that I would have you as my lover. I adore even the soles of your feet. And, although I know you will never want me in the way I want you, I will always Love you and be your dear and truest friend. Never again, I promise, will I bring discomfort to you by my feelings or actions as I have just done. I would never try to persuade you to my bed. Forgive me, Morgan, for loving you... but it is something I cannot help. Perhaps it is the crafty acts of the Trickster God, the One who shifts from Fox to Man, who has made these cruel jokes, to entangle and test us. But, we are taught that we each have to play out the pains and responsibilities of this life – which we chose for ourselves from the Time before our conception. We have chosen our paths and we must accept these obstacles and trials. Nay, we must bless them, for they lead us ever closer to the Spiritual Enlightenment which we seek."

She let me go.

"Oh Makyr, I do Love you well and all the more so for your Wisdom. You astound me. Never worry about our friendship. I only hope, one Day, to live in faith and assuredness such as yours. You will never know just how much you have helped me today."

Then, I kissed her mouth – a chaste kiss – in return.

That Night the Wind howled like a pack of Wolfs. The Treetops were swaying from side to side; their great boughs groaning, singing their own song. The Bel-fires – both at the top of the Tor – amidst the ring of Standing Stones – and at the bottom, in a large clearing surrounded by deep Woods – were burning wildly, their Flames whipping in every direction. Two great Fires, sparking high the sexual energy of the Antlered God of the Wild Dance, along with everyone else's. It was portentous, and all who were there, were joyously filled with the thrill of anticipation.

Everyone would play tonight the age-old mating game. Many of the women would take their pleasures throughout the Night with any man – or woman – they chose to. Although, I must note here, that there are always some couples who would only ever lie with each other, because of their great Love for and devotion to one another.

Most everyone was drugged or drunk on fermented juice of Berries, honey mead – or purely on lust! But there would be no rape! A rapist would be torn apart and cast into the Fire for their treachery! For, this was a Night of Sacred Love and of pleasure – to bless the Earth and Her productiveness and to ensure that babies, both Human and Animal, would come to birth and thrive during this coming year.

Any child born of this Night's frolic would be one of the "Blessed Ones," born of the Gods – wild and free.

All was in readiness:

Vivianne entered the pavilion that had been erected as my dressing quarters at the top of the Tor – not far from the Circle of Stones.

"The Fires have been lit... It has begun! Here, Morgan, drink of this Sacred cup, which I, myself, have prepared for you."

"Yes, Mother," said I. And so I did. It was warm and bittersweet tasting. I began to feel a weird sensation in my whole body. It was a pleasurable feeling. There was a tingling in the small nub of flesh near the opening of my vagina. So, this was part of the Mystery, too...

"My dear Morgan, I place this veil over your head and face, so that you may be the Goddess and every woman. Yet, truly Goddess you will be. She will enter your body, thoughts and Spirit. Her words and Wisdoms *you* will utter. This, Morgan, is the greatest privilege on Earth. Go out now and dance the Fire! Dance as you have never danced before! The young Stag is well drunk, and drunk, too, is he with the cup of lust for the Goddess. So that, woman to man, Enchantress to King, Goddess to God, you two may bless the Grain, the land, and Her children."

As I had been instructed, I entered the Ritual circle...

I called to the Goddess:

"GREAT GODDESS of Nine, You with so many faces: On this blessed Night, I call to You as The White Moon Goddess... I, Your Priestess, humbly entreat You... that You cast your light upon and within me... I ask that I may be Your vessel... Your chalice... Your Well... That my Lord may drink deeply of this Night's work... Oh, Great Beauty of the Night sky, fill me with your power and your Love. Let your words, your Wisdom, your blessings – and your pleasure – be mine upon this Night... And may all of Your children be blessed with fertility!"

I danced around the Fire as the Goddess Veiled. All of our third and forth level Priestesses and Priests were there dancing with me – conjuring up the Spirits of the Night.

Makyr and some others were drumming for the dancers and everyone was clapping their hands in a steady, persistent beat. The Merlin was there, too. He had accompanied Lady Vivianne to the top of the Tor. Only *he* did not dance, but stood aside, playing an eerie melody upon his flute.

Everything surrounding me – even the Air itself – was filled with a sense of Magic and surreality... No, it was more than that – Oh, words fail me! But I knew that within that Circle of power, the Ancestors danced amoung us.

A great horn sounded somewhere at the bottom of the Tor. It was to be the first of two. A very loud cheer arose – we heard it all the way up here! Then a mad rush of people was running up the last of the spiral path from whence they had been waiting. The closer they came, the louder and louder they were. Finally, fifty or sixty or more bodies were dancing, clapping, and cheering around the circle – awaiting the arrival of the Stag God.

They were becoming more and more drunk on drugged wine and lust – all but for The Merlin. Everyone was Chanting, except for the Goddess Veiled.

The Chant was this:
"The Stag and the King are one!
The King and the land are one!
Tonight, tonight it has begun,
The God, the King, and the Stag are one..."

Over and over in a more and more hypnotic rhythm they Chanted, and then the sound shifted, to just the drumming and the clapping of hands...

A new Chant arose:
Where is the Stag who comes to the rut?
To unveil the Goddess,
Bless all with good luck...
Oh, where is the Stag?
Come quick as you could...
For then may we all run into the Wood!

The Chant continued to change and become bawdier and bawdier, until the second great horn sounded... The Time had come for Arthur and his companions to race up the final section of the path to the top of the Tor...

Then... there He was! The Stag King! He was magnificent! His body completely naked, blue dots painted upon His forehead, on his eyelids, and over His cheekbones. So strange was it when He closed His eyes – to see the dots, where a moment before had been eyes of piercing blue... His whole form, so chiseled – yet in ever-changing motion... And, of course, that which all were awaiting... His mighty cock, standing straight up as the Giant of Cerne's! He wore the traditional full Stag's headpiece complete with great antlers, which covered the top of His head and down to the middle of his shoulder blades. Seven tines each had the antlers, for the seven Sacred directions.

I was to hide myself from Him, within the circle of dancers, ever weaving in and out amoung them. He was to proclaim Himself as the "God" and pursue the Enchantress who would be His lover... until I was caught. Then He was to throw back the veil, to look upon the face of His Goddess – and kiss me with great passion.

Arthur

Betrayed I was by my body, just as Morgan had told me I would be. I was inflamed with passion, ready for the rut...

Oh, it was not desire for an Enchantress or anticipation which had brought me to this state, but the drugged wine my men had bade me drink. Not only was *I* well drunk, but also Bedwyr, and too, all the men who were in my company at the bottom of the Tor. Only Gwyddion had abstained.

More and more had we toasted, then gibed – they taunting me with licentious suggestions for the Night's doing. The more we drank, the hotter grew the Fires of our loins. But none would relieve themselves until the appointed Time – and even then not until the Stag God had captured His Goddess and whisked Her away.

I had planned to please the Enchantress well – She who would be the Goddess to me this Night. For as King I must care for and please my people. This was my honour and Sacred trust. If I was to be King, I must be King first and man second. Or were the two one on this Night?

Yet I knew that it would be Morgan's face I would see behind my closed eyes, when my climax was reached.

"Oh, Morgan..." I prayed, "Hear me when I call out your name. For this Love will always be for you, as you will always be the face of the Goddess to me."

The great Fires had been lit. We heard the drumming and Chanting coming from the Tor, then echoing off of the Water of the Lake. There was a throbbing in our ears like the throbbing in our loins.

The women were there in the circle already, of course. For, each woman would be the face of the Goddess to the man or men they lay with this Night. We, the men, must pursue them until they let us catch them. When we heard the second horn sound, we shouted one great cheer and raised one last flagon in salute! Then we were all making our way up the spiral path to the top of the Tor. When we were almost there, we heard the women already in the circle clapping their hands and Chanting:

Where is the Stag?

Where is the King?

Where is the Antlered God?

We men all sprinted the rest of the way up the path and jumped into the ring of dancers and danced as we called out:

Where is my beauty?

Where is my Love?

Where is my Dream for this Night?

I held back for a moment... Then, when I entered the circle, all became silent. Only the Wind and dancing flames could be heard.

To honour that part of my blood that was of the Clans who I would serve as King, I chose as my call to the God the words of an ancient poem. As I pranced round the circle, feeling more and more like the God within me, I cried out:

I am a Stag of seven tines...
I am a wide flood on a plane...
I am a Wind on the deep Waters...
I am a shining tear of the Sun...
I am a Hawk on a cliff...
I am fair amoung Flowers...
I am a God who sets the head afire with smoke

All the while I was strutting the circle – trying to find the hiding Veiled One. As soon as I stopped my Chant – with the power of the God coursing through me – I saw her. Dancing wildly, I chased and pursued her, weaving in and out of the spectators standing in the circle, and calling out to Her until She was caught in my arms.

When I lifted her veil to kiss her, there was an audible gasp from all the participants seeing who She was... Morgan!!! I was speechless... horrified... and thrilled beyond what I could bear! I could not move; I could only stare into the face of my beloved.

She had invoked the Goddess to enter herself before the Stag God was summoned to the Tor. It was not now Morgan's, but the shifting face of the Goddess looking back into mine. I saw eternity in her eyes...

She began to speak, in a voice both terrible and beautiful. Quoth She:

"Face to face in a Time that is not a Time... and a place that is not a place, I hail and welcome you, Great Horned One... My consort of the Eternal Present... Drink of this cup... Goddess to God, Enchantress to King, Woman to man..."

I thought, but did not say aloud... "Drink of this cup? Cup of Death?" In stark realization I thought – *I am the sacrificial King of old*!

She continued...

"As Enchantress and King we honour the Great Ones of Creation... But upon this one Night, as Goddess and God, we shall lie in the throes of ecstasy, to bless this land and all who dwell herein... On this one glorious Night, we, together, will conjure the Magic of Creation! Here – In the Land of Myth, In the Realm of Magic – In the Beginning of all – we stand... you and I, my King, waiting to be joined in form."

At that moment – for the first Time, I fully realised that we were the hands of Creation Itself.

I answered: "Goddess and God, female and male... We are the perfect polarity of life – the breathing in and the breathing out of the Cosmos!"

These were the ancient words that I had memorized. Yes, but when I spoke them, they and all of this – the Tor, the Stone Circle, the dancing flames, the Ritual – became the only true reality... as though the daily lives we lived were but a Dream without substance... shadows only in the thoughts of Man.

Morgan

Arthur spoke as if Entranced...

"Hail and welcome my Goddess, my Love..."

He hesitated!!! Another intake of breath came from those all around. He had *forgotten* the last ancient words!

Silence...

Then Vivianne raised her hands and said:

"All that is, is... and yet everything changes. She changes as She wishes, and as She wishes, all things change. I beseech You, Goddess – Go now and change the world! Make a King! – one such as the world has been waiting for. 'King of the Holy Blood'." Vivianne wavered, almost collapsed. Then she hissed – "Go now!"

At her words, Arthur and I ran down toward the Wood. A few moments after we left, another great shout came from amoung the celebrants gathered at the Circle. So then did everyone else atop and around the Tor, run down the spiral path and into the Greenwood for the merrymaking.

Only Vivianne and The Merlin remained at the Bel-fire.

Lady Vivianne sang the Chant of Acceptance, with tears falling down her cheeks. Her words were:

Shake the bones, grind them to dust
If live we will, then die we must
Shake the bones, stir the soul
If laughter is silver, then tears are gold
Round and round, the Dance of Death
Moment to moment and breath to breath
Ashes to ashes, beginning to end
Death to Death, to live again!

Ceridwen's cauldron
Hecate's keys
Ishtar's Dragons
Innana's Bees

What will be, will be, will be...
What will be, will be, will be...
What will be, will be, will be...

We had to run deeply into the Woods to arrive at our destination.

Although it was only I who knew the way, Arthur followed quickly down the path, which had been cleared for us to make the going easier. Arthur was running so fast! I was flushed and out of breath – he, of course, was Warrior trained... This run and ten Times more would not have affected him. Yes, he was *all* of what a Warrior and the Horned God should be. The Consort of a Goddess! He was beautiful! And he was desirable...

I was holding Arthur's hand as we of a sudden came upon the clearing in the midst of a grove of Oaks. It seemed as though even what clouds had been on the Tor this Night – as well as the heavy Mist we had run though, had all blown away to allow my Lady, this first full Moon of Summer – to smile down upon us. There, in the clearing, had been erected for us a canopy made of Willow boughs, bent and braided into fantastical shapes of Stags, Dragons, Stars, and Moons. It had been draped with finely beaded and embroidered blood red cloth. The cloth had been woven on the Isle, of course, and was of such a delicate Weave that the Moon's light shone right through it. Gossamer as a Spider's web was it... Was that to remind us of the part the Weavers of Fate had played in all of this? The beautiful canopy cascaded to the ground from beneath the ornate finials and spread out in waves of soft folds at each corner of the bed. Long silk ribbons hung from the canopy's edges, as well as from the branches of the Oaks that hung around and above us.

The bed itself was made of straw with Wolfs pelts lain across it.

Sweet smelling herbs and early Summer flowers were scattered upon the bed and lay strewn on the carpet of leaves covering the Earth in the clearing.

Woolen coverlets were folded and laying beside our bed, in order to cover ourselves should the Night become too cool. Two white robes had been left hanging from a nearby Rowan, with which to clothe ourselves in the morning. A bottle of honey mead and one each of the two Holy Springs' Waters were there beside the coverlets for us to drink, along with some foods to eat as we wished. All this had been prepared by my brothers and sisters – all there waiting for the Holy Ones. We... the Goddess and the Stag God...

A place of such earthly beauty had never been seen by my eyes. More was it like a journey into the Otherworlds – the realms of phantasm – than our world of form.

We stopped and gazed into each other's eyes. Arthur pulled me firmly toward him and kissed my mouth with such an urgent and yet heartbreakingly tender kiss. This was the kiss of a man grown, not of a timid boy. He kissed me and kissed me again – my mouth, my throat, my eyes, my breasts – all the while murmuring unrecognizable endearments.

Then at once he stopped, raised my chin and looked directly into my eyes.

"Morgan, I could lie and say it is but the drugged wine or my Kingly duty or even the God's Spell upon me, but never will I have a lie between us. Even if you come to hate me for this Night's doing, you must know this – I have always Loved and adored you, not only as sister, but as a man Loves a woman. And I will *always* Love you so. Do you understand me, Morgan? To no one else will I ever give this Love. Tonight, I will have you as a man has a woman and I thank all the Gods for this one Time. If you think this wrong, Morgan, so be it – but please forgive me."

There were no words I could conjure – no *right* words to say to him. I suppose it was the Goddess within me who uttered the words that I heard coming from my mouth – for later, I barely remembered saying them: "Tonight we feast on Love's bounty, as woman to man, Priestess to King, and Goddess to God. Let us hold nothing back and let there never be shame between us on account of this."

We stood there motionless, in utter silence, holding back that which we both hungered for. I knew that *my* heart – *not* the Goddess' within me – but *my* heart, was of two houses.

"Goddess... Yes," thought I, "She is who I am tonight ... but I am Morgan, Arthur's sister, as well." One house held the memories of my childhood companion, the Bear, the boy I had so cherished and had taught to read and to write, to Love Nature, to understand the movements of the Stars, the boy who could never fill the Well of his yearning for the stories and Myths of the Old Ones. That house also held the memories of those balmy Days spent together in the Woods, whiling away our Time, with his head in my lap, speaking of our dreams and of things to come... Yet, I had not even seen that child for over seven years, but in the here and now, so near my body and desire, stood Arthur the *man*.

He was breathing heavily and trembling for me. Yes, *desire*... It had me in its clutches as much as it did Arthur... His burning was evident in his taught muscles, the rigidity of his cock, as well as the lust in those beautiful blue eyes. They were drawing me down... down... into some hitherto unknown, forbidden Destiny. Some uncharted Sea – a maelstrom... I was undone... over powered.

"Here Be Dragons, Morgan!" screamed the warning.

This voice came from the second house – that of my rational being.

"Could I really desire my own brother Arthur? Mayhap this is only the drugged mead... Or that I was only yearning for my first experience of carnal Love... Who was I trying to fool? In any case, these feelings are a secret I must keep to my grave..."

But by now, the house in which dwelled my childhood memories and all rational thought, was being pulled farther and farther into oblivion... We were on a course steadily falling into silence.

"Morgan..." was the last word spoken...

He slowly lifted my buckskin shift, as though relishing every moment of the anticipation *and* every part of my body. When at last I stood naked before him, he stared at my breasts. I read his thoughts – "Oh, my Goddess!"

Never did I know whether he meant me or *THE* Goddess. No matter now – She and I were one.

He was so much taller than I, that when I looked straight toward him, I faced his muscular chest and arms. My eyes followed the trickle of sweat that ran down his chest and clung to the scant line of curly golden hair there, down to the thick patch above his manhood. Then, I looked up again to his nipples that were as perfect and hard as a man's should be. I threw my arms around him and took one of them between my teeth. I kissed and sucked upon it. Arthur gasped. Then he roughly took my breasts into his mouth and suckled hard upon them. It almost hurt... Almost...

Then he lifted me into his arms and lay me down upon our Wildwood bed. He began to enter me at once, but I stopped him. I shook my head in a gesture of "no." His piercing blue eyes – which lit up my world – looked quizzically, almost hurt, at me.

"Why," he said – "have I done something wrong?"

"No, Arthur," said I – surprised by the strange hoarseness of my voice – "but the pleasure will last much longer if we play at Love by many different games."

I used every skill of Love and lust – as I had been trained to – to please a man, although I had no need to inflame Arthur. His Fire burned as hot as the blazing Sun must. It could not be quenched for hours. I, as well, was greedy for gratification, and with no shame... no shame... Over and over we clawed, bit, and caressed each other, rolling this way and that, ever changing the ways in which we would have each other.

At Times, Arthur seemed surprised that there was ever a new road to ecstasy and release, only then, to have the heat of desire rise again and again. I was like a she-Cat in heat! Ravenous! He was like a Warrior at Love. But the roughness and pain of his Lovemaking was only ever to the point of Love's pleasure.

Oh, it was true, that at his first entrance, I felt a sharp pain... Then the maidens' blood trickled between my legs... Then I was lost! In just a moment, the pain was forgotten. He filled me, then withdrew, then repeated his thrust to fill me again and again and again... I knew not which sensation I Loved the better. When we were joined – he inside of me – I saw the Stars. When he withdrew, I knew only the hunger to be filled again.

"Oh my Horned one, I see forever in your eyes!..."

Oh...
Your Eyes... Entrance me...
Oh...
Your Smile... Enchants me..
When you call my name...
It is a haunting refrain...
I am reborn again
In Your Eyes...

Finally, it was Dawn. I awoke to the songs of Birds and the coming light. Entwined in each other's embrace, arms and legs entangled and heart to heart, were we. I did not remember when I had fallen asleep. Arthur had covered us with several layers of the woolen cloth sometime during the Night. I had no recollection of this, either. It was chill and humid, with a great Mist filling the Wood and surrounding our bodies. But I was warm in our embrace.

In wonder I remembered how our bodies had responded to each other and had fit so well together last Night. But, now what?

"No shame" – She, the Goddess within me had said – "No shame..."

But, Arthur, oh Arthur, what of your great and tender heart – will it ever mend from this trick of the Weavers?

Poetry of the Stars entered my thoughts:

"I have awakened upon this morn, to see the sleeping form of my lover... The Dragon stirs within me... I adore his face, neck and shoulder... He is so child-like lying here that my heart sobs with delight of it! Oh, sleep a little while longer, my Love... for when you awake, the man will appear – and although I do Love the man... I worship the sleeping child..."

Sleep a little longer, my dearest brother...

Arthur

I opened my eyes and was looking straight into Morgan's. She began to speak, but softly I placed my fingers to her mouth.

"Please Morgan, allow me to speak first. Thank you for last Night... No... please... listen in silence, to what I must say. Allow me to finish. I know that you will never be mine again in the way that you were last Night. I am not a fool. If I were to satisfy my own desires, I would give away my Kingdom, Caledfwlch, and everything I have and am, to live in your Love forever as lover or Husband. But, I could dare not do it, even if you were willing – for I have been made King through The Merlin's Magic and by the Blessing of The Goddess. Duty binds me to bring forth an heir. And you, daughter of Igraine, have been made by the Ancient Ones Enchantress of the Isle of Apples. The Stars have crossed us in different directions... Duty binds us both. So there is no need for you to speak painful words of rejection to me. I know and understand all the reasons why... but no matter, my heart will always belong to you. So please, my dearest one, do not break me in twain."

Tears were streaming down her face. With great effort, she choked out...

"And I will always Love you, Arthur."

I kissed her forehead and removed myself from our bed. I brought one of the robes to her whilst averting my eyes for the sake of her modesty.

How I wished to gaze upon her nakedness again... But...

"Look, over there Morgan, they have left a cauldron of Water for us, so that we may bathe. Go, freshen yourself and be comfortable first. I will wait here."

My inner thoughts were challenging me. Did I really mean what I said about duty? Or am I a hypocrite who lies to the woman he Loves – as do most men? Were these simply words that I knew she had a need to hear? Curse me! For now I have spoken them... words which, in this life, bind her from my grasp. Morgan, oh, Morgan...

I am captured by your Spirit...
Delivered by your gift...
Redeemed within your silence...
Broken by this rift...
Beguiled by your laughter...
Enchanted by your song...
Haunted by sweet memories...
Will I be my whole life long...

It was then that I noticed blood on the coverlets. So, Morgan had never lain with a man before! More fool I, to have tormented myself with jealousy – Phantoms in the darkness of un-knowings, of trysts that had never been! I hurriedly threw the coverlet up to cover the stains. I would not add the insult of yet more embarrassment for her to suffer.

But, why had she not been with other men sexually? She had passed her twenty-forth year-turn! I knew that she cared not to have sexual relations with other women, for in conversation she had casually mentioned this to me. Not, of course, that she held disrespect for *any* form of Love; but why, then, her abstinence? "Oh, fool! Arthur," thought I, "will you now try to convince yourself that she has somehow waited for you?"

Soon she returned, looking as fresh as the newly opened blossoms. Still I saw that she averted her eyes from me... as she had *never* done before.

My heart cried, "Oh Morgan, I cannot lose you entirely!"

In silence we walked hand-in-hand toward the Order's cottages... Until I could stand it no more!

Pleading burst from my mouth...

"Morgan, please... Forget all I have said of duty and responsibilities, promises and plans. For my life without you would be an empty torment. Oh, my Morgan, marry me! When I am crowned King, none will go against my wishes. Beside which, half brothers and sisters marry in many lands, where Kings and Queens are involved. You could even live on the Isle, if that is what must be for you. I could not be here always, what with the Times that I must spend away on my King's work. But we could have a home here and..."

"NO, ARTHUR! You have given your word! You must give your Kingdom an heir! That is your solemn responsibility."

"But..."

"No! Listen to me Arthur; it is true that in other lands, it is a common practice for half brothers and sisters to marry, but those are not Christian lands. And although their numbers have been dwindling since the Romans abandoned our Isles, yours is still partly a Christian land. You and The Merlin have *promised* to treat all the peoples on these Fair Isles with equal respect, in return for their alliance. An heir, from what your Christian compatriots would call an incestuous and sinful liaison, would be a great affront to them; one which could break the alliance asunder. And – such an heir as that would never live to rule. Arthur, for these and many more reasons, I cannot marry you. What is more, what passed between us last Night will *never* happen again. I Love you Arthur, more than you could know... You and my – our – Lady Mother, have been the dearest ones to me in all of my life. But no, I cannot marry you. I *will* not marry you. I do not *WANT* to marry you!"

Those words, harsh words, killing words, pierced my heart and bruised me to the marrow.

"I... I am sorry Morgan; I will never ask it of you again."

We went each in the direction of our separate quarters. I prayed to all the Gods and Goddesses of the three worlds, that Morgan and I would not lose the closeness and tenderness which we had always shared. I could not lose her, even if it only be as her brother. But, I feared the outcome of this.

Some of my companions were there in my quarters, awaiting my return. Amoung them were Gwyddion and Bedwyr, of course. I was met by their tentative silence. But then Kai, the Red, cleared his throat, and began the traditional lewd jesting and jeering...

"Oh Night of Greenwood frolic
I kissed her on the lips...
But in my drunken stupor

Mistook her ears for hips...

My darling what fine ears you have
But I will hold them straight...
For not to miss my target of
Your lips and pearly gate...

I took my aim so gallantly
But then became abashed...
For where I thought smooth skin to be
Found her bearded and mustached..."

A roar of laughter went up...
"Come on lads, where is your Spirit? Join in the fun!"
And so I must. And so I did, although this was the most agonized
and bereft I had ever felt in my life.   Tradition demanded, so I
acquiesced.

All of my companions acted as though this morning was like any
other morning after the First of Summer Rites with each one of them
trying to top the other with stories of their own sexual escapades.
Meanwhile, I was dying inside...

Part Two
Arthur, The King

Chapter 10
Arthur Rex

Arthur

The crowning was set for three weeks past the Rite of Summer's beginning.

It was amazing how many people had come to attend the crowning ceremony and feast. An invitation had been extended to all of the most influential men and women of Our Fair Isles. Kings and Queens, Tribal Elders and Clan Chieftains, Dux and other military leaders, wealthy land owners and Merchants, and of course many Holy men and women. In addition to quite a few known Druids in attendance, there were several leaders of other religious traditions; such ones as the Seers and high Grandmothers of the Old Tribes, Christian Bishops and Monks, as well as some of Hengist's Priests and Priestesses of Odin, Thor, Freyr, and Freya. Many of the Picti, too, had come, including a strange and terrifying looking Picti Seer. They had travelled the length of Briton to witness the crowning. This in itself was an historic event. For, never had the Picti involved themselves in anything farther South than the Emperor Hadrian's great wall!

There were many Bards, Musicians, and Dancers too. Great men and women, all...

I remember noting how heady were the aromas of the feast – redolent with scents of flowers and smoldering Herbs in the hall. Large trestle tables were filled with delicacies of whole roast Boar and venison, Salmon, Trout, Quail, Geese and Swan. Savory dishes of Peas, Beans, Parsnips, Turnips, and Leeks were abundant. Flat Grain breads flavoured with Rosemary were served with butter, Berries, and honey. Amphorae of mead, ale, wine and of course, the Holy Springs' Water were placed conveniently for all the feasters use. Great flaming torches were hanging along the walls and many oil lamps had been placed along the centers of the tables. The Oak beams were hung with banners representing all the peoples who were here in attendance. The Great Hall was filled with merriment and anticipation.

I had chosen to be crowned, surrounded by a representative of each of the five cultures of these, Our Fair Isles, who had accepted me as their Over-King. The one thing that I had insisted upon was that Bedwyr stand with me for the crowning. Lady Vivianne would represent the ancient Dark Tribes as well as the Order of the Isle of Apples. Of course Gwyddion, The Merlin – a Druid – would represent the traditionalist Clans. As for the rest, Gwyddion had suggested that each of the cultures choose one of their own Holy men or women to represent them. I would also honour the seven directions.

Lord Ignatius Constantius, the Christian, would have the honour of representing the Roman-styled Britons. Of this I was glad, for, as Gwyddion has said, I must rule Christians in equality with all others. Aethelwulf, a Seer of Hengist's court, would stand for the Saxons. Drest, son of Erp, was chosen to represent the Picti. These, along with Bedwyr, would stand closest to me in the ceremony.

The ceremony began with Gwyddion loudly pronouncing for all to hear – "As Arthur has commanded, I place his brother Bedwyr by his side, to faithfully guard and protect this King."

Bedwyr stepped up and stood at my right.

In doing this, I had legally adopted him as my brother.

At the appointed Time, Morgan the Enchantress, who had *made* the King at the Rite of Summer's beginning, stepped up to give me her blessing. She was wearing the shell and Stone necklace that I had made for her when I was nine years old. I had to swallow hard and grit my teeth to hold back my tears. In formal language, she sang these words of blessing:

"Oh King, Great Stag – Lord of the Wild Hunt – guide and protect us well. And when the sad Day comes that the Stars guide you home, leave us with an heir as brave and strong as you. Leave with him or her the sword Caledfwlch and the Crown – and may their heart be as pure as yours."

She knelt before me. I raised her quickly...

"Sister, you will never kneel before me again!" My first command... She nodded in acquiescence and then she and Bedwyr backed away. "Morgan," thought I – "do not put this gap between us..."

The four other chosen ones waited aside.

Gwyddion then stepped into place, and said, regarding Lady Vivianne, "I place this Priestess of the ancients in front of you to remind you ever of this land's foundation." Gwyddion and Bedwyr each offered her an arm to aid in mounting the short stool that had been placed there for her.

Lady Vivianne stepped up to stand before me. She offered, "I place my counsel at your disposal whenever your need arises. May you always listen first to those who would counsel you – and thus might you never be rash."

"Behind you stands Drest, son of Erp, the Pict, our allies to the North who have pledged to guard your back and fight with you to defend our alliance.

"I place a comrade at your left" – Ignatius Constantius stepped to my left – "to remind you always that we are one people, one land, one King – each with our different and blessed ways.

"To your right stands Aethelwulf, of Hengist's court, who is gladly here as ambassador of the Saxons of Briton."

Now this was a ticklish situation, for we all of the alliance would fight to prevent any more Teutons from invading and stealing our lands. However, Hengist had been invited to Our Fair Isles by Vortigern – and thus had had the right to settle his Kingdom here.

"Beneath your feet, with every step you take, is our Mother, the Goddess of Earth – to remind you that the land and the King are one. As fare you, so will these lands and these Peoples.

"Above you is placed this circlet of gold – which is your crown – ever to remind you that every Woman and Man, Animal and Bird, Tree and Rock and Spring, are all ONE in the great circle of life – each with their own work and glory and worship of the great Ones of Creation and that you, who holds the God within you, are a willing sacrifice for these, your peoples."

Then Gwyddion held the golden circlet on high – showing it to all gathered in the hall – held it above my head, and giving it into the hands of the four... he stepped back. Then all four, each holding their directional quarters of the Crown, lowered it upon my head. I was King! A great cheer arose and did not cease for a long while... Gwyddion whispered, "It is done."

Then, I got very, very drunk and was eventually carried to the King's bed.

The politics...

The next Day – filled with introductions to every Chieftain, Minor King, Queen, Dux, and Lord of each of the realms, along with their wives and even some of their sons and daughters – plowed slowly onward. I stood patiently with Gwyddion by my side. Of course, I was expected to remember all of their names as well as the location of their land holdings. They were standing in a great line waiting to kneel, wish the King well, kiss my hand, or present gifts – which gifts were stacking into huge piles behind us. They were also there to remind me of favours they had done for me or my Mother's or Father's house and of course, of boons they were wishing for. I can think of no word other than *tedious* to describe it, but that word cannot even begin to reach the level of the thing...

At last, some very interestingly unexpected guests arrived... the first of whom had been unexpected by me because of the great distance they travelled. This was a large group of the wild men and women of the Picti, who had pledged their peace. Here they were in their colourful checkered dress and painted skin, coming to show, in front of all, their support for this alliance. This pleased me and Gwyddion well. I was so very pleased by their presence that I proclaimed:

"Once in every year, or as often as is possible, we should all remember our pact by feasting and holding games at Table Rock together" – to which it was a much lesser distance for our compatriots of the North to come. Another cheer arose at that – and much more drinking.

The very last supplicant, for *effect* I am sure, was Princess Rowena – she who was daughter of Hengist the Saxon and widow of Vortigern – Hengist with whom we held a shaky peace treaty.

Now, Princess Rowena herself was a very good negotiator and a brilliant politician. She had taken over Vortigern's estate, holdings and fortress, which, as she managed them, had become very prosperous. Yes, she was a strong woman – and a *very* beautiful woman as well.

Gwyddion whispered to me:

"I like this woman – listen acutely to whatever she says, for she is very clever, but also trustworthy."

"My Lady Princess Rowena – daughter of the great King Hengist – you will always be welcome at this court" said I.

She nodded her head, but did not kneel – showing herself to be my equal.

I nodded in acceptance, paying the same homage to her.

"King Arthur, I have come to pledge my support to you, to make a treaty of alliance, and to bring a very special gift."

"Speak, dear Lady."

"You have become High King of a great nation. It is understood everywhere, that one of your first and most important duties is to marry and produce an heir, no?"

"Yes..."

"Well, then, allow me to first give a gift to you, free of conditions – a golden gem-encrusted chalice made by Saxon goldsmiths, known the World over for their excellence in metal craftsmanship."

She motioned with her hand. The crowd of her people separated and out walked a girl of such unearthly beauty that a murmur ran through the entire hall. She was not as tall as was Princess Rowena, who towered over almost all the men present. No, but she was lithe as a Willow, small breasted – which was unusual in Saxon women – and she moved with the grace of a Swan, even her hands moved with the delicate beauty of the Twyla y Tag. Slender and pale was she and her hair was very light and brilliant as Sunlight. I caught a glimpse of her eyes – wide and turned up like a Cat's – they were so pale a blue that I was not sure whether they were blue or gray or colourless. So stunning was her beauty that whispered admiration grew and grew across the Great Hall.

I held up a hand for silence.

She was holding out before herself a magnificent golden chalice. It had emeralds, amber, and pearls embedded into it.

Princess Rowena said with a slight smile, fetchingly upturning one corner of her mouth, "Behold the golden chalice – fit for a King."

Now, everyone in that hall knew that the chalice was a symbol for woman – more than that – the womb of a woman. It was what held the blood of the line...

"May I present my little sister, whose name in your tongue is Gwenyfar? Behold – the chalice of King Hengist's blood. The *metal* one is yours as a token of our esteem."

Gwenyfar walked up to me, knelt and held up the chalice offering it to me with trembling hands. I took it from her.

"Beautiful," said I.

"Yes... Yes," said Rowena, now with a big sunny smile, which I knew was genuine...

"The gift is yours to keep... But the alliance offer is this: King Hengist, who fathered Gwenyfar upon his Cymru Queen, is offering to you a *permanent* peace, cementing the bond between our two families and sealed by your marriage to his daughter Gwenyfar."

By the Power of Three! A Spell had been Cast. Oh, not the truly Magical kind, but a Spell, nonetheless. Everyone could feel the tension – anticipation grew in the Hall.

I said, very carefully, "Your sister is a beautiful and most worthy girl. I thank you for the golden chalice and this most generous offer of alliance. You will understand that I must first meet with my counselors, but we will have an answer by tomorrow as regards King Hengist's generous offer.

"Please eat and drink – be merry all, on this Night of celebration. We are most honoured by your presence."

I signaled that this ordeal was over for this Day and left for my chamber with Gwyddion and Bedwyr.

My head was pounding with pain.

In my chambers I asked, "Now what, Gwyddion?!"

He responded: "This is a prospectively good – or dangerous – situation. Hengist is offering his daughter to you. If you accept, he pledges permanent peace. If you refuse there is a great insult to him and war with his Saxons will most probably follow..."

"But if I accept a marriage alliance with a Saxon Princess, what will all the other Chieftains and Dux of my army think?"

"Yes, yes... I see your point... Probably a number of them are planning to ask the same thing of you – to tie you to them with a daughter or sister. *Whichever* one you would choose Arthur, the rest would be upset.

"But Arthur, this girl is half of Clan blood. Rowena made a point of that."

Bedwyr butted in – "Arthur, she is the most beautiful woman I have ever beheld."

"Bedwyr you know my heart, she is not my... *type*... at all."

Gwyddion retorted, "But, would anyone who would be offered to you in marriage please you, Arthur?"

"Probably not."

"But, Princess Rowena is right, your duty is to marry and produce an heir."

"So you are recommending that I take her as wife, Gwyddion?"

"Yes, I believe that you should. But rest this Night, Arthur, and tomorrow we will call council to discuss the matter. Sleep well, Arthur."

As he spoke these words, he looked at me with those silver spiral eyes of his...

"Sleep well, Arthur..."

His owl blinked and the next thing I knew, I was fully rested and it was morning.

After three hours of arguing back and forth, the decision was unanimous that marrying Gwenyfar was a most astute political move. So, I wearily acquiesced...

That was it, then, my life was no longer my own... I felt like a fisher's boat in a maelstrom.

"Morgan, oh, Morgan, what foul games the Gods sometimes play... for always and only did I wish to be your husband."

My heart was filled with tragedy...

When the festivities were over and farewells were said, everyone began to travel back to their various homelands.

The wedding was set to take place at Mid-Summer, when the Sun God ruled in all of his glory.

I kissed and hugged my true Lady Mother, Igraine. We looked into each others eyes and both knew that although there had been a lifelong association, never had she thought of me as her son, nor had I looked upon her as my Mother. My dear Mother, Tangwen was the woman who had raised me. She was here too, along with the man who I had known as my dear Father. I hugged and kissed them both and was so very glad to see them. I filled them in on everything that had happened.

Surprisingly, Morganna had come too... I had not seen or spoken with her since we learned that we were blood siblings...

When I had finished visiting with my family, it was Time for rest.

I was very grateful for that. I had drunk more in the last week than ever I had done in my life. But it seemed as something that was needed, if not appropriate, to the stressful situation I was in.

Just before retiring, my sister Morganna, already known and well feared throughout our land for her Dark Magics, walked up to me with a goblet and said,

"Here, my brother, take ye a drink of the Vine. I have flavored it with costly and exotic spices, so that you may be treated as a King ought to be. And there is a little something in it to aid you to rest this Night."

Never expecting she dare any foul play, I drank it.

I bade them all a good Night and I went up to my chamber.

I sent everyone away. I had no need of people dressing me and undressing me just because now I was King. I had been a soldier, I had been a boy who mucked the Horses, and I had been the student of a wise man and a worker for him. I had lived in a cave, for Goddess' sake... This being a King was a new thing to me and I decided right then and there that I would not take on a lot of the trappings, which were embellished upon other Kings. I wanted no one to guard my door, I felt this unnecessary...

But then Gwyddion knocked upon my chamber door and said, "Something is wrong, Arthur – I taste it on the air."

I said, "What?"

He anwered, "For once, I do not know, I cannot see into the thoughts of the one who may be wishing me – or you – evil."

"You cannot see into their thoughts?"

"Oh, perhaps it is only that I am so tired. But... will you not have a guard? For I feel a foul Wind approaches."

"If you wish it Gwyddion, I certainly will."

"I do wish it. Good Night, Arthur."

"Good Night to you, Gwyddion."

So, a guard was set at my chamber door.

I do not know when it was... perhaps some Time in the deep of Midnight, as I was in a fitful Dream of Morgan – always Morgan – a veiled woman approached the guard standing outside the door. She made a hand gesture and blew in his face, without uttering a word. He fell fast to sleep.

She crept into my chamber, dressed in a buckskin like the one that my beloved had worn on the Night of the Heiros Gamos and the veil as well. All I knew when I awoke in the darkness was that *she* was lying there... Sleepy as I was and feeling drugged – perhaps from the drink Morganna had made – when I looked up, there, as the Goddess veiled, was my Morgan.

"Morgan... Have you come to lie with me?"

She nodded her head and pressed her finger to my mouth for silence. I began to lift the veil from her head, but she put her hands up to stop me and shook her head "no." Still, there behind the veil in the deep shadows, I could see the angles of her beautiful face.

"Oh Morgan, you are wearing the robe that you wore on the Night of the Sacred Marriage..."

Although this pleased me well, she seemed bothered somehow by my mention of it, for she made a small growling sound in her throat. Her body pressed urgently against mine. She sat up on top of me and raised the buckskin from herself. There was her glorious dark body.

I was naked, of course, beneath the coverings of my bed. She had thrown them aside. She would not kiss me, although I tried hard to have her mouth upon mine... But instead she bit me on the neck as she mounted my phallus and thrust her hips forward. She scratched at my arms, and commanding me to submit to her will, gathered my hands into hers and placed them upon her hips. Roughly, she pulled my hips up to meet her. She went wild atop me.

If this was a Dream, oh, Gods, blessed be that I may live in this Dream forever. I had thought never to have her again like this. Could this really be? Will it be so forever? I was ravaged by her Love. Then all thought escaped me...

I lost myself in her. It did not take long for me to reach climax. I reached for her – for another joining, but she pushed me away. She said, "Shhhh" and shoved me back onto the bed. Wordlessly she got up, straightened her clothing and then walked out of my chamber!

I tried to go after her. Confused, I pled, "Morgan, wait!"

I stumbled when my feet met the floor. The room spun. I could not stand. Had I really drunk so much?

I lay there with my head swimming and my thoughts scattered. Soon I was asleep again...

In the morning my eyes opened to Sunlight streaming through the slits in my chamber wall and to a cool breeze. There I lay – naked and uncovered upon my bed.

"Am I always going to be blessed or cursed with Dreams such as this?"

But then when I looked down at myself and at the bed, there was the evidence and scent of Lovemaking.

"Morgan, you really *have* come to me!"

I did not know whether I was deliriously happy or just delirious – or terribly sad.

I lay in bed for hours.

Gwyddion came to me later that morning and said, "I woke up with such a foreboding – Arthur, has something happened to you in the Night?

"My head hurts badly."

He looked into my eyes, opened my mouth, looked at my hands and listened to my heartbeat.

"You have been drugged! What happened?"

I remained silent. I would not – could not – tell this thing of Morgan and myself, even to Gwyddion.

The guard at my door, when questioned, could not remember what had happened. When he awoke in the morn, his only thoughts were of how he had failed his duty of keeping watch at wakeful attention. When questioned, he spoke truthfully – as he remembered it – of incomprehension at how he had done so. I would later remember him for his truthfulness...

When I saw Morgan later in the Day, she walked up and smiled to me as sweetly as ever she had. As though nothing had happened... As though the world had not changed...

She said, "Good morning my brother, the King."

I held her by the shoulders and with desperate joy said, "Morgan!"

She looked up at me quizzically – "Yes?"

I could see in her eyes that she knew nothing of what had happened. A feeling of dark and dreadful doom passed over me.

Although I have not the Sight, there have been moments when flashes of something glinted in my head – and this was one of those moments.

Morgan, still looking at me, heard whatever Voices were trying to speak to me.

She gasped, "Oh, Arthur!"

"What?"

"Someone came to you in the Night! And you thought it was me?"

Damn her Sight!

I could not even look into her eyes... much the less speak... Finally I fumbled with my words and, falling to my knees, I said, "Morgan, forgive me!"

"No, but you must have known that I would have never..."

"I know... But, there you were, in the buckskin, and the veil. It *was* you!"

My words stuck in my throat...

Then both of us realised the horror of horrors that had taken place.

"Morganna!"

Morganna looked exactly like Morgan, although a bit older...

"But no and no again," quoth I... "I could not have been so deceived."

But wait! I tried to think – quickly going over all that had happened.

"That is why she would not kiss me – for I would have known the evil taste of her kiss."

"No," thought I, there could not be the sweetness of Morgan's kiss within that bitch Morganna. She could not have fooled me with her kiss – and she knew it!

Morgan was reading my every thought. I was so ashamed, for I had indeed lost my self in passion and lust – with Morganna!

"Forgive me," I begged.

"No, brother, no, there is nothing for me to forgive..."

"Yes, I have done a terrible wrong. And for what possible reason would Morganna use her trickery to lie with me?"

Morgan, calmly, yet intently, answered: "For you to get a child upon her."

"Oh, no! A thousand Times no! I cannot bear the thought..."

As my wits returned, Morganna's wicked scheme became clear and dawned in perfect light upon me.

"How much a fool could I be not to realise that her meddling – her machinations – would enter into all of this somehow? How could I have been so naïve?"

But then, Morgan reminded me that in the past, Morganna had sometimes fooled even Igraine and the great Merlin.

"Her powers are enormous Arthur. And they are not used for good and righteous intent. They are for the *Breaking*, rarely the *Making*."

I stood as if frozen...

Morgan began to slip into a Trance – right then, right there – right in front of me.

There was a glimmer in the Air, such as there is betimes on a hot Summer Day – how the Air shimmers and moves from side to side in a rippling effect... This shimmering was all around my innocent, beautiful, Morgan. I stood back with a great wonder and respect for whatever it was that she would utter, for I knew that it would be the "Voices of the Stars" who would speak through her mouth – through those beautiful lips.

The Voices spoke... and I *heard* them... their words branded into my heart... although they never spoke above a lulling whisper – it was as though the words came from her but were already inside my head, creating this eerie echo...

"Everything has a cost Arthur... Now you have tasted the cost of rulership. Too bad, so sad, so soon... For you have met the source of your doom... We see, in your future, many webs of treachery. Your heart, your desires, will ensnare you, Arthur. Although you will give good gifts all the Days of your life, what you gave and what was received last Night will be your strife, your greatest sorrow and the ultimate masque of your Death... Remember, Arthur – everything has a price, for everything there is a cost... "

Chapter 11
Morgan's Fear

Morgan

On the first Dark Moon after the Heiros Gamos, my Moon's blood did not flow as usual but was only spotty. I gave it little thought... However, when upon the Dark Moon following the Crowning, I did not bleed, I wondered if Arthur and I had made a child. I was distressed although I knew it was completely inappropriate to not count this potential as a blessing.

I spoke with Lady Vivianne about it. I have tried never to be a hypocrite and so I told her of my fears. She, as it was her station to do, reminded me how Sacred any child born of the Fertility Rites was. Then she spoke to me as lovingly as if I were a daughter of her womb.

"Morgan you have been put into the middle of a dangerous and sorrowful intrigue. Ye, The Merlin told me of Morganna's treachery."

"How does he know? Arthur would never have exposed my shame to him..."

"Your shame? No my dear, Arthur would never betray you in any manner. For true, he said nothing to Gwyddion whilst he thought it was *you* who had come to him in the Night. You know that Arthur would protect you at all costs. But after he spoke with you upon the next morn and realised that it was Morganna who had come to him, he told The Merlin everything."

"Everything?"

I felt my face heating... I blushed again. I could not hide my thoughts...

"Oh Gwyddion... How can I ever look into your eyes again if Arthur has told you everything of my passion in our Sacred Marriage bed?"

Vivianne looked right through me.

"No, Morgan, not *everything* – everything of *Morganna's*

treachery."

"But still, Mother, how can I be ... how can one thing be separated from the other? Is this how it will always be – that I will never be allowed my own private thoughts or feelings? Must my inner, shadow self be exposed to all just because I am the King's sister?"

"Morgan, you are ill from worry and fear. Many Times such emotions will disrupt our body's normal flow of Moon Blood. You must rest and relax. To this end, I relieve you of all your duties here at the Order – except for your Bee tending, for I know that their keeping is not like work to you, as they are your beloved companions. Still, I suggest that you temporarily turn most of your chores with them over to your helper Kia, so that you may spend some of your Nights away. For one entire Moon's Dance you will rest... And then we will see what happens.

"But Morgan, my dear, just think of this: what a blessing and protection to Arthur's Kingdom it would be if a child of his was conceived by and born of a Goddess – and this child having been conceived *before* what Morganna brings forth from her evil Magic!"

"Oh Lady, do you '*See*' that Morganna is with child?"

"Do not worry about that now Morgan, just rest."

I was not blind to the fact that she had not answered either of my questions...

"Just rest..." she had said. Reluctantly, but successfully, that was what I did.

I visited the people of the villages surrounded the Tor and even some of those across the Inland Sea. I watched them Weave their Summer baskets as adeptly as the Robins had woven their nests at Winter's End. I gifted the folk with honey from our Bees and cheese from our dairy. They in turn invited me to eat, sing, and dance with them at their evening relaxations.

I realised that my Days in service to the Order were far different from the lives these people led. These precious Days reminded me of my childhood with my dear Mother. How I missed her now...

The villagers shared their innocent gossips with me and even told stories of legends – which had grown and, I am sure, been much embellished over the centuries – of the secret Cave whose entrance is in the bottom of the Tor. Which, they said, no one had entered since Time out of memory – for it led directly to the Underworld.

"And no one *will* ever enter it!" quoth they.

They continued, "There have been a few great Magicians in the long ago past who had dared to enter... but they were never seen or heard from again.

"The legends of the 'Cave of Nodens' say that, 'He and his minions of the lowest levels of the Underworld had filled the Cave with Crystals, encrusting them into the walls and ceiling – as a lure to all who were bent toward temptations of riches – or were pridefully unable to resist a challenge.

"But... at its deepest, darksome recesses, just beyond the brilliant sight, is a Whirlwind – which it is said – draws the seeker ever farther within...'

"So, no one would ever dare think it worth the cost to enter, my Lady!"

I gravely agreed, all the while smiling on the inside of myself.

But then a prickling of my skin began... I felt the wooziness come upon me... Then the "Voices" spoke: "A good place to hide what must not be found. *Remember this*, Morgan of the Woods."

Then all the world was back to my listless Day, and to my enjoyment of the company of the villagers.

I also drank each Day from the two Sacred Wells and asked the Spirits of the Springs to calm me and to help insure that everything "lead to a good outcome."

On the Night of the Full Moon I lay myself across the green Star Stone atop the Tor. As I lay there my thoughts drifted into less tense regions...   Whilst trying so hard to relax, I thought of many diverse things; such as the one I have written below...

Hidden away in our Order's secret library are manuscripts designated as "Books of the Knowledge of other Mystery Schools." Many of these books and scrolls are very old and fragile, as they have been in our library since before the Time of the Roman invasion. And so, long ago, because of their great value and irreplaceability, one of the Ladies of the Lake set our scribes to the task of copying the entire library of manuscripts that we hold. This work continues to our Day.

Not long after I had attained my Enchantress status in the Order, I asked Lady Vivianne if I might have access to some of our copies of these writings. She granted permission. I cannot express what a thrill this was to me.

One whole section of our vault is a collection noted as: "The Scrolls of Khemet." The land of Khemet, now called Aegyptos in the tongue of the Greeks – or, Ageyptus in the Roman – meaning 'the land South of the Aegean,' lies far to the East of Our Fair Isles.

Within the pages of these books I found diagrams and explanations of many Magical and medical techniques, along with other scientific knowledge, far advanced beyond what Western cultures now understand. Most of these had been written and copied in the Greek tongue and so was I able to read them.

I was especially interested in the books of the "House of Life of the Memphian Priesthood." Their school and Temple, which they termed a "House of Life," was dedicated to the teachings and disciplines of their creator God, Ptah – and of their great Lioness Goddess Sekhmet, whose name means power.

One of these is entitled: "Discipline of the Understandings of the Five Bodies of Humankind." In this book I found detailed explanations of these five bodies.

They teach that there are 'Light Spheres' – in the Spirit energy fields that surround every Human, Animal, Tree, Stone, and all other living things.

The book says that every *Human* has five *bodies* – each one with its own energy 'Light Sphere' system. They are:

The Body of Flesh

The Body of Thoughts

The Body of Dreams

The Body of Magic

The Divine Spirit Body

Each of these bodies, in succession, is more ethereal, less knowable or controllable than the one before it.

The "Body of Flesh" is, of course, important, for it is what *binds and defines* us as Humans. Most people think that it is their *only* body.

The second is the *"Thought Body."* It is the *self-conscious* body. This body believes *itself* to be the *Only One*. Whilst what it is, in truth, is only that part of us that "thinks." It believes only that which it perceives – can see, hear, taste, touch, or smell... It believes that *It is* the whole self.

The third body is the *"Dream Body."* The Dream Body is the *gateway* that allows *entrance into* our true selves. It is the Body that *receives* messages, Visions, and Dreams. It is the body through which the "Voices" speak. Some call the ability to know and use this third body – "Having the Sight." Yet, Dreams come unbidden to all people.

The forth body is the *"Magical Body."* It is the first one that is capable of *'Making,'* creating, or *manifesting*... It can, at will, reach out into the Otherworlds to use the stuff of 'The Making' to effect change in the perceived reality of the world of form. This is what is called 'the bending' or 'Magic.' It gives the Adept – at their *will* – access to communicate with Gods, Ancestors, Spirits, Animals, Trees, Stars, Stones, Springs, and so forth...

The fifth body is the least accessible and most ethereal of all. It is the *"Spiritual Body."* The *"Spiritual Body,"* as the old tome quotes, is the *becoming*. It is that which enables one to *join* with the Divine Ones at will or need: To walk amoung the Great Gods and Goddesses, even the Great Mother GODDESS, in the Land of Myth – in the Time of Making, when the First Word was sounded, which Time *was and is* the Eternal Present... Few Humans – whilst alive in flesh and bone – will ever reach the level of Enlightenment necessary to access and use the "Spiritual Body."

I will share a Sacred Secret with you. That secret is that the Cosmic Creation did not come *to be* in one great event, but is *continuing* even unto our Day... It is *becoming*, and will continue to do so until the penultimate word of the *Unmaking* is sounded at the Time of the Great Dissolution... This Secret came to us by way of my Mother's Ancestors.

But back to the Khemet books...

Those Adepts who have obtained the level of knowledge and competency to first be aware of, and then use, *all* of the five bodies, must *align* the energy Spheres within *each* of these bodies first – and then accomplish the ultimate achievement, which is to *align* – with each other – *all* of the five Bodies. This, it is said, is the state of perfect Human balance, harmony, and Spiritual ascension – from whence comes our term En-light-ened.

I have read in the old tome that the Priests of Khemet call this quality Maat... Maat is depicted in their Sacred glyphs as a woman with a Vulture feather atop her head. She is the Goddess of truth and justice. The *principle* of Maat, the book says, is and always has been the foundation and goal of their culture. It means, as I understand it, order – the proper way of things – of *all and everything*.

Theirs is an interesting philosophy...

Their true culture, it is said, has lasted, with little change, for many and more millenniums, even through Greek and early Roman domination. Their longevity speaks well for their "Maat."

Now, it is not only the Aegyptian Priests who have sent emissaries to the Isle of Apples with ancient scrolls and books to be left safely in the Order's keeping. The Magi of many traditions have known of and revered the Wisdom of our Order. How blessed are we to be entrusted with their precious volumes.

Perhaps it *is* as my Tribe's legends tell – that one of the one hundred boats, such as that which arrived on these Fair Isles, went to Aegyptos, to bring the same Wisdoms to them... and one to... Well... or, perhaps it is simply that the Mysteries are the Mysteries and truth is truth.

It is a fact that I have heard many stories of great Christian Mystics who understand these same Truths, as well. I have wondered many Times if these Mysteries are written on the hearts of all Humans – there, awaiting our discovery.

Perhaps that is what The Merlin means when he says that "All the Gods are ONE."

These things – which passed through my thoughts whilst lying upon the Star Stone – seemed to lighten my burdens. Then I realised that I was not *resting*.

"Rest?" I laughed at myself. And to my surprise that laugh, in and of itself, was very healing. It has always been hard for me to silence my thoughts, for they relentlessly roll over me as do waves upon the sea...

The next two weeks went by in pursuits of seemingly decadent pleasures.

Upon the Day that the Dark Moon would be seen – or rather *not* seen – in the Night Sky, I fretfully wrung my hands and generally fidgeted the hours away.

Then, blessing of all blessings – as I saw it then – it happened. My blood began to flow.

Now, it is our custom that during our Moon Blood Time, that we would go to each of the Sacred Wells to cleanse ourselves with the Holy Waters. Great jugs were left at the Springs for this very purpose. As it was my wont to do, I would scoop up a small gob of red iron soil around the Red Spring – and with this I would cover my face and hair.

Our Healers tell that the clay will draw out of ourselves sickening poisons – *and* will make smooth our skin – whilst nourishing our hair so that it may be lustrous and strong. It is also a *symbolic* Rite of banishing all painful emotions that we have held within ourselves.

Then I lay in the Sun. This I did for a long Time that Day, for it was warm and beautiful. However, it was the custom of my sisters on these occasions to spend at least the Time it took to Chant an age old round:

"Oh Lady of darksome and ancient fame
At the crossroads of the Moon we call Thy name...

Aft' Thy bow hast flown arrows for Love's sweet repast
And Thy deepened long shadows upon Earth hast cast...

Whence Thy quicksilver dance hast waxed and hast waned
The Magic of women can ne'er be o'er reigned...

One Day and one half whilst Thy face ne'er shows
Black be the Sky... whence our Moon blood flows..."

We do this, not for any idea that we are "unclean" – as is the thinking of some during this very natural function of our womanly bodies – but more it was as an honouring of our feminine Magic and gifts of Motherhood. By partaking in the goodness of the Holy Waters, we are reminded that all life sprang forth from the great Cosmic Sea. In this we may share in the realization that even fresh Waters are a Sacred representation of the gifts of the Mother of all.

And so my life continued on as usual. I tended my Bees. They buzzed with me. I sang to them. And all had returned to normality.

I must admit that my personal feelings would have been devastated if I *had* been pregnant with Arthur's child *and* had to face Gwyddion with this news. This would have embarrassed me so...

My feelings toward Gwyddion were... complicated.

A feeling of freedom had overtaken me. I once again felt the Spirit within me of the child – "Morgan of the Woods."

Chapter 12
Of Names, Blood, and Other Topics

Vivianne, Lady of the Lake

Many people wonder how I came to have such a foreign name. They wonder because, I am – as are most of the women here at the Order – of the blood of the ancient Tribes, who lived on these, Our Fair Isles, before all others. It is obvious that we are of this blood because our skin colour is much darker than that of the Clans, Romans, or Saxons, who live about us, and we are smaller of stature.

The "Old Dark Tribes," as they are now called, live in vast and darkling, almost impenetrable Forests, so as to keep themselves hidden away from "The Others" or "The Strangers," who, as they see it, are invaders of their lands.

Mostly now are the Old Tribes gathered in the area known as Dumnonia, near to the craggy coast of the Western Sea. There are formed the fabled Forests whose Trees grow into beautiful, frightful, or grotesque – depending upon one's perspective – gnarled and knotted twisted giants. From Time out of memory these Ancestor Trees have stretched their limbs higher up into the foggy Mists than the eye can see. It is perched within these boughs that most of their dwellings are found.

However, it is well known that the Tribes also have far reaching outposts, isolated here and there in the virgin Forests from the far South to the far North of the main Isle of the Britons.

It was in one of these Dumnonian villages that I grew from infancy to young childhood – although truly, I can remember very little of that Time, or of the intricacies of their culture.

Our worship and Sacred Philosophies here at the Order are based upon long held Wisdoms, passed on generation to generation – yet are ever-evolving because of our interactions with the Magi of other Sacred Traditions.

Time changes all things...

However, it is said that those of the Tribal society of my Father's kin have never changed their ways – and this, we of the Order greatly honour. Some people of this world may consider the Tribes' way of life primitive – primeval even – but *we understand.* Their ways are the ways of the Gods "In the First Time." They live in a Sacred World, where all things are ONE with Great Nature. That is why long and long ago they chose not to sully their hands, or their Spirits, with the ways of "The Others" – with whom they did inevitably come into contact.

As our legends tell it – long before any of Briton's known invasions:

At the Time of the great catastrophe, when the one hundred boats sailed away from their sinking Island – out in each direction of the Four Winds – they were filled with their civilization's most gifted Philosophers, "Seers," Holy Ones, Astronomers, and Teachers of all other Arts and Sciences in an attempt to save their vast knowledge of the Cosmic Mysteries. And so, these women and men were sent as emissaries to lands across the Earth, so as to aid in the cultural development of less advanced peoples.

However, our original Ancestors were mindful of the value of all people, not just the well-educated or successful: For, the GREAT GODDESS – in her expansive Love, gifts and protects all of her children – those of simple lives, who hunt and gather or sow and till, equally with the city dwellers.

So, yet one hundred *more* sailing vessels were hurriedly put to Sea, bringing the Island's simpler village folk to wherever the Goddess should blow their sails; for there was no Time left to teach them to navigate by the Stars.

The Elders of the Original Land did, however, set within each of *those* boats a small cargo of Sacred items, each of which held Symbols of the Cosmic Mysteries.

To our knowledge, at least one of those second one hundred boats survived... From that original stock, come the village dwellers of the "Old Dark Tribes" of the Britons.

It was by the educated travelers in one of the *first* one hundred boats set to Sea that the Order here on the Isle of Apples was formed.

Our school of the Higher Mysteries has educated our postulants, Priests, and Priestesses in the sciences and Arts of Writing, Mathematics, Astronomy, Sacred Geometry, Healing, Animal husbandry, Herbology, Mineralogy, History, Rituals, and Magics.

However, we also *use and treasure* the ancient ways of the Tribal "Walkers between the Worlds" to Heal, "See," seek, and Divine answers to questions unavailable in the world of form – and to communicate with the Spirits and Ancestors. For after all, how else but through the Walkers did the Gods of the *First Time* impart the knowledge of the Mysteries and of all other things to their Human family?

I think that this combination of Arts and methods is not unique to our Order... for I have heard it said that in *all* lands wherein there are Great Mystery Systems with vast Temples, Universities and Priesthoods, there are also the "Walkers," such as ours, who work simple Folk Magics and journey into the Otherworlds for the everyday personal needs of the common folk.

Perhaps these Gifts of the Arts Magical dwell in every Human's Spirit as a heritage from the common Ancestors of all people – there, but awaiting awakening.

My Ancestry

My own blood ancestry is only *partly* of the Old Tribes' stock. I have kept this fact a silent secret until now...

It is a long and complicated story of how a child would be made by such an odd coupling as my parents. But regardless of length, and because I think that these are important facts which should be added to my dear Morgan's histories, I will write of them now:

My Father was a man of the Old Dark Tribes of the Britons.

My Mother's is a very old family, whose land is on the continent across the Eastern Sea and far to the South of Briton. They are known to the Roman world as the Bergundian Affalonians, living in the area called Aix-en-Provence. However, of late, some call their Kingdom the land of Merovia.

My Mother's people are obsessed with keeping genealogies. Their meticulously kept records show that they have lived in the same area for almost as long as the Romans have been in Gaul.

There had been connections, in the long ago past, amoung the Romans, the Clans and my Mother's family. However, each is a very different culture from the others.

Her maternal Ancestors originally came from the East, where they had lived in the city of Old Jerusalem.

You see, their legends say that a distant Ancestor of my Mother's was a man named Yosef of Arimathea. He was, it is said, a Holy Man and a Tin Merchant.

This man, in his first sojourn Westwards, came all the way to the land of the Britons, and *here*, to the Isle of Apples. His purpose was to visit the Tor and the Sacred White and Red Springs, as well as to ply his trade. For it is known near and far that this entire area, which includes the Giant's Dance and the other, larger, Stone Circles, as well as the great mounds of the Ancestors – and all places within – are filled with the Magic of the Gods. With this man Yosef came a young boy.

Some say that the boy was his nephew – some say his brother. Yet, I find a great contradiction in this... If Yosef, as a man full grown, brought a *boy* with him, and he was the boy's brother, then Yosef would have been the elder. If he was the *elder* brother, *he* would later have been named King of the Jews...

Oh... I go ahead of myself...

Yosef had come from the city of Old Jerusalem, whose name means the "City of Peace." It was, in fact, anything but that.

Years after his visit to Our Fair Isles, the Time came when the Romans were in pursuit of his immediate family, accusing them of sedition – and so he fled his ancestral home with his small band of fellow travelers, to live amoungst the people of Narbonne.

This land is still inhabited by some of my Mother's family.

There are many other stories about this man and his family. What is fact? What is legend? I do not know. But some of the stories are quite fanciful...

As it is, through the twists of Fate, my Mother was a hereditary princess of this line of Yosef's family.

My Mother was given in marriage to Merovech, King of the Salian Franks, and now reigns as Queen Vivianne the first, or, as some call her – Verica.

But, before her marriage – unfortunately for her – she fell in Love with a man of the Old Dark Tribes of the Britons. This man – whose name was later forbidden to be spoken in her Grandfather's court – left his Tribe and travelled to her land as a mercenary soldier, which was indeed a very unusual thing for a man of the Tribes to do.

Apparently he was rebellious too! –

Princess Vivianne gave to him a forbidden Love and she became pregnant with me. So, you see, I had tainted blood – unworthy of her family's *pure* royal blood.

The "official" story that was put about was that: "Vivianne had been confined to her quarters for the period of six months due to an illness..."

Every helping woman and Midwife who had attended my Mother through her confinement and birthing were sworn to silence about the whole matter – upon the threat of their own Death and the immediate exile of their families.

I, *who did not exist*, was given into my Father's hands upon the third Day of my life. My Father brought me across the Sea to Briton when I was only four weeks old.

I was told – when I was old enough to understand – that my Mother had sorrowfully begged and pleaded that I not be taken away from her. Furthermore, she vowed that she would not eat a bite until finally her Grandfather relented and promised that my wet nurse be sent along with my Father and me to Briton – with gold for passage and proper provisions.

My Father brought me to the Dumnonian Woods to live with my paternal Grandmother. She kept me for five years, whilst I was being nursed by the girl who had arrived with me from my Mother's court.

But I was not of the *pure* blood of the Old Dark Tribes *either*. In their eyes, I had come from a race of literate, city people – wise in the ways of the world and political intrigue – with whom my Father had carelessly bred and, because my Father had chosen to leave his life as a Tribesman, it was decided that I should be given to the sisters here on the Isle of Apples – *if* they would receive me... They did.

Mine, though, is not the only strain of this Hebrew *Royal Blood* on our Island...

But what do I care what blood runs through my heart? I am a child of the GREAT GODDESS, as are we all!

Of my life...

When I had passed twenty-nine year-turns and had been an Enchantress of the Isle of Apples for more than eight years, a great Chieftain of one of the lowland Clans died childless. And so, the Clan's best Warrior and Seer was chosen as their new Chieftain. After he had been elected by their Clan council and the approval of their Druids, and after having received the blessing of the Lady of the Lake, all that was left to do to for his officially becoming Clan Chieftain, was to take part in the Ritual of the Heiros Gamos – the Sacred Marriage:

"Priestess to Chieftain, Goddess to God, woman to man."

I was selected by The Nine High Wise Mothers, at the behest of the Lady of the Lake, to become the Goddess in that Ritual.

She who was the "Lady" in those Days was a Priestess named Madrcsicsrgst. Her name meant – in the tongue of the Old Tribes – Bird Song. She had been like the Mother I had never known. But Bird Song seemed very old to me at that Time. I thought that, surely, soon another "Lady" would be chosen. I prayed that it would not be *too* soon. It proved not to be, for she remained alive for thirteen more years, after which *I* was elected to her position.

As for the Sacred Marriage Rite, when she told me that I was the *chosen one*, I felt so honoured and joyful.

Sexual encounters were nothing new to me. I was a worshipper of the Goddess and as such I knew that: "All acts of Love and pleasure are HER Sacred Gifts."

We of the Tribes, and all those of The Order, have been taught that: "To eat, to work, to sing, to dance, to plan, to Cast seeds, to harvest, to make Love, to bring forth children, to Heal, and to die... all else which is – and is done – under the Stars, is Sacred..."

Nothing, to me, was profane.

For, after all, did not the Gods of the "First Time" give us the example and teach us how to do every action under the Stars? In all of our Rites, are we not only reenacting what THEY did at the Cosmogenesis, thereby ensuring – as long as the Fates will allow – the continuance of all Creation? We keep the Great Wheel circling, one cog at a Time. Our Rites bring us into the "Land of Myth." Through our Magic, we become co-creators with the Gods – "In the beginning."

Perhaps, for some, this Idea of a Ritual place and Time which is *not* a place *or* a Time of this world, yet, at the same Time *is* – is a new Idea... But in many, many lands, this concept is well understood.

I held no foolish modesty of my beautiful body – of the Goddess who dwells within me – nor of what pleasure I could give or receive. So when the wondrous Night came, all was as it should be.

I had known for a long Time that a daughter would be born to me someday. I prayed that this wonder of all wonders would be a child of the Bel-Fire Night. If that were to be the case, then no Father's hand could claim her – no husband's rule would tame her... This is not to say that she could never marry, if she so chose, but that no man would ever control her.

Finally the Night of the Heiros Gamos was nigh...

First came the traditional bathing, anointing, dressing, and veiling, then the drinking of the spiced herbal wine, then the drumming and the Enchanting.

Then the Stag God appeared... I hid from him – he caught me. He kissed me with a great passion at the very first. I did not know whether this was the usual thing, but it was thrilling to me. He was handsome... Good! I spoke the words. He spoke the words. We ran to the Woods and I had the best sex I had ever had.

I never saw him again, though he tried a few Times to visit me. I might have continued a relationship with him, for I did like him very much, but the Goddess had blessed me with a child and I wanted no one to know of it. Except, that is, for the Lady Bird Song. She was to be the only exception. When I explained my wishes to The Lady regarding my child, she understood and allowed me to leave the Isle of Apples for an entire year's cycle. When I came back with a girl child in my arms, the story was put about that I had found her in the Woods and did not have the heart to let her die.

My daughter, I named Nimue...

Nimue was raised and taught by all of my sisters and brothers of The Order. Lady Bird Song made sure that I was the one who taught her to read and write in three languages. This was a means of Nimue's spending much Time with me, as her lessons required her to be with me for a while, almost every Day.

Nimue was not told until the Night of her Enchantress initiation that she was my daughter – or of my plans for her. Because of the fact that Nimue's training had begun at such a young age and that she is such an intelligent creature, by the time of her eighteenth year-turn she was properly prepared to become an Enchantress.

I was so afraid that she might feel betrayed or hate me for not letting her know until then. For all of her childhood she had believed that her family had abandoned her and left her to die in the Woods...

Of course, I – who was by this Time Lady of the Lake, since Lady Bird Song had passed through the veil five years earlier – extracted a promise of silence from Nimue to never reveal this truth to anyone, until the Time was right. I required this complete confidentially before I could tell her the truth of her family.

When I told her, I stood back and waited, holding my breath. She just stood there, staring, blank-faced at me. My voice broke when I said, "Nimue?"

I, who am thought of by many as being stern, even cold, could not hold back the tears from falling down my face. What would she say?

She rushed into my arms with such a tight embrace that I thought I could not breathe!

"Oh, Mother! I have always wished that you could have been my true Mother. Everyone here was kind to me, but you were the one to give me strength, knowledge, honour, and language. Also perhaps... a Mother's Love?"

Then she sobbed and I sobbed as I stroked her lustrous, long black hair.

Yes, some may think me hard-hearted, but this I can assure; that I Love Nimue as much as any Mother could ever Love a daughter.

She was perhaps the most intelligent and driven girl I had ever known. I can even say this objectively.

Before I conclude my writings for this Time and return quill to chest, I feel that I must add one more comment to these pages...

Having said all that I have about our initiates of the Order being mostly of the Old Dark Tribes, I must add that with every generation, more and more Clanswomen, of Briton and Gaul, have come to live, learn, worship, and work here at our Order. This has especially been so since the Roman ravaging of the Druidical Universities. Even has a Picti girl – and one boy too – travelled from the far North, through the lands of their hereditary enemies to ask admittance to our Order's school. It will not surprise me if, during my lifetime, a Saxon girl seeks admittance.

And why not? After all, are the Goddesses in *their* colourful sagas, not similar to our Nine Mothers?

This has been the story of the bloodline of Vivianne, Lady of the Lake, written for Morgan, by my own hand and seal, in this the forty-eighth year of my life on this Earth.

A Note from Morgan...

Now, before I die, and as I compile these histories, there is another way to view what my dear Lady Vivianne had written...

There were some folk of this theoretically "Royal Line" of the Hebrews, who ended up in Briton as she revealed. Down through the various strains Arthur, Ambrosius, Uther, and Gwyddion were all of this Royal blood, through the line of King Hen Coel. My Father Gorlois was, as well, through his Mother – whose paternal lineage had come directly through the matrilineal line of the original house of Yosef of Arimathea.

So, when Morganna tricked Arthur into begetting a child upon her, that child, Mordred, had many and great Royal claims – not only upon the Britons, but also upon the line of the now-called Merovingian blood.

By now the families have multiplied to great extent, with Royal heirs in many different lands and Kingdoms.

Perhaps it will be helpful to say, that for those who do care, detailed copies of these genealogies are not only kept by my Mother's family, but also by people who call themselves Coptic Wisdom Seekers, living in Egypt. These are held safely in their hands.

I hope that someday, someone will write them in a picture graph form, so that they may be seen and therefore more easily understood. But this is a work for someone *else*...

Chapter 13
Nimue, the Enchantress

Nimue

I know that Morgan will have written and compiled all that my Mother tells her. However, there may be some things that The Lady Vivianne will have held until the last... She is just that way.

When my Mother is approaching the hour of her Death, she intends to pass on to Morgan the mantel of Lady of the Lake. This, I do not think she has told Morgan. However, in the event that she should die suddenly, she has given into my hand a signed and sealed manuscript, naming Morgan as her successor.

I say this here and now, to illustrate Morgan's special place in my Mother's heart.

I have always felt that my Mother secretly wished that I was more like Morgan, at least in terms of devotion to the Gods. Always that is, since I have known that The Lady of the Lake *was* my Mother.

My Memoirs...

Since Morgan has asked that I write my *memoirs* – if you will pardon my Languedocien expression – I have been delighted by the task.

I am called an Enchantress of the Isle of Apples. I was never to obtain Mother of Wisdom status in The Order and, to be true, I cared not to. In fact, I have never considered myself to be a very religiously inclined person. The level of Enchantress I did attain – by the skin of my brow.

There did come the Time though, when my continued learning of the *Mysteries* was to take a turn into a *far* different direction.

Some say that I enjoy intrigue and adventure to excess. What is excess?

My histories – if you will – will be truthful, on pain of embarrassment... all the more adventurous, no?

Perhaps my Mother knew me better than I had thought she did, when I was a young and rebellious girl. For I had always placed more value upon my own will, plans, and desires, than upon any obligations to – or needs of – others. Yet, in the outcome, my Mother had *plans* for me. And in me she was to place great trust.

My Mother's plan...

I was to leave the Isle of Apples to travel incognito through the Mainland of the Eastern Continent, thence to find the fortress of my Mother's Mother, which lay in the heart of King Merovech's Southern lands – with the ultimate goal of being granted admittance into the court – and confidence – of my Grandmother, Queen Vivianne.

The gaining of my Grandmother's confidence, most especially regarding the closely guarded and accurately kept genealogies of the families and blood lines of Yosef of Arimathea and of Miriam of Magdala – who, it is claimed, was the "companion" of the King, Yeshua Ben Yosef – was not an easy task.

I was always to wonder how my Mother had attained such wealth as she lavished upon me and my endeavours abroad... Was it from her Grandmother's Tribe? Of course, I had heard the stories of the almost limitless wealth held by the Old Dark Ones... Could this really be true? Or was the *Order* really that wealthy? And was our Order – and not only my Lady Mother Vivianne – financing my espionage for some benefit to which I was not privy?

Perhaps it was entangled with the royal bloodlines of our new King, Arthur... And did my Mother have a plan beyond that, which I could ever know?

So, when my journey was to begin, I purchased Horses to ride and pack, which would take my company to the Sea. Also, I procured Clansmen mercenary guards to protect my person and property – in the case we were to encounter trouble along our way.

We took the route toward the Eastern Sea, which would lead us through Hengist's Saxon territories. As we were at tentative peace with his people, I felt it safe enough to do this.

We stayed amoung them for the span of two Moon Dances. Quite hospitable they were. Jolly folk.

I Loved hearing their tales of the Bandersnatch and other monsters and otherworldly realms such as Alfheimr, the world of the Elves; Jotunheimr, the realm of Giants; Nioavellir, the land of Dwarfs; Muspelheim, a world of Fire; and Niflheimr, a world of Ice and Mist into which the wicked dead are cast and so many more tales...

From them I bought beautiful golden and silver torques, rings, braces, goblets, plates, and many other things wrought by their excellent Metalsmiths.

I also bought nine beautiful cloaks – embellished with Saxon embroidery of Wolf's heads and fierce rampant white Horses. Fox tails, Wolfs claws and teeth, and strips of Horse hides were laced to their shoulders. I never knew whether these were talismans of protection, or for extra warmth. Regardless, they were gorgeous!

With all of these to sell I could easily pass as a wealthy Merchant.

When we arrived at the shore of the Eastern Sea, we sold the Horses we had bought for our travels.

My Mother's plan was in the works...

The Voyage...

When we were wont to cross the Eastern Sea, it was deep into the Time of Red and Gold Leaves... I learned that this could be the worst season of the year to sail – few shipmen had the heart to do so. Finally, we did find a hardy bunch who agreed to attempt it – albeit for three Times the usual cost of the crossing!

We could not just sail straight away from the Eastern shore of Briton to the continent, for that would have landed us in a very dangerous country of the Gauls – for, as of late, they were ever fighting amoungst themselves – each for domination of the other's land. No, we would not chance that. And so we angled South, then Southeast toward the Southernmost Gaulish lands, to shore at the closest port of Bordeaux, from whence we would travel overland through the Aquitaine to the territory of the Bergundian Affalonians. This route made the crossing many Times the length it would usually have been.

The passage was beyond a Nightmare...

A great storm arose; a gale of such magnitude that it seemed as though the thick dark Sky was boiling. The swells of the tempestuous main rolled and heaved, hurling up waves taller than the ship, crashing the bows and washing to their depths men and cargo alike – pulling and drawing all to their Watery grave – all but that which was securely tied down... Everyone who could was bailing Water, even were my own guards. It was a terror!

Everyone began to beseech their Gods... Even the seasoned Saxon Shipmen yelled – arms outstretched to their Thunder God, Thunor, to save their ship and their lives, lest they die not with sword in hand – and thus be not accepted into Woden's halls.

Above the roaring Chaos, I heard one man who bellowed –

"All-Father Woden, save us...
Let us die not in disgrace...
Lest we be doomed to a wat'ry grave
If Thee turn away Thy face...

Weel our eyen ne'er seen your halls
With our feet not on the ground?...
Like weed o' the Sea, ne'er aught we be
White bones lying – they be drowned...

Let our good wives ne'er be taken
Nor raped, nor slain nor bound...
Let our children ne'er be orphaned
With nay guidance to be found...

Let our names ne'er be forgotten
So wandering souls we be...
Let our bodies be not eaten
By the Giants of the Sea..."

I even heard, above the roar, some of the more Roman of my own guards calling out to their Lord of the Sea:

"Oh Neptune, oh Poseidon,
See how thine Ocean raves
We call three Times, we toll three chimes...
Toward thy mighty waves...

Ride thy gilded chariot with Horses white of foam...
Ascend thy dark realm's secret depths...
Above thy Kingdom's dome...

Raise thy mighty Trident, oh Ruler of the Sea...
Three pointed tines, three Magic Times
Command the swells to silent be..."

All my own thoughts were disgorged from my very core and vomited out through my mouth, along with whatever contents of my stomach were left, until there was naught else but yellow bile... then nothing... but for the empty violent retching.

But somewhere, through it all, I do have a glimpse of a memory... Did I truly sing out with a Siren's voice, to calm the Chaos to peace, as I was later told? If so, it did not work.

The old Sailors had known what was coming. They had bound themselves with thick ropes to the masts in the center of the deck or to anything sturdy, in hope of saving life and limb.

I, too, was tied with a rope to some part of the ship, so as not to be dragged off into the unfathomable Deep.

I was not bailing. Only was I was vomiting uncontrollably. I had been doing so even before the storm, at the first rocking of the ship. That was when I knew that I had the Sea sickness.

Oh, what a bother this has proven to be. But perhaps it was what saved me from murder – for the superstitious men began to stare at me with murderous eyes. Then one voice called out: "*She* is the cause of this tempest... A witch... An Enchantress of the Isle of the Old Dark Ones!"

Then another... "I weel do it... throw 'er overboard I weel!"

Then the Ship's Master yelled above the howling noise, "She is not causing this, you fools! Look at her... She is about to die from the Sea illness. If the tempest was her doing, well, we would be dying, not her! And she would be fine! Stop praying! Keep bailing!"

For hours we were ravaged like this, tossed this way and that. The wooden hull of the ship was groaning with so much stress that I could hear it above the roar. I do remember thinking that perhaps the groaning was from some Great Sea Monster of the Darksome Deep, calling us to our Watery grave.

Then thought I...

"Nimue... for shame... if you are going to die, at least drown with dignity! You do not believe in Monsters as do these simple-minded Saxons."

But, I did believe that surely the ship would crack to pieces at any moment. However, it did not. And it seemed as if from one moment to another the storm passed us by. The Sky brightened, the Water calmed and we were alive.

So weak from vomiting and retching was I that I was just hanging from the ropes tied around my stomach and arms. I could not stand on my feet. I felt terrible pangs in my stomach and my head ached as though an axe had rent it! I could not tell how much of this was from being bound by the ropes or how much was from my violent illness.

The Shipmen untied me, avoiding my gaze in shame... I must have looked like Death herself. Someone tried to give me Water and I vomited again, then wine, and again. Then they let me sleep. I had Nightmares of Water Dragons and huge Serpent-like Eels – I *hate* Eels – and Visions of Mer Folk with canine teeth tearing at my flesh.

Finally I awoke.

One of my personal guards was holding me up to a part sitting position and cooling my fevered forehead with a fresh cool cloth of Water.

"You are safe now, my Lady. We are to shore. Please drink some of this broth."

So I did. And as soon as we offed the plank, I held it in.

This man's name was Owen. He was a kind man, a gentle of heart man. I liked him. I looked into his eyes and laughed.

He said, "What makes you laugh, my Lady?"

"I suppose..." said I, "I missed my chance to really see a Water Dragon."

Owen laughed with me. "Oh, Gods! You have beautiful green eyes!"

On a windless Day, we had actually landed in Southern Gaul. So we found lodging, care for our wounds, and baths – Roman baths. AAH!

Never had I felt so grateful...

Before the Ship's Master left, I gave him a golden torc, as an offering of my gratitude for his saving my life, and for his excellence in ship mastery. He gave me a hearty Saxon toothless smile. He was grateful to be alive too.

Nimue the philosopher...

We rested for two weeks, at which point we were approaching the worst of the Winter weather. I was unused to being at leisure for such a long period. On the Isle of Apples everyone's hands were busy all of the Time. Not that we did not play, but even then, there was activity.

However it is different for those who had reached our "Dark Moon" Wise Mother initiation. They had frequent and long rests – periods of seclusion. These were for meditation and journeying into the Otherworlds.

Whilst speaking of the "Walkers," I will mention here that there *are* a few of them – who are not so highly elevated within the Order as to have been taught these methods, but who were "chosen" by the Spirits Themselves. Mostly this "Calling" comes in young adulthood – but to some while yet children. Their works are the same as those which the High Mothers practice in their Trances. In addition to those works, they Divine future events, find lost objects, Animals or people, and locate the herds for the hunt. Oh, yes, and they "En-Chant the Dying to Rest" and help the newly dead – who might not yet realise that they are in fact dead – to peace. Some of these young ones can even reunite people with their own lost "Spirit Pieces." One such of these "Walkers" is Morgan of the Woods.

I suppose the Christian Mystics accomplish these same works – as do the Magi in other traditions. Walkers are as old as Humans themselves and are in all the known cultures of the world, or so I have been told.

I believe this is how the Mysteries have arrived in the hearts of Humankind. For this work of *gaining the Mysteries* is one of the primary works of these Walkers.

It is even said that the plants and herbs – or actually their Spirit forms – revealed their Healing functions to Walkers. I suppose this is where the Healing Arts began and how all knowledge of the Mysteries and sciences came to people in the beginning... then this "first knowledge" was honed into various Mythic Rites suited to fit each culture.

I also believe that the old stories of the sunken Island and the one hundred boats bringing all true Cosmic Knowledge to people of the Four Winds, is but a metaphor for the work of the Walkers.

Vivianne says that I am too much of a realist. Well, probably so.

Of The Druids...

In the past there were many Women's Orders affiliated with the Druids' Mysteries. They were part of great scholastic centers. Most of the women who lived and were taught at these were of the Clans, our close neighbors. We honour their Wisdoms as they do ours.

We, of the Old Tribes, on our Isle in the Inland Sea, are the last and only school of our Order. But long ago, there were many.

Time rushes by and the old is lost or assimilated, and the new glimmers brightly, until another yet newer Philosophy comes along. This is happening now to the Druids – and to the Order.

Enter the Yeshuites...

Long and many years ago, a few early Yeshuites came to the Isle of Apples. These, it is told, were very kind and Mystical people. Some of them still remain in the lands of the Britons.

But then my Ancestors heard it written upon the Winds that things began to change amoung the Yeshuites in Rome.

History says that:

First they began to argue amoung themselves as to the very nature of Yeshua – should he be King, Prophet, or God? – and of the place of women in their religion.

Next, emperor Constantine in the Roman year of three hundred and twenty-five, or so, beyond the birth of Yeshua, had a "Vision" to create a new Roman religion – and to proclaim it the only legal – or *permitted* – religion in the entire Roman Empire.

Long before Emperor Constantine, the Romans thought the Druids a political threat in our lands.

It was said that the Druids taught subversion to the Clans of the Britons – who held them in highest esteem – and still counted their say as final law.

So the Romans tore down their Universities, cut down many of their Sacred Oak Groves, and put all the Druids they could find to the sword.

This is still impacting the Druids, even to our Day, for it is said that many of the Druidic Priesthood are becoming Cymric Christian Monks. Although I hear that their Druidical ideas and ideals have been interjected thoroughly into this non-Roman Christian Church.

This is why The Ceasar of Constantinople and the Pontifus Maximus of Rome sent Germanus of Auxaire to our land to quell the so-called "Pelagian heresy."

Now, Pelagius was the great leader of this Druidically inspired Christianity; teaching these ideals to a great many followers. So, at the Pontifus Maximus' order, Germanus – backed by The Caesar's own troops – under his royal standard of the Purple Dragon, held a great meeting regarding Pelagius.

As the legend goes, Thirteen Druids – two of which were women – were questioned by Germanus and his Roman court, as to the nature of some of their teachings, philosophies, and social structures, so as to compare these to Pelagius' teachings.

The findings of this Tribunal council were: That many of the Pelagian teachings were identical to those of the Druids. Such as: that the sexes should be equal to each other in honour and law. Also, this "heresy" taught the doctrine of transmigration of the soul and that Humans could come to Spiritual Ascension, or a state of goodness, by their own works – not *only* by the grace of God – thereby effectively denying the need or purpose of the Human sacrifice of Yeshua as redemption for their imperfection and the inborn sin of all of Adam's decedents. Man, he taught, was a perfect reflection of God and therefore was not flawed.

After the "trial" and all the great fuss, Pelagius was murdered as a heretic.

However, I do not know, nor can anyone guess, how all will come to be in the future. There are certainly fewer Christians amoung the Britons now, than even two generations ago. And the tides of people's hearts have turned back to the old Gods and the old ways. But, will it remain so?

Ah... There, you see what happens when I even *think* about resting. Vivianne says that my thoughts never stop; that they are like the buzzing of Bees on a Mid-Summer's Day.

She is right, of course. I suppose it was the best thing for me to leave the Order. I think my *own* thoughts too much. And to be true, I think that I am not like the other Enchantresses. I crave adventure and challenge. And I am wanting in the devotion, yes, even the spirituality of the others. I crave the things of this world. I know that Vivianne saw this in me and knew that I would never be meant for a monastic life.

So now I will serve my Mother in the way that she has asked of me. Even though I really must interject here that I personally could not care any less about ancient bloodlines or their more ancient origins.

I do realise that this idea of being a High King means a lot to Chieftains and military Dux, their people, and to *my Mother* – who hopes that The Merlin's Arthur will unite in peace all the factions and peoples of the Britons and of the whole Island, as far as even into the old Picti lands. Of course, I wish this mighty and noble plan of theirs works. But as for me, I will believe it when I see it come about.

Nimue the Merchant...

So now, I am a wealthy Merchant – of indeterminate origin – secretly sent by Vivianne to infiltrate the people of her Mother's blood, the supposed descendants of the Fisher Kings of the royal line of David, the Hebrew.

But to go on: after resting for two weeks and recuperating from our arduous Sea voyage, for the next two full Moon's Dances my guard and I busied ourselves with learning the language and customs of the people in that area, as well as laying in all the needed supplies for the months-long overland journey we would take to reach my Grandmother's lands. Of course, we had to procure clothing that would not mark us out as foreigners! We were outfitted with sturdy Horses – and beautiful beasts they were. I bought a new wagon in which to transport my belongings. It also was beautiful – but only on the inside, so as not to display too much wealth, for dangerous and robber-filled Woods would we traverse. I travelled with a heavy guard for these reasons.

The inside of my wagon, sides and floor, were covered with great carpets from Byzantium that I had bought from traveling Merchants. They kept me warm on Nights when the cold winds blew and we could find no safe lodging. Amazingly I had lost very little on the Sea voyage – and none of my gold.

I must admit here that I do Love luxuries. It is just the way I am. For this I offer no apologies – and mention it only to explain why I was so thankful that my clothing was safe from the passage. You see, my Mother, with the help of Makyr and some of the other women on our Isle, had spun, woven, dyed and stitched the most beautiful underclothing and cloaks for me that I had ever seen. Also, Makyr had made three pair of boots for me; one for very cold weather, which were fur lined, one for warmer weather, and a pair which was for any instance of wet, muddy, or rough terrain. That pair was twice as thick and heavy as the others and simple looking. The other two pair were fit for a Queen. She had made a great red Fox skin muff to wrap my hands or feet in case we were in frozen lands.

But my best-loved thing was a red Fox-lined cloak with a hood, which was very heavy and of tightly woven wool on the whole outside of it. It had two Roman clasps on it – one was at my neck and one just below my breasts, to keep it closed for warmth when the Winds blew. But the thing I Loved so much about my cloak was that the wool had been very richly dyed with madder. It was a scarlet red; also patterns of vines had been embroidered upon it with threads of deep brown and green. Nothing I had ever seen could compare with my red cloak. And everywhere I was to wear it, it drew attention and many compliments and much comment.

I think perhaps my physical appearance will not have been described in my Mother's or Morgan's histories. Well then, I will do so here. Like Lady Vivianne, I am much taller than the women of the Tribes, but not quite as tall as the Saxon or Northmen's women. My skin is also lighter and I have green eyes. Men watch me as I go by. And, I have been told many Times that I am beautiful. I do not believe that my beauty can compare with Morgan's, but it is hard to honestly compare, for I have a different look than that of any of the peoples living in Briton, Saxony, Alba, or the far Northlands of the wild Picti. My teeth are strong and white. My hair is very long, thick, straight, and black. I think that my hair is my best feature. I would not call myself slender, for my breasts, hips, and thighs curve well, but other than these things, I believe myself to be unremarkable. My hands are small, long fingered, and graceful. I do like my hands. Some say the way I move into gesture when I speak or sing is Enchanting. This I put to my own good benefit. They are also all the better to display many rings and wrist works.

I did say that I Love luxuries.

So, enough about the way I look – except that no one can guess my Ancestry from my features and this suits my Mother's plan very well.

The farther inland we travelled – and as we entered the Time of longer Daylight – the more predictable and warmer was the weather. There were many more balmy Days filled with radiant sunshine and blue skies.

It seemed that with each passing Day, the Trees – their blossoms of pink and white drifting on the breezes, falling upon our Horses, catching in their manes and tails, and settling on the wagon and the track upon which we rode – became greener and greener and the tiny buds on their branches grew into leaves. Everywhere our Mother the Goddess – She who *is* the Earth – arrayed herself in beauty. Even in the deep Forests – where the sunlight is filtered through the thick growth of overhead branches – the Mosses on the Stones, the wild Ferns and wildflowers, were richer and more lush than had they been the Day before.

New life was everywhere. How it lifted our spirits to see the Mother Does and their young Fawns walking through the Woods. Here and there were families of Hare and Foxes. And then there were the Birds – beautiful Birds of every description. Many of them were exotically coloured. They filled the Trees and the Sky above. There was one kind in particular which had become my favourite – although I have never learned what was their name. They had blue and grey feathers, yellow chests, a short bill, and vivid blue collars, wings and tails. Sometimes there were little markings of white on their faces and heads; I suspect these were the males. They seemed to be curious of us, too. I could see the intelligence in their eyes. Their songs and chirping filled the Air all around us and added much to the enjoyment of our travels.

All this loveliness of the season brought to my mind a song that had been taught to me as a child on the Isle of Apples by a visiting Greek Scholar. I cannot remember his name – as it was so long ago. But I never forgot the words or the haunting melody of his song:

Persephone, Arise and Cast your seeds
Dry your Mother's eyes, for you she grieves
For all the Winter long, she has lain asleep while you were gone
Persephone, Arise and Cast your seeds

The Birds of every kind they wait to sing
A song to celebrate the birth of Spring
For every little Worm and Bee with bated breath await to see
Your Magic wand of Love and warmth's awakening

Persephone, Arise and Cast your seeds
All the good Earth's sons and daughters wait in need
For they must clear and till and sow –
For this they learned and this they know
We reap all blessings of The Mother through our deeds
Persephone, Arise and Cast your seeds...

As we passed by villages and towns, their cottages were different than those on Our Fair Isles. Their roofs were more compactly thatched and had hints of designs on their edges. The wattle and daub exteriors seemed a bit more refined somehow. As many cottages were square as were round. The villages themselves were more symmetrically organized... as compared to the generally haphazard, randomly laid out manner of villages back home. The overall effect was quite pleasing to my eyes. The folk of these villages had a greater variety of sweet smelling herbs planted in their gardens – in front of and around their cottages. Of course, because of less frequent rainfalls it was much less muddy which made for an overall cleaner appearance – as well as affording more comfortable and easier travelling on the roads.

We stopped as often as we could so that I might ply my 'trade' and develop a good reputation as a Merchant, for word spreads far and fast of such things.

After some long and languid months we finally reached the land of my Grandmother's people without incident.

During that Time, I had developed a great fondness for Owen – the one of my guards who had so kindly cared for me in my Sea illness.

Although we, the company – who had shared such companionable and lighthearted Times together had all formed a bond of friendship that was to last for years – it was with Owen that I had become entangled in a sweet and lusty liaison. Never did I perceive a jealousy or resentment over this coming from the others. For that, I was very thankful. I am sure that each of the other men found many warm and inviting beds to visit along the way.

It was not a great once-in-a-lifetime Love between Owen and myself – not, at least on my part; and I believe not on his either – but an abiding respect and understanding had we. However, beside our tenderness for each other, what there *was* between us was a very hot, intense sexual attraction. To my great benefit, he was quite simply an exquisite lover.

Our relationship was to last until our return to the lands of the Britons where I did meet the great Love of my life. Always though, did Owen and I remain friends.

Chapter 14
Gwyddion's Dreams

Gwyddion

The Night before I was supposed to escort Gwenyfar to Princess Rowena's fortress in Dumnonia, I had a great and sorrowful Dream. Brennos was calling out to me to me from his Deathbed. When I told Arthur of my Dream and urgency to reach Brennos, he was distressed on my account. I begged his leave to go – of course it was granted.

"Gwyddion, there is nothing of a pressing enough nature to keep you here. I will send Bedwyr to escort Gwenyfar in your stead. The Time has come now for you to ride!"

That morning, as I was about to leave, Arthur gifted me with one of the most beautiful Horses in his stables. She was a golden with a slightly darker mane and tail. She had wondrous eyes, which showed her alertness and intelligence. He gave immediate orders to his stable boys to quickly outfit her with everything I would need for my travels to the Snowy Mountains.

Now, I did *know how* to ride a Horse before that Day. It is just that I have always preferred walking or running to wherever I would go, which is something I can still do, even for long distances. I suppose my walking everywhere is just one more of my eccentricities for people to make much about – which people will do – when they have not enough of their own affairs to busy themselves with.

When I was a child, the man I had called Grandfather had taught all of the other boys of our household a great deal about Horses, as part of their training in War-Craft. Of course, as I was "The Bastard," I received naught from him but disdain. I was not allowed to join in their Warrior games. However, on numerous occasions, I had hidden out of sight so as to watch these exercises and catch whatever words of knowledge were spoken of them. I did not learn much of the nature of Horses that way – much less how to ride them.

However, years later I had ridden Horse with Ambrosius and Uther, but then only when the need presented itself.

The Night I met with Uther, in the great Valley of the Cymru, so long ago – and "*Saw*" the Bear – when the Voices first had spoken to me of Arthur – I had had to run all the way to the Dumnonian Woods to warn Igraine and Gorlois of Uther's wicked plan. I ran Day and Night for many Days to reach them. I had to, for I did not own a Horse at that Time and Uther was surely not of a mind to give me one. Of course, I was much younger then...

On this occasion there was a great need for a speedy arrival. I thanked Arthur for giving me leave to go to Brennos, gave him a blessing of peace and protection, and was on my way within the hour.

Feverishly I rode – hard as I dared push the Horse, not stopping at all, save for that I must stop for such things as relieving myself, a bite of food, and to sleep a bit each Night. That first Night's rest came earlier than I had hoped. Exhaustion had undone me. Beneath a Rocky overhang, I huddled within the warmth of my mount's blanket.

I Dreamed again...

When I awoke in the morn, so filled was I with my sorrowful Dream, that I could eat nothing. My head ached.

On I rode in dreaded anticipation...

I arrived at Brennos' Cave before Sundown on the fifth Day. All was quiet. There was no grave – nothing was different than ever it had been.

So, were my Dreams not prophetic Dreams? Were they only the Dreams men Dream out of fear, need, or desire?

I rushed into his Cave – my boyhood solace, my foundation and my strength. I hurried to his bed. My Owl Chronos flew to a familiar perch. There was Brennos, lying silently and in Deathlike stillness. Oh, Gods, was I too late? I threw myself to my knees beside him, and said, "Brennos!"

His eyes popped open as though he had never slept at all.

"Gwyddion... Hello my boy! You have surprised me. I have always known in the past when you were coming. What brings you here when you are so busy with Arthur? Is everything alright?"

Startled out of my wits – thinking to have found my dear old friend dead, I said...

"Brennos, you are not ill! But I Dreamed... I Dreamed that you called me! I have been sick with worry the whole way here..."

"My boy, you look terrible! Allow me to prepare an Herb simple for you! Why, you look as if you have seen a ghost!"

"Oh, no – Brennos, I am so happy... you are well!"

"I assure you, Gwyddion, I am well and fit... *and* I am so glad to see you as well! Will we talk now or must you rest first?

"Oh no, I could not sleep now, my relief is overwhelming. And yes, I would have your Herbal drink – if it is not fermented... Thank you."

"Good, good... Now tell me of this daunting Dream."

"In my terror of the Night, I heard you calling me: 'Gwyddion... Gwyddion... Come to me soon, for I am unwell...'"

I paused, for even the memory of it pained me.

"Was that all, my boy?"

"No... I mean yes... I mean... There were two Dreams..."

He sat quietly and thoughtfully, as I related the whole of what I had seen.

"My first Dream was this: You were calling me... but then, instantly I was at your Cave... The Horse – which I did not *yet have* in waking Time, but who was the same Horse that Arthur gave to me upon the very next Day – slid to a stop at the mouth of your Cave. Dust and Rocks flew everywhere. I jumped from the Animal and ran to where I saw a *woman* – but only from her back. She was piling Stones in a great heap upon your grave. Over there..." – I pointed for Brennos – "outside, to the right of your Cave's opening. There, too, were your two old Ravens, Night and Raven. They were fretting above the very top Stones of the heap.

"Then I cried aloud... 'So, I am too late, he has died...'

"Without turning, the woman, who was piling the Stones, said...

'Are you Gwyddion, The Merlin? I have been expecting you...'

'Yes, I am... But who are you?'

"She ignored my query... But quoth, 'The two old Ravens will soon follow Brennos across the veil into the Summerlands. The small one upon my shoulder, Chance, has chosen life... But be comforted, Gwyddion, The Merlin, we are all fated to meet in Death... She awaits us all.'

"All of this transpired without her ever turning her head to let me see her face; then all vanished into black and I awoke with a start, covered in a sweat!

"I tried so hard to get up and come to you immediately, but some greater force than my own will made me fall back into a deep sleep in moments!

"As Arthur had permitted, I left the next morning.

"After racing to get to you the whole of the next Day, too early that evening I was stricken with such fatigue that I had to rest awhile...

"I Dreamed again. The second Dream was this: and so strange it was...

"I was here again and all was as had been before in my first Dream. There she was finishing her piling of Stones upon your grave. But this Time your two old Ravens were high in the Air circling widdershins above your cairn.

"'Who are you?' I said again, 'What is your name?'"

"She spoke it... It was as the sound of bells. Yet, I could not understand what she had said. Or mayhap it was only that I could not hold it in my remembrance?"

"This Time she stopped, turned around, and looked at me."

"She had the most beautiful green eyes I had ever seen, which pierced straight through me. In that instant, Brennos, I was changed – on the inside – how I cannot say – but I was."

"I appraised the way she looked: long graceful neck, high round breasts, straight square shoulders, luxuriously thick, long black hair. Her lips had a sensual fullness. My eyes drifted downward toward her hips, which curved out from her slender waist. I looked upward again. Her angular face had a knowing smile upon it, not quite – but almost – mocking me. I began to look downward once more... I could not resist her allure.

"I knew my behavior to be impudent, but there was no help for it!"

"'What is this?' thought I..."

"Even in my Dreams, never have I noticed a woman in this way."

"I must have been staring at her although I had willed myself not to! She spoke – but at first I just stood there as though stricken dumb. The whole of her beauty had captured the breath from me. 'You are Gwyddion, The Merlin? I have been expecting you...'"

"'Yes... Brennos called me two Nights ago.'"

"'I know,' said she, 'he called me two weeks ago. It was too late for Healing but not for comfort.

"'He has left his Cave and Ravens to me, but to you also has he left a great gift, the value of which is beyond all earthly measure.

"'Come inside Gwyddion, The Merlin... I have prepared a stew for you and there is mead for your drink; or warm honeyed Water if you prefer...'"

"Upon entering your Cave, Brennos, I felt wretchedly woozy, not aligned in normal Time or place. My head was spinning... my vision blurred... and then I saw it! A Dragon! *A Dragon*! Not *quite* in the world of form... but real nonetheless... Then my Dream faded...

"The Dragon, it was right over there Brennos..." I walked over to the spot to show him exactly where – "Really... right here!"

"This is all very interesting and I believe portends things to come. You have seen the future Gwyddion – the unchangeable future."

"Then I have seen your Death."

"The woman of your Dreams was right, my boy – Death awaits us all, but not too soon I think – rest easy."

"When this eventually comes to pass, Brennos, I will grieve the loss of you most sorrowfully."

"Never fear for the Death of my body, Gwyddion, for I will never be lost to you. I will live in your Dreams and in your memories. Besides, all you have to do, my boy, is come and find me... Have I not myself trained you to be a *Walker*? I will meet you in the Otherworlds..."

"Now, tell me all about this Dragon you saw. Was it male or female?"

"How could I know?"

"Trust your instincts, boy – and your feelings! Close your eyes and 'See' it again."

"Yes... Well then... she was female."

"A good start! Now what size and colour was she? And, did she look into your eyes? And, if so, what were her eyes like?"

"I do not remember."

"Yes, you do, Gwyddion – think! Was she winged? If so, how large were they? Did she have fur or down on her skin, or scales? What shape was her head? Did she have bony spikes? Think, boy!"

I sat and closed my eyes, focusing on the sound of my breathing and the Water trickling down the walls of his Cave. I made a hand sign, just as Brennos had taught me to do – I remembered: "Breathe in, and then out." And so I breathed in and out, and in and out, and in and out... and soon I was Entranced. I began to "*See*"... I was *inside* my Dream now – reliving it. I slowed all motion down... Now, understand that when I am in this state I am wholly in the place that I have gone to; in this case back into my Dream. Yet, at the same Time I always know where my fleshly body is, as well; thus I can narrate what I am experiencing to those around me. And so I began to tell Brennos what I was seeing.

"She is perhaps twice the size of a Human; dark golden cream in her colouring, mostly, but with some brown. She does not look directly into my eyes, but I see the colour of hers in a glance... They are gold... with vertically shaped pupils, which are very dark, but not truly black. More than this I cannot see."

"Yes you can! Try my boy."

I breathed some more and soon my Vision cleared...

"The Dragon, she has a beautiful face, somehow. I have never thought of a Dragon as being beautiful before – but she is! She is mesmerizing. The glow of the life energy around her is larger than that of Humans or other beings of flesh; but I see now she is *not* here in flesh and bone – not quite solid – more made of the stuff of Visions, Mists, Spirits, and Gods."

"A Spirit, a God... as you wish... But *what* does she *look* like?" asked Brennos.

"Well, there is one bony nub on the top of her head – half a hand's length high. It is covered in skin and fur, very soft short fur – in fact most of her body is thusly covered. So soft looking... I am being drawn to touch her... seduced by my own desire to feel her. She has seven spikes running down the length of her neck. They seem like bone. Her head is somewhat square with a long and graceful snout. She has wings, held close to her breast now, so that I can neither tell what size nor shape they are. She has four muscular legs with great feet – five toes on each one; four in front and one on their insides – with heavy curved claws.

But wait, my focus is changing... shifting... I cannot hold this Vision... It is lost. All I see – all I care about are the black haired woman's green eyes. They that taunt me... Her eyes... It is only they which draw me in... draw me in... I am enthralled... Lost... I am lost... I only want to live in her eyes... Her eyes... Her eyes..."

He shouted, "*Gwyddion*! Gwyddion! Come back! Awaken!"

Brennos was shaking me – but to no avail. I had fallen downward – into the Sea of her eyes...

Finally he pulled me back to this world.

"If it is the future that I have seen, then she is there, too!"

With nothing more to say, we sat for a while in silence.

When I had recovered, I asked...

"But Brennos, truly... *Dragons*???"

"Yes, Gwyddion, Dragons *are* real; God-like Creatures of the Spirit Realms, they are. Great guides, teachers, companions, and protectors are they. Somewhat like the Creatures the Christians call 'Angels.' But... not always are their lessons easy."

"Tell me..."

"Well for one thing, they are more intelligent than Humans, still they are fascinated by us. And although they communicate in thoughts similar to Human thinking, they are *not Human* – they are Dragon. And it is very, very wise always to remember the difference.

"Dragons are literal beings and great caution must be taken when requesting their help in some matter. For, if they choose to grant your spoken desire, only do they take care that the outcome accomplishes your wish – and only that the final outcome be in your ultimate best interests. Now, this may sound like a fine idea – but think – in the event that they do your bidding, they will arrange that all circumstances in your life fall in such a way as to lead you down the straightest path to your desire – giving little or no concern to the consequences.

"Oh bother, my boy! I am not expressing myself clearly... Here, let me give you a true example, which befell one of my old friends:

"Now as it was, this man had a nagging and unreasonable wife, who from Time to Time threatened to leave him to go back to her family – although he tried in every way to keep her happy. This made my friend very sad and he lived in fear and misery all of the Time. For he did, in fact, so very much Love his wife, regardless of her ill treatment of him.

"So, after much thought and consternation, he made up a song of great sadness, for to sing in the Woods or on the Hilltops – anywhere that he might be alone – calling out to an old Dragon with his mournful plea to return joyfulness to their lives. He, not really believing in Dragons, thought that his singing at the top of his voice would, of itself, relieve his sadness.

"'For after all' – he told me – 'I knew that, at the least, I had Mother Nature to sing to of my plight... I knew that *She* would listen and bring some comfort to my aching heart.'

"Well, Gwyddion, that is not how things worked out at all. For in his song, he was calling out to Dragons and *they* heard his anguished plea. So, they granted his request.

"Within three months from the first singing of his song, his cruel wife found another man, whom she fancied – and joyfully left with him, never to return.

"Oh, how he wailed and moaned at first – thinking never to recover from her loss. When he told me of it, he said, 'This is the worst thing that could ever happen to me in my whole life. Should I live to be old, I surely will never heal from this hurt!'

"But in a much shorter Time than he, or I, could ever have imagined, he too found a woman he fancied, and they fell in Love.

"I knew this man for thirty more years and he and his 'new fancy' were still joyful in Love – and they treated each other with all tenderness and respect.

"There is a lesson to learn from this. Dragons – although they do Love – do not *fear* the pain of loss as do Humans.

"If what is best for us would cost the loss of a wife or a house or our Animals, fields or crops, then we would walk a winding path around these perceived obstacles, avoiding the *pain of loss*... But it is not so with Dragons! They clear a *straight path* between us and what we need or want.

"So... the moral of this story is: Never ask a Dragon for something if you are not willing to pay the cost... For, as I have taught you from the beginning, 'everything has a cost.' Never forget this, Gwyddion! And, be careful if ever you entreat a Dragon!"

Confounded by these new revelations, I blurted out – "But I have ever thought of Dragons as imaginary fabrications of superstitious and delusionary fools."

Brennos replied, "I believe that the tales told of Dragon sightings, wherein they are perceived as flesh and bone in this world of form – walking through the countryside or flying above the Mountainous ranges – are misunderstandings by people who, perhaps someday in this life or perhaps in their next life, will be *Dragon called*, but are not yet ready for that communication... I believe they are granted 'glimpses' of that future relationship.

"Have you *never* seen a Dragon before, Gwyddion?"

"Never... Well, only in my Dream...

"Brennos, why did you never tell me or teach me of their existence?"

"Because you never asked...

"You see Gwyddion, the brother and sisterhood of Dragon Callers is a silent tradition. Only those who are *called* may speak of it – and then only to others who have been 'called.' You probably know several, perhaps many, people who are Dragon called, or Dragon Callers – Bedwyr, for one."

"Bedwyr? Yet, I never knew!"

"We Dragon Callers seem to feel each other – or each other's Dragons. I call the one in your Dream, Brandon – which means 'From the Dark Valley'."

Trying still to digest this knowledge, I responded, "Then Dragons are *truly* real?

"Bedwyr!? My student – no less dear to me than a son – with whom I thought was held no secret; yet I never knew!

"Brennos... I can read his faithful heart in all other things! I shake my head in wonder, for I am called a great Seer and yet sometimes I cannot *see* a truth that is right in front of my eyes.

"But you said, 'Dragon called' or 'Dragon Caller'? What is the difference?"

"Ahh, now you have reached the boundaries of what must remain silent. Only if we learn these things from Dragons themselves may we speak of them."

"But, you were giving to the woman with green eyes your Cave, your home. Then she must be a Dragon Caller, too?"

"That might be so. To give her my home... then yes, she must be a Dragon Caller and perhaps much more. In that case I might bequeath my Cave and what material possessions I have to her, but more importantly, the care of my Dragon, Brandon, and my Ravens three."

"I see.

"But her name, Brennos? I can almost hear it. I have been crazy with fear for you and yet, it is her name that haunts me. Her name... So sweet, it is... Elusive like the song of a bubbling Brook, almost here now, then gone – it changes. Gone from my memory... Like a Faun; so gentle, a beguiling little thing, yet always just beyond reach..."

"You must rest now, Gwyddion. Sleep well."

The last thing I remembered was his Humming an old tune. Then into the land of peaceful sleep went I...

Chapter 15
Riddle of the Ages

Gwyddion

After a good Night's rest I felt more my old self again.

The next morning, whilst sharing a cup of honeyed milk with Brennos, he said that he had barely slept the Night before for thinking of what I had said about not seeing a *truth* that is right before my eyes.

"Gwyddion, if you truly believe that you have this weakness, there is something that can help you see the truth in all things. For, as King Arthur's counselor, we both know that you must *always* be able to discern truth from lie. The safety of these Fair Isles is at risk if you cannot!

"This *something* of which I speak, you must yourself find. On your way back to Arthur, seek a broad but shallow Creek, whose Waters are swiftly rushing. Look there in the Water for a Stone with a hole in it."

He held a Stone in the palm of his open hand.

"A Stone of the Twyla y Tag – A Faery Stone?" asked I.

"Yes... Yes, some call them that, some call them Goddess Stones – whichever... I call them *Truth Stones*.

"But listen, you must choose one pulled from the Water by your own hand.

"This Stone would best have the insinuation of a face upon it, with the hole forming its mouth.

"Now, there is but one real test to determine whether you have found the right Stone – and this is of the utmost importance. It is regarding the thin boundary of life force, which emanates from the entire surface of every living thing in and on this Earth. Of course, you know of what I speak... You will recognize your Stone by the extraordinarily strong ring of life energy encircling the interior of its hole. Only so will it serve your purpose.

"Hold it up to the light... Now look – not through it, but – at the surface of the hole as if it were a bronze mirror. You must see that the ring of its life force is much wider than all other Stones you may find. Take your Time – look until you find the perfect one. Only then can it serve you well in this manner.

"Then, of course, as you know, you must entreat the Spirit of the Stone to serve as your Truth Seer.

"Once the finding of it has been accomplished, you must wear it always – hanging from a braided twine cord, fastened with seven Magic Knots, and hung around your neck.

"But know *this truth*, Gwyddion – when one as wise as you cannot see the lie in something or *someone*, the cause of it can only be that your own *desire* has placed a veil before your eyes. This conundrum can happen to any of us. We refuse to believe the true nature of someone because we do not wish to. We have allowed ourselves to be *Charmed* by this one beyond our own reason. Do you see what I mean?"

"Yes, I do. Thank you, Brennos...

"I saw such a Creek on my way here. I will stay at that Creek until I have found my 'Stone of Truth,' just as you have charged me to. Once found, I will wear it always.

"Brennos, it has been wonderful finding you alive and well. I am more grateful than I can express. How I would Love to stay longer here with you, but as you said, Arthur needs me. I should be leaving soon."

He leaned back in the chair that he had fashioned for himself of Wood, straw, and pelts. There he stayed with eyes closed and head bent forward – the weight of it seemingly being held up only by his ancient, arched hands – fingertips pressed together – for ever so long. In this pensive position, I would have thought him fast asleep, but for the ever so gentle, rhythmic tapping of his forefingers against his bottom lip. I waited...

"I was just remembering a Day, long ago Gwyddion, when you came rushing into my Cave with your right hand held up – fingers splayed before your face – utterly astounded and fascinated. You blurted out to me: 'Brennos... I... I can see it! The line of clearness – that is all around the outside of my skin – brighter and clearer is it than everything else I see in the whole world! And... and... just beyond that 'clearer than clear' line, is a wavering, white edged line of cloudiness! Oh, I mean, although it is slim, it is thicker by twice, or sometimes even by thrice, or *more*, than the clear space. Farther out, beyond where the changeable white cloudy edge fades from my sight, I see no more. I can only *feel* – or perceive – the rings of colours, which, as you have told me, many Wise Ones see. But this... these life force lines I can *see* with my eyes!'

"Yes, your every word was seared into my memory... Maybe it was for this very reason that I had spent twenty years learning to memorize...

"Do you remember that Day, Gwyddion? Should I say, that month?

For, I think your eyes beheld nothing else around you during that Time, save your *clearer than clear*."

"Of course I do, Brennos... I remember everything of those years.

"Just now I am thinking of the Day upon which you taught me of the 'Grym Hudol' – of Magical power.

"How I had wanted to believe in Magic, but in my Grandfather's house, even the word *Magic* was forbidden to be spoken. You were the spark that ignited my curiosity, my intellect, and my hunger to learn. You were the one who *believed* in the 'Grym Hudol.' You were the one who believed in *me*. No one could ever have had a better teacher than you, or a better friend. No... much more than a teacher, you were like the Father I never had."

"I wonder Gwyddion, was I the teacher or the apprentice? Yes, I was a Druid; having studied for the full twenty years... I had the most renowned teachers known to be about. Wise and venerable were they. Still, in my old age I deeply respect them and am very grateful for all I learned from them. But you, my boy, shine with an un-earthly brilliance, which has confounded me since first we met.

"As an example – and perhaps the greatest one – I believe you were only ten years upon the Day in which *the Voices of the Stars* spoke their 'Great Riddle' into your thoughts. It was all those years ago, yet I remember every breath of it as though it had been today.

"I will never forget your telling of the *Great Riddle*. The Riddle of the Ages...

"You said, 'One afternoon whilst sitting beneath the boughs of my favourite Oak, heavy with its Summer greens, *Voices* entered my thoughts – the One, yet the Many, all speaking in perfect unison; interrupting what thoughts I had been thinking – busily intent upon another subject – with a RIDDLE... the most confounding Riddle in all the Worlds...

"'As if They were beginning in the *middle* of something... The Voices said, '*BUT*... WHAT WOULD THERE BE IF THERE WERE NOTHING?'

"'I beg your pardon?' – was your response."

"Yes, Brennos," I laughed. "There was naught but silence... No answer... only the question... Truly, I expected nothing more... or less... You know, I did indeed take that quite literally. I knew they meant NOTHING – *NOTHING anywhere*!

"I laugh now to think back on how it was with me during those first few Months; of my almost complete absorption in trying to deduce the answer. Night and Day it haunted me... I even remember stumbling over boulders and walking right into Trees – so obsessed was I with The Riddle... 'IF THERE WERE NOTHING?'

"I also instinctively knew that, once blessed with the challenge – a chance to solve such an enormous Mystery, the chance would not be offered twice. I knew that I must remember every word of what They had said. I must hold on to it... keep it in my thoughts... lest it blow away into the Sands of Time, forever irretrievable. I knew that I must clutch it fast to my heart, never allowing it to flee from me.

"At first I began the whole method of deciphering in the wrong direction... I began to go backward... As in: there would be no Forests, no Streams, no Animals, no People, no Spirits, no Ancestors, no Earth, no Sun, no indigo Starry Sky, no Gods... No Universe at all! But how could this be? If everything were to be gone, all that would be left would be empty space! But then again – NO! A void – empty space – could not be counted as *space*, lest it fill something – lest it have boundaries to lie within! And boundaries are *something*...

"Always I absolutely knew that it was a *true* Riddle, not a trick. There *was* an answer! A *REAL* answer! Not just a philosophical one, but a truly *scientific* answer. And, I knew that they meant for me to find the answer, even if it be my whole life's work... Strangely, I always knew that I would."

"Yes, yes, I, too, always believed that you would somehow solve *The Riddle* one Day."

"Then illumination... or at least recognition... came upon me.

"'Just wait here a moment...' I had commanded my thoughts: 'The RIDDLE did *not* ask; what would *NOT BE* if there were nothing... But, 'What *WOULD there be*, if there were nothing?'

"Yes, I was tormented by it... Each Day I would ponder it, to no avail...

"I, of course, had told no one else of it – only you, Brennos – lest they believe me daft!

"Then my whole life changed and changed and changed again... My studies with you, then my years with Vortigern, then Uther and Ambrosius, then the boys and so forth and so on... Still, at least once or twice in each half of a Moon's Dance, I pondered the seemingly unsolvable Riddle... I never found the answer... no matter how hard I sought it.

"But in the end, so many years later, The ANSWER to that which I had fretted over for all of that Time – the answer to the Great Riddle was *given* to me in the flash of a moment... All it took was two words...

"*THEY* need not – nor have they ever – put all the rest into words! For there it was – the answer to all and everything! When the two words were spoken, I knew instantly what they meant. No preamble was necessary. No; 'Gwyddion, remember US? Here is the answer...' No repetition of the question...

"Well, you know the rest, Brennos... For, again, I could not wait to tell you – which I did upon our last meeting..."

"Yes, Gwyddion... You know I was just thinking as you were recounting this to me, that it is akin to a device of memorization taught in the Druidical Tradition. It is a tricksy twist of rhyme recounting the theological gulf between the old religions and the new; regarding the question of *eminence* or *immanence*. Is GOD a pre-*eminent* and *separate* Being, '*out* there' somewhere in the vast Universe – a GOD who '*rules*' Nature? Or is GOD an *immanent* Being who's Presence '*is*' Nature – the ONE, the ALL?

"It goes like this: The Hebrews and the Christian Fathers say that
The name of GOD is
'I AM.' also...
'*He causes to be.*'
We say: SHE/He... Causes to be...
THEY *Are*...   THE ALL...
Therefore are we...
Therefore we *Are*...
Therefore *I AM*...
It is all in the name of GOD...
The Making, the Breaking...
Creation, Destruction...
Expansion, Contraction...
It is All is in the name of GOD...
'ALL' *is* the name of GOD..."

With this having been said, we resumed our companionable silence for a while, during which I reflected on how it came about that *the answer* to the Riddle was given to me.

Not so very many years ago, I was alone save for Chronos, reading one of my precious books. This reading had nothing at all to do with the subject of the Riddle, when, in the middle of a sentence – out of nowhere – the "Voices of the Stars" whispered the ANSWER into my ears – two words!

"INFINITE POTENTIAL..."

I felt the blood drain from my face...   I called out, "*I have it!*" ...although no one was there to hear me, save for Chronos...

His feathers ruffled...

But the moment I tried to speak them, the words tried to flee my memory...

"*No! No!*" I cried, "*stay with me – I must remember!*"

Then, blessing of all blessings and wonder of all wonders, the words came searing back into my thoughts. "INFINITE POTENTIAL..." Two words: And I understood... everything!

Immediately upon my great epiphany, I closed my eyes. When I did, just off to the right of my face was a hand, seen, then unseen, unfurling the pages of a great book, at a humanly impossible speed... No, not *a* book – *THE GREAT BOOK*! Pages were whirling by, in seemingly never-ending succession – each holding concepts of Cosmic Truths... of EVERYTHING! And all of it was being implanted deep within my consciousness somehow!

When I came back to myself I knew that I had been given the answer to the RIDDLE – 'WHAT WOULD THERE BE IF THERE WERE NOTHING?' – INFINITE POTENTIAL, the what and how of it ALL!

Oh, it is not as though I have ever, since that Day, expected to be able to retrieve *all* of this great knowledge at my own will or in my own wanted Time, but there, within me, it lies, awaiting "remembering." Piece by piece, as in a puzzle, understandings come, not as words, but just as quiet knowings. And these I hold as absolute truths!

Remembering that first moment of my epiphany is the easiest thing I could ever do – so concretely in my thoughts it is! But, explaining its meaning to others... now that is a different story – although, I have indeed tried to, for it is a Sacred trust and a knowledge given to me, which I must share.

So... here is what I "knew" from the moment "They" first whispered the words to me and the *Great Book's* pages sped before my closed eyes...

The Great Initiator's Diagram...

At the First Time, In the Beginning, at the Cosmogenesis, from out of the *Infinite Potentials* that SHE holds – or is, and with a *great vibration* – which diverse Myths call the *'Word,' 'Sound,'* or Rumble – SHE *caused to be* an infinitesimally small spark. Within that spark was held the seed – the *pattern*, the mathematical equation, the Architect's design, the diagram – of the Universe, of everything that *would* come to be. But not everything that *could be*... From the moment of that first vibration – and onward – as the Cosmos expands outwardly, from the center, which is HER, it grows and multiplies according to HER sequence. However, it must always and only *stay within the boundaries of the finite building blocks, potentials and laws* of HER pattern for this particular incarnation of the Universe. Beyond these boundaries, nothing in this Creation can ever expand... All things had then, and have now, *great* – but *finite* – potential.

Oh, the brilliance! – It is far beyond the frail reasoning of Man or Angels – that SHE could put all eventualities within that first *seed*... But just so is a Universe born!

Think of it this way:

As everyone knows, any plan has a beginning point and a completion – an ending.

If you or I were to make a plan to build and furnish a house – taking all of the Time we needed to decide upon everything we wanted of, and in, that house, we would first make a list of our desires, then a plan, and a drawing. Next we would accumulate all tools, supplies, building materials, and furnishings that were needed. Then we would proceed to build and furnish it according to our plan.

But when the last bit of wattle and daub were set or the last of the rushes were strewn upon the floor, and the last bit of food filled the cupboards – or whichever was the very last thing to be done to complete our plan – having accomplished our goal, all of our work would be done, for there would be nothing more left to do but to enjoy our house.

The thing is that the Earth would remain beneath our house, the Rain and Sunshine would still come to grow our crops, the Wind would still hit our shutters, and our Wood Fires would still keep the chill from our bones... This is all because the GODDESS would still provide for us, because the world – and Her Cosmic Creation – will not have come to a completion, just because we have built our house!

However, when HER 'Great Plan' for *this Time* is successfully completed – and by this I mean that all Creation will have achieved its perfection – all outward expansion will have reached the boundaries of HER diagram. Then, with nothing further to do, nowhere else to go and no further design, motion or energy to support its existence – *this* Universe will come to an end.   ALL things, concepts, design, mathematics, powers, and laws in this Creation will return to HER. Even the existence and form of the Gods and Spirits must return to HER, for They are, as well, a part of her diagram for *this Time*. This then, will be the *Penultimate Contraction*, the perfect, necessary, complimentary polarity of Expansion.

SHE *is* that which exists, *before, beyond, between and after, all* epoch cycles of Cosmic Creation. SHE holds within HERSELF Infinite Potential – all possibilities, Universal laws, concepts, Elements, and powers – from which all things in *form, Spirit, and energy*, come into being.

SHE is "*what there will be, when there is nothing.*" SHE *is* "Infinite Potential!" SHE is Chaos – the swirling, enduring, fathomless Sea of potentials – without form. SHE is The Great Initiator... a pure Consciousness of profoundly brilliant intelligence.

Cosmos, on the other hand *is form and motion* – the active, created Universe – the Male polarity. So, Chaos and Cosmos, Female and Male, Darkness and Light, Contraction and Expansion, are the Breathing in and the Breathing out of all existance. All are compatible polarities – and necessary for life to continue. One Creator, but many expressions – all beautiful and perfect. How could we and everything we see and perceive *not* be perfect? We all are expressions in form – and Spirit – of the Great One's desire.

The Sacrificed God...

In the same way goes the Mythic round of the young God....

There is a Sacred Secret in this... For in all of the known world's Myths, the sacrificed God... the Grain God – the Son of the Great Mother Goddess – is born and then grows to the full bloom and perfection of his manhood, only to be cut down as the Corn of the fields at Harvest... his seed resting in the womb of the Earth until She awakens at the budding of Summer, when He will grow once more to the fullness of life. As does the Grain, so does the God. Just so, will be the pattern and the fate of this Universe, as well as all others to come...

When He is likened to the Sun, He is born in the depths of the Longest Night – a babe – to grow to his full brilliance and strength at the pinnacle of Mid-Summer – the Longest Day. Then he is vanquished by his Brother/Other Self, his Divine Twin – God of the diminishing Light, to rest in the arms of his Mother/Lover – She who births him once again as the Child of Promise, at the next Longest Night.

It is my belief that all cyclic Rituals based upon these myths are the means by which all Humans beseech, appease or co-create with the Gods; in Sacred places and in ecstatic states of being, to the end that the continuance of the Wheel or cycles of life will go on.

Somehow this pattern must resonate deeply within all Humans. We must all feel this instinctually.

There is a great comfort in these thoughts to me: That all the worlds we know and beyond are of an order, a suitability, and although it seems right to me to call the Great Initiator "Mother" and "She," I realise, of course, that Infinite Potential means the holding all possibilities – and that in reality, this must be Mother and Father, female *and* male, all and neither. How else could it be?

What boundaries of potentials SHE places upon the *next* incarnation of the Cosmos – when the next Word is spoken, when the next Sound vibrates, what is held within that seed, that spark – are entirely her prerogative. SHE may wish to make it all completely different from that which has been this Time. Perhaps nothing will be the same – or would even be recognizable to us.

As to the *method* of the dissolution of all in existence... who under the Sun could know? Will a second Vibration sound, to, in an instant, collapse all inward – back to the Origin? Or might everything just fade as though it never was at all?

How will it all end and how begin again? The explanation of this is absolutely unknowable... Except by HER – SHE who is the INFINITE POTENTIAL.

I have heard that the Greek and Babylonian astronomers and mathematicians have hypothesized that all things begin and end in nothing, yet they have no numerical symbol for nothingness... Funny that... Perhaps someday, this Mystery, too, will be revealed."

Blissful silence – all but for the flickering of the flame in the lamp, the sound of our breathing and the trickling of Water somewhere in the back of the Cave.

His eyes opened, and as Brennos so often did of late – without skipping a heartbeat, he resumed our former conversation, returning to the topic left behind... sometimes repeating himself.

"Well then... Remember that the hole in the Stone you seek will have that life force emanating from it. It must be very pronounced, my boy. Remember, too, to look, not *through* the hole, but *at* the hole's surface. If the ring of its life force is indeed very strong, then you have found your Stone of Truth.

"Oh... have I repeated myself again? Well, no matter... Use it in good Magic, my boy."

We embraced.

"Farewell my boy, it is always good to see you..."

"*See* you," he had said. I wondered, by then, what, if anything, he could still see. If he was totally blind, no one could tell it. And "boy"... He still called me boy, although I was past my fortieth year-turn.

There is one further observation I must quill to page, and that is that, although I did not know it yet, I would never again think of 'The Dragon' as being merely the central spiritual force of Earthly Creation – as I had believed and was held in Druidical thought. Perhaps some of the Druids that I have known know much more than they will tell to those who are not Dragon called.

Funny that – I just wrote *merely*, as if the whole of Creation were no more than a thought in the Psyche of the Great One. Well, then again, perhaps it is.

Or could it be that all things written in these pages of our histories have been woven into the Weavers' Web long ago, to be thought, said and written now, without volition, to reappear somewhere in the distant future? I wonder...

I wonder, too, if my speculations will lead me off a precipice someday – into a "Dark Valley" of oblivion. I laugh at myself. But I have come to know that Dragons are Dragons, and of this I can say no more.

Chapter 16
Bedwyr and Gwenyfar

Bedwyr

Preparations for the royal wedding were amazingly complicated. Everything was a Beehive of activity. Fulfilling all the protocols, such as who would sit where and who would do what... Thank the Gods that I was not expected to be a part of those decisions.

At the first, Princess Rowena wanted to pay for the whole wedding and feast, including all of the week-long festivities, games, and entertainments.

"I *am* Gwenyfar's older sister." quoth she...

But her fortress, which had been designed by Gwyddion for Vortigern, was thought of as a bleak, albeit marvelous, military tower built for defense and war, not suitable for such a large and gay affair.

Hengist himself wrote, "She is my daughter; I should host the wedding feast in my long hall."

But of course, the rest of the Chieftains, Queens and Kings, who voiced their opinion of this, would have none of it. The collective thought, as put to Arthur by Maelgwn, one of the Kings of Gwynedd was, "Peradventure, going into the thick of potentially hostile Saxon territory would be dangerous. So, no – an emphatic no!"

This having been stated, with a majority of those present nodding their heads in agreement, Arthur opened the floor for other offers to host the event. There were none forthcoming, as the cost of hosting a royal wedding was enormous.

In the end, it was decided that the wedding festivities would be held at Lady Igraine's fortress.

Arthur sent a large chest of gold and silver, as a token of his thanksgiving, to his prospective Father in law, Hengist, for his gracious offer – hoping to placate any offense the decline may cause. Along with the gift, Arthur explained that his Lady Mother, Igraine, so very much wished to have the affair at her beautiful fortress on the rocky coast of Dumnonia.

"What is more," wrote he, "although Dumnonia is not evenly convenient to all, the great old Roman Road, the Ermine Way, runs from Northeast to Southwest, connects with many other good roads and runs in close proximity to Lady Igraine's fortress. This will make travel to Dumnonia easier, safer, and much more comfortable for most who wish to attend. Besides which, Lady Igraine holds one of the largest and most beautiful of the great halls of the Britons – more than large enough for a royal wedding."

Arthur also pointed out that Igraine could provide sleeping arrangements for two hundred people *inside* her fortress.

This assurance – and Arthur's treasure – had made sense to Hengist. It also meant, of course, that the extreme cost of the whole affair would fall upon Igraine and Arthur – not upon Hengist – and so he agreed. The matter was settled.

Arthur had arranged for a heavy Royal Guard to escort Princess Gwenyfar and her company whilst travelling from Gwynedd, where she was with Princess Rowena.

Everything was in place for Gwyddion to have the honour of leading the troop there and back to our family fortress in Dumnonia. It was agreed that Princess Rowena would then follow, in good Time, for the required three Day isolation of the bride and her attendants.

However, upon the Night before their leaving – The Merlin had a *Great* Dream.

His teacher, Brennos, was calling to him. He had seen him upon his Deathbed. The next morning he told Arthur that he must go to Brennos immediately. Arthur bade him safe travels and said that *I* should go in his stead to collect Gwenyfar and her retinue.

Of Gwenyfar...

I suppose I had fallen in Love with Gwenyfar the first moment I saw her – walking as she was through the midst of the parted company – that great and raucous crowd – to present Hengist's golden chalice to Arthur. Trembling and pale was she, a little timid, perhaps... but brave... so brave. She was the most beautiful girl I had ever beheld. Never – even in my Dreams had I imagined one so beautiful. I felt protective of her. I wanted to run up to her, clutch her to my chest and shout: "She is not a Ewe to be put up for auction in men's political games."

But I also knew that Arthur must feel the same. We had talked many Times about this sort of thing. Our Mother, Igraine – for she was truly *our* Mother – would *so* disapprove of this.

I remember then that Igraine had been there in the great hall of council that Night, to see Arthur receive the golden chalice. She *and*

Morganna had come. Never could anyone have suspected what evil Morganna had planned for that Night's doings!

However, I do remember noting Morganna's presence... She was leading her vicious Wildcat, Terror, by a silver chain and collar. I remember fearing for Gwyddion's Owl. But then thinking: "How foolish of me, Gwyddion needs no protection from Morganna."

Those were the Days of pure naïveté.

Woe and woe... More is this trouble to my heart... I knew she was Arthur's... Oh, how I need a good Night's sleep!

On the way to Gwynedd, I thought much of Gwenyfar – delicate, sweet, perhaps fragile – Gwenyfar. Would she be afraid to live amoung people with such different ways? Would she miss the Holy Places and colourful Rites of her Saxon Goddesses and Gods? I must speak with Arthur of allowing a Scald or Priestess of her religion to come to stay with her. Surely Arthur would not mind. The Merlin had taught us that "all the Gods are one," so why not?

Arthur had made arrangements to allow Gwenyfar to bring whichever of her ladies and Animals she Loved the best to come to live with her in Dumnonia, where he had already set up her apartments. I thought surely she would Love this beautiful place where Arthur and I had spent our childhoods. Jutting out over the Western Sea as it does, the sunsets are magnificent as they gild the Water. Even the Storms are thrilling; with thunderous waves crashing the cliffs. Well, they were for me. But I wondered if this would be so for timid little Gwenyfar.

I wondered, too, if she feared Arthur... and the marriage bed. Although I gathered that he would not impose upon her much in that way – only in so much as he must, to bring forth an heir.

I tormented myself...

"Oh the sorrowful games the Weavers play with us. For, if I had truly been Igraine's blood son, Gwenyfar would be mine and Arthur could be with Morgan."

Yes, I knew the depths of my brother's loss regarding Morgan. He could not hide his tragic Love for her from me.

But, if so, I would be King in Arthur's stead. Yet the crux of the matter is that there exists not one man who could be so worthy, so honourable or so great a King as my brother Arthur. I am no King – nor would I wish to be. All I can do is to stand at his side, as his most loyal, faithful, and beloved friend – brothers of the heart, are we. This I *will* do at *any* cost. No, never could I betray him. I would rather slit my own throat and bleed out my life's blood, than ever to see a loss of trust in my brother's eyes toward me.

"Everything has a cost." This, The Merlin taught to me, early in my life.

Of the Fortress That The Merlin Built...

We, the guards, travelled with great haste toward Gwynedd, as soldiers always do. We arrived at Princess Rowena's fortress upon a clear Night and a Full Moon. A chill had fallen.

Stern, powerful, and terrible did look the fortress that The Merlin had built for Vortigern. Impregnable and menacing was it. But of course, that was what The Merlin had intended it to be. Well done, Gwyddion!

Inside the Great Hall was a completely different matter. Although not nearly as large as the one in Dumnonia, it was warm, comfortable, and very inviting. We had been greeted at the gate of the outer courtyard and escorted there by Princess Rowena's guardsmen. We waited... Then without pomp, in strolled Princess Rowena – both beautiful and charming was she. She greeted us and set servants to fetch wine, bread, cheese, and Fruit for our refreshment.

After the protocols of greetings and salutations were observed, we stood gazing around at the Great Hall... Dragons and banners hung from the lower rafters – Stag, Elk, Bear, and Boar's heads lined one wall. Displays of Vortigern's swords, shields, and javelins were prominent on another. Colourful, vivid tapestries – probably imported by Rowena from Byzantium – decorated the wall nearest the permanent feasting trestle. At both ends of the long table were three-legged armed chairs, whose backs and arms were heavily carved in Saxon knotwork with intricately entwined Animals and mythic Creatures – they were stunning! Princess Rowena said, "A gift from my Father's court..."

My eyes then fell upon a most amazing and unique feature: instead of a great round Fire pit in the center of the hall – with a hole in the ceiling far above it to draw much of the heat and most of the smoke upward and out of the hall – there, on opposite walls, were TWO Fires that roared – each in a stonework box against the wall, with a tall column-like feature traversing the distance from it all the way through the ceiling. Each had a square, open front, which was as wide as two men were tall and as deep as could hold the largest of cauldrons, and then some. Like a small chamber, they were. Each held beautifully wrought iron "FireDogs," with great flaming oaken logs lying upon them. Nearly the height of a tall man were the frontal openings! The stonework encasing the Fire chambers narrowed at their tops to form the square columns, which were hollow, so as to convey the smoke within their confines. The smoke was then drawn all the way upward and through the roof of the hall! Amazing! The heat remained in the entire hall, yet, did very little smoke. Wonder of wonders, Gwyddion! How ever do you think of these things?

"Amazing, is it not? said Princess Rowena. "And, if you were to climb the stairwell to the next level, you would see another like them in the master sleeping chamber – aah, the warmth on cold Winter Nights..."

Then, we were led to a large opening in the Western wall, and shown a spectacle that was hard for my thoughts to accept. This was as though a window in a cottage, but SO much larger! Sealing the opening was a substance that looked as if it were of great, flat clear Crystal. But, as tall and wide as it was, it seemed no thicker than vellum. I mean that one could see straight through it to view the Mountainside dropping away to reveal the distant Sea.

"Beautiful is it not?" – asked Princess Rowena.

"We are on a high enough Hill, and have a tall enough tower to see the Ocean from here." It was then that I looked around and noted how much light there was in the hall – surely it was not all from this crystalline opening... I said, "The light? ..."

"Oh, yes – another innovation of Gwyddion's. There are polished brass mirrors strategically placed in order to reflect and spread the light coming in through the window.

"Quite a splendid idea, yes?" said Princess Rowena.

"Absolutely! I have never seen nor heard of wonders such as these."

"Oh – did he not tell you? Such is the brilliance of Gwyddion, The Merlin – for he designed and built this fortress for Vortigern while he was yet a boy.

"But, my Lady, I notice that even here – far away from the Fire chambers – the hall is almost as warm as near to them... How can this be?"

"Well, when Gwyddion was drawing the plans for this fortress he remembered something that his Master Brennos had told him... that the Romans had built – in Aquae Sulis, amoung other places – what is called a hypocaust, a means of heating the floors of the great hall by using a Fire pit in a small building just outside of the hall and then forcing the hot Air through lead pipes running beneath the floors, thereby heating them. Here – feel the floor... you see... it is warm."

"I do see.   Tell me – what other fantastic contrivances did he incorporate into his building?"

"Well..." Her cheeks turning the faintest shade of pink, she continued, "The privy – beyond the stairwell – has Water running beneath it, to sweep away the... err... you can imagine what a help this is. This Water is carried in a small aqueduct which runs beyond the Hill's edge and flows down to the Grain fields beyond the pool of the Cows' and our drinking Water. Of course, it is propelled thusly by the pressure of the Waterfall running off the top of yonder Hill. I will also show you how the fall is split in two so that what is not piped into the aqueduct may continue to flow to the pool.

"Look over here, too..."

"Why, it is a small Well... inside..."

"Yes. In the heat of high Summer its cold Water refreshes and puts a constant source of fresh drinking Water to hand. In Winter it adds a bit of moisture to the Air and is quite a convenience when it is cold enough outside to freeze the other Springs and to make the downhill climb to the pool perilous. It is the source from which we keep our cauldron boiling. Vortigern told me that Gwyddion had said that its Water was cleaner and more healthful to drink than that which is in the pool."

"I see..."

"Come and sit down by the Fire, all of you, and rest from your travels. Let us eat and make merry."

Just then, two Wolfs ran up to Princess Rowena, danced with her, then fell into her arms as she sat, giving her many kisses, as Hounds will do.

"Have no fear of my companions," said she... "Only, do not walk within an arm's length of me. They are good and kind beasts, but very protective. Other than this, they are amenable and will even play with you."

They were magnificent Creatures, finely groomed and pampered, yet wild and free – so like Rowena herself. Such perfect compliments to her, were they.

"Princess Rowena," said I...

"Oh please, my dear boy, simply call me Rowena whilst in companionable conversation. Save the formalities for functions of state..."

At her words, I completely forgot what I was about to ask... But answered, "As you wish, my Lady."

She smiled...

We, weary travelers all, greatly appreciated Princess Rowena's warm hospitality. We ate and drank, then bathed in the heated Roman-style bathhouse – another of The Merlin's fabrications. Then came a much-needed slumber. As was the usual custom, all guests slept along the walls of the great hall.

Everyone, it seemed, had slept well and long through the Night, except for me – fretful was I with anticipation of seeing Gwenyfar in the morning – and cursing myself for my desire. I thought it never to happen, but sleep finally came.

I was awakened by a bustle of clamorous activity in the great hall, by the noises of seven tables and benches being readied for the breaking of our fast – and by the exotic aromas of foods, the like of which we were unaccustomed to being served. Thick Saxon-style round loaves of bread had been baked in Stone ovens and would be served with cheese, honey, butter, and ale. These loaves were not at all like the hard, flat breads we Britons ate. All of the Teutonic peoples were known to be great feasters.

I ran my fingers through my hair, wiped the sleep from my eyes, splashed Water to my face from the jug offered to me, bit my lower lip, and waited.

Vortigern, cousin of Ambrosius Aurelius and of the one later called the Pen Dragon, had married Hengist's daughter, Princess Rowena, not long before his Death. He left her with child. Their daughter, who was one half of his blood and one half pure Saxon, was about my age, or perhaps four years older by this Time, yet still unmarried... She was a beautiful woman with golden hair, light glowing golden skin, and bright blue eyes. She was clever, too – well-spoken and poised – very like her Mother. Her name was Ribrowst Ardora.

Rowena presented her daughter to us first... "May I introduce Ribrowst, my beloved daughter and sole heir," said Rowena, with just a touch of challenge in her voice.

"It will be very hard," thought I, "for any man who craves Rowena's wealth and thinks to acquire it through a marriage with Ribrowst!"

Princess Rowena, being the astute Politician that she was, awaited the perfect moment for Gwenyfar and her ladies to enter the great hall to be presented.

My breath caught in my chest when she entered our company. Her hair had been meticulously braided and tied with pale blue ribbons. Her gown was a slightly darker colour. It was surprisingly simple. But then, why would she need ornament? Her beauty could not find its match in complement. The only thing she wore as adornment was a small strand of pearls, hanging just at the bottom of her neck.

Gwenyfar had the same effect upon each one of the Royal Guard as she had on every man. Her beauty; her slender, graceful body, the haunted – was it sad? – look in her pale blue eyes, her pale skin, and her shy demeanor – was it all of these things, or was it some other inexplicable Enchantment about her that turned every man's knees to butter?

What is the word to describe Gwenyfar – ethereal, perhaps? Could we see right through her like the Twyla Y Tag – the Faery Folk? Or mayhap, a she-Spider's gossamer web. She seemed barely there. No... but real flesh and blood was she.

Then she spoke...

"I welcome and honour each of you, companions and Guard of Arthur, the King. I thank you for coming to provide a safe and comfortable journey to Dumnonia for me and my ladies."

So it had been a memorized speech...

Was there a question in the words 'my ladies'? Of course! It was my responsibility to tell her that Arthur would welcome *any* of her ladies or pets to Dumnonia. So I stepped toward her and told her so. A look of the greatest relief passed over her visage. She grabbed the hand of the girl standing closest to her, who seemed as thrilled at this news as was Gwenyfar.

The girl's name was Branwen, which means White Raven in the tongue of the Clans. She was a redheaded girl with creamy white skin and golden eyes.

"Good," thought I, "then dear Gwenyfar will not feel all alone."

Procession to Dumnonia...

It was one full Moon's Dance before the wedding, on a beautiful Day in the warmest month of Summer, when the procession of the Royal Guard, Princess Gwenyfar, her ladies, and her Greyhounds – Günter and Greta – left Gwynedd, to travel toward Dumnonia.

The Woods and fields were covered with lush Wildflowers, with each village and cottage garden filled with Herbs and bursting with fragrance and colour, all ready to be harvested.

Princess Rowena had commissioned her Smiths and Craftsmen to make a beautiful canopied wagon for Gwenyfar. It was fitted with great silk pillows and curtains of green, lavender, and golden coloured silk cloths, which Princess Rowena had purchased at great cost for Gwenyfar's comfort, as well as to protect her lovely fair skin. Gwenyfar's wagon was followed by other pretty wagons for her ladies and all of their belongings. These were surrounded by the rear Guard, to insure a safe trip to my Lady Mother's fortress.

I, as Commander of the Guard, and two other of Arthur's Companions led the caravan. I rode beside Gwenyfar...

All things needed had been provided. In our caravan were enough nuts, Fruits, ale, pickled eggs, breads, honey, cheeses and Spring Water to last the trip for the whole company. Only must we hunt for fresh meat. It was said by all that I was the best archer in Briton. Whatever the case, I Loved to hunt and my hunting was rarely in vain. So, there was a good Time had by all the men as well as the ladies.

At her insistence, we left Princess Rowena in Gwynedd to have the final touches added to her sister's wedding gown. Rowena would come later, in Time for the wedding – probably un-attended and riding her own war Stallion to Dumnonia! The thought of her fearless independence made my heart smile... I liked Rowena very much.

We stopped often to rest and while away the Days in pleasant games, hunting, and conversation. This was a very different sort of travel for me, for Warriors always keep a swift pace.

Much too soon for my heart, we saw the towers of my home looming above the Dumnonian Forest.

Arthur and my Lady Mother – for thusly will I always think of Igraine – greeted Princess Gwenyfar and her company.

After all the introductions, I kissed Igraine and excused myself.

I felt it only proper that I bid hello to the woman and man who were my true blood parents.

They lived in a fine house adjacent to Igraine's fortress. I cannot say why it was so awkward to stand face to face with them, but at the first it was. And not only for me, it seemed, but for them as well. This discomfort had probably been caused by the fact that we had not seen each other since we had all learned of Gwyddion's switching of Arthur and me upon the Night of our births. What an entanglement!

You see, while I was a child, Tangwen and Marcus were a great part of my life. They and the Bear lived in Igraine's fortress and were considered of our household. I had known and truly cared for them. Tangwen had always seemed to like and treat me well and goodly. I was their son's – as they had believed the Bear to be – best friend. Markus had taught the Arts of war and of hunting to me. Tangwen, thoughtfully and lovingly, always had something savory simmering in the cauldron or a sweet-scented pastry baking in the ovens for the Bear and I to eat once we had finished our games – for all of which I had been exceedingly grateful. Almost as a son was I treated by them... almost. But in everyone's thoughts in those Days, I was regarded as the young master of Igraine's fortress.

There we stood, each not knowing what to say to the other. But of a sudden, a flood of childhood memories, of the Times we had all shared, washed over me. I suppose they felt the same, for we all smiled at each other in wonder of how oddly twisted life can be. From that Day forward an understanding stood between us. Arthur would always be the son of their hearts – as Igraine would hold me to hers. And all was good.

Gwenyfar and her ladies settled in. She had *insisted* – which of itself seemed odd for her – that Branwen have her own private chamber and that it be very close to Gwenyfar's. Igraine felt this a small indulgence that she was happy to extend to Gwenyfar. The two young girls had grown up together just as had Arthur and I. It was good that they not be separated now. So, Igraine had their chambers changed to the only two in the fortress that opened onto each other by a door. Of course Igraine had first asked Arthur if he minded having his bridal chamber that close to Branwen's. Arthur seemed absent from their conversation and said, "Oh no, Lady Mother, whatever she wishes – I do not care."

The Village...

Knowing of Arthur's trepidation over his upcoming marriage, I thought it would be a splendid diversion for us to ride to the village, which was not far from our home, to drink and wench together. I knew that my loins ached for a woman. As for Arthur... It was high Time for him to live as a man – as well as a King.

It is an irony that on the way from Rowena's fortress in Gwynedd, one of Gwenyfar's companions, a girl named Freidl, was doing everything she could to capture my attention. She was a very pretty, blue-eyed Saxon girl, with full voluptuous breasts and a small waist. The latter was unusual – for she also had very round buttocks. Then there were her glossy golden braids falling almost to her knees. The whole, put together, was quite alluring. But I, as if in a Dream when one knows they are Dreaming yet want never to awaken, felt my body's loyalty was to Gwenyfar.

"Fool!" I had chided myself. I knew she was not mine... nor would she ever be, for she was Arthur's. But I would live out this sweet Dream of pretence while it lasted. So, I had not responded to Freidl.

Now that my feet were back on solid ground and I was with Arthur – I felt well again.

So, that first Night of our being together, I pushed, prodded, and playfully shamed Arthur into riding to the nearby village with me.

It had a very large trading market alongside it – with a drinking hall where you could sup and let a room with a woman for the Night. I had heard of this place when I was a boy and had always longed for the adventure of it.

However, I was only twelve years when The Merlin took us away from our home, so I had never the chance to bed a woman until I was past sixteen years. Since then I have tried to make up the lost Time. Tonight, I expected, would be all the more fun with Arthur there.

We laughed and drank so much that I do not even remember the woman I was with. But Arthur did join in – and a woman did warm his bed that Night, as well.

When I awoke I was alone of course, the room was dank and dingy and smelled like soot, piss, and old sex. I have always been very clean with my body, as clean as was ever possible. I shuddered at what small beasties might have invaded my hair from that filthy bed. I quickly dressed, went outside to the Well and splashed Water on my face. I thought we had better find a Stream to bathe in before we saw Igraine again. I waited for Arthur. I was offered some meat with ale and flat breads, which I gratefully paid for, ate and drank.

Still no Arthur... So I went up the ladder to the two rooms the tavern rented and called out in a loud voice – "Arthur!" I heard something like a wounded Animal... a groan... "Arthur?"

"I am here..."

I pulled back the curtain to find him on the floor with his arms wrapped around – and head resting against – the chamber pot.

I laughed, "You drank yourself sick! I hope you can remember the best parts of last eve's frolic – that is if you could get *your* parts to work!"

"They worked." He smiled.

"Let us go get some ale for you."

"Oh no!... No more ale."

"Oh yes! It will help... I promise you Arthur."

We found that Stream, bragged about our sexual prowess and the world was aright again.

That was to be the first of many years worth of wenching and such frolicking that we did share with each other.

The Wedding...

Arthur had sent out messengers to all the lands of the confederacy, to invite those Chieftains, Kings, Queens, Elders, Dux – and their wives or husbands – to come to the wedding celebration.

In these missives was an alternate invitation: To make plans to meet at Table Rock in Alba, in three Moon Dances, to celebrate with those who were otherwise detained or too far away to attend the wedding and crowning. This was wise of Arthur...

To the Day of my writing these pages, Arthur has kept the knack of keeping his subjects satisfied – in as far as his remembrance of, and respectful words and deeds toward them.

Chapter 17
The Royal Wedding

Arthur

Dumnonia was a bustle of activity. Never in my life have I beheld such an elaborate affair.

Each new party who rode in was more pretentious than the one before. Every woman, man and youth was dressed in costumes of the finest cloth their family's wealth could purchase. Each one of them had brought gifts for Gwenyfar and me. All were vying for my attention and speaking in great flatteries to Igraine and Gwenyfar. Of course, each family in attendance did have hopes of future favours from their King.

Oh, let me not be so cynical. Many true and loyal friends of mine were there, too. And as far as flatteries spoken to Igraine and Gwenyfar, well, none of these were exaggerations, as they both *were* very beautiful.

I greeted everyone, returning their compliments:

"My dear Lady, have you grown younger than when last I saw you? And is this your daughter? What a beauty... Why she looks just like her Mother!"

"Who has sewn your marvelous tunic, my good Sir? I must remember their name when next I am in need of a new wardrobe..."

"Are these your sons? What fine, strong men they will become – Perhaps, one Day, future Commanders – Goddess willing?"

And so on and so forth...

Just as soon as I felt that I had satisfied protocol and good manners, I fled the scene!

My eyes kept searching for Morgan and Lady Vivianne. Two young Hunter Priests had arrived the Day before to assure us of their coming! I wondered what was keeping them.

I went outside to the Sacred Well, drank some of its Waters and splashed some on my face.

"Oh Morgan," I thought. "What a farce this is. Why could not all marriages be as was ours?" Then I caught myself. "But no... GREAT GODDESS, I mean no offence. I know that the Sacred Marriage in the Wildwood was not that of Arthur and Morgan; it was the Stag King and the Great Mother. Regardless, the memory of it – of its beautiful simplicity and true Love's expression – takes my breath away."

I sat for another while longer at the Well... Then I heard their voices, and the jingle of the bells on Morgan's and Lady Vivianne's ankle braces. My heart leapt. My stomach ached. I ran to meet them.

Proud and stately were they. Morgan grew more beautiful every Time my eyes beheld her.

They were guarded by only two older Warrior Priests. Why so few? But then I realised; why need *they* ever fear? Their Magics alone are but all they need for protection! Not to mention their *unseen* Guardians.

By the Time I reached them they had dismounted. I ran up to them and smiled. As protocol demanded I greeted Lady Vivianne first. She bowed her head to me and said, "May the Goddess bless you, my King."

"And may she always hold you in her Love, my Lady."

Then I embraced Morgan.

"Sister..."

What more could be said?

On the Day of the wedding...

All who entered the fortress that Day must come through the main gates, which led them directly past Nodens' Well. As soon as all arrangements had been meticulously overseen, Igraine met and welcomed them there. Many wished for her blessing as Seer of the Well. All who asked were blessed by the Waters of the Spring and I am sure many were Healed of their maladies.

My Lady Mother Igraine had prompted her folk of the Old Dark Tribes to come out of their twisted Forests to pay homage to her son's and their High King's wedding, which they did. Twenty of them came, dressed in all their gold and finery. Igraine had painted the Tribal black dots on her own forehead and cheekbones to honour them. How stunning she looked.

I looked at her in wonder – still so beautiful – she must be near to her fiftieth year-turn by now. Would Morgan be like Igraine in this way too?

A realization made me smile... I knew that Morgan would always be beautiful in my eyes. If I am to live long enough to see her face wrinkled and marred by the ravages of Time – or if her long black hair be streaked white as Snow or silvered like the hair of the Star Goddess in the Heavens, or if her deep eyes be clouded over from the blindness of old age – no matter what changes must be endured, I will always be dazzled by her beautiful, exquisite Spirit.

Oh, Morgan, I am doomed and blessed to suffer this Love in silence.

I waited until Igraine was alone at the Well, then I went to her.

"Lady Mother, can you or your Well Heal me of that which consumes me?"

She looked deeply into my eyes. I lowered them in shame. I felt my face flush.

"It does you no good to try to hide this from me, Arthur. I have seen this Love in you since you were a boy. I had hoped... But never mind that. The Waters of Nodens' Well might give you the strength to live with this burden, but no, they will not *Heal* you of it.

"Here, drink Arthur; know that these Waters, my regard, and yes, my Love for you, my son and King, will be here always. As I can help you, I will. Even after I have passed through the Veil, you will always be able to find me here. As for now, I will do what I can to help you pass through this Day and the next few as easily and with as much comfort as possible. Do you want me to prepare some of the Herbed wine, which is used at the Sacred Marriage – the fertility rights – for your wedding Night?"

"I thank you, but no... I think Gwenyfar will need it more than I – she disdains me. She cringed when I kissed her cheek in welcome. She is afraid of me! I wish that it were not this way. Now I am to ravage this young maiden to get a child upon her..."

"I can read her, Arthur. She has her own reasons for avoiding your touch and they have *nothing* to do with you."

"What then?"

"These reasons I may not speak of. This problem is between you and your royal wife. But remember Arthur, why we are doing this."

"I know... I know – it is political – and the Kingdom *must have an heir*..."

"You must get through this somehow... But mind my words Arthur – there must be blood on the sheets tonight! Do you understand?"

"I will not rape her! Surely you could not condone this, Igraine? I mean... My Lady Mother..."

"No, of course not Arthur, use your vast intelligence along with your great and compassionate heart – find a way Arthur... blood on the sheets."

Soon after, I was taken by my companions to my personal chamber, dressed and vulgarly given much advice about the marriage bed. The jesting was all very funny! So, my spirits lifted a little and I drank; but only a bit, so as not to offend Gwenyfar.

Many and more Gifts...

Princess Rowena had arrived three Days before the wedding. She had ridden her war Stallion, with only an axe, her long dagger, and one guard – all the way from her fortress in Gwynedd. She had brought an extra Horse along to carry – rolled and covered upon its saddle – a beautiful Saxon wedding gown for Gwenyfar. It was the same in which she had been married to Vortigern. Of course, the seamstresses hastened to shorten it substantially, for Princess Rowena was a much taller woman than Gwenyfar. So that there be no bad luck in our marriage, she had cleansed it in the Well Water at her fortress and hung it in the light of Sol to bless it – for she had had little Love for Vortigern.

She had brought two more wedding gifts: a silver and amber ring for her sister and a solid gold brooch for me, which was emblazoned with the Pen Dragon standard on its front. On its back was engraved, in Latin, "Rex Regis of Totus Nostrum Populus." "King of all our People." How delicately tactful a reminder was this to me of my vows of showing equality and tolerance towards all the Tribes and Clans of our Islands – including Hengist's Saxons.

The Priestesses of the Isle of Apples gifted blue and purple dyed cloth, which they themselves had woven. They had been sent by courier to Igraine at Mid-Summer. Igraine had then fashioned my tunic and breeches from these with Magical stitches and knotted threads. She then embroidered many symbols of the Tribes upon the front of my tunic. Upon the back – with threads of pure gold – she had embroidered the Pen Dragon sigil. The sleeves were fixed with vertical lines of scrollwork of the Saxons, Picti, and the Clans. In addition to the fabric, the Lady of the Lake sent many clay jars filled with the Isle's fabled honey and many baskets of early Apples from the Order's orchards.

A Picti Chieftain, from the far North had brought a wood and leathern shield – with many of their strange pictures etched into the leather, as a gift for me.

From the Clans of the Cymru had come a silver wrist torque for me of a style similar to the ones I had seen on their War Chieftains' wrists. For Gwenyfar, they presented fanciful iron Fire Dogs, similar to the ones in Princess Rowena's Great Hall.

By the Northern Clans, from just South of Table Rock, in Alba, a ribbon of checked cloth was presented – which had obviously been woven by hand with much finesse. Many hours of labor had been spent upon it. It was vibrantly coloured in scarlet, purple and blue. I tied it to the braces of my wedding outfit.

It was so like Hengist to have sent his son – Thüringen Red Wolf, his youngest – in his stead and with no excuses for his absence. Still, it has never been said that Hengist is a stingy man; he sent with his son a short dagger with a gold and silver Boar's head hilt as a gift for me. It came with a fine handcrafted leather scabbard. This I slid into the side of my right boot.

A Christian Monk representing a male Monastery of ten men arrived thence with a Cross for me. I was greatly offended in my heart.

Although everyone knew that I honoured each one's leaning toward the Gods of their desires, they also knew that I worshiped the *Old Gods*. I could not help suspecting it as a trick – or was it a trust? Trust that I would indeed defend and treat all on these, Our Fair Isles, equally well? In any case, I graciously accepted it.

One of the Monks then asked if he might have the honour of meeting Gwenyfar one Day. I, of course, did not refuse – that was "entirely at Gwenyfar's discretion" said I – then quickly excused myself.

The list of gifts went on and on...

Later that Day, I asked Igraine "Lady Mother, what am I to do with this cross?"

"I think you must place it on the Christian Altar, which Gorlois set up in the back corner of the courtyard. Did you ever realise that he had done that, Arthur?"

"Yes, but I had forgotten."

"He, like you, was a man who kept his word. When he agreed that *all* were welcome at the Holy Well, he realised that those who had travelled from long distances would require hospitality, a bed, and food. He said that if Christians wished to partake of the Water for Healing, they might also want to pray to their God – or Angels – or Saints. He, being kind and thoughtful, set up a lovely and comfortable haven for any Christian who would wish to pray or make offerings to their God or to the poor. There he erected a small Altar.

"He and I had spoken of this when I first arrived here, as his wife. We agreed with each other that the Holy Spring had been revered for thousands of years, perhaps even before the Old Tribes – my people – had arrived and long before the Clans and the Romans.

"The Well is owned by no one and everyone. He said that, perhaps someday, even a Christian Holy person might be Guardian of the Well. At this I inwardly laughed, but then wondered... for Gorlois was a very wise man. I had said nothing.

"At that shrine and Altar – that is where I think you should put your Cross, as a gesture of good will; after all, you *are* King of *all* the Britons."

"Igraine... I mean, Lady Mother, wish for me that someday I have but a portion of your Wisdom."

She smiled... "You must go now, Arthur, it is near to the Time."

Much fuss was made over Gwenyfar, and she and her Ladies In Waiting remaining in seclusion. Those who would be dressing Gwenyfar were: Branwen, Freidl, my Lady Mother Igraine, and Princess Rowena. They were the only ones who were allowed into the bride's presence. The doors to Gwenyfar's chamber remained barred all Day. The only contact with the world outside of this sacrosanct conclave was through a spy hole in the door – from which requests for anything needed or desired could be spoken to her "Outside Court" attendants, included Tangwen, the Mother of my heart.

Igraine had tried to persuade Gwenyfar to include Tangwen into her Inner Chamber ladies – explaining that she was the only woman I had known as Mother through my childhood and even unto less than two years past. But Gwenyfar protested – stating that it would not suit, for Tangwen's being of a lower station than she. None argued the obvious – that Branwen and Freidl were but servants to Gwenyfar's household.

Much later it was expressed to me – with no excuses made – by Princess Rowena that she and Igraine had greatly disapproved of Gwenyfar's pompous attitude. I hoped this was only due to the stressfulness of the occasion.

The Wedding Feast...

It was nearing the season of the First Harvest – of Grains and of Herbs. The late Summer Flowers were heavy with their blooms. They were lush in their bounty. My Lady Mother had transformed the Great Hall into a Magical land of a Mid-Summer's Dream. Sweet scents perfumed the Air and everywhere I looked, a bounty of Flora bewitched the senses! Even the oil torches were lightly scented with Rosemary.

Hung from high up in the smoke blackened beams, were banners representing – in one way or another – every Tribe, Clan, and Great House of our alliance. Grey doves and Tree Finches flew 'round the rafters.

The processional path, upon which we, as well as the six Holy Ones and the Sages were to walk, was carpeted with sweet and spicy scented gifts of the Earth Mother. Where had Igraine found so many? Never had I seen, but in the wilds of Nature, such beauty.

And Gwenyfar, I must say, seemed to spring from the same source. She blended in as if a delicate white Flower had sprung up between the wild Ferns and Mosses.

She *was* beautiful – in her pale way.

She was dressed in the gown that Princess Rowena had gifted to her. All a-shimmer was she in its Lavender blue chemise, with a long, open weave, light grey sleeveless tunic atop it. There were pearls and amber beads sewn to the tunic in a pattern of Vines. She wore the ring of silver and amber which Rowena had given to her and an exquisite twisted golden neck torque with Saxon Horse heads sigils on each end, identifying her as a royal Princess of her Father's line. Her long flaxen hair had been braided and put atop her head, with many white flowers, Lavender Herbs, and delicate ribbons woven in. The only adornment upon her skin was the extract of boiled juice of berries, carefully staining her perfectly formed lips.

It was expected that when the right moment came in the wedding ceremony, I would place upon Gwenyfar's head a circlet of gold – claiming her as King's Wife.

I had commissioned one myself from a master Goldsmith. It was a very thin one, as I thought that would well suit her delicate beauty. Engraved all around it was an incredible pattern of entwined Dragons. I had always thought the knot work of the Clans to be the most beautiful.

The Handfasting...

Everything was set. The moment had finally arrived. No turning back now. This, then had been inevitable – since I had agreed to become King.

We stood there waiting...

For all the fuss and costly trappings, the actual ceremony was to be relatively simple. This was because of my disgust at the lengthy and heated debate about who would perform the Rites. Who would pray? Who would sacrifice? Who would stand in the center?

You see, every tradition of the peoples amoung us has each their own proscribed customs of Marriage Rites. Since there were no laws here to require any one or another ceremony, I invoked my right as King – as per Gwyddion's counsel – to use none of them, so as to offend none.

At last, when I had had enough of the pushing and pulling, I said that Gwyddion, my Mother, Princess Rowena, and I would write the ceremony.

It was determined there should be six Holy persons standing in front of Gwenyfar and Me. These would be:

My Mother Igraine, the Lady Vivianne, The Merlin, a Priest of Odin from Hengist's court, a Christian Monk – who was of the more tolerant sort – and the High Druid from the newly reorganized Druidical University on Ynys Mon.

The companions I had chosen to be my men-at-arms for the wedding – to stand with me – were the ones most beloved by Bedwyr and me. They were: Bedwyr – of course – Fergus Macroich, Branbleidd, Kai, Beddryd, and Ddalon. They were my most trusted companions – we were the original "Seven of Battles."

Feeling as I did that I was about to walk into a never ending, dark and perilous labyrinth – from which I knew no escape – well, it was good to have them near to remind me that most things in my life would remain the same. After all, I was King! This marriage would change nothing; or at least I prayed it so.

When the ceremony was about to begin, the serene delegation from Igraine's Tribe walked toward Gwenyfar's ladies and my men at arms – who were already waiting near to the officiates of the Rite. As they walked, they began to Hum and Drum – in rhythm with their ankle bells – in their hauntingly beautiful and mysterious way.

To the slow and steady, quiet beating of their drums, Gwenyfar and I, hand in hand – hers cold and clammy as the Mists of the Highlands – walked the long way across the Great Hall to where my companions and Gwenyfar's ladies waited with the Holy Ones. I heard an intake of breath from the onlookers as we came into their sight. I suppose that we were resplendent. That walk, across the Great Hall, seemed to last forever.

Time slowed...

I heard "Voices" again – but not with my fleshly ears – it was as if they were visitors inside my head. Were they really the "Voices of the Stars," as Merlin and those others with the Sight called them? How could I know? They spoke with such benevolence and compassion; within them I heard the Wisdom of the ages.

"There," said they, "behold the frightened young girl who walks beside you. She fears a great loss in her life – as do you. Be kind and forgiving toward her, Arthur, for she does not have the strength of character that you possess. Fear not this marriage and remember whichever way the North Winds blow, let it always be said that Arthur was a fair and great King. Treat her with honour. Do nothing ever to besmirch your name. Let there be faith and hope amoung the people. For, one Day you will be gone from this Earth. But, so long as hope lives, men will always await the return of a King such as you and a new Time of peace..."

Then they vanished.

Had we only taken one step while they spoke? My cold heart – as cold as her hands – had been warmed toward Gwenyfar. I turned my head and caught her eye; I squeezed her hand lovingly and smiled at her. I whispered, "Gwenyfar, have no fear of me. I know this is hard for you. It is hard for me as well."

She looked surprised!

"I promise always to be kind to you and give you your say in matters of your own desires. Always will you have my respect as a Princess, a woman and therefore a representation of the GREAT GODDESS Herself; for it is my belief that any man who worships the Goddess must recognize and honour Her in every woman. I will force nothing upon you."

Her hand began to warm and did not tremble as it had.

Then we had arrived.

I did not let go of her hand through the short ceremony.

The six celebrant witnesses all spoke in a Chant:

"Hail King Arthur and Princess Gwenyfar! Hail to each God and Goddess. Hail to our Ancestors. Hail to Air, Fire, Water, and Earth. Hail to the four Winds and the four directions. Hail to each of you witnesses who stand in this hall."

After each statement they paused, allowing a resounding response of the same words from the crowd of onlookers.

Again spoke the celebrants, "May each and all bear witness to the vows exchanged this Day between Arthur, the King and Princess Gwenyfar."

While holding tight her hand, I began:

"I, Arthur, by my right as Over King, through acceptance of the Clan and Tribal Chieftains and Councils, with the blessing of the Lady of the Lake and Wise Mothers of the ancient Order of the Isle of Apples – as well as by my blood through Lady Igraine, great Seer of the Dark Tribes; and of Uther, called the Pen Dragon, descendant of King Coel of old renown, through Constantine the Great and Macsen Wledig – and by design of the Goddesses Nine and the Great ONE – do offer myself as husband to Gwenyfar, daughter of King Hengist the Saxon, son of Witigislaus, son of Witta, descendant of Woden; and of his wife, Arwyn of the Cymru Clans."

Now these words I was expected to say, but I went on...

"With this marriage alliance, should she accept it, I also ask Princess Gwenyfar, to accept the crown as my Queen consort."

A murmur arose, for I was not required to title her Queen. However it was not for goodwill's sake alone that I extended this offer to her, for I had vowed to myself that this was the only Time I would ever marry, as Gwenyfar lived.

The six, again in one voice, asked:

"Prince Thüringen Red Wolf, this once and last Time, as you stand here in this company, as proxy for King Hengist, Princess Gwenyfar's and your Father, does he agree to this marriage?'

"He does."

"Then Princess Gwenyfar, do you agree to be wife to King Arthur, the Pen Dragon?"

In a very quiet and choked voice she said,

"Yes... I do."

Lady Vivianne stepped forward with a long, thin, braided leather cord, with which to wind our hands together at the wrists. She tied the knot and said, "You are now Handfasted – husband and wife."

A great and long cheer arose around the Hall.

Bedwyr held the gold circlet out toward me. I faced Gwenyfar and with my free hand, placed it upon her head. Then, unscripted and truly from my heart, I said, "I crown you Queen Gwenyfar... honourary Lady of many lands. As you are High Queen of these Isles, may the comfort offered to you here on this Day grow within you, so that one Day all these Islands will become as home in your heart."

The six then offered their benediction, "May the blessings of the Great Divine Ones – one voice said 'Only One' – be with you always."

Another raucous noise arose, with much foot stomping and clanging of daggers against shields.

I leaned over toward Gwenyfar and kissed her forehead.   She squeezed my hand.

When all was silent again, Lady Vivianne removed the cord, without breaking the knot. She would, as Priestess, keep that cord, for as long as she – or we – lived. This was to remind us of the vows we had made to each other.

That was it!

Another great cheer swelled, followed by the fastest setting up of feasting trestles and benches I could ever have imagined. I watched as the trestles were covered, all at a Time, with long patterned cloths. To me, it seemed as if a dance... Two attendants – one at each end of every table, lifted the billowing fabrics and then pulled them down to smooth them across the surfaces. Then the feasting began.

It was the beginning of the first Harvest and a very rich one at that. Great pits had been dug to roast whole Boars, Sheep, Hare, Swans, and other fowl of many kinds, which were brought to the tables upon great trays of silver and gold. Oysters, Mussels, Cockles, and Eels had been smoked in Lady Igraine's ovens in quantity to accommodate as many as three hundred guests. In addition to these, there were jellied Eels and pickled Quail's eggs, Larks' tongue in aspic and stuffed Dormouse – all seasoned with various exotic spices, such as salt from the lands of the East, Pepper, Cinnamon, Cloves, Nutmeg, Ginger, Cardamom, Coriander, and Mustard. Even were Vegetables served: Rape, Onions, Garlic, Carrots, and Leeks. In addition to these were the Apples, which had been sent by the Lady of the Lake. Igraine's tables were also graced by woven baskets filled with rare Fruits and nuts, which she had had shipped to Dumnonia from the Continent.   Loaves of Manchet and trenchers of Barley and Rye were placed upon silver plates – with which Dux Gorlois had set his Roman tables. And, at every plate cutlery of bronze spoons with carved handles were set. Of course, as was expected, everyone had brought their own daggers.   Mead, wine, and ale were drunk in copious amounts, all served from silver goblets, flasks, and cups. Decanters of gold and painted pottery were filled with the different wines that accompanied every course and brought 'round to all those seated. A group of Musicians, Drummers, and Singers – with beautiful voices all – played and sang sweet melodies of joy and sadness.

A young Cymric Bard sang a saga of the Gods in the First Time – a story of the making of Blodeuedd – the maiden made of flowers and of her betrayal of Lleu – her husband and his uncle Gwyddion... Lleu had been cursed by his Mother Arianrhod – the Moon Goddess – that no woman would have him as her husband and so, Llew's uncle fashioned a beautiful maiden of flowers and gave her – Blodeuedd – to him as his wife. She had no say in the marriage and Loved him not. This led to much scheming on her part – and as Love cannot be commanded, she found and Loved another. The Spells and machinations of Blodeuedd and her lover eventually caused the Death of Lleu. The Bard's song was far too long and I far too drunk to remember all of the words, but the refrain of it was "...And all did she for Love."

"Was this Gwenyfar of whom he sang?" I wondered... "Made of flowers from the body of the Earth Goddess, fragile as petals, but 'treacherous as the thorns of a Rose?'"

Well, no matter...

I feasted and drank with my Companions. Good intentions aside, I was quite drunk. After a goodly Time of all this, I found myself surrounded by the smiling, mostly sotted faces of men who were demanding my bedding. This was it, then... the hour of reckoning... I laughed at myself! This was not my execution, nor Gwenyfar's. "So be it then," I thought as the crowd of men pushed and pulled me up the winding Stone stairwell to the bridal chamber.

Blood on the Sheets...

The women had brought Gwenyfar up to our chamber first. To follow custom, they would have un-plaited her long hair, brushed it to fall across her shoulders and down to her waist, then removed her gown and rubbed oil of Roses onto her throat, wrists, belly, and feet. A white shift of the finest weave – beautiful in its simplicity – is what she was wearing when I entered the Chamber, although it could not be seen, for she lay in our great bed of state, covered up to her chin in pelts and coverlets. She was visibly shaking; her cheeks were tear-stained and her berry-tinted lips were smeared. 'That is odd,' I thought, for I knew that she had not eaten or drunk anything.

It had been a hot Day – hot in the Great Hall, too, with all those people. The blessing of it was that, here in my home, high upon the rocky cliff jutting out over the Western Sea, there was always a cooling breeze and sometimes, very strong Winds. In Summer we removed the boards from the window slits to allow in the coolness.

"We should be comfortable here" – said I to myself – "for this chamber faces Westward, toward the Sea."

I laughed at myself again. At this moment in my life, here I was talking to myself about breezes. An escape, I suppose, from the reality that I dreaded.

The custom was, that with lewd and loud descriptions of what was about to take place in our marriage bed this Night, the men and some of the more fun loving women would taunt us and even try to stay in our chamber. At the very least, a large crowd would wait just outside the door. The more demure women did finally leave, just before I was stripped naked. Others stayed and watched as I climbed into the bed with Gwenyfar. At that point I raised my voice and insisted that we have privacy. The room emptied and most of those who had been standing just outside the chamber door removed to the Great Hall's festivities. Of course, two or three men would wait a bit down the hallway to guard us. Really, this was all to be sure that we did indeed spend the whole Night together.

When the chamber had emptied I got back out of the bed, latched the door for her comfort and turned off all of the oil lamps but one. When I returned to her, I sat on the bed – above the covers, whilst nonchalantly keeping my manhood from her view.

"Gwenyfar," quoth I in a kindly voice, "Please do not be afraid of me."

At that she broke down and cried in great sobs. I tried to hold her in my arms as would a brother. I shuddered at *that* thought... 'Oh, my Morgan, are you lost from me forever now?' Gwenyfar pulled violently away to the head of the bed until she could get no farther away from me.

So this is how it would be, then...

"Gwenyfar, I would not rape you! I would never force myself upon you. I only wanted to comfort you."

"Thank you, Arthur," she sobbed.

Was that the first Time she had ever spoken my name?

"It would do us both well if you would trust me..."

To my great surprise she threw herself into my arms. However, she continued to cry. Perhaps this had been building within her for months. When finally she calmed, I said, "Can we try to be friends, Gwenyfar?"

She actually smiled at me, a crooked little smile, between her gasps for breath.

"Gwenyfar, listen to me, there is no rush to make an heir. Sometimes babes do not come for a very long while. Knowing that you have this fear, what kind of a man, or friend, would I be to rush you into this, or to force you? Let us get to know each other well. I have many other friends who are women. We could talk, or ride, or play games together, and with your ladies and companions nearby, as well. Our life, while we are together, could be pleasant. Besides which, I will be gone to battles and other business for much of the year. I have told you that I will make sure you have everything you need and want here. Is Igraine not good to you already?"

"Yes."

"Well then, can we agree that we will not rush things?"

"Yes, Arthur, but... but what will happen when there is not blood on the sheets this Night? I will be shamed and they will want you to put me away. Then my Father will beat me badly and perhaps banish my Mother and... and..."

I got up again and went to my boots where I keep the short dagger Hengist had sent as my wedding gift. I brought it back to the bed. Her eyes widened. She looked terrified again, but I winked at her, then I threw off the covers, and cut my arm where I could hide the wound, whilst wearing a sleeve. At the middle of the bed I let my blood drip onto the sheets. She looked amazed. She hurried for cloth to hold against the cut.

"You would do this for me?"

"Yes."

"This is not my own idea – I have heard of this in lore."

Then I wondered, ironically, how often this ruse had been perpetrated by Princes and Kings in the past...

"But, it is not done yet. You must cry out."

She did. We bounced around on the bed. Then I groaned. And to my great surprise, she cried out again, this Time in a much more lusty way. We covered our mouths to hide the sound of our laughter. Then I went to the chamber door with the blooded undercover bunched in my hands and threw it out into the hallway. A small cheer went up from the men awaiting it and then they ran down the winding stairway to bring the evidence into the Great Hall. All the way up here we could hear the ruckus made over this by those feasting.

"Well, Gwenyfar, will you now trust me to sleep on the bed with you – above the covers, of course? For the Stone floor is uneven and very hard..."

Chapter 18

Harvest Festival on the Isle of Apples

Arthur

I could hardly wait for the Festival to begin, not only because it meant that Bedwyr and I would compete in the Games with many mighty and noble opponents, but that I would also see Morgan again. I felt a great need to speak with her. Truthfully, I must add that being away from the pressures of my marriage was a very welcome change.

My situation with Gwenyfar had remained the same. Well, perhaps things were coming closer – albeit slowly – toward the eventual begetting of an heir. I remember thinking 'At least Gwenyfar does not hate or fear me now.' I suppose I should have counted lucky all the Stars above me for that.

The Harvest Festival is the one and only Festival held on the Isle of Apples that is open to people of all lands – all other Rites being held as Sacred Secrets. The thought was that all people equally benefit from the Harvest and that it is a good thing when people of many countries come together, and can join with each other in celebration. And the people do come, from far and wide, even from as far away as Rome and Asia Minor!

At one Time, long ago, the Ancestors of all the peoples living on these Fair Isles and all lands surrounding them celebrated the Grain and Herb Harvest with Human sacrifice. A young man, once having been selected, would live as King for one whole Moon's Dance – with his every wish or desire being granted – until the next Dark Moon, when he would be cut down like the Grain; a willing sacrifice. Then he – who embodied the Sacrificed God – would be buried with the seeds of the Grain, or cast into the Fires with the first sheaves harvested. This was all with the understanding that the Harvest King's Spirit would enter into the presence of the Gods to present the value of his sacrifice and the needs of the Tribe, Clan, or village to them. But that was long ago...

The Old Dark Tribes discontinued Human sacrifice hundreds of years ago. Now their Harvest "Killed Man," in order to be worthy, is chosen by his showing exceptional skills in Archery, storytelling, and the hunt – just as he ever was. Except that now he is laid – alive – in the Forest, on a bed of Blue Bells – with his arms and legs bound, as if he were a Stag. Then the women Gatherers and the men Hunters, sit around him, extolling his prowess and their thanksgiving to the Goddess for a plentiful Harvest – all the while feasting upon Sacred Mushrooms, Berries, and venison and drinking copious amounts of fermented Berry juice.   After the celebratory Feast, the "Killed Man," having been released by the Sacrificed God who had possessed him, re-joins the Tribe as their equal.

The Druids of the Eire observe their Grain and Herb Harvest Rite as "Lughnasadh" – which name means the Games of Lugh – by holding competitions amoung men of many diverse skills. These include: games of strength, archery, horsemanship, ax tossing, spear throwing, swordsmanship, and poetry. The Druids of the Cymru call him Lleu Llaw Gyffes – Lleu of the Long Arm. Lleu – or Lugh – is the God of Light, Magic, poetry, and of many skills.

Long ago, one of the Ladies of the Lake began the tradition of staging the Order's Harvest Festival on the Isle of Apples. Anyone who wishes to may attend. Even men from the continent, across the Eastern Sea, come to join in the Games. So that, in this way, once a year, *all* the peoples of these Our Fair Isles or elsewhere – who do in fact share the lands' Harvest – may join in celebration together. It is the largest Festival on the Isle of Apples – and for that matter, anywhere on these Our Fair Isles.

By their very nature, the Games of Lleu are male focused; it is only the men who compete in the Games against each other. At the end of three Days, a Champion emerges. This man, in Days of old, is he who would have earned the honour of being the Human sacrifice.

Now, this Champion is honoured on the Night of and for three Days after the Games and is given every desire of his heart. He may remain on the Isle of Apples, should he wish to, being given the full hospitality of the Lady of the Lake and the Order, until it is Time for the final Ritual. But stay or go, he must vow to return upon the next Full Moon for the Harvest Ritual – not at the bloodletting Dark Moon as long ago – there to present the *value* of his Human sacrifice to the Fires.

For the final Ritual, he will have made a bread from the first sheaves – by his own hands – in the form of a Man, symbolizing the life and body of the Grain. The Lady of the Lake will have whispered the needs of the peoples of these Isles into his ear; which he then writes, or intones into the bread. He then offers the loaf as sacrifice, in place of his own life.

The First Seeds of the Grain in hand after the Harvest is gathered are buried at that Time, there to await, deep in the Earth, the Time when the great Wheel has turned and warmth has returned to the land – when they will sprout through the soil as the next year's new growth.

The idea of a Sacrificed God, or King, is a very ancient one, yet Gwyddion tells me that this pattern keeps playing out in ever-new ideologies. The King/God of the Christians was said to be in the ground, or a tomb, for three and one-half Days in a Death-like state, then resurrected in full glory – just as was the Grain! And this was in the season of planting, in the first month of the Jews' year.

Even the length of three – or three and one half – Days, has been used symbolically in many cultures. Gwyddion thinks that this number might be a part of so much Myth and Magic because a Lunar month is about twenty-eight and one half Days in measure, with eight phases, making each recognizable phase about three and one half Days long.

Gwyddion once posed the question to Bedwyr and me, "Boys, why do we keep these Sacred Festivals?"

Of course this was a rhetorical question, so he continued: "It is because, as long as the Sun rises again each Day and the Earth, Trees, Grain, Animals, Humans, and all other living things continue to turn the Wheel of the Year by performing their annual Ritual rounds of necessary tasks, the World will go on. This is why we keep these Sabbats. It is the right thing to do. It is our Divinely given endeavour and function upon this Earth.

"Let me ask you this, boys: What do you think would happen, if upon one year, all the Trees refused to do their dance – refused to blossom, leaf and drop their leaves – refused to honour the great cycles of life in the Wheel of the Year? Why, all life on Earth would die! For all things on Earth are interdependent.

"Well then, let me ask you this: What if all the insects or Animals or Birds – and so on – did the same?"

"All life on Earth would die!" quoth we.

Gwyddion continued, "We as Humans must do our part in keeping the Wheel of the Year turning. We must enter the Land of Myth – the Realm of the Gods – and do as they did 'In the Beginning' and have taught us to do; we must keep the Holy Days and perform the Rites. By doing these things we keep the seasons turning – one notch at a Time. For I tell you truly, if the Day should ever come when all Humans refuse to do their part in this and keep the Old Gods' ways, all things as we know them on Earth will come to an end. Yes, we keep the Holy Days because it is the right thing to do!"

The Order's lands...

As a very generous gesture on the part of the Order, the footpath –
beyond the gates of entry, which leads to the beginning of the Tor's
spiral climb – was open to everyone that week, in honour of the Games.
No Human guards stood there to intimidate visitors.

The pathway is kept in a state of natural perfection. Throughout the
growing season, sweet smelling Herbs, variously coloured Flowers and
bushes with medicinal properties, wild Ferns and green Mosses, all grow
along its sides. It is a beguiling delight to the senses. Once having
walked its length, never have I forgotten its haunting beauty. Like
strains of an Incantation does it come ever unbidden into my thoughts –
maddening yet comforting all at a Time. Every so often, a Willow, Oak,
or Ash Tree stands beside the foot path, to offer shade from the Sun or
shelter from the often sprinkling Rain. Stones to be seated upon have
been placed beneath those Trees – a rest to the stiff bones of the aged or
unwell pilgrims who have traversed to the Isle for Healing.

This same path also passes beside the two Holy Wells of the Red and
White Springs. A Thorn grows by each of them.

At Summer's Beginning, in the season of fertility and then again at
the Grain and Herb Harvest, folk who live near and far come to *dress* the
Wells with Charms. Coloured ribbons of wool, flax, and silk hang in the
Thorns, billowing in the breezes, carrying prayers of worship,
thanksgiving, and supplication to the Four Winds. Small White Quartz
pebbles are tossed into the Wells, for requests of blessings and for
Divination. Gold coins sparkle in the Water, where they have lodged in
the Stones containing the Wells. Of course no one takes them – no one
would dare rob the Gods.

That Day as I walked by the White Spring, I saw that bread offerings
had been made as well. It was understood that these gifts, which had
been left on a Stone offering table, would be used by the sisters and
brothers of the Order, who maintain this place of beauty. Fruits,
Vegetables, mead, ale, honey cakes and such things were sometimes left
there too. And these things, although appreciated by the Order, were not
needed by them due to the bountiful harvest of their gardens and fields.
So, these food stuffs were given to the poor, the widows, and sickly folk
living in the vicinity of the Order.

To walk the pathways of the Order's gardens, to drink from the Holy
Wells and to continue up to the top of the Tor, changes one from their
ordinary state of being to that of the world of Seers and Mystics – at least
in the way one feels – whether Gifted in these Arts or not. Even a man
such as I, who has been passed by in the way of the Gifts of my Mother's
blood, can feel a sort of floating motionlessness and a profound silence
of peace. It seems a Spiritual Ascension of sorts – yet was I more in

touch and connected to everything in the Earthly world of form, as well as in the realm of Spirits. The path to the Tor was filled with the Dragon's Breath – a Mist. It seemed a Time out of Time. As I walked the path up the Tor, I felt as though I was walking the path of my Destiny – and all was well and right.

Might my final rest be here in this realm, or perhaps on this very piece of land? I do pray so.

As always, there was a basin of pure Well Water standing at the top of the spiral path, there for any who needed refreshment. I washed my hands, neck and face. After thusly refreshing myself, cleansed of heart and thought, I went to Morgan.

She was with her Bees, of course. Like a child I hid in the bushes to watch and listen. Buzzing and humming they were. Morgan and her Bees in some great sympathetic song, or was it really a conversation? Of a sudden she turned and smiled at me.

"Bear!"

I ran to her, wanting so to embrace her as a lover, of course I only held both of her delicate hands and kissed her forehead.

"Morgan, it seems so often I come to you in need. What I wish is that each Time would only be a joy, but now again..."

"Arthur, is it regarding Gwenyfar?"

I blurted out, "Oh, Morgan, how can I be husband to her? If I like her at all, it is only as a friend."

Recovering my composure, I recanted, "But this is not your problem. Truly, none of my problems are. Please, once again, forgive my neediness. I will be here for six Days. Let us have pleasant Times together. Tell me! What has your life been like this season?"

"Simple, as always, Arthur."

"Oh, but talk of your 'simple things' is like music to my ears. I will wait here until you finish your work for the Day and if it is all right with you, then perhaps we can walk together in the Woods as we used to do so long ago. If it pleases you, would you tell your tales of the Myths to me?"

"Oh, Bear – I think you must know them all by now!"

"It would not matter if I heard them one hundred and one Times! The joy is in the listening; you have surely been told what a wonderful storyteller you are, Morgan!"

"Well, yes I have."

"Then after we walk and sit in the Woods, would you like to fish in the Lake with me?"

So I spent three blessed Days in Morgan's company, then on the fifth Day – the second of the Games – everything changed...

The Games...

Great sport and fun was had by all contestants, I believe; those bested as well as those besting. There were Champions competing under the standards of many Kings and Chieftains; from as far away as the Languedoc in the far Southwest of the Continent. Even as far as from Rome was one man. His name was Lucian – "Of the light" – and so he was.

This next is difficult for me to quill to page. But it is so, that many people speak of the good looks of their King – handsome and well-built, light wavy hair, clear skin, good teeth, brilliant blue eyes and on and on and on. It is tedious to me how often they speak of this.

At first, when I was a boy, comparisons of my looks to other young boys hurt me for Bedwyr's sake, for he was small, dark and well... just plain. And I would not have his feelings hurt for anything. Of course, at that Time he was thought to be the young Lord of Dumnonia, so no one dared to openly compare us. But as years went by, Bedwyr changed. Every year he grew more comely, with a smile sly like a Fox. He was clever, agile, virile, charming. His Magic seemed more and more to attract women, and so does it still.   Now, it only makes me uncomfortable for my own sake when people go on and on about their "handsome King."

The reason that I write of this here, is that this Warrior – Lucian – was all that I am in these ways and *very much more*. He was taller and more muscular. His hair shone like gold on the field when the Sun lit it, and to my eyes, he was much more handsome than I. In fact, I do not remember ever seeing a man so beautiful as he. Like a God he looked – out there upon the field of Games.

In addition to this, he had the same Fox-like smile and charm that Bedwyr had. No woman could keep her eyes from him. No woman... not even Morgan. She watched him with a fascination that made my gut churn. It was a jealousy that burned me. I could not turn my thoughts from it. Even when I played the Games of wit – in which, indeed, I was wagered on and expected to win – I could not concentrate. I brooded between events and chided myself for a fool. Why had I not realised – expected – Morgan to want and Love other men? My thoughts raced, "She is a Priestess of the Goddess. She will express Love in all ways. I have no right to her... I have no hold upon her."

Finally, I was pitted against this Lucian. I shouted within myself: "Arthur! It is a Game! Let not yourself be dishonoured by anger – by jealousy." Then, just before we were to meet in this pretend combat, he walked right to where Morgan sat with Lady Vivianne and Makyr and gave her a bow, a smile, and a piece of cloth from his under tunic. In a Latin accent, he loudly proclaimed, "My Lady, you are *so* beautiful..."

My blood boiled. I grabbed a real sword and put off the wooden one I was supposed to use for this game. The crowd went silent.

I called out to him – "Arm yourself Sir; let us put more spice in this Game. First cut?"

He called back, "So be it – first cut."

I had angered and offended him. So we each, with heavy breath, threw ourselves at the other. We thrust and parried back and forth. "Evenly matched – Good!" thought I. I might have beaten him, but for the ache I felt at the loss of Morgan. Loss! Yes, it was on that Day, on that field, that I felt I had really and finally lost her.

This painful realisation and the thought that – "Even crazed as I am, I cannot be so disreputable as to deliberately endanger our lives. I am King, after all, my life is not my own to waste" – caused concentration to slip from my grasp.

He was quick. I had not even seen it coming. Of a sudden, I felt a searing burn at the top of my left arm. He withdrew from me and held down his blooded sword.

"Sir, you are High King of this land; to your right as King, I bend my knee."

His words stung much more than did his cut. He had said: "To your *right* as King" – not "To your *honour*."

I had not behaved honourably. I was so ashamed. He rose, turned and began to walk away from me.

I called to him, "Good Sir!"

He turned to face me.

"A good and honourable man you are," said I, "Much to my shame and dismay I let my heart rule my behavior toward you – you who have not wronged me. I give my apology to you with the hope that you will accept it."

I held his gaze. He deserved as much. I would not look away. He returned it.

"My Lord, King Arthur, whatever led your heart in anger toward me, I do not know of it. I have only held the deepest respect for you, for the stories of you are all of 'a great and good Lord.' We men are not Gods, none of us, but mere Humans – fallible and prone to missteps. You, King Arthur, have a great heart. You, as King, apologized to me – one who has in some way offended you... Of course, I accept your apology."

Attendants began to rush toward us as I swayed upon my feet.

"Leave us!" I called out.

Everyone backed away.

He continued, "But will you not allow someone to assist you? The cut is deeper than I intended."

"Good Sir, Lucian, the cut is deep, but you hold no fault in it."

He motioned for help as I lost consciousness, lying in a pool of my own blood.

The next thing I saw was Morgan's worried face and the morning

Sun streaming through the doorway of her cottage – to whence I had been taken from the Field of Games.

She and two other Healers had cleansed my wound the Night before, but after using a medicinal herbal salve made from honey to keep it from festering she had decided to sear the wound with a hot iron rod anyway. However, I had still raised a slight fever in the Night. The fever worried Morgan. She had run to the kitchens to find some bread mold, then, having used just enough – not so much as to be poisonous – in a potion, she had tried to make me drink. It tasted horrible – I gagged and choked. This was what had awakened me from my stupor. In my wild Dream, Morgan was calling to me, "Bear... Arthur! Come to the world of form! Awaken!" Whether she had said these words in reality or just in my Dream, I could not tell. Finally she shook me. The pain in my arm from the movement was terrible. I remember thinking, "How can I hurt this much from one cut?" She helped me to drink the rest of the potion.

"Lie still."

As if I would, or could move; drugged as I was... The pain then began to subside... I slept again.

Morgan

After I was assured that Arthur would not die from his wound, I returned to Lady Vivianne's side. In order to justly honour the Games and all of the contestants, my duty was to be present, watching until a Champion had emerged. This was now the third Day of the Games.

At the end there were two with tied points – Bedwyr and a Scald of Hengist's court. His name was Cuthbert. He had the most beautiful voice I had ever heard in a man. Yet, it was more than just that. He had composed a song of such loveliness of phrase that tears rolled down my cheeks in the midst of it. When he had finished, the strangest thing happened. Where I would have thought that everyone would be cheering him, everyone was still and silent. A pause... for at least three breaths, he stood there with his head downcast, holding his lyre to his right side. Then, of a sudden, a cheer arose to wake the dead! Everyone was standing, stomping their feet, and those who had them, clanged dagger to shield or staff to ground.

Bedwyr forfeited the Games to him. It was done. Cuthbert the Scald was this year's Champion.

He walked forward to stand before Lady Vivianne, to make his vow of offering the representation of his life in sacrifice and Thanksgiving to the Gods. This he did, then he looked at me.

"Oh, my Lady of the Lake, may I ask a boon of you?"

"Yes, of course. You will be granted the every desire of your heart... as long as it is something within my right to grant..." said Vivianne.

She was no man's fool. She looked at me and then back toward him.

"What is it you ask?"

"I ask to be introduced to the lovely Lady who is beside you, if I may."

Lady Vivianne made the introduction and he asked if he might later walk with me for awhile.

Of course, our walk had had to wait, for there were many congratulations and other introductions to be made before his Time would be free.

In the meanwhile, I was flushed. I was enthralled. Had he captured the Muse within me, or my heart? Eventually the beating of my heart began to slow toward its more usual pace. It was his Art that had captured me – not the man. Yet somehow it was hard to separate the two. What would I say to him?

He had awakened my Muse from her long drowse. I hurriedly found a piece of reed to dip into a muddy puddle and then scratched some words onto my undergarment, which I had stretched over my lap.

Before very long, Cuthbert was back at my side. I was still Enchanted. I could do naught but smile at him like a silly girl.

"Oh, my Lady Morgan, I hold nothing but honourable intent toward you – may I touch your beautiful delicate hands? They are the hands of an artist. I noticed how gracefully you held them in your lap, when I approached the Lady. I know that you are a Priestess of the Goddess, but I do not know what work you do here at the Order... surely nothing of hard work – for your hands look as soft as an infant's. May I touch them? Only if it would not make you feel uncomfortable..."

"Cuthbert, you may hold my hands. But you must understand that it will go no farther than that between us."

"Oh, my Lady Morgan, I hold no expectations..."

There was a very awkward silence...

I could not help but to wonder why I had said that? I thought, "I am bound to no one man. Lucian – whose ribbon I still held – had raised desire within me when first I saw him on the field. What would I do about that?" Nothing, I suppose, for I had seen Arthur's reaction and shameful behavior in response to my accepting Lucian's cloth and granting my favour to him.

"Cuthbert, I was enthralled by your poetry and your beautiful voice as well as with the deep tenderness with which you sang it. Truly, I am unable to explain the depths to which you have touched me. You have inspired me. I thank you for this gift. Should I live to be one hundred years, I will always remember it – and you. I wrote these words for you, in the hope that they may express my feelings better than I could speak them at this moment."

He held my hands then. It was as if a spark had jumped from a Fire onto them... "So then," thought I, "I am still swept away..."

These are the words I sang to him...
"How I Love your Dark Music,
Passionate Vision,
Words so bitter-sweet...
Haunting, yearning, exquisitely burning
My heart falls at you feet..."

I have not seen him since that Day...

Lucian

It was upon that Day that I met Arthur – Arthur, in all of his colours and passion. It was then, too, that I first laid my gaze upon Morgan. I was so young then... How could I have known that my life – or the better part of it – would be spent entwined in Arthur's glory, as well as in my Love for Morgan. That Day is as clear to me as if I were re-living it. First, I was to meet the one man in this world that could have made me willingly leave my family and my beautiful home in Rome to live in the dreary, Misty land of the Britons. Yes, this I would gladly do for the young King whose rising star had already been so brilliantly acclaimed, near and far.

The Games were thrilling. Oddly, the weather was perfect. I could not have been more excited.

Then I saw her... She was sitting in one of the seats of honour, just beside the Lady of the Lake. She was the most beautiful girl – well, perhaps I should say young woman – I had ever seen. I still remember what she wore. She was dressed in grey, which somehow enhanced her flawless, dusky skin and vibrant black eyes. I thought: "Have I been stunned by the brilliance of the Sun? The Sun, yes, it must be the Sun that makes her long, black hair glisten so." She stood out in contrast to all others around her. My heart has been hers ever since.

But, my heart holds Love for another, too – Arthur, my King and my friend. In all the world, he is the man I hold in highest esteem.

Yet, later, on that very Night, I was to learn of their tragic Love for one another.

From that Time until this I have honoured Morgan's stated desire that we be no more than friends. Yet, I have always thought that I saw more than friendship in her eyes that Day... I had offered a strip of cloth to her – torn from my tunic – as an emblem of my desire to know her better, and she had accepted.

Arthur

"How long? How long have I slept?"

"Three Days. You lost a lot of blood. You could have died! And a good thing it is that this is not your *sword* arm..."

She was angry. When I was just a little bit better, I knew that she would not hold her feelings back from me.

I tried to remember – had she ever shown anger toward me before this?

Oh, yes, I remember. When I was seven, she found me swimming in a deep Creek, with very swiftly rushing Water and many large boulders. Yes, I remember everything.

The next Day I awoke feverless. Morgan was still there. She had fallen into sleep on a pallet on the floor beside me. I tried to raise myself. The pain was still severe, although a bit better. My head was still swimming. "...still drugged, then..." thought I. I fell back with a groan and Morgan awoke.

"Arthur? Are you better?"

She felt my head and my hands.

"Good – no fever. Thank the Goddess, you will be alright."

She looked pale – with dark circles beneath her swollen eyes. Had she been crying for me, then? What more harm have I caused? She smiled at me, but it was forced; I could tell...

Then she said, "Lucian – he has asked about you every hour of the Day, so sick with grief is he over the cut he inflicted upon you. But, Arthur, he is not to blame for this. What were you thinking?!"

So here it was – her anger – about to bubble over like a boiling cauldron. Fair enough – I knew that it was deserved.

"I know it was my fault Morgan, but why do you find the need to protect Lucian so?"

Puzzled, she said, "What is wrong with you, Arthur? I asked you what you were thinking to behave as such..."

"As such a fool? Morgan, you do not want to know what I was thinking."

She looked surprised and then became silent. She was staring at me – through me – comprehension dawning in her eyes. She held my gaze. Large tears began to roll down her face. So, then – she had read my thoughts and felt my feelings.

"Oh, Arthur, what will we do?"

"Let me say it then, Morgan... I Love you more than everything and want you more than life. This I have lived with, but you, you could not keep your eyes from him and when he expressed his desire for you... I just went mad. Mad with fear and jealousy. I have been a fool – a fool to not realise and accept that you will be Loved by other men. It is your right. I cannot have you in the way that I want to or try to keep a hold upon you. You are not mine as wife or lover, nor will you ever be. I know this well. But in my heart... in my feelings... I am tortured by the picture of you in someone else's arms – and bed."

"But Arthur, we – this land – needs you as King. And I *do* Love you!"

"Yes, I know," I interrupted "As brother."

"But I do Love you, Arthur. I could not bear your Death. There is an old adage, which says: 'The King is the land and the land is the King.' You are our shining hope. What if you were to lose your concentration on a real battlefield, or if you let your troubled heart lead you to recklessness? All would be lost."

"Morgan, without you, all *is* lost to me. I know that I will ever be tortured by this."

"It cannot be, Arthur!"

"Then, Morgan, what I beg from you now, is that you use your Magics to remove this all-consuming, overpowering Love I hold for you. Make this Love go away. Let me only Love you as my dear sister – for truly I Love you that way, too."

Morgan looked at me, sadly and wearily.

"I do not desire Lucian, Arthur."

"That is not the point, Morgan. You will Love someone, someday. This, I do not think I can bear."

"Arthur, there is no Magic to *cure Love* and no Mysteries which can extinguish it. The Flame of Love burns brightly – Sometimes eternally."

I felt woozy, faint. I exhaled and fell back onto my bed.

"Oh, Arthur, I would do anything for this not to be so. Forgive me for scolding you, especially since you are still so weak. Give me your leave to go now and I will ask the Goddess what can be done for our great trouble. Here, I will leave young Gwenda to watch over you."

Chapter 19
An Eternal Love

Morgan

So profound was my sadness and worry – for I could never in this life give to Arthur what he wanted of me. I knew this. He knew this – but how to fix it?

He must never learn of my feelings for Gwyddion, whatever they are, for Gwyddion is like a Father to him. Oh, but mine is not a great *Love* for Gwyddion – surely not in the way a woman Loves a man. Perhaps it is more an infatuation with his intellect and Spirit. I may never fully understand my feelings for him – only that I feel a-flutter when he is near. Then there is the fact that Gwyddion seems to have no desire for the flesh of women, or if he does, he has chosen never to express it. Perhaps he has buried it so deeply beneath his vast and complex genius that even he knows not the whys or hows of the thing. I have often wondered if Gwyddion believes that he is like the hero Samson of the Hebrews, who lost his strength through the cutting of his hair by a faithless lover. For, this is what I think I have read within him – that he fears the transfer of his Love – his energy – into another and that somehow that act would drain him of his Magical powers. Betimes I have wondered too, if this may not be more than an irrational fear of his. He could be right, if this is indeed his fear. I have wondered if he could feel a premonition of some distant Fate he may suffer.

I chided myself: "Perhaps all of this musing on my part is a way of putting off what must be done – to leave my own sadness and desires behind and to seek the Wisdom of the Voices."

So, I dressed in my Enchantress robes, brought along a long and pointed Crystal that I had found at the mouth of the Cave beneath the Tor, and then climbed the spiral path to the Stone Circle at its summit. There I built a Fire and upon it offered the Crystal as a libation to the Spirits of Fire. When – and if – the Fire intensified enough to shatter the

Crystal, I would have the sign that my entreaty had been heard. This being done, I shed my clothing; and naked as at my birth, I laid myself, once again, across the Green Star Stone.

Always there is a Wind upon the Tor, and although it was the warmest Time of the year, I felt chilled. Was that a feeling of foreboding? I tried to relax.

About the Time of my seventeenth year-turn – in my second year of training – the Lady Vivianne herself began to teach me how to, at will, go to a place of my own Creation in the Otherworld. She taught me how to use deep breathings which, when combined with a certain hand gesture and the closing of my eyes, would transport me to that place – *my place*. This method was to be used whenever I must traverse the Other Realms when alone, with no one to Drum or Hum for me.

"And" said she, "there will be many such Times."

She painstakingly worked with me to lead me through the Creation of my own place of entrance into the Otherworlds, one chamber at a Time...

"It should be everything that you imagine a magnificent chamber to be. Create it in what dimensions and in what manner and with what furnishings you would most desire it to have. Begin with an entrance – a gateway or a doorway."

To this I had given much thought. The entryway into my chamber was an arched top, rough, wooden door. From there, this chamber eventually grew from "my chamber" into "my world" beyond form.

So, when I laid myself down across the Star Stone in the deepening of twilight that Day, I made my hand gesture and began deep breathing. I continued... eleven, twelve, thirteen breaths – knowing that upon the closing of my eyes during this practice, I would be transported into pure other-consciousness and, once there, to be held to my flesh by an imaginary "Silver Cord" which would keep me alive – for if this "Silver Cord" were to break, my breath would leave my body and fly with my Spirit to the Stars. So, I closed my eyes and entered the world of Trance.

Whenever there, I find myself in an enormous Cavern on a footpath. The pathway follows the curvature a great rocky outcropping jutting from the wall of the Cavern. This outcropping is itself the size of a small cottage. The edge of this outcropping lies to the left of the path, and just to the right of the path is a great precipice, falling into the depths of the Cavern. There are wooden posts running along the right edge of the footpath – with thick ropes tied between them – to prevent one from falling over the precipice into the deep unknown. Far below is its floor. It is immense... dark... and yet I can see as if on a clear, Full Moonlit, Starry Night.

My Bees await me on the footpath. They speak to me in *words* here. The Fawn that I had Loved so very much as a young child – who

Morganna's Wildcat, Terror, had torn to shreds and half eaten – greets me. I pet her.

Across the breadth of the Cavern is another, seemingly wider ledge. Animals play there.

Always it is the same.

I see that, not far ahead, the path ends abruptly where a narrow ravine interrupts its progress. There is a swinging rope bridge to allow passage across the ravine to the far ledge. At the bridge's end there is another footpath, at a perpendicular angle to the bridge, forming a crossroads of sorts.

I take two steps forward, crossing the path. There, in front of me is an ancient, rough wooden door, with iron brackets, crossbars and an old rusted latch.

Always there needs be a key... I say, "Where is my key?" The key appears before my eyes. I put it into the latch, pull the latch down with my hand to open the door and enter. As I step into the first chamber I see that just to the right of the doorway, hanging upon the wall of entry, is an oil lamp. I raise my first finger to make a motion toward the lamp and the Flame flares. I close the door behind me. Now I am ready to begin my work.

I look around the chamber. This is my library. On the left there is a long wall with wooden shelves filling its entirety – floor to ceiling. The shelves are filled with leather bound manuscripts – books and scrolls of vellum and woven pages, containing the Wisdom of the Ages. They are all here for the reading; all here for me. Yet, I have never opened one of them to peer inside. Each Time I wonder, "What am I waiting for?"

There is a trestle table in the middle of the room, with a three legged stool pushed beneath it. Behind the table and stool, on the far right wall there is some straw bedding with woolen blankets tightly wound around it and Wolf pelts covering it. I have yet to lie upon it.

Beyond the trestle table, toward the opposite wall from the door of entry, there sits a large chest. Upon it, leaning against the wall, is a polished bronze mirror.

Things change in here sometimes. It happened once upon my being here that suddenly, atop the chest – which had always before been bare wood – lay a long cloth of finest gold and scarlet silk, embroidered with fanciful Animals, flowers, and leaves. Long fringes hung from its sides. Upon that same Day I saw sitting there a golden sphere, with indentions all over its surface. I, as yet, do not understand the function of this strange sphere. There also appeared at that Time a wooden box on the floor in front of the chest. I feared to open it. It seemed somehow a portent of some evil yet to be visited upon me. "Why?" I asked myself, but never have I gained an answer. The box remains there, unopened.

To the left of the chest and mirror is an open doorway into a dark, short corridor. I walk through it and one step down then turn to my left and yet another doorway faces me. This one is always open, too.

Through this passage is a great chamber, with a red mud brick floor – which bricks have been baked hard and buffed to a low sheen. This is a vast chamber – spacious and never crowded. It is always cool, dim, and slightly humid. All the walls are made of grey Stone.

On the long left wall, there is a kind of Waterfall or fountain. Its stream is narrow yet more than a trickle. The Water falls from ceiling to floor, into a short, round Well or basin, which lies beneath it. It makes a delightful, melodic, splashing sound. I have always Loved the sound of falling Water. Perhaps that is why it is here.

On the right side of the hall is a seating area, with a coloured wool rug from Byzantium, spread upon the floor for warmth and comfort. Two low benches face one another on either side of the rug. On these are carefully placed Bearskins, to provide softness whilst sitting upon them.

Against the far right wall is a great Fire chamber, large enough so that I can stand within it, reaching both arms out from my sides – or reaching up – without ever touching the Stones of its inner walls. Mind that I have never before seen such a Fire chamber in this world of form – only have I heard of the one that is in the fortress of the late Vortigern, which Gwyddion, The Merlin designed. Within the Fire chamber a large cauldron is hanging from a strong iron arm that swivels. There are forged Firedogs to support the logs. They are ornamented with Dragon's heads on their fronts.

The whole back wall of this Fire chamber is a secret Stone doorway. If I were to push this door open, I would find behind it a deep cylindrical shaft made of dirt and Stone, which is twice as wide as I am tall. It extends far upward as well as downward beyond sight. Every now and then, within its walls, there are open portals. If I were to jump into this shaft – which I have done on many occasions before this Day – I would float like a feather on a breeze, gliding downward or upward at will – there awaiting the one portal which most intrigues me. When found, I can enter it by reaching out to grasp the post and lintel opening, then pulling myself toward and through it. And there, as I enter through the opening, I would find myself in another Time and place; sometimes in another life in the distant past, or sometimes in a future realm. However, this is not the working for this Day, so I pass the Fire chamber and its passage by.

Walking toward the great hall's back wall, I see through its large arched openings a perfect Forest and hidden garden, which is strewn with Standing Stones – some erect, some fallen. Although the light in this great chamber is always subdued – like mid-twilight, somewhere between light and darkness – the Forest – which is deep, lush and completely covered by a canopy of branches and leaves has a very different light and season each Time I walk into it. Sometimes it is Day and then in the blink of an eye, Night. Or Winter and then Summer. At this hour a beautiful Snow is falling in my Woodland garden. Perhaps, by the Time that I have my answer, it will be early Summer here, with petals falling, or perhaps the season of Red and Gold leaves. My Forest ever changes his face.

I exit through another passage on the far right of this wall, leading out to my sanctuary. There, in the distance, is a Spring, bubbling up between the exposed gnarled roots of a Birch Tree. All about I hear the whispering of the Wind through leaves, Bird song, and the rustling of small Creatures. There is a small clearing in the middle of the Forest where there is another Spring feeding a Well. It bubbles up in great, large, persistent bubbles coming from far beneath the Earth's surface. It makes the sound of "gu-glug, gu-glug, gu- glug." Beside this Well stands a monolith that is indwelled by the Spirit of the Spring.

It is here – amidst the Waters springing up from the depths of the Earth – that I will ask for the answer that I seek and listen for it.

So, I laid myself upon the Mossy ground near to the Well – for it had indeed turned to Summer in the blink of an eye. I aligned my Dream body with my body of flesh and bone, which lay upon the green Star Stone on the Tor – back in the world of form.

I prayed: "Great Mother, Goddess of the Stars, of the Sun disc in the Sky, and of the Fire in the belly, Healer of wounds, Great One of Magic, Granter of desires – please answer my entreaty.

"My questions are these: Why does this overwhelming Love between Arthur and I take each of us upon a different path – for so strong is our bond, yet we each feel it in our own and different way? And how may be prevented the dire consequences of Arthur's jealousy over me? Speak to me, oh Lady of comforts; give answer through the sparks of this Fire – of this, my libation to you. For surely, the not knowing will drive me mad."

I began to Hum an ancient tune... waiting. Then did the Voices of the Stars speak: "Morgan..." whispered they – "Yours is an eternal Love. You and the Bear have been together through many lifetimes in this world of form and so will you be for many more – and even when you have each accomplished what works have been fated for you upon this Earth will you be together amoung the Stars. There in the breast of the GREAT GODDESS will you be together and still will you Love. For there is a Sacred Secret; that once Love or anything else exists in this Cosmos, it can never die completely and become nothing. For all things, once in existence, become a strand of thread in the fabric of the Weavers' great Web – the ONE, the ALL. Even beyond the next great dissolution, perhaps Love will remain. For when all returns to the MOTHER, SHE – who *is Love* – remains. This, however, is only a supposition on our part, for we, too, are part of *this Time* and can see no farther than what will be in *this* incarnation of this Cosmos.

"Morgan – at Arthur's birth, the Stars were crossed. In this life, each of you has a great work to do, albeit different tasks, one from other. In each your own way, you will work towards the same objective. Arthur will make History and you will be its Keeper.

"You must be the Stone from which his sword finds its voice. And his must be the voice of the people, of peace, and of saving the old Gods and the old ways from extinction. So write, Morgan, collect your histories, thereby you may save the knowledge of the Mysteries.

"As lovers reveling in the gifts of each others' souls and flesh, both of you would be distracted from these grand works you are about. For this reason the Stars crossed, but only for this Time, Morgan – only for this life, only for now."

The Voices disappeared into the laughter of the bubbling Waters.

"Oh, Arthur," quoth I, "then I am truly barred and forbidden to desire you in the way that you desire me. But my dearest one, never will my Love be barred from you."

Tears wet my cheeks.

"But wait, do not leave me – please come back!" I prayed. "Oh Spirits, I have not yet gained the answer to the most important question of all...

"How can I be the Stone from which his sword finds voice and what must I do to protect him from this obsession of wanting me – from the dangers and distraction of it? His dread of my ever loving another could kill him, this I know. I would do *anything* to protect him. So please, what must I do?"

Once more they crept quietly and slowly into my awareness.

"Morgan... Morgan..." whispered They.

"Yes?"

"You know what you must do. Do we really have to tell you? Have you not yet learned, Morgan, that you must be careful of what you ask for? Everything has its cost. For everything there is a price. If we tell you what to do, you will obey us because of who and what you are. Do you really, then, want us to say it?"

"Yes," said I, "because I would not have the courage to do what I think must be done without your direction."

"Well then, if We must say it: If you would insure Arthur's safety from the distraction of his jealousy over you, then you must never share your Love – your body – with another man while Arthur lives, and this you must vow to him.

"But be warned, although this *will* save him from his distraction – his obsession – and you *will* save his life for a Time, you cannot save him from his desire for you, or from the grief he must surely feel over what he has caused. He will loathe himself always for what price you will pay. Remember, Morgan, everything has its cost. We are sorry for you... We are sorry for you... We Love you..."

The Voices faded. I lay there softly crying with the gift of understanding.

I exhaled and opened my eyes. There I was amidst the Stones of the Tor, in the cold Midnight Air, with an aching back and a broken heart.

Everything has its cost.

Arthur

An entire rising and setting and rising again of the Sun had passed. She was gone from me, yet I was feeling better somehow.

On the Day past, Lucian had sent a request to speak with me. I was embarrassed to see him, but of course, I did let him come. Not a word passed between us of our combat – only did we speak of the Games and of who had been named Champion this year.

It had unfolded like this: At the very last, when all other contenders had been eliminated, the contest was between Bedwyr and the Scald Cuthbert of Hengist's court.

This Bard had done well in the Games, in both strength and wit, but had saved his best for last. He bragged that no valiant acts of Archer, Swordsman, Ax Thrower, or Wrestler's skill could compare with the wonder of the story he was about to tell.

With his marvelous voice that could be heard by all participants around the field and the audience of the Games, he told of the mighty adventures of Thunor – the Lightning and Thunder God of the Teutons. On and on he went in a great song of power and beauty, as the Sun moved one sixth of the way from horizon to horizon. Never did his voice tire, nor did he stumble over a single word. All in rhyme was it, and all held within his memory.

Although the story was old and honoured, he himself had made the poetry and the melody and put the words together in rhyme. And, although he was Saxon, he had composed and sung it all in the tongue of the Clans. I believe this to have been the first of their sagas ever to have been translated and rhymed in Cymric.

Everyone was so rapt in their attention to him that for the whole while he sang and spoke, no one else uttered a word. Not a sound was heard but his enthralling performance. When he was finished with his story, many women and even some men had wiped tears from their eyes. None could but name him Champion.

Bedwyr was the first to call it. He said, "I bow to your greatness, Cuthbert the Bard; you are indeed Champion of the Games of Lleu! I concede to your brilliance."

When Lucian described all of this to me – with his infectious charm

– I had to leave my concerns and mad jealousy behind me and call this man 'friend.' I asked if he would stay here with us, in Our Fair Isles, as one of my Companions. This, he said he would gladly do.

As Time has gone by – until the hour of my writing this – he has become one of our greatest Warriors and truest of my friends.

He left me after a few hours and then I rested, awaiting Morgan.

When Morgan returned, I was fast asleep. She sent my attendant away and sat beside me.

For the first Time in my life, I had Dreamt a Dream that seemed more than just a Dream. I saw Morgan in a deep Cavern and then, abruptly, she was in a Forest by a Well. It was Snowing. I thought I heard voices whispering to her – then it changed again and she was on the Tor, crying. I awoke to find her beside me.

"The Dream I just had, Morgan – it was so real."

I told her about it.

"Arthur, you were there! Did you hear what the Voices said to me?"

"No."

She smiled sadly at me, held my hand in hers and said, "My beloved brother, listen to me – for what I tell you now is my Sacred, unchangeable, vow."

A feeling of foreboding began in my heart and spread quickly to my arms, stomach, throat – where I felt that it might choke me to Death. She continued: "Please do not speak until I have finished. You are our King and the one who will bring peace amoung the peoples. Your great Vision as well as your acts of honour and valor will become part of history and because of my efforts in saving the true history of this Time, the old and true ways will not be forgotten. This has been promised to me Arthur, and this I believe. And so, I vow to you: as you live Arthur, I will Love no other nor to any other will I give my passion or body. You need never fear or imagine this again, for there is no one that I could ever Love as much as I Love you, my brother – my Bear."

"No, Morgan! I will not be your bane – your ruin... I forbid this!"

"No, Arthur – this is my decision and my vow. You cannot change it."

"Oh Morgan, no... I never meant for you to sacrifice your happiness for me. It is unthinkable."

"It is unchangeable."

"Oh, GREAT GODDESS, say it is not so. I have ruined your chances for Love and happiness. I never meant to hurt you, Morgan. I have been so blind and selfish. I loathe myself for this."

"Arthur, I *am* happy, and I have much Love in my life. I live here, on the Isle of Apples, in peace. I have my work, my sisters and brothers of the Order, my bees – and I have my Love for you and our dear Mother..."

"I am cut to the bone by this. I will never recover from this wound. I am punished for my selfishness. Then, Morgan, I will also vow to you. Never will I..."

"Arthur! Do not dare to copy my vow! You will be mocking the cause of it and making my vision of you untrue. You are speaking from pain and self-imposed guilt. Stand strong, my King, this is the way it must be. It is Time for you to put aside your fears and put your Kingship before your feelings."

I opened my mouth to say something else...

"Stop! On your Love for me, do not dare say what will or will not be. I have *seen* it...   And I have *seen* your bedding many women in the future..."

"I could never... not now."

"Long ago, Bear, before you were born, my wise and kind Father admonished me: 'Never say, 'Fountain – I shall not drink of thy Waters.''"

I felt the Wind from her energy blowing my hair back... so powerful had she become. I sat staring at her. Her eyes... they held me captive, and they were shouting at me: "Arthur this would be unforgiveable folly!"

She was speaking...

"What did you say?"

"It must become known that you can desire a woman who is not your sister. No insinuations of perversion can tarnish your history."

"Perversion? You are but my half sister and we grew up not knowing. Do you, Morgan, call my Love for you perversion?"

"No, I will never think of it as such, Arthur. But in years to come, stories and legends will grow and change. They will be coloured by the values of those telling them.

"You will have an heir, a bastard like yourself... This, too, I have seen."

"Oh, Morgan, will you ever forgive me?"

"My Bear, I Love and honour the man you are. You have done nothing for me to forgive. Let us vow to each other here and now that we shall allow no wedge to separate us or tear us apart – not ever."

"I vow it, Morgan."

"And I vow it too, Arthur."

Morgan's eyes – or those who spoke through them – had said: "You will have an heir, a bastard like yourself." "Perversion... an heir? Morganna! Why had I never thought? Of course – *Hers* is the perversion. She will raise her child to hate me. Will he – or she – then Spell my doom?

For some strange reason, just as these realizations dawned in my thoughts, the ancient words I should have spoken at the Heiros Gamos

Ritual – while I had instead just stood silent – came flooding back into my memory:

> I am the great Stag
> The hunted and the hunter
> I am the Grain of the Barley
> Full and ripe in my prime...

> I am feral
> I am hungry
> I will taste of the ecstasy of your body
> We will be as one...

> Ever knowing I will be cut down
> Like the Harvest at its prime
> Devoured by you
> Great Mother of the Earth

> And there waiting in your belly
> For the good and proper Time
> Will I rise again as does the Grain
> Another King, another son...

> For from you all proceeds and all returns...
> The Stag, the King and the land are one...

So now I knew. An heir... cut me down in my prime.

"Then indeed, I have much to accomplish while I live.   Again Morgan, your Wisdom leads me. Thank you, my eternal beloved."

Post-scriptum...

If I have got a bastard upon Morganna Le Faye, then in all urgency I must beget a legitimate heir upon my wife Gwenyfar. Pray the Gods I may persuade her understanding and cooperation in this...

Chapter 20
Return to Gwenyfar

Arthur

When I healed from my wound, I took leave of Morgan, Lady Vivianne, and the others of the Order and began my return to Dumnonia. However, first I veered in a more Northerly direction to visit the great baths of Aquae Sulis, which the Romans had built. The entire setting was magnificent! Great marble statues of Roman Gods and Mythic beings stood everywhere I looked. Even the interior of the pools themselves were covered in smoothly fired pottery tiles – depictions of Neptune, Jupiter, Minerva, and Nymphs of the Seas. Around the old Roman town and baths, a great city and marketplace had sprung up. Once, there had been whole streets of Iron Forgers and Gold- and Silver-Smiths, Merchants hawking exotic Herbs and even Fruits that did not grow on Our Fair Isles; also were there wines from the Roman vineyards of Gaul, silks from the East, and beautiful woolen carpets. Virtually every luxury that one could hope to purchase had been available. But, that was in a Time past... Now the baths were not as well manned as they had been; where once had been a great city, there was now a mean town. Yet, it did still support a thriving market. Of course, this was the high season for travelers and therefore also for Merchants. Surely before the Days grew colder and while the passage was still good, some of these Merchants would cross the Eastern Sea to the warmer lands on the Continent.

However, the hot Healing Springs would flow all year long – intensified by brilliant Roman engineering. And there I was, fascinated by it all.

My plan was to bring a gift of great beauty and worth home to Gwenyfar. The gift must be something personal to praise and enhance her beauty – a husband's or lover's gift.

I searched every Merchant's tent or wagon for two Days, walking through dusty streets filled with well-kempt tents and ramshackle huts and smells of all sorts – sweet and pungent as well as the stench of overripe meats, fish and refuse.

Finally, following the scent of an exotic perfume, I looked into the open entrance of a pavilion, the ceiling of which spiraled upward into a pointed cone shape. The light wooden frame had strange letters from the desert lands of the East etched into it. I had seen these letters before in one of Morgan's books. Within was a man with brilliant white teeth smiling at me and welcoming my presence.

I paid close attention to the Merchant himself. He had a dusky complexion, was well dressed and groomed with perfectly clean hands – even beneath his fingernails. In his youth I suppose that he had had dark hair, but now it was mostly white, and very curly. His intelligent eyes were large and almond-shaped – and he was somewhat corpulent, which is taken as a sign of prosperity amoung his people. This would be fun. I entered.

My eyes were drawn to a table of glittering silver, gold and gems...

The moment I saw it, I knew that I had found the perfect gift for Gwenyfar. It was a delicate neck torque of hammered silver with a perfectly matched pair of clear red Rubies set into each end. It was lovely. I knew that it would be costly.

Before the Merchant would quote a price for it, he offered a small glass of wine to me, which, he said, had travelled with him all the way from his Tribal homeland. At first I declined... However, quoth he, "To quench a thirst... to feed a hunger... to console a loss... these are the customs of our hospitality. So I pray you, linger a moment in the comfort of my humble pavilion, so that you may accept my offer and that we may speak of something pleasant before discussing trade. Will you?"

Intrigued by his softly spoken words and genteel manners, I decided to accept the drink and sit as he had invited me to and to linger awhile to look around the inside of his beautiful tent.

The walls were hung with carpets, most of which were coloured the natural colouring of Sheep or Goats. But then, around the borders were woven intricate patterns of green, red, blue, brown, and yellow wool. On two of these carpets, in their center, were oddly intertwined geometric patterns. Upon another carpet were two figures – a Man and a Woman – also entwined. When he saw that I admired them, he said that they were called 'Wadd' and 'Suwa.' These, he told me represented the Magic of 'Manly Power and Mutability' – as best I could understand – and of womanly 'Beauty.' On another carpet were a Bull, a Horse, and a Vulture. These he said were named: 'Yaguth,' 'Ya'uq,' and 'Nasr,' respectively. These images, he said, imbued his travels with 'Brute Strength,' 'Swiftness,' and 'Sharp Sight' – or perhaps 'Insight.'

About the images on yet another carpet – he said with a beaming smile, "These are the Three Goddesses... 'Al-Uzza,' whose name means 'The Mighty One,' the Goddess of the Morning Star;   'Al-Lat,' the "Mother," whose name means simply 'The Goddess'; and 'Manat,' the Dark Mother of 'Fate' or 'Time.'

"This carpet was made by my wife's family, as our wedding carpet, to pass on to our children and grandchildren... It has long been filled with 'Baraka.'   This I believe you would call Luck or Divine Blessings..."

"What does that smaller one portend?"

"Oh, that my friend, is a ward against 'The Evil Eye.'"

I paid to the Merchant what price he first asked for Gwenyfar's neck torque.   Somehow to me, haggling over the cost would lessen the sentiment with which it would be given. The Merchant was so surprised at this that he bade me stay to see his other works.

"Perhaps you might bring a smaller gift to each of her ladies. That is a way to a woman's heart."

I thought about that. Yes, his was a good Idea. So, for her best and favourite – Branwen – I found an amber ball with an insect caught within it. My eyes then caught sight of a wooden box with intricate designs deeply carved into its sides and a Raven carved and painted onto the top of it. Perfect. He wrapped the amber in a silk cloth and placed it in the box.

For Igraine and Tangwen, I bought silver clasps for their hair. For the rest of Gwenyfar's ladies I purchased thin wrist torques of plain silver. They were delicate and fine enough to show my willingness to please, but not so fine as to compete with Gwenyfar's gift. Satisfied that I had fulfilled my purpose, I thanked the Merchant for his goods, his wine, and the sharing of his traditions.

After taking in the baths, I left for Dumnonia, making a promise to myself that I would return to Aquae Sulis as often as I was able.

Bedwyr had returned to Dumnonia as soon as I was sure to be out of danger from my wound. He wished to visit with Igraine and his birth parents. Gwyddion travelled with him.

It was an hour past twilight when I arrived and all was quiet. To enter into the main courtyard, I passed the Sacred Well. Ribbons hung from the branches of the Tree that grew beside it, swaying in the Wind. Torches were burning brightly at the entrance of and inside the courtyard.

I was well and truly home.

After using some Water of the Holy Spring and fresh Rosemary which lay in a basket next to the well with which to cleanse myself, I dressed and joined the others in the great hall.

Gwenyfar, Branwen, and Bedwyr were playing a board game, gaily laughing. Igraine and Gwyddion – who I had not expected to be here –

were deep in conversation. Two others of Gwenyfar's ladies were in a far corner of the hall doing needlework. I entered and went first to Gwenyfar. She was, after all, my Queen and wife. I thought it wise to do so. She stood and said, "My Lord." I embraced her and kissing her hand said, "Greetings my wife and queen." We smiled at each other. "Greetings Branwen" – she arose and bowed her head. Then I greeted Bedwyr, Igraine, and Gwyddion and nodded at Gwenyfar's two other ladies. They 'bent the knee' to me.

"Sit down everyone, continue your pleasures," said I. "This is our home. Please, let us not stand on formality." This, of course, only addressed those to whom it applied. Never would I let The Merlin or my Lady Mother bend a knee to me – and as to Bedwyr, only at state affairs where it would be expected of him.

My Lady Mother called to the attendants to serve food and drink. They did and we all – save for Gwyddion – drank newly made honey mead and ate flat cakes with dried venison, Apples, and cheese.

After a couple of hours, I whispered to Gwenyfar that I wished to join her in her bedchamber. As ever, she stiffened, but then complied. We bade all a good rest and retired.

All I would do upon this Night would be to give her the silver and ruby torque in private. She Loved it and put it on – right then. It did look perfect with her Moon-lit beauty.

"How lovely you look in it, Gwenyfar. Will you wear it tomorrow when we go riding together? It should be a warm and sunny Day."

"Yes, I will, Arthur, if it please you."

"Then I will bid a good Night to you. Sleep well."

I gently kissed her lips, turned away from her in our bed and bothered her no further.

So it went every Day and evening for a week. We rode or walked and talked of her childhood, our Mothers, Princess Rowena, and so forth.

We also talked about – as she did seem genuinely interested in – all of my youthful adventures. Slowly the wall of Ice between us melted.

Then the Night came when I would speak to her about Morganna's treachery. It could not have been more uncomfortable and awkward. What could I say?

Inevitably, she asked.

"How could she trick you so? You *saw her*, veiled or not. How did you not know her as your sister?"

So here it was, the dreaded accusation, the moment of reckoning. I *had* vowed to Gwenyfar that I would never lie to, or deceive her.

"I thought she was Morgan."

"But Morgan is your sister, too!"

"My *half* sister, Gwenyfar, but we did not know this, nor did our Mother, until I was a man and chosen King."

So I told her the simple truth. I also told her how, at the Rite of Fertility, I had only found out that the Goddess had chosen Morgan to represent herself in the Sacred Marriage, just before it had taken place. I held nothing back. Why should I? Then I told her that now I feared I had got Morganna with child and that now there was an urgency to make a legitimate heir. She stood, wide eyed with her hands held to the top of her chest as if in protection of her heart and throat. I waited. To my relief, she seemed not scandalized by all that I had told her.

"I am sorry for you, Arthur."

"I am sorry for you, as, well Gwenyfar. I know that you did not want this marriage, but now we must make a child."

I smiled.

"I know that you do not Love me but perhaps you will even enjoy our bed frolics..." said I, trying to be light hearted. "Have no fear in answering this, for it matters not to me. But have you ever been with a man in this way? No? Well, I promise to be respectful and treat you gently and lovingly."

Large tears began to drop down her cheeks.

"Oh, Gwenyfar, you might even like it. It might feel very good if you could relax and try to enjoy my body. Please do not cry."

I wiped her tears and gently – but as a lover – kissed her mouth, then her ears and neck. She was stiff and cold. So, I gave her some wine. I was not going to trick her – I told her it had some passion-exciting herbs in it. She drank heartily. When she seemed a bit drunk, I undressed her, carried her to the bed and covered her. Then I removed my clothes, drank another whole flagon of the drugged wine and lay beside her. I caressed her. She *was* beautiful and soft. The drugs in my body were working. I pulled her atop myself and felt the full length of her naked body and her soft breasts upon my chest. I kissed her more passionately and caressed her between her legs. *I could do this.* I rolled her on her back and sucked on her small round breasts and slowly I ran my mouth down to her belly all the while rubbing her between her legs. When finally my mouth grasped the nub of flesh just above the entrance to her womb, I sucked on it to please her. She screamed out, "No, no!"

Her body was wracked with trembling.

"No, please, no. I do not want this, please!"

She jumped out of bed. I sat with my head in my hands. My member was as soft as her pillow.

"Stop screaming, Gwenyfar. Everyone in the fortress will hear you."

"I do not care!"

"I will not *rape* you. Have I moved too quickly?"

"I don't know – perhaps. Oh, I am sorry, Arthur."

I covered her naked body, wrapped it in a blanket, kissed her forehead and said, "Goodnight then, Gwenyfar."

I let the Night go by. Upon the next Day she seemed truly contrite.

The following Night I tried again. She only lay in bed stiffly, crying softly. But this Time, drugged wine or no, I could not become hard enough to enter her. I knew that it was no use. How could I spill my seed if I felt numb? I slept chastely in her bed again that Night.

I thought I heard weeping in the next chamber...

By the end of the week, my patience had worn thin. I had to leave upon the next Day as there was word of enemy Saxons on the move and their boats coming toward land near *Lindisfarne*. So, for one last Time, I tried again. This Time my body responded – perhaps from desperation and a bit of anger. She spurned me again – vehemently saying, "You just do not understand!"

I got up, threw my tunic on, and said, "No, I do not! I do not understand!"

Then I slammed the door behind me. I did not get very far down the hall when I stopped and put my head against the Stone wall. "Breathe, Arthur," I told myself – as The Merlin had taught me to. What had she said? "You just do not understand"? What did I not understand? Perhaps she had been violated somehow. Perhaps even in her childhood. I stood there composing myself for a few moments. Then compassion overtook my heart. I strode back to her chamber door, flung it open – prepared to say, "What do I not understand Gwenyfar?" But my voice only got as far as "What do..."

To my complete astonishment, what I beheld answered everything. Gwenyfar and Branwen stood in the center of the chamber. Gwenyfar was completely naked and they were locked in a lover's kiss and embrace. Gwenyfar's back was to me and Branwen held her head and beautiful blonde hair in a caress of such Love that it took my breath away. I said nothing, speechless. They broke their embrace and Branwen pushed Gwenyfar behind herself in a pose of protection.

"Do not hurt her! Kill me if you must, but I beg of you – do not hurt her."

She dropped to her knees.

"Take your sword and run me through but by all the Gods do not hurt her."

"You Love her!" I said. "Truly Love her..."

"Yes – since we were children."

This I understood well.

I smiled. So now I knew.

"I will never hurt either of you, and I will never make Gwenyfar cry again."

I walked toward them.

Please, lord, do not put her away. Take two wives, but do not shame her."

"I will do neither. Your secret Love is safe with me. I kissed both on their foreheads.

"There is no shame in Love. It is the Goddess' greatest gift."

I turned and left them to their privacy. So it was settled. There would be no legitimate heir.

I got Bedwyr up from his bed.

"Tomorrow, Bedwyr, we ride to battle. Tonight, let us drink, laugh, and go wenching."

He looked surprised.

"I will be dressed in a moment, Arthur."

We rode to our usual village tavern. However, before we paid our gold for the rooms and the wenches, he said, "Arthur, let us talk a moment."

"Alright."

We were served ale and he began...

"Is there trouble between Gwenyfar and yourself?"

"No." I laughed. "Not anymore, Bedwyr."

"I do not understand – you were just in her chamber, are you not spent?"

The reason Bedwyr dared speak so frankly to me of such intimate things was because of the closeness of our hearts. He knew that I would not be offended by his query.

"No, my brother, I am not spent.   The marriage has never been consummated. Of course you must give your oath of honour to me that this conversation between us tonight will never be repeated to anyone."

"Yes, yes, on my honour and my Love for you... But the blooded sheets?"

"A trick to save her honour... What is wrong Bedwyr?" asked I as his face paled.

He blurted out "Is she just *afraid* of sex?"

"Oh, I think not..." said I, with a chuckle of laughter.

Incomprehension filled his eyes...

"But then, what?"

"It is a sensitive issue, Bedwyr."

"But Arthur, it is also a sensitive and very important matter that you must get an heir upon her! Truly, there must be a way to persuade?"

"You are missing a great piece of this puzzle, Bedwyr. The Weavers play seemingly cruel tricks upon us all."

I looked deeply into his eyes. It did not take the 'Sight' for me to see into his troubled heart. I had always known that he desired and perhaps even Loved Gwenyfar. I saw a sudden dawning realization in his eyes. Had he just read my thoughts – that I knew of his emotional attachment to her?

"Arthur," said he, "You know that you can trust me with anything."

Yes – it was true – never would he betray me.

"Of course I trust you Bedwyr, as much as anyone else in this world. So, to satisfy your burning curiosity and worry, I will give the missing piece of this puzzle to you.

"First I must tell you that I will *never* put Gwenyfar away and I will not take a second wife as do some other Kings. While she lives, she will be Queen of our realm. My voice trailed away, deeply into my thoughts.

"You see Bedwyr, Morgan's Voices have told her that I already have a son."

"What? How?"

Silence hung between us for a moment.

"Oh, Gods... Damn Morganna's trickery!"

"Never to worry, Bedwyr – I myself am bastard born and this has not stopped my gaining the Kingship."

"But *why*, Arthur, does Gwenyfar refuse you? Surely she could not hate you so much, for you have ever been kind to her."

"No, she should not. And hatred is not the problem; rather – Love is the problem. We may even become friends someday, I believe... I hope."

"Arthur, this *is* a puzzle. I feel that there is much more to this than you are saying. So tell me... Why?"

And so I did. I told of all my efforts, patience, and cajoling; of the events and revelations of this very Night and of Gwenyfar and Branwen's Love.

Round-eyed as a Buck surrounded by a pack of Wolfs was he. Shocked, Bedwyr was sitting before me in disbelief of the unfathomable truth that had evaded us both for all of this Time. When I had finished explaining this to him, I felt a sardonic smile growing upon my face, although I tried – for the sake of his feelings and for Gwenyfar's honour – to seem a bit grave. Ah, but my efforts were of no use, for in the telling of it all, I found it ironically humorous. I could not help my expression any more than my sense of relief.

Bedwyr was just staring at me, blank faced. I looked down at the wooden table at which we sat, save I break out in uncontrollable laughter. I took a draught of ale, swallowed it, and played with a knife that lay upon the table in front of me. I spun it with my fingers like a nervous child. I bit my bottom lip and then looked up at him. I was still hopelessly grinning and trying ever so hard not to laugh.

When finally he found his voice, all he could say was, "Oh..."

Such a small word... just, "Oh..." a word of total comprehension and clear vision of the changing of his world and mine forever.

I said, still smiling with that fool's grin, "*Indeed!*"

"Drink up, Bedwyr, and let us find the two most plump, alluring, and desirable wenches with whom to quench the Fires of our loins this Night.

For, on the morrow, we ride to battle."

To my dearest Morgan...

I have written what is above for it is truth. However, if you think these words of a too scandalous nature – I mean that they should not be left for posterity – well... I will defer to your judgment in this. Remove them at your will...

Chapter 21
The Genealogies

Nimue

Just past the Time of the Earth Mother's fertility, but not quite yet to Mid-Summer, I arrived in Bergundian Affolonia, there to seek audience with my Grandmother, Queen Vivianne the first – of the court of King Merovech. I immediately sent word to her in the guise of my being a traveling Merchant, offering to her extensive and beautiful wares.

Theirs was obviously a very wealthy court, but beyond that, it seemed as though the wealth was shared by all in the land. There were no grasping beggars; no starving people to be seen and no shabby huts with leaky roofs were evident, either. Everyone was, to some measure, clean and comfortably clothed.

My preparation and guise had worked perfectly. I was admitted into my Grandmother's house and soon into her affections. After I had been there for two years and believed I had earned her trust, I told my Grandmother who I was and all about my Mother. I had not been sure of how she would feel to be reminded of her transgression and perhaps her shame. But she said, "My granddaughter, my heart. Always have I grieved the loss and the robbery of my beautiful daughter, my baby girl, ripped from my arms – rending the foundation of my whole. And now, here you are, in the fading Days of my life, bringing the joy, the answer, and the peace with which I may go to my grave."

Her clouded eyes beheld me as though I was her life's greatest treasure. My fears of rejection had been completely unfounded. My existence would always be our secret, to be kept between us – and from her people. She had bidden me to send word to my Mother, Vivianne, of how happy she was to know of her wellbeing and successes. This news of her daughter and her relationship with me filled the rest of her Days with joy.

I soon found out to my astonishment that many men there – and women too – were literate, some still in the old language their Ancestors had brought with them from Old Jerusalem. Others spoke Greek, as well. Their Holy Men – both Hebrew and Christian – had some books in the ancient tongues of Greek and Hebrew, the latter being close to Aramaic. I learned that these related tongues had originated in the land of the Chaldeans, wherein was the city of Ur – from whence their Holy Books say Father Abraham had come.

These people, secretly, yet exuberantly, shared their histories and legends with me. They have an "In the beginning" Myth or actually two – depending upon how Mystically oriented was the person telling it.

Creation Myths always interest me, for in a very basic way – albeit culturally coloured – they are all similar: "In the beginning," "Once Upon a Time," "In The First Time," "Before the Fall of Man, when everyone was a Seer or spoke with the Gods, the Animals and the Birds," there was a Paradise on Earth.

This makes me wonder whether the legend of my Mother's people – about the one hundred original boats sailing away from their doomed land – is not just another such Myth of origins... origins, that is, of their original Ancestors and therefore Divine right of Kingship.

Oh, it is not that the propaganda of Kings and their lackeys of all lands have not claimed the special support of their Gods at Times, but it has ever been understood that their enemies or competitors have their own Gods, just as alive – if not as powerful – as their own. I had very much hoped that the old Jews, as well as the Christians here, were more tolerant than others, and they were.

However, they all strictly keep hold of their belief in their God's chosen bloodline of Kings, through Father Abraham and King David. And here, most Christians and Jews alike claim descendancy through Yeshua, Miriam of Magdala, or Yosef of Arimathea.

Legends of the origins of these people abound, and some are quite complicated or fanciful. I will relate the one held as truth by my Grandmother:

The man named Yeshua, the King – the Christ – had been killed. His followers had immediately dispersed after the crucifixion, for fear of persecution by Roman and the Jewish Sanhedrin "powers that be." However they rallied soon after, with the advent of Mystical stories of Yeshua's arising from the dead and being whisked away upon the wings of Angels into the heavens – as had their legendary prophet Enoch, long before.

These followers became many – as Yeshua had not only been a great Wise Man and Philosopher, but the anointed and accepted King of the Jews through the line of King David of the Tribe of Judah. They called themselves "Nazarenes."

When the dreaded persecution did begin, Yosef took the woman

Miriam, Yeshua's companion – which is what the Jews called a wife – Miriam's young daughter Sara, two other women, and three male friends with him – and fled Old Jerusalem.

They sailed across the great Southern Sea – which the Romans call Mare Nostrum – in a Merchant vessel, to its far Northwestern coast. There they established a community in the area of Aix en Provence.

Roman historians have written that "After the Romans sacked Old Jerusalem, the Jews were forced to live with much tribulation." Most of them eventually fled the immediate Roman environs Westward across the Mare Nostrum to live with their ever-increasing population of kin.

...and perhaps the Royal Family?

Miriam of Magdala was of the royal line of King Saul of the Tribe of Benjamin. This is important; because as my Grandmother's people reckon it, the only true GOD of the Jews, and the great Father God of the now called "Christians" had *Himself*, first chosen Saul to be King of the Jews. Then, changing His decision – no doubt due to the rebellious nature of Saul – bade his Prophet Samuel to anoint David – of the Tribe of Judah – as King of His "chosen people."

This created a problem for many, for according to their cultural tradition, the Kingship was supposed to be *hereditary*.

Many people of the Tribe of Benjamin had held resentment that an heir of Saul's had not been anointed to the Kingship after Saul. Apparently, this resentment amoung them had quietly lingered for all of the centuries that passed until the Time of Yeshua Ben Yosef!

This long rift would be healed by the joining of Miriam of Magdala and Yeshua, the Nazarene – thus uniting the royal lineages of David and Saul.

It has been speculated by some that the reason for Yeshua's great support amoung the people and his acceptance as their King, was because of this joining.

It is the Jews' centuries' long tradition to keep very strict genealogies, for they hold it of the utmost importance that the true Royal bloodlines of King David, King Saul, and of their rightful heirs, be kept safely in written form.

These genealogies state that my Grandmother, who is now called Queen Vivianne del Acqs – Queen of King Merovech – is a direct hereditary princess through the matrilineal line of Miriam of Magdala and Yeshua, the King.

I know that a list of every generation since Miriam of Magdala and Yosef of Arimathea has been kept in secret – and in many houses – by my Grandmother's family's genealogists to preserve it; one Day to claim the sovereign Kingship of all the lands they be worthy of. Yet, in my own thoughts, I wonder, "What lands are these? and, why does this matter?"

The most important aspect of this was the right of Kingship.

This concept of Kingship by Divine right is widely held. Most royal houses and even Clan and Tribal Chieftains try to legitimatize their claims by faking their genealogies back to an original Ancestor or to people from the Stars or to the Consort of the Goddess or even – as in their case – to the one HIGH GOD.

Perhaps some legends do hold truly historical memories from the distant past. There may be seeds of actual truths in these tales.

Yes... I suppose my Mother was right, I am a cynical realist.

But to continue the story...

The following are the words of my Grandmother Queen Vivianne, wife of King Merovech: "My Mother was the hereditary princess of the royal line. Her Mother named her Sara, which means 'Princess.' That had also been my Grandmother's name. My Grandmother had been so acclaimed for her Wisdom – even at a young age, that her Grandfather had taught the Magic and the Mysteries of the Secret Books to her. This was a thing forbidden. She was sworn to keep this knowledge to herself, as tradition held that only married men could know such things. After her Grandfather died and her daughter – my Mother – had begun her menstruation, my Grandmother could not bear to keep these secrets silent, so she taught my Mother all. My Mother was a rebellious girl – she would NOT go along with her Father's wishes regarding anything. One Day, in a rage, she told him that women should not be treated as inferior to men. "I hold the Blood Royal within me through my Mother, so why should I obey *you* in all things?" Then she spat forth "I know the Mysteries of the Secret Books!"

Her Father asked, "Who taught these things to you?!"

Of course, she would not hurt her Mother for anything under the sun, so she never answered him. This only made his anger and hatred towards her grow. He retorted, "Sara, you hold the Blood Royal, but so does your sister. You must be removed far from our midst. I have made a marriage contract with the King of the Svars, Gundaharius, so that you will not be able to contaminate our families of Burgundian Affalonia. Gundaharius is desirous of your Holy Blood for his children."

"I will NOT marry this man!"

"Oh? Well, then – you do have another choice. My men will take you – bound upon a Horse – far from here into unknown territory, untie you and leave you with only the clothing you are wearing, a flask of water, a loaf, and one gold coin. This I will do so that it may not be said of me that I caused your Death. Which is your choice?"

Of course, she married the King of the Svars and went to live in his land – far from her family. There was one stipulation that her Father insisted upon in the marriage contract with Gundaharius. This was that she never be known as 'Sara' in his land. Her husband agreed. Now, in the families of the Svars, women are treated much differently than in Provence or Burgundy. There, women fight alongside their men and have their say in all things. Of course, my Mother was happy to hear this! Also, in that land, the Arts Magical are revered as were the Magicians, Seers, and "Knowing Women," perhaps too, a little feared.

When my Mother first saw her husband, she Loved him and his long, thick, fair hair, which fell over his shoulders in waves. And so did she Love his blue eyes!

Seeing how things were, my Mother told her husband of her great knowledge. He said, "Then you will be named Brunhild – 'She who knows'."

I was born of their union – Princess Chlodeswinth, later called Verica and now Vivianne. It seems that I was too much my Mother's daughter, for at fourteen I met a young and handsome archer for hire from the Old Tribes of the Britons and fell in Love with him. We made a child together – she who is your Mother, Nimue. My Father hid me away from sight of all until I gave birth... then... well, I suppose that your Mother has told the rest.

When I was seventeen, I was married to Merovech and came South into his land and thence here, were I was reunited with my Mother's family... My Mother – 'She who knows' – had secretly brought a scroll that was a copy of the genealogies of every generation from Adam –the original Ancestor – through her Mother Sara. Every generation! As I was leaving her land with Merovech, she gave it to me. I now ask you, Nimue, to write my name, your Mother's name, and your name onto the scroll.

I have heard of the Library of Secrets of the Order on the Isle of Apples. I ask you to have a copy of this scroll made, leave the original in the keeping of my family here and then, please, give the copy into the hands of your Mother to place in the library."

I remained in her land for six years, then she died. I grieved her loss, yet I knew that she went to her Ancestors in peace.

I felt it Time to go home then, so Owen and I, as well as those of our company who had not made new lives in this wonderful new land, returned to King Arthur's Misty realm.

Of course the first place I went was to my Mother on the Isle of Apples.

Owen had family that he would see too, so we went our separate ways. I stayed with my Mother for three months, giving into her hand the written account of her Mother's ancient bloodline. By that Time, I had to get away. Their peaceful, quiet lifestyle at the Order was not what I was accustomed to. I longed for my freedom. My Mother understood. So, we said our farewells and I began to travel Northward.

Chapter 22
Nimue, the Dragon
Caller

Nimue

I had never really seen much of these Fair Isles, so once again I began sojourning into unknown adventures as Nimue the traveling Merchant. I went as far as the land of the Picti, a wild and craggy land – a land of Bracken, Thistle, and Heather, of dangerous rocky shore lines, of splendorous Lochs and Mountains. There were Islands off the mainland in the choppy Sea, where there were many ancient Stone Circles and monuments. Once I saw the great swirling coloured lights in the Northern Night Sky. I watched the Full Moon dance between a row of monoliths, high upon a ridge. The Lady's Dance, they call it.

Here in this wilderness I came to know the painted barbarians – they who practice very primitive, ancient Rites. There was amoung them a woman – a Seer – who was very old and powerful. Her sagging jowls, the deep lines around her mouth and eyes, and the creases in her forehead betrayed her age, but more than that, they seemed to tell the story of her life's journeys and her Wisdoms. Her hair hung matted nearly to her knees. The palms of her hands were stained red. The tongue she spoke was hard for me to learn at first, but I did learn it well enough to get by. I have always been gifted in languages. She trusted me for some reason and eventually allowed me into their Ritual circle of power.

Upon one of those occasions, strong and chaotic Spirits – of something – moving, dancing around me, were brushing my cloak and hair. I even saw and experienced their Ancestors in these Rites and many other wondrous things. They painted me blue, even tattooed their symbols upon my back – symbols so old that even they had lost the meaning of most of them.

It was here in the far North that my Great Teacher called to me – to me – the cynical realist, the skeptic, the one who had all but scoffed at the Gods!

One Night, the old woman led me to a blazing Fire amidst a circle of Stones. There, standing calf deep in the heavy Snow, which had been falling since Sundown, the old woman presented a staff to me. It was as tall as I and had the same symbols carved deeply into it as had been tattooed onto my back. A black Serpent spiraled down its length. She told me that it was to be used to call the Great Teachers to me. She related to me and the six others who were observing, that she had spoken with one of these Teachers while in a deep Trance that had lasted for three Days and Nights. She said it was especially momentous 'to be by the power of three.' Have I not heard this expression somewhere before? She said that she had made the staff exactly as *my* Great Teacher had instructed her to do in her Vision. My teacher? The moment I held the staff in my hand, I felt an opening up of myself. I was as one with all around me. Even the Stars were reaching down to me. The Rocks, the Land, all Animals, all People – everything – everything was a piece of me as I was of them.

Words fail me to explain what I felt and what changed within me, but at once I knew that nothing in my life had ever been this real. She called to my Teacher, in words I did not understand. I told her so. She smiled a broad toothless smile and then laughed.

"I will let *Her* tell you," she said. Then, all the observers backed away from me and vanished into the heavy frozen Mist. I waited. I cannot say for how long. Hours? No Time at all? Slowly a hissing whisper came to me.

"I claim you, Nimue… but only if you accept me. This *one chance* you have. Only *once* will I call to you. Will you be claimed or no, Nimue?"

"But, what or who are you?" I asked.

"What do you think, Nimue? What do I feel like to you?"

"You feel different – not Human nor Ancestor nor Animal."

"You are saying what I do *not* feel like. I asked what I *do* feel like. Stop using the body that thinks, Nimue. See and feel through your Magical eyes and tell me what I am. Time will come and Time will go, but only now may you answer – or I will leave you forever."

"No… No, do not go, please. You are…you are…"

I had to fight to hold onto what was almost in my consciousness, but was tearing itself away from me. Moment by moment I was thrown out into a dark and churning Sea, yet in the same moment I was falling… falling into an eternal, benevolent darkness. There was no Time, there was no place. I surrendered to primal extinct.

"You are a Dragon! But I do not fear you – no one could. You are

Wisdom, you are goodness and you are the Great Teacher of my Spirit. You Love me... I Love you... I only now know that I have been waiting for you all of my life."

"Many lives, Dragon Caller."

I wept and wept. The Tribal people surrounded me again. They rattled, drummed, and called out. They seemed to glow in the Mist. Were they all Dragon Callers too?

Then I saw what the churning and swirling energies were. Many, many Dragons, all beautiful, but especially was mine, and so to me she would always be.

In the weeks to come she told me what to call her – and that I *may* call her, and that she would come whenever I did.

No one had to tell me that this was a silent tradition. Only should I tell their Mysteries to another one touched by – or called by – Dragons or to another Dragon Caller. I knew without a doubt that I would recognize these ones when they came into my life, as I knew they, too, would me.

As years went by, I would call for Dragons and whole chambers or Fields or Forests would fill up with them. Many became lifelong companions, but only one was my own Great Teacher.

Never could I learn from whence they have come, or what exactly they had been before they all ascended into Spirit form. Once I made up a story about them – my myth went thusly...

Aeons ago Dragons had been the dominant and most intelligent race on this Earth. But the Time came about that they had all served their required incarnations of life on this Earth. And so, all together they had ascended to the Stars – save for one Dragon.

This one Dragon was broken-hearted to leave this place. She could not bear the thought of leaving this world behind without the stewardship of a race of beings as – or at least almost as – intelligent and wise as Dragons. She knew, of course, that within the great Seas were Creatures such as the Whales and Dolphins, but as for the land...

Now, really she should have known that the Mother Goddess would leave no void – that She would provide. Besides which, intelligence might not be as valuable as the Love, Spirit, and instincts that the other Animals had. But this Dragon would have her own way. So, as all of her race flew towards the Stars in one mighty flock, she stayed behind.

She had a plan. She rolled up a ball of wet mud made of Water and Earth and she rubbed two Stones together with her mighty front clawed feet to create a spark of Fire. Taking a living branch from a Tree, she lit the branch with the Fire and blew her breath upon it to create a very hot Flame. Air, Fire, Water, and Earth had she used. Then to gift her Creation with life, she cut her wrist and bled out her life's blood upon the wet muddy ball. She became weaker and weaker – still she nurtured the muddy ball, determined to give it her last drop of blood.

As she bled and as her mud ball cooled, she lay herself down beside it to keep it warm and safe even whilst the burning branch had extinguished and turned to ash.

She continued to weaken...   But before she breathed out her last breath, she saw to her joy and great amazement that the ball began to crack open as if it were an egg. There inside there were two Human babies, one male and one female. They looked very strange to her.

Then an awful thought came to her – who would feed them? Who would teach them? She fretted mightily. But just before she died, a great Idea came upon her.

You see, Dragons bleed in great large drops of blood – so as she had just enough strength left to drop her last drop of blood, she dropped it into the babies' hungry open mouths. Then she hissed, "Eat the bloody mud and ash, oh my Creatures of earthly Elements." Then she howled a beautiful Deathsong with her last great breath. Within this Magical song she left knowledge of all of the Cosmic Mysteries to the babes as well as the gift of creativity and Love of music, poetry and dance.

All of the other Dragons looked down from the Stars in great sorrow, knowing that their sister had sacrificed herself for the babies. They held counsel together and vowed to protect this new kind, which held the last earthly drop of Dragons' blood.

But as ages passed, the Humans became less and less like Dragons. That is to say that although they had been gifted with Dragon intelligence – well almost – they lost the Dragons' heart.   Most of them lost the ability to see and feel the Spirit Realms and could no longer hear the Dragons' call. Even worse than this, they became haughty, vain, and selfish. So far away from the first Humans' nature had they become, that even the gifted and sincere could only see Dragons when Dragons made great effort to be seen. As Time went by less and less did the Dragons care to *be* seen.

Realizing this, the Dragons held that they would fervently guard their own treasures – which are the Wisdoms of the Ages – by Flame and by terror, to assure that only true seekers could breach the entrances of their Caverns.

Or so does my imaginary tale go...

Still I do wonder sometimes if there is not a remnant of Dragon blood in me – for I have felt its Humming and Drumming every moment of my life since I stood in that frozen Mist in the center of that Fiery dance of Stones and heard my Great Teacher's call.

Chapter 23
The 12th Battle Strategy

Arthur

In the eleventh year of my reign...

Should I have to account as to where the years have flown, I would surely fail.

In my own defense, I have been very busy running a Kingdom and fighting battles.

Some things, it seems, never change: my Mother's beauty – she looks as young as when I married Gwenyfar – oh yes, my marriage does not change, my friendships – all but for the fact that two of my Companions of the "Seven of Battles" have lost their lives in skirmishes and battles against the Saxons. All has been well with my dear teacher and councilor, Gwyddion, and with my brother Bedwyr. The alliance still holds strong.

Almost every year we have travelled to Table Rock for games and political talks. Every year I have supported the Games of Lleu on the Isle of Apples, and upon three of our year-turns I spent the Longest Night with Bedwyr and our families at Dumnonia. The other Longest Nights I have spent with Morgan and the Lady, celebrating and being included in their Sacred Rites atop the Tor, and for all of these I am grateful. But, history? No, these years have rolled by in the mean events of a plain, mortal man, not warranting historical measure – not, at least in my way of reckoning.

However, we have fought eleven battles against marauding Teutons.

By the fourth year past my crowning, it proved not only to be Saxons who thought to eat up our lands. No, they had been joined in ever-growing numbers by Angles, Jutes, and other Teutons who we have been unable to recognize. Most of these battles we had won – if they can be called wins, for I saw no purpose or gains in them – and some we had lost. In losing these we had lost men and a few villages – only later to regain most of the ravished lands.

Of course, by then, these villages were filled with the living blood of these Teutons. Simple folk were they, just wanting to live their lives being able to house and feed their children. I had not the heart to slaughter them. So they remained – under the laws of our alliance of peace.

Beyond these events, my life seems as if every Day has been lived in sameness.

I thank the Gods for Bedwyr as he is the one who keeps me, shall I say, social. We have continued to frequent taverns and ladies of the Night whenever the occasion was to *arise* – much to our fun and pleasure, save for the fact that never has there been even a rumour of a woman with child from my philandering. To tell it true, this was a disappointment to me on some level. Even a bastard might become my heir some Day, if he – or she – be worthy. But this fact has also given rise to the hope that Morganna did *not* become with child from the Night of her treachery toward my body. And – no one has heard from, or of, Morganna since that Night.

Perhaps I am just tired or overly sentimental, but for whatever reason I am writing this tonight; it is a good and long overdue thing.

Regarding our twelfth battle called *"the battle of Baddon Hill"* – which battle was *not* at Baddon Hill at all...

There came the morning when we were to leave for battle against a new and deadly influx of combined Teutonic forces. We thought that it should be a decisive battle, for never before had we received reports of so many of their long boats coming toward us. We, of course, had our spies in the thick of the continental Saxon lands to warn us of such a threat.

I awoke at Dawn, dressed, and went down to my Lady Mother's Great Hall. The Merlin was there drinking warm, honeyed Spring Water and speaking with Igraine. A Fire of Oak and Ash was burning strongly and it was warming them well, despite the very cold Dawn. Great billows of smoke rose straight up through the round hole in the center of the roof, ascending in an almost perfect spiral pillar. Outside, the Wind coming from across the Western Sea was angry and howling. It was not yet the beginning of the season of Red and Gold Leaves – barely into the Vine Harvest in fact, yet it seemed as though it would ride in '*with the Teutons, like the Hounds of Hell'*...

So ironic was it – or perhaps so Magical – that Gwyddion, The Merlin always arrived at my side just at the point of his being needed... and this with no warning or summoning! He would just appear at my side – no preamble or explanation, just... "You needed me Arthur?" or "I thought it best to arrive today." This was the way of it, although sometimes weeks had passed since last we had spoken with one another.

Igraine and Gwyddion held a long and deep respect and friendship for one another and oft' Times, when together, were engaged in fervent conversation. This morn was one of those Times. Gwyddion held her hands. This was the scene I saw as I intruded into their private moment. Had she been crying? I abruptly stopped. There was Igraine, with her great Gift of the "Sight." Had she *seen* calamity for us in the upcoming battle?

"Good morning Mother... Gwyddion... I am sorry; it seems that I have interrupted your privacy with one another...

"Gwyddion, again you come precisely when you are needed – thank you for that... I received word of the true location of the imminent invasion just yesterday. Has Lady Igraine brought you up to date on what is happening?

"But, my Lady Mother, I see that you are upset! Pray tell me you have not a foreboding toward the outcome of this battle."

"Arthur, my tears are not spent only for sake of this battle – but also for a more personal loss."

Her words smarted me. She knew about Gwenyfar and that there would be no legitimate heir of my body. Had she always known about Morganna's nocturnal visit to by bedchamber, too? The Gods only know what she knows – about my heart or my sexual desires, failures or betrayals... There had never been any logical point in trying to hide anything from Igraine. Had she not said on the Day of my marriage to Gwenyfar; "She has her *reasons* and they have nothing to do with you as a person" and that Gwenyfar had much to lose through this marriage? Perhaps she had known all along. But then, why had she not told me? I did remember that upon a long Time ago I had overheard her say to Morgan, "There are Times – for those of us who have the *first Gift – the Sight* – when we 'See' what is to happen and if we give warning regarding those events which *might* come to be, and if in those cases people pay heed to our warnings the future might be *bent* toward a more favorable outcome. However, there are other Times when the Weavers have woven unbreakable threads into the carpets of our lives – for reasons only They know. In those cases, although we have *seen* what *will be* before it happens, we can only stand still and watch events unfold into the un-changeable future. The second *Gift* in these circumstances is to know the difference between the two seeings – at which point we must weigh the loss and gain of making these events known. The *third Gift* is to have the *grace of silence*, even when our heart screams out to sound the warning. Do you understand, Morgan?"

Had my marriage been one of those unbreakable threads? Evidently so...

"But Mother, what do you *See* of this battle?"

"Many men of good heart – friend and foe alike – will die on the killing field – and women too. In war, as in all other things, nothing is ever all one way or the other, Arthur. As for those we call enemy, theirs are warring and aggressive cultures. They have only ever been exposed to their Motherland's ways. Their beautiful, golden, braided women fight as ferociously as do their men. Violence is their creed. They know no other way. It is also so that the soil in their colder countries is not as rich as ours and many of their children starve to Death for the lack of what grows so prolifically here. So, for the people who have allied themselves with us, as well as for those who are invading our Islands, I weep. I weep for the Fatherless children and the widows who will be left alive in a strange land – some with no family, friends, or comfort. Arthur, there can be no battle without losses on both sides. And yes, I have 'Seen' many of your good and brave companions die or be horribly wounded in this battle."

"Not Bedwyr, Mother! Say it is not so!"

"Oh, no my dear one, Bedwyr will not die, nor will you, Arthur. But I do *beg* of you to keep a watch on Gwyddion and Chronos, so that they be well guarded on their every side. I know that Gwyddion always watches from a Hilltop or dense grove of Trees – far from the thick of battle – yet I have fear that some treachery is afoot, aimed towards his person on the morn of battle."

"You never need *beg* anything of me. I will heed your warning well. Gwyddion, I will personally choose those who will stand your guard. Or... perhaps you should help me choose them."

"Yes... yes Arthur, I will..."

"Lady Mother, I do not want named to me those who will be lost. But I pray you *Hum* Magic songs for us and beseech the Great Mother Goddess to let this battle be a worthy beginning of true peace."

"I will, Arthur."

"Gods' will it be so..." said The Merlin and I in unison.

"Good. Let us retire to my personal chamber, out of anyone else's hearing, to allow me to share my strategy for this battle with both of you."

As we entered my personal chamber, I poured some Watered wine for my Mother and I, and some more honeyed Water for Gwyddion. In our privacy we spoke of many things. The most pertinent and unusual was about a Dream that I had had.

The Dream...

"In the early hours of a morning, near two Moon's Dances ago, I had a strange Dream. It went thus wise...

"I awoke from my slumber, arose from my bed, left my bed chamber and walked all the way to the very precipice of the high and rocky outcropping over the Ocean, upon which this fortress stands. All the while I was, in truth, still fast asleep. Deepest darkness had descended the land. But then I saw what could not be... The Sun began to rise in the West, to glint the Western Waters. "No" cried I, "the Sun rises in the East!"

"Nay, but I twist all around" – said a sardonic voice – "I am Loki – God of dis-order and confusion. I have used my foolery well for in such tricksy ways I always find delight. This Time it was by making a wager with Sol – which I won – then collected Her forfeit by summoning Her into your eyes...

"Now come closer, oh blinded one, so that ye may stumble and fall into the churning deep... For it is said... 'What danger thou cans't see, thou cans't defend thyself against.'"

"Of a sudden, I cast my eyes downward, with my hand blocking out the light, and lo, there was my bronze long body shield lying on the ground beside me. I thought, "What is *that* doing here?" and then, "Oh yes, but this is only a Dream." So, I picked the shield – which of a sudden was polished to a high sheen – and held it in before me to reflect the Sunlight, which was then thrown back at Loki, who hung suspended over the Sea in front of me. The reflection hit him with full force and tumbled Him head over heels and spun Him round and round, back to the Sun, who then swallowed Him up whole.

"Then all was dark again and I was back to my bed, sitting full upright.

"What could it mean? Upon this I pondered for seven Nights and seven Days. Then understanding dawned upon me.

"So, five weeks ago I sent the order out to all of my Guard and Shield Bearers, to polish and buff their long-body shields 'until they shine like mirrors.'

"Most of my Guard and Shield Bearers lived close to our fortress in Dumnonia. Some lived in re-fortified old Roman barracks and some, who had families and lived in cottages, were spread as far afield as Aquae Sulis, but to all had my word been delivered.

"Great caution must be taken in all matters regarding this battle. It is our twelfth and I pray our last for a long and long Time. Because, remember, the number thirteen, which signifies our Moon Mother, is also the most Sacred number to the Teutons' powerful Goddess Freya. I have felt her energy myself, in my bedchamber escapades with Saxon women." I blushed. "Pray excuse me, my Lady Mother... But powerful is She. It is said that **half of the souls of the bravest Warriors who** die on battlefields belong to Freya – to keep with Herself in *her* realm of the dead! Were She to be a greedy Goddess, a thirteenth battle may go awry for us. So, let us not tempt Fate – all must go as I have planned."

The Strategy...

"The formations will be thus... Bedwyr will lead the Vanguard. Two rows of Long Shield Bearers will take front line. Behind these will stand two rows of our Archers, who will be ready to let fly – or to run left and right out of the way of our Cavalry, as needed – at my command. Last in the Vanguard formation will be our finest Foot Warriors, just to the rear of the Archers.

"Lucian will command the left flank, where the Picti will be – we hope – and Kai will lead the right...

"Gwyddion, you will watch from a protected Hill and do what Magic you will for the right outcome – and that all be over with as few Deaths as possible on either side.

"Before the action commences I will remove myself to some elevated point that is in clear view of all of my Commanders – where my Standard Bearers will already have been stealthily waiting. I will be a-mount of course in the event that I am needed upon the field.

"Hopefully I will find the terrain suitable to these formations.

"At our last skirmish, my Companions overtook and confiscated three Saxon ships from the defeated and fleeing invaders. These were very interesting in the fact that, while many were built only to be rowed, these were to be sailed by the power of the Wind. Of course, Roman Ships have always had sails, but most Saxon Ships have not. One of these confiscated Ships had a Boar's head and two had Dragon's heads at their prows. They were in good seaworthy condition.

"Whilst examining the long boats for possible later use, my men found hiding in one of them two enemy Saxon men, two children, and one woman – all of whom were alive and seemed well although hungry. Even so were they terrified for their lives! The two men were speaking bravely, albeit nervously, in Saxon words, which were fortunately understood and translated by one of our own Saxon men.

They tried to reason that even though *they* were enemy Warriors and therefore expected to be executed by my men, the Woman, dressed in battle garb, was only a Shield Bearer and had not killed anyone. They suggested that she be kept as a slave. As for the children, they said that these were not their sons, but were slaves, taken aboard to do service for the Shipmen – and so were also not deserving of Death. All of our men standing there laughed at these assertions, they being obvious lies. The two boys looked exactly like one of the men and in fact very similar to the other... their Father and their uncle perhaps? Yet my men did not run them through, for I was not far from them and they would wait until I gave orders regarding this matter.

I, taking opportunity, whilst it be given, bought for a price the service of those same two found Saxon Shipmen – who will sail aboard these recovered ships, so as to act as interpreters or spokesmen, should our ships be called out to or challenged during the battle. To these men, I promised great wealth and safety for themselves, the woman, and their captured children. I also promised to them a plot of land, oxen, seeds, a Goat and a cottage – *if* they comply with my orders – or at their choice, immediate Death to themselves *and* their woman and children, if not."

"Arthur!"

Both Igraine and Gwyddion expressed their shock at my words.

"Oh, do not worry. You both know that I am not a child slayer. I only used this threat to keep the men honest. Of course *they themselves would* be run through immediately if they were to cross me... I am counting on their not doing so.

"I recognized, on that moment, that these Ships should us well to trick the Teutons.

"We have completely outfitted these three ships and have copied every contrivance that we have ever seen on other Teutonic vessels. We found that we must replace one main sail on the Boar's head ship, and so, painted it in typical Saxon colours, complete with their knot work and standards. Now they are fit to sail and will be awaiting our arrival at the expected site of battle.

"As to the site of battle, I have had an itching in my stomach and in the back of my neck that their whole clever plan is to confuse everyone by spreading rumours that they will invade in the South. But you see, the rumours are too wide spread to have allowed them a surprise attack. Their Commanders are ruthless and passionate but they are not stupid!

"First we heard that they would invade from the East Coast going up the River Witham to anchor near a great mound called Baddon Hill, at the site of Lindum, in the old Briton Kingdom of Lindes. Next we heard intelligence that they would try the daring venture of navigating the Southern tip of our main Isle and then Northward, coming inland to Aquae Sulis via the Afon.

"Either would indeed have been a good site for a battle. The very name of Lindum leaves much room for conjecture. For, as we know, in the tongue of the Clans 'lindo' means 'pool,' and *dd* is sometimes pronounced as the Teutons pronounce *'th'* and so the 'dd,' as in Baddon Hill, could also refer to Baths – such as are in Aquae Sulis. There is also a pool in Lindum made by the River's end. However the *pool* might also refer to the pools made by their many Springs. In fact, at the settlement atop Baddon Hill, the old public Baths, which the Romans had built, can still be visited. However, unlike the baths in Aquae Sulis, they are not still usable, having fallen into rubble. This ruse would have been very clever – had it worked. For because of this linguistic confusion I would have had to leave half of my army at Aquae Sulis and half at Lindum to be sure to protect both areas.

"As you know, traitorous ones who deal in espionage for gold are always to be found. We, of course, have paid the price to them, to even the score with those of our enemy's purchase. We trust the joke will be on them."

I raised my flagon... "Hail to the spies!

"According to the latest information received by our spies, all of the Teutonic alliance's long boats will in fact be anchoring far to the North in the shallows of the Eastern Sea, hidden behind the ragged cliffs of Alba, in the territory of the Votadini. Through this same espionage I have also learned that this attack will be lead by Cerdic the Saxon, acting as Superior Commander of the combined Teutonic forces in collusion with Osla the Angle, Cissa the Saxon, and Aesc the Jute – all of whom hold great ambitions of creating their own Kingdoms upon our lands, which they would conquer, plunder, and claim.

"In my thinking, they plan first to invade – then conquer – Alba and all those who therein dwell so as to confiscate their lands, thereby effectively splitting our alliance in two. After that they would invade the Southeast of our main Island as so many of their predecessors have done."

I took another drink of my Watered wine. I grimaced slightly – for last Night had been one of *Those* Nights spent carousing with Bedwyr and my head ached with a mighty ache. What a fine way to begin this Day.

"They are grossly mistaken if these are indeed their plans – for our ships will be waiting – anchored and hidden within the many coves that are out of sight from the main body of the Eastern Sea. When the hour is right our three confiscated ships will mingle into the midst of the Teutonic Fleet. Our Seamen will have to be cautious to go unnoticed by those aboard the other Ships.

"The trick is for us to know by then *exactly* where the enemy ships will beach so that by the Time our boats have reached the proper location and have melded into the Teutonic fleet, our land forces will already be there waiting.

"This Time we will have our best Archers *behind* enemy forces – at the Water's edge. The way in which I have planned to accomplish placing them at the shoreline is this: I will place forty of my Archers within each of our three vessels. Fifteen will remain aboard the boats, dressed in Saxon clothing. However, the ones who go ashore will be outfitted in total black, so as to go unseen. After they have stealthily waded to the shore and are well in place and yet un-noticed, our second group of Archers – those remaining aboard our ships – will be ready with pitch-dipped arrows. At the foreordained signal they will set them alight and let fly to burn as many of the enemy's fleet as they can. Then our camouflaged Archers – waiting upon the shore to the rear of the enemy troops, will let fly their Death-birds into the enemy ranks. This will synchronize with the first war cries. But this, although it should prove very effective and a great surprise to our enemies, is not the whole of my plan.

"Quickly after they have set the enemy long boats aflame, *our* Ships will flee Southward, planning for a cold North Wind to billow their sails as quickly as the messages of Mercury – or the lightning flashes of Thor."

I laughed...

"Gwyddion, I am counting on you to Weather-Spell the North Wind into Her dance at the good and proper Time. I am also counting upon the enemy's never suspecting that – or how – we have done this.

"You see, always do the continental North-men employ the same configuration of battle lines. They keep the few mounted, noble Warrior forces they have to the very rear. In front of these stand their helmed and chain-mailed Gedriht, who are the personal followers of the Chief Battle Commander and are sworn to die with him. These carry long spears and some of them have long slashing swords. In the front line are the Foot Warriors, carrying swords, axes, hammers, and long pikes. On one side-flank are a small band of unfortunates; the untrained men and women of the peasant troops, called Fyrdmen – farmers and Goat herders fighting with rakes and shovels or wooden axes, hoping to win a plot of land for themselves upon our Sunny shores. Fortunately they are few, because there is little room on the Teutonic long boats. These Fyrdmen, at the call, run towards their enemy – being used as a distraction to the enemy's forward push. Then the Northmen's few Archers, kneeling to the rear of the peasant lines and hopefully just out of range of the opposition's arrows, step up and let fly – killing many of their own who are in their way. Only when their Archers have spent their arrows do the bulk of their mighty Warriors – men and women – the Berserkers and the Gedriht – run to the clash. They will then send their few excellently trained, armored, and weaponed Mounted Nobles into the fray, followed perhaps by their Commanders. This is their standard battle procedure. Because we know that they always use these tactics, we are assured that that my plan will be effective."

I took another sip of my wine – my stomach souring all the more with my every draught.

"Remember my Dream of Loki and Sol and of the wager lost – that which prompted me to have all of our Long Shields polished? Well, on the morning of the battle, the Sun, rising in the East, will *not* be in our black-garbed, hidden Archer's eyes – as would it be in a usual defense from the inland side, for as I have said, they will have snuck up behind and therefore to the East of the enemy lines.

"Now, you may be thinking: 'But neither will the Sun be in our enemy's eyes – for they will be facing our inland forces towards the

West, with their backs to the rising sun...' and this is true. However, just as the first rays of the Sun rise above the horizon, my Shield Bearers – who will be hiding behind great boulders – will have positioned themselves in a double row, front line in a kneeling position, with the second line holding their shields above the first – thereby forming a solid wall of mirrored bronze to catch and reflect the blazing Sun's brilliance back into the eyes of the enemy. We, being above them on a Hill, will easily be able to angle this reflective wall into perfect position to blind them. Gwyddion, you and I will calculate the Geometry of the needed angle upon our arrival at the site.

"As Loki said... 'What danger thou cans't see, thou cans't defend thyself against.'

"If all goes well, their Mounted and Foot Warriors will become completely disoriented – what with Sol blazing at them from the West, Fire raging amoungst their treasured Fleet in the Sea behind them, and arrows assaulting them from behind. With their Horses standing together in tightly ranked lines, it will be impossible for them to turn their mounts in Time even to face their attackers, much less ever come close enough to slay our Archers.

"As for their Archers – to even get around the mass of foot Soldiers, screaming Noble's Horses and confused, wounded riders will also be an impossible feat. They will be picked off like Apples from a Tree by our right flank Archers.

"Our plan is to drive the invaders back toward their ships – although, by that Time – many of these will be a-blaze.

"It is inevitable that some of their infamous long boats will escape, and that is fine, for they will bring home with them the story of their defeat by King Arthur and his alliance and thus discourage future invasions."

When I had explained all to Gwyddion and Igraine, I said, "It is close to the Time. Let me give orders to the garrison to be ready to leave within the hour, as they have been preparing since yesterday morning."

Then quoth Gwyddion, "With your indulgence, my King, I took the liberty to rouse them three hours past. I thought it best to allow yourself and Bedwyr a bit of rest after last Night's revelry. A-hem... Indeed it will make the riding a bit easier for you this morning. Oh, yes, I almost forgot... here, drink this – it will also do wonders for what, um, urh, ails you."

He winked at me and smiled a wicked little knowing smile. No fooling him about our escapades of the Night past. I cuffed him on the shoulder. Igraine smiled too. No fooling her, either.

About then, Bedwyr, yawning, entered the chamber saying, "Why did you let me sleep so late? I must ready the troops!"

"Already done," said I.

"Gwyddion... of course, you are here. Welcome, my teacher. How do you do that? Always knowing *when* to be *where* in the perfect Time – you must teach this Magic to me someday."

Not long thereafter we were a-mount just beyond the gates of our fortress. All was ready. Bedwyr, Gwyddion, and I bade farewell to Igraine. I left word for my Queen to be well and have no fear. Then we were off.

We made our way to Aquae Sulis on rougher roads than are usual. This near to the Equinox, our Days have most unpredictable weather. This year it rained a little – or a lot – every Day and evening so that the roads were pockmarked with many holes, some treacherous to our Horses' footing. Caution slowed us down.

I began to feel anxious in the pit of my stomach about reaching our destination in good enough Time to put our plan into action. I need not have worried. By the Time we reached Aquae Sulis, where the old Roman road – the Fosse Way – began, the going was much easier and we began to make good progress.

We had decided to follow this road all the way up to Lindum, where the first reports we had received indicated that the Teutonic forces would stage battle. By that Time we knew for a certainty that these reports were untrue. However, just in case they happened to stage a false engagement there, I left a small Guard to take care of any problems – from Lindum on we traversed Northward on the Roman Ermine Way and Akeman Streets.

All along our way, our numbers grew larger and larger, for many farmers and villagers joined our main forces. My heart broke for the very bravery and loyalty of these, my people. How I secretly wished that none of these un-trained men or boys would ever have to feel the sting of battle... Yet I knew that by their honour, they, too, would protect their families and these Fair Isles.

Our Forefathers had long ago assembled a row of Hill Fire posts to be lit as signals, one to the other, in the event of attack. A very old contrivance was this, but useful. As soon as ships were spotted by watchers in the North or South – depending from whence they were sighted – these great Fires would alert the next in the chain of beacons and the next in turn would light their Fire... and so on. We also – usually – had swift Horsemen running from one Fire signal post to the next, where another Horseman awaited in hiding just in the case that foul play or trickery was afoot at one of the stations. These couriers would reach our outposts with orders to assemble at a given Time and place to meet up with us and our allies in the North. This double system never failed me. This Time, however, Fires would only have alerted the enemy forces of our whereabouts and so no Fires could be used.

Gwyddion had originally thought of the idea of runners from one beacon to the next, because my uncle, Ambrosius Aurillious, had died from a wound he suffered in a very small, surprise skirmish. The Saxons had killed two of the Fire starters at critical signal posts so that he had no warning of enemies encroaching. An ignominious end it was for one of Briton's most valued and capable leaders. "All Hail and Honour to you, my uncle" I silently saluted. "May you rest and be joyful in your peace."

It seems right to note here that, for years now, the rumour has gone about that Ambrosius still lives. When my Father, Uther, was named Chief Battle Commander, taking Ambrosius' place, the common folk were probably not even aware of the events leading to this change. Ambrosius had found a place in the hearts of the Britons, as well as now in folklore and memory.

But my Father Uther had not been Loved. By this Time in my life, as I write these histories – the two of them are combined and confused in stories and soon to be the stuff of legends. Perhaps someday *I* will be entwined in Ambrosius' glory too. But this is why Morgan compiles her histories... for truth's sake.

From Caesar Hadrian's wall Northward to just South of the great Stone Hill called Table Rock was quite an expanse. For true – we as yet felt uncertain as to the exact location the Teutonic fleet would land.

As I was silently fretting about this, Gwyddion's Owl Chronos hooted in his ear – a something only he could understand – giving him the true location. The Merlin's eyes – his spirals – began to glow – or was it a brighter misty gray they became? It was always a frightening, yet wonderful thing, to see him thus. Was his *"Sight"* now in the distant future? ...seeing events as they *were* to be? Or was he more present than ever, more aware and more conscious of all around him? Were the "Voices of the Stars" whispering to him?

"Arthur," said Gwyddion, "Mistletoe is deemed the Druids' most Sacred and Magical Stuff of Great Nature. It is neither Tree, nor Moss, nor Herb, although it is connected to each. No, but it is a *parasite* clinging to Oak, Ash, and other Trees... a thing that is not a *thing*, but a great living wonder. Oh, how do I explain? *Here*, ride to battle with this piece of Mistletoe on your person. I myself picked it and cut it with a Golden Sickle at the most propitious Time. Let this be a Magic of *sympathy*. May one thing stand for another. Let King Arthur and his troops become a parasite, devouring the greedy inclinations and desires of all the Angle, Saxon, and Jute invaders who would take our lands as their own dominion. Let this battle, there on that Hill, settle once and for all a lasting peace and comfort for our peoples..."

I think that it was at *that* very moment that I knew we could not lose this battle. My whole body thrilled and my heart beat faster. I felt invincible.

"But wait!" – said Gwyddion with a frown... "I am corrected... Oh yes..." said he with a smile of benevolent comprehension overtaking his face.

"I am reminded of the GREAT GODDESS – She who changes everything She touches. All things come in cycles and nothing lasts forever – neither we, nor this Time of peace and pleasure soon to come, nor the Earth nor the Stars. Nay, not even Her consort, the God of the Wild Dance. So let us be content with a good and lasting peace for a long and fair Time. And for so long as it will last, let this be remembered as *Arthur's Time* – the Time of the Summer King!"

Then his eyes changed back from Prophet's to man's.

At perhaps two hours before Dawn on the morn of battle, the energy in our camp was tangible, like something heavy hanging in the Air around us. But the thrill – yes, the battle lust – was bubbling under, swelling our chests, and stiffening our cocks. Was that what I was feeling? Yes. The battle lust *and* the compelling desire to keep our homeland ours. We were still in control of ourselves, though. We must remain quiet and stealthy. But all knew the mania that would overtake us at the first battle cry.

It was then that first I thought I saw three familiar Mainsails.

"Look to the sea, our Archer ships are safely hidden within the fray of perhaps sixty or more Long boats of the attackers. Their small boats are awaiting their silent slipping to shore."

All of a sudden one of the Long boats let an arrow of Flame fly into the pre-Dawn Sky. Was that a signal from one of our ships that the Archers had slipped to shore? It was a foolhardy thing to do, if so.

"But look!" said I...

At once from the surface of the Sea, to higher than the boats' masts a dense Fog had arisen. None could know from whence came the flaming arrow.

I looked at The Merlin. He was grinning.

"Was this sudden Mist caused by you?"

"To raise a Mist is a simple Magic, Arthur. To best this vast army – three Times the size of your own – now *that* will be real Magic. And that is for you to accomplish!" Then Gwyddion made a little pun: "But win you will – even now the anticipation *is rising* in all your Warriors and Archers."

He, of course, was alluding to the battle lust. He could be cleverly humourous at Times.

But then, perhaps the arrow *was* the signal. If so, this meant that all of our enemy's long boats had stopped and those not beached had angled away from the shoreline, giving each other a fair breadth, so as to not to collide with one another. This meant that all was in readiness.

Chapter 24
The Battle of Baddon Hill

Arthur

In silent form we stood.

Many of our men of the Clans had shaved the hair from their heads – all but for a narrow band from the front of their scalp straight down to their necks – which hair was kept at a hand's length long and stiffened with egg whites to stand up like the hackles of Hounds. Many had stained their hair red and painted their faces with black or blue bands or ancient symbols of spirals and other geometric shapes. Yet, there were some of our Warriors who were still more Roman at their heart and practice. These kept their hair cut short and with no beards or other hair at all on their faces.

Most of the ancient Dark Tribesmen – my Lady Mother's kin – were tattooed with black Serpents on their ankles or five- six- or seven-pointed Stars on their chests, arms or faces. They wore their black hair long and free, with Bird feathers woven into it. Black as Ravens, free as Hawks, and dangerous as Wild Boars were they! They wore no armour – they were covered only by short, kilt-like loincloths.

Then were there the "Painted Ones" – the Picti – who had come to join us from the far North. Terrifying beast-men they were; mud matted hair, wild-eyed, completely naked... intimidating and fearless. I knew that at the first war cry, these Picti men and women would scream – blood curdling screams – never ending until Death or triumph. Besides their terrifying demeanor; they played droning reed pipes that were maddening with their shrill tones, and drums which they beat in wild abandon. These were as frightening as the worst of Night-terrors. Some tales later told that the fight was over at the first sight and sounds of the

Picti alone.

So we were ready; many Kingdoms, Tribes, and Clans joined with one purpose – one beating heart.

Of a sudden I remembered something Morgan had read to me in my youth – of a great rousing battle speech made by an ancient Grecian Commander. Be it truth or legend, so stirring it was as to turn the battle's outcome by sheer might of will and valor.

So, pulling the threads of my memory together, I – there on the moment – found my Words of Power to rouse the men to their finest hour. I unsheathed Caledfwlch and rode the front lines.

"Is this truly the Day we become forged into an alliance of brothers – no longer strangers – held together only by our mutual need of repelling invaders?"

And then, a rare and wondrous thing happened. I closed my eyes and when I became silent – just as Gwyddion had taught me to do – I heard Voices from deep within. I am not so bold as to think that these were "The Voices of the Stars", but peradventure, this was the voice of my own deep will? Whichever the truth – I heard "This is the Time of action, Arthur... Say the words."

My white mare snorted and by her own volition galloped to the left end of the front line of the Vanguard. I held my sword on high. To my astonishment, Caledfwlch began to glow, first green then into blue Flame.

From left to right I saluted my Warriors by slapping the broad side of Caledfwlch against their polished bronze Long Shields. Never in my life had I held the reigns of Kingship so firmly in my grasp.

From the depths of what Well the words came, I will never know...

"My brothers... we were forged in the Fires of necessity... and moulded as though metals through skill and strength – be *it by Gofannon, Vulcan,* Weyland, Dark Moon Mother, the Cailleach... or the Seraphim...

"Out of the Chaos we have grown, into a confederacy of equals of mutual purpose and regard. We have put aside the differences that had separated us for long generations. Together we have created a world of peace, a world of prosperity, but a world that has lived in the shadow of threat.

"Now, here we stand, at this hour, *ready to fight, side by side, for the* sovereignty *of our Islands. Individually, we are strength. Together, we are power! On this Day, that Power is to be tested once more. I, Arthur, believe with all my might and do swear to you by all the Gods and Ancestors, and by the honour of Caledfwlch, that while we stand united and stand fast, we cannot lose the Day.* My brothers, we are invincible!

"Destiny is not a matter of chance; it is a matter of choice! Our stories will be told from Father to son for generations untold. And those who *have* not – or *could* not – come to fight by our sides, will, when they have lived to be old and grey, always remember this Day with regret and say 'I was not there with Arthur on that Day, when he and his compatriots fought so bravely and made a lasting peace upon the land of our peoples.'

"So I ask you, would you have rather feasted at your hearth, getting old and fat on the heels of heroes – or would you become the stuff of legend?

"I have chosen Freedom! I have chosen honour! I have chosen to become a dread and a horror to those who have killed, pillaged, and raped our land...

"I say – on to victory! What say you?"

Our combined troops had been ordered to silence – to preserve our stealth. They all, as with one hand, raised their shields and weapons in silent salute of agreement. First did the Vanguard who had heard my words and seen their Long Shields touched by the blue flame of Caledfwlch. And then, as my words were translated into speech comprehendible to our loyal Saxons, Picti, and Tribesmen, so too did they salute their agreement.

Then we waited...

As soon as the Sun's rays hit my eyes, I shouted the call to battle. At that, a deafening cheer went up; a wail and a keening, banging of shields and drums, screeching of pipes, blowing of the calyx and eerie two tonal Humming arose, loud enough to reach the Star Goddess. Then came the jeering insults hurled at the enemy – all of which did not cease until the Day was won.

I suppose it was as the Weavers had spun events that I was not to take the field upon that momentous Day, for the Battle was won before my eyes, in less Time and with fewer losses on our side than I could ever have imagined. An odd thing it was that, for this of all battles, I was reduced to playing the role of King, astride my Mare, upon a Windy Hill with my Standard Bearers.

As Bedwyr led the Vanguard, I will have him write of how the field of conflict was.

Bedwyr

When the first rank of our enemy's brave fighters were dead or wounded, their second flank of famous strong-armed and courageous ax-Warriors attacked us. Incredible fighters were they. Their Gods of war were mighty and ruthless. I swear by my honour that I saw and heard their Valkyries screech and fly amoung them – egging them on to feats of valor – perhaps conducting their fallen to the Halls of Paradise. Finally my frontline had broken. But little had they known that the great shield wall and Sol's blinding light had hidden the fact that just behind our front line was our entire combined cavalry – none on foot to meet them as equals... I was at the very front of this formation. My mighty sword lopped off the heads of many of their famed Warriors. I thought to have found exhilaration and joy in this. Though I remained in the fervor of the battle-lust while it was happening around me, there were a few lucid moments – and moments only were they – in which that part of me that is man and not killer found no joy at all in this.

Cunningly and brilliantly had this battle been planned by Arthur and then executed precisely. We were vanquishing a vast army of men – only, men such as we. Did I hear the weeping of their women? But then, no Time to think or feel... Women – yes, so fast in the thick of battle did things move, the faces were barely seen – all was skilled action and reaction. Once I noticed the shocked, still expression on the face of a braided Saxon woman whose severed head lay face up on the ground as though looking in eternal challenge at me. ...one of the heads I had lopped off? Then one my officer's War Stallion stomped its hooves down upon the face and crushed it... Gods! What a horror... His rider never realised... My concentration faltered... Then the most irrational thought flitted through me: "Where did that beautiful face go?" – knowing all the while that I had just seen it smashed like an egg – an explosion of blood and brains... I had been distracted – that was dangerous... "Keep awake, man!" I warned myself.

Yes, the Horses – they were as bloodthirsty as any of our Warriors – their hooves kicking and teeth tearing apart faces, arms and bellies. From the slaughter of the Ax-Warriors on foot, the Earth had turned red and green and brown with pools of stinking slime of Human offal, blood, and brains. So much was there, in fact, that our Horses began to slip and fall, crushing more and more men and women. I suppose that this is always the way of pitched battle. I steadied my mount's footing. My heart and breaths, which were racing beyond my control, gave rise to an all-encompassing sickness within me, but I could not let myself vomit or fall, so as to show weakness to the men I led. This, then, was the hardest moment of my life.

Finally, I heard a low and mournful horn giving the Saxon and companion army the signal to retreat. Now, these retreats could be the most fatal part of any battle for those on the losing side... dangerous to turn your backs on your enemy and run. But, Arthur, watching now from his heavily guarded Hilltop command post raised his hand. His royal standard was waved in the signal for ceasing battle. No one was to chase the escaping enemy. All fighting was to stop. The second signal was given to hold prisoner any King or Chieftain, but if they would not be held, then to kill them.

"Hail to the victors!" – how ironic, how empty those words on that moment... Then I noticed a searing pain in my left calf and looked to see a stream of blood rushing from it. How much blood had I lost? Was that why I had felt ill?

So, everything has its cost... the evil and the good, but, which was which? I was never to know.

The next conscious thought I had was in Gwyddion's tent.

The Merlin

I left Arthur's presence as soon as the first Fire arrow had signaled the ready.

I awaited the Dawn on an adjacent Hill, heavily guarded by an escort of six men. And a good vantage place from which to observe the battle it was.

Igraine's foreboding thickened the Air around me. Never would I ignore *her* premonitions... So, from whence would my attackers come?

My guard and I were well hidden in the *Glamour* I had Cast about us. We could see all on-comers, but no one could see us.

Of a sudden, Chronos puffed out his feathers and began rocking himself from one foot to another. Something was amiss – but where? My guard instinctively pulled in closer to me. Too close?

With the ear of my thoughts, I heard the howl – the cry of a Wildcat... Morganna!

In the blink of an eye, I looked into the faces of my hand-picked guard. And I saw it! Eyes glazed, lips curled in a snarl. Swords and knifes out and at the ready for the kill.

I waved my hand and used an *old Magic*: The Magic of the Walkers from Time unknowable. I slowed... Time... down... Not in half, or in a quarter, or an eighth, but by the power of thirty-two – so that one breath or one movement of mine would cover the span of thirty-two of theirs. Such a thing of beauty it was... Such a graceful dance.

While unsheathing my knife, I watched even as their muscles rippled like undulating waves of slowly building Water. Each one of the six I cut down with a stroke to their throat that was never even seen or felt by them. And down they fell like feathers, slowly gliding on a breeze. I had all the Time I needed to watch their bodies bounce as they hit the ground. Then it was over.

I looked around at the leaves swaying on the branches of Trees, Birds flying, landing and chirping – all in the true rhythm of the Earth. Everything was back to normal. Everything except that I stood on the bloody ground surrounded by six corpses of men whom I had known and trusted – and slaughtered in the blink of an eye, the sway of a branch or the chirp of a Bird. *Nothing* was normal...

I vomited and wept.

Morganna had not succeeded in killing Arthur's councilor and protector, but I had been woefully distracted. I must bring myself back to balance – never to falter again. What had I missed of the battle? Was all well? But – oh, yes... it had all happened in the blink of an eye...

The battle raged...

I focused my Grym Hudol and placed myself within the moment of the Britons' victory. I 'saw' what was left of our enemy fleeing the battlefield towards the shore, hoping to escape to their ships – most of which were being consumed in Flame... I cried "And so it is!" as I pounded my staff on the rock upon which I stood.

And so it was...

Lucian

I waited upon the ridge of a small Hill just to the North of the Vanguard. The Picti were under my command – if indeed anyone could command them to do anything.

It was the Time of the Ides of September, as my Roman kindred reckoned it, near the Autumnal Equinox and the Vine and Apple Harvest. In the land of my Forefathers the Elysian Mysteries Festival would have begun. More importantly, the Days and Nights at this Time of year are near an equality of hours, with the Sun rising closest to the East.

Under usual circumstances, the enemy, coming from the East, would have had the advantage – our being blinded by the rays of Phaeton's Chariot blazing toward us in the early morning Sky. But Arthur's brilliant plan placed our Archers at the shore *behind* the enemy lines – their backs to the Sea and so to the sunrise – turning the advantage to our forces.

Bedwyr led the Vanguard. The entire front line held highly polished long-shields in front of themselves with pikes protruding between them. All were ready to turn their shields ever so slightly so as to catch the rays of the Sun and reflect them back into the eyes of the enemy forces.

It was almost Time...

The Mist that had been so dense just moments before had cleared, the North Wind having carried it away.

The Sun rose above the horizon...

Arthur's battle signal went up and all hailed Chaos.

At that moment the Sunlight hit the Picti. Their rage and terrifying visage could be clearly seen by all. Fearless, savage, Picti beasts and unstoppable killers were they. Then began their howls and screams along with their pipes' drones and wailing.

The enemy hesitated momentarily. I imagined their breath taken by the perceived enormity of the strength they faced. They hesitated just long enough for our blackened Archers – who were positioned behind our opposition's mounted Nobles and Foot Warriors – to strike them down with their Death-birds. Horses and men alike began screaming in rage, confusion and agony.

So tightly formed was the line of their mounted Nobles that very few were even able to turn to face their attackers. Those who were able saw to flames spreading amoung their fleet. I wondered if they heard the screams of the men left aboard them.

Their peasant lines were then shoved forward. Many within their ranks were cut down by their own Archers, who were blinded by the reflected Sunlight coming from our polished shields. Of course, as was inevitable, some hit our men too.

After their Sword Wielders and Ax Throwers had finally crashed into our Shield-men, our closed front line began to falter and gap. But soon all would be over.

The Picti and I awaited Arthur's signal, but it never came. So we watched the brief and beautifully performed massacre begin. As I had expected, when the Picti leaders saw the raging conflict taking place on the field below, they could not contain their men to await my command. So off they ran toward the melee, almost foiling Bedwyr's Horsemen's attack upon the Teutonic Warriors – albeit with the best of intentions.

In the meanwhile, our Archers behind the enemy lines were now almost out of arrows. And so, Arthur's plan for their escape was carried out; they ran back to the small boats awaiting them and rowed safely back to our ships while the Archers still aboard covered their escape with a mass of Death-birds aimed into the remaining enemy troops. Then they fled Southward.

All of the enemy's long boats – including those already burning from our Fire arrows – were securely anchored, with none aboard of sufficient rank to make decisions or to give orders; they did not follow our ships.

Gwyddion

The next Day, Arthur was in my tent, hovering over Bedwyr like a Mother Hen.

"He will be alright!" said I. "I was able to treat the wound well. The cut was deep, but clean – it will mend. It did cut through muscle though, which I sewed together as best I could.   I brought some moldy breadcrumbs with me in my Horse's pouch, for just such a need.   I packed the mold against his wound, then covered the stuff with Horseradish leaves, then wrapped clean cloths around the whole, to bind it. There is no sign of potential festering or fever. Although it will take a while before he has good use of that leg.

"Arthur, I am sorry for the men you have lost. I knew them too. They will be sorrowfully missed by all of us."

"Yes. I thank you. I know that you, too, grieve for the six good men who were evilly Enchanted by Morganna."

"Yes, I do. They hold no blame in their actions, yet now they are dead. You and I personally picked them out to guard me and then I had to kill them – and all men with families..."

"But Gwyddion, you are safe and I thank all the Gods for that. I will take care of their wives and children."

"Thank you Arthur, but no one can give those men back to their families. What a senseless waste."

"Morganna – would that I knew where she hides... But let me not focus on hatred, despair, and gloom. In truth, fewer of our men were killed in this battle than I thought might be."

"Yes, Arthur... I see a long Time of peacefulness to come, with joy and prosperity for all – the Summer of our lives. You have achieved it. You have brought all of the peoples of this land together and chased off the invaders and, I am sure, have raised the hopes and dreams of all."

"You mean 'we,' Gwyddion...

"Let us speak frankly. You have ever been the driving force behind all of this. Without you, would I even have been born? I wonder... Thank you for everything, my dear teacher... my uncle.

"We have never spoken of this, you and I, but we both know that you are of the same royal lineage as I, and we were both born bastards. The sword, the Magic, the power, they were all rightfully yours first. Yes, I have always known it. I need not ask the obvious – why you are not King over these Isles in my stead. I know that you have never had a taste for battle. And you hold your privacy and solitude too dear for the demands of diplomacy and politics placed upon a King. Then, there is the duty of marrying and making heirs. No, you have ever preferred to stand in the background – yet you are the true maker and foundation of this alliance and of everything that has come to pass. You are the torch... I am but the carrier who runs before you and in truth am but the reflection of your brilliance, yet you stand in my shadow. If my reign is to be hailed as the 'Summer King's,' it is all of your making. I am but half the being you are. You walk the Earth holding the Wisdom of the Ages, Gwyddion. So many Times I have thought that, if not for your council my Kingship would be a Fool's endeavour. If left to my own devices, I fear that I would have stumbled through my life being led only by my heart."

"Ah, but Arthur, therein lies the answer. Your great compassionate heart is the heart of a Lion. All great Kingdoms, won only by the strength of a man's arm and the sting of his sword, are doomed to fall in Time, to a younger and stronger arm. And on and on it goes, generation after generation. Those Kings are ever competing, never striving for harmony, but only for power. It is your heart that has made our world what it has become. Even through the compassion you have shown toward your enemies have you engendered a deep respect from them. You could have vanquished every last one of the Warriors in this battle, raped and put their women to the sword – only then to face the next stronger arm. Because you have always put the good of the people before greed, lust, or Hero's fame, fame is what you will have and will leave behind as a beacon of hope. But you do not see this in yourself, do you? And that makes me Love and respect you all the more."

Chapter 25
Baldric the Bard

Gwyddion

Now, Arthur had in his court a certain Poet – and an excellent Scribe was he. This man's name was Baldric. I had met Baldric when I was still a boy in Vortigern's clutches. But his grace of song and phrase remained always in my memory. And so, when Arthur gained his power, I found and brought Baldric to him.

Baldric's Grandmother was from Swede-land. Her family had migrated South into the Jutland peninsula. She spoke a somewhat different tongue than his Grandsire, who spoke more similarly to the Jutes – for his family had come from North of the Saxon lands, where the two had met. There they married and made Baldric's Father. He, in turn had married a Saxon woman – fair of skin and golden blond of hair. Together they made Baldric.

Their family had been amoungst the earliest settlers on Briton's Eastern shores – those who had come when Vortigern first made bargain with Hengist and Horsa, to hire his Saxon mercenaries.

Of course, Baldric's grandparents had never been anything but farmers.

No, it was his Father who had fought the Eire when they came across the Western Sea to plague the Clans of Gwynedd, Cambria, Powys, and Alba. Baldric's Father had died in one of these early skirmishes when Baldric was yet an infant. His Mother soon followed his Father into Death, so Baldric was raised by his Grandparents.

He was taught to speak in both his Grandsire's and Grandmother's tongues. He was also taught the Runes and Magic by their village Thane. There he stayed until the beauty of his countenance and gift of voice came to the attention of Vortigern's court. Then Baldric was taken to Vortigern's fortress and educated in the Latin Language – both in spoken and written form – by a Scholar of renown.

While with Vortigern, Baldric had had much intellectual intercourse with Scholars of both Vortigern's and Hengist's courts, who, together with Baldric, eventually forged a transliteration of the Saxon Runes into the Latin alphabet by the use of phonetics – the perceived sounds of each other's written marks.

These were the Runes they used:

They were transliterated as: A B C D E F G H I J K L M N O P Q R S T U V W X Y Z . In addition to these, there are a few other Runes, which correspond to sounds in Saxon, these are:

= AE, then there is a Rune that looks something akin to two Xs – one atop the other, which corresponds to the sound NG. Also one for the Cymru sound of DD – or TH in Saxon – but in Latin there is not this sound. This Rune looks similar to a letter P.

It was not long after this great accomplishment that Baldric began to compose poetry in Latin and then translate it into the Runic characters. I know of these things because Baldric told me.

Just before I abandoned Vortigern, Baldric gave a gift to me. It was a small piece of vellum, which skin had been painstakingly prepared by his friend Swidhun, the Smith. Upon this vellum he had written the Runes and their corresponding Roman letters. So intrigued was I with his brilliance and so honoured by his gesture that I have kept it on my person, in my pouch, ever since. In fact, besides the clothes on my body, my cloak and brooch, my dagger, and some bread to eat, it was the only possession I took with me when I fled Vortigern's camp.

Arthur thought that Baldric could be of great political worth as regards this battle – to engender goodwill amoung his Saxon allies, by writing of it in their tongue – for it was well known that they were charmed and much enamoured of Poetic Sagas.

I am sure that Morgan had a great influence upon Arthur in this too, for she has ever been a great appreciator of the Poetic Arts.

Baldric
The Battle of Baddon Hill...
A great fog had arisen, so dense that I could not see my hand held in

front of my face. I heard not a sound but the lapping of Water against the sides of our Ship and the thudding of my heartbeat in my ears. We were under orders of silence. At Times our wooden hull groaned and creaked and in the distance there were other lappings, groanings and creakings, but the surrounding Waters ate up most of these. Or was it the impenetrable Darkness and eerie Fog that did so?

Expectant, with my stomach churning like the Sea beneath us, I wondered where we were? Surely we were anchored not very far from the Coast, but who could know? It gave a man Time to think of what Creatures might lurk in the depths beneath – great Sea Serpents a-waiting their chance to drag us down into the Deep to devour us – down and down, into a Watery grave.

Somewhere a man coughed. Was that man on our boat? Or had we drifted too close to another? Instinctively, I braced myself for a great bump. Would I next feel the icy breath of the Water Spirits upon my neck?

I chided myself – "Get yourself together, man..."

Just then, Rhodri, the lead Archer of Arthur's three boats, found his way over to me. He whispered, "When weell it begin?"

Gryffydd, the Shipmaster of the boat we were on – who was not privy to King Arthur's plan – sidled over to listen. But first he asked, "Rhodri, why are y'r Archers leaving our ship?"

"Now is't the Time I can tell ye Gryffydd," said Rhodri, "what be our orders. King Arthur 'as a great cunning for this morning.

"Ye 'ave seen the Archers, who'r staying a-board through th' battle, be dressed as Saxons – for as t' trick 'em what might call out t' us from a Saxon Ship. Then we 'ave a-board one o' th' two Saxon captives t' answer 'em in their own tongue if they ask a question from being suspicious. But as for th' rest o' th' Archers – them that's climbing o'er th' side of the ship now and going t' shore that is – an' sure ye've noticed – everything, ev'n their bows and arrows is black. Their heads be wrapped in black cloth too. An' they be all naked an' covered from head t' foot in thick black mud. Like the pitch it is. I ken ye must 'ave wondered why.

"Weel, me Archers 'ave been told t' not e'en look up or straight ahead – so as not t' 'ave the whites o' their eyes give 'em away. All a-quiet, not so far behind the enemy will they sneak their way t' shore... slinking as Deer t' their places."

Gryffydd muttered, "But when weell all begin an' what be th' trick 'o getting our small boats a-beach an' y'r Archers behind enemy lines without 'em bein' seen? Be it by Magic?"

Rhodri answered, "You know, I heard it whispered th' Enchantress Morgan herself cooked up th' stuff from Magic honey an' dust o' th' Tor an' dyed it blackest black from crushing o' the Walnut husks. Blacker e'en than pitch is this conjured stuff, 'though not so easy to a-light. For if t'were really pitch, th' men would go up in a fiery Death – if they be seen that is, an' hit by blazing arrows. She, the Enchantress – it is alike whispered – then added Magic't Flea Bane Herb t' her potion, for so t' keep th' biting vermin from bedeviling th' men. Don't know it be true – but t'wer what I heard."

Gryffydd crossed himself at that...

I said, "Look, the Eastern Sky is lightening, soon will be the rising of the great disk of the Sun across the Water. We must wait for those moments when the Water is aflame with Her brilliant golden light, blinding all who look Eastward from the shore toward us or from their Ships.

"All must be Timed perfectly! The battle cry will go up and just after the havoc is full on, those Archers who remain a-board will let loose their Fire-birds to torch the enemy long boats.

"When all is done and the Water is full a-flame with brilliant blinding light, you will raise anchor and we will wend Southward...

"But first Rhodri," said I "is it not Time to arm the rest of your Archers, as the moment is growing near. It will not be long now."

Rhodri gave the order and all were armed in quiet precision! Then he asked me...

"Baldric th' Scribe, how *weell* Gryffydd an' our other ships get away quick enough so as t' keep th' Saxon Shipmen – who are left behind t' mind their own Long boats – from torching *ours*?"

"The North Wind, Rhodri."

"Wha' Wind?"

"The same that has made the fog and then lifted it... The Merlin... He will call the Call of the North Wind and our Ships will sail swiftly to South."

At that Gryffydd made the sign against evil Enchantment, and hurried to follow his tasks. I did wonder then if he was a Christian? But even so, did not their Saints raise the Winds as well?"

Then Rhodri – after stealing the "Black Archers" to the shore, a-waited the agreed signal.

All there was left to do was to wait – but not so long. No matter... no Time... The cry went up... It was on...

To quiet the devils in my head, I placed quill to vellum and wrote...

No matter then... No Time was left...
The cry went up... The signal sent...
And who could tell how Wyrd was bent?

I saw it all transpire...

Did'st Hell's fury let loose... let loose...
Arrows torching Woden's fleet...
Ne'er did'st a one see from whence they came...
Only shadows did'st fall at their feet...

The Valkyries swooped with their Flaming helm's...
We heard their screeching cries...
Or was this the call of delirium –
Mortals meeting their demise?

Woden, Woden, the Terrible... The True...
Has't your fury abandoned you?

Where went your Warriors, Berserkers who,
In mad and frenzied lust...
Do slash and bend... Do kill and maim...
Do pummel, crush and thrust?

"Look, the Eastern Sky is lightening"
Said the Archer at the rising of the Sun...

I replied:

"Across the Waters, there be Sol...
So hold... hold... hold... trust...
Wait... the battle cry will rise...
Wait... Wait... Wait they must...

"When the Sea is't aflame... a-flame...
With Sol's brilliant golden light...
Blinding all who look to East
Then will the moment be right..."

The cry went up... and louder grew
Beserkers frenzied call...
How coulds't they know by high Sun's light...
They'd be vanquished one and all...

The Picti wailed and blew their pipes...
They beat upon their drums...
The Old Dark Tribes they shook their bells
Chanted, danced, and Hummed...

The Clansmen and the Romans

Shadows of the waning Night...
Didst shout vile insults, blasphemies
Ridiculing heart and might...

No matter then... no Time was left... the battle it began...
And all... unfolded... perfectly...
Just as King Arthur planned...

Some Time later, I travelled from the land of my birth, through all
the Tribes of the Teutons, Northward to the cold land of my
Grandmother's Father, all along the way speaking to my kinsmen –
friend and foe – jof Arthur's quickly won battle...

All did ask and meant to know:

"How is't that Woden did'st abandon his blood... men and women,
young and old? Did'st th' Valkyries fly their chosen to Valhalla? Or are
their corpses still gaoling their souls?"

How could I answer that they might understand? T'was a hard thing
for me myself, with so many Gods of Tribal difference, yet all seeming
as from one Well...

So I, Baldric, the Scop, composed this poem – and recited:

The Night of Woden's Shame

That Day I drank from Woden's bucket
The Mead of Poetry...
Then Wyrd demanded that I scald
The truth of memory...

Old Woden hung from Yggdrisil's bough
Wracked with hunger, thirst and pain...
For seven Nights and seven Days
In the cold Winds He had sway'n...

Oh, one eyed Lord of Asgard
He sacrificed his sight...
To gain the Wisdom that he sought
The Magic, Runes, and Rites...

The Gods serve not blood, nor desire, nor greed
Nor borders nor lands nor field...
Nor what seems just in the hearts of Man
But for honour their judgments wield...

Although when – as in this instance...

There are two lands, one blood, two sides...
Where in men's heart does Justice sing
And rightfulness abides...

When each man says in heartfelt truth
'T'is My way that is right...
The Norns must choose by their will and Wyrd
And Their unfailing Sight...

By Thor's all thunderous name
By Loki's devious game...
By Sigurd and ol' Heimdal
By Wulpur's Perfect aim...

By Baldur's Shining Day
By Frey's Lordly might...
By Nanna's lullaby
By Freyja's Long Night's Lights...

By Frigg... High Queen of Asgard
Who Weaveth all to Wyrd...
Yet in the fray of battle clash
Has't ne're She interfered...

Dark Lady flies Her black Mare
Hair whipping in the Wind...
Keeps count of all who have transgressed
Shone kindnesses or sinned...

Calamity... pain... Her Warriors' fall!
All hast She heard and seen...
But 'tis written 'Is't not Her task
To answer wail or keen...

True, Seaxneat and Ull bless sword or ax
If wise be he who wields it...
But with Woden's wizened sanction
Eostar slays the fool who shields it...

Who will judge, which side to fall?
Who is wrong or who is right?
Nay, but men alone must win their wars
By their own swords' mortal bite...

You asked if He abandoned us
T'was written in the Stars...
That we the men of Middilgard
Clash like insects in clay jars...

No right nor reason hath we all
To put Gods to the test...
For Brothers killing brothers
Is't ne're a noble quest...

True, Sigurd brave slew Fafnir
To claim the Dragon's gold...
Yet no squandered blood would'st Gods accept
In Middilgard's Days of old...

Who then can judge the "Eternal Ones"?
Or who can rightly claim...
A grudge against ol' Woden
Or curse his mighty name?

Does Woden care? Oh, yes, He does
His Love is't beyond all blame...
There never would... Nor ever could
Be a "Night of Woden's Shame!"

Part Three
The Summer King

Chapter 26
Rest in Peace

Gwyddion

The next few years breezed by in uneventful and blissful peace – for the most part that is.

With Arthur's leave, I settled back into the old Cave in Gwynedd that had served as a dwelling for Chronos, the boys and I, so many years ago. I rested, read, tended my Herbs, and wrote my journals whenever Arthur did not need me.

As for Arthur and Bedwyr, these may have been the best years of their lives.

Prosperity filled these, Our Fair Isles. Even the Harvests were more than usually bountiful. The land was well with her people satisfied.

Igraine's fortress and surrounding village prospered and ever more and more people were coming to honour and be blessed by Nodens' Well.

Bedwyr finally had Time to oversee the refurbishment of both.

Brennos was aging, yet still enjoying his Ravens and Dragon, as well as my more frequent visits.

Sometimes I would visit with my friend Princess Rowena. She was still sharp as a dagger. Her beauty had changed but not left; she was aging in the loveliest way. Her daughter, Ribrowst, who had always had Rowena's beauty and her wit, married a Cymru man soon after the battle – which even by then folk insisted upon calling *"Baddon Hill"* – and began to bear children.

Gwenyfar and Branwen had been moved from Dumnonia to an abandoned Roman coastal villa, which they themselves had chosen. Of course, Arthur had had to spend a small fortune on it before it met with Gwenyfar's approval. There they lived unbothered by all around them – except for the fact that a certain Monk, who had been in attendance at Arthur and Gwenyfar's wedding, had taken to visiting and talking with

Gwenyfar on a regular basis – he seeming to be her only contact with the outside world. In the most charitable way possible, Arthur let me know that he would have done most anything to relieve Igraine of Gwenyfar's presence in her fortress. He, of course, in addition to providing everything they needed or wanted continued to make occasional visits to their villa, in order to keep up appearances. For, true to his word, Gwenyfar was still his Queen.

Lady Vivianne's health was declining, as were her years. She, of course, faced all with dignity and grace. On the one occasion that I had seen her, it was obvious that her limbs were becoming stiff – as does so many Times happen with age.

I saw or heard little of Morgan through those years – much less than I would have liked to, but I felt that all was well with her.

Much to everyone's relief, no one had heard from Morganna Le Faye.

The movement of Time meant little to me in my pleasant, sometimes solitude.

Then one Day a courier arrived at my Cave. He looked as if he had been chased by the Cwn Annwn. The missive told that Igraine's health was sorely fading and that she was asking to see me one last Time. She warned that I must not tarry, "but" she promised, "I will wait." I rode my horse like the Wind. Arthur and Bedwyr had also been notified and were on their way to her side from Aquae Sulis. We all made great haste to reach Igraine while she still held onto life – which we did.

She must have seen this coming, for we later found out that she had been suffering general weakness, difficulty breathing, and occasional pressures in her chest, but she told no one until the Day came when she no longer had the strength to walk to the Sacred Well. At that, she had sent word of her ill health to the Grandmother of her Tribe, to Morgan, to Bedwyr and Arthur and to me.

She was only perhaps sixty-one or -two years old, which, it is true, was more than a long life for the mean person. But I had always considered Igraine one of the Magi... an enlightened one.   Her meditations and Magic should have given her longer years even than that.

She had looked so young and beautiful the last Time I had been with her, but now I was shocked to see her. Very little flesh covered her withered, yellowed skin. Her eyes, which had always been so beguiling, were dull. The moment she spoke, albeit hoarsely and quietly, I found the woman I had known.

"My dear Igraine, why did you not call sooner?"

"No matter, Gwyddion, you are here now."

"The breaths left to me are few, so please listen carefully to my words. Call my Scribe here to my side so that he can witness what I say."

Her words were obviously well thought out. I silently thanked the Gods that at least her memories and Wisdom were still with her.

"My beloved husband Gorlois would have expected me to leave his Dumnonian fortress to Morganna, according to his family's hereditary customs. However, it is fact that he made *me* owner of all that was his before his Death. It is written and let it be remembered, that to Morganna – she who is called "Le Faye" – I leave nothing."

She winced, and had to stop speaking for a moment. She looked at Morgan and asked, "Morgan, do you want this fortress? You could take my place as Guardian of the Well..."

"Thank you, Mother, but no. My life is on the Isle of Apples."

"I thought so. Then I bequeath one half of my great wealth to your Order. To you, my dear daughter, I leave my blessings and all of my personal, Sacred objects.

"Arthur and Bedwyr, my two boys, only one of you is of my body and blood, but you are both mine, with even a stronger tie than..." She coughed, and then winced, "blood... with a Love... that is greater than blood... Always care for this fortress and for the birth Mother of Bedwyr and his Father. Let them keep their cottages and land, keep them happy and well fed. Of course, I know that you would do that without my asking. I bequeath all I have – not already left to Morgan and the Order – to both of you, which includes this fortress, lands, Horses, livestock and all else within. You may decide between you what you will do with it all – but with this one stipulation: that for as many generations as can possibly be, Nodens' Well will be tended by a Holy Woman or Man... Promise this to me."

"We do... we will, Mother."

"One more thing... I wish for my Tribal Grandmother to choose the first Keeper of the Well. Lay my bones near the Well when I am gone.

"My dear ones, I am always with you.

"I must stop talking, for I have not the strength to go on, but sit by me, my beloveds and keep vigil until my Spirit has gone from this body..."

Those were her last words, spoken with her last breath.

We kept vigil until the third Day, when her kin of the Tribes arrived to lay her bones to rest.

The Holy Men – the Raven Men – came to her fortress dressed in their bells and black feathered cloaks, with Raven and Owl feathers braided into their long black hair. From a distance we heard them coming, but it was only their bells and anklets of gold jingling that we heard, for beyond this they were silent.

First they covered her in honeyed beer and then rolled her body in sweet Herbs, grasses, and seeds. Then, as was their custom, they carried her to a clearing in the deep Wood, upon a Hill where the Birds of prey were allowed to feast upon her flesh for three Nights and three Days, after which they retrieved, cleaned, then washed her bones and brought them back to the fortress, where they wrapped them tightly in many layers of woven cloth.

From the Time of their first arrival, not a man had spoken a word. The women had ceaselessly Hummed, Night and Day, their voices taking up one from another to create an exquisite, unending, drone.

They buried her bones in a shallow grave next to Nodens' Well, 'returning her to the womb' – as the Tribal ones say. Large Stones were stacked above the grave and then packed with dirt to form a mound upon which new grasses would grow.

Then a rhythm of persistent and steady drumming was added to the other-worldly Humming of their song, so ancient and beautiful that even the Birds did not mock it.

We wept.

Everything has its cost...

Two more years rolled by in peaceful succession and it seemed that without the driving force of challenge and accomplishment, our Loved ones, one by one, having fulfilled their predestined works of this life, faded through the Veil into the Summerlands – there to refresh and await a rebirth. Some, perhaps, would ascend to the Stars, to join those of their Ancestors who have not the need to return to life on this Earth – those who have done and learned all they must in their Human cycles of lives. We earthly beings never can know who these might be. We mortals may be inclined to elevate certain ones of our peers, in our own thinking, as being amoung the ascended ones. But I have learned through my own experience and have been taught that many things may cause a person's return to life on this Earth, again and again. An unrequited Love or desire, an obsession for a person, a goal, a place, or a thing – even loving this Earth too much... Any of these things can bind a Spirit to seemingly endless incarnations. One may also be bound by some shadow fault, held so deeply to themselves that only they know of it. A secret heart, an unspoken shame... I know that I have mine.

The next Death was an unexpected shock, indeed. It was Princess Rowena's daughter, Ribrowst Ardora.

She had married a man much younger than herself, named Rhodri Nau Caw – whose name means, 'the seventh son of a ninth son – full of joy.' She had chosen him for Love and had born three red-haired sons to him. The oldest, Huail ab Nau Caw, was thirteen years upon her Death, the second son, Celyn ab Nau Caw, was ten and the youngest, Gildas, later known as "Sapiens," was three. Ribrowst had given birth to two daughters, but they had died in infancy.

She had waited until after her twenty-forth year-turn to marry. This was at a much older age than was expected of a sole heiress. But Princess Rowena would let her do as she pleased in all things. Unfortunately this one thing proved to be a sorrowful mistake.

Although Ribrowst was a good wife and loving Mother, her husband was given to rages and unkind words. He drank too much and too often. Oh, he knew how to beguile and charm all whom he wanted to, so no one around them really saw how he treated Ribrowst when the two were alone – no one, that is, but Princess Rowena. It would have taken a person of much more wit than he to fool Rowena and so she despised him. And because his two eldest sons became more and more like their Father, she did not Love them much either.

One Day Rowena rode to their house without invitation or warning, to find her daughter, Ribrowst, bruised and swollen. He had beaten her. Rowena threatened that she would take Ribrowst away from Rhodri to live at her fortress if she ever heard of his cruelty again. What was more, she said that for as long as he lived, he would never personally own so much as one gold coin of Rowena's great wealth – and that only Ribrowst would ever live in her fortress.

Rowena told Rhodri that from that Day on her spies would be watching him always. She also insinuated in her politic way that she would dispatch his life promptly if he was ever caught beating Ribrowst again.

Ribrowst begged her Mother to not be so hard.

"He only hits me sometimes Mother... when he drinks too much. There are still some good Days too."

She still Loved him! This infuriated Rowena all the more. Rowena shook her head in disgust. She kissed her daughter goodbye and rode off.

Rowena always remembered that Day too well, for it was the last Time she saw Ribrowst before the 'accident' that caused her Death two weeks later.

She told it all to me when I went to comfort her. There had been a Storm the Night before...

"The husband" said she, for she would not speak his name, "went to assess the damage to the roof of his stables. Apparently a timber had been knocked loose and was precariously hanging from another. Ribrowst had gone with him to see that the Horses were unhurt. When she walked to the stall where her Horse was to stroke, comfort and bring him from harms way, the timber became dislodged and fell on Ribrowst. "She was dead at once" – had said her grieving husband. "Look at how it caved in her head. I pulled it off of her, to try to save her, but she was already gone. Oh my God... She is gone."

They buried Ribrowst at the fortress of Vortigern, which I had designed, and much later had come to Love as the home of my dear friend Princess Rowena. But never again did it seem as bright and alive with warmth as it had been before. There were no grand funerary Rites for Ribrowst. It was a small, somber affair for family and closest friends only.

Queen Gwenyfar came for the burial of her niece, but to my surprise she was not accompanied by Branwen, but only by Arthur, Bedwyr, and Freidl. Oh yes, and by a certain Monk named Collin – who had come uninvited, except by Gwenyfar – and never left her side.

I noticed with disdain that the Monk declined to sing the Saxon Death song with everyone else or even to stand at the Ritual site in respectful posture.

Perhaps because of my sadness for Rowena or that joyful little blonde haired girl I had once so Loved, I felt my anger rise hotly – and this is very rare for me. One thing I do pride myself on – and I will probably pay for my pride someday – is that I can control myself very well. But that Monk almost made me lose myself. How dare he place his jealous God so far above all others. Where is the compassion, the Love, the humanity in that? Why come to a funeral Rite at all if only to make a spectacle of his bigotry?

Thankfully, not all Christians are like him. In fact, most that I have known were not. They were good people. Theirs is a God of compassion and Love, offering the bread of a covenant of peace, of redemption from the sorrows of this world. Their King, leader, and teacher has been quoted as saying great words of comfort and Wisdom. It is written that others of the Magi came to his birth to recognize him as one of their own – and they tell of his birth as being expected by the great astrologers of Persia and that he was born at Winter's Longest Night, just as were Cernunnos, Balder, and Mithras – the Children of Promise. These are not so different from all other cultural beliefs. The Mysteries are the Mysteries, after all. Cosmic truths do not depend upon what we believe. The truth is the truth, regardless. And the truth is that we all must mourn our dead – and be dead someday, too. It is unseemly beyond words to disrespect such a thing. But no, this Monk is of a new breed, and I like it not.

I made my hand sign and began even and deep breathing. I calmed down and regained balance.

While I was thinking of all this, I wondered if my brother Uther had been grieved at all? Well, I had grieved his loss. And I had grieved the sadness of his not being grieved by anyone else. Regardless, grieve I did, but as for the why's, I do not know – for he left not much to commend him. Someday I will weep for Uther and every other sadness of my life – of which there have been many and which I have for too long held fast under my control.

Chapter 27
The Nine Mother
Goddesses

Morgan

During those years The Merlin has written of – the Summer Years – the years of peace and tranquility, most things remained as always on the Isle of Apples. One Day breezed into another, Moon into Moon, then into a new cycle – on and on did go our works, pleasures, worship, and Rites. But there were some notable changes…

Makyr, who was about five years older than I, was elected into the circle of The Nine High Wise Mothers. I was so happy for my dear friend. The very old Priestess who had died, thereby creating the vacancy in this position of honour, had been called Anuit – 'Of the Stars.' I believe she had passed ninety years, but no one knew for sure. She died peacefully in her sleep. "May she be joyful in the 'Realm of Rejuvenation' and may she choose her next life well."

Makyr had been the youngest to be elected into the circle of The Nine in several generations. Her strength of Wisdom and devotion were unquestionable, but I wondered what had made her Moon blood cycles end at such a young age. I was by that Time past my thirty-eighth year-turn, so Makyr must have been about forty-three years.

Oh, my… well… perhaps we were not so young anymore… Still – she was young for a woman to be elected one of this position.

She was initiated into the Circle of Nine on the Dark Moon before the end of the year. It actually was almost a month before the great Fire Festival at the Time of Red and Gold Leaves. The Clans call this Samhain. We have a secret name in our ancient tongue for it, too. But either way, the Dark Moon fell right before the leaves came into their full colours that year. The ceremony was a closed and private Sacred Rite of

Passage. Only The Nine have knowledge of its Mysteries.

Perhaps, to lend understanding to you who will read this one Day, I should tell one of the Old Tribes' Myths that my Mother's Mother had told to her and that she told to me... 'May those who have sight, See...'

My Mother said:

"In the beginning, there were nine Mother Goddesses – in the beginning of Human reckoning that is...

"Once, before Time began... from out of the Chaos – which was formless, a breath was breathed. That breath formed the Air, which became the first Mother Goddess, She who floated in freedom. Eventually She became aware that She *was*... That was the first thought... From then on She was always thinking...

She named herself Shi-Zikru... Breath... Thought... and Beginning...

After a Timeless eternity, her thoughts became so enlightened that She began to glow... So She formed Herself into the first silver Crescent Moon hanging in the Air... She wished to show herself to her children – but She existed in aloneness and there was no one to see. Shi-Zikru thought about this. After millions and millions of Thoughts, one gave birth to Desire – a Desire for companionship. And so was born the second Mother Goddess.

The daughter of Shi-Zikru named herself Desire – who, because of her passionate, Fiery nature shone in the darkness as a great white sphere, dancing in Her cloak as the Full Moon. Her dance was to light the desires, passions, and will of all Creations – which were yet to be. She named herself A-ama... Full Ripened Womb... White Moon Goddess... But her twirling frenzy was so brilliant that it would be impossible for her never to rest. A-ama realised that she must sleep. As She fell into her slumber, she began to dim. As She began to Dream, She became distraught, for She was unwilling to lose her glowing beauty – yet even in her Dream she could see that her light was dwindling. She uttered the first prayer:

"Oh please, Mother, have I been selfish? Haughty? So delighted in my own beauty that I thought I needed no one else? Will my Fire now be extinguished forever?"

In her sadness, and regret, one teardrop fell, which became the third Mother Goddess, who was Emotion.

Her name was Mudi... Oracle... Enchantress... Secret Keeper. She became the Western gate into the twilight – the land of Trance – the Seer, who passed on her knowings to her children as they slept at Night. She became the great empathizer who draws all into herself, showing herself as the last Crescent Moon, waning into darkness. She gave all of herself until she was no more – plunging into Death and sweeping along with Her all She had taken in.

So the Spirit of Mudi gave birth to the fourth Mother Goddess – who was Wisdom. But remember, to enter Death is to enter the gateway into re-birth.

The fourth Mother Goddess' name was Elat... to Become Black... Death... Night... She was the cold North... Winter... The dirt and the bones. Elat never showed herself at all. But She allowed herself to be honoured as the Dark Moon.

She, in her unnamable compassion, great Wisdom, and deep heart, received the dead unto her bosom, there to hold them fast and unfold to them all Cosmic secrets – which, of course, only their Spirit Bodies would remember in their next life.

She was the Full Moon Mother's silent twin; never could they touch, or be rejoined to each other until the end of the Cosmos – each drawing to and away from each other, pushing and pulling in flux and flow – mirror images in polarity – as above, so below – darkness and illumination.

These first four Mother Goddesses were the Cosmic Elements. Each one holding up one Quarter of the known realms, which were suspended between their voluptuous arms... ever spinning in cycles.

The fifth Mother – who was born between the thighs of the first four – was the Star Goddess, Mother of spatial dimension, the Mother from whose belly and outstretched body would come – in a boat through the Starry Night Sky – the Original Ones, the Ancestors, and the Ancestor's Ancestors, bringing their seed, their culture, and their knowledge to our homeland.

She named herself Nana... Beauty of the Stars.

The sixth Mother burned as a great Fiery disk, outshining the light of her sisters and turning blackness into Dawn and shone in the clear blue Sky. She was the Dependable Light, She was to bring ever a new Day. She warmed her children's hearts with playfulness. Even once in a while, did she too play 'Hide yourself from me.'

She named herself Sud-Ma... Sun Mother.

The seventh Mother Goddess named Herself Kia... Earth. She walked as one with her children – all beasts, and Creatures of green, Stone, feather, fin or flesh, including Humans. Her robe swayed in Summer as the Grain of the fields and the dance of the leaves in the Trees. In Winter She was silver, brown, and grey. In wakefulness or slumber, Kia was always beautiful and abounding with life.

The eighth Mother was Goddess of the Seas... Mysterious one of unknown realms and Creatures. She undulated to mimic the White Moon Goddess' dance... then became Entranced by Her ever changing tides, becoming the place and Being of Magic. She was and is the gateway into the twilight of the three otherworldly realms. She named herself Na-Amu-Ma... The Deep Sea.

And then there was the ninth GODDESS... However, SHE was only the ninth in so much as SHE became the ninth in Human awareness. For, when we Humans had become enlightened enough to understand that there is THAT which is not understandable or to perceive that there is THAT which is imperceptible, we began to *See* that there was – and is – The GODDESS *before* everything... THE GREAT MOTHER... THE ONE...

SHE is the ABZU-AABBABA... The Primeval Source...

SHE is TIME... As designer and implementer of the great ONE, SHE alone holds the secret of the epochs of Cosmic Time... SHE is ETERNAL... Before, after, and ever – existed, exists, and will exist.

SHE is FATE... who Weaves and Spins with HER gossamer threads the pattern and Creation of all the Cosmos... As such, SHE is sometimes called "The Weavers."

SHE dwells in the center – The center of the Cosmos... the center of our Temple, and the center of ourselves.

HER name is AIXIA...

We understand!

Thank you for listening..."

And so it is that in our Order, the Circle of Nine High Wise Mothers reflect these original Mother Goddesses – the how and why of this is only known by and passed down to them as Guardians of these Sacred Secrets.

Makyr was the first in my experience to be elevated to one of The Nine and so was the first one in whom I was to see "the Change." The Change is what happens to one who has ascended to Spiritual Enlightenment, while yet in a body of flesh – a Holy One, a Magi. I, of course, could feel the difference between ordinary mortals and those of the Nine. But then and there, to suddenly experience this change in Maker was... was... I find no words. Perhaps my tongue is bound from the utterance of something that must remain unspoken.

When the Moon was Dark that month and cast no shadows, the Nine met alone upon the Tor to induct Makyr into their ranks. What Rites were performed I did not then know.

Later in that Moon's Dance, under the Full Moon, the second part of Makyr's elevation was to be completed. Upon that beauteous Night, all initiated males and females of the Order met at the Tor, within the circle of Stones, to celebrate and honour the White Moon Goddess as well as her consort, the Stag God – God of wild Nature, the ecstatic Dance and the Hunt. If you have read the entirety of these histories, you will well know of Him.

Although I am forbidden to reveal certain parts of that Full Moon Ritual, I can relate some...

On that beautiful, crisp Night, dressed in our long, hooded, green cloaks, we women walked in silent procession through the Woods, upon an ancient Deer path, toward the Tor – each of us holding a small flame. As we walked, only the sounds of Nature and the jingling of the bells on our ankle braces could be heard. This we call *"The silence of Man."* I remember well that in that silence all the world around gently hummed and buzzed, whispered and howled, a song of such great beauty that for those wistful moments I felt that I could live my whole life in that silence. One of our women pulled a cart with a large skin of Water, a wool blanket, and a sack of dirt – this in precaution of a Fire running out of control, which of course, and thankfully, had never happened. And so did we wend our way to the bottom of the Tor's spiral path.

The men of our Order awaited us atop the windy Tor. Many Times since have they told me that we appeared to them as elusive as Wood Spirits, gliding through the Forest – disappearing and reappearing twixt the Trees – our flames small in the distance, twinkling as though Summer Glow-flies.

They, being so high upon the Tor, could watch the Mist roll in across the inland Sea. Mostly the Mist covers all but the Tor by Sundown, but that Night the Mist came later than usual, reaching the bottom of the Tor just as we, the women did – and it had been full twilight when we began our procession. Stars filled the deep blue-black Sky above. Our Lady the White Moon Goddess was rising as we walked. To our vision, it was She who danced between the boughs, winking at us as She went higher and higher in her arch of beauty.

When we reached the Tor, our silence broke. We, all together, began to Hum the ancient tunes of our Foremothers and Forefathers. The Bees were sleeping so they did not join me in this, but a family of Wolfs in the distance howled their song of greeting and celebration to the White Moon Goddess. The men drummed as we spiraled up the Tor.

Later I was told that the Lake carried our songs as far as to the Marsh Folk. They – though of strange customs and unknown origins – regarded our voices as a blessing of the Gods. Just, who their Gods were we have never been never told...

There is always to me a shift in the worlds, a dizzying change of something – my usual consciousness dropping down through my feet as if it must remain at the bottom – whenever I walk up the Tor. And so it was upon that Night.

Even after all these years – when now as I compile these histories, and am so old that I must be assisted or pulled in a wagon up the narrow and perilous path – I still feel the same familiar shift. Although I leave behind – or lose – some part of my consciousness, what I gain is overwhelming in the balance. I enter the realm of the Divine Ones. Oh – not only of our Gods and Goddesses, but of the great ONE – the Spirits of those around me. It brings to my memory the Chant:

"We are all One... We are all one...
My brothers and sisters of the winged ones...
Of Stone and Brook, of flesh and Tree...
All are ONE with me...

My fingers are branches they reach to the Stars...
To all beyond and in-between,
Heard, touched, tasted, or seen
All is ONE with me...

We are all ONE... We are all ONE... We are all ONE..."

I always know this, of course, but rarely am I as aware as when I climb up the Tor.

Oh, I digress again... I *am* getting old.

But back to that blessed Starry Night, when we all began to Hum and Drum and drone a single low note with our voices, which, at Times purposely clashed against the tunes we Hummed – to bring Chaos. Then as our notes changed, their droning became sometimes a melodious harmony of Cosmos – of form – thusly stirring the energies of... Oh... Perhaps I should say no more to the uninitiated, except that amidst the Stones and Firelight, we danced in wild abandon.

Whoever you are reading this, please feel no offence. Here I speak only of tradition, not of value. The Divine One who breathed life into you is the same who did to us. "May the peace of that One be upon and within you forever."

It is enough to say that our sisters and brothers performed a Rite of great sincerity and worship to the White Moon Goddess and the Stag God – and then all who were not of the Nine retreated down the spiral path to await them at their finish. Then we feasted and danced in honour of Makyr's becoming – all congratulating her with deepest reverence.

When it was my turn, I held her tightly in my arms, and kissed her cheek. I whispered in her ear; "My dear friend and sister, I Love you." She smiled at me, but without the trace of sadness that had always been there before.

Although I am compiling these histories many years later, the remembrance of my experience of Makyr's elevation and Change is burned into my Vision forever.

Chapter 28
Branwen

Morgan

Not long after the Death and mourning of Ribrowst – which in itself made me aware of my own mortality – an unexpected visitor arrived at the Isle of Apples. She came from the West, riding a very fine Horse – with only a few clothes, a bag of gold coins, and her gold Saxon lyre. It was Branwen.

Branwen was the daughter of Gwenyfar's Mother's closest friend and handmaiden. She and Gwenyfar had always been inseparable. They had been children together, raised in the court of Hengist, when Gwenyfar's Mother had been in great favor. There were rumours, of course, of the sexual nature of their closeness, but I had paid little attention – there were always rumours. Gossip is a cultural pastime, I think.

But now, Branwen stood before me with haunted eyes – the unmistakable look of someone mourning a great loss. She broke with protocol by not presenting herself to Lady Vivianne first. She had ridden quickly and directly to the small cottage in which I lived and had found only Gwenda there. Gwenda – who had nursed Arthur through his injury from the incident with Lucian years ago at the Games of Lleu – was still sharing my cottage with me.

Branwen would say nothing but to ask for me. Seeing her state, Gwenda hurried to bring me to her. When I arrived, with no preamble she fell into my arms and wept bitterly. I spoke not a word. I knew that there is a Time for words and a Time for silence. I held and comforted her as a child. She needed only to cry, and cry she did – for so long. Through her unbroken sobbing and the racking of her body, without words I knew she had suffered a life tragedy. Finally, late into the evening she composed herself. I had sent Gwenda away for our privacy and prepared some warmed spiced honey mead to help calm her down.

We both drank, for I had a feeling that what I was about to hear would shake fortresses to the ground.

Branwen knew that whatever she would confide would be safe with me. I could see already within her the whole story, but of course I listened attentively to all she must say. The floodgates opened and so she talked for hours.

Her whole life she had Loved Gwenyfar more than anyone or anything. She said that she would tell me – with my oath of confidence that never while she lived would I repeat what she was about to say – of a certain tragic event in Gwenyfar's life. And so she began...

It seemed that while Branwen had never so much as looked at a man or boy with sexual desire, it had not always been so with Gwenyfar.

"When Gweny was only twelve year-turns, she fell in Love with one of her Father's guards. Uthbert was his name. He was a good man, with a hearty sense of humor. He was also twenty years older than Gwenyfar. But she threw herself at him at every opportunity."

Branwen went on to tell me that she still believed Uthbert never touched Gwenyfar, for even if he had Loved her, it could not be. She was a beautiful Princess, and therefore, a political pawn to Hengist. Uthbert knew very well that Hengist would kill him if ever he had touched her or even spoken of it.

"I am not even sure he ever wanted her at all," said Branwen, "but then who could not? She was – is – so beautiful."

Branwen went on with the story.

"I tried to warn her even for her Mother's sake and mine, to leave Uthbert alone, for Hengist was a fierce and cruel man. But Gwenyfar would have her way, as always. I do not know how she managed it, but one Night she crept into the guard's hall where Uthbert was sleeping. She awakened him and offered herself to him. She told me later that he refused. Well, the desperate whispered commotion awoke another guard who came, *so he thought*, to Uthbert's rescue. What he saw was the Princess in tears, with Uthbert's hands on her shoulders. Shocked and thinking to protect the fair little Princess, he shouted an alarm and Uthbert was taken to the dungeon and chained to the Stone wall.

When Hengist heard of it, he went into a rage. He would listen to no explanation – especially from Gwenyfar. Of course, Uthbert was as good as a dead man and would not die with a sword or an ax in his hand. No one was surprised at that. And by their thinking, that would mean that he would never be allowed into the Halls of the Warrior's Paradise. It was a horrible punishment. Hengist wanted to severely punish Gwenyfar too, but not to leave a physical mark or flaw on his prized possession, so the very next Day, at Midday, he ordered *all* in his household and guard – even the children – to stand in the outer keep courtyard, to watch Uthbert's execution. Gwenyfar was placed a few arm's spans in front of Uthbert, who was naked and tied to a pole. Hengist himself, walking up slowly, took a Saex – a curved dagger – and cut off Uthbert's manhood – all of it. There was so much blood... Uthbert, a battle worn Warrior, could not keep from wailing. Gwenyfar began to faint, but Hengist slapped her face, to rouse her. His hands – covered in blood – left a dripping handprint on her face – Uthbert's blood. But this was not enough for Hengist. He had Gwenyfar held – just out of harm's way – and he beheaded Uthbert. His head rolled to her feet. She could not stop screaming, and then Hengist picked up his hairy, bloody man parts and held them up to Gwenyfar's face. "Here," he said, "enjoy him all you want to."

"Well, she was never the same..."

Branwen let her head hang in silence for several moments... then continued:

"My dearest one – so full of daring and Spirit – diminished before my horrified eyes.

"From then on, she clung only to me, afraid of everyone but me. Even her Mother she could not be with, knowing that *she* was still allowing herself to be sexually ravaged by this monster who was her Father. That is why – I could not believe my good fortune, nay blessing – when she spoke up that I must accompany her to Arthur's house and then again, to ask Igraine so straightforwardly to place my chamber next to hers. When she refused to lie with Arthur I thought I had my Gweny back forever."

Branwen sat quietly for a few moments, looking down at the floor. I rose to warm some more spiced mead.

She looked around my humble cottage; the walls of baked mud and straw and at the plain and scant furnishings. Then her eyes caught the beautiful, scarlet woolen blanket on my straw bed. From there her gaze went to the cozy hearth Fire then to my chest that was covered by a doeskin with ancient Tribal symbols burnt into it. Upon it were my Crystal and other personal ceremonial tools – also my short bladed knife. For the first Time I saw her eyes as they really were – clever, intelligent, inquisitive, and thoroughly heart sick. Branwen talked all Night long. She told me everything, even what Arthur had said to them. She quoted:

"My lady, there is no shame in Love. It is the Goddess's greatest blessing."

"So like Arthur," I thought.

By late into the Night, she had exhausted herself, and finally slept on my bed.

Branwen awoke a few hours later. I had had Gwenda cook Apples and honey along with pieces of broken flat bread for her to eat. Also some cheese from our dairy and warmed milk. I thought perhaps Branwen had not eaten for a few Days and surely this meal would tempt anyone. She ate it heartily and smiled her first smile at me.

She was a pretty girl in a boyish sort of way. Really she was past her girl years. Still there was an air about her that made her look much younger than her years. How she could have kept any of her innocence with all she had been through was beyond my understanding. She would be perhaps twenty-six or twenty-seven years old by now, I believe – about two years younger than Gwenyfar. But I was realizing that she had seen more than enough violence and pain for a lifetime. I had asked about her Mother and Gwenyfar's Mother. She said only "dead." Something in her look made me pursue this no more. But now, eating and still sitting up in my bed, she seemed so much more peaceful than upon the previous Night.

I told her that today she should be presented to Lady Vivianne to receive her blessing of welcome. "You will be welcomed to rest here for one full Moon's Dance, or longer if you will," said I.

"And Branwen, even though you are much older than our usual postulants, you may be given the opportunity to learn our Mysteries, if you wish. If you do wish to stay here with us, perhaps the Lady will allow it. Of course you need not – nor should you even – decide this now. No, you must wait at least through the first Moon's Dance spent here. You are simply our guest for now. I only mention this to give you hope for your life. There is also the possibility of living amoungst us as a worker for a season or two while you learn where your heart will lead you."

I knew as I said these things to her that it was a lot all at one Time, but there was something or someone that bade me speak.

Then my eyes caught sight of her golden lyre leaning against my chest of Sacred things. You see, I had positioned everything in my hut so that the chest could catch the morning Sunlight through the small open window in the front wall near the doorway. I had been blessed in that the front of my cottage faced relative East. The Rosemary and lavender bushes which Arthur had brought to me from the continent thrived in that setting, and while in bloom emanated a lovely fragrance that wafted through the open window. Well, when my eyes happened upon Branwen's lyre, it was at the perfect moment. The Sunlight was gleaming on the surface of its polished gold. It shone brightly, even casting a ray of light across the room to Branwen's heart and breast. I think she was unaware of this, though. She had called her lyre a harpy, or herpie, which is the Saxon name for it.

"Branwen, will you grace us with your lovely voice and lyre this Night at our bonfire and evening meal? Music soothes the heart. We have many talented Singers and Storytellers here, both male and female, but none I think, quite as gifted as you. Do not tell anyone that I said that. Art is wondrous, especially in the way that its quality can be judged only by the eye or ear of the one beholding it. There are such seemingly endlessly diverse ways of expression and each is beautiful in its own way."

Somewhat to my surprise she said, "Yes, I will."

"Good then, I will leave you to freshen yourself to see Lady Vivianne. Do you have clean clothing?"

"Yes, Lady... Thank you for everything."

As I left her to walk for a while by myself, I tried to comprehend the ramifications of all she had told me of Gwenyfar's decisions and actions. Queen Gwenyfar had renounced the old ways and taken Christian vows and baptism. This was after a many-cycle-long mentorship and friendship with a certain Monk. She had told Branwen that their Love and sexual relations were a great sin and an abomination and that she dreadfully feared the Fires of Hell – the torment of punishment in the Christian afterlife. So Gwenyfar would never see Branwen again. Just like that – No kiss of parting. No consolation.

Then she had written a letter– *a letter* – to Arthur, explaining that this Monk had told her that she and Arthur were not really married. This, he said, was because the marriage bed had never been duly consecrated or consummated. Gwenyfar's letter went on that she feared the loss of honour to herself and to Arthur because of the deception of the *false* blooded sheets on their wedding Night, and that she would keep this their secret *if* Arthur would allow her to retire from her position as Queen and live with the sisters of the small Christian monastic center near to our Order's land.

Eight Days later, Arthur arrived at the Isle of Apples...

Arthur later told me that she had signed it and sealed it with the ring her sister, Princess Rowena, had given to her as a wedding gift. How ironic! No other words, apologies nor salutation, simply signed – *Princess* Gwenyfar – retaining only her Saxon title. The letter and ring were delivered to Arthur in Aquae Sulis by messenger.

"She acts like a mad bitch – or perhaps more like a snake – heartless, no concern for the harm she has done," was his reaction.

He had immediately sent word to Gwenyfar upon his arrival at the Isle of Apples – too angry to go himself to the small Monastery. His message said, "Queen Gwenyfar. You will *never* be relieved of your title as Queen, but I do give my permission for removing yourself from court. Signed, Arthur Rex."

"Oh Morgan, what more can I do?"

"Arthur," I said, "I hope this causes as little embarrassment as possible to you. I know that *you* hold no Love for her in your heart – but poor Branwen."

"Yes, she did not deserve this ill treatment from Gwenyfar... Can I do anything for her?"

"I know not what, Arthur..."

These were my only words of comfort to him. I thought it best to let lie this twist of the Fates.

And so it was that Branwen, during her first Moon's Dance here, sang and played her harpy for us, in bittersweet and haunting melodies on many fine evenings 'round the Fires, in the coolness of early Summer. During her Days, she spent much Time with me, learning how to care for my Bees, shear the wool from the white -aced Sheep, tend the dairy Cows, make cheese, and to build and repair the cottages. She especially Loved the crafts of the Thatchers and Weavers. None of these tasks had she ever done before. At Times she seemed to be fine and to find some peace here. One Day she came to me and said, "How I do Love to thatch the roofs, Morgan."

I had given her leave to call me by my familial name, so as not to stand on protocol.

One of my brothers called "Wolf Eyes" accepted her as his apprentice.

Excitedly, she shared her enthusiasm with me.

"First we collect the materials of Water reeds, straw, and flax from the Marshes or the fields; these being Water reeds, they are not very heavy and are easy to roll to the building sites on our wagons. Then the thatch is tied in bundles and laid in an under layer upon the roof beams. And then they are pegged in place with rods of Hazel-Wood. Added to this is an upper layer – which is very thick – laid over the first, and a final reinforcing layer is laid along the ridgeline.

I was told that when, in Time, the roof leaks it can be repaired by rethatching only the badly damaged portion of it. But I could not see how that would work, for each of the original layers formed a solid barrier over the entire roof. Then, when one of the widows' – living in the nearby village – roof leaked buckets at a Time, the Order's Thatchers heard of it and came to help. Wolf Eyes showed me how to Weave a repair together with the original thatching. It worked! And very fine work I did – if I may be allowed to say so.

On the continent across the Eastern Sea, Thatchers have taken to decorating the edges of roofs with beautiful designs. I would Love to see that done here. Might I try it, Lady Morgan? I have asked my teacher – I know that it would take extra Time... But all things of beauty are a reflection of the Goddess' Love, are they not?"

To see her enthusiasm did my heart good. Perhaps she was finding her light again. At the end of that Moon's Dance, she decided to stay with us.

She so Loved the Weaving. She was also fascinated in the Art of Weaving wool into yarn and then dying it and quickly learned to be an excellent Weaver in a short Time. With most of our Weavers it had taken much longer to learn how to spin, then much more Time to achieve the finest perfection of regularity in the Weaving of the yarn. Branwen was gifted in so many ways and, it seemed to me, that she was finding some joy here at last.

But then there were her dark Times when she was so distant, lonely, and seemingly out of place. Though surrounded by friends, there would be a hollowness of Spirit about her. I so often wondered how she could create such beauty with such an empty heart – but she did. Perhaps the answer to this is that her Muses sang and played *through* her, just as sometimes the Voices speak through me.

One Night, over a year later, at the beginning of the First Harvest when all of those who had worked so hard were tired – yet joyful with the blessing of the accomplishment of a ripe and full Harvest – we built a great bonfire. We would celebrate that Night by dancing and drinking honey mead – all in our own good measure – and the morrow would be a Day of rest. Near to the end of our revelries, Branwen stepped forward to play her harpy and sang a song she had just written. Branwen's song had a Magic of its own, the power of it seemed to circle and fill our whole grounds. When she sang it, all Creatures – Animal and Human – hushed, but the Air stirred as if she had called the Winds. Heart-piercing was the melody, and her words cut to the bone. I knew... yes I knew what her song was about.

"I sing a song macabre
A dark and restless tune
A woeful tale of sadness over Love...

Oh-oo-oo-oo-oh...
All over Love...

How once the Raven sang more sweetly than the Nightingale
Her Spirit soared more joyfully than a Crane in flight
Her heart was full and peaceful as the Dove...

But then you clipped the Raven's wings
Now she no longer sings
Her heart a lonely fortress... over Love

Oh-oo-oo-oo-oh, all over Love...
Oh-oo-oo-oo-oh, I'm over Love..."

Of course, there were other Seers amoung us who felt the hollow hopelessness in her song as did I. But the others – overwhelmed by Branwen's golden mask and dark shadows, equally devastatingly beautiful and disturbingly mysterious – stood to their feet, applauded and cheered her. She smiled, bade us all a good Night, and thanked us for all of the Love and kindnesses we had shown to her.

The next morning when she did not join us in our song to the Sun Mother at her rising, I went to the hut which she and three of our men had just finished building for her. All was quiet. Not the usual sort of quiet, but a vacant stillness. I hesitated a moment outside her doorway.

Shielding myself with courage, I knocked and then entered. I half expected to see her hanging from a beam, but no, she lay peacefully in her bed. In her hand was a written note, addressed to me.

"Morgan of the Woods, Enchantress of the Bees, dear, kind friend... you have done everything you could do for me. Have no regrets, dear one. Please accept and care for the only thing of beauty left of me – my lyre, my harpie. Perhaps, Morgan, you will play it, and if not you, then Gwenda.

Thank you and Goddess bless you...

Branwen"

An empty vial lay across her belly.

I never sent word to Queen Gwenyfar. Perhaps that was uncouth of me, but I had no words lacking anger and distaste for her that I could say. I tried to keep my thoughts away from Gwenyfar for as long as she lived, for my thoughts have power and my wishes *can and do* manifest in this world of form. I would not soil my Spirit by wishing her to Death, so besides the writing of this account, I have never spoken her name again, nor will I ever.

Now, before I write of the events that followed, I must say that I am not a superstitious person, but I do have great respect for the interaction of all life forces, even emotions such as grief and fear. I consider them living entities that can swell like a great wave of the Sea, covering all in their path, consuming everything. And so the despondency of Branwen, when released from her living body, spread all over the Isle, including the land of our Order. It hung in the Air with a powerful heaviness. Two of our milk Cows could give only spoiled milk. One of them died over Night – she was very difficult to move. When finally we were able to move her, she had to be buried right where she lay outside the dairy's entrance, which of itself was a sadness and constant reminder of Branwen. The Cow's name had been Marigold. The milkers wept. The Horses were agitated in their stables. A Hound who visited us from a nearby village had formed a bond with Branwen in the short Time of her life here. The Hound wailed at her grave until his owner came to bring him home. But he kept coming back. Even my Bees felt the heaviness. They were quiet and listless. You see, none of us had ever experienced anything like this before. In our known history, no one had ever taken their own life here.

Oh, it is said that Time out of memory ago, the Harvest Kings, Human males, had been Sacrificed at the Grain Harvest Festivals, but that was a very long Time ago. And besides, every Harvest King had been a *willing* and honoured Sacrifice to the Earth Mother – a joyful thing, not a waste of life for sadness sake, as was Branwen's.

Even the weather was unusual. It was so hot and humid, so stifling, that our Harvesters had not enough stamina to complete their tasks, and so, some of the Grain and early Apples withered and rotted in the fields and orchards. The green lands began to turn brown, but of course, I knew it was the same in all the lands around us, as well. The decline of all around us was not caused by Branwen's Death. It could not be, could it? But still it added to the general ill mood.

As I have said, I did not contact the Queen – but Arthur insisted that she attend Branwen's burial. He sent a heavy guard and a messenger to fetch her here by royal command. She could not refuse on penalty of treason! Her standing on our blessed land made everything even worse. I spoke not a word to her. Arthur asked me to acknowledge her, but I said I would only under his royal *command*. He smiled, stroked my hair and said, "Do as you will, Morgan. Never will I command anything of you."

So I did as I would, not even sharing eye contact with her. Once, though, I snuck a glance at her face as she stood behind Branwen's open grave. When they lowered the box that held Branwen's body into the hole, the Queen stood dry eyed and blank faced. The moment it was over, she turned to Arthur and sarcastically said, "May I go now?"

My kind hearted Bear could not believe it. Branwen had been her lifelong friend and devoted lover. His face grew stern and cold, something I had only seen twice before in him. He said, "Go then, never let me see your face again!"

To my knowledge, that was the last Time Arthur and Gwenyfar ever spoke to each other.

This one Time, Arthur's guard had not included Bedwyr. Bedwyr held hatred to his core toward Gwenyfar – for his Love of Arthur.

Bedwyr was a powerful Seer and Magician, raised and taught by Igraine, my Mother. Something told me that he was prudent in his absence, so as to keep his Spirit unstained by *his* Death wish toward Gwenyfar. I am sure we all tried to keep our thoughts pure, but ironically on the ride back to her small Monastery; Gwenyfar's Horse shied, stumbled, and fell upon her. Oh, she did not die, but lived with deformity and pain for the rest of her life.

The next Day Lady Vivianne called a council with all Initiates of our Order. She and the rest of the nine Mothers had planned a great cleansing Ritual, which we were all to participate in. Her proclamation was: "This needs be done; to cast out and away from the land – and all who inhabit Her – the dismal forces of sadness, anger, confusion, and despair, so that the Order can be restored to balance and once again be filled with the Spirits of joy."

Although this Ritual would not be held as being of great importance in the years to come, it is a memory – Sacred and dear to my heart – for which reason I write of it here in these histories.

Perhaps I should begin by sharing my observations of Magic workers in many other cultures. It seems to me that with most, the more passionately they try to banish or rid themselves of some evil, unhealthy, or dangerous forces – or as we perceive them, Spirits – the more angrily, puffed up, and loudly they command these to be GONE! They hold their breath, tense up every muscle in their bodies, and then expel all of their powers in one great BOOM! –

such as does an Archer releasing an arrow held too long for the aim – believing that the surge of power will force the desired action to occur. I have heard that some rant and rave and threaten in very dramatic gestures, shaking their fists, staffs, bells, or swords to the Four Winds – proclaiming an eternally dreadful outcome for the Spirits who refuse to leave. Oh, but listen to my mocking... My apologies.

"Remember to respect all paths, Morgan..." came a vague breath whispering into my ears.

I mean no disrespect to my peers and I cannot say with certainty that they do not gain the desired results in their works. But it has come down to us, from our Ancestors, that there is a simpler way.

You see, our tradition teaches that the great Astronomers who came here from our Motherland discerned that it is not the Sun Mother who traverses the Day and Night sky, but rather it is that the Earth Mother dances a spiral dance, so elusively and gracefully around the Sun that we cannot detect her motion.

Just so, does it look to us, when the White Moon Goddess arches the Sky from our left to right if we are facing South, that her dance is so subtly slow, that we can watch Her moving betwixt Trees and Hills to beyond the horizon; always moving vaguely in the same direction as does the Sun. This is all because the sphere of our Earth spins in a widdershins direction.

This may all be very confusing, because people in many other lands have very different understandings of the Cosmos than we. Perhaps, one Day in the future, when someone – like you – is reading these histories, these scientific observations will be recognized as truth and understood by everyone.

But back to our Magic making...

A component of *raising* Magical or any energy is *friction* – such as rubbing two sticks together to spark a flame – or how your hands will warm on a Winter's Night when you rub them together, back and forth in hard and swift motion. Friction equals *building* energy. Energy "changes" things; which equals Creation. Expansion is the *male* polarity of the Cosmos – the "breathing out," the pushing force – hence, manifestation or the coming *into* form.

But the allowing of all things to go *with* the natural flow – not against it – is the *female* polarity. It is the Cosmos' "breathing in," "the contraction," "the draw," the" pull," the "reception."

Heat is always drawn into the absence of heat. When you touch your cool hand to the Fire, heat will be drawn into your hand, burning you. It will not be that your hand will cool the Fire.

Perhaps I am saying too much of things that may never be understood, accepted, or proven, but these things are our teachings. It is from this science that we obtain the understanding of how to use the natural currents of the Earth – and all within Her – to do our Magics of the making, Creation, the coming into form – or the breaking, destruction, the coming un-done.

So, when we wish to *banish* ill forces or Spirits, we do not create the friction that is necessary when we wish to *create* something – bringing it into form. No, we simply move *with* the flow and motion of the Earth. We circle, we glide, we dance – always widdershins, drawing these energies *with* our 'dance,' *allowing* them to spiral with the irresistible natural widdershins flow of Earth. No huffing and puffing and anger and threatening, which only *feeds* these unwanted forces with the energies they thrive upon. We simply deplete them; drawing them down into the Mother. We *release* them.

And so, on the Night of the Black Moon, we assembled – all cloaked in our dark leaf-green mantles, with our hoods pulled over our heads. We held each other's hands and gracefully danced, weaving back and forth like a great long Serpent, completely circling the whole of our lands on the Isle of Apples. Three Times around did we dance. It took from twilight to Dawn. As we traversed this path of beauty, we all sang a song of entreaty, release, and comfort – a way out for the Spirits we would banish – gently, but thoroughly. With the contraction and flow, we drew them irresistibly along. To an ancient tune – passed down from generation to generation – these were the words we sang...

> I dance thee out of my home...
> Feelings of anger, betrayal and pain...
> Unwanted emotions, my dance be thy bane...
> I dance thee out of my home...
>
> I dance thee out of my home...
> Words rashly spoken, malefic intent...
> Want and frustration – thy power be rent

I dance thee out of my home...

Fly through the cracks in the doors and the windows
Follow the breeze towards the boughs up above...
Then circle and circle, way down to the Mother...
Whence the Earth will embrace thee, and turn thee to Love.

I dance thee out of my home...
I dance thee out of my home...
I dance thee out of my home...

I dance thee out of my home...
Unwelcome intruders, we utter thy name...
Forces of discord, our peace to reclaim...
I dance thee out of my home...

I dance thee out of my home...
We banish thee now from our own fields and livestock,
Our homes and our hearts, our Springs and our Wood...
Gently we Charm thee way down to the Mother...
Where Her Love will embrace thee, and change thee to good...

I dance thee out of my home.
I dance thee out of my home.
I dance thee out of my home.

It is so simple to dance, circle, move, spiral, Charm, banish, release, and disseminate, with the widdershins motion – the flow of the Earth, where all is absorbed and absolved into her draw.

Do you understand?

There is an old parable that says: "Power lies not within the strength of the arm, but in the quality of the sword."

Like a leaf flowing downstream, peace retuned and the years of the Summer King continued. Not even a whisper of war was in the Winds on Our Fair Isles.

Chapter 29
Bronte

Gwyddion

In about the second year of peace I reminded Arthur of his promise to the Picti and the Highland Clans that he would periodically return to Table Rock to meet with his allies there. So, at my request, all was arranged; messengers sent out, and provisions packed for our journey.

On the first Day out toward the meet, Arthur, Bedwyr, and Lucian all expressed the desire to visit the great Stone Temples and Dragon lines on an Island far off the West Coast of Alba. And, as well, they said that they wished to go to the extreme North in the wild and craggy Highlands – for none of them had seen that country and they had heard of a beautiful Loch of renown wherein, it is said, lives a great Sea Dragon. Bedwyr and I chuckled and winked at each other. How could Arthur and Lucian know that Dragons travelled everywhere we went? Or so Brennos and Bedwyr had told me and, in fact, I had begun to feel them myself.

Bedwyr said, "I would like to see a Dragon in the flesh, though I hardly believe the tales that are told. It is probably a very old and grumpy Salmon."

We all laughed.

The Picti, along with some of their neighbors, such as the Southern-most Highland Clans, had planned great games of strength in honour of our meet. A bit different and singular to their culture were these games. They had felled Trees, cutting off the tops and bottoms, keeping only the main trunks, which were smoothed. They drew a line in the dirt and each contestant picked up and held one of these huge trunks straight upwards in their hands - the great beams being supported by stewards or fellow-competitors while being placed into position. Then, they must balance it just right and toss it with a great heave toward a second, third, or fourth line away in the distance. Wherever it landed was marked, so that the next man would try to toss it farther. It was amazing! I learned that the third and fourth lines marked the distance former Champions had tossed the beam.

These men were stout and muscular; more squarely built than our more Southern men. That was one reason they were such frightening Warriors. But far from the impression these men gave in battle, they were a good-humored lot. Lucian tossed a Tree and did get it many arms' lengths away – not bad for a first try. He paid for this the next Day with aching arms, shoulders, and knees, though.

At the end of the Games whilst everyone was packing up, a man engaged Bedwyr and I in conversation. He told us that his name was Mohaw, which meant "Lost in the Mists of Time." A poetic man was he, with a poetic name. He introduced himself as being of the Gododdin Clan and a member of the Council of the town of Din Eidyn.

"Din Eidyn is just over there, my Lords..."

He was pointing toward a nearby promontory overlooking the Sea, which seemed to be – as a Crow flies – about two Roman miles away. He asked if we had made arrangements for this Night's lodging before continuing our travels. When I said that we had not, he asked if we would honour him by staying a Night or two – or more – at his humble farm.

"My cottage is comfortable and there is enough room for the four of you to sleep inside. Your Guardsmen can find room in our stable, where there is fresh hay. My farm is farther down yon Hill on the outskirts of Din Eidyn. It is not far."

I asked Arthur if we could stay with him. Arthur replied that it may be a good thing, as there would be many others seeking near-by lodging too. Arthur... still so humble and un-pretentious – as if the King could not command lodging anywhere. Arthur told Mohaw that we would gladly accept the hospitality of his comfortable cottage.

On our way to his farm, Mohaw told us that he was a widower and that he lived with his three daughters, "...all of an age to marry."

Bedwyr lowered his head and smiled ever so slightly...

Mohaw went on, "My three daughters have talked about little else since I told them that King Arthur and his Companions would be at the Games."

The youngest of his daughters, whose name was Cleur, was fourteen years, the next, whose name was Ahna, was fifteen, and the eldest – whose name was Bronte – was past her eighteenth year-turn. They looked to have much more Clansmen's blood than Picti – although Mohaw had told us that his wife had been of the Picti.

A diary...

I have interjected this next bit of writing, which – unlike most of my written histories, written well after the incidents involved had actually taken place – were written upon our fourth evening at Mohaw's farm. I think the events – as well as the hitherto uncharted feelings arising within me – so unexpected and poignant, are worthy of being written down before they slip away into my ever *so well-guarded* self...

Feelings... Yes...

Bronte... I would her call a comely girl, in a simple sort of way... although she has not the mysterious dark beauty of Morgan or Igraine. Neither has she the strong, golden, Sun-lit beauty of Princess Rowena nor the vulnerable, pale allure of Arthur's wife, Gwenyfar. She is of an average size. Her mouth is a little too wide – all the better to smile with. Her hair is brown, her eyes a light hazel-brown – with green flecks in them. I suppose that most folk would say that Bronte is a plain girl. Yet there is nothing *ordinary* about her. She is charming and very intelligent. From the first moment I met her, I began to recognize a power within her.

Bronte has not kept her eyes from me. She has used every excuse to see, to speak, or to walk with me all Day long for the four Days that we have been here. Is it not longer than that that I have known her? I am over fifty years now – older than her Father. Does she desire me? Could a young girl like her want me as her lover? Or am I just an old fool lying to myself just as young fools do? Love? Desire? What business have I toying with such ideas anyway? Long ago I decided that sexual Love was not for one such as me. Yet... all the while we have been here I have felt a hunger within me.

Oh, I am confused and a little embarrassed – even to write these things in my own secret pages.

No, it could never be... But then, what *does* she want? Illumination dawning... "Ah... She wants the Magic from me. Of course."

Those were the only words I had written whilst there...

To Continue -

Upon the next Day she raised her courage to ask me, "Please, take me with you on your travels, my Lord Merlin – if only for a Moon's Dance or two. I wish... I want to go with you."

"My girl, your Father would not let you travel with four men and their Guard."

"Yes, he would! He said so!"

She blushed.

"My people hold no value in virginity, so..."

"My girl! Are you suggesting...?"

"No, no, I only meant – why else should he have objected? This is what I have always wanted – to learn!"

"To learn WHAT, exactly?"

"To Heal people and other Creatures and to travel the Three Realms. My Mother knew the Herbs and she knew other things, too. Like... like... my Mother taught me how to stir the cauldron:

Three Times widdershins, seven by the Sun
A bag o' bones an' holey Stones
An then ye ha' begun
Bitter Herbs an' Mouse's tails – poison Mushrooms, too...
Bubble, bubble, boil the pot
Ta make a pungent brew
Chant a song o' seven words:
A Hi le Broch 'n doodle dee
Chase ol' evil, pain an' Death
Awee, awee, awee
Twirl aroun' th' cauldron unteel the Charm is done
Three Times widdershins, seven by the Sun

"She taught me until she died, when I was ten years. Since then I have done the woman's work at home and what was needed for my Father and sisters. But now, my sister Ahna is fifteen and old enough to care for our home."

"But do you not wish to marry and have children, Bronte?"

She answered thoughtfully.

"Perhaps, someday, but all in good Time, my Lord Gwyddion The Merlin."

"Bronte, I must think about this. It is a lot that you ask."

"But even if only for a short while? I will be a very good student. I will *never* forget anything you tell me. I will do anything you require of me..."

"Never is a long Time." I smiled. "We barely know each other Bronte."

"But, if I may be so bold as to contradict you, my Lord – this is not the first Time we have met. Ever and never go in both directions. Have you, my Lord, The Merlin no remembrance of Time we have spent together in other lives?"

My head began to spin, an itching I could not quite reach. Shadows of memories were rushing through my thoughts – or, well, no – better said, my feelings – three steps ahead of me, but which I could not catch. I felt faint and ill, but it was just a sickness which most Seers experience... as if I had been in the hot Sun too long without Water. Slowly, I came back to myself. Who was she? Or – who had we been to each other?

"I do not quite remember," I said. "Will you tell me, Bronte?"

"Yes, my Lord... Will you take me with you?"

"It seems that I must..."

Bronte – the name means "Bestower." Now, I wonder what Wisdom you might bestow upon *me*?

It seems I had spoken it aloud. She responded:

"It is I, my Lord, who will receive the gift of your company and teachings. I humbly thank you."

And so Bronte came with us.

First we went beyond the West coast of Pictland and across a stretch of Sea, to the Isle of Stones. To say that I like crossing any stretch of Water would be like saying that I like a toothache. I was ill from the moment I stood on the rocking boat until an hour after disembarking it.

We found there a wild and craggy Island of breathtakingly beautiful shorelines, sparsely inhabited by people of a primitive way of life. The natives called it something that sounded like Haibowdai. Bronte said that her Father called it Skye.

We did see a couple of crude villages – with round huts of Stone – and there, saw some people. Mostly they avoided us, but a few were friendly and helpful. Bronte understood their dialect easier than the rest of us and this helped us to find food, drink, and lodging. One man acted as guide.

Our guide also took us to their ring of Stones. Of course we, the men, had all walked amoung the Giant's Dance, the great Henge near Sorviodunum. But it all seemed different somehow on this majestic, yet lonely place – seemingly so removed from Time and humanity's imprint.

I wondered what sort of Magics, sciences, and Rituals had been practiced here down through the Ages. It is now so desolate, but once it must have been awash with people – Priests and Priestesses perhaps – and Merchants plying their trades and wares to all those coming and going. Perhaps it was thus, once. Still the echoes of brilliance linger – the awe and spectacle, the energy and the Magic. My heart rejoiced.

I thought – "If I should cross the veil today, I have seen and felt more than enough for three lifetimes."

I must have said this aloud, too. Bronte was standing next to me, though I had not noticed her until that moment. She said, "You have seen enough for many more than that – even before you were born into this life."

"Bronte, please tell me now – here and now, in this place – what you remember of our lives together."

"Yes, My Lord, I will.

"You were an Architect, a designer of buildings – buildings of Stone, a Temple of the Sun. For our people were Sun worshippers. Or well, perhaps not really. We worshipped Gods as symbols, or symbols as Gods. It is hard to explain – the Sun was the symbol, the outward manifestation of the Gods. We worshipped the God of the Sun, at its zenith in the Sky. I seem to remember that His name was Hora or Haru...

"A Great Age was passing into a new one. This I cannot explain, but, somehow I know.

"It was taught that our God of Wisdom spoke the first word, which set all Creation into motion. This is all I can remember of that...

"You were a wise and powerful man, the King's man, yes, even then. I was... a Water Healer... There was a Ritual of the Cool Water.

"I saw you many Times, but we never met, until an accident happened. A large Stone fell upon your leg and crushed it. They brought you to the Healing Temple. There the Physicians cut off your leg. They burned it with red hot Stones and covered the stump with a tar-like substance mixed with many Herbs and Flowers, which had been ground into it. You raised a great fever. They brought me to you, to perform the Magic of the Cool Water. I stayed with you Day and Night, along with many Priests coming and going to say their Magic Words. After seven Days, you awoke – feverless – and in great pain, so I gave you wine mixed with the oils and essence of the large red flowers that grew in great abundance in this lush land. I spent a whole season with you, my Lord. I Loved you."

She blushed...

"Then one Night, you died.

"I have been waiting for you for so long. Now I have found you."

"Bronte, I am astounded... I have known others who were *born remembering*, but your memories are so clear. Pray, tell me more. Do you remember their Words of the Making? Or of the Breaking? And what was your name – or mine? What did people wear? Tell me all you remember."

"My Lord and teacher Gwyddion, my Sacred name was given to me by my mentor in the Temple University. And I may never speak it. I cannot remember your name, but I think it had the Sun God's name within it. As to their secret Words of the Making and the Breaking, I cannot remember a one..."

Most of our land's terrain was as the Sand of a shoreline, but there was no Sea – only a great River running through the length of it like blood through the channels in our arms. Extending Eastward and Westward from each bank of this River was lush and fertile land – but only a little way out from it on either side. The people lined their eyes black for beauty, as some of the Tribes in our lands do. We – or was it they? – had Priestly trappings for Ritual and official works.

Once and only once, did I see a very old Priestess – and a very important person was she. Perhaps she was Royal too. She wore a robe of black with small, white, five pointed Stars spotted all over it – like the Starry Night Sky. I believe very few – and only the highest ranking of those in the Temple Schools – wore a robe like this. Yet this memory is very confusing... Mayhap I only Dreamed of her. I thought I *was* her, for I saw that robe as if upon myself – from my eyes looking outward. Perhaps I am confused... I do not truly know what this all means or even if this memory is from the same life we shared, my Lord. That is all I remember. When these Visions or Dreams come upon me, it is as though it is happening just then, at that very moment. So *many* Visions and Dreams have I had about that land..."

Her voice trailed off.

I, the so-called *great* Merlin, stood cold and shivering in her presence. She was so much more than I could ever have known. Bronte was like a sponge of the Sea. I could never quench her thirst for knowledge. Always would she have more and more. True to her word, she remembered every drink from my cup. So quickly did she excel in the Arts that before our travels of four Moon's Dances had ended, she was as one who had studied for years.

Bronte was not all seriousness though. She had a wonderful sense of humour, witty and quick of tongue, a joy to be with – we all thought so. We all Loved her, each in our own way.

I have ever wondered if Bedwyr wanted her as his lover. But if so, to my knowledge he never acted upon it.

Time flew by... We did go as far North as the uppermost Islands – to the land called Orkney, which, Bronte said, her Father called Arcaibh. This entailed yet more Sea rides for me. But, all in all, it was worth it. Once, we saw the great Northern Lights in the Night – albeit twilit – Sky.

This Time was to me as if living in a Dream. But all Dreams must come to an ending. The Day came when we knew that we could tarry no longer. It was Time for Arthur to return home, to get on with the work of ruling his Kingdom.

Bronte begged us to go, one last Time, to Croft Moraig. She so Loved that Stone Circle. Well, really it was not a true circle but was shaped more like the Roman letter C. There were round markings on the Stones. Some called them cup marks, but Bronte said they looked like flowers to her. She told us that her Father had taken her and her Mother to see Croft Moraig not long before her Mother had become ill and died. Always, she said, she had felt closest to her Mother there.

Croft Moraig is near to the Southeast edge of where the River Tamia splits in two. It is a hard Day's ride from her Father's home. We agreed to go there.

Nothing had ever been spoken between Bronte and me about the future. It was as if we had been frozen in Time – one Day blissfully flowing into the next. But now what? Could she be content to remain in her Father's house, caring for the aches and pains of whoever lived nearby? After all of our long and wondrous talks of Magic, Cosmic

Truths, and our shared past, we must finally speak of the future. But when we arrived at Croft Moraig and set up our camp, we, being weary from the long Days' ride, went promptly to sleep.

When Dawn came, Bronte went a-ways from the camp to a Stream where she could bathe herself as best she could. As I have already written, Bronte was a half Picti girl, while we all, or at least most of our company, had very Roman trappings about ourselves and our Horses.

We will never really know and will only torment ourselves as to what happened next and why. Perhaps some of the Picti thought her traitorous to her kin by traveling with Roman men – who can know? All we heard in the early morning peace was the soft whooshing sound of an arrow through the Air, a blunt hit, and a moan.

We were all up and out of our pallet rolls in a moment and at our fallen Bronte's side.

She did not die at once, but we knew that it had been a fatal blow. We were already stricken with grief while she lay there with laboured breathing.

Her attackers were gone – fled like Harts into the surrounding Woods. No one was in sight or hearing of us. No matter... I held her head in my arms.

"Bronte..."

She looked up at me.

"So it was not to be..."

"Bronte... Bronte..." was all I could think to say – I had no words of comfort or Wisdom.

She whispered again, "I will wait for you. No matter how long... Always..."

It was then that once again, the Voices of the Stars shook the Earth beneath my feet. They said, "No, Gwyddion, she must not wait. She must not be bound to waiting because of her Love for you. She must return – and soon – for she will come as a Child of Promise – a Magic child – she has a great work awaiting her. Tell her, Gwyddion! Let her go!"

But, she was already gone.

Still I called out to her again, this Time to her Spirit, which I perceived was hovering just above her lifeless body.

"Bronte, my dear one, before you leave you must know what the Voices told me. Can you hear me?"

Silence... Naught but silence. Yet, all around us, hanging in the Air, was a mighty presence – rich, heady, transcendent, powerful, beautiful. We all felt it. I hurried before her Spirit fled.

"BRONTE! They told me..." I whispered what they had said. Then suddenly, the presence was filled with the sweet smell of Summer Flowers although there were none around us anywhere. We each spoke at once: "Flowers." Then, all was gone. She was gone.

Lucian said, "It is said by the Christians in Rome that the Saints – their Holy Men and Women – are followed by the scent of Flowers and that by this they are known to be Holy." Then the realization of her Death hit him.

"The Flowers... they are gone... she is gone."

I wept first and then did Arthur, then Bedwyr. Lucian and the men of our Guard each walked away to their own privacy, with heads hung in sorrow, lest we see them weep.

"We will bury her here by the Northernmost Stone," said I.

"Hurry, ride like the Wind to bring this sad news to her Father. It should take you one Day's ride there and one Day to return. We will prepare for her burial. Tell her Father of her sweet memories of this place. I believe he will agree to bury her here. Now, go!"

To preserve her privacy, we did not remove her shift, but only washed the parts of her body that would be proper for our eyes to see. She had just bathed the parts she had felt essential for her comfort. But her sweet face, arms, hands, feet and legs, we washed and rubbed with Oil of Rosemary, which I always carry with me for the sake of offerings and consecrations to the Gods. I placed her boots upon her feet. I removed the arrow and tried to clean the blood from her shift as best I could.

My thoughts carried me to so many conversations that Bronte and I had shared. Know that they were not always about the Arts. Many talks did we have about her own feelings and observations of life, her own peculiarities and the like. Like how she Loved Frogs and other Animals usually disgusting to other people. She had Loved to observe the complete life cycles of Tadpoles into Frogs in her family pond and how Snakes shed their skins. She said that she thought it akin to Magic how at Night, there were no Mushrooms in her Father's Field, and then in the morning she would see, in what had been an empty field, rings and whole bunches of fully grown and perfectly white Mushrooms. She would pick them for medicines – for she knew which were and which were not, the poisonous kinds – only to find that new rings had all grown back the next morning. She said she never picked Ferns, Tree leaves, Heather, Flowers, or Mosses for her own pleasures, because they were the adornment of our Earth Mother and were to be shared with all of her Creatures. Only those used for Healing were suitable to be picked in her way of thinking.

Many Times she had spoken to me of freedom – a strange kind of freedom, which could only be felt from within and could not really be defined by a name or a word. With difficulty she tried and tried to explain this freedom to me. Indeed, she could not define it. But, to her it was the most precious treasure she could have.

What was it she had said? Oh yes, she had said that "To stand upon a Rocky ledge high above all else with the Wind blowing my hair – or even to walk barefooted without my boots – these are things of my freedom. To swim naked in a River, the draw pulling me and my not resisting it, becoming one with it and going wherever it might take me, these are things of my freedom. Traveling as I have with you and our merry company – this, too, is freedom. My freedom is to be able to read and write, to search and find, to be kind but not to live for anyone else's feelings, needs, or demands. My freedom, my Lord, is a *being* – not a *having*."

It was the freedom of her Spirit I suppose, a sort of independence. She said that without it she would wither and die. Was that why she had died – because she would have had to go back home now to a plain, boring, and ordinary existence?

"But Bronte," I cried, "you could have stayed with me."

Then I remembered that I had not offered. Oh Bronte... Was my solitude as precious to me as your freedom was to you? I am so sorry.

Her grave was dug. A thing of rectangular perfection, three arms lengths deep so that no wild Animal could disrupt it. We laid her body on its side with her hands cradling her head, knees raised as a sleeping babe. That was how I had seen her whilst she slept at Night. We could not wait for her Father to lay her in her grave, as the Deaths' stiffness would set in. We covered the bloody part of her shift, where the arrow had pierced her, with leaves that had fallen from the surrounding Oaks, Ash, and Rowans. Nothing had been picked. All had fallen – like you my dear, beloved child. This covering we did for her Father's feelings and all the more so of the fragile feelings of her sisters, should they come as well.

Of a sudden I remembered what she had said about her freedom. It struck me that I could honour her freedom by removing her boots.

"There my dear one, fly in your freedom..."

I kept vigil by her grave. I did not sleep. Neither did Bedwyr nor Arthur. It was almost three Days before the riders reached our camp, just at Sundown. Her Father came alone.

"Too hard a ride for two grieving young girls..." said he.

He must have Loved Bronte greatly. Hurting too much to weep, he just stood stoically looking down at her body in the grave. After a long Time he said, "Thank you for your waiting."

When he felt ready he said: "I would cover her body with Earth myself. It is all I may do to honour her for now."

Something was missing... Her name! I never gave her a Magical or Sacred name – as it was my right to do, as her Teacher. When her Father had finished covering her with dirt, he asked me to say some words for her.

"Freedom... Saoirse!"

I yelled it to the four Winds and pounded my staff onto the ground, twice.

"Saoirse... may you be blessed by this name which I, Gwyddion, your teacher, bestow upon you. So must it be and so it is!" I hit my staff upon the ground a third Time... The Earth shook. Then silently I said to her, "On an Isle of Mist you told me who we had been, but may you return quickly and may you not be lost in the Mists of Time. Find your way back soon, Saoirse. Do not wait for me in the Otherworlds. For, you have a great work to do. Bring with your Spirit this Child of Promise."

Chapter 30
The Fortress & Liaisons

Arthur

After Bronte's Death, I saw Gwyddion diminish. I thought hard and long of what task I could set him to to take his thoughts away from her – as much as was possible. I came upon an Idea that just might benefit everyone. So, I set The Merlin to drawing the plans and excavating for my fortress. I was as excited as a little boy.

Until now, I have kept large barracks for myself as well as for my Guard in and near Aquae Sulis. I have also made arrangements for meager yet comfortable dwellings for those of my Warriors who have families with whom they wish to live.

Aquae Sulis is still a truly amazing city. Yet it has always been sorrowful to me how Time and the course of history have affected the ruin of such powerful and magnificent edifices as the Roman Baths and the Temple of Sulis-Minerva.

The Romans built the Temple of Sulis – whom they equated with Minerva – sweet Goddess of Wisdom. The baths were still supported with Roman money until they abandoned the Britons well over one hundred years ago. Then, for another long while, our wealthy Briton men and women kept both in operation.

It falls now into disrepair – the heating system is breaking down – but, no matter to me. These Waters are heated from deep within the Earth. What Magic of the Goddess is this? Nowhere else on our Isles is there another hot Spring. The Waters relax my thoughts as well as my body, but it is not only for the baths that I Love this place.

Its surrounding lands are beautiful. The River runs just beside the baths. Rundown market stalls still do business on market Day. Small cottages and huts dapple the countryside – and then, too, there are grand Roman-style Villas. It seems that, no matter what, life goes on. "She changes all She touches... And all who are touched by Her, change..."

Are these the right words? I heard these words – or some alike them – in an old Chant being sung by those sitting around the Bel-fire one Night upon the Isle of Apples.

I can still feel Sulis' and the Gods' presence here. I am sure their Spirits have indwelled these Springs from Times uncountable. I have walked deep within the Holy Sanctuary of the lofty, yet reachable image of Sulis-Minerva. Although her statue is now defaced, Her power and her presence are still there lingering. This place rings with echoes of Divine Love.

Perhaps long before the masters built the Stone Rings and Star Temples, they too came to the Sacred Waters for health or to ask for their desires to be fulfilled. I wonder by what names they called their Gods? No matter that. I believe that those Gods are still here along with all the others brought by subsequent waves of believers...

Gwyddion

The Time of the Summer King – those years of peace, abundance, and prosperity of the land and of the people continued. But why must there have been so many Deaths?

Of course, by the Time of my writing this, there have been ten years of peace. Where have they gone?

Bedwyr married Freidl not long after we returned from our travels to the North-lands. It proved to be a good and happy match. Freidl has had two sons by him. They came a year apart from each other. Both children lived and they are a contented and happy family. They live in Bedwyr's Dumnonian fortress. Not long after the second boy had been born both Bedwyr's Mother and Father died. Their graves are near to Igraine's, by Nodens' Well.

Arthur had had many lovers, but the liaisons never lasted long at all – and never had there been a hint of a child being made from any of these. Of course, he was kind and generous to all of these women, but there was only one great Love in his life. His pain and longing for her had never healed.

Lucian had Loved or lusted for several women over the years but none of these liaisons lasted for more than a year or two. Something always held him back from commitment.

Remembering back now, it too was not long after Bronte's Death that Chronos, my old friend, had flown away one Night to hunt and had never returned. I missed her. I still do. Later that year another Owl came to stay with me. I named him Chronos as well.

Soon thereafter, Arthur asked me to design a Fortress of State for him. As he put it, "It must be a place where we can offer to as many visitors as we wish a comfortable stay for as long as needed – just as large as Bedwyr's fortress in Dumnonia, where I spent my childhood. It must also be a place that I can call home."

The fortress I would design for Arthur was to be in a more secluded place than the bustling town of Aquae Sulis, although Arthur generally liked to stay there. A Day's ride – with everyone on Horseback, or two if with wagons – away from Aquae Sulis, there was a most perfect site. It was near to the old Roman Civitas of Venta Silurum, which still has a market and many dwellers.

Within sight of Silurum is an enormous Hill, with a very flat plateau covering its whole length. I was very excited upon first seeing it for it looked to be just what Arthur wanted as a site for his fortress.

This site was also interesting because it is, as well, near to Isca, where Arthur had long before established housing and a training area for his troops at an abandoned Roman amphitheatre and barracks, which he had renovated.

When first excavating the Hill, I found the ruins of an ancient fortress and village upon its summit. I saw that the ancient fortress' Stones lay in rubble but that they could be re-used for Arthur's building. This was an excellent thing for it did save a great deal of labour in not having to haul that many Stones so far up-hill.

Now, upon this great Hill – which seemed almost as high as a Mountain – was a most unusual feature. There was one standing Monolith at the Northeastern edge of the Hill's summit marking an active Spring rushing with cool Water. It would be plenty for a main source.

Arthur named his Hill Fort Llan-y-Gelli. Some have begun to shorten it to Celliwig – both of which names mean Forest Grove.

After I had drawn the plans, excavated and made sure that the foundation was well laid and the building of the inner keep was well on its way, I asked Arthur's leave to return to my Cave in the Snowy Mountain for a Time.

"For you have little need of me now. Your fine Builders can complete the fortress as I have outlined in my drawings. Of course, I can come to their aid whenever I am needed."

He did not prevent me, although I knew that he would have rather that I stayed with him.

I was more than ready now for my much longed-for solitude. I went straight to my old Cave. Everything was as I had left it – in near perfect order – except that I would have to do something about the dust and cobwebs.

I had paid a nearby Farmer and his wife to look after my Cave and keep things safe and in good repair. This they had done until the Farmer had died a year before. I had received word of this, but continued to send their annual stipend. After her Time of deep grieving had past, his widow continued to look in on things as often as she could. After my return, this same widow and her two daughters came once a week for a full Day's work, to renew the Garden and clean the rest of my Cave. Even this Time I resented for the loss of my solitude, but cleanliness and order began to be restored to my surroundings and that added to my peacefulness. So, all things considered, it was good.

Chapter 31
Into the Halls of
Paradise

Gwyddion

The Time came when I knew that I must visit my old friend, Princess Rowena. What state I found her in gave me much to be concerned about. She had aged more than I had expected. She was thin and frail. She no longer rode her Horses and could not walk unaided. Did she not have the breath for it? She would not speak of it and said only, "It is much too late…" when I offered Healing.

"But you always come at the right Time. Gwyddion, you know that there is a Time to live and a Time to die. I have lived very well. Now I will die well. Come with me tomorrow to see what my Builders have finished for me. Perhaps in this way you can help me. It is a bit of a trip, especially now when I must ride in a wagon. My endeavour is waiting at the Western shore. I have been waiting for this. I am so glad that you are here."

Before we retired I saw that she was coughing blood, although she tried to hide it. I said nothing, but bid her a good Night's sleep.

The next morning, Rowena, her whole household, Guard, and I rode to the gates of her fortress together. But there, most of her household had been instructed to remain. Each one bid her a tearful farewell.

It was indeed a long ride from Rowena's fortress to the Western Sea.

As we approached the Coast I could not believe my eyes. There, moored and anchored, was a beautiful golden Boat. It was a very small replica of the great Ship that Rowena's Father, Hengist the Saxon, had originally rowed to Briton in, complete with a Horse's head carving jutting out from its prow and banners of many colours waving in the Wind. Flying highest of them all, as its first standard, was the Pen

Dragon banner, in honour of Arthur. Just below it, the banner of her own blood, the two standing Horses of Hengist and Horsa, flew proudly. After these were the banners of Gwynedd and the Snowy Mountains. But the most spectacular thing about this tiny Ship was that it was almost completely covered with thinly hammered gold. Gold! The mast, the railings, the Horse's head prow, the Helmsman's rudder, everything!

There was one thing added to this small boat that had not been on Hengist's Ship – Rowena had added a sail. Mind that by this Time, many Saxon Ships have sails, but in Hengist's youth, most had not. In the middle of this boat with no oars was a raised pallet, the pedestal of which was covered in gold as well, but the top of which was covered in Wolfs' pelts, which appeared to be over a great bed of straw.

We stopped at the quay, near the entry plank. She smiled brightly at me and had one of her guards pull a beautiful short sword and a battle ax from the trappings of one of her splendid Horses. An exquisite wool mantel was placed around her shoulders. "A gift from Morgan" – she said.

She was helped from the wagon and over to her two Horses where she kissed and stroked the sides of their faces tenderly.

"Walk with me, Gwyddion, to examine my beautiful boat. Will you?"

"Of course, Lady."

I looked around at her entourage of softly weeping women, three Archers, and four guardsmen. Princess Rowena carried a small box in her hand. She said, "What is held in here is to quicken my voyage and to state in writing my final wishes – which I will entrust to you, my dear friend."

We boarded along with the Guardsman who held her sword and battle ax. A foreboding – no, a horror – filled me. It showed on my face.

"Oh, no, my dear old friend – this is a joyful voyage I take. Please do not be sad."

I understood...

"My dear Gwyddion, will you give me your blessing and pray to your Gods for my Spirit's joy?"

I choked out, "Of course I will."

She laid herself upon the Wolfs pelts and had the Guard lay her battle ax at her side.

She opened the box and withdrew a page of vellum bound with ribbon and gave it to me.

"This you must keep to ensure that the other copies, which are in the proper hands, are rightfully administered."

Then, from within this same box, she withdrew a vial of poison. The vial she held in her left hand whilst her loyal Guardsman opened it. Then he laid her sword across her belly at an upward slant and laced the fingers of her right hand in a clasp around its hilt. He withdrew his own sword and carefully clanged it against Rowena's.

So she was to die a Warrior's Death, with sword in hand, to be taken to her Gods by the Valkyries.

Ravens were circling above her. She smiled at that.

"I assure you, Gwyddion, this is a sleeping potion which brings Death quickly and painlessly. Goodbye, my dear friend."

She drank the contents of the vial. No pain. No struggle. She just closed her beautiful eyes and went to sleep.

"Quickly" said her Guardsman with a heavy voice and ushered me off her boat.

He raised the message flag. We jumped off. The anchor was cut away, the moorings released and the Wind and current pulled her out to Sea. Shortly thereafter, the Archers – with pitch-dipped arrows – lit them and let fly to her boat. Silver birds with golden Fire. The Flames caught. The boat was soon engulfed and Princess Rowena sailed to her Ancestors in full Saxon honours and dignity.

Then a Scald played his harpy and sang a heroic saga – a dirge of his people. A clear and beautiful voice had he – such a contrast to the coarse spoken Saxon language.

I whispered "Thank you Rowena, for enriching my life. Perhaps we will meet again someday."

I opened the vellum page that she had given to me as per her instructions. The page told that she was leaving a large share of her vast wealth to her three grandsons with some stipulations: that the first female child of their blood to live safely to adulthood be named Rowena – that she be legally considered her own great-grandchild – and that while growing up this Rowena would never lack for anything. Then, when her adopted great grand-daughter, Rowena, reached the age of sixteen years, she would receive one quarter of Princess Rowena's wealth and be the sole heir of her fortress and that she be declared "A woman in her own right," meaning that she could marry, *or not*, as she chose. Regardless, the fortress and her fortune would remain her own – still leaving half of Princess Rowena's wealth – with the exception of her fortress – to be divided amoungst the three grandsons. Furthermore, if these qualifications were not met – if there be no female heir or if the girl should ever die of unnatural causes, all of her fortune then left to her grandsons would be forfeited and bequeathed in equal portions to her dear friend Tudno, who had built a place of worship near his hut and Well at Cyngreawdr Fynydd "there beside the Druid's swinging Stone of Judgment," to the Order on the Isle of Apples – for charitable works, and to the local Bishopric – also for charitable works. The fortress itself and the lands immediately surrounding it would then be given to the Clan Chieftain of the area, that he and his descendants might maintain and protect it.

The young Rowena's wealth was to be held in assurance by Tudno until she reached her majority. He would disburse all necessary funds to the grandsons, as needed to keep the fortress, village and grounds in good repair – again, until the younger Rowena's majority. In return for his help, she gave to Tudno two hundred acres of prime Sheep lands.

She trusted this man well, of course, yet Princess Rowena – being who she was – had the fail-proof plan that Tudno – or his successor – must give an accounting of her fortune to the Bishop nearest the fortress.

I left with the strange sensation that the world had somehow lost some of its brightness.

Chapter 32
A Dream Realised

Gwyddion

Back to my Cave...

Chronos, the second – as I had named him in honour of my old companion – seemed to be perfectly comfortable in my Cave. He went straight away to old Chronos' perch. Funny, that.

Now I had Time... Time to think about my life... Time to read my books again and to write my histories for Morgan, my lovely girl. Time to rest and to sleep as long as I wished of a morning on my warm pallet. Although, by then, I was of an age that my bones were beginning to get a bit stiff on occasion and so it seemed that I must rise with the Cock anyway. Yes... Time steals away youth and beauty. It moves us inexorably toward Death. It is the golden Times we must recognize and live to the full, for all of our golden situations stay so briefly. Things change. We can no better hold fast those golden Times than a handful of Water, so fleeting do they seem when looked back upon. Yet, although we know this, we do not always recognize those Times whilst in the midst of them. We let them pass us by... slip through our fingers. Years go by that should have been wondrous, pleasurable, treasured, but were spent in mediocrity – worried over or involved with things that, in the end, were unimportant. These are the thieves of life – the not savoring of life fully but only in flashes of memories gone by.

This I will write in my letters to Morgan, for it is a Wisdom that would do her well to follow. I wondered how she was. Fine, I was sure, for I would have felt something or somehow known if anything was amiss.

I lay awake that Night thinking of Bronte with these words playing over and over again in my thoughts – and when I slept, in my Dreams:

How it makes me cry
When I think of all the Golden Chances

That have passed me by...
Longing so to Love you
But too proud, too shy...
Longing so to tell you, that I feared to die...
Golden Chances slipped right through my fingers...
Why?
Bronte – your name means "Bestower" – is this another Wisdom you have bestowed upon me?

I awoke the next morning feeling better. I made a promise to myself to seize what moments of Love and joy come to me – if ever they come again...

One more Moon's Dance in blissful peace passed. Then one Night, I had exactly the same Dream as I had had so many years ago when I was to escort Gwenyfar to Dumnonia. Brennos was calling to me. Why had I not gone straight away to him before settling into my home? He was dying and calling to me!

I awoke and rode swiftly to his Cave. But when I got there – not the first, but – the second Dream unfolded exactly as I had Dreamt it so long ago.

My Horse came sliding upon the rocks up to the entrance of Brennos' Cave. There was the woman, placing Stones upon his grave. She was standing with her back to me. My heart was full of more oppositional feelings than I had ever experienced in my life. Brennos! I was too late! My worthy and learned mentor, Druid of the highest degree and the only Father I had ever known, was dead. But what had he said?

"Walker, come, find me in the Otherworlds. I will be waiting for you."

"I do trust that you will always be with me, but – oh, Brennos..."

Tears flooded my eyes. But then, she spoke... "Are you Gwyddion, The Merlin?"

She turned to face me. There she was, the woman in my Dreams – she who was to be the Love of my life. There was no denying what I felt. She saw right through me, her green eyes overpowering my thoughts and feelings.

"Come," said she, "I have made a cauldron of stew for you and we have mead, or I can make hot honey-Water if you prefer."

My head, my whole Spirit was spinning. I looked at Brennos' grave... His two oldest Ravens were perched atop it.

"They will not leave him to hunt," said she. "They will soon die. But this one, Chance, has chosen life. She will stay with me."

The still, smaller Raven was upon her shoulder. She had a leather contrivance covering her shoulders for Chance to safely perch upon.

"Come inside the Cave, Merlin. It is for the living. Brennos lives on within it; you will feel him there. Be comforted: he was not afraid or sorry to die. He left a letter for you."

My Dream unfolding... I went in with her.

"Who are you? In my Dreams you told me, but I could not hold your name in memory."

She said; "Why Merlin, I am Nimue, Enchantress of the Order of the Isle of Apples, Daughter of the Lady Vivianne, Walker through the Worlds, and as you already know, Dragon Caller. I am the one to bring you solace and passionate Love for the rest of your life."

I marveled at her words. We had just met moments ago, yet she could speak so openly and frankly of passionate Love – to me who had never allowed myself to experience this kind of Love at all! She arose from her chair across the table and came toward me.

"Yes, Gwyddion, The Merlin, we have only met in the land of Dreams, now we meet in the flesh; but I have Loved you in my Dreams, and I think, in many lives past. I am the gift of great value that Brennos has left for you; me and his Dragon."

"That is right!" I exclaimed, "The Dragon!"

Nimue touched me. Stars burst in my head and their fragments fell to Earth all around me. I felt a heat rising in my loins, and a weakness – a dependency – and a longing for another, which I had never known. But I was not losing myself; I was gaining her. I thought, "Am I now entwined in a Thorn Tree whose thorns awaken my senses with every prickling? Are these the pangs of Love – the sensual pains of Love?" If now I was lost to the Creature I had been, so be it! I will never look back."

In that moment, when she touched me first, I lived forever... forever in the eternal present.

"Love... Was it the Gods' Spell?" She had read my thoughts, and laughing – not a demeaning laugh but a laugh of tenderness and of knowing – she said, "Gwyddion, The Merlin, highest in renown of all the Druids – I have a riddle for you."

She held a basket of loaves and cheese before me and asked, "What is stronger Magic than Mistletoe?"

I was awash with images of the Ritual of the cutting of the Mistletoe with the golden sickle, with the pomp and ceremony of it. Mistletoe is, to us, the most Magical of all Creatures of the Earth, a thing of naught... neither Herb nor Tree nor Grass nor Root, neither in the Earth nor in the Sky, hanging in a Tree, but not a part of it. I had been taught that the strongest of all Magics were bound up in the Mistletoe.

"What is stronger Magic than Mistletoe?" I repeated like a child. "I do not know."

Nimue leaned in toward me allowing me to see the full roundness of her breasts, her lips held so close to my ear as if to brush it with their softness.

The answer, she whispered in a husky voice: "Desire."

Her lips moved to mine and she kissed me with a lingering and moist kiss. Nature compelled me and I arose. She dropped the basket when I pulled her full body close to mine – lips, chest, stomach, loins – even her legs she wrapped around me as she gently writhed like a Serpent against me. My breath was coming in deep gasps. My cock was so hard against her softness. A fleeting thought – was I hurting her? But then she pressed herself harder against me and rocked herself back and forth, side to side. Our kiss had never broken but the kiss became more internal. Our mouths open now and suckling upon each other, my tongue gently exploring her tongue, the insides of her cheeks, and she did the same, but with more fervor. She took my hand and placed it beneath her shift to cup her breast. Her nipple was hard; I had never known... Our kiss apart, she was leading me to the pallet. When, as it seemed, we were torn apart so abruptly, I felt bereft of the intimacy of our embrace and the kissing we had just shared. But even her hand in mine sent waves of feelings and power to my loins. Desire...

At the pallet's edge, she kissed me again, but briefly. Then, she stripped off her shift and stood naked before me. Oh, Gods, she was so beautiful. She took my hand and rubbed it between her thighs. She was wet and pulsing somehow. Quickly she and I removed my tunic and boots. She appraised the way I looked – up and down. For the first Time, I felt embarrassed – like a trapped Animal. But then she smiled and said, "Remember, you have Loved me in your Dreams."

"But," said I, "I have never..."

"Shhh... I will lead you as I must, but your nature as a Man will show you the ways."

Fully naked now, no more words passed between us as we embraced again, she pulled me to the pallet and laying me on my back, she climbed upon me. She leaned forward so that we were, once again, belly to belly, chest to breast, lips sucking. She moved her head to lick my ear. Oh, my Goddess! She reached down between us and positioned my manhood right at the Gates of Paradise. She thrust her hips forward gently – her hands gripping the front of my shoulders. Then, she began to rock. I entered her completely. We were as one body, one being. "This," thought I, "was the moment of pure, inescapable, breathtaking Love." But only for that one, brief moment of Time did I think at all. That moment is seared into my heart forever. Then, the dam broke. Thrashing about like Wildcats, we clawed and moaned for each other. Harder and faster my body jerked into hers as if there were more – what could be more? I swear that I heard the Humming of the Dark Tribes surrounding her. She hissed, "Slowly, my Love. It will last longer."

"Longer than eternity? For that is what this Magic holds."

I opened my eyes to see her thus – her face contorted yet smiling, the very image of lustfulness; her beautiful, long, black hair, wet and thrashing about us. I closed my eyes again, "Oh, blackness, blackness, take me. Let me be a being of only feeling."

But then, as I was about to reach the summit, she cried out and her body jerked convulsively, four, five, six Times and a rush of moisture covered me. This, then, pushed me over the unknown precipice. I believe that my heart stopped once and then pounded like the drums of the Ancient Ones. My head felt as if it would burst from my neck, and the rapture of my very being sent me into a rush of convulsions, as well. The force of it amazed me. Had it hurt her? It seemed not. That was an odd thought. I think too much.

If my semen had had no way to rush from my body, I would have shattered like the Stones of a fortress under siege from Catapults. I chuckled. Then I looked at my Love, my heart, my Nimue, and I wept...

She did not speak. She knew. I had waited for this all of my life. So be it then. If I am changed, if The Merlin's Magic is lesser, then I am so much more.

She lay beside me and cradled my head against her breast, caressing my hair and kissing my brow.

"I Love you," I said. "Take care of my heart, Nimue, for you are the one who holds it in your grasp. Yours is the face of the Goddess to me. You are the source, you are the image of my worship, and your body is my Altar."

Later, in the middle of that Night, I wrote these words:

Lost... without a trace...
There is no Time there is no place
Yet there is nowhere I would rather be
Let your sweet Love wash itself all over me
I am lost...

Lost... beyond concern...
Far past the point of no return
Still I hunger – still I burn
If I am caught within your web then let it be
I am lost...

On a dark and Windswept Sea I drift and I am tossed
Oh, Starless Sky above you are the only light I see
But I am yours no matter what the cost
Although I fear the fatal cost is all of me
I am Lost...

Lost... Without regret...
All of my fears I will forget
Nothing really matters anymore
Have the Gods now opened every door for me?
Or am I lost?...

Chapter 33
Morganna Le Faye
Returns

Morgan

When Mordred, son of Morganna, was past his seventeenth year-turn, Morganna intruded into my life once more.

She made her grand entrance just as I would have expected – had I known she was coming – with luxurious pomp, of course. An escort of eleven black war Stallions, affixed with decorative trappings and each mounted by a leathered and armed Guard, arrived at the Isle of Apples. Mean and dangerous looking were these men in their full black battle armour. Behind the first contingent of riders was a tall and handsome, solitary young man a-mount a solid black destrier. The standard bearer riding behind him flew the Pen Dragon emblem. The symbolism was not lost to me. Twelve followers and the one leader – this has played out in many a Myth, far and near across the world.

In the middle of the grand entourage was a canopied litter of golden beauty, which gleamed in the mid-Day Sun. Flying above the litter was the Dumnonian banner of Blue Ocean waves and black five-pointed Stars upon a field of white. Save that, to this, Morganna had added one large pearl, visually reinforcing her claim of being the true heiress of Dumnonia. Long ribbons of brightly coloured blue and white silk trailed behind the litter, fluttering in the Wind. In this rode Morganna Le Faye. Was Morganna playing the role of the Goddess, then? At her back rode four more heavily armed Guards ceremoniously carrying wood and leathern shields, also bearing Dumnonian colours. Were these, then, the four Elements – also under Morganna's power?

As no one was allowed to enter the Order's grounds whilst armed for battle, the entourage was stopped at the gate.

It had been a warm breezy Day. The blue Sky above had not a cloud in it. It was now mid-Day and everyone on the Isle was busy with each their own works. What a gift was a sunny Day, for our weather was always moody and changeable. Why, in the space of one whole Day and Night, we might see Sun, warmth, Snow, sleet, strong Winds, hail... None of this would have been unusual, except for the circumstances that transpired.

It was at the very *moment* that I was standing just inside the doorway of Lady Vivianne's quarters speaking with her about the beauty of this Day and attempting to plan a special evening's bonfire gathering – should the weather hold into the Night – that a runner was fast approaching from the gates to announce Morganna's arrival. I looked outside even before the runner had had the chance to speak, for I heard an ominous rumbling. I looked in the direction from whence the rumbling came. The whole Sky down to the Earth's floor was a wall of darkness; I saw a swirling mass of black and Thunderous clouds swiftly rolling in from the West – while moments ago the Sky had been clear.

The runner gave Lady Vivianne the message: "Lady Morgan's sister, Morganna Le Faye, has come to visit with her. Also, she says that she has brought along another very special guest. However, now, they have not the Time to fully unarm and follow all protocols because of the great gale coming in behind them. She asks if they may be sheltered quickly before the Storm ravages their party..."

I had never seen the Sky so black. Everyone was coming outside to stare at it. Then I heard a great howling noise and felt a great change in the pressure of the Air. Heaviness hung all around us.

Hail began to beat down upon us in ever increasing measure. Then it began to fly sideways, clinking against the Trees and the outside walls of our cottages. Everyone ran for shelter.

I looked at Lady Vivianne.

"We cannot let her onto our Sacred ground."

"Morgan! We can do nothing else. A Tempest is brewing!"

"Go to the gate and give them leave to enter," she told the runner – "but take care."

Just then I saw Morganna's entire entourage riding in a fury toward us. So, she had not even waited for permission.

"Curse you, Morganna!"

"Morgan!"

"I beg your pardon, Lady Vivianne."

"Beg nothing of me, my girl, but take care for your Spirit in the Halls of Justice. She is not worth a scar on your measure."

"She has already scarred me from my childhood on, Mother."

"Yes, yes. But those inflictions have been written on the great scrolls to be weighed against *her*. She will owe the debt for her wickedness, Morgan. Everything has its cost."

Just then, Morganna and a beautiful young man, burst into Lady Vivianne's cottage. She hollered orders to the rest of those with her, to seek shelter in the stables.

A very cold Wind blew through the cottage, scattering scrolls and vellum pages; knocking down the Lady's Altar and precious things.

Then she slammed the door shut, fell into a deep bow and said, "Forgive me for the intrusion, Lady Vivianne."

When she arose and looked into my face I was shocked. She had not aged one Day. She looked as young as she had at Dumnonia, before Arthur's crowning. She smiled sweetly with her lips, but her eyes betrayed her inherent evil.

"Sister..." quoth she, whilst nodding her head in acknowledgement.

"I would like to introduce you to your nephew, my son; Mordred *Pendragon*" I noted the shift in her pronunciation of Pen Dragon... as if it were a name that could be inherited.

He stiffly nodded at first – but then he smiled, with the sweetest of smiles.

Was he Charming me? Or could this young man really be of good heart, as would seem? When he caught sight of his Mother's gaze his face suddenly became stoic again. Fear... Was that what I smelled upon him? Was he then, in total subjugation to Morganna? Or did he simply hold a son's natural devotion to his Mother?

Of course, she had shielded his thoughts from me totally. Morganna was the most adept person at shielding thoughts that I had ever encountered.

"If only I had the key to breaking down her fortress of Dark Magic..."

Then... right there...at that very moment... the Voices whispered to me, "If there is a way in, there is a way out, Morgan. Always, you must only find the *key.*"

Now, as I think back upon those words, they, of themselves, do not relay the layers of meaning that fled through my thoughts. Or rather, more were they like *knowings*. Through these words, I gained a deep understanding of a Magical truth, which had heretofore been held secret from me. Now I knew... And in years to come, I would find this key.

"Someday Morganna, I will be your undoing!"

I had not even tried to shield that thought from her. Morganna's lips curled up on their sides, and slowly, almost imperceptibly, she shook her head in a gesture, which acknowledged that a battle line had been drawn in the ground between us.

The Storm hit with a fury. The cottage walls were trembling – or was that just me trembling in anger? For a few moments I feared that the Lady's cottage might be blown asunder. But no. Lady Vivianne and I began quoting the words of an ancient Chant of protection, invoking the four Winds to keep us safe. Of course, these words were said in silence – for never would we have allowed Morganna to hear our Sacred phrases spoken aloud. The Storm quickly passed, causing no harm.

'Difficult' does not begin to describe Morganna's and Mordred's visit with us.

Regarding her son – Arthur's son – so torn were my feelings, that I could not get a grasp on them. He was so like Arthur – not only in the way that he looked, with his golden hair, his radiant, dimpled smile, his broad, square shoulders and guileless blue eyes – but in his obviously generous heart. A part of me wanted to Love and protect him. Yet, whenever Arthur, or anything vaguely related to him was broached, those eyes turned hard as Stone and filled with vehement rancor. I recognized his as a murderous hatred.

"Why?" I wondered how many venomous lies Morganna had told to make him despise Arthur so. On the one hand, I knew he was to be the only son that Arthur would ever have. On the other, I knew that he was fated to be Arthur's doom.

During their visit, and the flaunting of the trophy of Morganna's treachery toward Arthur, I realised the extent of my own hatred toward Morganna. There was no use in my denying it.

As I watched Morganna fawn over Mordred's every capricious whim, showering him with more favours than he could ever have thought to ask for – coquettishly teasing him as she would a lover... *A lover?*

Just as that picture entered my consciousness, remembrances of Morganna's unspeakable perversions swept all other thoughts away.

"*No! No!*" I told myself, "I have no basis to even suspect such a horrible thing."

It is known that some men sink to their lowest, base Natures, against all cultural and moral taboos, by having sexual relations with their own young children. This is to me an abomination beyond all others. But never have I heard of a *Mother* doing so. Yet, somewhere, some Time – although surely, very rarely – there must have been women who... My thoughts trailed off.

A chill ran through my blood as I was stung by a flash of murky memory from my own childhood... perhaps from a Dream?

I was very young, three or four years old... A dark room... alone in my bed... awakened by heavy breathing... Morganna saying "Shhhh..." in a hoarse voice. Fear overtaking me. She said "Shhhh!" more vehemently – then I was slapped. She was touching me in a way that made me cry. I was afraid and confused. I cried out loud, "Mother, Mother!" Morganna fled.

My Mother hurried into my chamber.

"Morgan, what is wrong?"

She sat upon my bed and took me into her arms. We rocked back and forth together – she, caressing my hair and murmuring soft endearments into my ear.

"Hush now, my dearest, you must have had a bad Dream. Everything is all right now."

My Mother had always known the truth of a thing. I knew that...

"So then, it *must* have been a Dream..." thought I.

She spent that Night sleeping in my chamber and I felt safe again.

Perhaps it *was* just a Dream. But it was Morganna's *touch* that had made me cry. After that Night, I had never again trusted being alone with her. However, as the years went by, the image of that Night's events had faded into oblivion. Until now...

I looked deeply into Mordred's eyes. No, he was an innocent, spoiled and doted upon by a Mother who had very real ambitions for him – and for herself. She could not threaten his confidence in her by allowing him to know the true depth of her perversions.

Morganna and I never really engaged in conversation with each other after that first Day, whereupon I had asked where she had been all these years.

"Well, in Breton Breiz, of course. It *is* to where the *more cultured* Britons have been re-locating. I lived there with my two lovers – a very rich man and his wife. They both claim descendancy from Conan Meriadoc, the founder of the House of Rohan.

"Nothing but the very best was offered to me and Mordred whilst living in their house. For Mordred, that included being taught by the best instructors their money could buy in the Games of War, political diplomacy, hunting, writing, and manners. Mordred is fitted to be a King. After all, he is a Prince, no?"

She had accomplished her mission. Mordred – King Arthur's son – had been announced to the world.

A week later they were gone.

However, before they left, Mordred sought me out to say goodbye. I saw him, through the open doorway, approaching my cottage. There, walking toward me, was a square and straight, muscular young man. He was walking slowly and looking around whilst obviously admiring our environs. When he reached me, he said, "How beautiful and peaceful is this Isle."

His eyes and expression were wistful.

"Yes," I replied. "We are happy here."

"I have come to bid you farewell, Aunt... and one other thing as well... My Lady Morgan, Enchantress of this Isle of Apples, you of my own blood, I put myself at risk in trusting you with what I am about to say, yet I believe that I can trust you."

"My dear nephew, so like your Father..."

He winced when I mentioned Arthur. I continued; "I pledge to you on my heart's honour, that you can always trust me."

"I believe that, Lady... It is an odd thing – you *look* so like my Mother, yet there are some things missing in your countenance, which are constants in *hers*..."

He did not say what things these were, but for the first Time, I detected a note of disapproval in his voice toward his Mother.

He continued: "There is a waving beauty of Spirit that hangs in the Air around you. It is filled with colours. I see much violet and white about your head – and then, moving flashes of scarlet, blue, and green. I see nothing of this in my Lady Mother.

"I feel a bond of friendship toward you, Aunt Morgan. So I am asking; if ever I have need of seeking your counsel, confiding in, or warning you of something, may I?"

"Yes, you may. But does that go both ways between us? Mordred, your Mother has ambitious plans for your future. There may come a Time when you and I find ourselves in opposing lines of a great battlefield. There may come a Time when we see the issues at hand differently. But no matter what may come, as my blood, my nephew, and my *friend*, I will be there for you, to guide – or to reason with – you."

The world began to spin around me. Had that just been prophecy?

Of a sudden, I knew that the next Time we spoke, he would, somehow, be out of Morganna's clutches – yet it would be a black Day of mortal doom. This I knew within – deep within.

As my head cleared, Mordred was mounting his splendid black Horse. Had I missed something?   He rode away with a nod of farewell. So like Arthur... but ruined by the bitch who was his Mother.

Market Day...

About a week later it was market Day at one of the villages across the Inland Sea to the Northwest of us. It was our wont to go and so I and one of our young novices carried cheese, mead, honey, Apples, Plums and cloth to it in our sturdy wagon, pulled by one of the work Horses from the Order's stables.

Long ago the Marsh Folk had built a village in the Marshes. Their huts and their walkways from one hut to another were built upon tall wooden stilts. They were all made of Willow, Hazel, and Reeds, which they had covered in pitch to protect them from the Water.   Their walkways were unlike anything else I have ever seen. That Day we must use these to cross over the Marsh.

I must admit that I so preferred crossing by punt, but the punts of the Marsh Folk were small. They could perhaps hold three or four people plus the Punts-men, but not a Horse and wagon. Since we had to cross this way, I would greet and share news with some of the Folk living there, so as to be polite and to ask their assistance in safely crossing, whilst using their paths.

By the Time these histories are known again, perhaps things will have changed. The Marsh Folk have lived as they do now for unknown hundreds of years or perhaps longer, yet they are not as many now as when Lady Vivianne was a child. I want to write of them – for things can evaporate into the Mists of Time.

The Marsh Folk are very ingenious, although ignorant people. They know nothing of the lands, peoples, or cultures beyond the area immediately surrounding their unusual world. They are excellent rope makers. If and when they trade with others, it is their rope that is sought after.

These people are small and dark as are my Mother's race and so their dwellings are on a smaller scale than others. Their huts and walkways are above the Water's level at high Water Time. The walkways are also supported every now and then by pitched wooden pole foundations – but most sway – or float – between the posts, held up by thick ropes, wound and tied to the wooden structures above them. Oh bother... I hope that I am describing this clearly enough. They are like bridges, but not at all like the Roman bridges made of Stone. These, they walk on a daily basis to socialize with their kindred. Each family, of usually two or three generations, has their own separate dwelling.

For generations unknown they have marked with lines the highest and lowest Water levels of each year upon a very tall pole with carvings of ancient symbols, which pole stands nearly in the exact center of their village. I asked what the ancient symbols meant, but none of them seemed to know.

The conical roofs and outside walls of their huts are made of reeds tied tightly together with rope and then also washed with pitch. When I asked if they kept warm on Winter Nights, they nodded "Yes" – but I wondered how, for on all the land surrounding the Tor, the Winds blow hard in Winter and it seemed to me that the Winds must blow right through the Reeds of these walls.

I had been honoured by being invited into their homes. Of course, I always leave gifts of honey, cheese, and mead for their hospitality for never have they asked to be paid for punting Priestesses across the Lake or Marshes. This Time, we had Apples to leave for them, as well. I enquired if all were well or if Healing was needed. They responded, "Only your blessing, Lady."

In their hut they all sat on the wooden planked floors, although there were one or two crude benches for their eldest family members. They offered one of these to me out of respect, but I saw that there was a very old looking woman and an old man living in this hut, so I declined.

Their expressions changed. I wondered if I had broken a social taboo, so I quickly said, "Thank you, we have not the Time to sit and talk, we must be on our way now. I only wanted to greet you and to be sure all was well. Please accept our gifts and may they increase your health."

Before leaving, I looked around. In the center of their hut was the hearth Fire, built upon a flat Stone foundation, several layers high. Then atop that hung a large cauldron of iron filled with Stones. I looked up to see that the roof had an opening in its center, not unlike other cottages. This was a very practical design, as the tall cone shape drew the smoke upward; of course I had seen other conical roofs, including the one above my own cottage at that Time – but mine and others were shorter and less even. All the reeds went upward in vertical lines – perhaps that caused the better draw. There was very little smoky odour and not much black soot either. They said this hole was the Spirits' door and that they, the Spirits, came and left through it. I asked them of which Spirits they spoke.

"Why... our Ancestors and the Spirits of sickness and Death and bad luck and strife."

But their eyes said... "You are a Priestess and you do not know this?" Of course they only smiled. So only did I smile and offer my benediction...

"May your beloved Ancestors come often to bless and comfort you. And may the Spirits of ill fortune not enter through your Spirit door. Yet should they get in by some other means, may they be cast out as soon as they enter."

They liked this speech very much.

I knew that they usually lived on a poor diet of mainly Fish and I knew that what I had brought would help them. They smiled toothless smiles. So all was well. I had not offended or at least I had covered my blunder over.

Just before I left I looked around for their Ancestors' shrine, there it was – just by the hearth-Fire – with pieces of shell, bone, dried Herbs and knotted twine upon it. I suppose a knot for each of their Dead? I did not ask, but bade them farewell.

Two of the young men insisted that they aid us with our Horse and wagon across the Marsh walkways until we landed on solid ground. Of this I was grateful, for it was a tricky business.

A world unto itself was this. But the Marsh Folk lived and continued to bear children and faired as well as did others, I suppose.

Rumours...

The girl and I arrived at the village market, well before mid-Day. I stayed with the wagon to disburse our goods and let the girl go off to amuse herself. I remembered when I was fifteen years and came to the

Isle as a novice – I Loved it all... but sometimes I had the wander-lust. I suppose all the young ones do. I told her to meet me in an hour as we already had lodging arranged in the village. By the Time she returned to me, the wagon was empty. We retired to the cottage, whose inhabitants had offered their hospitality and shelter.

A nice couple were they, with three grown children of their own and five grand-children. So, for the first Time in their lives, they lived alone together. We shared surprisingly bawdy talk engendered by the mead I had brought. We laughed a lot too.

"We are old and do little more than sleep in our bed together now, what a shame we did not have this privacy when we were younger!"

They both laughed and he patted her hand. They shared some innocent gossips of the village including some of improper relationships amoungst some of the women in the Christian Monastic order.

"Improper – that is – according to the rules of their Church. You know the one close by where Queen Gwenyfar is retired?"

A knowing look passed between them...

"Oh, do not mistake our meaning – we are worshippers of the Goddess and all Love is Sacred to her. But not, they say, to their God. Yet people *are* people, right? And Love may be found by whoever truly seeks it..."

I nodded my head in agreement. People are people.

I had not noticed the girl drinking as much of the mead as she apparently had, for *her* tongue was loosened too. Wanting to be included in the adults' conversation, she began to speak, "Lady Morgan, I heard gossip in the village today too! The villagers told that when your sister, Morganna Le Faye, with her son and their guards stayed in this village, they were passing it about that King Arthur, your brother, was begotten upon your Mother, the Lady Igraine, through a brutal rape by Uther the Pen Dragon. But then, they said, Igraine fell hopelessly in Love with Uther and lay with him often as she could and allowed poison to be given to the Dux Gorlois, your Father, to kill him so that she might have Uther for her own!"

I stared at her in horror.

"Child... how dare you speak so of my Lady Mother? She who was a great and powerful Seer? These are all lies... lies!"

"Oh, Lady, I am so sorry! I was only saying what rumours go 'round... only what I have heard – not what I believe!"

"Yes!" I snapped at her, "and with much relish in the retelling!"

She burst into tears. I pursued it: "What else have you heard today?"

"Oh Lady please... I cannot repeat it!"

"Where does your loyalty lie, girl? Must I send you back to your Mother in disgrace?"

"Oh Lady Morgan, my loyalty is to the Goddess and to my sisters and brothers of The Order; to you My Lady... and to Lady Vivianne... but also to my King Arthur!"

"Arthur? What about Arthur? Tell me – right now!"

"Oh I cannot say it!"

"Speak, girl!"

Almost did I strike her... but regained my composure in Time.

"They say... Oh Lady! They say that upon the Night of King Arthur's acceptance celebration he... He violently raped his own half sister Morganna Le Fey – *your* sister, my Lady Morgan! And he begot Prince Mordred upon her... and then... then he banished her to Lesser Briton. But when... they say... he heard of her being with child from his crime against her he sent some of his companions to find Mordred and to slay him! But Morganna's Magic was too strong so she killed his two companions who sought to kill her son. Then it is said that King Arthur lied and said these men were killed in battle. And that The Merlin knows all of this, yet still he serves King Arthur – to his own disgrace. Oh, my Lady, *I* do not say this is so! Only that it is the rumour that is being passed from village to village. I am so sorry, please, please forgive me!"

"Magic so strong... yet she could not prevent her own rape?"

"Oh, you speak wisely, my Lady... how could this be true?"

"Be silent girl."

So now, everywhere Morganna went she was dropping seeds of her poisonous vine. How many would believe her slanderous lies? Did Mordred believe her?

Of a sudden, a cold North Wind picked up in the cottage and blew in a harsh spiral around me. Dried leaves were catching in my hair, stinging my face. Where was I? So cold and empty! Where was this place of dolorous doom? ...this ancient darkness revisits men as thrashing down come their highest aspirations, their lofty plans, and their most valorous moments. ...the wounding of a dream, the pains of Love lost, the fading of Gods... it was the chill of the White Lady of Death.

But do the old Gods die, too, when they are forgotten? ...or when the dreams of men are lost? On that moment, that was how it seemed. But what of the Goddess... will She too withdraw beyond the Veil one Day – unreachable to her earthly children?

So cold was I, so utterly alone, falling... falling, somewhere into the Night of Time. In total silence and near blackness, here I was, hiding behind an old Oak Tree and some bushes in the Wood. Morgan of the Woods – watching. Watching what? Then my Vision faded away. I came back to myself, hearing the last of a terrifying scream – my scream. Arthur? Was that what I had screamed?

The old couple were kneeling on the floor next to me, white faced and worried. As my sense of where I was came slowly back to me, my hearing returned as well as my sight. The couple were clucking over me like Mother Hens. The girl that I had brought with me was cradling my head in her lap – her copious and genuine tears were falling onto my face and eyes. She was muttering, "So sorry... please forgive me!"

When I had my thoughts together enough, I said, "I will be alright – hush child. You did not cause me this pain; it is the 'Sight.'"

A benediction or a curse? No... No, it is a gift, one to use as we may. The troubling thing of it is that sometimes we can see things that are to come but cannot change them. They are written in the primordial script of the Weavers' web. Pray the GREAT GODDESS and all the Gods that this Vision just past is not bound thusly. For I fear it beyond all comprehension.

I slept fitfully that Night. Always running through my thoughts was an old theological quandary: Being as idealistic as I have always been since my childhood, I was wont to believe that psychic Gifts came from the Gods as a reward to those of great and good spiritual merit. But then, there was Morganna. She was the only one I had ever met whose thoughts or motivations I could not read, and for that matter neither could anyone else! From whence and why have come her powers? Had she been born wicked? Or were she and other wicked Seers born good and with great potential? Have they been gifted in this life, perhaps on the merit of one past, only then to choose evil as their path? This concept had always bothered me greatly; could the Weavers not foresee these things? Was evil a random potential lurking within us all, awaiting our own secret will or unholy desire to release it? This, then, was my great doubt and conflict. Were Mystical abilities not really Gifts at all? So saddened was my heart at the thought.

The child stayed with me, never leaving my side through the Night. I slept, I awoke. Again, I slept – off and on – fretfully. With the Dawn we left for our Isle.

It was from that Day forward that I began to find silver threads in my long black hair. I fear I will take this lack of understanding of – no, I must admit it, lack of agreement with – the Gifts of the Bestowers with me to my grave. I fear that this judgment and criticism of Them may be the unraveling of my ultimate ascension. Yet, if this is, I am allowing Morganna to hold the power of my undoing. No! This I must not do. I suppose that there will always be some things beyond Human comprehension.

Chapter 34
Bedwyr – A Man of Few Words

Bedwyr

So many years have passed since last I placed my quill to vellum for your histories, Morgan. But I promised to you, my dear sister, that I would write of my life and Times. Where do I begin?

So much has happened – I cannot write of everything. We forget the Day-to-Day happenings of life. It is only the exceptional moments we remember, of joy and of beauty – or of pain and sorrow.

So, I will begin by listing those I Love.

First, my Lady Mother, Igraine, now with her Ancestors – she awaits me at her Well. Beyond that knowing, there is a hole in my heart, which I am unable to fill.

The Bear... my brother of the heart, for whom I have lived this life, and for whom I would die.

Gwyddion, The Merlin, my teacher of the Arts and Wisdoms; the only true Father I have ever known.

Morgan... raised we were as sister and brother. Who could but Love her? We share the Sight, she and I.

Bronte... So short a Time I had with her, yet I believed I Loved her. I held back from declaring it – perhaps for Gwyddion's sake – but he held back, too, and then she was gone. So briefly did she bless our lives. The Voices have said that she must return soon, but I know it would not be soon enough for us.

When my carousing Days were over, I married Freidl – after all these years. I suppose I enjoyed wenching too much to ever commit myself to her. But eventually comes, or at least it came for me, the longing for a deep and comfortable, committed Love. This was, is, and will always be, my Freidl – who had first caught my eye even while I was as if Spell-bound to Gwenyfar. What a waste were those years in-between. We have two children now and I am satisfied and happy with her beyond measure.

All in my life would be perfect except that I sorrow for Arthur's old wound – his Love for you, Morgan. It keeps him from ever having the kind of Love and joy in his life that I share with Freidl. I grieve for him.

Morven, my Dragon... I hope he does not dislike my mention of him, but with the way things are changing, especially on the continent with the new One God – who knows but that in centuries to come, the Dragons will abandon us Humans and will be forgotten entirely. Already they have become extremely particular regarding with whom they will communicate. But know this, they are real, and to all who may ever read my words, they live in the Spirit Realms. They live! If ever they should feel enough distrust or disgust for Humans to impel them to withdraw entirely from our world, it would be the loss of the aeons. And it would entirely be the fault of unenlightened, suspicious, and Spiritless people. Already I am forbidden to speak more of their great Magics and Mysteries – save to another Dragon Caller – or, to some extent, to one Dragon-called. But perhaps people, or at least some people, far into the future *will* remember the old ways, or the Great Truth. Perhaps even the Dragons, by whatever form they take, will remind them that we are all one, there is only ONE.

Morgan, I suppose you wanted me to write of battles, political intrigues, and deeds of heroic proportions, but I am no Poet. Yes, I fear that he Bardic skills have passed me by. Yet the "Sight" forces me to see what is to come.

We and all our deeds are like Grains of sand in the Seas. Really, I think we individually mean very little in the passing of the ages. So what does it matter? Only that now there lives a dream of fairness, a dream of beauty for all people. The true Christians have a beautiful dream as well; the words of Wisdom and Love from their Teacher and King. We, Arthur's people, mostly are believers in the old ways – of the Old Gods – of honour and respect for our Ancestors, our brothers and sisters of "Tree and Bone, of Spring and Stone, of feather and fur and all who creep." All our dreams and beliefs, our Kingdoms and Tribes – our worlds even – are no more or less than Grains of sand or particles of dust.

It is my own wish too, that the old ways and the Old Gods will be remembered. That, whenever there is need for a new dream and the Time is right, a new King, – a Summer King or Summer Queen – will again arise.

These are my Loves, my sorrows, and my hopes. They are the only things of any true importance in my life.

Morgan, perhaps towards the end of this life I will write of the endings – which I have already 'Seen.'

I mean no disrespect to your dream of true histories, Morgan. Perhaps my inability to express feelings with quill upon vellum will confuse you as to my true meaning – however it is only that I believe that the Time of wonder is now. So I will honour our dream, now, in this life – for it is a good and worthy dream.

I will say this one more thing – I well know those who have given their histories to you, and I absolutely hold faith in their complete honesty. So by my word of honour I support and recommend them and their words to who-so-ever reads them.

May you, Morgan, live each hour you are given to its richest fulfillment.

Bedwyr, Arthur's man

Part Four
The Final Conflicts

Chapter 35
Growing Threats

Lady Vivianne

And so, AIXIA had Spun her gossamer threads and we all were set in our places and Time.

Word reached me that Hengist had died. But his Saxon Kingdom on our Eastern shores was well established – flourishing and growing. Other Tribes of the Horse, Wolf and Boar people – the Saxons, Angles, and Jutes – were slowly migrating to join Hengist's lands, albeit peacefully so far, and so stealthily that they were hardly noticed until one blinked and saw their spreading.

We heard that Hengist died with a sword in his hand and all rejoiced that he was now in Paradise – feasting, drinking, and enjoying his women. They had not sent a flaming boat out to Sea with his body and funerary goods in it. They had chosen to put his corpse, his crown, personal treasures, armour, sword and shields in a great boat and buried the lot on the land he had won and had been given by Vortigern.

So then – he is forever a part of us.

Lucian came often to our Isle of Apples to visit with Morgan of whom he is very fond. I read more than friendship in his eyes when he looks at her. I had seen it from that first Day – now so long ago – when he and Arthur battled. He had bowed to Morgan with his flirtatious smile and given to her a piece torn from his tunic. The light of desire that I saw upon that Day still shines. But Lucian, knowing of the Love that Arthur bears for Morgan, has never spoken of his feelings to anyone. A good man is he, loyal to his King and friend.

Funny how the Human heart is; although I truly believe that Lucian never allowed himself feelings of jealousy toward Arthur over Morgan, it was not that way regarding Arthur's Love for Bedwyr. Bedwyr was so protective and possessive of Arthur, always having to be first of his men. This, of course, always kept a thin wall between Bedwyr and Lucian.

Both men, in small and not too obvious ways, were always competing for Arthur's Love and attention. Of course, Lucian had to have known that Arthur and Bedwyr were as close as twins, for blood aside, they were. But next to Bedwyr, I think Arthur favored Lucian above all of his other companions.

Now Lucian has grown from the seventeen year old boy-man I first met to a self-composed, dignified, intelligent, and cool-tempered man. He is loyal and honourable way beyond the measure of most folk. Only when it comes to competing for Arthur's attention do I always see the boy again in him.

I do not include Gwyddion into these comparisons, for he was as a Father and more to both of his boys.

There is one more thing about Lucian. I read in his hand and eyes a very long life. Also I know he has a part to play in some great journey. But this, I think, will be beyond my earthly life.

I believe that I am beyond my sixty-third year-turn now. Sometimes I forget things, so I am not sure. I also have pains in my knees and hands and sometimes in my back as well. I do not complain for it is just old age. I have, long ago, chosen Morgan to replace me as Lady of the Lake upon my Death, whether she has already become one of the Nine Wise Mothers or not, by then. She can always replace me on our council at the Time of my Death if none of the others cross the Veil before me.

In all things but name, Morgan is already acting High Priestess, for I tire so easily. But our tradition says I must remain the Lady of the Lake until my Death. All will be ready for Morgan to take over at that Time.

I am very happy in my old age. My true daughter, Nimue, has lately returned to live at our Order with her lover – Gwyddion! They say they have come here for just a while to refresh their Spirits and bodies. But I know they have come for my benefit – to help me as they can, while I live. She, of course, wants no Priestly duties here – as she follows her own path. That is just fine. I am so pleased for her. How wonderfully strange the workings of the Fates are.

Last week I learned some troubling news – new aggressive bands of Teutons have been attacking small villages on our Southeastern shores, trying to dispossess our native folk. Or perhaps Mordred has broken the pact of peace by beginning aggression against the Saxons aligned with Hengist's Kingdom. Rumours of Mordred trying to usurp his Father's crown have been spreading like a great Fire across the lands.

The younger lords aligning themselves with Mordred complain that their armour, swords, and pikes grow rusty with disuse. They hunger for the glory of battle which their Sires had... fools! They think not of the costs of war! Because of Arthur, Bedwyr, The Merlin and all of the loyal Chieftains and Companions, we have had peace for... is it almost ten years now? Blessed peace! These young fools remember not what it was like before. Pray Morganna's machinations do not prove to be our undoing.

Is this now what she has been waiting for? It is said that each year Mordred becomes more devoted to her and caught up in her Glamour. Some even say it is a perverse and unholy relationship.

I tire now...

Morgan, below is the genealogy so hard to come by, of the almost five hundred years of the Hebrews of the Languedoc.   It shows that Arthur's lineage, and thus Ambrosius Aurelius' are linked with an ancient King of Jerusalem. Please, Morgan, while you live, follow and add to this if you can, until your histories are hidden – as have you planned – for a future age.

May the truth of these matters be known and may someone care. But remember this... distasteful as it may seem to you, Prince Mordred is of these same blood lines, in fact, through your Father – Morganna's Father – he holds yet another strand of rightful Kingship, even beyond that of Arthur's.

A lesson for you Morgan – perhaps the last I might teach you: Sometimes things do not go the way of our wishes, but then, new gateways open beyond our hopes and expectations.   Keep track of Mordred's blood, of his descendents, if there be any. This is not just for me, Morgan. This I have been admonished to tell you. Somehow the Spirits of the Crossroads have new wonders yet to unfold. But these works will be yours and not mine.

These genealogies are now held for safe keeping in the Order's library. Upon my Death, or at the Time of your handing your Histories down to the next Keeper, you must include these into them.

Chapter 36
Oh, Mordred

Morgan

By one Moon's Dance after the turning of the year our Lake was frozen solid, which made things very difficult for everyone living on the Isle and all those who depended upon our foodstuffs. As it so happens, the Marsh folk have devised a means of using woven mats covered by heavy Sheep pelts, pulled by ropes and pushed by reed poles, so as to bring these supplies to the villages around us, as well as to the Christian Women's Monastery and to the old Monk's cell. Our brothers help to convey foodstuffs such as Apples, honey, mead, cheese and the like to these.

The last thing our brothers did on their charitable journey was to visit the old Monk living in his nearby cell – which was nothing but a very small Cave with no real closure or heat source. Our Brothers, at great length, persuaded the old Monk, who was a hold-over follower of Pelagius, to come to our order for the Winter so that he would not freeze to Death.

When they returned it was with the news that Queen Gwenyfar was on Death's bed. I immediately sent messages to Arthur, but due to the Ice and Winds, they did not reach him in Time. When Arthur and Bedwyr arrived, Arthur informed us that the Queen had died a week before he got to her. She had already been buried. I wondered if the world would remember that there had ever even been a Queen Gwenyfar – much less take note of her Death.

While Arthur was here he confirmed that already he had been informed of the ill rumours of impending War.

"Just as a plague, they spread from village to farm to town..."

Bedwyr, too, had warned Arthur of a dreaded battle to come – led by "Mordred the Usurper." Arthur corrected him; "*Prince* Mordred, Bedwyr – my son and heir.

"I must try to make peace with him. But, let it be understood now between us – as I have already written and placed in the care of The Merlin – as well as Lady Vivianne and Morgan – that should my peace-making go awry and should Mordred kill me, I have named you, Bedwyr, as my heir... and your sons and daughters after. In that case, his treasonous actions will have proven that he is no lover of our so hard fought for alliance of peace."

I made great note that Bedwyr did not contradict or try to reassure Arthur of a good outcome. A look passed between them then; a look of a deep acknowledgement of an end.

Bedwyr finally broke their silence – "But what of Gwyddion?"

Arthur smiled...

"He could have been King all along, if he had accepted it. We all know that *he* had the best claim of blood! Caledfwlch was rightfully his."

"Yes, but he did not have the blood of the Tribes. No, you, Arthur, are our true King, you are the one ordained by the Weavers – The Summer King, the promised one – Caledfwlch sings for you. Even though a man may be High King beyond your life Arthur, he will never be this."

Bedwyr wiped his eyes and sent a dagger straight through my heart.

Arthur replied thoughtfully – "My dearest ones, I have often and diligently pondered this question – If everything exists as part of the Great ONE, then it would follow that everything including our thoughts, words, deeds, even feelings – once experienced – is a thread of the great fabric of HER Creation... that which is ever expanding until the end of this epoch. Well then, my question is this: Is Love not a piece – a thread – of this Cosmos also? Once made or felt, it has been given life, breath, substance... I have heard a lover say of another in their weeping and moaning – 'My lover Loves me no longer. Their Love for me has died.' Their meaning is that their lover's Love has vanished into nothingness, has un-become. How could this be? Do you understand my meaning? A living thing cannot vanish, as all things of the Goddess return. So where does Love go when it 'dies'?

"Nearing now the end of this earthly life of mine... No, no, do not protest, Morgan... Bedwyr... I am no Seer but I see it in both of your eyes and I know that you know my Death is nigh. So, having had the Time allotted to me to ponder this question, I have come to the conclusion that Love *never* dies. Once created between people or Spirits it always lives and remains. So I ask this, will you two share a pact with me? That ,so far as we may remember – I mean hold it in our power to remember – we will always Love each other in future lives? I make this promise of forever and a Day to you, my beloveds. By whatever form this Love takes, I will give it to you. Will you promise this to me, as well?"

So stunned was I! ...that Arthur knew what I had known for years – ours was an eternal Love.

"Yes," said I.

Bedwyr choked out, "Yes Bear, I would Love you as well."

"Then you two, who are far more Gifted than I in these matters, will have to help me find you and remember!"

This broke the tension and we smiled. Bedwyr and I knew better than to argue with Arthur about such things. His shining greatness was accompanied by humility far beyond what was due. Arthur was brilliant! And not only in his thinking abilities... but in all that is of most value regarding Human worth.

That very evening, two unexpected visitors arrived; Gwyddion and Nimue. They were together, I mean, as *one*. They told us of their Dreams, their meeting, and their great and passionate Love for one another. So, Gwyddion had found Love at last! If it is right, and the will of the Gods – and for their sake, I hope this is true – what a wonder and great blessing it is for both of them.

"May you Love and be joyful in each other forever."

I knew that this blessing that I bestowed upon them would not be granted to me in this life.

My Fears...

Political tensions had swelled like a wave in an angry Sea. Not a usual wave as from a Storm, but the kind that comes so rarely – and why and from whence no one knows – a great wave that builds and builds in strength and height until it devours and devastates everything in its path – coastal farms and villages, even cities – leaving nothing in its wake. Once in my life, when I was a child, I had heard of one of these. In my great, great Grandmother's Time there had been such a one, which came in from the South-Southwest toward our lands. The storytellers still speak of it. Just so, for the past three Moon Dances, a great line was 'being drawn in the dirt,' between cousins, uncles and nephews, brothers, Fathers and sons, and even Grandfathers. Some were remaining loyal to Arthur's Alliance while others were beguiled by Mordred and Morganna's promise of the young overtaking Gaul and the wiping out of three generations of Hengist's Saxon Kingdom on our lands. War fury and battle lust, violence against innocent farmers and herdsmen who refused to side with Mordred was becoming a daily deed. A black fog was spreading across our lands. Even rape and pillage was on the rise so that no one felt safe. Then the murmur began, that "King Arthur and his Merlin were not protecting the people against lawlessness – so perhaps the Gods were taking their revenge upon them for past wicked deeds."

I was heartsick, how could things have turned this way? But, of course, it was all of Morganna's Making.

Upon one Twilit evening, I ran to the Stone Circle atop the Tor. I prayed fervently. Angrily, frantically I beat my fists upon the Altar Stone. Then I looked up and raised my voice. With hands open in supplication I asked – "Great Star Goddess, Divine One of Fathomless Beauty, could these things be written as such in the movements of your Heavens? I was told once by the Voices that upon the Night of Arthur's birth his Stars were crossed. Each living being has a lifespan, this we must all respect, but – The Dream – is it to die too? Tell me this is not so!"

Are Humans less honourable than Beasts? Beasts kill for food and to protect their young – never for greed, envy, or sport. Men fight and argue over who owns the land... but no one owns the land! The land owns Herself and shares Her bounty and shelter with Humans and Beasts alike. Arthur and his companions of men and women, Chieftains, Kings and Queens, sought only for peace amoung all peoples who shared these lands, even the folk of the Saxon Kingdom who had been invited here to live peacefully amoung us. Morganna Le Faye has blinded Prince Mordred to the truth.

So I, Morgan, now, at this place and Time, do take the risk – at the peril of my future lives – by the power of my will, by the power of three, at whatever the cost, do command Prince Mordred to speak with me, one more Time before our Deaths so that I might right the wrongs he believes of his Father. Whatever the price, so must it be!

Lightning struck the oldest Oak in my sight and rent it in two. Then the Thunder boomed and rumbled. I felt the Earth quake beneath my feet. The shaking continued and the tall Stones around me wobbled to and fro. I was thrown from my feet and back down upon the Altar – the green Star Stone – belly up like a sacrifice awaiting the slaughter. One by one the tall Stones in the circle began to topple and crack, the Stars above me began to spiral as if in a whirlwind. A face emerged in their patterns: the Star Goddess! Fearsome and utterly beautiful was She. Strands of her long hair slung around her, or were they Stars? Her eyes opened and stared at me, her gaze burned me to ash, my consciousness hung above my ruined body. Looking on in utter amazement as Time flew by... centuries later... A Christian tower stood where once the Circle of Stones had been, it had been built atop the Star Stone, now deeply buried beneath its foundation.   But the Tor itself was indestructible. Its Dragon Lines were strong as ever. Here, there was peace.

Fair haired and fair skinned people walked the dirt path spiraling upward. There were very dark skinned and very dark haired people too... people from the Far East, people from the exotic land of Morganna's great pearl, people of all kinds, some who were totally unrecognizable to me, climbing the Tor to pay their respects – seekers every one.

Then I was lying atop the green Star Stone again, in the Circle of Stones, staring up at the Stars. My Bees had all flown buzzing and fretting to be around me, even though it was Night Time. Through their buzzing loudness I thought I heard Her speak.

"Whatever the price, Morgan? So you have vowed. So will it be!"

What had I done?

Arthur

I had sent word to Mordred three Times. Three Times I had asked to speak with him face to face, man to man, Father to son. I had never even looked upon the countenance of my own son's face. He did not even pay the honour of an answer to the first or second request. On the third I had written that I lived by the Rule of Three, which says that to request or refuse something of someone the first Time is an entrance into parlance or negotiation. To ask or refuse the second Time is to admit that Humans may fail to properly communicate or to understand the request. But that when the third request or refusal is given, it must be the last, for the matter should be clear by then. Because, as The Merlin taught me long years ago – To refuse a request more than three Times is to demean yourself by acknowledging that your word means nothing to the other person. 'No' means 'No!' Likewise, if one requests a thing more than three Times, they have entered into the realm of begging – thereby also demeaning themselves. And, too, one would be insulting the other person by as much as saying, I know your word means nothing.

So, upon the third request I wrote – "Prince Mordred, I think it fair to explain this to you, this is my last request. Your failing to answer I will take as a call to arms. I pay to you this respect. But if, my son, we could talk, perhaps all of this senseless killing could be avoided."

He answered.

Somehow his spies stole one of the entrance gates' Wind banners from my fortress. It arrived at my headquarters, wrapped and drenched in the blood of a Sow, with its head rolled up in it – and then rolled in the dirt. The young courier, with shaking hands, gave it to me with a brief note: "Father – Uncle, I will have your crown and I will wield Caledfwlch. May your head rot as this sow, for your perversions stink as does it!" – Prince Mordred, Brittanicus Rex.

I gave the courier two gold coins for Morganna Le Fey. The young lad's terror abating, he said, "My Lord... why?"

"For the ferryman."

Realization dawned in his eyes and he bowed,

"May I leave in peace?"

"Yes lad, and here is a gold coin for your bravery, go – no one will harm you."

I was heartsick. Not because I feared Death, not even the Death of my remaining beloved brothers in war – for we had all lived valorous lives – but because I never thought it would come to this. Oh, Mordred.

Chapter 37
Hiding in the Perilous Wood

Gwyddion

Vivianne, Lady of the Lake, Nimue the Enchantress, and Morgan of the Woods – the women – the Priestesses all insisted upon traveling with me to Alba where we knew that in one Moon's Dance the decisive battle would be fought.

It would fall upon the first Day past the Full Moon, one Night past the peak of power for the Great Cast of Magic – Magic to gather in, Magic of manifestation, of culmination... the Cast of highest power! We all knew that Morganna Le Faye had planned it thus.

The first Cast of Magic should be done upon the Dark or Waning Moon. Its power is that of endings – banishing all obstacles, removing all threats, or cursing an outcome. The second Cast is done upon the Waxing Crescent Moon – the Archer Maiden. Her Magic is to place all matters in order for beginnings, to plant the seeds of our desire, and to set our needs and desires into motion.   But the third and most mighty Magical Cast is made upon the Full Moon Herself. When that which we desire has been envisioned and the end of that desire has been 'Seen,' we use our Grym Hudol to Cast the 'Spell of Making.'   And then we... well... the rest is a secret...

Then, we rest well in the certainty that with this *it is done*, and that the perfect outcome of our desire has already been created in the true reality of the Other-realms – there awaiting its most beneficent Time to manifest upon this earthly plane – *to be* – to mirror that which *already is*. As above, so below...

Something was scratching at the back of my neck. I did not mention it. But of course – how foolish of me! – these three traveling fellows of mine all had the Sight and could read me like a book – albeit not completely.

You see, for many years I worked on the Magic of Secrets, endeavouring to devise a way to shield my inner thoughts – keeping them to myself alone – for the sake of privacy or to ward off treachery. This knowledge is a Gift of the Gods. It is not taught in Druidical Universities or by any other tradition I have heard of. The way of it is this – in order to shield my secret thoughts from being read by other Adepts, I must Cast a shimmer of invisibility over my true thoughts – while at the same Time giving those Adepts something else to read. It would not do to just leave a hole in my thoughts, or other Seers would suspect me. And so, I have mastered a way to place simple everyday thoughts into the hole left by my shielded, private thoughts. These are thoughts that I am not really thinking, but only allowing to float there to fool those who would attempt to read me.

The knowledge of how this Magic of Secrets is accomplished will die with me. For, of what use would it be if everyone knew how to use it?

But as to the scratching at my neck...

Morgan approached me quietly upon the second Night of our sojourn to the site where we would meet Arthur and his Warriors.

"Gwyddion, something concerns me greatly. Why – on the Night *past* the fullness of the Moon? Morganna would, of course, bring the most drama possible to all matters. It would just seem more like her haughty self to attempt to cause a victory over Arthur *upon* the Full Moon – for her legend... her fame. I cannot bring thoughts together to make sense of why this bothers me so much. However, when I think of it, an odor of fear and distaste fills my nostrils. That is all – as if there are pieces missing from a puzzle game."

"Morgan, I feel it too."

There was nothing more to say of it.

Travelling North at the pace we had to maintain was very hard on Lady Vivianne. Nimue and Morgan gave potions of Herbs mixed with wine to her along the way – just enough to relieve some of her pain but not enough to tax her with Visions.

Inland from the Bay of Puffins, we passed the Vallum Aelium – the Roman wall. There we found Mile Forts, which are very small, gated fortresses. We found no army – neither Mordred's nor Arthur's... not even the ghosts of the Romans. I supposed they had faded long, long before and flown to their sunny homeland of Grapes and Olives.

Upon the second Day after, we performed Divinations to learn where we would find Arthur's army. By this we ascertained that the Battle would be staged somewhere not far to the East of our present location.

When we arrived at Arthur's encampment, there was no sight of

Mordred's army. Good. We would have at least a little while to rest.

"Bedwyr," I thought – "my dear, dear boy..." I laughed at myself. They were... what... forty-two years by now? Talking to myself, I said, "You and I, Bedwyr, have spent our lives for Arthur – a worthy expenditure for sure. Yet, I fear that I have not taken enough Time over all these years to tell you how much I Love you – how proud I am of you. I know Arthur has named you as his heir in the event of his Death. A King... But, of course, it is not that easy. You would have to reunite the people and be claimed and accepted. A good, kind King you would be. But I know that you would like this not. Here, in my own thoughts, I see you better as a Druid, for as men go in the Arts Magical, I know of none in your generation so gifted as you. Well, anyway, I cannot see beyond my own Death. Perhaps that is a blessing to me.

I was startled by his voice... Bedwyr stepped out of the Shadows and said, "Gwyddion..."

We embraced, but he held me longer than usual as he whispered in my ear: "You are the only Father I have ever known. As for my real parents, well, we did not know. I have Loved you and been in awe of you most of my life. And never worry – I have always felt it returned. As to being King or a Druid, this I have not seen. Only the Weavers know what lies beyond this battle. I do not wish to know. I think I will not die today, nor will you. But when we are beyond this Day and its fell deeds, let us make Time for one another."

Our embrace broke. His eyes were glistening with tears, but I knew they were not for me.

I crept into Arthur's tent.

"Ah, ha!" said he – "Here you are – right on Time."

We embraced. I had sworn by my honour not to tell him that the women had come – and so I did not. Better for him to believe Morgan safe on her Isle of peace. I knew that I must warn Bedwyr – to keep silent, as well...

"Gwyddion, please come over here."

Arthur had his battle tactics all drawn and neatly spread upon a roughly constructed trestle.

"See, here is our plan..."

Chapter 38
The Scarlet Fields

Arthur

Frozen in the pre-Dawn Fog, we sat atop our mounts. There were only the four of us left now of the original Seven of Battles. We were Lucian, Fergus Macroich, Bedwyr, and I – Arthur the King.

"King of what?"– I thought – "a land torn by disagreement, separate visions, sons against Fathers, and now in the end, Clan against Clan? Has Time run backward? The younger seek for the glory of Empire... Rome! What idiots! Rome abandoned us three generations before the Time of my birth. Rome is not even Rome anymore. Constantine, almost two hundred years ago, abandoned what was then left of the greatness of Rome – changing everything.

These romantic notions of reinventing what is crumbled are a fool's endeavour. The Picti, who had joined in compatriotism with the other people of this great Island – when first we met at Table Rock – have not answered the call to arms. I cannot in my heart, blame them. Stubborn and primitive as they may be, they are not fools. This is not their fight.

The Eire from across the Western Sea have taken advantage of our civil unrest by raiding our shores in great frequency and numbers. Many of the Cymru Chieftains have sent their words of apologies and excuses for not standing with us – some to "protect our lands from the Eire," and some to maintain solidarity within their family Clans, by remaining neutral rather than killing each other. These Clans will never tolerate a pretend new Rome, but will save their Warriors to fight against Mordred should he win the Day and invade them. They must think – "If Arthur wins, all will be well anyway – so why risk it?"

More the fool I – to have thought that they would risk all to defend me. But it is not about *me*, it is about The Dream – The Dream we all shared and realised against all odds.

Then, instinctually, I reached for an amulet that hung from a silver chain about my neck. I had worn it in every battle I had fought for the past twenty years. Morgan made for me, just after she had heard about Morganna's treachery toward my body on the Night of my crowning celebration. She had told me "When this is needed most, throw it into a body of Water. At that the Curse will be activated..."

The words written upon it were – "Adixoui Deuina Deieda Andagin Uindiorix cuamenai'" – "May I summon to justice the worthless woman, oh Divine Deieda."

She said this old Curse would bring justice to Morganna – and she never explained farther. Of course, I have always trusted Morgan with my life. The thing was that I could never find the heart to throw it away. But when I reached for it, the amulet was not there.

"Oh yes," I remembered. As my troops were passing Aquae Sulis, on our way toward this battle, I felt that *the Time* had come. I stopped for a few moments to pray to Sulis-Minerva. Then I threw the amulet into the River.

"It is lighter now, almost Dawn, my King." quoth one of my Guard.

I came back from the depth of my thought.

The blackness was a bit lighter than it had been a few moments ago. Light enough now to see around us – campfires on both sides were beginning to be extinguished.

It was then that we all saw a strange phenomenon. A murmur passed through the ranks. A giant bank of frozen Mist, tall as the Oaks and seemingly impenetrable, was rolling and billowing, unlike anything I had ever seen. It was coming toward us and toward the enemy lines, as well. For all the Gods, it seemed as a Misty giant mouth, eating up all within its path. A thing of such magnificence was it, that for a moment I forgot all else.

When it reached us, it engulfed everything – every blade of grass, even the beards of the men who wore them in the Clans' style. Our Horses' manes and ears were covered in an instant with Ice – as was our armor. Visibility was gone. We could not even see to the Horse ahead of us. Our marvelous Archers would be of little use in this. My heart cried – "Merlin, where is your North Wind Magic? Have even *your* Spirits abandoned us?"

I had positioned myself at the front of the Vanguard but had asked Bedwyr to accompany me. This put me out in front of all but the Archers, against the pleading of my companions. Lucian would lead the Left Flank and Fergus the Right. Our scouts reported that we were outnumbered two to one. But then a great cheer arose from our men. A swell of gladness filled me and a pride for all that we had and still stood for: the Picti had come. At that, I decided to throw off whatever pieces of metal armour I wore to fight like my long ago Forefathers had – lest I turn to Ice, too.

As these conditions made sight impossible, I thought for sure the battle would be put off until we could see. And it might very well have been that way but for the Picti, who yelled, drummed, and played their Battle Pipes – without a command to do so, of course. No matter, it was on.

From Mordred's command position we heard "Archers, let fly!"

The first round of Mordred's arrows flew into our ranks. These were probably meant to hit our Archers, but they over-shot them. So – they were closer than anyone knew. I quickly ordered our Archers to "Aim very low and let fly three rounds" – which they can do in three breath's Time. They had aforetime been instructed, "...then run behind the lines."

The arrows thumped into flesh and leathered wooden shields, but the sounds were dull, as were the Death screams. That was when I noted that the Fog – and now Snow – impaired our hearing as well as our sight. Everything sounded as if we were swimming beneath the Waters of a great Lake.

So much for strategy... No one knew who or what they were lunging into with sword or pike. "GREAT GODDESS, let us not kill our own."

"Stop!" I hollered. "Do not press forward. Let none get behind you. Stand your ground!"

I heard my orders repeated to left and right, each Time drifting deeper and deeper into silence. But I believed we were holding.

I felt my Warriors falling beside me. All thought of command left me. I *was* the battle, the killing, the wounding. At once all my other senses; smell, taste, and touch, especially touch were somehow heightened. They say this is true of the blind. Each Time Caledfwlch hit something it felt different. Still I kept pushing – through flesh, fat, muscle, guts, eyes, throats – I could not tell what anything was. "Had that just been a shield or was it a man's bone that I could not completely pierce?" Quickly I tried to pull Caledfwlch out by putting my knee upon the dead man's thigh. I had not enough strength to do it. I looked for another body to steady one foot against for leverage so as to release my sword.

Never had I been so aware of the sensation of pulling sword through flesh, although it is always a hard thing to do. It takes strength to run a man through. Flesh and bones do not yield easily. Is this only because of the way we are made? Or could part of it be that our will to live gives our flesh the strength to battle against sword and pike?

Then the too-familiar odors were here again – the stench of blood and of dead men lying in their own shit, piss, and vomit. Men foul themselves when they die. Is it from fear alone, I wonder, or simply the release of Death?

I think I killed two Horses. I heard them scream – poor, innocent beasts. I prayed, "Lady of Animals, give them solace." Then I felt a burning in my left arm, sharp and hot as an iron poker in a forge.

"I will be alright – I wear Makyr's scabbard. I am invincible as I wield Caledfwlch." I assured myself. "Is that fair?" I wondered... But the Goddess has willed it so.

I heard low moans and whimpers, or were they prayers? I am sure I heard women's names called out. Lovers? Wives? Daughters? Once I heard a young voice call, "Mama, please, Mama, I Love you."

Then I cried. Not just tears, but with my whole body wracked and shaking in uncontrollable sobbing. Never have I been so sad. How had it come to this? "Must I kill my own son? Could I?" This was insanity – all of it.

Finally I heard a horn blow from across the battle line. It was Mordred's call to cease. So then... we would wait for the fog to lift. But it was already well into the afternoon. The battle would not resume this Day.

I write these words in my quarters on this cold, still Night. I do not know what the outcome of all of this will be.

"Oh, Goddess of the Starry Black, bless my beloved ones and keep them safe through whatever calamity might come."

To you Morgan... I hope this reaches you: I Love you.
Arthur Rex

Morgan

Gwyddion, Lady Vivianne, Nimue, and I hid in the Woods on a Hill, from whence we thought we would have a view of Arthur's command. But a great, thick Mist had rolled onto the battlefield. Within this shroud, we could barely see each other, much less anything that was going on far from us. This was frustrating beyond measure!

But then we did hear the Picti proclaim their fearsome and so welcomed selves. Hope was renewed!

"So my brothers have come," said Nimue. "I sent word through the Spirits of Deer, Raven, Seal, and Wolf. I knew they would hear my plea.

"I thank you great Cailleach, Goddess of war and Death, Dark Mother, my Lady of Storms and Ice."

Then, in a tongue that seemed so familiar, yet just out of my reach – so that I could not make sense of the words – Nimue intoned a Chant of praise to this ancient, Dark Goddess, by naming her attributes.

She needed not explain to me the reason for her words. I knew that she was invoking this GREAT GODDESS *into herself.* The fog was impeding my vision of course, but even so Nimue seemed to grow far beyond her physical stature and beyond her Human power. The power coming from Nimue pierced through me and Gwyddion and Lady Vivianne too.

"I am the Well the chalice, the womb
I am the ashes, the maggot, the tomb
I am the end, the contraction, the fall
I am the Death, and beginning of all
I wear a necklace of skulls and of seeds
I wait in the crossroads with Dragons and Steeds
Some call me Raven, or Vulture and Asp...
But the Universe breathes while held in my grasp"

So beautiful... I know this One by many names. Had I not heard Lady Vivianne speak these same words at the Rite of the Heiros Gamos so long ago?

Gwyddion leaned against me. Face to face, eyes to eyes, I saw his silver spirals mesmerized and mesmerizing. Then somehow he, too, was the Goddess. He added to the Incantation:

"I am the Star, the Lotus, the Rose...
Out from my breasts, the Milky Way flows...
The Cosmos spins with my spiral dance...
Mother of Time, eternal romance... "

As if from the cold Goddess Herself, a great Snow began to blanket the Valley. Snowflakes as large as half the size of my palms were falling at a pace that I had never seen before.

Gwyddion, Nimue, and I held to each other as if we were no longer three, but one – as lovers entwined were we, affixed to each other, in a whirlwind of power, frozen Mist, and heavy Snow.

Time had passed. How much? None of us could ever say.

Vaguely in the distance we began to hear the clashing of swords and cries and groans. All was as if in a Dream.

I thought I heard Nimue let out a terrible, high-pitch scream. Had she? Or was all of this only the stuff of Visions?

Then I saw Her... the Washer at the Ford, washing the bloody clothes of the dying. But who's clothes? Arthur's? I, the woman, Morgan, dared not look.

I heard The Merlin speak in the voice of a God – his words getting louder and louder with every phrase...

"By the power of three, as above so below...
To the front, so the back, to the left, so the right...
By the power of each of the seven directions
True Wisdom tells 'all things have a price'

An equal and opposite restitution...

By the power of the pipes which began this charge...
I call for the blasts of three horns to rescind it...
By the power of command that began this charge...
I summon a command to end it...

An equal and opposite restitution...

By the Powers of Darkness, the Powers of Light...
By the powers of Fire and Ice...
By the powers of complimentary polarity...
By the powers of all sanity...
I summon an end to this lunacy...

ZAMILAK!!!"

At that very moment we heard the sound of horns from Mordred's command post.

"A call to retreat – yes... yes..." sighed The Merlin.

"But it is only a respite from the eventuality of all things."

I looked over at Lady Vivianne. She seemed more diminished and frail with each passing moment.

"Mother Vivianne" I pled. "I must go with Gwyddion to help Heal the wounded and Sing the dying to Death.   There are not enough Warriors skilled in the Healing Arts to care for everyone."

"You cannot Heal everyone, Morgan, have you not yet learned this? And what about Arthur? We agreed he would be more comforted to think you safe at home."

"Mother, please, I must go."

"Then if you must, I give my permission, my dear."

I looked at Nimue. She said, "I will stay to care for my Mother."

Gwyddion grabbed my arm and we sped toward Arthur's camp.

The King's Encampment

Arthur's encampment was spread out over many hectares of land and was mostly comprised of tents covered in hides. It lay in the Woods to the West of the battlefield.

I could see that the field was almost completely soaked in blood. Of what did this remind me? Red blood on white Snow... Yes... our Sacred Red and White Springs. Were they the Gods' foreshadowing of blood on Snow – mingled in their sacrifice to opposing opinions? Must it always be this way?" No, this was now and the Springs were for as long as the world lasted and since its beginning. How many battles, how many lives and Deaths and how many lost dreams had they existed through? Perhaps we truly are no more than a flash in the Sky. If so, are my histories merely a vainglorious attempt at immortality? Perhaps I am weary.

A knowing came suddenly upon me. We, on these Isles, can never again separate our bloods one from another. This is a truth. A hope rang in my heart that, even though through the Ages men will come, bring forth their ideas of glory and then die... once mingled, our bloods – our descendants – are one. Agreement or disagreement over policy can never change this.

I had been taught to hold great respect for the Balancer of the cycles of life. So, when I saw the Death feast begin, I should have sung blessings to the feasters. But as I saw a Raven poke into and suck out the broken eye from the cadaver of a young boy – of perhaps fourteen years – I felt the gorge rising into my mouth. I quickly looked away. I knew that I would have enough horror in seeing the living, wounded ones being sawn apart, then their flesh being burnt to ward off festering, pestilence, and Death... It was Time to leave the scavengers to their endeavours and turn my eyes toward the work ahead.

It was very cold, but I could pay no attention to that, either. I rolled up the sleeves of my simple robe and pushed my cloak back behind my arms. I was ready.

Gwyddion and I worked together, sending runners to find the most damaged ones – but only those whose Death was not inevitable.

Other runners had already been sent from Arthur's command post that were combing the field to find the mortally wounded ones. Their orders were to speak words of comfort to these, listen to *their* words, if any, and then to hasten their Deaths by humanely slitting their throats. As to the ones who might live, they were to be brought to the Healers in the camp.

All the Healers worked for many hours, struggling against their own exhaustion and frailty. Gwyddion and I worked on into the Night by torchlight.

When finally we were forced to rest, the scene and conditions of the encampment were thus: Many bonfires had been lit to try to ward off the Clutchers of Life and the cold. But with the fog, dampness had penetrated into everything, even where Firewood had been stacked and loosely covered. Where rain could not have wetted, the tendrils of Fog entered. There was no protection from the merciless damp. The Snow had ceased now, yet all the Firewood was wet and slow to catch and so each log popped, sputtered and smoked a great deal. The stinging, acrid smoke, which was everywhere, burned my eyes, my throat, and the back of my nose. I could not stop coughing and tearing. Gwyddion told me that he had experienced these same conditions on the Night before the first battle he had ever seen. Most people were coughing, which caused much pain to those who had been run through – or had a chunk cut off or out of their bodies. But there was nothing we could do for it. We needed the Fires for warmth and cauterizing.

There were moments when I thought I could not go on because the fingers of my hands were so cold that I could barely feel them. This was bad, as there were many cuts to sew. But I did go on until slowly I realised that there were fewer Warriors crying out than had been. Had we mended so many? Or was it just that Death was dealing her silence. I realised that I was needed more now to "Sing the dying to Death" and to give the gift of Love and peace.

"Gwyddion," I said, "it is Time..."

"Yes, I know, Morgan. Go."

The first man whose bloody hand I held whispered his name to me.

"I am Rhodri ab Llewellyn, from Rowen in Gwynedd. Please," he coughed – a stream of blood coming down his chin from the corner of his mouth – "tell my wife, Enead, that I leave all I have to her and I Love her. Tell my daughter..." He coughed once more, grimaced, and his expression froze.

"I will, Rhodri."

He wore a silver ring on his hand. I took it off to give to his wife. I would find her somehow. I felt his Spirit watching from above. I turned my eyes upward and repeated.

"I promise Rhodri ab Llewellyn. Now let you rest easy and be joyful in the Summerlands."

I Hummed an ancient tune for a moment and then went to the next dying one.

This man was of Clansmen blood and beliefs as well. His leg had been cut off at the thigh.

There is a powerful river of blood that runs through that area of our bodies. The Healers had tried to stop the flow by burning it with hot irons, but it was too late and of no use... I wished that they had not tormented him further by doing so. I also knew it had been well meant. The river had slowed to a trickle, but he had lost too much blood not to die.

I held his head in my lap, brushing the dirt from his face and caressing his hair with my hands. I saw the light of life yet clinging to him. No words passed between us. I sang his song of Death.

"I Chant your song of Death
Let it float upon the Air...
Way high up to the Starry Night
I sing it as a prayer...

I sing it as a comfort
I sing it soft and low
I will sing 'twixt twilight's mystery

Rowena Whaling

And new Sun's golden glow...

I sing it with respect
I sing it all in care
To lead you to the Misty light,
'til Loved ones meet you there...

Until you loose the cord of life
In this thing you can trust
I will sing it on and on and on and on and on I must...

I Chant your song of Death
Let it rumble in the Earth
Way down below the roots and rocks
To celebrate your worth

I sing it as a comfort
I sing it soft and sweet
I will sing twixt Daylight's first Birds call
And Sundown's Lambs do bleat...

I sing it with respect
I sing it all in care
I call your kin in the Fields of Green
That they will meet you there...

Until you let your Spirit go,
In this you can believe
I will sing it on and on and on until you leave...

Until you loose the cord of life
In this thing you can trust
I will sing it on and on and on and on... I must..."

He clung hard to life and so I sang the old song again and again. Finally his eyes caught mine in a look of wonder and recognition. Good... he understood. He smiled so faintly that I almost missed it. Then he inhaled and was gone.

"Bless you, brave sir, and your Loved ones wherever they are..." I began to walk away, but then saw a strip of dyed cloth tied to his neck torque. Was it from his lover or wife? I hesitated, but then removed them and took them with me. I would journey to the upper worlds to ask the Spirits where to find his lady, to tell her he had died bravely and give to her this token he cherished, that she might wear them to keep him close.

So on and on I worked until I realised that it was getting late. I knew that Arthur must know by then that I was here and that he would wait up for me upon this Night that he most needed rest. My heart needed to see him, too. I went to his pavilion.

I opened the flap and entered. Gwyddion was there with him. His cut was clean, sewn, and bandaged of course, but he was lying down resting with dark circles beneath his eyes.

"Bear," I said in a soft voice. He kept his eyes closed but smiled.

"So they could not keep you away? Still so stubborn a rule breaker, I see"

"Me? I have always seen myself as a stanch traditionalist, an obedient..."

"Oh, yes, yes – when it suits you. Even when we were children, Morgan, would you not bring me to your Woods to teach me the Latin and history and the ways of other peoples. Did you ever tell Igraine how you spent those Days?"

"Well," I said, "Not completely."

"Are you angry with me for coming?"

"Angry? No. I fear not for your doom, Morgan. Gwyddion will protect you, if even you need protecting by another. Oh, Morgan, let me hold you in my arms."

I went to him, knelt beside his pallet and lay my head upon his chest. He caressed my hair.

"You know, now that your hair has so much silver mixed with the black, I think that it is more beautiful than ever."

I laughed.

"No, I mean it. You will pass your forty eighth year-turn this year, no? And you are just as beautiful to me as when we had all those blissful Days in the Woods together, so long ago."

"Time has dulled your memory, Arthur. You were but a boy when I left for the Isle of Apples."

He grew serious.

"Morgan, please, no more pretenses. I have always Loved you. I remember every moment we have shared. I have watched you grow and change in Spirit, strength, and body, and your beauty grows deeper and deeper in my eyes, as does my Love for you. You know that all of these years I have contrived every way of staying close to you. The first years of training I spent with Gwyddion were the longest Time I have ever gone without seeing you. So think what you will – as I know you will – but your beauty never fades, nor does my Love."

I sighed but had no retort.

"Does it hurt much, Arthur?"

"The cut?" he smiled... "No, not the cut.

"Morgan, there is so much to say yet I have not the words. I have heard all the rumours. I know that Mordred's heart and feelings toward me have been warped by Morganna. He believes all her despicable lies to be truth. Time has run out. Will I kill my only son? Could I?"

"Is that rhetorical, Arthur, or do you seek Divination?"

"No, no, Morgan. What will be, will be."

"I tire you Arthur. You must rest now. Gwyddion, have you a simple?'

He shook his head yes.

"Here, my dearest, drink this – be valiant and strong tomorrow."

"Never fear Morgan, I will meet you in your Dreams. Goodbye."

"No, no, never goodbye – only goodnight, Arthur" said I.

I could not run from there fast enough, beyond his hearing, if he was not in fact already asleep. I fell to my knees in the Snow with my hands covering my eyes and face, as if to block out the world... and broke into deep sobbing.

"It will never be goodbye, my Bear. Never."

Gwyddion found me thus. His long graceful hands were wrapped around my arms, pulling me from the frozen ground.

"Come my sweet, you have need of a simple too – and a long rest as well..."

Lucian

The horns of awakening sounded on both sides of the perilous field. It was almost Dawn of the second Day. A clear, beautiful morn it would be.

A clanging and a roar of bustling and talking filled the camp. Armour, weapons, and shields were being made ready.

I was to command the left flank, which stood to the Northwest of the Vanguard.

The Picti, who were more numerous than any could have guessed, were crowding my men out. They were ready for a fight. What a spectacle they made – their faces were painted blue with Woad and red with Madder. Black symbols covered their necks, backs, buttocks and faces. Seeing them standing there – so proud and naked, with matted hair standing straight up and out from their heads – reminded me of our last great battle against the Saxon, Jute, and Angle invaders. Our greatest campaign, our great victory – what a Day of glory that had been!

Now I fear that the outcome of this Day will bring naught but sorrow.

Rome, where I had grown up, was as if another life to me. Seventeen years old I had been when I came to these shores to participate in the great Games of Lleu.

There had been my *so-called* battle with Arthur and then my absolute loyalty to him. How long ago was that? Arthur was not yet twenty at the Time of his crowning, so now he must be forty-two years. That would make me thirty-nine...

I have only been back once to see my family in Rome. It was during the seventh and eighth years of peace. There had been a plague in Rome and almost everyone in my immediate family had died. Only my sister, who had been two years old when I left home was still there. Of course she did not know me, nor I her.

I did see some of my Father's and uncle's military friends and even their sons, who had followed in their Fathers' careers. One was a statesman of high degree. They all asked me to stay but I declined. The stories of Arthur — or was it Ambrosius? who could tell?... had even reached Rome. They all told me that I would be welcomed back at any Time to resume a career with them there. I thanked them, but I returned to Arthur.

I must admit that there have been many Times during this long peace that I have found myself bored. I had always been used to discipline, training and battle, or at least competitions. A few Times I had thought about returning to Rome to take them at their word, but I did not. I could not.

Now, as I await the call to the field I wonder if anyone — but perhaps Morganna Le Faye and her whelp, Mordred — would find pleasure in this. If Arthur falls then... no, I will not even think of that. "Gods above and below, may it not be so!" I spat on the ground.

To be truthful — as I write this sitting astride my mount, waiting — I do this only for you, Morgan. You will find it if I am dead. Or I will give it to you when the Time is right — if I live.

My true Love and loyalty for Arthur aside, everything I have done, I have done for you. I first desired and then Loved you from afar. Never would I speak of it. Did you know? If so, we are both good secret keepers.

I know of the sad twist of the Fates that has befallen you and our beloved Arthur. I know of your undying Love and loyalty to him. I also once thought I caught a longing in your eyes for The Merlin — no? Now he is with Nimue. I wonder if ever you, or I, will share a Love like theirs with another.

I am forever caught in a web of conflict. I dared never wish you could be mine, for the fulfillment of that wish would probably mean that Arthur had gone to his Ancestors. Perish that thought. I Love Arthur better than any other friend, brother, or Father. And yet, for this Love of him, I have never even spoken of my Love for you. There it is. I have given it voice.

I give this to the boy helping me.

"Go, boy. Should I fall, give this to Lady Morgan of the Isle of

Apples. Put this in my quarters for now, where none but she will find it."

Morgan's note
I have inserted this here for the chronology of this being written, however I never saw it until two years after Lucian returned from his second visit to Rome, which was many years later.

The Merlin
Naught but sorrow...
I now have the third Chronos. Owls do not live the span of a man. They have been so like each other that I have many Times thought that perhaps my old first companion, Chronos, had come back to me in new flesh each Time – and I do believe that this might be true. Had she not said that we would be together for the rest of our lives? Or else, perhaps I am a foolish old man, always wanting things to be the way I would have them.

The way I would have them? Upon this cold, clear Dawn, awaiting this battle, nothing is the way I would have it. Nothing, that is, but for my heart, Nimue. And even that you, my Love, felt the need to be here on this saddest of Days, is not the way I would have it. But of course, I have known from the beginning that you are a woman of your own desires. I have given thanks for each moment that you have been with me. Never a one taken for granted.

In this moment, frozen in Time, with bated breath, I await an outcome that can bring no joy – no matter which way it turns.

Arthur is devastated. If he wins, it means he must kill his only son and perhaps his sister too, for neither of them would let it be made right. If he refuses to do what he must, he will either be dead, or disgraced and broken.

I have read this in Arthur's thoughts, over and over: "How has it come to this?"

But never is there a satisfying answer. We thought we were doing the will of the Gods. Morgan believes the point of all that we have done, is that men remember The Dream. I hope that men remember *to* dream.

Of a sudden there arose a dreadful din of yelling, drumming, horns blowing and Picti war pipes and then the whooshing sound of thousands of arrows.

I could *see* clearly – with the Sight – two great thick walls of men, shaking their spears, beating their defiant swords against their shields and yelling curses toward their enemies. Then they began to run, like two great waves rolling ever closer to one another. With a shock of unbelievable impact, they clashed together. I saw men's bodies fly into the Air from the force. Yard after yard they pushed the one ahead of them ever deeper into the fray of carnage. There was nothing else for them to do but to kill or be killed. It was so like the first battle I had seen, long and long ago...

On and on it went, with the advantage seeming to shift first to one side, then the other, for hour upon hour – maiming, killing, crushing, then more maiming, killing, crushing... it was horrid.

Then from Mordred's side came the Horses and their riders. They were so impatient that they rode over their own men – beating living Humans into the ground by massive hoofs and muscular legs. Their wounded howled in agony and rage to be betrayed thusly – but Mordred's Commanders continued to send up signals as more and more war Stallions stomped, tore and bit everything in their way.

Arthur did not send his Horsemen into the battle. Instead he ordered a daring counter-attack.

"Ride around to the South! Attack from the side, where the ground is open!"

Most of the melee then turned to the South and still raged on. But Mordred had spotted Arthur and his Guard – who always stood staunchly at Arthur's side. He saw that they had dwindled by then to only eight.

I watched as Mordred, with his core Guard, moved closer and closer to Arthur.

Morgan and I fled through the Trees toward Arthur, staying always behind Mordred, lest his company see us.

By then, it was well into the Day. A low Mist had risen again. It hovered close to the ground, in places only to the height of a man's knees. It was a thing of such beauty in this hour of judgment and finality. Do the Gods mock us? – or do they remind us that all things, such as happenings, beginnings, and endings – when seen from Their greater view – are never as important or stupendous as they seem to us?

Morgan

We were running as quickly and quietly as we could behind the Tree line, toward what I knew would spell the final outcome of the Day. The Woods were growing thicker. Finally we came upon a clearing just ahead of us and to our left. If we hid here amidst the Trees, we would be able see everything clearly. So there we stopped.

As the last rays of Sunlight were streaming into the clearing, shadows were descending between the branches overhead, to then be swallowed up by the knee high Mist. They cast a menacing look. Everything was quiet. Everything was wrong... *wrong*! Chaos! Even Great Nature seemed as though masked – turned inside out – just as were my breath and stomach. Was the God of Misrule holding court over this Day? Had I heard someone laughing... an evil laugh – a laugh of triumph? Morganna! It is so like you to have your seven directions covered – just in case.

Oh – Arthur, my Bear, be strong and do what must be done.

Suddenly intruding upon the silence was a rustling and a crunching. It was the sound of Horses approaching. They were coming toward the clearing, where we waited. But, we would not be captured – for Mordred's band would encounter Arthur before coming upon us.

A silver Bird whooshed through the Forest – then a dull thump – and the man immediately to Mordred's left fell to the ground with only an "ugh." He was shot in the middle of his forehead, by a skilled and prized Archer, no doubt.

Then, with an amazing amount of bravery or perhaps bravado, Mordred and his five remaining Warriors slowed their Horses to a walk and rode out into clear sight. I knew that Mordred would be dead if Arthur had wanted it so. Mordred, who knew this too, yelled out to Arthur –

"Father! Uncle! Will you hide in the bush like a coward, behind your Archer's kilt, while we are picked off one at a Time like Pheasants for the King's table? Or will you face me, man to man, now – at last?"

"I will come forward to speak with you, Mordred. On my word and honour, my men will not interfere. You and I alone can settle this."

"You ask me to take you at your word and honour? I attribute no honour to you, Father – you incestuous rapist. You son of an adulterous, murderous Mother."

Arthur dismounted and walked into the clearing.

"You go too far, Mordred. How could you come to believe these things of me when you have never even so much as faced me man to man to question me or to hear words of denial or defense? Are we not civilized men? You condemn without rebuttal. Where is your proof? Your Mother's word? Should we speak then of *her* honour?"

Mordred said, "Let it never be told that I slew you while mounted and you on foot."

At that, Mordred and all his men dismounted. Arthur's men stepped into the clearing but kept their distance.

My breath was caught, held within me. In those few moments of silence, the Ancestors Hummed an ancient tune within my head. No words. There were not then, nor are there now, words for this. Were my Bees buzzing, too?

I called to the Queen of the Starry Night's Sky. "Oh, One of great comfort, did you think you could prepare me? Take away the pain? Make me accept what should never have been?" I pled to the Powers of Darkness and Light – to the Elements four. "Let Arthur live."

Still no one moved. Then, without a word being spoken, with no command from Arthur or Mordred, Mordred's men made a move. With a great clash, swords and shields came together in the Dance of Death.

Everything, including my breath and heartbeat, slowed, slowed, and

than I. I go to my Ancestors, befouled... disgraced... destroyed..."

A great chill ran though me. "Mordred?" But his eyes were lifeless.

"Oh, Mordred... Why could I not have let you die in peace? Oh, child – who could have been mine. Nothing mattered but my own selfishness, to prove my sister's wicked agenda. You were always a victim, drowned in the poison of Morganna's evil cauldron. I am so, so sorry. I pray you hear me."

I tore my robe asunder. There, let them see my bare, dry, childless breasts. I scooped up dust and soil from the blooded ground and smeared it upon my face and chest. I took my blade from my boot and cut off my long hair. I howled and rocked back and forth upon my knees... – "I am withered... I am regret... I am a hollow ghost..."

There, for a long while, I knelt with Gwyddion silently weeping beside me.

It was Nimue – who had finally found us – who spoke: "Look, Arthur breathes and does not bleed – he lives."

Vivianne still lay upon her pallet in the Wood far away, yet we all heard her whispered voice in our heads – "It is the Spell of Makyr's scabbard. He will never bleed out his life's blood nor die whilst he wears it. The sword brought its bearer invincibility and Kingship, but the scabbard keeps him alive. Bring him to me and we will travel by Saxon Ship to the Isle of Apples so that he may rest while Briton awaits the return of its Summer King."

Vivianne's word was law, so we obeyed.

Before we left that blooded grove, Lucian and Bedwyr buried Fergus Macroich in the center of the circling Trees – the last of their original Companions. They lay a pile of Stones over his grave, with his bow and quiver standing upon it. His sword and dagger, along with a bag of gold would be taken to his family.

Chapter 39
Endings

Vivianne, Lady of the Lake

My daughter Nimue is writing these words for me as we sail home to the Isle of Apples.

I saw it all happen, even with eyes closed. I am sure that Morgan will write of the events leading to Arthur's wounding. I am so tired now...

I have held to this life only to put in place my edicts, which by our tradition remain law even after I am gone.

For many years now, I have watched Morgan grow in Spirit and power. I now proclaim her elevation to High Wise Mother upon my Death – one of the Nine. Also, when I die, it is my fervent wish, desire and recommendation that she replace me as Lady of the Lake.

I have wondered for a while now if I was hasty in making this decision. Should I have chosen Makyr? Yes, it is true that Morgan is fallible and too emotional. She takes upon herself what responsibilities and what debts belong to others. She sacrifices what is due to her for the comfort of others. She Loves completely and unconditionally – at Times tragically and perhaps even unwisely. Yes, she Loves... The great cup of her heart is seemingly endless. That is why I have chosen her. Yes, she is Human, but no less perfect than any of us. Nimue will make all this known when Death claims me.

To you, Nimue – daughter of my flesh and of my heart, write this down too – for I would have it in my history; You have not disappointed me. You walk your own path and it is a wise, venerable, and Magical one. I have always and will always Love you more than anyone on this Earth.

Soon I will rest with my Ancestors. I cannot stay to give Morgan her Initiations, but the others of The Nine must not let more than one and one half Moon's Dances of burial and mourning go by without having all in place. They must elevate Morgan quickly.

Morgan, you must leave your heavy grief behind you. So much I ask of you. Yes, I have always asked a lot of you, as has the GREAT GODDESS. I have Loved you well. Do not disappoint me.

Vivianne, Lady of the Lake

A note from Morgan

The Day after we arrived at our Order's lands, Vivianne, Lady of the Lake, passed through the veil.

Lucian

I write this on the Saxon ship sailing Arthur homeward to the Isle of Apples.

When I saw Arthur throw Caledfwlch to Bedwyr, I knew it was the end. When I saw Mordred impale himself upon the long pike, I stared in revulsion and yet wonder. What courage – or insanity! When he pierced Arthur, I fell to my knees and vomited but then strangely I could not weep. I just felt cold. I am still cold. The center of that coldness is my heart. Then I saw Morgan's grief. Oh Gods, how can you be so cruel?

No, I am not a religious man, full of Divine Spirit as are most of my company of friends. So, although I do not curse you, my Gods, I want an answer – Why? I stay silent to listen, but they remain silent, as well.

For now I have no other words.

Bedwyr, the Heir

I knew they had me when my sword was flung from my grasp. I was prepared to die. The thought came unbidden – "At least I will not have to watch Arthur die..." And then, the immediate next thought was – "But I need to be there for him until the end, always!" So quickly did everything happen that my thoughts fell behind the happenings. One moment I was as good as dead and then Arthur hurled Caledfwlch toward me. In that instant my thoughts caught up and ran ahead. I gasped at all the significance. Arthur could be bested without the sword of power. He was in mortal peril – but I was invincible. I would live. By this one act of Love and unselfishness, he saved my life *and* made me his heir. He would have me as high King!

But quickly I must pay heed to my attackers – to kill them.

Then the drama began. I turned back to see the unthinkable.

Mordred... Arthur... the long pike... Arthur had fallen.

My Spirit cried – "Oh, my beloved brother, my childhood companion, when at last all is said and all is done – it makes no matter to me if you be High King, companion, or brother – nothing really matters but my Love for you. Bear, I have lived for you. What do I do now?

Can anything ever fill this deep Well of my emptiness?"

Arthur, will I forever be the shadow you have left behind? I do not want to be King. This, even for you, I will not do. Those Days, those Dreams, have passed.

I wept.

Oh Lady of the withering Dream...
The potent Art remains...
Yet is ever receding...
From Mankind's world of fame...

Oh, beauty of the Moonlight's beings...
Your shadow's kiss now wanes...
Forgotten, abandoned, Enchantments
In ruins they lie unclaimed...

Oh, Lady of the countless Stars...
Do men forget your dance?
They march to the drums of War Gods,
Devoid of all romance...

Oh why is this thing happening?
Will you ever return again?
Oh Radiant Light to spin and twirl
To ancient Love's refrain?

When I regained some composure, I remembered that my Freidl and my children were at home, awaiting me. All was not lost.

I have decided to give Caledfwlch back to the Lady of the Lake, when she is established. I now know that Lady Vivianne intends to name Morgan as her successor upon her passing, so Morgan will have to decide what to do with it. Really, it belongs to The Merlin... He found it. But the Lady will decide and the Lady's word is law.

Morgan, Lady of the Lake

We returned to our blessed Isle to find the Water levels high and so were able to travel farther inland on the Saxon ship than we had expected to. But finally the Time came to thank our sailing hosts and transfer to the Punts of the Marsh folk.

A dolorous Day it was for all. We had to face the reality of our beloved King having been cut down. The Lady Vivianne was near death and everyone was deeply concerned about The Merlin.

The King maker, the strength beneath the tower, was somehow quite diminished. Grief? Hopelessness? Age? He who always knew the secret of the right words for everyone and everything, was mostly silent now, vacant even. For the first Time, in my eyes he seemed far too old for Nimue. I wondered how she felt. Nimue the Enchantress – Dragon Caller and Walker between the Worlds... I respected her far too much to try to read her, so I could only guess. She and I had never been close, but I admired her greatly. I had always thought of her as strength personified. Or was that only the Full Moon of her outer visage? ...the way she would have us see her? I wondered... The Mother she had only discovered in adulthood was near to crossing the veil. Her beloved was now becoming an old and ailing man who was withdrawing into some realm only he knew. But I myself felt too lost for compassion, too lost to comfort her, even if she would have allowed it.

Yet I knew that I had not the luxury of rest or self-pity.

Some Time later...

Vivianne the Great died and was buried with full pomp and ceremony. I was elevated to Wise Mother by our ancient custom and was unanimously accepted by the eight remaining High Mothers of council into their ranks. Then on a blue-Skied Day of benevolent Sun and Winds, with all the Stars in their most propitious positions, I was made Lady of the Lake, High Wise Mother of the Isle of Apples, and leader of the Order.

According to Vivianne's written wishes, for the first Time ever, all Druids as well as the Tribes' Folk who dwell in the Forests were invited to the post-initiation celebration. That Day should have been the proudest and most resplendent Day of my life, but...

Now, do not misunderstand, it is not that I only went through the motions of this Divine Rite. In some ways it was the most beautiful and empowering experience of my life – perhaps all of my lives. While living the hours and moments of it I was truly transformed beyond this world, this life, this flesh. But when all was accomplished, the deep shadows of my inner sorrow blemished the memories of it. I feared it would be so for some long Time to come.

Bedwyr left soon after I was elevated to Lady of the Lake. He stayed long enough for the ceremonies and then he gave Caledfwlch to me. He relinquished it along with any claim to Kingship.

From here he went to his fortress in Dumnonia where he lived happily with Freidl and his children.

Lucian bade us all farewell soon after that too, to return to his family in Rome. But before leaving, he said that he would not be gone for very long, for it was his desire to finish his life here with me on the Isle of Apples.

With me?

Arthur was bedded in a humble cottage with open windows, a

brazier, a chair, and a chest with an oil lamp upon it. My loom sat next to his bed.

I wanted to vow that every Day until the hour of my Death I would spend some Time there speaking to him and caressing him. But, of course, I had many responsibilities that kept me from being with him *every* Day. But almost... Even though he lived with his heart and breathing greatly slowed, and seemed beyond all awareness, I hoped somehow he would feel my presence, my Love and perhaps even hear my words. So, when my work for the Day was done, I went to him and Wove my Magic into the wool of our white-faced Sheep.

Gwenda aided me in Arthur's care. She was a well-trained Healer by then. For more than twenty years she had dedicated herself to this Art. Arthur was rolled from side to side and front to back twice a Day to prevent skin sores. His scabbard, which was keeping him alive whilst on his person, was often moved in position for the same reason, but never removed. I nourished him, although I never really knew if this was necessary or even helped. I knew it could not hurt, so every evening I dropped one Enchanted drop of my Bees' honey upon his sweet lips and three drops each of the Sacred Waters of the White and Red Springs. This was a simple enough thing to do for my Bear.

I went to the Springs myself or sent others to fetch fresh Water each Day.

I made sure that the White Spring, running out of the Cave's mouth, was kept freshly dressed with pretty cloth ribbons and Herbs, as well as leaving bread for the Birds and Squirrels and milk and cheese for what other Creatures might come to accept the offerings. This in thanksgiving for its Magic – all according to the old ways.

As for the Red Spring, it had of late been named Chalice Well by the women's Monastery, and was visited more and more by the Christian folk living in the environs. Mostly they were the ones who dressed it now – still according to the old ways. I told my children of the Order to allow this to them. Of course, we were not banned from its beautification either.

The Christians have added yet another layer of significance upon it – as representing the Carpenter's cup from which their God's earthly son, Yeshua, had drunk wine with his faithful companions on the evening before his Death. They, all having been Jews, celebrated their oldest Ritual of a meal shared in honour of being passed over by an Angel of Death – long, long ago. What a beautiful tradition. As they practice their Blood Mass, the cup or Chalice of each Church holds the blood of Yeshua the Christ – their Priests having said their Magical Incantation, turning wine into his blood.

Yet others believe that the Chalice symbolizes the womb of Yeshua's companion, Miriam of Magdala – who came from Old

Jerusalem to Vivianne's Mother's land with her child, and that they were brought here by Yosef of Arimathea to honour our Sacred Springs. Whichever way they believe, the Red Spring has now become a Holy place to Christians, too.

Chalice, cup, Well, womb, blood, Creation, destruction, salvation, and the Child of Promise – are all very old themes with ever a new twist. Blessed be the Creator of all Sacred Symbols. To us the Springs remain – red and white, Moon-blood and semen – the eternal hope of life renewed.

One Day as I walked up to the source of this Magic – the Chalice Well – there were two of my sisters already sitting there in silence, as well as were two of our brothers. Stars' Son was quietly filling a jug of Water and sitting upon the Dragon's Stone was my brother Ember, who officiates as Priest in many of our Rituals. He is one the kindest men I have ever known. As to the rest of Ember's name, "Keeper of the Fire" – well he does that too, and in more ways than one. He keeps many of our sisters' hearts a-flame whilst tending our evening Fires – and after – and seemingly all are happy with these dalliances.

Two young women from the Monastery were there also, collecting Water from the Well. They said their names were Mahr and Arrianell. They were all quite comfortable with one another – as was I with them.

With quill in hand now, I wonder why I thought to write of this encounter.

Perhaps it is because it seems to me that far too much is made of the differences between people and not enough of the similarities. I hope never to fall into this trap of disrespect and prejudice, as it has been the ruination of many a culture.

Lying just beneath my grief for the loss of Arthur and of our Dream is my great concern for The Merlin. For month after month he has lived within himself; sitting slack mouthed and unaware of drooling or mumbling unintelligible words meant only for himself. Our once-great Merlin – diminished to a demented old man. Still, Nimue helps him to their bed each Night where I am sure she holds him close to her breast for their mutual comfort, although I seriously doubt that there are any sexual acts between them. So sad... So sad is this – an obviously lusty and passionate, great Love such as theirs, fallen somewhere between the cracks of earthly matters.

Poor Nimue. So fleeting is life's experience. Golden Days come and we live them ecstatically taking for granted that they are forever to be ours. But holding onto these Times and situations is like trying to hold Water in our hands. Inevitably, irreversibly, they slip through our fingers, never to repeat themselves. Were these thoughts for Nimue and Gwyddion, or were they for Arthur and me?

It is said that the Goddess changes all she touches. This is just the way of things. Truth is truth, and this is one of the most bitter truths. I should be able to embrace change by now.   At least, this is what is expected of me. Still, it is so hard. Is everyone fooled by what and who they think I am? Truly I am but a child inside – Morgan of the Woods. Still I sing with the Bees and the Birds. But more and more of late, my child's song is a dirge. Where has the joy of living gone?

Chapter 40

Awakening of The

Merlin

Morgan

One Night, Nimue came running to me.

"Gwyddion is dying!"

"What?"

"His hands are cold and he has the Death rattle in his chest."

"I will be right there, Nimue."

I ran to fetch Caledfwlch from where it lay wrapped in skins beneath my bedding – thinking all the while – "Caledfwlch, oh Caledfwlch, what greatness and what catastrophe you have caused." Quickly I ran back to Nimue's cottage. "The sword should be his" – said I, motioning to Gwyddion. Nimue began to respond. I interrupted – "No, Nimue... I have decided. Help me move him to a more seated position."

She obeyed. Then, with words of great power, I lay Caledfwlch across his lap and wrapped his left hand around its hilt. His left, as that was his Making hand – the one he used to write with. As I stepped back, I noted with some alarm that I had placed it so that the blade read "Chaos"– representing the Great Originator and the forces of drawing in.

"Chaos..." I gasped.

Nimue answered, "The Dark Mother calls him home..."

Just as the last echo of her voice faded, Caledfwlch began to glow. The room filled with an emerald hue, then changed to Flame the brightest of blues. The Air surrounding us became heavy with heat and moisture and all became Misty. Here were Ancestors. I said so, but Nimue smiled wryly.

"Dragons, Morgan – and Ancestors, too."

Just then The great Merlin opened his eyes. No longer were they vacant, but filled with excitement and life.

He looked at me, then at the sword and then at Nimue. He smiled a smile filled with Wisdom and power, Love and humility.

"Where have I been?"

Nimue answered, "Within yourself, my Love, or in the Otherworlds."

"But I am here now!" He looked at me – "Why do I hold Caledfwlch?"

"Because it is yours. Bedwyr relinquished it to me and now I, Lady of the Lake, have given it to you – or perhaps as it is glowing so brightly, it has willed itself home to you."

"Yes, I believe you are right.

"Nimue, my heart, my beloved, my desire, I am only here in the flesh these few more hours. I can feel it. It is the sword that has awakened me. No, do not argue or pretend. This you know, as well. Come, quickly – make a scabbard from one of your shifts so as to wrap Caledfwlch upon me. Do not tarry. We three will go to the Cave within the Tor."

"But…"

"Do not take the Time to question me. Our moments together in the flesh are precious and irreplaceable."

Something in his absolute determination of cause bade us follow his every direction. Nimue tore one of her shifts into a useable scabbard, long enough to tie the sword to Gwyddion and then we leapt into action.

He grabbed her hand and she mine and then we ran to where the White Spring flows out of the Cave's entrance – the Cave of Gwyn ab Nudd or of Nodens, the crossroads betwixt life and Death, the place where worlds collide – the entrance to the womb of the Dark Mother.

Outside the Cave, the Waters of the White Spring – all dressed in her ribbons and Herbs – bubbled an ancient tune. To be here gave my countenance a moment's respite. But to enter the forbidden Cave…

"My girls" – said Gwyddion – "The tales told of this Cave are but superstitions, which will serve me well, for where even the Magi fear to enter is a place well met for hiding a thing."

"What is your plan, Gwyddion?" I asked. "What will you hide in the Cave?"

"Listen, my darlings, it is my Day to die."

Nimue groaned. He continued.

"But only in the flesh. I will live on in your Dreams, where I will come to you as often as I am able.

"Morgan, my body and the sword of Kings will be hidden here together. You must let out the word that Caledfwlch was returned to the Watery realm and lives at the bottom of the Inland Sea, awaiting the true High King's return. Oh, that is – if you will, my Lady" – allowing deference to me.

"What is your reasoning, Gwyddion?"

Just then, as I spoke, a flash of lightning and a long low rumble of thunder menaced the land.

He responded, "The sword in the wrong hands would spell disaster. None but one chosen by the Gods will ever find it here, buried with my body."

Nimue gasped, but she covered her mouth quickly, so as to be brave – or to seem so.

Gwyddion continued: "Perhaps the Time of Enchanted swords, Merlins, and Dragon Callers is coming to an end. Only the Weavers know and the Stars can tell. But I believe that they will live on in legend. We must do our parts to let the dignity, honour, and innocence of our Days – our Time – live on in the hearts of all true romantics and Dreamers. Let them live on through the quill of the Poet and the voice of the Bard. You must choose, Morgan, what of this you will say in your histories."

We entered the Cave and then walked along a path through a dark crevice, which led us into the bowels of the Tor – and a chamber completely covered in Crystals.

Gwyddion spoke: "Nimue, I will fill you with all of my Grym Hudol and Wisdoms. Let this Magic be through an act of Love – our last coupling in this life's flesh. This Magic of all Magics, I bestow upon you, my beloved, if you will accept it, for you are deserving of it."

There was a question in his voice. As the lovers' eyes locked into eternity with each other, I heard her whisper, "Yes." His silver spirals began their mesmerizing spin. They embraced each other and lustily kissed.

I quickly looked away and turned my back to them to give them their privacy. How childish of me to feel embarrassed. This was pure Love, the Goddess' greatest gift, and all the more so in this Rite of uniting woman with man, Goddess with God. The transfer of all the power, knowledge, and Wisdom of the one Druidical Merlin of our generation, to Nimue – Walker, Dragon Caller, and Enchantress of the Isle of Apples – was a joining of blood, peoples, and traditions.

The chamber was small, about the size of Nimue's hut. I could not get far enough away from them to not hear – even feel – their Lovemaking. I stood as still and as quietly as I could so as to not remind them of my presence. I leaned my forehead against the Crystal wall. My senses were heightened, my head spinning. I heard the sound of moist lips kissing, sucking, the murmurs of passion rising, two entwined lovers breathing ever more rapidly – the sounds of hands groping, caressing, Loving. My own breathing began to rise. "Stop it!" I told myself. But I could not help being swept along by their tide. Then, at the height of it, a steady rhythm began – the thrusting of his phallus into her wet, yearning entrance. I swallowed hard. "Be quiet!" I reproached myself again.

Were all things in this Earth in tune with the rhythm of their Lovemaking? Was this the rhythm of life? The Humming and Drumming of my dark kin, the creaking of the boughs of the Trees, the buzzing of my Bees, the Wind in the leaves, the bubbling of the Sacred Springs, the dance of Wolfs, the running of Deer, the calls of Birds, the vibrating of this Hill, this Cave, these Crystals – everything? Was *this* the song of the Goddess?

Now the sounds and their tempo became more and more frantic. I heard the suction of a sweating chest against breasts. Their sounds echoed and swirled about the chamber and when their Lovemaking seemed almost to reach its climax, I heard her whimper –

"No, slow down. Stay still. If this is our last Time, do not let it end so soon."

As though frozen, everything stopped still – except for their breathing and her quiet weeping.

Gwyddion whispered hoarsely through his gasps, "I will always Love you, Nimue."

My thoughts repeated... "Last Time... Always Love you..."

I flew like an arrow backward in Time. There I was again beneath a canopy in the Woods, adorned with flowers, experiencing once more the ecstasy of what I have pushed farther and farther away from my thoughts...

So safely and deeply had I kept this memory locked away so as never to threaten a reawakening of its passionate desire. Of course, it was the memory of Arthur's and my ecstatic Lovemaking.

Oh, no – I could never let loose the binds in which I held safe my predictable life – my own judgment of what was right and what was wrong and what was all in a proper order. I could never have wanted my own half brother as lover. Perish the thought! Arthur was the child – albeit not six years younger than I – whom I had always Loved and felt such pride in. He was my Bear, a cub, until I was confronted with the man – the man who has never stopped loving and wanting me. What had the Voices of the Stars said? "Yours is an eternal Love..." Eternal?

Had I thrown away my golden chances? I remembered the words of Gwyddion's poetry...

How it makes me cry
When I think of all the Golden Chances
That have passed me by...

Yet I am taught that this world and all things in it come to an end with each new epoch of the Cosmos and then return to the Mother. Does this mean that Love lives on within Her?

Here I was again, my thoughts taking shelter within the Cosmic Mysteries. Who was I lying to? I suppose this had been my refuge from what things I could not allow myself to acknowledge or explain. But now, standing in the naked harshness of realization, I must acknowledge and embrace my own Human frailty. I am now Lady of the Lake – no longer do I have the liberty of living a lie.

Pushing my self back into the here and now, I again became intensely aware of Nimue and Gwyddion. I could barely breathe for the heat in the chamber.

Finally their natures overtook their desire to make their Lovemaking last forever. As all came to the final pitch and frenzy, Gwyddion said hoarsely "With this climax, I, Gwyddion – The Merlin, give to you, Nimue – Dragon Caller and Enchantress, all that I know, have, and am." Then she wailed like a Beast, an enthralled release, and he groaned a very masculine expression of paradise found. But at the end of his groan came a smaller, higher pitched moan. With this, his life force left his fleshly body.

Nimue sobbed...

I have, in my life, heard the sounds of agony and loss, but never have I heard anything so sad to me as this. I ran to embrace her and we both cried and cried for all we had ever lost.

Some long Time later, Nimue arose and laid his cloak over his body. She asked me to place Caledfwlch upon him. This I did, wrapping his hands around the hilt. Then Nimue took over. She bade me step back into the crevice through which we had entered. I silently obeyed. She came to stand in front of me, then stretched out her hands and sang the song of Dragons. "Eee-Ah-Oh!" I saw and felt Fire power coming from the open palms of her hands. She made a gesture as if drawing or creating a bubble of protection around The Merlin's body. Next, she screeched a note higher in pitch than any Bird. With this, the Crystals that covered the ceiling, walls and floor of the chamber began to vibrate. The longer she held this note, the more they vibrated and shook until the whole chamber imploded to completely cover and surround The Merlin – yet they did not crush him nor dent the sword. It was a mighty, terrifying, and wondrous thing to see.

When she silenced her voice, all things settled. She then, to my further amazement, held those hands filled with power – her own power, which now included all the Grym Hudol formerly possessed by The great Merlin – up and out toward the mound of Crystals. Almost imperceptibly she muttered in a tongue I could not understand. Then she focused a searing heat toward the mound, one spot at a Time and then broadened the focus. Was that the shadow of a Dragon I saw hovering above her? I watched as she fused all the Crystals together. By this action the great Merlin's body and Caledfwlch were sealed in a crystalline grave – the heat of which had dissipated in an instant.

We walked toward it. She peered inside and beheld her lover. She laid her hand against it and said, "Farewell, my beloved."

I touched the Crystalline shroud. It was as cool as the Waters of the Inland Sea in deep Winter. In utter wonder I looked into her eyes, and in that one moment, without a word spoken, we two – who had never been close to one another – formed a bond that I knew would exist for as long as we lived. I also knew that soon she would be gone back to the Picti Dragon Callers, who she had embraced as family.

Then I remembered Chronos. "Where is...?" I said. She pointed toward The Merlin's far shoulder and there was Chronos, also sleeping in Death. How had he come to be there? Well, so be it and good, thought I.

Nimue and I, hand in hand, left the Crystal Cave, never to return.

Note: I have decided, after much long thought and fretting, to write this in my history. For you see, now in my very old age, evil rumours about Nimue have already begun. I heard the song of a Bard one Moon's Dance ago, which said:

"Nimue the Enchantress befuddled the thoughts of the old man Merlin to make him fall in Love with her. But she had Loved him not. Only did she want his Magic. So she stole his power and made him a fool. Then, when he taught her all that he knew, she tricked him and Spelled him into a living sleep."

One of my sisters told me that they had heard a different tune, but that it, too, named Nimue a wicked Creature. So, for your honour, Nimue, I write the truth.

I have only heard from Nimue twice in the long years since she left the Isle of Apples. Both Times was by courier, but never have I seen her face again.

Chapter 41
Nimue's Letters

Morgan

Gryffydd and Ahna arrive at the Isle of Apples...

About four years after The Merlin "disappeared" – as folk reckoned it and Nimue the Enchantress stepped out of our lives and into legend – a finely outfitted wagon, pulled by two exquisite Horses, arrived at the entrance gate of our Order's lands.

By then we had posted guards and a large and loud clanging bell to alert us to visitors' – or foes' – arrivals. Sad as it was that this had become necessary, we all slept easier at Night because of it. You see, within the less than six years since the breakdown of the federation of the Dux' authority, more and more Saxons, Angles, and Jutes had sailed to our shores, especially into the South and East and had violently pillaged and taken lands which had been inhabited by Britons for millennia. Whole villages had been razed with their inhabitants slaughtered.

Perhaps I write too harshly against the invaders. Even I, who have been taught since childhood to honour and find the good in all cultures, have my biases.

When the Clans had first come to this land, it is told that they came as intruders, not murdering invaders. Or so it is told... Who knows now?

The true fact of the matter is that at least the Teutonic Clans do not kill the children. Even some of the more "cooperative" young women are assimilated into their families. I should not make them sound like murderous barbarians, for it is just the way of the world that conquering people move the older race out of their way.

The Saxons do have a high culture and are very creative, with talented craftsmen and Poets. Their fine work in gold gives testament to this. Some whom I have met are very warm, friendly, and generous folk – albeit they drink and eat overmuch, compared to my kin, but who am I to judge?

Still, they are, in general, a warring, strong, and lusty people. They have vengeful and violent Gods and Goddesses as well – or so their sagas and Myths tell. One of their most respected Gods – Woden, Wotan or Odin – was a "Walker between the worlds" who had sacrificed one of his eyes to gain Wisdom and the Mysteries. Hel is the name of their Dark Mother of the Underworld, and Baldag, or Balder, is their Child of Promise – not unlike Yeshua or Mabon. So, I suppose, they are not so different from the Gods and Goddesses of the Britons.

Their Seers are well-respected amoung them, so they have shown respect toward the sisters and brothers of our Order – at least for now. Still, we felt the need for caution.

But the young man, his wife, and baby who arrived at our gate in the wagon that Day were not Saxons.

"My Lady," said the runner from the gate, "Here – they have given this to me for you. They said you would recognize from whom it has come."

It was an Owl's feather and a Raven's claw holding a finely wrought medallion with the same Picti symbols as were tattooed on Nimue tied and wrapped around a vellum scroll.

"Nimue!" I excitedly proclaimed.

"No, my Lady, not Nimue, she is not here – just a young family from Alba – a man, a woman and a young child. Very wealthy they seem."

"Of course... Nimue," I mused.

He looked at me as if I had not understood him.

"Go now, allow them entrance and bring them to my quarters immediately."

By the Time they had arrived I had already arranged for food and drink to be prepared and waiting for them. There were flat breads, butter, cheese, honey, Apples, and Water. I also had a basket filled with fresh straw and soft woolen bedding for the child – and Goat's milk too, not knowing how old the baby was. The brothers of our Order are not very accustomed to determining the age of young children.

It had seemed that as in a flash of Lightning after my request, the stuffs were there. I laughed at myself. Have these six years of authority turned the manner of my spoken requests into commands? It was probably my heightened excitement – but whatever the cause, my usually serene, relaxed, even slow moving sisters had jumped into action like Horseflies. By the Time the visitors' wagon had pulled to my cottage door, everything was in readiness.

Then a thought struck me. How far North were they from? Would I understand their speech?

There came a knock on the wall outside my doorway, and the words, "My Lady Morgan, your guests have arrived and are awaiting your welcome."

"Thank you, D'twain."

I walked to the doorway of my cottage and pushed aside the ironclad wooden panels, which opened or closed the entrance to my quarters.

"Welcome, travelers!" said I. "May the Goddess bless you. Come in from the Sun. I am Morgan, Lady of the Lake. So, do you come from Nimue?"

"Yes, Lady. And be ye blessed as well."

Good, I understood them. They spoke the language of the North Britons.

"I forget myself, please sit and be comfortable."

The child was perhaps a year old. No Goat's milk needed, then.

"Will you partake of food and drink? If you wish, the babe can rest here." I pointed to the basket.

"Also, my sisters can prepare vats of warm Water in which you may bathe yourselves clean of the road dust, and perhaps then you can tell me all about your travels and how you have come to know Nimue. Is she well?"

"Yes," spoke the man through an already full mouth. "And thank you much for your welcome, M'Lady."

I leaned back in my chair, smiled and took a cup of mead for myself. We all relaxed then. They were quite companionable folk, as it turned out.

The young woman, Ahna, told me she was the eldest of the two sisters of Bronte, "the great Merlin's apprentice" – she said with pride.

A plague had ravaged their small village and almost everyone had died. Her Father – who had been Chieftain of their small Clan – as well as her younger sister had died of this pestilence. I had received news of this plague. "May the Spirits of illness keep it North. Well, that was not a very kind thought" I mused.

After her Father's Death and burial, those left of the Clan had Cast lots to vote who could or could not be the new Chieftain. The vote could not be ratified. So the local Seer had Cast the Bones. The decision of the Gods was that her cousin Gryffydd, of the same name as her husband, would become Chieftain.

Another of Ahna's cousins, Dealbrihl, had married Gryffydd, and was with child when Nimue had come to visit the family of Bronte. All she had found was famine and Death. Nimue saved Ahna and her husband from these eventualities by giving them "a great deal of gold" and arranging for them to take her wagon filled with blankets, food stuffs, Well Water, medicines, and all but one of her Horses. They had tried to refuse these gifts saying that much less would still save their lives, but Nimue would not be argued with.

"Accept some as gift then, and some as payment for a task and long journey you will make on my behalf."

"She taught us how to travel by the Sun to come to the Isle of Apples, to deliver this letter to you, M'Lady.

"Nimue stayed in our village to mend and Heal the sick. We gave her my Father's house, garden, and one Goat. It was all we had to give her. She did keep some food, mead and medicines. She said that the worst of the plague had passed – and thankful of that we were.

"Huge black boils, coughing blood, sometimes shitting it – oh excuse me if I have offended, but the stench of the ill and Dead was the worst – all but for the wailing grief of their Loved ones, that is.

"Nimue told us that she would be alright. She would help tend the ill, bury the Dead, and do her best to restore the Clan as needed and then continue her travels Northward. This, Nimue said, she would do for Bronte, whom The Merlin had Loved.

"That is all, my Lady. Here we are, well and fine. And now you have the vellum scroll Nimue bade us place into your hands – and your hands alone."

I clutched the medallion, feather, Raven's claw, and vellum to my breast. "Nimue..."

I gave Gryffydd, Ahna, and their baby a warm and clean partitioned area of our dairy to live in and suggested they build a house beyond the Lake, on the other side of the Christian monastery.

"In the next few weeks we will help you, but for now, be comfortable in our dairy."

We bade our good-Nights and I had them helped to bring their belongings into the dairy, bathe, and get settled in. The central Fire had been lit for weeks now so the dairy was warm and dry enough for their comfort as well as for the Animals'.

I waited for my privacy to read Nimue's correspondence. I relished the Love and energy that lingered in the vellum from Nimue. I felt it in my hands and in my heart. I put my feet up on a cushion, relaxed, and read her words:

"Greetings Morgan. I am sure that if you have this letter in your hand, Gryffydd and Ahna have told you the whole story of their Clan and family, and of my meeting them. They left with no sign of the plague, and I knew if it did strike them down, they would be dead long before they reached the Isle of Apples. So, either way, my sending them to you would be safe enough.

I am well and trust that you are too. As to my history, I wish to add these words to it:

My heart so shattered, my body scattered – the cup that holds all that I am was cracked, leaking and almost empty. That is how I left you, the Isle of Apples, and Gwyddion behind. I thought only to return to the Highlands of the far North, where I had first truly found myself.

You see, Morgan, I had forgotten that I am never alone. My guides and my comforts have never left me. Even Gwyddion has walked into my Dreams. The first Time he did, I cried for two Days at the passing of that Dream.

But the next Time he came into my Dreams, he said, "You are asleep and I have come to you in your Dream. Everything will be alright. I Love you. I always will. I will definitely come to you on the Holy-Days, but look for me always."

When I awoke, all was different. He was there in my heart, alive again. Really, all around me his Spirit walked. Then I remembered that he had told us he would live in our Dreams. The next Time he came to me he said, "You know, I am not really dead. Why, right now I am sitting at the craggy bottom of Vortigern's failed Hill-fort, even now some have begun to name it after me – The Merlin's Hill. Why did Vortigern pick this spot, when so many others were more suitable? Yes, it would have been quite defendable and the views are spectacular, but the land slides!"

The Dream faded. The next Night my Dream continued from where the last had ended. He said, "Nimue, funny that some men name it for my brother Ambrosius. Men remember him and that is good. No finer man has Briton seen. I remember working all of this out in my living thoughts.

"This is a Sacred Secret: I see not only the past but some of the future. Someday, long and far into the future, as men reckon it, people of learning will say that there never was a King Arthur. They will believe that you, Morgan and I, and the Isle of Apples lived only in the realm of Legend. Yet, even in those scientific cultures, which will have erased most sacrality from their lives – where all things once Sacred are then profane – there will be some who, filled with Spirit and hope, will believe. For the sake of the Dreamers and believers then, continue to write your history, and send it to Morgan.

"I also *See* that Bronte, the Magic child, will come back into Morgan's life as a girl in whose body her Spirit will live. She will protect Morgan's histories. She is the one Morgan must know and find and recognize. By twists and turns and guidance, these truths will come to light when most needed.

"Long and far from now when the Stars and constellations make their next great shift into a new Epoch, when the Water Bearer's coming is soon to be established, Morgan's compiled histories will light the world with the Dream renewed – not only with our Dream, but with the knowledge of the Mysteries and of thousands of Human generations of Earth's Tribes and Cultures. This knowledge will light the world!

"Good Night, my beloved."

I awoke enthralled in joy, and with three missions. First, to finish my history and send it to you; secondly, to tell you these words of The Merlin; and thirdly, to honour Bronte's grave and speak with her. My thinking was that if I could wander to wherever her living Spirit was, perhaps she would know and tell me who this Child of Promise will be.

I journeyed into the Otherworlds to find Gwyddion. Three Times I went there. The first Time, my great Teacher in Spirit appeared to me. She said, "Are you Nimue, Dragon Caller, Enchantress, Seer? Or are you, Gwyddion, The Merlin?" I answered, "I do not know who I am. Will you tell me?"

"It is for you to remember who you are."

"But I do not know" I answered.

She vanished and I awoke from my Trance. The second Time I went there my great Teacher appeared again, but this Time in a deep Wood, filled with Apple Trees and Oaks and Hazels, Birds, Insects, and Animals of all kinds. Streams rushed, Winds blew, Fires burned – but not to harm. The Dragons were there too, all watching me. My great Teacher asked again,

"What are you? Who are you?"

"I have forgotten..."

In an instant, everything turned to the blackest of blacks, and utter silence. I was lifted far above, then I was left there alone – but only for a moment, or was it a lifetime?

"I will not give up!" I screamed as I awoke to the world of form. For a third Time I journeyed to the Other-Realms. Once more the Forest was overflowing with life of all kinds.

My great Teacher pointed her finger up to the Sky. It was Day. It was Night. It was Dawn. It was Dusk. All at once the Sun shown with the Full Moon beside it, then a Mist came upon the Forest and She said, "I will ask you one last Time. What are you? Who are you? When is today – and tomorrow and yesterday? And what are we all?"

Then her bony finger pointed across a clearing that had not been there a moment ago. Out of the Mist walked my beloved Gwyddion, with Chronos. Gwyddion's eye winked at me and then he raised his first finger to his lips to signal my silence. For what? To listen! Then Chronos said, "Whoo... Whoo..." All at once everything spun and spiraled down to the Earth, even the Stars fell from the Sky, and all things became indistinguishable. My body became as sand in a Whirlwind. My flesh and my bones dissolved, as did all else around me. I became merely a part of the whole.

Suddenly – I remembered... I yelled at the top of my voice:

"What am I? I am alive! Who am I? I am everyone and yet myself! When is today – and tomorrow and yesterday? All Time is now! What are we all? We are all One!"

"Yes, my girl," said Gwyddion, spreading his hands and arms out into a sweeping gesture indicating all in the world around us, he continued – "and you are never alone."

At this, the Mountains were filled with a choir of Elves, and so haunting of voice were they as they sang:

"Live and laugh and Love and sing...
Sharing the beauty is a Magic thing...

Time will come and Time will go...
All Time is now, this we must know...
Time will come and Time will go...
All Time is now... All things must grow...

Dance and twirl and spin and fly...
Kiss me my Love... Do not sit and cry...

Time will come and Time will go...
All Time is now... All things must grow...

Celebrate the life we share...
The touch, the smile, the breath of Air...

Sleep and Dream and hold me tight...
All Time is now... All things are right...

Shhh... Ooooh... Sleep and Dream...

All Time is now... All Time is now... All Time is now...
All Time is now... All Time is now... All Time is now...
All Time is now... All Time is now... All Time is now..."

Their Voices faded into the Hills...

I had fallen deeper and deeper into nonexistence, a shell with only emptiness inside. But, my beloved caught me from my fall and lifted me back to the realm of the living. He had awakened me from the sleep of grief and reminded me of what and who I am. Thusly reawakened, I fully remembered not only what Wisdoms I, Nimue, had known, but all that my Lord, The Merlin of Briton, had known. These I have reclaimed from over the precipice of living doom. I am whole again. My Dragons and Ancestors, my Spirits and Gods are with me, as is the Great Mother of all.

I write this to you, my dearest Morgan, not to brag – for it is the most humbling experience one could ever have. For, even as I am One with all, I am but an infinitesimal pinpoint of light within the countless others of this great Cosmos – each one being the center; each a Magi un-awakened, each a blade of grass, a bubble in a Brook, a mighty Oak, a gentle Fawn – yet un-remembering or un-aware.

I write, also for those in the distant future, those who The Merlin spoke of who will re-awaken, as well as to assure you that your histories and your life's work are of the greatest value.

Every person is a Star.

Nimue..."

In some way, hearing from Nimue was like opening the door and window of my cottage on a breezy, sunny Day. I was refreshed and renewed.

Life rolled by from one Ritual to another, one season to another, one year to another – the great wheel of Creation turning.

To my surprise our Order kept growing. I had thought it would dwindle like the ambition and the joy of our people and as had my life. Oh, I still had my beloved Bees to work with and once in a great while the folk of my Mother's Tribe would visit. My sisters and brothers of the Order still sang and danced the Fires at Night, told the legends of our Ancestors and gossiped – all for our common pleasures. Each Day was filled with the same work of running the monastic business and keeping everything in good order and repair. Each morning, without fail, I would spend an hour by Arthur's side, sharing with him the plans of the Day. Then, when my duties had been accomplished for that Day, I would go again every evening to be with Arthur, to give him the Sacred drops of the Water and honey and to En-chant the wool I would spin into yarn, always telling him of my Day. So, on and on, had many years of Time passed.

I thought never to hear of Nimue again. But, eventfully, on one glorious blue-Skied Day, near the Rites of Summer's Beginning – the season of the Heiros Gamos – amidst the bustling of preparations for one of our biggest Festivals, another courier arrived.

It was Owen, Nimue's old lover and companion – of what seemed all so long ago. I could not believe my eyes. Nimue and Owen had always remained friends, this I knew, but I had not seen or heard from him in... I cannot remember how long. He had come to bring another letter from Nimue.

"It is years old. It came to be in my hand, passed on by the Old Dark Tribesmen – your people." He blushed as if the term would offend me.

"Yes, yes, go on," I said, a little more impatiently than I meant to.

"How they finally found me and gave it to me is unbelievable. My home is in the Eastern lands, South of old Hengist's Kingdom – near no city. There – on a farm, with my wife, children, and grandchildren I live peacefully. But find me they did, after three years of passing it intact, undamaged and unopened from Tribal village to village. No one had broken the wax seal, as you see. The condition of it is almost perfect. It had come from an Island far to the North of the mainland, in the land of the Picti. How this found its way to me and now to you..." His voice trailed away.

I suppose he saw the hungry look in my eyes to hold and read it. He handed it to me.

Nimue told of a wondrous journey Northward. The first thing she had done – as she had set out to do – was to honour Bronte's grave and to relive, as best she could, the beauty of Gwyddion's experience there, to touch the marked Stones, to walk upon the very soil as had the company of travelers and The Merlin's apprentice. She wrote:

"In this country, there are no Roman roads or mile markers. The last evidence I passed that showed Rome had ever existed is what is left of Hadrian's wall – a failed endeavour at best. Already one can see houses, barns, and Wells, built using the Stones of the wall. One Day perhaps it will vanish entirely. This country and its people are virgin. They stand on their own – fiercely independent and proud of their blood ties.

But I am welcomed amoung the Picti as, in fact, are many Clansmen who have peacefully mingled with them, even intermarrying and bringing forth a new blending of language and customs. Mostly these marriages are in the Southern lands of the Picti, of course. But let any others come as worrying invaders and the Picti will slaughter them – for such is their honour and their sense of the Sacredness of "place" and of "blood."

As I have told you, Morgan, these people – who are my brethren of Spirit and heart – are powerfully Magical. And, although primitive – or because of this – are more *aware*, as a race, than any other people I have experienced. They have only an oral tradition, no Mystery Schools or Universities, just the living counsel of the wisest and most gifted ones amoung them. You see, Morgan, with no written tradition – just as the do Druids, yet differently because of their refusal of an organized hierarchy – they must learn and repeat their Mysteries and Myths in the presence of their Elders.   No mistake is allowed in their exact pronunciation – not even in their inflection, tempo, and tone. But more than this, they remember them by repeating and quoting them to their kindred and children in every endeavour of their daily lives. Always are they aware of what the Gods did and said "In the beginning." They live by their strongly held beliefs.

As it is amoung our Southern Clans and Tribes, Christian Monks have taken to writing their histories, Myths, and Sacred Poetry, but they take away or add to them as suits their Christian perspective.   Even though many of these Monks are still followers of Pelagian ideas – in fact, many Monks are really old Druids in new robes and head shavings – because of an ever more centralized power structure in their Church they must be very careful of what they write. In fact, I have heard that soon all such writings will have to be approved and *edited* by their superiors.

I heard it said in my Grandmother's court, that all history is written by the conquerors. Even though Rome never conquered the North Tribes, the Church has begun their infiltration – not that there are many Christians, for in fact there are but a few. But, these Priests and Monks are literate – they hold the power of the quill. I have *seen* that your histories, Morgan, will remain untouched. This is why I add my words to them.

As I am on the subject of Christians, there is a man I wish to tell you about. I learned of him on my travels Westward after helping Bronte's village and paying honour to her grave. His name was Columba. It is told that he was a student of a famous Abbot from the lands of the Eire, named Finnian, who founded a large Monastery and school there. As it happened, Columba had a bloody disagreement with his mentor in which tempers rose to the point of violence and where many men died. Columba, as a penance, was banished from Eire to Pictland. No doubt Finnian thought this to be a Death sentence for Columba. Columba was told he could bring twelve of his brothers with him and that he could only return when he had completely converted, as they say, one soul to Christianity for each man killed in their dispute.

So Columba and his fleshly brother, Oran, came along with eleven others to build and establish an Abbey Church and Monastery – albeit quite a small one – on the Isle of Iona, which lies off the West coast of the Isle of Mull. They work diligently, going from farm to farm and village to village to bring "the way of the truth" to the Picti. So charismatic and kind was Columba that soon there were several followers. Some even left the Old Gods to serve Yeshua, who Columba calls Jesus, and the cross.

People tell that Oran sacrificed himself because Columba wanted to consecrate the building of their Monastery with a burial and somehow it was deemed necessary for someone to be buried alive. So, after a lengthy dispute with his brother about the nature of Heaven and Hell, Oran descended alive into a pit, which was then filled in with dirt. After twenty Days, the pit was opened and when they uncovered Oran's head, it spoke to them, saying, "Heaven is not what it is said to be, Hell is not what it is said to be. The saved are not forever happy. The damned are not forever lost."

But upon hearing this, Columba was convinced that a demon had possessed his brother and quickly had him buried again.

Hmmm, I wonder...

Still other stories are sung that it was his head alone that was buried.

Yet others say that after being buried whole for twenty Days, he was dug up fully awake and filled with the Mysteries, speaking prophecies – all through the grace of God – and at this, Oran was embraced back into the Love of his brother.

But in the end, Columba was killed for his trouble. It is said that not long before his Death he called Christ his 'Druid.' He *did* predict the hour of his own Death. Although most say that a painted warring party stormed the Church and laid him open, others say he fell peacefully into the arms of Death in his Church – in the presence of the cross, his God's Spirit, and his Monastic brothers. Who knows which stories are true, if any? Still their legend grows and many powerful, Magical acts are attributed to Columba – as well as to his brother Oran.

Curious, I went to visit Columba's Church, Morgan, and I will tell you this – I did feel the Divine presence of Love there. I think that he must have been a very good man – regardless of the stories – with nothing but good intentions. I do not believe a man like that would bury his own brother alive. His small group of brethren slowly grows on Iona.

While there on the Islands I visited all of the great Stone monuments and observatories. My very favourite is the White Lady's Dance, where one Night every fourteenth year, when the Full Moon's arch across the Sky moves just above the horizon, She "dances" between a long row of Standing Stones high upon a ridge. When this Night comes, She shows her full beauty off and on, by hiding behind each Stone, then peeking out again – over and over. I, of course, waited there in that territory to see this beautiful phenomenon. The Fates blessed me in that I had only to wait less than a year.

I saw all of the Western Islands in my travels – ever Northward I went through the mainland and beyond, to what was to be my final destination – the Isles of Orkney.

I live on the Southwestern coast of the second largest Island – which Island lies just to the North of the largest one. It is from here that I am writing to you of my adventures.

This is a land of drama. The stark terrain, the eerie light, the Sea – which is at once breathtakingly beautiful and overwhelmingly, terrifyingly alive with Her undulating force of motion – seemingly posturing Herself to engulf the whole world in Her dark and restless depths.

In Summer it is Daylight almost the whole Day and evening long, with but a very short twilight and no true darkness at all. In Winter it is a harsh, freezing, and gale-ridden place, with very few hours of light and a long Night of darkness. Yet, I Love the Winter best because of the frequent show of the phantastical Lights above the horizon. To me, the exquisite display of the Lights is the great celestial Goddess' way of allowing us to see the glory of Her eyes watching from the darkness.

Out of the bounty of Her unquestioning Love, we catch glimpses –
momentary, infinitesimal flashes of revelation and Love from them. I
pray that she never in this lifetime Loves me enough to reveal herself
completely – for I would surely die and be absorbed into nothingness if I
were to look fully into the eternity of those eyes and thus be forever gone
from this Earth. I do not wish to leave this Earth, which I so dearly
Love. Not yet – for there is one more great and wonderful work for me
to fulfill in this lifetime.

Oh, perhaps I am overmuch influenced by my surroundings, in that I
have become so poetic.

But I have digressed. We are all getting older, are we not, my sister?

I have yet to see a Tree on this Island – it is so strange. But there are
many beautiful flowers and much good vegetation to eat and of course,
many Fish, too. No one ever goes hungry here, for there are so few
people and much abundance. There are many Birds and other wildlife
too. At Times the shores are covered with Seals. Funny Creatures are
they, but with an apparent, devoted sense of family. Oh, I could go on
and on.

You will be astonished to hear that I live in a Stone house. This
house stands upon the Southwestern coast, at Water's edge, but because
of its strong and thick Stone walls – and that it is mostly buried in the
ground – it is quite sheltered from the Winds. Of course, it was not built
for me, but has been here for some long centuries past. I heard of it from
a Seer I had met in the first Moon's Dance of my being here. She lived
in the house and said that she welcomed us to live with her.

Oh, yes, I said 'us' – a white Wolf has become my constant
companion. To tell you how he came into my life, I must speak of
Bronte once more.

My beloved Gwyddion had spoken of her so often, always with a
fond, sweet sadness. "So young was she. We buried her by the
Northernmost Stone just outside the outer ring of the Stones at Croft
Moraig."

The site is ancient, and still powerful. The *cups*, or indentations, on
some of the Stones must have had great importance, but who can know
now of what or why.

I, of course, knew of where Gwyddion had spoken, for he had
described the way of getting there many Times.

"It lies close to the West coast of Alba, near to the town of Obar
Pheallaidh. Traveling Northward from Eidyn – the town closest to Table
Rock, where was Bronte's home – toward the old Picti town of Pert,
there is an ancient trade path. Arthur, the Companions, Bronte, and I
travelled upon this until we came to Pert. Then we veered North-
Northwestward from there, still following the path until it turns due
Westward. We stopped at a small village to ask the way to Obar

Pheallaidh. A good neighbor led us to the great double horseshoe of Standing Stones. It took four to five Days by Horse for the entire journey".

He said that we should go there together one Day. So, there I went.

Sitting upon her grave... – what an amazing feeling it was to be closer to Gwyddion through Bronte. Whilst there, I was at peace. I closed my eyes and said, "Bronte – the Bestower – are you the bestower of this peace I feel, as well? How I wish I had known you. Come back, sweet child. The Voices of the Stars told that you have a great work to do. 'Saoirse,' claim your freedom soon..."

I have added these written words to your letter Morgan, so that in case the site of her burial has not been recorded in your histories, it may be known and remembered.

A Day's walk or two hours on Horse, from Croft Moraig, there is another smaller circle of four Standing Stones, with one very large one at the North-Northeastern end of the circle. Gwyddion had told me that whenever we went to Croft Moraig we should also visit it. So I did. It is so peaceful there. A sweet kind of peace, as if the Stones are Elves, dressed up as Stones. I remember thinking, "I wonder if these Stones are Star aligned. Had this perhaps been a grave, too?"

I tied my Horse to a small Oak Tree growing right near the center of the Circle, then laid myself down to a beautiful sleep.

Gwyddion came to me there in a Dream of reassurance. "I will Love you forever and we will meet again," said he. When I awoke, still in the wonder of that tiny Circle on its small Mound, I thought that I wished I could just stay there until my flesh was absorbed by the green. I remember thinking, "This might just be my favourite place in all the Earth!"

The next Night, while still there, I fell to sleep again within the ring of Stones, beneath the midnight blue Sky. I felt many Spirits encircling and comforting me. When I awoke, I walked in the chill Dawn. A thick Mist covered the ground, which was usual there. Someone or something stirred just behind me. I jerked quickly with my heart pounding and my knife at the ready. I could barely see him. All white, in the white Mist, lying near to me... was a young Wolf with golden green eyes. He stood up quickly, but with no harm intended toward me – I had startled him too. He was a bit shy at first, but I stooped down to his level and called to him in a soothing voice. He came right to me to lick my hand. That was it, Morgan. He travels now with me – my faithful companion. His name is Mist.

As for my Orkney home – I am happy here. Here I feel closest to the Gods. The Sea has become my Mother – all-be-Her dark at Times – and the cold North Wind is my brother.

Perhaps you will come to visit me in your sleep or Visions

sometimes? I would like that very much.

My dear Morgan, as I sit here in the in the long twilight writing to you, I know that all life is a gift and a wonder and that peace and contentment cannot be found without – for it dwells within.

These are probably the last words you will hear from me. Have strength, my sister. We will meet again in the Summerlands, if not sooner.

May the GREAT GODDESS always keep you in her Love.

Nimue..."

Owen had waited so quietly that I had forgotten his presence. Perhaps I *am* getting old. When I had finished reading, he made a sound in his throat like "a-hem."

"Oh, yes, I am sorry – I forget myself. Sit here with me by the hearth. Will you have some mead? Tell me of your family and how your life has been."

"Yes, Lady Morgan. But first, there is a reason that the Old Tribes came to fetch me. You see, long ago, Nimue entrusted me with the true genealogies of her Grandmother, Queen Vivianne, of Merovech's Kingdom, and it is even more complete than that which Nimue gave to her Mother. Its tendrils reach deep within the royal families of many lands – here and on the Continent. Nimue sent word to me to bring them to you, to use as you see fit.

"This is and will always be controversial information. You must choose the value or harm of bringing this knowledge to light"

Chapter 42
Queen of the Bees

Morgan

Nineteen years after the final battle, the Death of Mordred, and the ruining of Arthur's alliance, I began to hear disturbing rumours again. These were of sightings of Morganna Le Faye – returned from oblivion, arisen to the land of the living!

"Cloaked through Woods and villages, she walks in silence, my Lady, young and beautiful as she was when she vanished."

"And they say she is even more powerful in Magic than before."

"She did not walk by my door, she floated in the Air."

"She felled an ancient Oak by calling a bolt of lightening down upon it."

"This is ridiculous" – thought I. "Superstitious people!" Yet I wondered what prompted them to these tales.

Why... she would be seventy-three years old by now. Most of the generation who were old enough to remember the Days of Arthur's crowning and of Morganna's youthful beauty are long dead, so how can they compare? Yet these stories persisted.

One bright afternoon, while I was with my Bees, one of the brothers of our Order came running up the Hill toward me.

"My Lady," said he – puffing and holding side for the stitch in it – "a courier has arrived. This man says that he has come with a message from your sister."

"My sister? Morganna?!"

"Yes, my Lady."

"Well, let him come, then."

My sister... No one had heard a word from her since the battle when Mordred died. Most thought her dead. But somehow I never did. She felt to me as one locked between the worlds, hiding. Sometimes in my

Dreams, I had heard quiet but malicious laughter mocking me. In Trance journeys I traversed the Underworld, place of the newly dead, and the Summerlands, but nowhere was she to be found.

Even, I went as far as the Land of Forgetfulness, where the dead, when ready, go to leave all conscious memory of the life lived before, so as to be reborn into a new journey of life experience. I knew that that place is a danger to those Walkers who dare to go there. One could, it is said, not be able to return at will because of the of that place's function of forgetfulness.

Most of us have heard tell of some folk, who although alive in this world, sit open-eyed yet unreachable to the people around them. For years they can live like this, within themselves – yet breathing and eating and drinking, if fed – being moved from one place to another yet seemingly unaware or unconcerned of all around them. The Merlin had almost been there. Being condemned into this state, it is said, could be the danger to a Walker who dares journey to the Land of Forgetfulness.

Once only did I go there – shielded by powerful Magics – seeking the fate of Morganna. But she was not there. I sought to fly quickly from that world, through the dark, gossamer barrier – leading back to the Land of the Living. But, I began to forget why I must go.

Of sudden my Queen Bee appeared to me – only she was mighty and much larger than I. She buzzed so loudly that it seemed her voice could shake the Worlds. She spoke: "Come, Morgan of the Bees. Return home with me."

She flapped her wings, creating a tempest and then dragged me through the barrier into the Realm of the Peaceful Dead. On the other side, I was myself again – that is to say my *Spirit* self. I looked at her with Love and wonder. She was still as large as before. Then she spoke again: "Morgan, spend not yourself in any way for Morganna Le Faye. Though of your blood, she is evil. Hear what I am saying, Morgan – never forget. I, Queen of Bees, am yours to command. I will always protect you – as you have so lovingly cared for and protected my Ancestors, my children, and my children's children."

Even if it be by our own sacrifice, we will keep you from harm. Do you understand? We will also keep your hands free from the blood of the evil Morganna. Blood for blood, we would pay to rid our world from the living blight that she is. Even you do not know the extent of harm she had done toward this Earth and Her Creatures – both Human and Animal. Blood for blood, Morgan. It will be done."

I was disturbed from my thoughts when my brother arrived with the courier.

A beautiful and very young man was he, almost too beautiful not to be a girl. But there was about him an eerily strange countenance. His Spirit's Colours were a swirling, changing cloud. Then I saw him eye to eye. He looked as if possessed by a God. But no, this was no Ritual of worship to elicit beatific expression. Around him were not the fragrance of flowers, as befits the presence of a Holy Man. Instead he had about him a sweet, nay, sickly sweet odor of evil Enchantment. Of course, Morganna! His eyes were staring at me now, transfixed to mine, as if I could be drawn in by them. Lesser and pointless Magics were these.

"Yes," said I – "give her message to me."

The courier handed over the waxed scroll. It read: "Greetings, Morgan. I have a great surprise for you – a beautiful surprise. As befits the occasion and the monumental nature of my surprise, I want you to meet me at the Giant's Dance, upon the Night of the next Full Moon. Morganna Le Faye..."

I sat there for several minutes in silent thought.

"Is there a reply, my Lady?" asked the messenger.

"Yes... Tell her that the Lady of the Lake will meet her as she requests and will come to her, unescorted by man or woman, and unarmed."

If she thought to trick me, it would be best for her to think longer. I was finished with her surprises.

It was then that I knew without a doubt, that even if it meant that I must take upon my Spirit the condemnation of the Scrolls of Judgment for the murder of Morganna Le Faye, my blood sister, child of my own Mother – she must die!

"I pray the Goddess to forgive me that I do harm, knowingly and willingly, to another."

I told Arthur when I visited with him the next morning that soon I must be gone for a short while.

"But I will make sure that Gwenda brings the drops of my Bee's honey and the Holy Springs' Water to you everyday while I am away. Perhaps she can play Branwen's harpy, and sing for you as well."

I stroked his golden hair, fine as ever.

Still he does not age...

"Oh, Bear, if you could see me now. My hair is almost all white, and my hands, which you always said were so delicate and beautiful, are lined, spotted, and old looking."

Funny this – inside myself, I feel as young as when you were crowned. Mind I said, *inside*...

But then, my bones ache and my vision fails. Time ravages all things – except for you, Arthur. I hope with all my heart that you can hear me somehow. That is my greatest prayer – my dearest one – that somehow you know I am near to you. Know this Arthur: I will never betray you to this eternal silence, no matter what – for you do not deserve to be chained to this prison of emptiness...

Night of the Full Moon...

Full Moon and almost Dusk... How dramatic, Morganna. You make me wait...

Then, suddenly, walking from behind the shadows of one of the largest Stones came a figure, cloaked and hooded. But as she came closer to me, she threw back her hood and shook her head to reveal long and lush, perfectly black hair falling to her waist and the one large, perfect pearl given to her upon her name Day.

"Morganna?!"

"Yes... Morganna."

She looked as young and beautiful as she had the last Time we were here together. I took a moment to put my thoughts together. That last Time was when our Lady Mother was bringing me to the Isle of Apples, to become a postulant.

Igraine had said, "Before you are gone from me, my girl, I want you to see the Giant's Dance – even though it is much out of our way."

"The Giant's Dance, Mother? What do you mean? I thought Giants lived only in little children's tales. You know – to frighten them on a cold, stormy Night. You remember, Mother – just as you used to tell so that we would scream and run into your arms at the telling."

"You will see for yourself, Morgan. There are still wonders, even in this world of form."

Yes, in the world of form. Here was Morganna Le Faye, as beautiful – no, perhaps even more so than when last I saw her. But, how?

Then I smelled it, the unmistakable stench, the scent of feral Wildcat. No! This is lie, not truth!

"So, Morganna, have you used up your Magic thusly?"

This I spoke, not looking at the girl that stood before me, but up at the near dark Sky. Then with a chill, I remembered Mordred's words – Mordred's last words.

"She may be with child."

"Run home to your Mother, girl! You do not fool me. Although you are her likeness in every way, you hold not within you the power or the evil of your Mother. Tell her her game does not work on me. She must try much harder to fool the Lady of the Lake."

So the girl, wearing Morganna's angry face, turned and walked away into the darkness.

I stood alone, wondering what would come next. Yes, there I stood within the center ring of the Giant's Dance, waiting.

All of a sudden, a great wooden Fire burst into flames upon the Altar Stone, where there had been nothing a moment before. Or had I just not seen the Wood before this? It *was* now full dark save for the Moon's light.

She made her grand entrance. From behind the portal, through which the Sun disk shines upon its rising on the longest Day, walked Morganna Le Faye.

"Morganna," – I said, in mocking amusement. – "Do you not wish your Magics were potent enough to keep you looking as young and beautiful as your daughter? Oh, did I just ruin your surprise? Mordred, son of your flesh, as he lay dying in my arms, told all."

A look of deep-seated anger and hatred came upon her face, contorting it into a truly ugly and dangerous looking one. But wait – was that also a pang of deep grief showing – regret even?

I sensed it about her. How could I still feel my childhood pity for her? I disappoint myself.

Because she was so furious, she hesitated to speak. I took advantage of her momentary silence to say, "Why, Morganna? To what end? Why this now? For that matter, why everything you have ever done?"

"I will tell you why! Because I, and not Arthur, was the first born of Gorlois, who held the blood royal of the Clans – and of Igraine, who held the true blood of the Old Tribes. Gorlois was Dux, Second Battle Commander of the Britons under Ambrosius Aurelious. Gorlois' true, first-born heir, should have become King *or Queen* – as Uther left no heir of his body. Without The Merlin's meddling and plotting, I could have married into the Roman strain – say Uther Pen Dragon himself, or even Gwyddion The Merlin, the half man I could have made whole, at least long enough to get with child. But then Arthur was born, and all was ruined. But, as everyone knows, I gave birth to his only child, Mordred. Prince Mordred was trained and groomed to be a King. He should have been... and should still be."

"Then what went awry, Morganna? Did he hold Arthur's goodness as well as his looks and intelligence?"

She visibly flinched.

"He meant everything to me, but... but..."

"But what? He would not, could not, go along with your plot to kill his Father?"

"Yes. Yes! After all I had done for him!

"The week before the battle he said he would *speak* with Arthur. We argued bitterly. The selfish little sanctimonious retch! He was going to ruin everything – all my plans for all those years. I knew Arthur would name Bedwyr and not my son as King after himself. So I drugged Mordred, with aphrodisiacs – a potion so strong he would have fucked a Boar. That was the Night before the battle, upon the Full Moon. He awoke to the knowledge that he had coupled with his own Mother, and that after me, no woman, or man for that matter, could ever pleasure or satisfy him as I had. Not only once, but six Times we performed every act that could be performed between a man and a woman.

"When the drug wore off he slept. He awoke with a rage that befits a

Warrior. I thought he might even kill me. So I waved my hand in a certain gesture that I had prepared... just in case. I had used this same gesture many Times with Mordred, from his early childhood on, to hold him under my power and my every suggestion. The Spell he came to be under that morning was this: He would hold his rage, it would be forgotten, until the battle began, at which Time it would return to him. But as rage, not only for me, but for the perversion of our family – which I had convinced him of. Rage toward Arthur, toward himself.

"I knew that I was with child, a glorious, royal child to equal Mordred.

But, I had Loved him more than anyone. It was not my fault... This was all caused by his own rebellion against me and our plans."

Then, Morganna broke down and cried. Was this the first Time in my life I had ever seen her shed a genuine tear?

She came back to herself.

"Now I have a royal heir, with *all* the royal bloodlines. Morganna the Second will conquer and hold all in her sway. Because all will believe that she is me – Morganna Le Faye, the greatest Seer and Magician the world has ever known!

"For you see, Morgan, I will return to my hidden dwelling place, and no one alive will know that she is not me – the immortal, ever young, ever beautiful, Morganna Le Faye."

Then I knew that she had completely lost her wits. How long ago? I wondered. Had she always been thus? ...and through our weakness or blindness, we all had never allowed ourselves to see it or accept it?

"No one alive will know? But I know the truth, Morganna."

She laughed an ugly echoing laugh. It seemed to come from the branches of the Trees behind me. But wait! – there are no Trees... was that only her laughter I heard? No! My Bees! My Bees were here.

At once her blade flashed in the Fire light. She was running toward me across the inner circle holding a dagger. But my Bees – their buzzing was so loud! I looked behind myself. They were swarming toward me. No – toward Morganna! I remembered their vow:

"Blood for blood, we will sacrifice for you, Morgan."

I held my hands to my ears, so their angry buzzing would not drive me mad.

Morganna, realizing her peril, jumped upon her Horse, who had appeared by her side at the sound of her whistle. But how could he hear her above the deafening buzzing? Perhaps her Magic *was* that strong.

She and her Horse flew like an arrow across the Windy plain. My Bees swarmed past and around me. There were hundreds – no, thousands. I watched as they overtook her. Around her body they formed a grotesque mold. She fell from her Horse, arms and legs flailing convulsively, for the seemingly endless moments from when the Bees had first caught up with her. I heard her screams – screeching and wailing like a rabbit caught in the talons of a Hawk. They were unforgettable.

The Bees never harmed the good beast that ran out of sight, away from Morganna.

All that could be seen by Full Moon's light was a huge, seething mound. Then silence – except for the gentle sound of my Bees flapping their wings...

I ran as best I could toward her. Why? I do not know – morbid curiosity perhaps. I knew it would be a horrific sight. By the Time I reached her corpse, the Bees had done with her. Already she looked as if all of her bodily fluids had left her insides and rushed to just beneath her skin. This hideous swollen mass of dead flesh was unrecognizable to me.

I gagged, then retched, then held my hand to my mouth. I just stood and stared, not only at her, but at the hundreds of dead worker Bees.

"Blood for blood," my queen had said. Would I, too, have to pay the cost of this? of their blood? The Merlin always said, "Everything has a cost."

It did not matter. Feelings washed over me like an angry Sea, wave after wave, all changing, all un-nameable. I could not catch my breath. Would I drown in this? This, what... was this sorrow? Regret? Pity? Relief?

Vivianne had warned me. "You cannot Heal everyone, Morgan."

Remembering her words, I wept. I fell to sitting upon the ground beside the only sister of my flesh. The sister I could not save.

This was the end of an era. Everyone I had known of my generation was either dead or far removed from me. Gone... everyone was gone, even Arthur. Yes, at that moment I accepted the truth: I knew as a certainty – beyond all doubt – that Arthur would never return as King to the land of the living. His Kingdom – his Dream – was gone, too.

Then I remembered what the Voices of the Stars had told me long ago – "Yours is an eternal Love, Morgan..." But how could Arthur and I be together again if he was never to die?

I had promised not to leave him suspended between Death and life. At that moment, I knew what must be done, and I vowed to do it.

There I sat in vigil beside her until way past the Dawn. The sounds of the Day had begun.

I looked up to see the Ravens wheeling above. They awaited their feast.

Part Five
The Child of Promise

Chapter 43
Pieces of a Puzzle Game

Morgan

I have always thought that the Weavers were very clever in their web making. Things, people, and happenings which seemingly have no pattern come together like pieces of a puzzle game in the strangest of ways. This, I was to realise all the more at this late stage of my life. Yet coincidences – too odd, too strange to really be that – fall into place as neatly as a felled Tree hits the ground. The improbable is turned upside down by the inevitable. Or, is it the other way around?

You may ask, "Could these incidents not just be as leaves blown by the Wind, making beautiful art in a meadow? Or could it be that we see pictures in the Clouds because we want to see them there?"

Yes, you may ask... But the truth of this is that we will never really know. There comes a Time when random coincidences reach their point of no return, and then... 'There be the realm of Dragons' – we enter the uncharted, unknown territory of events that will change forever the course of history.

I had thought that Night on that windy plain there at the Giant's Dance, that all of the histories that would matter enough for me to compile had come to an end. I was so wrong...   for the tale of the keeping and hiding of these histories is as important as the writing of them.

So, as strange and unlikely as what I will write on these pages sounds – it is the absolute truth.

Rhodri had been a widower now for over twenty-five years.

When Princess Rowena, the daughter of Hengist – the Saxon King – died, she had left an ironclad agreement between Rhodri, his three sons, and herself regarding the inheritance of her vast wealth and fortress. Three copies of this agreement had been left in good hands.

One copy was given to The Merlin who passed it on to me, Morgan – now Lady of the Lake.

One copy was entrusted to her most Christian – and literate – friend, Tudno, who had built a place of worship near his hut and Well at Cyngreawdr Fynydd. This location was, she noted, "There beside the Druids' swinging Stone of judgment." Tudno was a kind and generous man. He had settled into the area to aid and educate the impoverished locals. Rowena was of the habit of visiting with Tudno often for some intelligent conversation and a game of Fidchell. She considered it worth the cost of the long ride from her fortress and Tudno's polite, occasional prompting of her toward the Christ. She trusted this man.

The third copy was held by Rhun Hir, the Chieftain of the Gwynedd Cymru surrounding her lands.

According to this agreement, Rhodri's sons were to inherit one half of all of her vast wealth and lands, with the exception of her fortress. This was provided that the first female child born – and this I quote – "to their blood, who survives into womanhood, is to be named Rowena in honour of myself, Princess Rowena – the Saxon."

It continued to read that if the first female child died – under any circumstances – then the second daughter born would also be named Rowena... and so forth. Also, that this girl, upon becoming a woman at her sixteenth year-turn, would "inherit one quarter of all of Rowena's monetary wealth – that she would inherit the fortress and lands immediately surrounding it and that she be declared "A woman in her own right" for as long as she lived – no matter who or whether she married. It would then be up to her own sense of charity whether any of her family would be allowed to continue living in her fortress. The document went on to say that – "All this must be accomplished within twenty-five years of my own Death."

If this heiress were to die of 'unnatural causes,' or if no daughters were born and lived to obtain their sixteenth year-turn by the twenty-fifth year, the fortress and ten hectares of land immediately surrounding it – including the village – was to go to the local Chieftain to maintain and protect. The rest of her vast wealth was to be equally divided amoung the Order on the Isle of Apples, Tudno's Church, and the Bishopric nearest the fortress – with the understanding that these assets be used for charitable works.

Princess Rowena did not trust her son-in-law, or for that matter, her two oldest grandsons. She had always suspected foul play in the Death of her dear, beloved, daughter, Ribrowst Ardora. This endowment would not only protect any female child born into this family from possible dangers at the hands of the men, but it would permanently enrage Rhodri, the man she so despised. In this way she could get to him even from her Watery grave.

Rowena was like that. I Loved her so. She had always made me smile.

It is now over twenty years past the final battle between Arthur with his Alliance and Mordred with his Roman Revivalists in the conflict that had broken up the Confederacy of all the Tribes and Clans upon these Our Fair Isles. Since that Time all hope of keeping our Island to ourselves was gone.

The whole Eastern side and much of the South below the highlands of the Picti were now Saxon, Jute or Angle territories. They came in beautiful ships across the Eastern Sea and swept over us, pushing us ever Westward like a great wave. But, of course, their history will be told by others.

Not long after the Death of Morganna, I began to think – to fret even – about Morganna's daughter. She had obviously been completely overwhelmed by Morganna's evil works. Did she even know that she was not really Morganna Le Faye herself? Had she ever known the world outside of Morganna's lair? I thought not.

For the little Time I had known my nephew, Mordred, I had Loved him. Could I come to care for this girl too? She was now my only blood, outside of Arthur, who is caught somewhere between the worlds. I had never given my Mother Igraine a grandchild and, of course, now being past sixty-seven years old... my thoughts trailed off. Igraine's blood.

"Princess Igraine," others would have called her – those who did not understand the social structure of the Old Dark Tribes. But to everyone who had known her, she was Igraine the great Seer, Guardian of Nodens' Well. Morganna's daughter was her granddaughter and also, her great-granddaughter. I shuddered...

Upon that dreadful Night at the Giant's Dance she had just walked away into the darkness. Not a word nor rumour has been heard of her since. The decision was being made in my heart that I must find her.

As those who read these histories will know, I wield a great deal of influence and authority. Also, my Order holds wealth beyond measure – whereas we need little of it. Therefore, I had come to the decision to finance many parties of men and women to search the length and breadth of Briton for Morganna's daughter. For years they searched to no avail...

Unbeknownst to me at that Time, this is what had been unfolding:

Rhodri had become lonely. Oh, for years there had always been young servant girls to warm his bed and cool his loins, but since Ribrowst had been killed by the roof timber that had fallen upon her head in the barn, he had missed her constant presence – or so he later told.

Had he forgotten the frequent rages he had focused toward her? How he had beaten her? I am sure that by now he had come to rationalize that it could all be blamed on Ribrowst's meddling Mother, Princess Rowena.

When Rowena disinherited him from her great wealth and said that only Ribrowst would ever live in her fortress, Rhodri had lost his wits in hatred. Then Ribrowst was dead and gone from him forever.

But he had Loved her and at first they had been happy – or so he told himself and so he said. She had given him three healthy sons. He missed all the things she had done for him. He remembered the fine smells of her cooking, the always joyful greetings for him whenever he arrived home. And she had truly Loved and desired him, so that their sexual play had been more satisfying to him than with any of the wenches since.

But Rhodri, being a very practical man, had a plan.

The Bishop – with whom Rhodri had become quite entangled through commerce, as well as due to his sons' and his own conversion and baptism into the Church – had found the "hole" in Princess Rowena's document. He had noted that Rowena's letters of inheritance had not specified whether Rhodri's sons alone could make the daughter, or daughters, to be named in her honour – for the wording had only said "born to their blood." Thus any of their blood, including Rhodri's, could make this "child." Rhodri believed that the Bishop, who potentially had a great stake in this, was only protecting his own chances of some wealth coming his way through Rhodri, his sons, and a female Christian heir. He also believed that it would suit the Bishop well if Tudno, who had been Rowena's friend, lost out on his potential gains from this whole affair. If the daughter was Rhodri's, and not his young sons, the Bishop's purse could be better filled.

By that Time Rhodri's eldest son, Huail ab Nau Caw, was known to be a great hunter and as violent as Rhodri was he. Between his carousing, gambling, and drunken debaucheries, he had little Time and no desire for a wife.

As to the middle son – Celyn ab Nau Caw, much to the surprise of all who knew his treacherous nature had decided to live out his life in a Monastery. Of course, his Father's friend, the Bishop, had in short order used his influence to maneuver things so that Huail was placed into position as the Sacrist – the one in charge of the Monastery's money and treasures. Granted, this so-called Monastery, which had been established by a Monk named Cadfan, was very small, being comprised of only eight men and had been newly formed on the Isle of Ynys Afallach. Ynys Afallach lies off the Westernmost point of the Llŷn peninsula of Gwynedd. It had been, from Time out of memory, an Isle of Druids' Bardic training.

Interestingly, it is said that the Isle was named for a God known as Afflach, the "Orchard Lord," who in Cymric myth, is the Father of nine sister Goddesses, who tend the Sacred Cauldron of Annwyn – hence its moniker "Orchard Isle" or "Isle of Many Apples," which was, incidentally, the same as attributed to Ynys Mona, where the Druids' renowned University had been before the Romans destroyed it.

The truth is, in fact, that Celyn's 'relationship' with the bishop allowed him many opportunities for being away from the monastery.

Sildag, Rodri's youngest son, who bade everyone call him Gildas – and was later known as Sapiens – had also become a Monk. But as things were to play out, it seemed that his faith was genuine.

Rhodri decided that it was Time to find a new wife.

One Day, near Sundown, as Rhodri was riding through the Woods at a pace, deep in thought, he of a sudden realised that he had taken a wrong turn somewhere. He saw smoke rising in one or two places above the Tree line, not far from where he was. A village then... But he had never known of a village a Day's ride East of the fortress. But then, he was not completely sure in which direction he had veered.

The village seemed quite primitive to him – five houses, a barn, a chicken house, a Well, a muddy pond, a few Pigs, and a Goat. The place was poor and filthy. The settlement was of the Clans. "Good..." thought he.

He was about to ride on and then he saw, walking from one of the hovels to the Well, the most beautiful and exotic girl he had ever seen. He hid in the Wood to watch. She was of the Old Dark Tribes. He crossed himself. They rarely were seen anymore. Her skin was dark, her hair and eyes black, not at all like his golden haired Ribrowst, but what a beauty! She had about her a quiet sensuality. His loins stirred.

People said that old King Arthur had been one-half of this race and the other half Roman and of the Clans. But he had come out with golden hair, blue eyes and fair, golden skin. Together, he and this girl could make a Golden haired Rowena, he mused.

He remembered this later and told her that he had wanted her from first sight because her beauty was so Enchanting to him.

He had not relieved himself sexually since the Night before last, when he had taken Llanwen, the cook's fourteen-year-old daughter to his bed. He began impulsively to rub his man-head to quell the itch, but it only served to heighten his desire for this dark beauty.

He decided to ride into the little settlement and speak with her, but when she saw him, she became frightened and screamed.

An emaciated old man with a crooked spine and yellow discharge draining from his red nose came running from one of the hovels with a pitchfork, hollering, "She's mine!" – but then stopped abruptly when he saw this well-built, handsome, and obviously rich man on a Horse, holding the girl by her wrist.

She looked at Rhodri, then again at the other man. She stood silent.

The villager said, in a pleading tone, "I have fed 'er fer a year, my Lord. Surely you will pay something to a poor man for a prize like 'er."

Rhodri's impulse was to kill the man, but he did not want the girl to fear him. He threw a small sack of coin to the man and said, "Will that do then?"

The man smiled – his brown, rotted teeth showing.

"G'bye girl! Be well!"

Rhodri looked down at his beauty and smiled.   She saw his handsome face, straight teeth and red-gold hair. She smiled too. Rhodri dismounted and lifted her to his Horse's blanketed back with great gentleness, and then he arose to sit behind her. They spoke not a word until he found his way home.

When they arrived, she was bathed thoroughly and dressed in whatever clothes would fit her and then her hair was braided and oiled. Rhodri bathed as well and burned both of their flea – and who knows what else – infested clothes and Horse blankets. When she was well prepared, she was taken to the great hall for cheese, honey cakes, and ale.

Rhodri had wondered if she had been spoiled by that wretched man. Could she be with child? Surely not! He had been too old for that. Well, he would have the first answer later that Night when he took her to his bed.

To Rhodri's surprise, when she spoke, he found that she was very well spoken – in three languages even, two of which he did not understand. He asked who she was and how she had been educated. She shook her head and a tear dropped down her face.

"I do not know, sir. I only remember walking and walking and being very hungry. Then a Merchant couple found me and brought me North. They fed me. I gave them the fine cloak I was wearing in exchange for food and shelter in their wagon. Sometime soon after they said they had no more food to share and put me off in the Wood with no cloak. Again I walked and walked. This Time I was so very cold without covering. When I thought I could not go on, I stumbled upon the farm village where you found me. The old man's wife and son had just died from an illness that had come upon them suddenly. He said that if I would work helping him with the garden and Animals and carrying things for him, he would give me shelter, food, and his wife's woolen cloak. There I have been ever since. I remember not who I am, where I am from, or if I have a family – only walking in the Woods and being hungry."

Rhodri leaned back into his chair.

"Are you spoiled? I mean – did that old man bed you?"

"I know not what you mean, sir. He gave me what had been his son's bed to sleep upon, if that is what you ask."

Rhodri exhaled; not having been aware of holding his breath.

"Think naught about it," he said. "It matters not."

He approached her to touch her hair.

"Do you have a name?"

"The old man called me Donella – "Dark-skinned Elfin one.""

Rhodri made the sign of the Cross...

"Well, we will do much better than that. You will have a Christian name."

"Christian?"

This she said with an uncomprehending question in her voice. He laughed.

"All will be well, girl, I will take care of you and please you as well. Trust and obey me in all things and you will be happy."

"Happy?" her voice faded.

Then he kissed her mouth. She responded, shyly at first, and then in kind. That Night when he bedded her, he found her unspoiled, a virgin, as the Christians say. Like a whore from the Temples in Aquae Sulis she satisfied him in every way. She performed his every suggestion. "Had all the Gods come to bless him?" he laughed to himself at his old ways. Perhaps he would name her for the Christian God's virgin Mother, Mair. Yes, that would be her name.

Rhodri delighted in her as if she was a toy to play with. They married the next week at the Church. The Bishop himself performed the Rite just after her Baptism.

Both Rhodri and Mair had told the story to me more or less with the same details, when, six years later, I was first in their presence at the fortress The Merlin had built.

To whoever is reading this, you have probably already concluded that this Mair is the very same girl who had walked out of my life into the darkness – my niece, Morganna, the daughter of Morganna Le Faye.

But why, you may ask, was she deceiving him thusly? Is she more her Mother's daughter than she seemed? No. She had lost all memory, and what follows is why.

Mind well that I am writing all of this account many years after these events took place. For, at the beginning of my newfound relationship with my niece, all I knew was from what I had been told by the searchers who I had hired for years to find her and that this information had come to me in many sketchy pieces.

First, my searchers accidentally met the traveling Merchants, on a road from "one place to another," very near to the great outcropping of rock in Manaw Gododdin, near to the place called Table Rock Hill. A very large village had begun to spring up upon and around the largest outcropping of rock where ancient Briton Chieftains had met to hold counsels and where Arthur had been presented by The Merlin as battle Commander and Over-King of these Our Fair Isles. Towns such as this were good "fields of plenty" for Merchants. When the Merchants were questioned by my armed Horsemen and women, they were, at first, too frightened to speak of the girl, but when they were offered gold for information, they pulled the beautiful hooded cloak from their wagon and showed it to the searchers. It proved to be the very one in which I had last seen her. Having had the description of it from me, the searchers obtained the story of how the Merchants had found "the girl" wandering cold and without food or drink.

"Oh, we saved 'er, we did, from a certain Death. Fed 'er 'til we 'ad none left fer ourselfs. We left 'er somewhere far to the Southwest o' 'ere. Can't say where 'xactly. She left the cloak fer payment. T'is ours by right!"

So my searchers paid a couple more coins of gold to acquire the cloak. They knew I would want to see it, and so I did. When the Cloak was finally in my hands, I brought it up to the top of the Tor to lay it upon the Altar in the center of the Ring of Stones, for it was there that I thought to discover the nature of Morganna's Magics woven into the cloak. There I stayed with others ministering to me for three Nights and three Days. Many deep Magics did I perform – yet I was unable to unravel the Mysteries of it.

Then I knew then that no ordinary Magic could reveal the source of Morganna's Spells, or give me the power to un-make them. And so I vowed to traverse beyond the darkness, into the bottomless depths of the Land of Naught – for these, I perceived, had been the playing grounds of Morganna Le Faye. I knew all the while that I must pay close attention at every moment not to disturb or to change anything whilst there.

Mind, that I do not mean by this that I journeyed into the Beautiful Dark – the Caldron of Potentials from whence all Creation has sprung. Nor do I speak here of darkness as opposed to light – for these principals are equal necessities in keeping the whole of Creation advancing within its circular cycles of birth, life, Death, dissolution, and rebirth – for great science and great Magics are these. No, I speak not of these principles, but of the darker – let us call them the darkest – Magics. These dwell in the Land of Naught – the realm of possibilities of the un-raveling of the Cosmos itself. These also lurk in the halls of our deep unconsciousness. Magi of all great Mystery Traditions know of what I speak.

There are sounds, vibrations and words of the Un-making, which I would never dare to utter, for they are not to be toyed with – not unless it would be to restore order to the Cosmos should it be split apart by one who is an emissary of the Land of Naught. But, knowledge is power, and this knowledge I hold – all but for the knowledge of the penultimate word of the Un-making, which no Human will ever know... And I thank all the Gods for that!

Morganna Le Faye had somehow found and played with these powers. It cost her her sanity as well as who knows what debts her Spirit

Rowena Whaling

must repay in the Halls of Justice.

Chapter 44
The Seven Keys

Morgan

Now... do have patience with this telling of my story – for it is quite complicated.

I feared the possible ramification of causing my own Death whilst within the Ring of Stones journeying in the Land of Naught. I knew that I must not risk sullying the soil of our most Sacred Temple – and so instead, upon the next Midnight I knelt beside the Well of the Red Spring. I held my arms around it tightly to keep me from being swallowed up by whatever monsters might confront me. I said a quick prayer to Nodens and Cast a Circle of protection about myself.

"I am Morgan of the Woods, Morgan of the Bees, and Lady of the Lake. Allow my entrance into the Land of Naught..."

I will write no more of the invocation I quoted, lest these words fall into untrained or unworthy hands.

Once spoken, down, down, down – or was it within, within, within? – I went that Night in search of the root of Morganna's Magic. I was dragged into the channel of the Red Spring for seemingly hundreds of miles – but I did not drown. I did not come to an end of it, either. Somewhere along its murky red depths I came upon a portal veering off to the left. Hundreds of fingers and hands rushed out of the portal, grabbing hold of me and sweeping me from the Spring into a deep Cavern of grey Rock and red dirt. I stood upright. Then suddenly the fingers and hands turned to dust and an unfelt Wind blew them away.

When I looked down at my feet, they were standing on some clear, solid surface – such as glass from the lands of the East. I could see right through it.

I was looking down, down – at the Star-filled Midnight Sky. Quickly I looked up again.   All about me were underground Mountainous heights. I could see no end to this. Fathoms and fathoms of petrified mineral columns had been formed by thousands of millennia of single drops of Water, drip, drip, dripping upward from the bottom. I looked down again and then I looked at my hands. With a start I saw that they and the rest of me were inside out.

Of a sudden I saw the flesh of my hands and arms and the rivers of blood running through them. There, too, were their great ivory bones. I watched in awe and fascination, being wooed into acceptance of my changed state of being. Then I remembered... "No!" I shouted, "Nothing can change here! I came as one Creature, I will remain as such. You have no power to change me!"

In that miniscule fraction of a second, while I awaited the outcome of my declaration of un-changed nature, I closed my eyes, held my breath, and thought, "Will this Land of Naught vomit me from its bowels – if indeed that is where I am? Will I now dis-integrate and be turned into chalky dust as did the grabbing fingers and hands, then to be blown away by the Wind with no presence?"

I waited... I felt nothing.

When I opened my eyes I was outside out and inside in again – I had kept my wits enough to pass the first test.

A Key fell out of no-where into my hands. Along with it fell a ragged scrap of Animal hide, with these words written upon it: "Let no one influence your perception of who you are. Let no one diminish you. Let no one change you without your desire to be changed. Whoever they are, do not let them! You know your value. Be what you know yourself to be."

I had gained The First Key, which was made of Mercury – and unlocked the first Gate of understanding the powers of the Land of Naught. But from whence had the Key come – and from whom?

The Key itself had immediately melted before my eyes, yet I knew that I would henceforth hold its power within.

Then I noticed that I finally felt stability beneath my feet, yet for some reason I was hesitant to take a step forward. Insecurity enveloped me. If I stepped away from the known, would I fall into terrifying unknowns? My gorge began to rise. Confusion had weakened me; every moment, terrifying fear was clutching me tighter. Fear – almost panic – my every hair was standing out and away from my skin.

Then I smelled it – the pungent odor of Wildcat. A voice came from out of no-where...

"Fear is the destroyer! – destroyer... destroyer... destroyer..." His voice echoed away from me... – "Say it Morgan!" he ordered.

I swallowed hard and firmed up my resolve. I said it aloud: "Fear is the destroyer! So I will un-chain myself from it!"

Next I took a step forward, but when I did, my position had not changed. Whatever solidity was beneath my feet had moved with me in sympathetic motion. I could gain no distance from my starting point.

At once I realised: "This is a game."

A voice spoke again. But it was not the same voice as I had heard before. This voice sounded very annoyed: "It is THE Game!

"Yes, Morganna played our Game to control others – because she had learned these skills from us. She knew how to manipulate the powers of confusion, fear, and loss in everyone – to weaken and destroy your world's solidity – the natural order of the way you think things should be. She broke your shields and downed your defenses. That is how she dragged everyone into her drama and held them under her sway. She used their own fears to camouflage her moves. For, this is one of the secrets of the Land of Naught."

I sarcastically retorted – "But confusion and fear of what? Loss of what? The loss of her? Of her Love? The loss of her immortal Soul? The loss of any good results that could possibly come of the efforts and Love spent upon her? I think not!"

"Oh, really?" returned the voice, "Loss, yes, and your fear that she could have been born without a conscience... fear of her beautiful madness. Yes, Morganna kept everyone's feelings confused and turned inside out. And, as to confusion... in your world the effects of the Land of Naught are in-comprehensible – thus comes the confusion. Thoughts such as these wind their way insidiously around you.

"Could this beautiful young girl really be so wicked? Could she have been born this way? Or could it be our fault? But no, surely my daughter – my sister, my friend's daughter – could not truly be as she seems. If she were, she could bring down the walls of this house and the halls of this Kingdom – and that is un-thinkable!   I/we must be mistaken... I must be a horrible Mother, sister, friend, to think of her this way. I do not want to believe it. I do not believe it! Or, do I?

"The breaking down of your shields and defenses disables your Gifts and strengths. This is how, on the Night of Gorlois' Death, Morganna could slink near to the presence of The Merlin and the great Seer Igraine un-noticed. This is also why she was un-readable. It was all in The Game..."

Then realization struck. I called out, "The Land of Naught – it is itself a game! But if a game, then there are rules... If rules, then there is law, if law, then pattern, and if there is pattern... then there is order. And if so, this land of Naught – this land of dis-order – is deceived, as well as a deceiver. I can win its game if I do not give in to fear and confusion, if I dis-allow the draining of the un-certainty of what I know to be truth."

"Ho-Huck!!!" shouted the voice disgustedly. Now you are not playing by the rules! You have un-tangled the mystery of The Game."

Begrudgingly he continued – "With this recognition, you have won the Second Key.

The Key to the Second gate: To know the truth; that to some, life is a game and the world is a board upon which they use others as pawns – breaking their shields, downing their defenses, sapping their strengths, all the while knowing that others will keep on giving and forgiving, for the sake of Love and the fear of loss. This Key was made of Lead.

I felt stronger.

Then for some reason I began to wonder... "Morganna... Le Faye... She had named herself that... Why? Was a part of that name itself one of the words of the un-making?" On an impulse I yelled, "Morganna Le Faye!"

Rushing by me, through me, above, below and around me, were fragmentary pieces of crushed and mutilated bloody tiny winged Gods – the Faye. Oh, no! Had I just destroyed them by speaking Morganna's name? Oh, retched Spirit of mine, I had spoken it – I killed them. Beautiful Creatures, helpers, and guides, I felt as if my heart would break – in reality. Then my stomach, my throat, my whole insides were shattering in slowed motion.

Pity, oh pity! I mortally pity you, dear winged Ones. Great sadness... I am drowning in my empathy for you. Poor Faye... Poor, broken, mad, Morganna! You were the only sister of my blood. I idolized you when I was a very young child. But even then I felt such sorrow for you. I mortally pitied you – pitied you unto my Death and my own undoing. Oh – winged Ones, I cannot Heal you. Morganna, I could not Heal you, either. I have failed you. I should have tried harder. I should have understood that you were ill. I should have Loved you more.

I wept bitterly, all the while knowing I was shattering myself – just as I always have. Then from one small place deep within me, still left un-shattered, I remembered Lady Vivianne's words – "You cannot Heal everyone, Morgan. Have you not learned this by now?"

I clung to that one small, still whole memory. It began to grow and un-shatter the rest of me. Fragment by fragment, I came back together into solidity. When enough of my pieces had returned, I noticed – really noticed and remembered – that the Faye are not helpless, diminutive sweetlings, flitting around with Dragon-fly wings. These pictures and symbols are the stuff of Faery Tales – old wives' and old men's stories, first told to fill and delight the hearts of children and others gathered around their hearth Fires on cold or otherwise boring and empty evenings. But, because of the ways of Humans, down through the generations these stories have been believed and have hence become 'truth'. The real truth is that the Faye are mighty beings, who have retreated from this world of men to the realms of Spirit. They need not wings with which to fly. It is all a lie!

Perhaps truth, here in the Land of Naught, is not truth at all, but untruth and the crushed winged Ones were only the catalyst to reveal my deepest tendencies, flaws, and weaknesses: my empathy, my pity. Oh, not simply to the extent of Human kindness, of course, but to the shattering self-destructive extent – by which I have allowed myself and my life to be ruled. I have been found out and made to look into the face of my own un-doing.

So this was the Third Key: It reveals to its holder their deepest shadow selves – those traits that keep them off-kilter in this life. Knowledge is power. I can understand and so I can change. This Key was made of Tin.

But her name... I had raised the power to kill – or so my eyes had told me – by the use of her name. Yet, Morganna was named as a babe, after a gift of great value, a pearl. It had been given to her by a kind and wise man. He said it had come from his land of great Magics. But she had added 'Le Faye' to it...

I suppose that is why she always proclaimed or announced herself when she entered anywhere. We always thought it was a somewhat charming, supercilious self-aggrandizement, but she knew what she was doing. By adding the Gods' name – Le Faye – to hers, she was adding greater power to it.

Are the God's names, then, the Words of the Making and the Un-making?

I remembered too, that I never saw her, Day or Night, but that she was wearing that pearl, held by a ribbon around her neck. Never except for the last Night I had seen her alive. Then it had been around the neck of her daughter. I remember because it caught the glint of the Full Moon's light, when she had thrown back her hood at the Giant's Dance. So then, had Morganna thrown her Magic into this pearl and had it grown and grown with every breath she took and every step she made?

But what about the sound of the name of the pearl? What makes Words of the Making and of the Un-Making? Is it their meaning or their tone and vibrational value, as I had been taught?

So I dared it – I hollered, "The Pearl!" Nothing...

But then, a huge, deep rumbling voice sounded as if it came from within the endless Cavern's boulders themselves. The walls shook. Some of the Crystals and mineral cone-shaped columns were loosened and fell – upward. The voice shook my bones. My teeth were chattering. I held my mouth tightly closed so that they would not chip or break. I pressed my hands tightly to my eyes to relieve the pressure, but to no avail. I knew the massive voice was echoing within my very being.

"Do you toy with me? Calling me a pearl? Your impudence could cause me to stir and arise. Do you want me to begin the un-raveling of all that exists? Do you want to be the one who causes it, the one who says the word – the penultimate word of the Un-making?"

Was this the Fourth Key?

Intimidation! Feeling undue responsibility for causing another's actions. This had come along with my empathy, which I could now fight, for I had been given the Key of Understanding with which to Heal it. Now I must take this enlightenment one step farther – now that I knew how to use the Un-making – the Naught – to turn this pattern of claiming what is not mine aside.

I responded with courage – "I have not intoned the penultimate word of the Un-making. I have not disturbed the state of being or the function of this realm – this Land of Naught. I cause you to do nothing! Thank you for the Fourth Key – now let me pass your gate."

"Who demands passage?"

"I am Morgan of the Woods! Morgan of the Bees! Lady of the Lake!"

"Hmmm... All right. Pass, Lady of the Lake."

Realizing that he had only acknowledged one part of me – she who is Lady of the Lake – I responded... "I will only pass whole and restored. I claim all of who and what I am, I will let none intimidate, diminish, or demean me. I am Morgan of the Bees, Morgan of the Woods, as well as Lady of the Lake."

"Well... All right..."

The rumbling ceased and there, at my feet, lay the key. I was stronger – this Key was made of Iron...

As quickly as I noticed it, it vanished.

I took a breath and closed my eyes. Immediately my eyes were as though sewn shut. My hands and arms snapped to my sides, and my legs closed together. Feeling like an arrow shot from a high tension bow of Divine proportion in an arc through the Air, I felt motion and great, great speed – yet, no Wind. No resistance. My being was passing through total blackness. After what seemed like a long while, I felt as if I had been gently laid in a pool of Water, only a wand's length deep. I opened my eyes and then stood. I was on a shoreline, but in place of Sand, the beach was covered in Water. Then I heard a strange sound and looked toward where I thought to see Sea waves. Waves were coming to the shoreline, swelling, then cresting and rolling to the shore into nothingness as the undertow was drawing them back into "Sea." But the waves – they were sand. Quickly I looked up. Everything was upside down again. What should have been Sky was the surface of the Earth – with long tendrils of roots and soil hanging down from beneath it. My head spun. I looked far ahead to an endless Sea of sand – then side to side: an endless shore of Water. Frustrated, I spun around to look behind me.

Normality...

There in front of me was a beautiful Forest. I could hear the calls of

Birds, the rushing of Springs and Creeks, and the quiet creeping of small Animals. Then a solitary Butterfly, beautiful in her elegant midnight blue iridescent wings, approached me. She spoke: "Welcome, Morgan of the Woods. We have awaited you forever. Are we not beautiful in your sight?"

I looked at the fragrant blossoms of the Trees falling gently to the ground. The rays of Sunlight were filtering through the branches to form a dappled surface of light and shadows on the pathway at my feet.

"Yes," I said, "you are."

"Then follow me Morgan, into the 'Wood of Tranquility,' where you will learn that all is well and as it should be. Will you do this for me? For even though you know we live in the land of Naught, you will feel our beauty and the safety of our company."

In my own thoughts, I wisely repeated, "beautiful in your sight, all is well and as it should be..." knowing in my rational thoughts what you are, yet being deceived by your beauty and my desire to feel safe.

She laughed a laugh as enticing as a bubbling Spring.

"Why did she laugh?" thought I.

"I will tell you why" she answered. My thoughts hung written on the breeze before me, spelled out in ever-changing letters of many languages – sometimes even my own.

"You can hold no secrets from me," said she. "This, too, is the Magic of the land of Naught"

"I am not fooled! Your Magic has given to me the Fifth Key – the Key to resisting seduction and false security – the ability to recognize the turning of the Glamour inside out and being used for ill."

She withdrew from beneath her wing a tiny, brilliant Copper Key and tossed it toward me. It spun through the air, but just at the Time I was about to catch it, everything froze into stillness.

The Butterfly hung motionless before me. The leaves and branches stopped in half sway. The dappled light on the ground, which had been ever shifting, was now still. A silence had fallen over the Birds and creeping ones. The Glamour had faded...

I have not ever – EVER! – felt so alone and heavy. No! I must not change whilst here. But how does one not change with every new thought, experience and feeling? I became insecure with this realization.

"Doubt!" I said aloud.

"Yes, I am here. Who calls me? I looked before me to where had been the Wood of Tranquility. It was full dark now. An old hag stood bent before a foul smelling, bubbling cauldron seething with unthinkable things of evil.

"I asked you, who called me?" said the hag.

"I am Morgan, but I did not call you."

"Yes, you called 'Doubt,' and here I am."

"Why do you show yourself thusly? Why as a hag with a long crooked nose, pussy boils upon your face, and a green discharge oozing from the corners of your cloudy eyes? The skin rots on your hands as on a leper. I have always been taught to Love and respect the Grandmothers, yet now you appear to me as something vile and untouchable. I have ever only heard of one such as you from the repeatings of Saxon tales of horrors.

"Have I shaken your trust in what you hold as truth? Are you prejudiced by my appearance, Morgan of the Woods? Do you hold within you the potential for hatred of what is unfamiliar? You, who have always held yourself in such high esteem as a woman who holds no prejudice? Do you now doubt who you are and all you have believed and been taught? Ha ha ha!" She cackled. "Have I rocked you from your foundation – your stability? Does the Earth quake beneath your feet?"

I thought for a moment and then answered: "Doubt! Doubt is the great distracter. Doubt kills Magic. Even if you doubt for only a moment, it is long enough to take away the Magic you hold in your hands. Doubt kills Trust and without trust, Love dies too."

"Ha ha ha! Banishing Doubt is the Sixth Key," she declared. "The Sixth Key!" And as she vanished, a great slimy bubble was spat forth from the cauldron. Captured within it was a finely wrought Silver Key. It was mine, but I dared not touch it... The bubble popped and all was gone. Illusion... perception... – such is the stuff of our doubts and prejudices.

With no warning a hole opened beneath my feet. I was swallowed by it. Deeper and deeper I fell, sometimes sliding within the narrow opening this way and that. It curved and turned – the roots and tendrils jutting through the walls tore at my hair and clothing as I bounced about down the passage. Finally I hit the bottom.

I found myself standing in an ancient, twilit Wood.

Before me stood the seventh gate, but this Time it was an actual gate. Wrought iron, gold and silver was it, with massive, beautifully turned ornamental designs. It loomed tall as an Oak Tree. The mighty beams that enclosed the doors of the gate were enormously thick and appeared to be covered in solid gold. Their simplicity contrasted the ornateness of the vertical bars of the doors and the whole was utterly pleasing in its artfulness. There, in the center of the gate – upon the doors, at just about my eye level – was a bold square of polished gold split in two vertically. In its center was a Silver Star with an Enchanting keyhole in it. Written upon the lintel, above the doors, in an unknown script, which somehow I was able to decipher, were the words: "All who would enter this gateway must solve The Riddle."

"You jest." Thought I, "This is ridiculous..."

"What riddle?" I said out loud with some irritation in my voice.

"Why, the Riddle of the Ages, my girl."

I started. It was The Merlin's voice. I spun around searching, but no one was there.

"Riddle of the Ages? Which one? There are so many. Perhaps the riddle is just that – to know which one to solve? The Riddle of the Ages... let me think.

"It would be the one The great Merlin was set to by the Voices of the Stars: 'What would there be if there were nothing?'" quoth I.

"No," said the voice of a woman of strict authority. "You have been taught the answer to that riddle by The Merlin. It is no longer a riddle to you."

It was Vivianne's voice.

"Oh, how I have missed you, my Lady!" said I.

"You must think hard, my Morgan of the Woods."

"Mother, Mother!" I cried. "I thought never to hear your voice again. I Love you, Mother!"

"If the answer were a Viper, you would be struck, Morgan" laughed Nimue.

"Wait – this is all deception – I know it is... It must be. All of you whom I have Loved are gone from me and beside that, you would not be *here* in the Land of Naught! Do I only hear your voices because I long to hear them? Am I ignoring the truth because of my desire?"

"Yes, desire..." said The Merlin.

"Obtain one more Key and you can return to the land of form, if that is what you wish to do."

This Time the voice was attached to a tall and straight young man walking toward me from a distance, but behind the golden gates. Arthur... Bear... Now I could see his brilliant smile, his golden hair and his teasing blue eyes. He walked to just beyond an arm's length from me on the other side of the gate. I reached through it for him, but he stepped back.

"Morgan, my beloved, behold: the Seventh Key."

He held in his hand an actual Golden Key.

"Morgan, when you attain this Key, you will hold the powers of Naught. But this Key is real... If you wish, it can be yours forever."

"At this Time you may choose to stay here with me, where we will not die, we will not grow old and we will be un-made brother and sister. Does not the desire of your heart lead you to me?"

I looked at him hesitantly...

"But Arthur, my Bear, you hold a key in form. The other six have been Keys of the Magic of the Land of Naught. I was not meant to stay here."

"Has your Love for me died, then, Morgan?"

"My Love... died?

"That is it! That is the answer to the Riddle of the Ages."

Gwyddion had once asked – "Where does Love go when it dies?"

I shouted! "The answer is – It does *not*! Love never dies!"

The gates opened toward me. I stepped inside. Arthur held the golden Key in his hand.

"Take it my Love, you know your desire."

With each step closer toward him, he receded and I began to forget where I was and why.

When my own desire had thoroughly Enchanted me, I reached for the Golden Key and for Arthur.

Just then – incomprehensible wonder of wonders and blessing of blessings – I heard them... the Voices of the Stars. They whispered into my thoughts, heart and Spirit...

"Morgan, daughter of the Goddess, you must not accept this golden Key. If you do, you will effect a change here in the Land of Naught. The only Keys you must receive are the Seven Keys of understanding. The Golden Key must remain here. It is a thing of Naught."

"I had forgotten..." I answered.

"But wait, how do I know that you are not also aspects of my own desire? How can I be sure of anything anymore?"

They chuckled – a coarse, yet Divinely beautiful amusement.

"Morgan, Lady of the Lake, you have found the true seventh and last Key."

More exquisite laughter...

"The truth is always there for truth seekers. You know the truth when you hear it and when you see it. Only your desires can keep the truth from you. Hold to the truth always, Morgan, even when you desire the lie...

"This is how Morganna held power over others. This is how she even fooled Igraine, to some extent. This is how Gorlois was beguiled by her. This is how she held her children and others captive. This is why Arthur believed she was you on the Night of his coronation celebration – and that you would lie with him again. Each of these ones accepted her lies – because Morganna used their own desires to wish these lies the truth.

"This power lies in the very roots of the Land of Naught. It is fed by the wisher's desire for an un-reality – holding to the lie as being more desirable than their truth.

"There is one more thing that you must understand. It is concerning the answer to the Riddle: 'Love never dies'... You have learned and understand that every thought, word and deed, *becomes a fiber of the Weavers' web* – a permanent part of the whole of our lives – a piece of the Cosmos. Yet of all things that will return to the MOTHER at the

Time of the great dissolution; Love, which is the reason – the impetus – for HER Creation of *any* Universal epoch – must return to HER intact. As such, it is the only force, of the *Infinite Potential* SHE holds, which must repeat into the next Universal Creation. Without Love, SHE would have no need or desire to create. Therefore, Love is the only thing of eternal existence – Love never dies.

"But you see, Morganna knew not the ways of Love, and therefore could not attain the seventh key, so that those gates would not open to her."

As the specter claiming to be Arthur said: "At this Time you may choose to stay here..." What it did NOT say was that one can also choose NOT to stay here. Upon solving the riddle, one can choose to go home. Morganna never solved the Riddle and her Spirit was thus stuck in the land of Naught. Living in the duality of the Land of Naught and the world of form drove her to madness.

"Come home now, Morgan."

"But how?"

"Accept this true Seventh Key of Knowledge and you will be home."

"But wait – how can you be here in the Land of Naught?"

More delightful chuckles...

"We are all One, Morgan. We are all ONE."

I repeated their words as a Chant.

"We are all ONE... We are all ONE... We are all ONE..."

My fingers began to hurt as I was grasping the Well so intently. I smelled the fresh clean Water. It sprayed upon me as it splashed against the Rocks.

I was home.

I also held within myself the Seven Keys of the un-raveling of the Human psyche – each Key being like unto the tip of what the Northmen call an Ice-berg – an Ice Mountain – with so much more below the surface than that which is seen. Now I understood the source and the ways of Morganna's Magic. Now I could un-ravel it!

The Seven Keys – To overcome the state and predicament of Naught...

The First Key – Oblivion of the self. Resist oblivion – let no one change or diminish *who* or *what* you know yourself to be.

The Second Key – Fear... Fear is the destroyer – recognize the game that is being played and overcome it.

The Third Key – Knowing the Shadow Self ... Claiming our hidden, inner tendencies in order to understand and overcome them. In my life, this has been my self-destructive empathy.

The Fourth Key – Intimidation... Be unyielding to it. Become the powerful one.

The Fifth Key – Seduction... False security – lying to ourselves – it is the Glamour turned inside out and used for ill.

The Sixth Key – Doubt... Foil self doubt – for it kills your Magic and sets your life upon a stage of failure.

The Seventh Key – Obsession versus Truth... Seeing things as they truly are – not as we *desire* them to be.

Now armed with these Seven Keys of the gates of the Land of Naught, I understood from whence Morganna's Magic had come – the *other side of the mirror*. It was twisted and bent toward the un-doing of all. Woven within the cloak she had mantled her daughter with was the tale of Morganna's evil intent and doings. Now I could read it. Her story began to unfold to me like the peeling of an onion.

Chapter 45
Morganna Un- raveled

Morgan

You see – through our Father, Gorlois, and after Ambrosius Aurillious and his brother Uther – Morganna had a blood-right of sorts to become a Queen.

Then Arthur had come along and eventually became High King.

Now, Morganna was always one to secure her bets. So she conceived the plan to trick Arthur into bedding her and getting her with child. This she accomplished. Mordred was born of this making and she raised him to hate his Father, telling him every foul lie that she could about Arthur. Mordred was to kill his Father to become High King in his stead.

But, when all her plans seemed to be coming to fruition and the battle lines had been drawn in the dirt, so to speak, something changed. She then "saw" that Mordred was, at the last moment, weakening in his conviction to kill his Father. Morganna saw that as treachery and disloyalty to her. Or, perhaps she simply realised that Arthur was a hard foe to beat and that Mordred might fail. For, although she had "seen" Arthur fall at his hands, she knew that "the Sight" is not perfect. Whatever her reasons, upon the Night before the last battle Morganna drugged and Spelled Mordred into lying with her. From this unholy coupling her belly had once again become filled.

When Mordred died in the final battle, Morganna grieved excessively and she fled North to the Snowy Mountain of the Clans. There she saw a strongly built house which was pleasing to her, so she conjured upon the house and family which therein lived a great Charm of invisibility and forgetfulness so that no one passing should ever see it again. And what is more, with her Spells and Incantations, all that ever existed of the house, family, and Animals that therein lived was forgotten by any who had ever known them. Further, if a hunter or a wanderer should, by chance, happen upon the house and walk into it, he would immediately forget that it had happened. That family and their Animals Morganna turned into her servants. And there, Morganna grieved – and waited.

As for the family living within the Enchanted farmstead – they forgot that their lives had ever been anything other than what they had become.

Morganna's plans for the fruit of her belly, her daughter Morganna, had been bound up in the truth that her blood contained all the royal bloodlines of these Isles, going back to Macsen Wledig, old King Hen Coel, and Yosef of Arimathea, or perhaps better yet to Yeshua the Jewish King and Christian God. I knew my sister's way of thinking... That tasty morsel would nullify and overcome, or at least smooth over, the concerns about the incestuous part in all of this. Of this she was convinced. But, even Morganna had to know that incest was a strictly and severely forbidden practice amoung the Christians.

Morganna determined to proclaim her daughter to the world as Arthur's granddaughter, through their son Mordred. She would win, regardless of the outcome. Then something had changed in Morganna's thinking. Had her madness finally completely overtaken her?

My niece Morganna had been born and raised in that house while it was under this Spell of forgetfulness and would never have questioned the lack of any outsiders in their lives. All must have seemed well and normal to her. When the Time had come to leave the house, perhaps she thought that she was indeed Morganna Le Faye, herself. Or perhaps her Mother had simply held her body and Spirit so captive for all of her life that she could do naught but do her bidding. My niece's glassy eyes told me as much at the Giant's Dance upon the Night of her Mother's Death and of the girl's vanishing, alone, into the darkness.

I greatly feared for my niece's welfare. If she was found out to be the daughter of the "Black Sorceress of Old" – as Morganna's legends had named her of late – she would be persecuted from coast to coast upon these Our Fair Isles. Her life would be worth little.

So, my searchers were set to a new task – to find the house that Morganna had Magicked into invisibility and forgetfulness. Out they travelled searching for word of strange tales of disappearing houses, people and the like.

At length, rumours led them to the family of the house that had disappeared. The folks who lived there told that one Night, they went to sleep and all was well, but when they awoke with the Dawn, the young couple they had been were old, bent, and gray. Their children were all grown up and their beloved Animals were gone. They held no memory of the nearly twenty years that had passed and no memory at all of Morganna Le Faye, or her daughter. All they knew and believed was that most of their lives had been lost in one Night's sleep. The searchers asked if they had Dreamt, but they answered "no." That long Night had been completely blank. The family asked if the searchers knew what had happened, but I had given strict instructions that the matter not be revealed.

I had sent gold to them through my searchers.

But gold cannot buy back twenty years of our lives nor missing the Love of our Animals nor missing seeing our children grow. It cannot buy back childhood memories of the adult strangers who are our children.

But gold and a blessing were all I could give – along with my sincere sympathies.

So, it was confirmed, that upon Morganna's Death, her Spells of forgetfulness and invisibility had un-raveled and reversed.

Chapter 46

The Complete Memoirs
of Morganna Le Faye

Morgan

I had arrived as quickly as I could. I went to speak with these poor folk. I asked if I might look around. They graciously allowed it. I found an old cupboard that they said had appeared in the morning of their awakening. They feared to open it or even touch it themselves as they feared that it was Black Magic. I asked if I might open it. They agreed.

What I found inside shocks me even now. In a secret compartment, I found a trick door that popped open at my command. In it, there lay scrolls, tied together neatly with red silk ribbons. I opened the bundle with trembling hands. It was entitled:

"The True and Complete Memoirs of Morganna Le Faye..."

With lavish strokes of quill and fanciful adornment of Magical symbols, of Animals, and dark and fearful portraits of things unspeakable – in Morganna Le Faye's own hand – was the true and full story of things she had withheld from me. Had she written it in her demented state merely for the pleasure of re-living it? More likely for the joy of thinking that I might find it one Day. I can imagine how she would relish shocking me.

Most of it was illegible. There were many pages rolled up in the scroll. Some were torn, smeared, or chewed away by rodents and other vermin, but then were followed by some which could be read – at least a word here and there. By some strangeness, a few pages, not far from the end, were readable – as if she taunted me from the land of the wicked dead.

These words were concerning the Night upon which my Father's pyre burned so hot and brightly – the Night upon which Arthur was conceived.

I thought just to burn it unread, but my curiosity would not allow that... for I noticed that this was a much longer version of those events than the one she had 'left' for my finding so many years ago.

Oh yes... my curiosity has led me into mischief and trouble all my life. I reasoned: What more could I hear, what could be worse than all that I already know of Morganna? So, I read it...

"I stealthily crossed the corridor to the steep winding stairwell, up and up, narrow and darksome was it. As quietly as a Fawn in the Wood did I go to my Mother's chambers. I hid myself behind a tapestry-covered wall, leading into her most private sanctuary. Her bed, it was lit by two small oil lamps. The chamber was just light enough for me to see all.

Finally! To see Igraine so disgraced and powerless – the Mother who Loved me less than her precious baby, Morgan, as soon as her precious baby was born. Did she ever Love me at all? I hated her!

Yet, as I watched her, so beautiful and desirable was she that I became short of breath and very aroused. I rubbed myself on the nub of pleasure between my legs in rhythm with Uther's thrusting and grunting. I have always been a good imaginer; it has done me well, and brought much profit and gain my way. Some would call it fantasizing, but do I not live in the realm of phantoms. All is real to me. That Night I shared the lust of Uther for Igraine, my Mother. I imagined squeezing her full breasts in my hands and sinking my teeth into her shoulders and neck... On and on did Uther thrust his thick phallus into her, turning her this way and that.

Had her body betrayed her? For as he came to his climax, she too arched her back and groaned through clenched teeth. My body quaked as well, over and over. Five or six Times I brought myself to rapture. I sucked on my fingers to taste the slimy cum. Finally, I had tasted of my Mother's Well...

Ever since that Night, it has always been the vision of my bitch Mother Igraine's body quaking over Uther that has enflamed my lusts. I offer no apologies for my luscious depravities. Men, women, children and even a few beasts – it mattered not to me – have I seduced into hours of sensual pleasures."

The next few pages disintegrated when I touched them... Her writing became legible again several pages after:

"...Days came to an end. When my son Mordred was to be born, I summoned a local Midwife. I would not trust her to pour safe wine to dull my pains, so I mixed my own posset and drank it before she touched me. I threatened her on pain of her life, that if anything go wrong, I would kill her myself. She looked terrified and began to leave, but I then continued – 'However, if you do your part very well, I will give to you gold, enough to build a new house and barn.'

She stayed...

My pains were hard and long – too long. Something was amiss! Finally, the woman said; 'Here it comes, but feet first. Push harder!'

'I am pushing, you idiot!'

Of a sudden, I thought my back would break. I felt a sliding... Then I heard a cry.

'Is it a boy?'

'No, my Lady, she's a girl.

I kicked her.

'What do you mean, a girl? I have *seen* my son in Visions.

I gasped... The hard pains were building again.

'Oh, my Lady, here comes another...

I could barely catch my breath. The pains were fast and furious. I felt a searing pain and a tearing. I waited to hear my son's cry...

'Oh, Gods! He is... He is a... His limbs are not right.'

Before I had Time to comprehend her meaning I felt a sliding again, along with the most pain I have ever experienced in my life.

'Am I going to die?'

Then I heard all three crying.

'No my Lady,' she smiled, 'you are going to raise three babes. The bleeding will stop soon and you will be alright. Just rest now while I sever the cords. Then I will clean the babies and wrap them in swaddling cloths.'

I did and she did.

An hour or two later I awoke. The woman was still there, kneeling on the floor beside the pallet she had made for the babies. She was humming a tune to them. Had I heard that tune somewhere before?

'Here, let me see them.' I began to get up. But sounding alarmed she said:

'No, my Lady – rest there – I will bring them to you.'

I looked first at the girl. She was small and dark. Her skin was all wrinkled and ugly. She looked like Morgan had when she was born. What need had I for a girl? Next she showed the last born, the fine looking boy I had seen in my Visions. His skin was fair but his hair was a reddish brown. I suppose I said it aloud: 'No, he has to have golden hair.'

She chuckled, 'Oh my Lady, babies are not born with the colour of hair – or eyes neither – that they will have later.'

Then she hesitated...

'Here is the first boy.'

She placed the bundle in my arms and then stepped away. It was a horror. Even its head was bent and twisted... Yet, it lived.

'Take it away. Go now and drown it in the creek!'

'But...'

'Do not "but" me! Take it away from my sight!'

She began to refuse. I got up from the bed, walked over to the central hearth Fire, picked the poking stick up, turned and stabbed her in the neck. All this so smoothly that she seemed not to realise what I was doing. She let out a blood-curdling scream. I stabbed her again and again, until my strength gave out. I could leave no one to tell that I, Morganna Le Faye, had given birth to a distorted monster.

My stable boy ran into my cottage.

'Are you alright? Oh! What has happened?'

Then he noted that I was naked, with only a woven cloth covering me and that I had delivered a child. It was well known, even by stable boys, that the birthing room was no place for a man. He just stared at me – not knowing what to do...

I yelled – 'Quickly, take this loathsome woman from my sight! She went to steal my baby and when I objected, she tried to kill me. But I got the better of her. Now I will be accused of murder!'

'No, my Lady Morganna, I will protect your name! Here, let me bury her now, behind the field of Barley. I will pile Rocks upon her grave so that none will know she be there.'

'Yes, yes, quickly! And never a word of this to anyone.'

'Of course...'

I knew that I would have to kill him too.

I looked at the three babies and then looked to see if anyone else was about. There was not. So I wrapped the twisted thing in a blanket, thinking to run with him to the swiftly flowing, deep creek nearby and there to drown and float him downstream.

I had kept myself hidden past the Time that my belly got too big to hide the fact that I was pregnant, so no one would suspect me.

My plan had been to disappear from this place, with my son, as soon as I could after the birthing. Then it occurred to me that travelling with two babies would be very difficult. Could I find a wet nurse with enough milk to keep my son strong *and* feed the girl? ...the girl that I had no need for and did not want, anyway? Certainly, I could not bring two nurses along with me. So, I determined to take the little, red faced, crying girl to the Creek as well – but she would not be quiet. I put my hand over her mouth but that did little good – she cried louder. So I strangled her. Then she was quiet.

That seemed to me a more efficient way of handling this problem, so I strangled the crippled thing as well. It was easier going from then on.

I laid the still bundles to the side, washed and dressed myself in a plain cloak, pulling the hood far forward over my head – just in the event that someone meet me on the path to the Stream and recognize me.

I had to leave Mordred – for that is what I named Arthur's son – by himself. I dared not leave him with my third beloved Wildcat, Terror, for he was past seventeen years old and almost completely blind. I feared that he might kill the child. So I led him along with me to the Creek. I would have to watch Terror carefully from then on.

On my way back was the cottage of a young woman who had given birth to a boy two years before. I stopped there and asked her to travel with me, as Mordred's wet nurse, to Lesser Briton, where I had land holdings. She – who had no possibility of ever being offered a fine life by anyone other than me – delightedly accepted. I instructed her to be ready in a week.

I knew that I must wait-and-see how it would be travelling with two children. But there was no other way – for to become a wet nurse, a woman must already be nursing a child.

As to the Stable boy, in the end I decided to bring him along instead of killing him. He was, after all, handsome and could prove to provide some pleasurable distraction along the way. Besides, he was obviously smitten with infatuation for me and would probable protect me with his life if that were what it would take.

Now I had my son – the Britons' next High King! I had been a very clever girl again..."

She signed it with lavish strokes – Morganna Le Faye

Morgan's Note...

I think that my hand might have been led by the Spirits to find these scrolls in that secret cupboard. For, if ever I had felt and allowed my empathy of my 'poor, demented sister's plight' to soften my anger toward her memory, this scroll was to prove to be the undoing of that possibility!

No one but me has ever known of its existence, yet now – with this copying of it – it has become part of my histories. No other lasting trace of her warped thinking and Visions of grandeur remain – or so do I fervently pray to the Goddess.

Morganna, wherever you are, do you just hate that?

Chapter 47
What of Morganna's Daughter?

Morgan

So it was that all of my suspicions of the nature of the inside-out Magics of the Land of Naught were confirmed. Upon Morganna's Death, her Spells of forgetfulness and invisibility had un-wound. The house that had been unseen was now visible, and what is more, the folk who had lived in it with Morganna, upon her Death, forgot all that had been.

But what of Morganna's daughter?

She was born within these Spells and lived her whole life under them until the Night of her Mother's Death. Thinking of all I had learned in my journey to the Land of Naught, I was convinced that my niece, Morganna, had no memories at all. In this I was to be proven correct – yet, that left unexplained why her Magic remained in the Cloak, for it truly had been bound in the Land of Naught.

It took more and more Time to find the old man of the village and, as with the Merchants, he was afraid and hesitant to speak of the girl, but finally, with his heart softened and his purse filled with gold, he relented.

"I cared for the girl, I did – like a daughter. At first it was only I needed help, an' she needed food an' a roof over 'er head, but then she was a kind girl with a sweet smile an' way about her. I felt sorry she could remember nay a thing. I thought sure she was a fine Lady, but what could I do? So when the rich man came and wanted to take 'er, I thought it would be best, for 'er, I mean. It was nay only for the coin I let 'er go, but then what could I have done to stop him anyway? Please, if you see the girl, tell 'er I cared about 'er."

The searchers said that they would.

I sent to him some Carpenters and Thatchers to keep his hut from falling in upon him and to keep him dry. I also sent two Goats, some Chickens, a work Horse, a plow and a wagon. From the Order's stocks I sent honey, Grain, mead, and a heavy woolen blanket with my thanks. Oh, yes, and great bales of fleabane for to scatter upon his dirt floor and the outside of his doorway – this done, of course, once the workmen had cleared out the old infested straw. I also sent some living plants and seeds from our gardens, so that he could plant a garden of his own. My guess is that that was the gift he appreciated most.

There was one more thing that he had asked of me; this was to have someone bury him near to his wife and son, whenever he died and to have a simple marker of some kind for all three of them. He had never been able to place one for his wife or son. For that, he said, he still grieved. Of course I agreed and would see it done when that Time came.

I felt so rewarded. We were getting close – very close.

While awaiting further word, I visited my kin deep in the Wood of the twisted old Trees and the Sacred Caves and rocky shorelines of the Western Sea.

I had come to ask when and why my Mother Igraine had had the two circling black Snakes tattooed upon her hands – for only some of their layers of symbolism had been revealed to me when I had received them upon ankles at my Enchantress initiation. Even as I became a Wise Mother and then one of the council of The Nine spiritual leaders of the Order, even as I became Lady of the Lake, I had yet to be taught the full depth of their Mystery. However, when I traversed the perils of the Land of Naught, I began to become more enlightened as to their meaning.

I was brought into the presence of the eldest Tribal Grandmother, and, after the expected greetings and words of salutation, she took my hands, looked at me and asked:

"So you have been there, too? You have earned the Seven Keys?"

I smiled. "Yes, I have." She smiled back.

"Then you now truly 'understand' the outside and the in, the making and the breaking, the fullness and naught..."

The seven of my kin sitting around the central hearth Fire repeated: "We understand."

No further explanation was expected or given.

A man of years beyond counting, perhaps one hundred – or one hundred and ten – took what looked to be ancient, but clean, tools used for tattooing out of a crude but elaborately painted rolled sack.

I sat upon a pile of dried leaves, which covered a log on the ground and laid the back of my hands across an Altar Stone, where he punched the black dye, one strike at a Time, into the palms of my hands. Of course I had been given a Mushroom to eat aforetime, to somewhat numb my sense of the pain. When he was finished, an hour later, the

Serpents were seamless, pristine, perfect, and almost alive. One circled Sunwise and the other contrary to the course of the Sun. Never in my life have I been so thrilled to receive a gift as I was then.

"Thank you, Grandfather."

I kissed the old man in the manner of Tribal custom. May I gift you in return?

"I need nothing."

His answer was traditional, but it was also tradition to give an exchange of energy. I removed a silver band from my finger...

"May this always keep us close, Grandfather."

He nodded his head, accepted the gift, and walked away. Now I was prepared for whatever lay ahead.

What a rich journey is life! Just when I had thought that mine had settled into monotonous duty, with a simple joy here and there, I find myself on an adventurous quest to find and save my beautiful niece.

"Be careful Morgan, be careful Morgan..." the Voices whispered.

It did not take long after that to find Morganna's daughter. There were not as many wealthy, finely dressed men in the environs of the West as had there been in Roman Times. There were only a few great fortresses left by that Time. One of them was the fortress that The Merlin had designed and overseen the building of – which had once been Vortigern's and then Princess Rowena's.

The Weavers are ever surprising. After questioning villagers and other farm folk, we heard of the beautiful dark bride – of six years now – of Rhodri, the former husband of Ribrowst, Princess Rowena's daughter.

"She came to him a head empty of memory. She was from the Old Dark Tribes, like you My Lady... Eyes like pools of black Water. She must be filled with the Magics – I thought when I first saw her. But she is a good Christian now. She is just a sweet thing, a good wife and Mother."

"Mother?" I questioned.

"Why yes, a daughter, must be past five year-turns by now."

"A daughter!"

My stomach was churning, as though a hive of my Bees was in it. Would my old age be blessed not only by a niece, but a child of my family? A girl child! I, who had never had children and therefore never had grandchildren... I had to be calm, to make myself remember that things may not come out the way I wish for them to.

Their introduction to me must be handled very cautiously. What reason would I state for my visit? I dared not mention Morganna, though surely everyone still remembered that I was her sister. Did Rhodri know who his wife was? He was, after all, a Christian.

Finally I settled on a small deception of sorts. I would not allow him Time to make an excuse, so I simply showed up at his fortress and begged admittance, on the merits of my having been very close to Princess Rowena as well as to The great Merlin, who had designed this wonder-filled place. I had instructed my messenger to say: "Lady Morgan, Lady of the Lake, would be very happy to be within its walls once more. She would also be grateful to meet Lord Rhodri and his sons – Princess Rowena's grandsons." It would have been a disgraceful discourtesy to refuse the Lady of the Lake, even though he had left the Old Ways to become a Christian, for the Order still held great political sway.

Rhodri – charmer that he was – and I mean that in the way of his good looks and charismatic veneer – opened the great gates. My company and I were welcomed with pomp. I was in.

How beautiful it was. I stood in the great hall taking in the spectacular architectural feat, which had been embellished by all the graciousness and style of Princess Rowena.

My thoughts travelled backwards to when our world was fresh and new – to the Days of Arthur's crowning. How beautiful and intelligent Rowena had been as she offered "The Golden Chalice" of her sister Gwenyfar to Arthur. How young we were and how innocent. But it was not only Princess Rowena's ghost who haunted my heart regarding the perfection and grandeur of that Night so long ago and the spectacle of Arthur's crowning...

My thoughts flew to the Night of Arthur's wedding Gwenyfar. That splendidly arranged event had taken place in another great hall – that of my dear Mother, Igraine, in Dumnonia. Did I feel her hand caress my hair? "Oh, Mother – no girl could have ever been blessed more than I. You showed your Love for me in every way. I still miss you so..."

Rhodri was speaking... "Lady Morgan, would you not sit by our great hearth and warm yourself from your travels? Here, my servant girl has brought Apples, Nuts, and warm spiced wine for you."

"Oh, I am sorry; I did not mean to ignore your warm greetings. I was just deep in thought of the long-ago past. Yes, that would be nice.

"I have heard, of course, that you have remarried after all these years and am glad for you. I remember Ribrowst as a precious and intelligent golden haired young woman. Such a beauty was she. I was very sorry for your loss when I heard of her fatal accident. But let us not dwell upon sad events. I look forward to meeting your new Lady wife."

"Yes," replied Rhodri, "she will come down soon. She sings our daughter to sleep each Night."

"How Enchanting," said I, "I mean lovely... Will your sons be here in the next few Days, Rhodri?"

"Gildas, my youngest, lives at a Monastic settlement to the South of Gwynedd, in the Monastery of Llan-Illtud, where he is being taught by the revered Monk and Wise Man named Hildutus – in Latin – or Illtud in our tongue. When Gildas finishes his studies there, he will be a Teacher and Cleric."

This, he said with great pride.

"I am not sure that he will be able to come.

"My second youngest is also a Monk. He lives nearby with our friend, the Bishop.

He spends his life in prayer and duty to the Church."

"My oldest son is hunting with his friends. If he does well, we will feast on fresh Boar or venison whilst you and your company are here. The hunting is good now that the leaves are falling and it is cooler."

I could read his lying eyes. I had also sent spies to learn all about Rhodri and his sons. Things were not as neatly bundled and honourably set as Rhodri would have me think. Everything I had found named Rhodri and both of his older sons as greedy, disreputable, and dangerous men. I had heard little of his youngest.

I drifted inside my thoughts again... "Yes, the Ancestors Feast will soon be upon us – the Time of Red and Gold Leaves, when the veil between the worlds is thin. It is less than one Moon's Dance until this year's cycle ends. I must be back home by then. So little Time... Already I feel that that Time is coming upon us as strongly as if waxing into a Full Moon. But the undertow pulls us down. Our Ancestors call. Our Loved ones intrude into our thoughts unbidden. Poor Ribrowst..."

An unsettling feeling came upon me – Morganna's daughter was near... I became agitated and worried. Will she know who I am?

Just then, Rhodri's wife entered the hall. There she stood. A more rounded beauty than the angular girl with haunted eyes I had met on the plain of the Giant's Dance. It was a woman who stood before me now – a well-satisfied and contented woman. She smiled.

"Hello Lady Morgan, I am so pleased you came to visit. My name is Mahr. It is so seldom we have visitors here. Perhaps you will share news or even old stories of the world around us?"

"Of course, if you would like that."

"I would like it very much."

So, there I was – finding myself in the midst of one of those "Golden Chances" that Gwyddion had often spoken of. It was my intention not to let it slip away. And so, Mahr and I did talk of news and of the glory Days of the Confederacy – of The Merlin, Arthur, Bedwyr, Lucian, Nimue, Igraine and, of course, Princess Rowena. I was careful to never mention Morganna. But then the inevitable happened.

Now, I was many years old at that Time, however I had kept my beauty – as far as anyone could at my age. The point being that I was still recognizable as myself. Although my skin was wrinkled and somewhat sagging, the features and shape of my face had not changed, as usually they do when youth becomes a long ago and far off memory. It was inevitable that Mahr recognized the resemblance between herself and me. I believe she thought that I may be her own Mother. I hated to deceive her so, although now looking back on events, I wish with all my heart that I had continued just that. Of course she told me of the loss of her memory. I divulged nothing.

She told that Rhodri's and her daughter had been named Rowena, in honour of Princess Rowena – "although she has no Saxon blood in her."

I knew of Princess Rowena's written legacy and its turns, but what I could not figure out was why. What did she care for Rodri's daughter, a child she would never meet, not at least on this side of the veil? But Rowena had never done anything without reason or plan. I knew that she had always disliked Rhodri – hated him even. She suspected him of causing Ribrowst's fatal injury. I wondered if that was so. Yet, Rhodri seemed happy with Mahr and she with him. I just wondered...

Chapter 48
Rowena

Morgan

Finally, upon the next Day, when I met my great niece Rowena, I saw that the child did not look the same as Morganna, Igraine, Mahr, and myself. She was tall for her age and her skin was fair as her Father's, not dark as ours. She had a look of the Clanswomen in some of her facial features. But her hair was black as a Raven's wing, as were her eyes. She had a strange beauty about her. She was a very unusual looking girl. She would be silent and intent, then upon the next moment she might burst out in childish laughter. She had an affectionate manner, which captured my heart. I could see her colours – they were beautiful!

"Rowena..."

I caressed her cheek and felt the Magic she was keeping to herself. A child of Secrets then...

Dare I hope that she was the Magic Child – the Child of Promise? Could she really be the one... the one I was waiting for?

She embraced a friendship with me as if she had known me for all of her life. Whenever we were alone together she would cautiously and calculatingly ask questions of the Isle of Apples – and of Magic. Oh, she tried not to let me know what she was doing, but she *was* only five years old.

She told me that she could read a little, but that someday she would read and write in Greek, Latin, and Cymric.

"My brother Gildas has promised to teach me. However there are no books in my Father's house except for the ones that Princess Rowena had owned, but he has locked them all away. I believe he would burn them but for their great value."

Rhodri was not a man to waste gold.

Four Days I had to spend with them... only four Days.

Of my first visit with Mahr, what more can I say? She was docile, sweet natured, and thoroughly in Love with Rhodri, but I could sense a hidden strength somewhere within her. What could I do for her? Did she even need my meddling? I wanted so badly to tell her who she really was, but to what avail – to what good cause? If Rhodri knew, he would despise her. He was a very superstitious man and he placed great value on his social standing with the Bishop and Clan leaders in his area. I believed he would be ashamed of this dark haired, dark skinned beauty of his if he or anyone else knew that she was the daughter of Morganna Le Faye. It was plain that he thought of her as a possession, a prize. His possession would be tarnished if anyone knew of her true parentage. Of all this I was sure.

Pride was a powerful force in Rhodri. When he had shown up with and married this much younger and exotic beauty, all the men around had him held a degree of envy toward him.

I had learned – during that visit – that one of the more powerful Clans' Chieftains had actually shown up two Days before Mahr and Rhodri's wedding, with a war party, to storm Rowena's fortress so as to steal Mahr, but that his efforts were to no avail. The Merlin had built this fortress to be impregnable, and so it was. The would-be kidnappers lost ten of their fourteen men, including their leader. Rhodri had the man's head piked and on display above the entrance battlements. I am sure that this was quite a gruesome welcome to the wedding guests. Rhodri still boasted of it and there it still was; a skull bleached white by the Sun. It had been there now for over six years. I wondered what Mahr had thought of this – she having no memory or knowledge of the wretchedness of man.

I, of course, do not exempt women from brutality or treachery. There was nothing lacking from *my* memories. It is just another one of those Human foibles.

Cruelty is not seen amoung the beasts. Healthy Animals kill only for food or to protect themselves and their young, but there is no premeditated, malicious intent in their actions. Even Cats, who *play* with their prey before killing them, do not seem to kill for sadistic pleasure. They live within the cycles of life, according to their natures. No, cruelty is only known amoung Humankind, only they take their delight in the agony and fears of others – sometimes for the sake of amusement or entertainment. Just look at the Romans and their gladiatorial theaters, teaching their young ones to laugh and feel joy in the tearing apart of other Humans by wild, starving, and tormented beasts or in the games of men and women fighting to the Death for purse or fame. Those were family outings!

Being as well educated as I am, I have heard of the writings of a self-righteous Caesar named Julius, who "shocked" his fellow Romans with stories of the Gaul's Human sacrifices! Hypocrite! Hypocrisy, too, is also only a Human trait. Of all these things, I am well aware. But Mahr was an innocent. So my Days went by, leaving her in her blessed ignorance.

I offered to Rhodri that I would be happy to sponsor a scribal tutor to teach Rowena to read and write, until her brother had finished his studies, as this was her wish. I offered, but Rhodri flatly and blankly refused.

"Why should she read and write? To what purpose? She is a girl. No, thank you, Lady Morgan."

And that was that.

When I was leaving, it was Rowena who ran out and across the entrance bridge to say one last farewell to me, or so was her guise. She climbed into my wagon where we were alone and out of range of all hearing ears.

"Lady Morgan, my Mother asked if you were her Mother. You look so alike. Is it true? Are you?"

"I am not."

"But she did not ask if you were her aunt..." said Rowena.

I froze. I thought quickly – "Are you asking me this, Rowena?"

She just looked at me intently, never losing eye contact. I answered her questioning eyes:

"Many people of the Old Tribes' blood resemble one another, as do your Mother and I."

Again, she sat still and stared at me, never backing down. Silence... Then, as though she had Timed it perfectly for effect, she said, "I mean no impudence, my Lady, but you have not answered. I *am* asking. Is my Mother the daughter of Morganna Le Faye, the black Sorceress of old? Your sister..."

How articulate she was! And only five and a half years old...

"Whatever would make you think so, child?"

"They told me."

"Who?" I asked.

"The Voices who whisper to me. Always kind are they. You will not tell anyone?" she said – with panic in her voice.

"No, I will never give your secret away, Rowena."

"But I always believe them," said Rowena. "Have they lied to me?"

Tears fell from her long black eye lashes, down her pearl white cheeks. She felt betrayed, heartbroken.

"No, Rowena. They have not lied to you, nor will they ever. They are your helpers, Rowena. Trust in them and in yourself. You know the truth when you hear it or see it. I will not lie to you either, not ever, so yes, your Mother is my niece, and you are my grand-niece."

"Oh! Lady Morgan! Thank you. I will never tell, either."

"Yes, Rowena, keep your silence in all of these matters. It may be best for the Time being that your Mother does not know who she really is. I believe she is with child."

"A baby!" she squealed.

"Shhhh... Let the Weavers unravel all in their own good Time. I do not think your Mother knows yet. When she tells you, be kind and act surprised. Do you think you can keep your silence?"

"Yes, Lady Morgan... Aunt... I will."

A secret keeper! Yes, I was testing her. If she was truly the Child of Magic – The Merlin's Bronte reborn – she would not disappoint me, but if she was only my beloved, Gifted niece, what matter? My life will have been blessed ten-fold just by her being.

When it was known that Mahr was with child I sent a messenger with an offer to send one of our Healers and Midwifes to stay with Mahr for the birthing and afterward to do the Winter Spinning, Weaving, and sewing, and to help to take care of the baby and Rowena. Rhodri refused again. I knew why. He wanted no part of the Goddess or her Priestesses. So be it. At least I was still welcome in his home.

Upon my second visit to Mahr, Rowena, and the baby girl whom she had born, I at last met Gildas. He entered the chamber just as his Father was showing the babe to me.

"Her name is Bridget."

Rhodri was very specific in telling me that she was not named for the old Goddess, of course, but for a respected Christian Abbess living on the Isle of the Eire, across the Western Sea.

"Our Bishop chose her name," said he.

I smiled and said, "I see."

Gildas had lowered his head when his Father said this, but I had caught in the twinkle and laugh lines increasing around his eyes that he was trying very hard to suppress a smile... a chuckle even? At that moment Gildas caught me looking at him. Our eyes held each other's. His were green and gold – a handsome colour, somewhat like Cat's eyes – they were also guileless, intelligent, independent and held more than a hint of a good sense of humor. He had his Father's red hair.

"Blessings be upon you, Lady Morgan, indeed upon us all, I hope. I am pleased to meet you."

I knew that he had meant every word.

"And I you, Gildas, or would you prefer that I call you 'Brother Gildas'?"

"Gildas is fine," said he. Rowena ran into the room just then and into his arms.

"Greetings my "Domina peradulescens," or as I see now, not as little as the last I saw of you."

"Domina peradulescens?" queried Rowena, "More new words to learn?"

"It means *young girl* in the Latin tongue."

I could see a genuine Love between them – half brother, half sister though they were. My heart felt a twinge – like Bear and me.

I wondered... "Perhaps... Do I dare hope that this Monk will be my ally within this fortress."?

On that very visit I spoke with Gildas about Rowena's burning desire to read and write. He said that he planned to teach her the Latin and Briton tongues.

"This will require a little subterfuge, for my Father does not approve. However, my Father will not go against his friend the Bishop's wishes and the Bishop has a need of me. I could arrange it, if only for their hope of Rowena's becoming a teaching Nun or Abbess one Day."

He then looked straight into my eyes again and said, "Of course, you know of my Grandmother's request. If Rowena ever took vows of poverty, as have I, our Father *and* the Bishop would gain much."

How honest of him to say this.

I was to gain ever more respect for Gildas as the next two or three years went by. I believe he knew from the Day he first saw me who Mahr really was, but he had the gift of silence, too.

Chapter 49
Correspondences

Morgan

One fine breezy Day on the Isle of Apples, about three years later, a messenger arrived. He was a close friend of Gildas,' although not a man of the Church. He gave to me a finely written and sealed letter from Gildas.

Everything had gone wrong. As the story had unfolded to Gildas, his letter went on to say, one of the nearby villagers had recognized that there was a close resemblance between Mahr and myself. He was an old man, but when he had been young he had seen the wedding party of King Arthur and Queen Gwenyfar, so long ago. He remembered how my Mother Igraine and I had looked exactly alike – but for the difference in our ages. He had always marveled at that. He had heard that my sister, Morganna Le Faye, also looked the same as we. It had made a lasting impression upon him.

It was "some Dark Magic," someone had told him. It seemed that the old villager had told only a friend or two about his thoughts that Mahr was really the daughter of the Evil Sorceress of Old – Morganna Le Faye.

"The poor, dear Lady – she doesn't even know it herself," he said.

Surprisingly, no one had spoken of it. It had not spread like a Fire – as tasty morsels of gossip usually do, wrote Gildas. I think it was for the Love and respect all held for Mahr, or for fear of my Father – and fear him they should.

For, when I was but three years old, my Mother met with a fatal accident. My Grandmother, Princess Rowena, sent a nurse to help care for me then.

Because of my Father's contrition for his abuses of my Mother, along with much grieving, Princess Rowena had had a large house built for my Father near to her fortress for my brothers and me to live in. I do believe she had done this so that she could watch over me, for she held no Love for my Father and little for my brothers. There I grew up in my nurse's care. Her name was Angharad.

My nurse and my dear Grandmother were both as Mothers to me. Of course, my Grandmother had told me everything of her suspicions as soon as she deemed that I was old enough to understand. Now, this was not done by way of revenge, but to protect me. My Grandmother also paid for Tutors to educate me. My Father did not object, as I was a male child.

I know that I can rely upon you, Lady Morgan, to keep confidence with me in regards to all that I write. I give this background of my family in order to protect you and my sister Rowena.

Nothing was said to my Father about Mahr's suspected parentage, but then, a plague struck. Well, first there was a drought at Winter's End, which did not cease through the Summer. All the crops failed, Wells ran dry, flocks died both from lack of Water to drink and from attack by starving Wolfs from the deep Woods.

That was when the illness hit. Now you know, Lady, how superstitious ignorant folk can be and although I have no ken why, it seems that my Christian brethren are all the more so than those who follow the Old Gods. They see Demons in everything. Evil lurks behind every Tree and Stone. Well, my dear sister Rowena, meaning only well, tried to tell my Father, the Bishop and the folk all around what was to come – before it happened. She was then not quite eight years. She said that Voices had spoken to her to warn them to keep large vats of clean Water for use through the coming drought. When the drought came, she told people that an illness was coming and that she had been told to stay in her house and keep herself clean.

Clean! That was what started it all. These people are not clean and besides, they said, "What does clean have to do with illness?!"

The Bishop, my Father, my brothers, everyone, questioned Rowena – violently questioned her. She cried and said, "The Voices do not lie! I only meant well."

That is when the villagers accused her of being the Grandaughter of Morganna Le Faye – hence Mahr's being Morganna's *evil* daughter.

My Father was enraged. He feared for his social position. Prideful man that he is he began to despise Mahr. He accused her of lying to him all along about the loss of her memory. He would not comfort or even touch her. He said, "I cast you away from me, Wickedness."

She was heartbroken and afraid. She begged him at first – reminding him of the Love they had shared. He spat in her face. Devastated, she finally got word to me as to all that had happened. I had been away for nine months and had known nothing of it. Quickly I returned home to find Mahr secluded and locked in the house in which I had grown up, whilst my Father and oldest brother kept Rowena locked in a chamber of the fortress, away from her Mother.

Lady Morgan, I tell you that the Air itself in the fortress seemed alive with an evil Spirit, yet at the same Time, it was as if there was no Air at all to breathe. I find it hard to describe these things. I am sure that you would know how to name it. Like a dungeon, it was.

You may not think of me as a man of God's inner Mysteries – or the Goddess' if calling God "HER" comforts you more. However, I believe that we all have an inner voice that speaks to us. That inner voice, or knowing, spoke "danger" to me in that fortress. My dear little sister, Rowena, is far more graced with these *knowings* than I, and no one in this world could ever convince me that there lies any evil in that sweet child. Perhaps they are jealous or envious of her, for more deeply has she been touched by God's Love than they. This envy and fear has martyred many of my own Christian brethren. I truly believe there is but one Divine Love and He – or She – leads none to violence or hatred.

I will do all that I can to protect Rowena and Mahr, but I fear a bad outcome.

Enclosed is Mahr's letter to you, as she dictated it to me.

Oh my dear Aunt Morgan, Lady of the Lake, why did you not tell me? Bereft of memory, family, and past as I have been, I would have been so honoured to know that I am your niece. You have only been kind to me and my daughter. Gildas has told all to me.

I have Loved – no adored – my husband Rhodri, only to find him a monster. Life holds no meaning to me. I am tired in soul and heart. I mean nothing in this world. I never have, except to have given life to my precious daughters, Rowena and Bridget. Please, I beg of you, protect them if you can. Gildas can be trusted, but I fear that my life will be coming to an end through violence. I believe that Rhodri will murder me soon, with the help or approval of his other wicked sons.

Do not pity me. I am so tired... I welcome an end, save that it leave my daughters unprotected. Do not cry for me, Aunt. Perhaps we will see each other again in a better world.

Know this – I have a bit of the Sight. I have kept silent about it. I have harmed none.

Herein is a song that I have written for my daughters. Please give it to Rowena when she is old enough to understand. Gildas also keeps a copy for Bridget, to give to her when the Time is right. Know this also, the high Bishop has heard of my being who I am. He has inflamed all against me. This saddens my stepson, Gildas, who writes my words as I say them.

Gildas will find his own way, Aunt Morgan. He is a good man. Oh, I know that to write this embarrasses him, but he is a Cleric, and like you, will write the truth as he sees it.

I think I will not see you again in this world. May all that is Divine bless you.

Here is my song:

I live in the tangle-wood with the Deer of the Forest
The Hunter watches over me...
I Weave in my Raven locks
Twine, twig and flora
Wood-heather, Thyme and Rosemary...

I break no man's peace and have Loved the Earth dearly
Covet not wealth... Covet not wealth... cause no calamity...
So why has this trial befallen me?

They call me The Creature...
I come it by Nature...
My Mother, Morganna Le Faye...

Creature...

The old King lies wounded – Gwenyfar's at Glastonbury
The Mist encroaches Affalon...
The Dux are all scattered
The land is torn and battered
The Merlin's Magic is dead and gone...

Great Dragon ships are landing
On our shores they are standing
So I would think, yes I would think
They would have better things to do
Than to burn me a Witch and stake me heart through...

They call me The Creature...
I come it by Nature...
My Mother – Morganna Le Faye...

Creature...

The Gods of the Old Ones, with their Spells and Incantations
They give me little peace of mind
And the Spirits of the Lakes and Streams

And the Stones in the cross-roads
Their gentle faces are hard to find...

The new religion's powers have me locked in these towers
But I care not, no, I care not
Their accusations are un-true...
And I laugh at their fear that I disappear in a smoke of blue...

They call me The Creature...
I come it by Nature...
My Mother – Morganna Le Faye...

Creature...

A daughter I am true and born not sprung from Witches' clatter
Like a child of Beltane, blessed free
No Father's hand can claim me
No husband's rule will tame me
If thus I die, then blessed be!

By trial and by Fire, fan the Flames ever higher
I will not beg, will not cry out
They will get nothing out of me...
But never rest you easy, behind thy shoulder I might be...

They call me The Creature...
I come it by Nature...
My Mother – Morganna Le Faye...

Creature...

I laid down the vellum scroll, cold as the North Wind – not
overtaken by fear, but by certainty am I.
"Is she murdered yet?" I wondered.
Suddenly I began to feel dizzy and ill. Everything was swirling, hot
and suffocating. I closed my eyes. Somewhere from a distance I heard a
thump and then I was no longer in my body. I was rushing through
darkness – no – it was utter blackness, again.
I must keep hold of the Silver Cord that binds me to my mortal flesh.
Then, as if seeing from above, I was looking at a woman with
beautiful, long, black hair – just as mine had once been. She was sitting
alone. No... she was holding a baby. Powerful and resolute was she,
singing her song, over and over again – "They call me the Creature..."
I watched as three men approached on Horseback. They were

carrying pitch-dipped staves... A Fire was lit. They torched the timbered walls and roof of the house. The Flames quickly spread. Knowing her Fate, the woman tenderly kissed her baby and then she covered her baby's face with a blanket and smothered her to Death. She was glaring at the men through the barred window slits with her head held high, all the while mocking Rhodri and his sons as they watched and heard her.

I noticed that she wore a great white pearl hanging from her neck by a ribbon. Had she kept it all this while? Had she known who she was all along?

She never stopped singing her song, louder and louder, cradling her dead baby in her arms. Never did she scream. She sang herself into silent Death.

Oh, Mahr! Oh, Morganna...

I awoke to find Gwenda's daughter Simu and two postulants cooling my brow and neck with wetted cloths.

"My Lady, you fell! Are you hurt?"

I immediately sent a small group of the Marsh men to my family's fortress in Dumnonia, with a message for Bedwyr. These were sturdy men, willing to fight if necessary, for me or for my kin. Bedwyr, although not my, nor Morganna's blood brother, must be informed of the details of my Vision – of my niece's and her baby's murder – also of the danger that Rowena faced. Always has Bedwyr thought of Igraine as his Mother, and Mahr was, after all, her granddaughter. I knew that he, even at his age, would round up a force of Warriors to bring retribution upon Rhodri and to protect Rowena – if we were not already too late.

I assured him that Gildas would be his ally in any way that he could, however I knew the danger Gildas could face on all fronts if he openly went against his Father and the Bishop. I asked Bedwyr to be mindful of Gildas' position.

Besides, something told me that even if Gildas would ever be willing to, or desirous of, taking arms against his Father and brother, he would not, because of his vows of peacefulness. These vows, ironically, were not required by the Church of Rome, who in fact had many Warrior Bishops and the like. Gildas had had long talks with me of his leanings toward the more Mystical followers of the Savior. "The first Church" as he had once called it – "as it was before the Roman Emperor Constantine quantified all Christian thought into Roman Christian dogma."

"Blessed it was," he said, "that later, many on these Fair Isles had been followers of Pelagian teachings."

I knew of Pelagius and his Druidical leanings. Of this fact, I do not think Gildas was aware. I remember smiling on the inside when he had said these things. But, more to the point, Gildas walked his own road and it was an astonishingly peaceful one. If he had any fault that I could see, it was that he was a bit critical of much regarding of his fellows. He was still idealistic... I wondered how these seeds would grow within him.

As it was to happen, Bedwyr's force arrived too late to save Mahr.

In the meanwhile, at the simple family burial of Mahr and her baby – Bridget, which was not attended by the Bishop or any other than Rhodri and his household, Gildas spoke of Mahr as a Christian woman, a good wife, and a loving Mother. He insisted that Bridget be laid upon her Mother in their shared grave. Rhodri, glaring impatiently at Gildas all the while, had adamantly refused to place a cross at their grave.

When it was his next opportunity, Gildas spoke privately with Rowena and gave Mahr's song to her.

"She read it stoically," – he wrote to me – "and without a word or tear, she burned it."

Rowena had already confided in Gildas that she knew who Mahr really was. At that Time, Gildas warned her that she was in danger.

"I know that, too," Rowena had said.

"I have thought of a way to keep you safe from all harm – a way our Father will gladly agree to."

His plan was to have Rhodri sponsor Rowena's keep and admittance as a postulant in the Christian women's Monastery at Bryn-y-gefeilian. He wrote to me:

It lies near to the old Roman road and bridge. The Monastic center is surrounded by a village. There are plans to build a great Abbey there one Day, although I doubt they will find the funding for such, in an out of the way place like that. The population is too small, but the great Roman road which runs not far from it is still much used to travel from one town to another.

Our Father will hold delight in the thought of her taking vows of poverty, after she has been taught and becomes of an age to do so. I told Rowena that it was the only immediate way out of danger that I could see for her. I said, "You are not yet ten year-turns. Your final vows will not be expected until you are fourteen or older. I will bring you safely to these women if you agree. The Bishop also has a vested interest in supporting the decision, and he will send his seal of recommendation. For, with you in vows of poverty, his Abbey will inherit large sums from Princess Rowena's wealth. Are you willing? I fear for your life, if not."

Rowena had been Christened not long after her birth, but now she was branded as Demon Spawn by all around her but Gildas. He had told her that the Saints had all heard Voices or seen Visions of things to come and that this was not evil.

Rowena had reluctantly agreed – and grieving sorrowfully she rode away from the only home she had ever known, the once great and beautiful fortress that The Merlin of legend had designed and which was to have been hers alone when she became a woman at her fourteenth year-turn.

Later she told me that she wondered if she ever would see it again. This she would accomplish, years later, only to find it in scorched ruins.

Chapter 50
The Brilliance Razed

Morgan

It took Bedwyr half a Moon's Dance to finally arrive at Princess Rowena's fortress with a force of men he thought equal to the task of besieging it. It was, of course, impregnable, but his plan was to surround it, and starve Rhodri out.

Rhodri had expected Bedwyr to do exactly that, so he had stockpiled enough dried meat and Grains to last a year or longer. There were three Wells within the inner courtyard, so he had no concern about thirst. That was his mistake... The drought continued on and on until the Water levels were so low in the whole of the land surrounding the Hill that one at a Time, the Wells had run dry.

Rhodri, besieged and defeated, knew that Bedwyr would never allow him to leave. I was later told that he had wondered why there had been no force of support sent by the Bishop, nor in fact was any help sent by any of the surrounding Chieftains. Then he remembered, Princess Rowena's bequest. I could only imagine his thoughts.

"That bitch! The Church and those heathen Priestesses would inherit all! The Church! That is why no help came. At least Mahr's wicked daughter would get nothing now."

So Rhodri vowed to a plan for himself, and he sent a messenger into the Night to Bedwyr, with word that "No one will ever hold this fortress if it is not mine!"

The messenger proved to be Rhodri's middle son, disguised as a stable boy – who could, after delivering the massage, flee to escape harm. Bedwyr, not fooled and knowing that this man had played a part in the evils done to Mahr and her babe – had him beheaded, just outside the walls of the fortress, right before Rhodri's eyes and just out of Rhodri's Archers' reach. Rhodri watched, blank faced.

Just after twilight upon the next evening, there appeared a strange glow in the deep purple, coming from the fortress, first here, then there. Then great billows of white and grey smoke crossed the Moonlit Sky and obliterated the Stars on this clearest of Nights. Next, rumblings and screams were heard. Finally pillars of dancing red and gold Flames engulfed the entire fortress. As the intensity grew, the screams silenced.

Bedwyr and his company watched, horrified, not only for the loss of humanity, but also for the loss of one of Briton's most splendid, magnificent, architectural achievements.

Bedwyr cried, feeling once more the loss of the only man who had ever been a Father to him – Gwyddion, The Merlin.

It was later reported that when Bedwyr saw the fortress in Flames, he said, "Oh, will there be nothing left for men to remember him by? No fortress of splendor – no act of triumph? No pillar of Stone? Only the songs of Bards – lest they forget too?"

He tore his garments and threw dirt upon his head and face as he watched – through that Night and into the next Day – the utter destruction of The Merlin's fortress. The Fire was so hot that his Company had to remove themselves to farther away. Even did many of the Stones themselves burst from the heat. At the end, there was naught but a charred ruin of roofless walls.

Rhodri had been insane, driven there by his own wickedness. He had determined to burn the grand fortress to the ground: Vortigern's fortress, Rowena's fortress, the fortress that The Merlin had built – killing himself along with his entire household. Not a man, woman or child was spared.

"Why?" Bedwyr had thrown his head back and asked the Stars. "Why?"

The Voices came...

"Fear not, Bedwyr. The Merlin will live in the memory of many peoples through the ages. Write all this for Morgan's histories – without which the true story of Gwyddion and Arthur would be lost forever, or *changed* into unrecognisable fable forever.

"Brave Bedwyr, it will not be long until you are reunited with them in the Summerlands."

The Voices faded.

Bedwyr came to see me at the Isle of Apples, to report all these things to me and brought with him another letter from Gildas, which told me where Rowena was.

"Bedwyr, my brother," said I – "go home to your wife and family. Live in peace now for the rest of your life. We are both old, you and I – perhaps this will be the last Time we will meet on this side of the Veil. Thank you for writing the account of all of this for me. You are a good and loyal man. Arthur would have never been who and what he was without you. No, really, Bedwyr, I mean what I say."

Bedwyr only smiled, in his old Foxy way.

"Farewell, my sister."

"Farewell to you my brother, blessings be upon you and your family."

He left our lives in this world one half of a year later – an idealist, a visionary, a supporter, a protector, *and* a Dragon Caller.

I began to wonder if his kind were a dying breed. My silent prayer was, "May you be blessed in the netherworld, Bedwyr, then awaken to a joyous new life."

And the world spins round...
And they all fall down...
And they crumble to the ground...

Chapter 51
The Would- Be Abbess

Morgan

One year later...

As I saw through my inner eye and as Gildas reported, Rowena had become a postulate to the Christian Abbess – or so she would be called if they could afford an Abbey. As it was, theirs was a meager and humble settlement of perhaps two huts – miserable hovels, really – with four women living in each, a small wooden Church, two stables, a garden and a kitchen, some chickens, two Goats, a Cow, and an old Mule.

The so-called Abbess had her own private quarters. In her cottage were three precious books, which her Father, a wealthy Roman-Briton Merchant, had given to the 'Abbey.' One had come all the way from Constantinople. He also sent a few pieces of gold every year for her upkeep, but the thing Mother Mair – yes that was *her* Christian name as well – treasured most was a sliver of wood from the true cross, which her Father had also bought in Jerusalem at great price. Mother Mair kept it in her own personal shrine in her cottage, next to her crucifix. When asked why it was not kept at the Altar in the Church, she said that she feared that thieves might come in the Night.

Mother Mair took her service to her God very seriously. She was organized, efficient, and very strict. She disliked Rowena from the first moment she laid eyes upon her. At their initial interview, even with Gildas there – bringing Rowena's large dowry, Mother Mair did little to hide her disapproval of Rowena.

"You are a beautiful girl." She accused. "Beautiful girls usually turn into beautiful women. It is said that your Grandmother, the Sorceress, was very beautiful. But not, of course, in our God's eyes. Beautiful women lead men to folly and themselves to damnation."

Mother Mair was a very plain woman without any redeeming features.

"That long black hair," she continued, "will be of no use to you here. I will have it all cut off today. You do understand you have come here to work, pray, and learn about our Lord?"

"Yes." Rowena replied.

Gildas interrupted at this point because he saw Rowena's lips quiver and one tear roll down her cheek. He drew the heat of Mother Mair's attention away from Rowena, to speak of future endowments to pay for Rowena's upkeep and of course to help towards the building of an Abbey.

At that, Rowena – as any curious ten year old would – looked more intently about her surroundings. First she noticed the great Fire in the hearth pit. Large logs had been placed upon it, seemingly sparing nothing for Mother Mair's comfort. Then her eyes alighted upon the books. "Books!" At a scorching look from Mother Mair, she became silent again. She patiently waited for a lull in the conversation to blurt out again – "Books! You have three books! Are they written in Latin? Are they wonderful? You must have read them many Times."

Gildas raised an eyebrow to Mother Mair as if to ask – "Well, have you?"

Mother Mair's distaste for Rowena must have turned to hatred on that moment. What is more, when she finally admitted that she did not read Latin, Rowena, trying to soften Mother Mair's obvious dislike of her, offered to read them to her. Of course, the child meant well, but not only did the offer humiliate Mother Mair, but she saw it as great impudence on Rowena's part.

"No!" she thundered. "You will teach me nothing, do you understand? Here, you are not the great-grandchild of a King, you are a servant of the Lord and of this Monastery – which I command."

The military term – command – coming so easily from her lips shocked Gildas. Perhaps it did even herself, but that ended the interview.

"I will come to see how she is faring soon," proclaimed Gildas.

Mother Mair answered, "That is not really necessary."

"Nevertheless," said he. "I will be back. You do not object, do you?" Gildas said as he placed the bag of gold on her table.

"No, I do not object."

That evening Rowena was bathed in cold Spring Water with lye soap that burned her skin. Her lovely clothes were burnt and her long black hair was shorn completely from her head. Even her leather boots, that were perfectly good and sound, were taken from her and she was given worn out felt ones with two holes in the bottom of them. In the windowless hut that she was assigned to, the floor was bare – no rushes – and the walls were in disrepair, allowing the cold to seep in. The bed that she would share with another of the girls was a thin layer of straw, covered with a blanket, also with holes in it – which the straw pushed through. A blanket too short even for a child was given to her to cover herself with, but it would not cover her feet as well as her arms. And, unlike in Mother Mair's cottage, the Fire to keep her and the other three girls she shared the hut with warm was little more than just a pile of warm ashes from dried Cow pats. The other girls explained that "to suffer was good for the soul. After all, our Lord suffered for us." A Fire was lit every other Night only, they said. Perhaps, Rowena thought, when I learn about their Lord, I will better understand.

Her work was hard. She churned the butter and pulled the wool from the Sheep. She mucked the stable of their one work Mule. Of course, she made mistakes. She was berated, made to go to bed hungry, or slapped, depending on the grossness of her mistakes. Such was her situation there that, for any made-up offense, she was beaten with a reed. Her every attempt at learning or questioning was met with charges of impudence, for which she was also beaten.

By the Time Gildas returned two Moon's Dances later, the pale, thin girl with stubbled hair and dark circles under her eyes was almost unrecognizable to him.

"Brother, I was told that I would work and learn – you remember Mother Mair saying that."

"Yes," he replied.

"I do not mind the work although it is very hard, but I have been taught nothing, except the prayers that is. Was it like this for you went you first went to the Monastery?"

Gildas thought of his first years.

"Well, to some extent, but not to the extent of what you have suffered."

This he said sternly as he removed the bandage on her arm to reveal skin torn from the lash.

He demanded audience with Mother Mahr. Soon, their raised voices inside could be heard by all of the girls.

"This child is filled with the Spirit of God." He told her. "She has the Gifts of prophecy and even Healing. She reads and writes Latin. She should be a treasure to you. Perhaps, even, someone to take your place in the eventuality of your being too old to continue – or should you die. As a Bride of Christ, there is no room for your jealousy of this child."

"Jealousy!?" said she. "This child is an evil one! She hears demon Voices – did you know that?!"

"How can you judge from whence her Voices come?" said Gildas.

"How can you?" she retorted.

"All I know is that she is my sister and I have known for all of her life she has only ever been good and kind. No evil lurks within her!"

"Then what about her Grandmother, Morganna Le Faye, and her aunt, the heathen Priestess and worshipper of Stones?"

Gildas shook his head in sadness. "Poor Rowena." Then he left. He kissed his little sister.

"Well, I will not be able to come back for about three more months. Please, just do as you are told... I will speak with my Bishop on your behalf. Perhaps I will be able to move you to another Abbess' rule."

Rowena cried – "Oh please do not leave me!"

"Rowena," Gildas admonished. "Pray to the Holy Mother for your comfort and protection. You are in need of a Mother's Love."

As Gildas rode away, he remembered the words he had used: "Abbess' *rule.*" It was then he wrote to me again.

"I had begun to see and feel the innate viciousness and hard heartedness of this woman."

I was sorry to read in his words the growing cynicism that I feared was in his nature.

Two more Moon's Dances passed, and several more beatings, as well as many missed meals as punishment for offenses that Rowena was unaware of committing. It was then, finally, that the Voices of the Stars spoke to her.

"Rowena, there is but ONE, do you know that?"

"Yes."

"Seek the Holy Mother as your brother Gildas has advised. Although She *is* here for many of the girls and women, this is not where you will find Her. Run to her, Rowena. Seek her at the Standing Stone of the Roman crossroad. She will send a way."

"How? I do not know where She is," said Rowena. But the Voices were gone.

And so, four Nights later – when the Moon was dark – Rowena took the holey boots and the largest of her two blankets and ran quickly and silently as a Hart through the deep Woods away from Mother Mair and that bleak compound that would be an Abbey – never looking back.

Yes – I later thought – perhaps it might one Day have been an Abbey, but for the fact that pestilence accounts no difference between the Holy "Bride of Christ" and "the servants of the Evil One." Nor, for that matter, the rest of us, who are neither Saint nor Demon. The plague passed through their compound and Mother Mair and every one of her "children" were wiped out. Countless people from the North to South and East to West of Our Fair Isles died. Many of my sisters and brothers had the plague that year, as well. But Rowena lived and so did Gildas – for the Weavers knew that they were both to have a great part in the histories of Our Fair, but troubled, Isles.

Rowena

To my dearest Aunt Morgan, Lady of the Lake...

I have asked my dear brother to bring this letter with him when he comes to visit you. My Gildas promised that he would do this for me. If you are reading it, I know he is with you and that he has fulfilled his greatest desire. May every God and Goddess bless him – and you, as well, my Lady.

Unfortunately, I have very little Time to write, yet wish to say so much.

I will begin with my decision to run from the cruel bonds in which I found myself. I am sure that Gildas has written to you of my sorry circumstances. Very worried was he on my behalf.

The Voices came – as a guidance, a comfort, a strength and to give me determination.

"Seek the Holy Mother at the Standing Stone – by the great Roman crossroad," they spoke.

"But where is that?" I asked.

They did not reply. I was completely disoriented as to where I was or to whence I should go. But, when the right Time came, I ran, fast and far away.

Aunt Morgan, the Christians speak much of faith, which is believing in something although you have no assurance that it is – although you cannot see it or touch it. Well, that is exactly the power by which I ran – the power of faith – Faith that the Holy Mother would rescue me and send "a way" as the Voices had promised.

For two Days and Nights I ran – cold, hungry, and frightened. I met one old man with a hay wagon on the second Day. He asked where I was going and from whence I had come. I hesitated to tell him anything about myself; for fear that someone may be looking for me. But then, again, I acted on faith. I looked into his eyes and saw there only compassion. So I told him that I must find and meet someone at the Great Roman Road where a Stone marks its crossroad.

He chuckled.

"My girl, you are on the Roman Road. As to how great it is so long a Time after it has been built and with no more Roman money or laborers to keep it up... well, as you see, the stones are here beneath your feet – with all this mud covering them."

I looked down. He was right. I was so excited! At least I had found the Roman Road. But to where?...

"Which way is the crossroad with the Stone marker?" asked I.

"Now, that I cannot say," said the man. "There is more than one such place. But if I were you, I would go the way we both go now. Several more miles in this direction is a small farm settlement with a Stream running through it. Not far from there are the old deserted Roman barracks and Fort. There is a wondrous bridge nearby – the Romans it built too – just beyond the barracks by a mile or so. A crossroad with a Stone marker is just before the Fort. Perhaps, someone in the settlement will help you, child."

He gave me a bite of cheese and a dried piece of flat bread. He asked if I would walk along with him for a mile or so, where he said he would reach the field where his hay was to go.

And so I did. Mostly we walked in silence, but at one point he noticed that I was limping and asked if I was injured. I showed him the bottoms of my boots, which by that Time had huge holes in them. The soles of my feet were blistered and bloody... He said, "Oh, poor Sweetling – here, I have a bit of leather – perhaps we can cut some for to line the bottoms of your boots..." He did – it was much better... A bit later, he asked my name. I became afraid to tell him, so I told him it was something that sounded in the tongue of the Britons like ro wen, which as you know, means the small white River or Stream Pebbles.

"White pebbles, how strange." he said.

"Why?" I asked.

"Because in the village near to the old Roman encampment, there is a Stream that runs through and it is filled with the ro wen. Folk gather them from the stream and use them for their Divining and offerings to the Old Spirits and Gods of the Wells or Springs – or to the Saints."

My Lady, then I knew I was on the right path.

I parted ways from the old man in an hour or so. I thanked him for his kindness.

"Be safe and well girl" he told me...

"Farewell" said I.

It began to get dark and cold again for the third Night. But upon this Night, the weather had taken a change for the worse. The Wind rose... The Night – it howled and thundered. Ice began to form and cover each blade of grass. The great boughs of every Tree groaned. One goodly sized bough snapped just ahead of me. It did not strike me though. On I went – although my feet were numb and my hands burning from the cold. I was covered with only my shift and the thin, holey blanket. I felt as if I would not live the Night through.

Then I saw it – a three point crossroad marked by a large Stone with Roman writing chiseled into it. It told the name of some long forgotten Commander. The rest was chipped away – probably by the Clan traditionalists who had spurned all trappings of Roman dominion long ago.

At the Crossroads...

There I was – alone in the darkness...

It was three Nights past the Dark Moon. I knew that She – as you would call the Moon, my Lady – would look like a Hunter's bow in the Night Sky, if I could clearly see Her, that is. But the Sky was clouded and violently churning. The Wind was up as high as ever I had seen and every thing that was frozen from the low hanging Mist was creaking and cracking.

The old Forest had been partially cleared here, I supposed to build the barracks and fort long ago – and had never thickened again.

I ran to the Stone as if it was the God... or an Altar... a Sacred thing. I threw myself down on my knees in front of it and wept. I wept for everything that had happened. Then I prayed a fervent prayer:

"Oh Holy Mother, Mother of us all, please find it in your infinite Love to look upon my plight. Oh great Lady of Compassion, You who wears the Stars as your cloak, embrace me as your daughter. As Gildas, my brother, has said, I am in great need of a Mother's Love. Please reveal yourself to me and save me. Let me come to know you."

Just then, I heard the sound of Horses – two Horses – and men speaking in the Roman tongue. They were close – on the road coming toward me. Lightning lit the Sky – I saw them! Waving in the Air beside them was... I thought I saw... a Dragon. Quickly, I ran to a bush and hid myself as best I could behind and beneath it. But just as they came to the crossroads, my hand leaned upon a frozen twig and it snapped.

Oh, the bell has rung for the call to repose... I must stop writing now. I will write more in the morn, if I am allowed the Time... If he must leave before I have been able to write more, Gildas can tell the rest of my story to you.

Know that I will ever hold you in my deepest respect and Love.

Rowena.

A note from Morgan...

I remember thinking – "My Goddess! What language for an eleven-year-old girl – or was she still ten? What a brilliant child!"

I wondered what this meant. She left herself in a dire predicament by a Roman crossroad. Yet she says the bell has rung for the call to repose? I looked at Gildas...

Chapter 52
Across the Continent

Lucian

I have never married. Although my life has been well and good, always at the edge of my heart is Briton and Morgan. Is she still alive? She was seven years older than I. I received a letter from Bedwyr four years ago. In it he spoke of Morgan being well and strong. However, I do not know when it was sent to me...

Pestilence, Barbarian raids, political wars and intrigues have all robbed the glamour and culture that was once Rome. Even when I was a boy – and it was well past her years of greatest fame – Rome still shone like the child of Apollo. She was respected by the entire world.

My family of both wealthy Merchants and nobles were proud people, refusing to accept the downfall of the Western Empire, which for the most part did not exist anymore.

But my head had been filled with dreams of glory.

A Warrior I would be, and so I was – but not for Rome.

It was to Arthur in Briton that I would give my blood. For more than twenty years I was his faithful companion.

After the final battle between Arthur and Mordred, the Confederacy crumbled. All seemed lost, so I returned to my family in Rome.

But, I did not stay long in the life of a Merchant and moneylender. My mouth drooled for the taste of military command. A Warrior was who and what I was.

So my uncle, who was highly placed in the Emperor's Guard, recommended me. I was immediately accepted and given a commission in and under my uncle's prestigious command. It seemed my reputation had preceded me.

For years, growing and much imbellished tales of King Arthur and his companions had spread across the blue Mare Nostrum and over the Mountains to Rome and Eastward to Constantinople and beyond. Some of these tales I hardly recognized. Yet with each mention of them, I was filled with bittersweet stirrings of memories. Always... memories...

I have grown many years past my prime. My once golden hair is all silvery white now. I have taken to wearing it long – as I had done in Briton so many years ago. My old military companions had all but tried to disgrace me for this – only with their teasing words, of course. I am still well regarded by them, even though I have left military service. Three years have passed since then.

Now, as I write this, I am past seventy years old. I remain fit and strong. I ride and train with sword, pike, and bow everyday – as if I were still a young Warrior. If I fool no one else, I fool myself, for I still feel as young as ever in my thoughts and in my heart – young and fit enough to have decided to return to Briton... perhaps to stay there, or at least to visit one last Time.

The top ranking of the Emperor's guard has very kindly and respectfully arranged for a personal Guard to travel with me and has honoured me by allowing us to ride under the banner of the Purple Dragon, the emblem of The Caesar's Elite Guard.

He offered four men, I accepted only one – but with gratitude. The man's name is Wilhelm. He is of Northern Teutonic stock. He is young and enormous. Both of my upper arms could make one of his. He looks terrifying – all the better to be my Guard. Despite his barbarian physique and facial features, his dress and manners are purely Roman. He is an intelligent man and we share good conversations and companionship. Our long voyage should not be overly tedious. We leave one week from the Day I am writing this.

Long ago, Morgan, you asked me to keep and write my history. I was so very reluctant to do so, yet since I left Briton I have kept a journal of all the events, feelings, and learned Wisdoms of my life. These I will keep for myself. But beginning with this writing, it will all be for you. Has some of your "sight" rubbed into me? For, somehow, I sense that the value of my history is not over.

Day five of the Sea voyage...

We are crossing the length of the "Mare Nostrum." Did you know that some refer to this as the 'Sea in the Middle of the Earth'?

Calm and sunny it has been every Day so far. The blue of the Sky reflects onto the clear Waters. "The paradise of Neptune," the Shipmen call it, although it is not *always* such. Many large ships have been swallowed by her waves when Jupiter sends his storm bolts to rouse her temper. On this sailing, I have seen Dolphins dance and play beside our ship. A peaceful and uneventful passage it has been so far – which has left Time for me to wonder how you, Morgan, and the Isle of Apples are faring.

I have heard you are troubled by Saxons, Jutes, and Angles. Worrisome thoughts are as useful to me as sand in my hands, and do me no better to pay heed to them. No, instead I will daydream of your Mists and the Standing Stones, the floating bridges of the Marsh Folk, and of you, Morgan, and your Bees. I close my eyes and see the Sacred Wells and the groves of ancient Oaks and Apple orchards...

My Forefathers, the earliest Romans who invaded the ancient Britons, fearing the power that the Druids held over the people, tried to destroy them. A good job they made of slaughtering and plundering their Sacred places and Universities. Yet the core Wisdoms and secret meanings have still survived to this Day, I am told. They communicate like a fisher's net across the lands. I wonder if still they choose a Merlin – surely so. Very glad am I that the Imperial Romans did not perceive your Order as a political threat. I pray that the Teutons respect the Order as well.

News has reached Rome – be it propaganda or not – that the Church regains some of its strength and numbers which had fallen in tatters when the Romans abandoned Briton. When I lived in Briton with Arthur, almost all had reverted to the Old Gods and native traditions.

No religion or Gods can be forced upon people and yet reach their hearts. I remember many conversations with you about this, Morgan.

Correspondences from old allies in Briton have told me that more and more Druids have become hermits and Monks, bringing their old Wisdoms with them and teaching them in the name of the Christ and that a steady flow of the old Druidical thought is accepted as a constant now – by more and more Christians of the Cymru. Yet this is nothing new – this sounds very much like the Days of Pelagius again, does it not?

I sent a letter to a friend there – an old King who had been allied with Arthur's confederacy. His name was Cadwallon ab Einion of Gwynedd. His son, King Einion of Lleyn replied, "I am sad to say that our Father has gone to his Ancestors. But please, do come to our fortress when you arrive in our land. It is very comfortable. We look forward to your staying with us for as long as you will while in Gwynedd. My brothers' and my fortresses, as well as our hunting lodge, are in the Snowy Mountains, not too far from where your old friend, Gwyddion, The Merlin's Cave was."

His brother Cereiod, he wrote, had – like himself – been but a boy when I left Briton. He is also a King now, Cereiod of Rhos.

"But you have never heard of our youngest brother. He is far younger than we by twenty four and twenty six years years. Our Father married a much younger girl when our Mother died, and indeed, they did Love each other. But she died in childbirth. Our brother Seiriol lived and grew strong. He was a wondrous child. His thoughts always were of the Gods. I forget, Lucian, are you a Christian? Well, no matter.

Seiriol, by the Time he became a man at fourteen, was already a 'Seer' and an 'Oak Knower.' He was taught by a very old man who had been the Grandfather of his wet nurse. The two were inseparable. The old man died upon the Day of Seiriol's fourteenth year-turn. Seiriol always believed the old man clung to life to see him a man.

"Our family is close of heart, Lucian. But Seiriol, our brother, is much younger than our own children. Cereiod and I have always been both brother and Father to him. So when he, at fourteen, told of his determination to go to the old Druid's Isle – Ynys Mon – to live as a hermit in a Cave cut into the side of a Hill, we were shocked, although in retrospect we should have seen this in him.

'I will spend my life in solitude,' said he, 'prayer and meditation. I will walk in the Otherworlds to Heal my fellow Britons.'

"Will you not be lonely, brother?" we asked.

'I am never alone. Fear not for me. This is what I must do.'

And that is what he did.

He sought his place of solitude on the Druids' Isle from whence he could look Southward across the narrow expanse of Sea toward the Snowy Mountains where he had been born. The old man who had been his teacher told him where to look for this place. He found the Well with the Stone beside it, as he knew that he would. It had been a place of worship of the old God Nodens. Nearby, he fitted out the Cave to sleep in – but with no comforts at all, not even a stool to sit upon.

"We begged him to accept our help, but he refused at first. Then, because he feared that we would worry too much about his safety, he finally relented.

"So we sent a group of workers to help him build a humble hut, with a proper roof and a little space in which to live. After our prompting, he finally allowed us to furnish him with six books, much vellum, writing instruments, a table, a bench, straw and pelts for a pallet, warm clothing, blankets and boots, and enough food and mead to last until we could get more to him, but other than these few things, he would accept nothing.

"I must learn to make my own way here," said he.

I saw the Wisdom in that. He did say that we were welcome to come – whenever we wished to see him.

Still, my brother Cereiod and I could not bear the worrying over him. So, when we heard that many people were coming to ask for his prayers and Healing, we contrived to build a Priory House for him with an Altar and some benches for prayer not far from his hut, the Well and the Stone. When he saw that more and more people needed his care and that three other young men wished to live the life he was living and to learn under his tutelage, he relented.

"The Priory has been in operation for three years now and its reputation grows. People call him Brother, Father, and Mage. Most of those who come to him follow the Christ – and so Seiriol set up a cross above the entrance to the Priory. He is of the thinking that there is but one God with many faces. Yet, now people call him a Christian.

"However, Seiriol still goes to the Well most every Day to pray by himself. Sometimes he leaves offerings for the ancient God there. Some of the folk, who still follow the Old Ways, leave food offerings there for the God of the Well – and for Seiriol, as they seek his counsel too.

"He is a good man of God – or as we would say, the Gods. So what does it matter?"

Indeed, Morgan, this I have wondered, as well. Does it really matter at all?

I remember the beauty and the sanctity of your Order of the Goddess. I remember the wonder of it all. Ancient Rites enacted in the same ways for countless generations, with the Ancestors looking on.   By comparison, Rome seems a pale, demoralized, and materialistic culture, riding upon the fleet wings of her past – which even then was but a shadow of the greatness that was Greece. Oh yes, Rome gave the world an Empire, an order, strategic warfare, law, magnificent roads, bridges and the like, but on your sweetest of Isles, in the Inland Sea, life is Art.

I tremble in anticipation.

Day nine of my voyage...

Wilhelm and I have been playing a board game called 'Tali and Tropa.' It is interesting and pleasant – sometimes challenging. It keeps the boredom at bay.

I have been thinking of the fact that you, Morgan, have never seen the Seven Hills of Rome. I know that you have heard many first hand descriptions, but you might find it garish and un-cultured. You see – Rome's city plan or layout was set many, many hundreds of years ago. It grew from nothing to one of the greatest cities in the world, but the organization and layout of the streets was anything but orderly, for they simply expanded in any and all directions. The myriad twists and turns of small streets and alleys with houses and later buildings built one to another, were and still are in many areas impossible to navigate. Therefore, when the great edifices, such as the Coliseum, the Temples, public buildings, baths, triumphant arches, and amphitheaters – all with their own promenades – were built, whole sections of the city were simply leveled. This was when the famed "order" of Rome was born. Rome has never been shy. The buildings were all copied from the style of the Greeks in their architectural form – and in the way that they are all painted in bright colours, of scarlet, Lapis blue, Carnelian, and intolerably bright greens and yellows. I suppose I should say it is intolerable to *my* senses, that is – because of my many years of living in Briton in earthly simplicity, where all man-made structures compliment and fold into the Nature of their surroundings. Even by the Time the great Roman building began in Briton – such as fortresses, garrisons and the like – a more utilitarian approach was taken by the Romans – building with natural Stones, found locally. Even the grand Villas were far more conservative in colour than those in Rome. When I compare Sulis-Minerva's Temple and baths at Aquae Sulis with public bathhouses in Rome, it is like comparing a serene garden with a competitive market place filled with hawkers, screaming their vulgar come-ons to all who pass. Perhaps I have gone too far in taking the other side of Roman society – with its false conservatism – too much to heart. Rome... Nothing is simple about her.

When I left Briton I thought it was to return home. More fool I. My home and heart is in Briton. My great hope is that I have not waited too long to return. I know that the whole Western world is shifting – and so quickly. Constantine changed everything. Now – centuries beyond Constantine, through two hundred years of tyranny and intolerance – the Rome that once was lies in moral ashes. But I do not weep for her. My eyes are set Westward, to the land of my Dreams and the Summer of my youth.

Day sixteen of my voyage...

My eyes behold the land at the far Northwestern Coast of Mare Nostrum. If I am not mistaken, this is not far from the lands of Lady Vivianne's Mother's people. This is an exotic land. Many traders of spices and silks travel here. I have heard that even Frankincense and Myrrh, as well as Cedar incense from Aegyptos and points East, can be purchased here – and much more costly than gold by weight are they. I intend to bring some to you. I know that you will enjoy them. I will also keep some. This is a luxury I will allow myself at the end of the Day, when all work is done and it is Time for the simple pleasure of peaceful rest. To be surrounded by the perfumes of the Ancients is as good to me as if I had my own Lyrist plucking the sweetest of tunes upon his or her strings. Do I sound more like a Dreamer than a Warrior? ...or even worse, an old romantic fool? Probably so, but I have learned through my years to savor what golden moments come.

Is that not what The Merlin called them? "Golden chances?" As in so many other instances, I have come to treasure the Wisdom of his words.

Morgan, my long Time dear friend, do not think I come to pressure you in any way. You know that I will always Love you. I write this only to relieve the uncomfortable moments that I might cause to you by saying it while looking into your eyes. By the Time you read this, we will be very comfortable old friends again, for I will hold this back awhile. Love is a Goddess with many faces and I will gracefully and

thankfully accept whichever face of Love you wish to show me. There
has always been a bond between us. Just to be friends as we were, so
long ago, would be one of the greatest blessings of my old age. But to be
your beloved... to finally – now at the end of my life – sleep in the
comfort of your embrace...

This will probably be my last entry until I reach Briton. Oh, yes,
although we reach landfall, far South and West of Briton, I feel, for some
reason, a calling to the North. I will traverse the lands through Gaul,
then sail North-Northwest to the land of the Southern Picti and Alba,
above Hadrian's wall, to Table Rock, there to sit upon that Rock one
more Time to relive my memories of Arthur. I hope also to reunite with
some of those long ago allies – such as the brother Kings I have written
of – who live near the West coast in Gwynedd. I was much younger than
many of them and I fear the Time is running out for such reunions. I will
stop there on my way to the South, but I will not tarry long, Morgan.

Chapter 53
Other Communications

Rowena

Her second letter...

I do have Time to finish my story.

And so, there I was at the crossroads, my dear Aunt Morgan, betrayed by the snap of a twig!

The two men on Horses abruptly halted in their tracks. They faced me. One of them was a well dressed man who looked as though he could be a Roman Dux. Funny that I would take note of such a thing. He drew his sword so swiftly that I saw nothing but the motion. Then they both held swords out, staring in the direction of where I hid.

"Come out and cast your weapon before you..." one of them called out, with his thick sword pointed toward me. "...or you will be run through in a blink of your eye."

This was not said by the more refined looking Roman officer – or something akin to that – but by the other, rougher looking man who was very large. Was he a giant, I wondered? I swallowed and said, "Please, Sir, I hold no weapon."

Then the older and finer looking man – who had long, thick, silver hair – raised his hand in front of the other – whose sword was at the ready to kill – in a gesture for abeyance.

"Wait," said he – who I, by then took as the superior of the two.

"Come out, girl, and show yourself – but no tricks."

I shakily crawled from behind and somewhat beneath the bush. Prickly branches clutched at my short hair and clothes, one scratched my face and I did feel a drip of blood running down my cheek. When I had untangled myself, I stood and looked into the eyes of the older man, who sat so straight and perfectly on his mount. When he looked at my face, he inhaled a sudden gasp of breath and in his expression there was the look of a question. Or was it recognition?

"Who are you, girl? Speak, have no fear."

He gestured for the man who was obviously his Guard to sheath his blade.

I stood before them, shivering and terrified. More gently this Time, he asked again – "Who are you? Who is your Mother?"

"My Mother is dead, sir."

"And your Father?"

It was then that my courage left me and I lost myself. I fell to the ground in a heap, weeping and shuddering from it. I could not speak. The words would not come out. I wanted to scream "No! Do not take me to my Father! He will kill me!" But all I could do was weep. The silver-haired man dismounted. His Guard was speaking a caution to him – to which he paid no heed. He picked me up into his arms and said, "I will ask you no more now child. Know that you are safe with me."

They wrapped me in both of their fine woolen blankets and my savior placed me upon his Horse, in front of himself, for travel. He gave me Watered wine to drink, to warm and calm me. It was good. It worked...

That Night he found a farmhouse in which we were given a place to sleep and food to break our fast in the morning. I was offered food that Night as well, but I vomited in a basin at its offer. He sat, sleeping off and on at my side, murmuring words of comfort as I kept awakening from my fretful sleep. The last thing I heard him say was "Everything will be well, girl. I will protect you. From whoever you have run, I will not return you, I promise."

At that, I slept the Night through.

I have a sense of knowing people. I trusted him. But why he would care for me, I did not know. Not until we reached the Snowy Mountains. True to his word, while we travelled, he asked me no more of my past.

When we reached the fortress of King Einion of Lleyn, my savior presented me to him and his family. King Einion looked very carefully at me, squinting his eyes. He asked "Lucian, who is this girl? She is much taller and fairer of skin, but she very much resembles the wife of Rhodri – the fucking bastard."

This last he said under his breath.

"She who was burned alive – locked in his house all alone, but for her infant child – who burned with her."

Lucian drew a sharp breath between his teeth.

"Most blame Rhodri. He was a madman. But I believe that both of his older sons had a hand in it. A small force came, under Bedwyr of Dumnonia, to try to prevent his hurting her, but they arrived too late.

"If this girl is who I think she is, she is the heiress of much of Princess Rowena, the Saxon's, vast wealth. Did you know Princess Rowena, Lucian? She was Queen Gwenyfar's sister."

"Yes. But this girl does not resemble princess Rowena or Ribrowst, her daughter."

"No, no. I forgot. You have been long away. Not Ribrowst – Rhodri's second wife, the daughter of Morganna Le Faye. It is said that her name was Mahr and that she was as lovely a woman as anyone had ever seen."

Lucian threw back his head and laughed – long and heartedly.

"Is this true, my sweet girl?"

I lowered my head, ashamed of my Grandmother, and in grief for my Mother. I said, "Yes."

"I know your Aunt Morgan, child. In fact I travel South soon to see her."

"Oh please bring me to her!" I pled.

But Lucian told me that he could not bring me to the order – at ten years old and uninvited. He explained that I must be at least fourteen years to become a postulate there. But he promised to speak with you about me.

Please, Aunt Morgan. I want to be with you, wherever you are. Please?

Lucian – who has given me leave to address him so – has contrived with King Einion, that if I stayed at the King's fortress, the Bishop might get word of it – and he is a dangerous man.

So I have been taken to the old Druid's Isle to live at the Priory of the King's brother, Father Seiriol. I giggle... He is but nineteen years old, yet people call him Father! He is very nice to me. I think he understands me well. He also hears the Voices and has Dream Visions. I am not so sure he is really a Christian though, such as Mother Mair or even Gildas. No, I believe he is of the Old Ones. But of course, this I will never ask him – I just feel it. He was delighted to know that I can read and write. He is very knowledgeable of many things and is also a Cleric, such as Gildas. He says that he himself will teach me for as long as I am here with him. He and his brothers will contact Gildas soon to let him know of my whereabouts.

I am well protected, Aunt Morgan, but I want so much to be with you.

I do not know how or where to find the Holy Mother on this Isle, but I will keep searching for her always. Please keep me in your heart.

Your niece, Rowena

Morgan

"Keep me in your heart?" My heart ached to be with her, to have her here with me on the Isle of Apples, but she was not yet fourteen year-turns. And, I had to know that it was indeed the Great Mother for whom she longed – and not only for me. For her to dedicate to our Order, she must truly want this with all of her being – not only the part of her who was "in need of a Mother's Love." I could show no favoritism to her, especially because she was of my blood.

I wondered if Rowena knew that Princess Rowena's fortress was to be hers and if she knew that it was in ruins? I felt sure that Lucian, Seiriol, and his brothers, would keep her in safe ignorance until she was old enough to defend her lands, if that was her wish. For this reason, too – that she stood to become an extensively wealthy heiress – I could not bind her to a simple life here at the Isle of Apples without her full knowledge of what and who she now was.

I read all of these correspondences to Arthur at his beside, as if he could hear me. Then I spoke to him.

"Oh, Arthur, do you not tire of this endless sameness? – caught between the worlds as you are? I have never been able to find you anywhere in the Other Realms. It was not really you in the Land of Naught – only a specter of my own desire. Only here, alone in my cottage, in your slumber, do I find you. If you Dream, Arthur, I pray you Dream well of your golden Times. And – if, or when, you Dream, do you see me there? Do you hold me in your arms? Do you know that you are not alone? Can you hear me, Arthur? Do you feel my presence and my Love? This is my only hope for you – for now. If you hear me, remember that I have devised a plan to break the chains that bind you to this emptiness. I have promised. I have sworn it. I will not forget. I will not leave you caught alone in this waste-land, my Bear."

I caressed his still golden, wavy tresses. Each Time was always the same. I kissed his cheek a good Night.

"Someday Arthur, we will walk the green Forests again, hand in hand. But not, I think, on this Earth, with you as a King, as Vivianne had hoped. For other Kings will be born, rise up, and will die. It is simply the way of things. Will there ever be another Summer King such as you? I do not know.

Later entries...

I received a messenger with a missive from King Einion, saying:

"Rowena did not stay long with Seiriol, for he recognized in her an itching for the knowledge which he and the other Brothers did not teach. I know that many Times in his solitude, he also itched for the Magic of his childhood training as an Oak Knower, but his work is here and now – and a good work it is. Seiriol has told me that there is a deep richness in the teachings of Yeshua. Words of Wisdom, such as – "Do to all others as you would have them do unto you." So many words and actions of compassion. But really, these were similar sentiments to those that were placed in Seiriol's heart by the old Druid who had been his childhood teacher. So, if he did not break the principals of his old teacher by serving a new master, what was the harm? These things he had taught Rowena. But as for her, he did not believe that she fit into their world. He told her, "You always go along with our disciplines respectfully, but I read the longings in your eyes, Rowena – a hunger for what you will not find here."

At first Rowena took this as a rejection, but Seiriol reassured her that she could do better elsewhere.

"You will better find what you are seeking amoung the Druids."

So it was that Seiriol wrote to Gildas, telling him all that had transpired with Rowena and of his thoughts that Rowena would do better with the Druids:

"There is a new Druids' school across the Island from here. There she will be well educated and can live in safety while she finds within her heart what path is truly hers. As Rowena is your half sister and you have been her protector – along with Lucian – I think it best that you take her there."

Gildas was very disappointed, but he had to see the logic in Seiriol's thoughts. He could not force Rowena into becoming a Christian, especially not in her heart, so he came to get her to bring her to the Druids' school.

"But she is a girl," he reasoned with the high Druid there. The Druid answered, "There are many women Druids, although many more here are men. Do not worry for the girl, for our teachings hold that there is no preeminence of men above women. All are taught equally in the Arts of memorization, writing, mathematics, Healing, and Herbal lore. Our Wisdoms are solid and hold Mysteries of an age-old Tradition."

"I see," said Gildas, for what else could he say?

"I have brought gold for her keep."

"That would be greatly appreciated, and wisely spent. However, it is in no way necessary, or expected. We care for our own. Many people bring gold, food, and other stipends to us because they hope for our success and longevity. If you wish to leave a gift, it will be spent to equally benefit all who live here. Fear not, brother Gildas, your sister will be in good and faithful hands."

"I understand," said Gildas, and he did.

As Gildas looked around at the High Druid's quarters, he noted that, unlike Mother Mair's, they were mean and humble and just as small as all the others' quarters in their compound.

He asked Rowena once more if this was what she truly wanted. She nodded her head in agreement. Tears streamed down her face. She told me when she related all this to me, "My tears were not for parting from the brother I so truly Loved, but for the parting of our ways. For this I knew from the very marrow of my bones – Gildas' and my paths had hit a fork in a road. We were traveling in separate directions now, never the two to entwine again."

She said to him, "I Love you, my brother."

"And I you," he had replied. Then he placed a bag of gold on the Druid's table and left.

As of the Time of my writing this, she has heard nothing more from him.

So many losses has my dear Rowena suffered.

She was eleven years when she began Druidical training. The High Druid wrote to me when she had finished her first year with them to relate his enthusiasm for her high intelligence and quickness of learning. He bragged of her many gifts.

"She far exceeds, in knowledge and practice, students who have been here four years to her one. Her memory is stunning. As you know, my Lady, we keep an oral tradition. It is forbidden and always has been for us to write of our Mysteries. Of course we are all literate here."

Chapter 54
Lucian Arrives

Morgan

A year! So long, yet so quickly has it passed.

It was well past Winter's End when Lucian arrived.

I remember chiding myself for foolishly worrying how old I must look in his eyes when first he beheld me. I fussed and acted like a young maiden trying on this robe and that to see which would better hide my sagging breasts and round belly, not that I was too plump – I was not – but age takes its toll.

I have always sympathized with our sisters who eat much less than I, but are always struggling not to become too fat. I admit I have been blessed in this way, for I eat all I wish to, I always have, but still – from my youth and many years beyond – I kept my beautiful body in fine shape. I am not conceited in this; my body was and is beautiful. All women's bodies are. We are all reflections of the Goddess. So, no matter what size or shape, all are beautiful. This I have been taught, this is what I know, this I teach – so I am a hypocrite! I must be – fussing like this as an old woman about my belly and sagging breasts! What was I expecting? – for Lucian to come riding upon a great War Stallion, to offer his heart to me? I must be mad. I am an old woman and Lucian... well, he is old, too. And is that what I want from him? Of course not. I must be very bored with my existence these Days. No, Lucian was my friend, and that is all. Yet I suppose women are mostly very vain.

So then, I would choose the blue robe... or perhaps the yellow one...

Lucian did finally arrive, and riding a War Stallion! I had left word at our guarded entrance to allow him passage.

Later he told me of his ride, following the Tree line path and stopping at every Stone and Stream on our Isle.

"It was a perfect blue-skied Day. The earliest blossoms were just at their point of falling with the slightest breeze. So elusive are they –

lasting only Days and then like large, gentle, fragrant Snowflakes, they fall."

Before he reached our cottages, dairy, and barns, he veered off the main path to climb the spiral walkway to the top of the Tor to the circle of Stones. There, I suppose to speak with his Gods.

He told me that he saw my Beehives on his way there. Yes, I still care for them, but with much help now. Sometimes they come to me, to my cottage window and as if to call me, they buzz. Who will care for them when I am gone? But no, I have no Time for sad thoughts. These concerns will be for the living. When I am dead I will see all the long gone generations of my Bees in the Summerlands – where my Queens await.

Finally, Lucian dismounted in front of my cottage. He called to me, and entered.

"Why, Morgan," said he. "I am shocked at your beauty – it has not left you! I expected... but oh, here you are – your long hair, thick as ever, only silver now, just as mine. We both smiled and embraced.

"Lucian..." I said with a crooked smile, "You *look* good too, even though it seems you do not *see* so well."

We laughed and laughed.

"Perhaps," he said through his laughter "it is a blessing we lose our clear sight when we begin to get old. The blurring softens the lines of our faces."

More laughter.

"Perhaps this accounts for why I think so well of my own looks. I wonder..."

"But really Morgan, your eyes are clear and are even lovelier for the lines that frame them when you smile. I am so glad to be home. Thank you for allowing me to come.

"When may I see Arthur? I have heard he still lives but has no consciousness."

"Yes, Lucian, Arthur still lives..."

I emphasized those words. A moment of silence hung between us. Our eyes met. He knew what I meant. "Arthur still lives." But now it seemed not to matter. We were old friends – the best of friends and always would be.

Chapter 55
My Earnest Desire

Rowena

Three years later my fourteenth year-turn was fast approaching. I asked audience with our blessed High Druid and expressed my desire to go to my Great Aunt Morgan on the Isle of Apples.

"There I may worship and thusly discover the Ancient Goddess of the Old Dark Tribes – those who have inhabited these lands from the Time before the Clans and the Druids. Father Druid, it is just that I hunger for the ways of my other Ancestors. My Grandmother – or no, my great Grandmother – was Igraine, the great Seer of fame and Guardian of Nodens' Holy Well at Dumnonia. I want to learn more about her from her daughter – Morgan, Lady of the Lake. Please, may I leave with your blessing, Father? – for it would break my heart should you not give it. You and everyone here have become my family. I Love all of you so much. I request never to be removed from our tradition. Is that possible?"

"Hmm, that is a good question, but one about which I must gain counsel. As for my blessing, child, of course – you have it always. You must know that this comes as no surprise to me. Your teacher and mentor, Gwern, has spoken of it for over a year now."

"Yes, I knew, but it did not seem correct for him to act as a messenger to you on my behalf – as I said, I Love and respect you greatly. I had to ask for myself."

"Rowena, you have passed your first initiations here. When you ask not to be removed from our rolls, are you asking for your Bard's Apprentice Initiation – which is due to you, according to your progress – before you leave?"

"Yes, Father, I am."

"And how would that title be, with the Lady of the Lake, I wonder?"

"I do not know Father, but I cannot leave behind what I have gained here. I do know that the Old Tribes are very ancient and they, as well as other races of old, recognize and hold in high esteem the Magi of all Traditions – or even a Magi's apprentice. I have heard also that the Order has a saying they live by – 'All paths are Sacred.' So I will hold this thing called faith that I learned from my Christian friends – and enemies – in the hope that the Lady will accept me as who and what I am."

"But Rowena, whose apprentice would you be? As if I do not know the answer to this already..."

"This, Sir, is the hardest thing of all, and this, my mentor, Gwern, the Bard and Druid, must speak about with you for himself.

"Thank you, Father. May I take my leave of your presence now?"

"Yes, Rowena, you may."

As I have had extensive memorization training, I am able to write this conversation word for word, as it occurred. This skill comes easily to me.

The hardest thing was that my mentor, Gwern – who was as a Father to me and I a daughter to him – wished to leave the Druidical school as well. He had trained as a Druid for over twenty years and had served this new school as a Teacher for seven. He had his own reasons for wanting to go now to become a wandering Bard and Druid. This was his right to do. However he would be sorrowfully missed here, as he has great skills and is an exceedingly wise man as well. But this is his dilemma to solve.

Actually, what he wishes to do is to first bring me to the Isle of Apples and stay there with me for a month or longer, if he is invited to do so. He says that he must be sure of my acceptance and happiness there. Then he would travel to Pictland and Alba, returning in one half of a year to assess my status and wellbeing again. After that he will fulfill his lifelong wish to travel to Greece, Aegyptos, and the City of Old Jerusalem.

The thought of his long-earned freedom both excites and saddens me for the loss of him.

Freedom! This desire I understand. I treasure my freedom above all things. Oh, do not misunderstand – I consider it my freedom to worship the Goddess and serve the Order, for this is my greatest desire.

Funny that. It feels as if I have lived this moment before.

But now, once again, I am to go and serve for a commitment of at least four years, to what is essentially another Monastic life – although from what I have heard, a much more lighthearted and pleasurable one than I have thus far experienced.

I am so excited about this opportunity, but also am I for my Bard's apprenticeship. Someday perhaps, if I diligently continue to learn and practice my art, I may be called a Bard, as well... In both meanings of "Bard" do I hold ambition and desire – in the singing and the telling of the traditional sagas and Myths as well as in the creating of Sacred Poetry. My Aunt Morgan does not know this of me yet.

Morgan's note...

Ah...but so wrong was she about what I knew of her. She forgot the Sight I hold, or did not think I cared enough to watch her grow – but I had and ever will.

Chapter 56
Rowena & Gwern the Bard

Gwern

My illustrious Lady of the Lake, High Mother of the Order of the Goddesses Nine, Lady Morgan – Your reputation and that of your Mother is legend in Gwynedd, as are the valorous tales of your brother, good King Arthur and his companions. Pray you not think I speak in flattery, I assure that I do not.

It is with me such an honour to think of being the recipient of your gracious invitation to rest on your beautiful Island for one Moon's Dance. The honour is all the more special for the knowing that Gwyddion, the late Merlin, rested with you as well.

I never had the privilege of meeting him, although I Dreamt of the possibility of it my entire childhood and into becoming a young man. But I never had the means to travel to wherever he was. You see – I was fourteen years when I began my formal Druidical education at a small school in a remote location near to the most Westerly tip of Ynys Mon. Once there, I had to commit to staying there.

I could already read by the Time my formal Druidical education had begun, as my Father had taught me at home. He had been trained as a Druidical Bard, as too, had my Grand-sire, his Father before him, and *his* Father before him. But that was in the Days when all must be kept silent for fear of Roman persecution.

After being accepted by the school, there I stayed for the next twenty years, until I had accomplished my Bardic Arts, Theology, and the Druidical Laws, after which I was initiated as a full Druid. I then began to teach at the new University on Ynys Mon, where I accepted Rowena as my student.

I Love her as a daughter, so perhaps I have not the ability to be unbiased – but in my estimation, she is the most brilliant Star in my Sky. That is to say that, my own pride laid aside, she is nothing short of the most intelligent, quick witted, inquisitive Human I have ever encountered. To add to these qualities, she has compassion for man and Beast alike, and although I believe her thoughts, beliefs, and conclusions will ever be her own, she is always anxious to learn those of all other peoples. She and I make a good compliment to each other in our searching hearts.

Yet now, I must relinquish my position as primary teacher of Rowena. You must know that this is not an easy thing for me to do; yet I truly believe it is exactly as should be. She has yearned for the GREAT GODDESS' Mysteries for as long as I have known her. Her blood calls to her. The ancients of these Isles beckon. She is as hungry as the Wolfs she so Loves to become an Enchantress on your Isle of Apples and a Seer of the Old Dark Tribes.

I write this letter to you not only as an introduction, but also to serve as a completely unadorned, truthful appraisal of what you might expect of Rowena.

She is restless... and her sense of what she calls her freedom is an overpowering force in her life. How this will play the strings of the song that will be her life there with you, only Time – or as is said, the Weavers – can tell. Do not think I call her fickle, far from it; she is loyal as the Stars spinning in the Heavens. She has vowed never to abandon any learning that she has embraced. Never will she turn her back on either of us.

Lady, I have spent much Time in studying the immense beauty of your tradition, as well as that of the Greeks. I am a seeker of the ageless truths and Cosmic Mysteries. Someday soon I hope to travel to Aegyptos, where – it is said – their Mysteries are as old as yours. Perhaps they both have sprung from the same source. The further I delve into these inner traditions – as well as any uninitiated might – the more I find the ONE. Yet, the intricacies and the diversity of method and symbol, Rituals and Rites, stun my sensibilities. I am filled with awe and humility. Humanity, it seems to me, has a great need and propensity for walking with the Gods in the Land of Myth. Every tradition, breathtakingly beautiful in its own way, seems to arrive at the same understandings. I know that Rowena embraces this quest as passionately as do I, but it is her will now to be with you. I am sure that each of you will be a blessing to the other.

May God keep and Goddess bless you,
Gwern, the Bard

Morgan

Rowena had been born on the Longest Night, which is a propitious Time to be born, for upon this Night, the Child of Promise appears – the newborn Sun. It was also upon that very Day that Arthur and Bedwyr had been born so long ago.

Rowena had been disappointed that she could not present herself to me upon the actual marking of her fourteenth year.

That Winter had been colder than anyone could remember. I had not expected Gwern and Rowena to travel all the way from the Snowy Mountains to our Isle in the cold Winds and frozen Mists. It seemed impossible to do so. But Rowena had cajoled Gwern into daring the trip. So, of course, the journey took much longer than she had expected. They had to interrupt their progress many Times due to downed Trees and high Snow drifts along the roads. Fortunately the Druids at the University had commissioned some Tanners, who lived and worked in a nearby settlement, to cover the top and sides of a two wheeled wagon for their trip.

Four weeks past her fourteenth year-turn they arrived at the Northern shore across the Lake from the Order.

The Inland Sea had frozen solid weeks before their coming, so that when they arrived they found it and everything else around it in that state.

It is not unusual for the surface of the Lake to freeze over in particularly cold Winters. Whenever this happens our usual means of conveyance – the Marsh Folk's punts and marvelous floating walkways – become treacherous and unusable and if there was no other practical means of crossing, this would leave the Marsh Folk and everyone else on the Isle stranded and unable to obtain needed supplies or be in a position to help others in need. And so, many long years ago – how many, no one can remember – the Marsh Folk devised an ingenious solution. First, at wide intervals they sank a series of tall, pitch covered wooden pilings deeply into the reedy floor of the Lake. These spanned the distance from their Marshy villages across the Lake to the Northern, as well as to the Southern shore. Along the tops of these great pilings, they attached large, taut ropes, connecting each piling to the next. The making of such ropes has, in fact, always been their main industry. They also devised flat, reed Ice boats – or sledges, as one might call them – with which to cross the frozen expanse of the Lake.

I waited...

Rowena

Gwern and I found ourselves stranded in a village near to the North-Northeastern edge of the Lake, not knowing what we would do. To our great blessing, we were taken into the home of a very hospitable couple, who were of the second generation of Saxons living in the small community of their fellows.

We were not like any sort of people that these Saxons had ever encountered. Our language – Cymric – the tone and lilt of our speech, as well as our clothing and features, were all strange to them. But kind and goodhearted folk were they, for they gave us shelter from the cold and fed us. These Saxons knew little of the Marsh Folk and not at all of their Ice boats. What is more, they knew not how to send word to the Lady of the   Lake.

The first Time I beheld the shore of the Isle of Apples, everything was so cold that my breath froze upon the Wind and then mingled with the Mist that was rising in tendrils from the frozen surface of the Lake. My nose ran and my eyes burned, still I looked around.

Snowflakes were falling in large, artful shapes and patterns. In the distance across the frozen Lake, I saw the outline of the Tor rising up, beckoning and teasing me... Every bough and branch near me was Ice-wrapped and everywhere I looked was an Enchantment of crystalline white, glittering with the Moon's light that shone through them. It seemed that I stood at the gates of the Winter Garden of the Twyla-y-Tag. The Wind whispered promises of the Goddess of Peaceful Dreams. A stirring arose within me such as I had never felt. Anticipation was winding around me like vine on Willow.

"So," thought I, "will I now have to wait until the thaw of Winter's End?" I fretted with frustration. All of my life I had waited to truly know the Great Mother. Of course, I had known of Yeshua's Mother Mair, Ceredwen, Brigantia, Arianrhod, and even the ancient Sulis, but these I had learned from Myths; from knowledge taught – not from inner knowing. I prayed that that knowing, once attained, would lead to Her awareness of me. I wished for Awen – as we children of the Druids call it – the connection with the ALL.

Since there seemed nothing for us to do but to wait, I thought to learn more of these good Saxon folk who were so full of life and joyfulness.

The goodwife of this household is named Hilde, her husband is Rwdroff, or something like that – I cannot be sure and they cannot write it for me. However, Gwern thinks it means "Red Wolf." Their children and their children's children are all grown and have gone away, but the other families in this small settlement look in on them often to be sure they are well and lack for neither food nor warmth.

Their house is square – not round – and it is partially buried into the ground. This seems to me to be a very practical idea – especially in the cold Winters. The outside walls are made of clay, straw and many tightly packed Stones, to ward off strong Winds. The roof is not thatched, but covered with dirt, reeds and straw. It is almost completely covered in Moss.

Inside, the walls are whitewashed. Their floor was dug deeper than the walls and then planked with wooden floorboards – over quite a good foundation it seems, as it has lasted three generations – and keeps the dust down and the whole hut cleaner than would a dirt floor. This is a very nice thing.

The door, which faces North – away from the Lake – is really two doors, which open from the center and are barred and latched together with iron. This provides for ease of bringing their Animals in. However, the only Animals they now have are a Hound and a Duck. There are no carpets so the Hound lies on the floor by the hearth most of the Time and the Duck has her own small pile of straw in which to lay her eggs.

As you enter, just to the right of the doorway, a stretching rack is leaning against the wall. Beyond it is where Rwdroff keeps his axes and other hand tools. Along the Western wall near the center of the cottage is a bench with a distaff and hand spindle attached to it by a peg in a hole. It has a basket of wool sitting beside it. In the far corner are some other baskets holding clothes, dishes, and boots. Just to the left of the entrance, along the Northern wall, is a stack of Firewood. Along the East wall is another, larger stack of wood, handier to the hearth. Above the stack – on a second rack – Rwdroff has a large Bear's pelt stretching, which, he said, was given to him by one of his neighbors. He gestured and spoke the word for eat, letting us know that there would be enough food for the Winter.

Across the hut, opposite the door, is a trestle table, filled with baskets, pottery bowls, a pitcher for Spring Water, and ewers that are always filled with ale. Beneath the trestle are baskets of Grain, Apples, and Onions – all at the ready for preparing their meals. Hanging on the wall close by are five drinking-horns, which Rwdroff proudly explained had been his Grandfather's. Or at least that is what I understood.

The central hearth is large and very warm. It is sunken into the ground with Stones walling it up to the height of my calves. The logs are placed across ironwork firedogs to allow Air to flow beneath them. The draw is good through the small hole in the center of their pitched roof so the Air in the cottage is not very smoky. Above the hearth is a sturdy three-legged stand with a large iron cauldron hanging from it. The cauldron is usually simmering with a pottage of oatmeal, Apples, late harvested roots, and perhaps a Squirrel or two.

Around the hearth are gathered one long and three short curved benches for seating. Some indistinguishable furry hides are thrown across them for warmth and comfort. On the floor beside each bench lie other neatly stacked pelts.

The old couple slept on a comfortable pallet in the Southeast corner of the hut. They offered that I sleep on the straw and feather, wool covered pallet that their children used to sleep on. I tried to insist that Gwern use it, instead of me – as his bones are much older than mine –

however he refused, so I obeyed. He slept on the floor instead – nearer to the hearth. It is really very comfortable in their home.

Each evening we all sit around the hearth with the pelts lying across our legs and feet. It seems a Ritual of sorts. We toast the Gods in thanksgiving for our food and health and then we drink our ale. Then more thanksgiving, then more ale. It was not long before Gwern and I were able to pick up some words and, between that and hand gestures, we could get the general meaning of their conversations... Rwdroff speaks of his plans for the coming Summer's planting, tending, and harvesting. Should he buy a Pig at Winter's Ending or should they build a coop and buy more chickens? After Rwdroff's ideas are spoken and while his goodwife spins her wool, she speaks of their children and of long ago memories.

When enough ale has been drunk we all take turns telling stories or singing; they in Saxon tongue, and we in Cymric. It is so much fun to hear the telling of their heroic sagas in their guttural Saxon tongue! Although I mostly do not know what they are saying or even how to copy their words, I do my best to mimic their words and sing along. This in itself leads to much more uproarious laughter. The Gods only know what I am really saying!

One Night, Rwdroff stood to enact a certain story – complete with exuberant gestures and expressions – as elegantly as any Bard's and mirthfully as any Fool's. It was a story of their Trickster God... I think he quoth:

"One darksome Night, on yon cold Mountain
The Frost Giants schemed their schemes
While all the while, did Loki lie upon his bed in Dreams
In his Dreams he travelled far, across the Bifrost Bridge
And there he saw four Giants meet upon a great white ridge
When he had heard all their good plans, of breaking down his House
He waved his hands and spun around, turning each into a Mouse
'Oh Loki, did you never know that you are of our blood?
Or did Woden say he sculpted you from Asgard's Holy mud?
No! We say to you, whose machinations are never nice,
Now you can claim not Giants' blood, but only that of Mice!'"

If not for my burning anxiousness to be with my great aunt, it should have been a lovely and fine Winter's spending.

Then one Day, a traveling Merchant came to the little Saxon settlement. Strange, it seemed to me, that a Merchant travel at this cold Time of year. This man spoke both the Saxon tongue and that of the Cymru, so Gwern and I could understand him well. He told us of the Marsh Folk's Ice Boats and when they would cross the Lake from the

Northern side of the Isle. Their crossing was to be in three Days. The Marsh Men were to meet the Merchant at the shore at a certain place to collect the goods he had brought for them and for the Order. When they did, they were told of our dilemma.

So a message was taken by them to Lady Morgan. Upon receiving this, she hurriedly sent stout men to help pull on the ropes for the sledges to cross the Ice and bring us to her. She sent along with the men many goods for the couple that had sheltered and fed us.

Amoung these goods were three heavy woolen cloaks; two in the natural colour of their White Faced Sheep and one, which was for me, heavily dyed in Madder and lined in Fox fur. It was the most beautiful scarlet colour I had ever seen and was fancifully embroidered with vines and leaves. Lady Morgan sent a note regarding the red cloak. She said that it had belonged to Nimue the Enchantress, who had been the great Merlin's lover, and daughter of Vivianne, the previous Lady of the Lake. She wrote that Nimue had worn and Loved the cloak for many years.

"It was, in fact, her most treasured possession. That, in itself, was something rare, for she had been a wealthy woman with many possessions."

Her note said that in the last missive that had come from Nimue, the courier who had brought the letter also brought Nimue's cloak. Nimue had asked that the cloak and brooch be kept for "Bronte's return." This, of course, was very quizzical to me. However, Lady Morgan said that she would explain all when I arrived at the Isle of Apples. "But for now," she admonished – "You must wear the cloak to keep yourself warm, Rowena, my dear."

With Hilde's cloak had come a braided rope of green wool – which was, of course, to tie around her middle so as to keep the Winds out – and a simple brooch of bronze for clasping it at her neck. I was later to learn that the Order's men and women who worked in the firing of metals had made the bronze brooch. Hilde cried when she saw it and although her expressions of disbelief and thankfulness were all uttered in her Saxon tongue, I knew very well what she would have me express to Lady Morgan.

My – or Nimue, the Enchantress' – cloak had a gold and jeweled brooch. It was a round disk of polished gold and upon it was a Gemstone and a six pointed Star, which had been formed by layering two equally sided triangles, then affixing one to other. The lower one was point down and the one laying atop it was point up. Gwern said that amoung many other things, the six-pointed Star was an ancient Hebrew symbol, known as the Star of David – he who had been their most beloved King of Legend.

He told me that many Philosophers and Historians have written that the six-pointed Star is a very ancient Mystical symbol – going back in

Time and fading into the origins of all known cultures.

Of course, the Druids use all geometric shapes as mathematical aids...

He said, "It is told that to the ancient, *Mystical* Hebrews, the six-pointed Star represents Cosmic polarity. Here is how: The top triangle, with its point up, is believed to be pointing to the Stars and to their God, the Celestial Father."

"Like Woden, Zeus, or Jupiter?" I asked.

"Yes, the Lord of the Cosmos, who lives in a Mansion and sits upon a Heavenly throne.

"The Hebrews have a Mystical tradition going back far into and beyond their establishment as a culture separate from their neighbors. Their Magi understand the Cosmic need for sympathetic polarity. So when the Star of David was conceived by them, they used the most basic symbol of the Mother, an upside down triangle – which of course represents the entrance to the womb, from whence all life springs forth – as a foundation. Then, with the upright triangle – which is an obvious symbol of male genitals – lain atop it, is formed the perfect representation of balance – male and female, in equality.

"It is whispered among the Magi of many lands that long ago the Sky Gods swept through the world of the Great Mother Goddess, joining her in equal power and then later subjugating her.

"As Time went by, some of the Hebrew culture went the way of the Greeks, Romans, Persians, and others by subjugating women and ignoring their long-held matrilineal genealogies. They created a male dominant culture. Even did they forget their ancestral Mother Goddess Asherah.

"Rowena, you remember, do you not, when I taught you that Aegyptian Temples had long before been built upon the same design as the later Hebrew Temple in Old Jerusalem?

The outer courtyard of the Hebrew Temple – as well as the older Aegyptian ones – were where most Vegetable and Animal sacrifices were made and where the common people could attend by watching from a distance. The first chamber to be entered beyond the courtyard is called The Holy. Only those of the initiated Priesthood could enter there. That is where most Priests and Priestesses perform their traditional Rituals and great Magics. Beyond The Holy chamber is the Inner Sanctum of the Temple – the Holy of Holies, where only the High Priest – or Priestess – and their attendants could enter. In Aegyptian Temples this chamber is reserved for the Idol that is indwelled by the God or Goddess. In the Holy of Holies of the Hebrew Temple originally stood their most Sacred relic, the Ark of the Covenant, where, hanging suspended in the Air above it between two winged Seraphim, was the Shekinah' light – or power – denoting their God's presence.

"When they lost the Ark, the Shekinah light was lost to them forever. But those Hebrews who still follow the Ancient Mystical Way – and there are still many who do – say that this powerful light was named for their ancient Mother Goddess – the Goddess of Holy Spirit and power."

"Rowena, your eyes are glazing over. Do I talk too much or bore you?"

"Oh, no, no... It is just that I was trying to 'see' it all. But I have no point of reference. We worship and do our seasonal Rites in Groves of Oak or Circles of Stone, but always Great Nature is our Temple."

"Well then, where is our Holy of Holies, Rowena?"

"Oh yes, I see, Gwern." I smiled. "It is the Inner Sanctum of ourselves – in our hearts and Spirits. But surely theirs is, too?"

"Of course it is – in everyone...

"But, our conversation has strayed far from old King David's Star."

"Gwern," I asked – "Will I ever go to Aegyptos, Greece, or Old Jerusalem? I know that you will leave me soon to venture upon your wonderful travels. Some Day perhaps I can accompany you... I will miss you so much."

"And I you," he replied, "but our paths have only come to a crossroads, Rowena – not an ending."

The next Day, we would cross the frozen Lake.

This is my first sight of the Marsh Folk. Small and dusky-skinned are they, with dark hair and eyes, but although they share these characteristics with my Mother and Lady Morgan, their features are sharper, rougher, and wilder somehow. Perhaps it was their more prominent cheekbones, heavier brows and squarer jaws. Their hair, too, is more coarse and straighter. Lady Morgan, just as I, had straight hair, but it was soft and did not look as if it would stand straight up and out if cut short, as does theirs. These Marsh Folk, the men anyway, who are all I had seen thus far of these people, had chopped their hair above their jaw and every one of them look like a prickly Hedgehog. I do not mean to be cruel or critical.

Most of the men I have seen have had longer hair. But then, having spent most my life within the boundaries of various sorts of Monastic centers, I suppose my knowledge of peoples of this world is very narrow.

I do still remember the man who was the Guard of my savior, Lucian. His hair was cut extremely short, to his scalp. The old Romans had begun this habit or discipline long ago, I was told.

Oh, enough about hair and the way men look... These Marsh Folk's hearts are as gold – as kind and attentive to us as they can be.

Now, it takes at least two very strong men to pull these Ice boats, hand over hand, along the heavy ropes. This is especially true since the Marsh Folk are very small people. So Lady Morgan had sent four of her men to help pull on the great taut ropes that were strung between the pilings. The Marsh Men used poles to keep the Ice boats from crashing into the pilings when approaching and passing them.

By the Time all was set – packed, unpacked and packed again – three Ice Boats were needed – two for the goods of the Merchant and one for us and our belongings.

The one Gwern and I were to cross in had short ledges about it on all sides, which kept one from easily falling out. Once, along the way of our crossing, the Ice Boats stopped to allow two of the men to relieve themselves. They were thoughtful enough to turn their backs to me. "So," thought I – "they are not as primitive or uncouth as they appear to be."

Just before our embarking, some men retrieved some Stones from a Fire that had been built on the shore and brought them to the boats wrapped in pelts. The Stones were quite warm, even through the pelts. They gave one to me and one to Gwern, gesturing to us to hold them close to our chests beneath the great coverings wrapped around us. Amazing! In no Time at all, the great chill I was suffering was going away. In fact, I began to feel too hot where I held the Stone, so I placed it beneath my feet, which I could barely feel. I mused at how thankful one could be over such a simple, basic comfort.

I have failed to note that the Night before our passage, it Snowed. Not too much or we should have had to wait for the surface to freeze and pack to hard Ice again. So here and there along our way we were compelled to stop to remove drifts of Snow that barred the way. For this, the front boat was equipped with a rigid broom of sorts. On our third stopping, of a sudden I felt the need to relieve myself of Water. What was I going to do? I whispered my dilemma to Gwern. He in turn, to my abashment, asked one of the young men from the Isle what I was to do. Without a word, I was handed a pot to piss in. With great effort to unwrap myself, I did finally piss. At that the men from the Isle began to sing in loud and humorous voices – I suppose to cover the sound of my pissing. The others joined in and Gwern winked at me. It was all too funny to remain embarrassed. When finished I poured the steaming contents over the side and rewrapped myself with the help of Gwern. The singing went on though, and the rest of the passage became a joyful celebration.

With a bump, we hit the shoreline. We were helped off the Ice Boat and onto the frozen shore. I was here – really here – on the Isle of Apples! I knelt upon the Snow-covered Earth. "Mother – pray I find you here…"

In that morning Mist, I wondered – had all of my life been leading me to this moment, or was it that my life was truly just beginning?

Book Two of the Voices of the Stars Series

"Rowena of the Glen"

Coming Soon...

Dylan, **son of the Waves**...

History, is it? Is it written on the Wind then, girl? Do the Trees read it? Can the herds smell it? Perhaps then, your Ravens remember... Do you believe the Wolf really cares who was his great-great Grandsire? They only live, my Rowena, they only live...

Live now with me, this one moment, this one breath, this one heartbeat, this one kiss.

Rowena

I was really here on the Isle of Apples! Standing upon this Sacred ground!

Early morning as it was, the Sunlight spilled through the boughs and branches of the ancient Trees. Everything glistened in its icy coating. It was to be a glorious Day.

The Tor was somehow not quite as big as I had imagined it to be...

I should not have been surprised, for I had already learned in my life that the perception – the anticipation – of a thing was always greater than the actuality. Once found, a hidden treasure was only wealth. Worthy, wanted, or needed as it may have been, once obtained – once solid and tangible – it is quickly taken for granted, leaving the worlds of imagination and mystery behind to be woven into ordinary life. Albeit a comfort, the actuality can never quite equal the dream and the quest... Sometimes even a treasure hoped for, such as my sanctuary with Mother Mair – the would-be Abbess – can turn a dream into a rotten thing, one which disintegrates into ash.

Ash... "Oh, Mother, my own dear Mother, you are ash, as is my baby sister. You should be the one reconnecting with your family here. You never had a chance at life, torn from all happiness and betrayed. But Mother, if you can hear me now, know that I share these, my first foot falls upon the Isle of Apples, with you. May you return to this Earth one Day to live a life of joy and peace."

As I arose from my knees, to which I had fallen to kiss this Sacred soil, I walked in the direction of the Tor. My heart grew lighter and lighter. Of a sudden I felt – no, I knew – that I was home.

Upon the first morning of our arrival at The Order, Gwern and I were taken to the dairy barn, which had two great hearths, one at each end. It was indeed very warm. There, we were bathed in luxuriously hot Water. While doing so my skin and hair were rubbed with fragrant oils and my hair was dried and plaited neatly by one of the women. Finally I was clean and comfortable. Next we were dressed in fine, lightweight, woolen robes, which were for our resting. All of these comforts were something I had not experienced since I was a small child at Vortigern's – or should I say, Princess Rowena's – fortress. Those days seemed to me as though a lifetime ago. How long had it been since I had really been warm – since before the Time of Samhain? I supposed so. I felt as if I could have bundled up and slept for Days.

Actually we did sleep through that Day and through the next Night.

When finally we awoke upon the following morn we found that new Sheepskin lined high leather boots had been placed near to each of our pallets. These had been fashioned to fit the size of our feet! An overdress of light green, loosely woven wool had been laid over a bench, near to the Fire for me. A braided cord was there too. My beautiful, red woolen cloak, as well as Gwern's hooded Druids' robe had been tidied up and hung to dry near the hearth.

That morning we were led to the cottage of my beloved great aunt Morgan, The Lady of the Lake. There waiting for me, too, was my savior, Lucian.

Morgan, Lady of the Lake

Oh, she was here... She was truly here! I had not realized just how apprehensive I had been over Rowena's arrival. Of course I knew that she would arrive safely, for I had 'Seen' many great things to come in Rowena's life. Still I fretted. I am human after all... Lucian was just as anxious as I. We kept each other in fine company.

When she finally entered my quarters, she ran into my arms, but then quickly into Lucian's. Gwern stood politely aside, until, with blushing cheeks, Rowena remembered herself and introduced him to us.

I knew at that very moment that I would like this man. I had wondered. You see, his letter had been so formal... But I was to find him very unlike what I had expected. He was clever, jolly, fun to be with, very entertaining, and a good game player. As far as I was concerned, he could have stayed here for as long as he wished.

I placed his lodging in the cottage that had been built for Rowena's coming. She could stay in my new quarters for the Time being. There was plenty of room for her here.

Arthur lay in my old cottage, where I still went most evenings to Weave and to sing to him. My hands are stiffer as of late, yet still I Weave the Wool, albeit much more slowly than I once had. Upon many evenings Lucian came to pass the Time with me there. How odd are the connections we make and keep in our lives. Lucian was my oldest and dearest friend now. Everyone else from our youth was dead, except for Arthur, of course.

Not one of the Nine High Wise Mothers of the council who had been of that station at the Time of my having been inducted into the position of Lady of the Lake was still alive. Some, I would think, had gone to the Stars to join the Ancestors, and some to the Summerlands to await a new rebirth on Earth. I wonder where I will go? Surely I still have many lessons to learn and failings to overcome before I need not reincarnate... I think that because of my foolishness and rebelliousness, I will be compelled to return again to Earth in many new lives. Besides, the 'Voices' had told me that Arthur and I would live many more lives together on this Earth...

Of course, in one way we are all perfect – as She has made us – each with our own foibles. This thought reminds me of a very funny thing The Merlin once told me... "I have a Christian acquaintance who often quotes; 'We are all imperfect, it is just that some are more imperfect than others." Well, one thing I do know is that wherever I go when I leave this Earth, Arthur and I will be together.

Yes, Arthur – I remind you once more that I will not leave you trapped forever between the worlds...

But what to do about Rowena? All of our girls come to us at fourteen or as close to that as they can arrive here, as has Rowena. I was over fifteen when I arrived. But the girls of the Old Tribes have already been taught well by their Grandmothers in the Arts of Herbal Healing and Humming and drumming up the power of all living things. They have learned the Sacred songs and some of the rudimentary Words of the Making.

In their first two to three years here, we teach them to read, write and Weave if they have not already been taught to, and to sow, tend, and gather. These Postulants also learn whichever of our Myths and legends the Grandmothers of their Tribe had not already taught them. Soon, too, they learn the simplest Mysteries of the Nine Mother Goddesses – none of the deeper Mysteries though... When they have accomplished these things, they are eligible for their first initiation, that of Huntress Maiden. Then later, after they have earned their next, Mother Initiation, they are eligible to teach all of these things to the Postulants and younger Maidens. Those who excel in the Arts will eventually become Enchantresses. The Enchantresses are taught the Arts Magical, the deeper Mysteries, Science, Astronomy, Mathematics, much more complicated Healing Arts, potions, and medicines, and to stand in Ritual as Priestesses. Those few Enchantresses who are exceptional in the skills of the Sight, or in leaving their physical bodies behind, become Walkers Between the Realms. They may remain here and continue to learn the deeper Cosmic Mysteries, perform the ancient Rituals, and then perhaps reach to obtain the fourth initiation, that of Wise Mother. At that stage of enlightenment they are taught the meaning of life, the incarnations of the Cosmos, and the secrets of all known things.

Oh, dear! Have I not written of all these things long ago? I suppose I really am getting old...

However, no human can teach another the love of and connection with the Great Goddess. This dwells or does not dwell within the heart of each individual, male or female.

Rowena did not fit the mold of the other girls at all. She had already been Druid trained. She read and wrote Cymric, a little Latin, and some Greek. She knew rudimentary Mathematics, Astronomy, and Herbal lore and had attained a Bard's Apprenticeship. However, despite her accomplishments, no Grandmother had blessed her with our ancient Sacred Words or Myths. And the Gods and Goddesses she had come to know were of the Druids' tradition. So, what to do with Rowena? Obviously we could not demean her accomplishments by insisting that she begin her education all over again with the other new postulants. No, she would need a very specialized education. I made the decision to become a surrogate Grandmother to her myself.

I will never forget how the eyebrows raised when I mentioned this in our Council meeting. I am sure that every one of the others of the Nine Wise Mothers would have raised impassioned objections to my decision – and some more heatedly than others – if they thought it would do any good. I could read it in their eyes and thoughts; "Why this is just not done, for the Lady of the Lake to take a novice – a Postulant – as her student! She breaks with tradition... again!"

Yes, again...although never would I have thought of myself as a rule breaker when I was younger and so full of obedience. But Time and circumstance have changed all of that.

"Yes," I said to their unspoken displeasure, "I will be the Grandmother she had not the opportunity to be blessed by. Will any of you challenge me in this? If so, let it be now – or forever after, keep your silence and peace about it. And, this is my final word."

No one spoke... I went on; "Then speak now to give your counsel – to aid me or to bless and encourage my intentions."

Silence again... Then one of the eight raised her hand in a gesture of salutation.

"My dear Sister, Morgan, who is there to challenge your Wisdom?

For my part, as a Sister who loves you very much, I wish more for your happiness than I do to follow protocol. If you judge this child to be so exceptional, who are we to argue? This is a great blessing that you would bestow upon Rowena. May the blessing come back to you, by the Power of Three."

They each in turn nodded their heads in agreement. I was relieved. Make no mistake, I would have had my way with or without their approval, for such is my right. But long ago when having a conversation with a Christian Monk who lived nearby, he quoted something from their Holy Book which I never forgot. I had then and still do hold there to be great Wisdom in these words. They were, through translation, something like this; 'All things are lawful, but not all things are advantageous.' I was gladdened to not break our peace.

When I told Rowena, it was as though I had given a Dragon's treasure – a horde of gold – to her. So thrilled was she that she capered about in joy. Then she took my hands and I was dancing too. "By what Magic is this, my child? You make me young again."

Rowena, my heart, by the Time you read this, my fleshly body may well have left this earthly realm, but never will I leave you, my dearest. So long as I have the power to watch over you, you will be protected. As for Arthur, we will be together too. I have a plan... By now you will know what I have done regarding Arthur. Pray you not judge me harshly.

"Always my love..."

Rowena
Being lead to my Mother Goddess...

Yes, the years have rolled by just as Lady Morgan had told me that they would do... nearly three and one half of them, in fact. This next Longest Night will turn my eighteenth year. Of course, discipline, study, and work – these are things not new to me, but the belonging, Love, closeness, loyalty, and companionable joy among the Sisters and Brothers here on the Isle are so much more than I had expected in the beginning.

By the Time of my writing this, I have had my Huntress Maiden and my Mother Initiations. Now I mentor and teach the young Huntress Maidens to read and write and to learn Herbal Lore and Poetry. I have learned of Spirit far beyond all of my expectations. Filled is my chalice – at the end of each Day it holds more.

Gwern had left a full Moon's Dance after we arrived. He came back as promised after six more and then again at the next Time of Red and Gold Leaves. Since then, I have not heard from him. I suppose he is in Greece by now.

But, for all that I have gained, I feel sorrowfully inadequate in one very important way. Just being told about the culture of the ancient Dark Tribes, from which the whole of our Traditions, Myths, Mysteries, and Seasonal Rites are derived, leaves me still with a worrisome lack of understanding.

I am of their blood. I feel the echoes of them in my bones. Yet, although I am told of the Old Ones who live amidst the Trees, I cannot feel their ways. I have imagined their primitive lives, the richness of their culture, knowings, and Spirit. But I hold no reckoning of their daily lives – things such as the odd way that they have kept their ancient, vast treasures of gold hidden in their Villages while never really using or needing any of it. They – who so long ago chose to vanish into the Woods, lest they be ruined or spoiled by other materialistic Cultures.

It is told that in primitive loin coverings or Star-speckled robes they *glide* through the Forests, never being seen by others unless they wish to be – never even being heard. No, not even with the jingling of the bells on their ankles. And, as does my Lady Morgan, many of them have tattooed Stars and Serpents on their hands and ankles – some upon their faces. Of course, the older they are and the longer they stay in the villages and the more Rite of Life passages they go through, the more Stars and Serpents cover their bodies.

I have heard about their great Walkers and Seers and of the deep Trances they enter when eating the Sacred Mushrooms that grow so prolifically in their deep Woods, even that some of them can float above the ground by their Magic Humming alone and that their Hunters Shape-shift into Stags and run with the herds. There are stories told in the Night by our hearth Fires that a few of them have gone so deeply into Trance that their fleshly bodies slowly disappear into a Mist. Actually, I find that a bit hard to believe. But it is said...

Theirs is an oral tradition carried down by their Grandmothers and Fathers, the same as has been the Druids' way. Most of their tribal Elders do not read and write at all, yet if their children wish to, they agree to send them to be educated at The Order. Their whole existence seems such a contradiction. They are hard to fathom. I feel a great need and wish to go to live amoung them for awhile. Perhaps there, I will truly find myself...

Finally I found the courage to ask Lady Morgan if I may go to visit with them at Summer's Beginning. I await her answer...

"Yes!" She said "yes!"

About Rowena Whaling

Born into the magical world of stage lights, sceneries, orchestras and Chorus lines, Rowena spent her childhood on the road with her theatrical parents.

Always looking to the stars to find her way home, she heard in them the music: and ever since then music and writing has been her life.

By the time she was ten years old, she was writing poetry and short stories expanding on the Classical Greek tragedies - adding characters and extending he story lines to suit her creativity.

She was also testing the waters writing her own musical plays, complete with dialog and songs, and she sang. She would sing for anyone who asked, - notably in the dressing rooms and hotel suites of many of the stars her parents worked with.

At age fourteen, her parents moved to New Orleans, where she immersed herself in the myriad cultural influences. By then, her parents were semi-retired and devoted much of their time encouraging Rowena to develop her singing talents and her 4 ½ octave vocal range. Her interest in traditional jazz and R&B was the beginning of a musical career, while continuing to cultivate her poetic skills.

Besides music and poetry, the secrets of the enthralled her and expanded her she knowledge as an amateur Egyptologist and self-taught cultural anthropologist, which remains constant in her life.

A highly spiritual person. Rowena's search for truths and the divine began at the early age of 6. As she grew, so did her interest in many of the world's religions—both modern and ancient, and continues to exhibit itself in her witchy naturalism.

As a very young woman, Rowena descended upon New York City with the intent of joining one of that city's opera companies, but despite her love of opera, her writing steered her in other directions. She was immediately discovered by several music business people who offered her songwriting and recording contracts, so she began writing songs for other people and recording her own albums.

Even though her major label recording debut met with much acclaim, she, like so many other artists, had her hopes dashed, and became entangled in a years long lawsuit.

During this crisis, her mother suggested she open a childcare center and she remains the maven and proprietor of an enchanting childcare run from her beautiful Victorian cottage in Nashville; which has been awarded with the highest of ratings.   Yet, through all the years, the Voices of the Stars spoke to her and inspired the exquisitely written first novel of the series "Voices of the Stars". She is currently engrossed in the creation of the second book in the series.

Rowena lives with her beloved husband - Joe Funderburk, and their little black poodle - The Mighty Mightor, in the greater Nashville area.